ENTANGLED

BRUTES OF BRISTLEBROOK
BOOK TWO

REBECCA QUINN

Cover by Artscandare.

Editing by Kate James.

Proofreading by Elizabeth Patrick at Headlight Fluid Press and Lilly Rayman.

ISBN: 978-0-6485031-2-5

CONTENT NOTE

Hello lovely Quinnksters,

I'm so freaking thrilled you've come back for book two. Thank you so, so much for all your support. Before we get started, I'd like to address a few important things.

Firstly, I would like to gently direct everyone to my website, https://rebeccaquinnauthor.com, where there is a list of all tropes and content warnings for this book. Entangled is darker than Ensnared, and deals with a wide range of scenes and situations that readers may find triggering, so I would encourage everyone to look those over before proceeding.

As with book one, I've tried to be as comprehensive as I could with that list, but please, if you have any questions or concerns, or believe anything should be added, contact me at rebecca.quinn.author@gmail.com

Secondly, on the above note, I'd like to specifically call out the fact that this book deals heavily with depression, the various ways people respond to trauma, anxiety, PTSD, and mental health in general. Your mental health matters, so please be kind to yourself and seek support if you need it.

Finally, this book also deals with a range of BDSM scenes and dynamics. As with book one, please be mindful that this is fiction, and shouldn't be taken as instructional reading. Liberties are taken for the sake of the story, events are dramatized, and relationships and dynamics move faster in fictional, apocalyptic worlds than they do in life.

In fiction, kink is seamless, there's no poop in the chute, first times aren't the uncomfortable equivalent of two bodies making awkward small talk, refractory periods are myths, characters *just know* how to make their partners feel good, and they already know exactly what to do for aftercare.

Must be nice, right? If you're inspired to try any new kink, please communicate extensively with your partner, research non-fiction, reputable sources of information, and always, always, keep things safe, sane, and consensual (or insert preferred kink acronym of your choice).

Okay, Becky's safety lecture is complete. Now go and have some fun!

Lots of love,
Becky Quinn

In memory of my Satisfyer Pro2
Rechargable Clitoral Stimulator.
I should have recognized the signs of burn out.
I should have stopped when you made that
weird, terrifying zapping sound.

It was either you or me at that point,
and I'm ashamed to say I chose myself.

You died with a hell of a bang.

R.I.P.

CHAPTER 1

EDEN

SURVIVAL TIP #136
*Loneliness won't kill you.
Violent men with guns? They might.*

L ucky. Jaykob. Lucky. Jaykob.
"Move it!" Sweat oozes into Sam's silver brows as he glares at me.

He yanks the rope chaining my waist and bloody wrists, and I stumble hard. I manage to keep on my feet, but my legs quiver under me, hot and gelatinous. Both of us stink, reeking of sour, anxious sweat and days-old soot.

Twigs scratch my hair and face as I stagger on, but I'm far too tired to avoid them. Yesterday, finally, my lower half slipped into a sweet, shaky numbness. I know the burst blisters on my heels and toes are rubbing bloody against my shoes and that muscle spasms must be arcing through my calves, but, blessedly, I feel none of it.

I hope my wrists go next. They're raw and swollen and fever-ish, my fingers stiff and blue-tinged. If I try to flex them, my arms throb and fresh blood seeps around the coarse rope, picking up shards of dried blood crystals. At least the pain distracts me from my thoughts.

Lucky. Jaykob. Lucky. Jaykob.

The first two days, while adrenaline still ran high, I tortured myself with my memories. Jaykob's barn engulfed in flame. Lucky's body jerking as he was peppered with bullets. Beau disappearing into the woods. Jasper trapped behind the truck. Dom's fear. A kaleidoscope of emotional lashes.

My mind is too foggy and vacant to bring them into focus anymore, but it doesn't matter. The names are enough to cut.

Lucky and Jaykob are dead.

Dead to me. Dead to the world. Dead and gone.

Dead, dead, dead.

The new word joins their names, circling my mind in a lurid carousel.

Lucky. Jaykob. Dead. Lucky. Jaykob. Dead.

I wonder about the others too, of course. But no matter how I turn through the details, not a single one gives me hope. I'm not prone to optimism, and the way I see it, there are only two options —either Dom, Beau, and Jasper are unable to come after me . . . or they're unwilling. It has been four days, after all. If a rescue were in the cards, it would have happened by now.

I'm not even sure they *would* come for me. I wasn't with them for long, after all. For all that my silly, inexperienced heart was growing dizzy and drunk with their touches and attention, I have no idea where I stand with them. Not really. And they've lost so much already—*Lucky. Jaykob. Dead*—I can understand them not wanting to take any more risks.

And that's if they survived.

I'm not ready to add their names to my carousel just yet, but, in any case, I can't count on a sexy trio of soldiers saving me a second time.

This time, I'm on my own.

At least, like my feet, my heart has grown numb. There's no

lump in my throat. No tears chill my cheeks in the bitter air. I'm not even afraid, though the possibilities of what Sam has planned for me *should* be enough to make me sick.

I've wondered before how much I could take. When it would all become too much. Too heavy, too lonely, too sad. I wonder now if that's what's happened—if my mind has fled from a body finally too battered and overworked to house it safely. Or maybe it's just that my poor heart was torn from my chest, bloody and still beating, when I saw the end of Bristlebrook, and I just didn't realize it at the time. Maybe this is just what living with an open wound is like, and all my pain and grief and fear are just spilling out of this hole in my chest and that's why I can't *feel* anything.

A hand cracks hot and hard across my cheek, the force of it whipping my head to the side. I catch myself on a tree, gagging. Something thick and metallic pools between my teeth, and when I brush my hand over my mouth, it comes away red.

Okay.

I felt *that*.

Sam grabs my shoulders, yanking me off the tree, and shakes me.

"What is *wrong* with you? I will kill you. Do you understand that?" He unholsters his gun and shoves the barrel under my chin. I force myself to focus on him. Sweat makes tracks in the dirt on his tanned face. "You stop again, and I'll shoot you in your stupid face."

I blink. Then blink again as the cold metal begins to register, almost seeping through my numbness. My sluggish pulse stutters.

I . . . don't . . . want to be shot.

Biting down on my cracked lower lip, I lick at the salty blood on my teeth and nod. It's wobbly, and it forces the gun into my neck, but it seems to appease him. Before he takes it upon himself to yank me again, I make myself lurch forward, and faster this time.

He pushes ahead of me with a grunt.

I want to live.

The thought presses against my numbness, testing its edges. It's too soon. I'm not ready to feel it all. Not yet, but . . .

I *need* to live.

It would be easier to give up—so much easier. It would hurt less, certainly. But survival is in my nature. I'm not sure I could stop clawing for life even if I were the last person clinging to this godforsaken planet. My life is just a checklist of awful people and places and positions I needed to push through.

I am prepared to do anything to live, to thrive. I *survived*.

And I will now too.

I stare at Sam's wide, brawny back, a spark of something hot catching fire inside me.

Sam is a thug—a brainless, cowardly bully. If I want to live, to give myself any chance at all, then I need to think. It's the only edge I have. The *one thing* that has kept me alive this long.

I need to outwit a dullard.

Sam hacks a glob of spit into the greenery, and I let the thought fester.

God, the dull vacancy behind his eyes offends me. It *infuriates* me. This? *Him?*

How did *he* cause this much carnage? This petty, unremarkable imbecile who spent twenty minutes clearing out his ears with his little finger. How is *he* the one who has me trapped and trussed? How is *he* the reason that Lucky and Jaykob—

No. *No.* They can't help me now. Not ever again. I need to save myself.

Whatever it takes.

"STOP."

At first, I don't hear him. I'm too lost in my useless schemes, testing the flex in my purple fingers, wondering how I can run away when I can't feel my legs. Two days later and, despite my new resolve, my body is worse than ever. At least I've managed to stop the carousel in my head. All thoughts of Bristlebrook—of *them*—are banished. The only way I've been able to keep them out is by trying to plot a way out of this nightmare.

Barring some kind of godly act of benevolence, I haven't found one yet.

Sam's meaty hand grabs the back of my head and shoves me down by my hair so I collapse in a heap. My shocked cry is muffled by another hand slapped over my mouth. Panic spikes, and I struggle, but he has me firmly in his grip. He must be tired too, but the difference in our strength is overwhelming.

"Stop," he growls again in my ear, low and barely audible.

Leaves crunch nearby, and I do stop then, instinct holding me taut and still as a hunted rabbit. The thought that maybe it's Dom, or Beau, or Jasper coming to get me flickers, but then is snuffed. Even untrained Jasper wouldn't make that much noise. And judging by Sam's reaction, whoever it is, it's no one he knows.

Should I struggle? Make enough noise for them to discover us here? I'm not sure if a change of captors would help me. Sam has been cruel, and I fear his plans, but he hasn't tried to touch me. Not yet. Can I trust the kindness of strangers? The only time that has ever worked out for me was with my Bristlebrook men.

Swallowing hard against thoughts of them, I focus on the new men as they push through the trees. This is the problem I need to focus on. Maybe *this* I can do something about.

The three men are armed and talking to one another in low, serious voices I can't quite make out. Sam reaches for his gun. I'm not sure how much ammo he has left, but it doesn't matter. He can't take on three, and I really hope he won't try.

Sam's hand tightens in warning on my mouth, and I nod, just slightly. I have a better chance at getting away from one exhausted, injured man than I do three healthy ones. Not that the odds in either situation are exactly in my favor.

As they pass by us, I catch snippets.

"... need to get it soon ..."

"... can't get in there ..."

"... don't care. I'll kill ..."

At the last, I shiver. No. I won't be begging them for mercy any time soon.

The three men disappear between branches, and we wait, poised and ready, for several minutes before Sam relaxes. When he stands, he shoves down on the back of my head to help himself up. It makes my whole middle section cramp, but I bite down to hide a sob.

"Get up."

I try to move, I do, but my legs just ... won't. They're puddles, and no matter how I will them to return to flesh and bone, I can't make them support me. I'm already cringing when Sam hauls me up by the rope at my wrists, and there's no way I can hide the screech that leaves me then. My hands feel like ripe cysts, hot and pus-filled and swollen to bursting.

"Get *up!*" he snaps again, dangling me by my hands.

Black dots pepper my vision, and my feet scramble uselessly under me, my knees too liquid to lock into place. I whimper, ready for him to hit me again. This isn't part of my plan. I'm meant to keep it together until I can find an opportunity to escape, but my body won't obey.

Then I'm wrenched backwards against a man's hard chest. His bitter sweat mixes with mine, and he holds me up, bringing his other arm around rapidly to catch Sam's gun before he can fire.

"*Mierda*! Stop, asshole. It's me."

I spot the coiled snake tattoo on the hand wrapped around my middle. He's one of them. A hunter. My stomach sinks.

"Mateo?" Sam pulls back, dropping his weapon. "Are you stupid? Why did you grab her? I almost shot you."

Mateo snorts. "You'll have to be quicker than that." His low, accented voice takes on an edge. "You're lucky I didn't shoot *you.*

Alastair told you after last time, he doesn't like it when you hurt the *chicas*."

Sam shoves his gun in its holster with too much force. He's a grown man, with a shock of white hair, a sharply cut salt-and-pepper beard, and lines at the corners of his eyes, but the way his lip juts out is almost a pout. "Alastair can back off. He does what *I* say."

"Whatever you say," Mateo replies, sounding amused. He lowers his hands to my hips to steady me, and I stiffen. "Hey hey, I won't hurt you. Can you stand?"

I test my feet and find I can, so I push away from him, turning so I can keep them both in view. Mateo has a gentle, angelic face, all soft curves and rich brown skin. But I don't trust it. The way he stands, the lazy tension in it, reminds me of my brutes—it speaks of training, and confidence.

That makes him dangerous.

He laughs under his breath as I eye him. "You're a smart one, pretty lady. You're a smart one."

Quicker than I blink, he whips out a knife. I can't help my flinch, but I set my shoulders and try to stay calm. He just stopped Sam from hurting me—whoever this Alastair is, Mateo seems to be following his orders. Orders that apparently include not hurting women. Making a quick, nervous decision, I lift my chin and hold up my wrists, meeting his eyes.

Mateo smiles and, just as quick as he pulled out the knife, he slices through the rope at the join between my hands. He doesn't even nick the skin.

"What the fuck are you doing?" Sam explodes, but I barely hear him. Blood rushes back into my palms, my fingers, it oozes from my wrists, and I sob through gritted teeth, squeezing my eyes closed as I wait for the worst of the shock of pain to ease. Breathing hard through my nose, I slowly bring myself under control.

Sam shoves himself into Mateo's face. He's taller, older, and heavy-set, and Mateo looks almost cherubic beside him, except for the irritated wrinkle in his forehead and that lazy preparedness.

"Get out of my face. Tying her hands won't stop her running away, you know? Unless you're afraid she's going to attack you? Bitty thing like her and all banged up? I think she could take you!" Mateo mock gasps, pressing a hand to his chest. Then he rolls his eyes. "You want her to walk, she'll walk. She doesn't need to bleed to do that, does she?"

I glance at the trees behind me but abandon the idea of making a run for it before it fully forms. I'm in no state to even try. Mateo catches the glance and how I stay put and smirks again. I lean surreptitiously against a tree and take a moment to collect myself, working my fingers as gently as I can to try and get some movement into them.

Sam spares a glare for me, then another for Mateo, but he edges back and crosses his arms as he sneers. "If I want her tied, then I'll tie her. Don't forget, Mateo, I can have my boys kick you and your boyfriend out of base camp before you can grab your green card."

"Ay. Homophobia *and* racism, no wonder you were voted president." Mateo steps into Sam's space again, and I'm not finding him so cherubic anymore. "Come back to the group with me, *presidente*. I wonder if you're still so popular after you got half of *your boys* killed."

A muscle flexes in Sam's tanned, gray-flecked jaw, and I see his Adam's apple work. I'm sluggish following the exchange, but I do see his uncertainty. It makes a nice change from his usual brash, blind rage. Sam's not sure of his men. I file that detail away; I'll think on it more when I remember *how* to think. If I can just get some sleep—lying down, not chained against a tree—maybe my brain will restart.

Awareness prickles at the back of my neck, and I glance around at the trees. Nothing moves, even as the feeling of being watched grows.

"What are you doing anyway? Why aren't you back at base?" Sam asks irritably, changing the subject with zero subtlety.

Mateo's brows draw down. "We couldn't travel that far. We're still by the lake. I just had to make sure those assholes didn't stumble over us." He lifts his chin in the direction of the three men who passed us.

Sam grunts. "They're from Red Zone. I've seen the tall one before."

"Well, they're crawling all around here looking for something." Mateo shrugs one shoulder, then lifts a brow significantly. "We'd rather *not* be found, hmm?"

Sam rubs a hand over his beard, then he smiles. It looks cramped and unnatural on his dirty, weathered face. "Lead the way then."

Mateo makes a short bow that makes Sam turn a hellish shade of red, then indicates for us to follow.

Chapter 2

Eden

Survival tip #66
*If you're trapped between two predators,
don't worry about taking sides.
You're probably dead anyway.*

When the sounds and smells of a makeshift camp finally reach me hours later, I almost collapse in dizzy relief, despite my growing dread. A camp means they're not moving, not immediately, and I *need* to rest. I crave it with a vicious hunger.

The day is fading into twilight, and the last filtered rays of sun burnish the group of men in a cozy gold. There are about a dozen of them scattered through the area, and I feel an abrupt wave of recognition. This is the spot I saw on Jasper's screens in his secret lair. I'm fairly sure, anyway. I'd been too preoccupied to examine them for more than a brief moment at the time.

The camp is curiously divided, with seven or so men set up by the trees and the remaining five opposite them, at the base of a towering cliff. I'm looking between them when I spot a pretty woman with coal black hair sitting on a blond man's lap. She's in the larger group by the trees, and even though I know it's terribly rude and I have far bigger concerns, I can't stop staring. It has been *so long* since I've seen another woman that I almost put us in the same category as Javan rhinos and mountain gorillas—bordering on extinction.

It's absurd, of course. I knew women were around somewhere, raiding tampons and bras and diapers, but *seeing* one? The kinship I feel is as sudden as it is surprising.

I'm not the last of a dead race.

As we step from the forest, tired heads turn and about half of the men reach for their guns. They take us in and several shove to their feet.

"Keep moving, *chica*," Mateo urges.

Sam grabs my arm, and I grimace, but he's looking at the group. Groups? "Why is no one on watch? We could have been anyone."

Mateo hesitates, looking at me in Sam's grip, then glances at the men in the camp. Their expressions are disturbingly dark. Mateo gives me an apologetic half-smile, then shrugs and walks over to the group by the trees.

"You've got a lot of nerve to show up here, Sam," the blond man says as he gestures for the woman in his lap to get off him. When she does, he stands so he faces Sam and me. He has a vicious bruise running up his neck and small cuts pepper his face and arms.

Sam stiffens. "Watch your tone, boy."

Two others shoulder in beside the blond man, hands on their weapons. Hot adrenaline begins to fire in my veins.

Sam's grip on me tightens. "You're lucky I'm alive! You left me for dead."

"If only," Mateo grumbles loud enough that his voice carries, and there's a rumble of laughter from the larger group by the trees.

A tall, narrow-featured man from the other group by the cliff spits into the dirt. "Sam's the only reason any of you made it in the first place. Show some respect." He tongues his lower lip and looks me over. "He even found us a friend."

"Is that the same bitch we were chasing?" someone asks behind him, elbowing a tattooed man sitting on a log, who squints at me. "Fuck me, it is too."

A cold weight slams into the bottom of my stomach. Sam confiscated my bloody little knife and bag of weapons when he captured me. I don't even have that to protect myself.

Though, given that I can't feel my fingers, I doubt it would have made a difference.

"What a waste of goddamned time," the blond man growls at the other group, not sparing me a glance. "Maybe if you'd spent less time chasing after her and more time scouting that stupid lodge, you wouldn't have killed us all!"

"How were we supposed to know they had bombs?" the narrow-featured man replies, bored, as if they've gone over this before.

Sam takes a breath beside me, glancing between the groups. He works up a rough smile. "We've had a setback, it's true. But the Sinners were born from the mistakes of our past—we can learn from this. We're forged by our trials."

The blond man unholsters his weapon. "It was meant to be bloodless, you stupid son of a bitch."

The cliff group leaps up, grabbing their guns from where they lay discarded around them. Then the men by the trees surge to their feet, crowding around the blond man. I feel a cold sweat gather along my hairline, under my arms. This is bad. I'm about to be in the middle of a gunfight, and I have no way to magically un-injure my body.

I wish Beau were here. He might not be magic, but he's the closest thing I've found.

Sam shuffles back as the men start shoving at one another, dragging me along with him, but the blond man breaks free and strides toward us, gun pointed.

Yanking me in front of him, Sam yells, "Back *down*, Logan. You need me! You all need me!"

My heart hammers against my ribcage like it wants to scurry to safety. I twist against Sam's grip, needing to escape, even though I know it's pointless. It's too late now. I'm caught.

I'm dead.

Logan barks a laugh. "You think I won't shoot through your new piece of ass? I should do it on principle after you got Ryder and Benji killed. Jonas, Carolos, Luke, Jamie, Lee, Slater. How many more names do you want?"

Cold metal bites at my forehead, and I freeze. My lids flutter closed.

In the new darkness, I see Beau's lingering smile after he kissed me. Dom's slow, shocked pride when I delivered the weapons. Jasper's dark beauty as I curled up at his feet. Jaykob's smirk as he fucked me. Lucky's laughter as we fled Dom's room with a bazooka.

I wonder if I'll get to see them again when I go—if there is an afterlife, after all. I wonder if they'll all be there, or if it will be just Lucky and Jaykob for a while. I hope so. I hope the others are alive, at least, and that they'll find some happiness together.

I wonder if this will hurt.

Taking a deep breath, I wait for the burst that will end my life.

"Enough, Logan." The thin, reedy voice comes from the trees. For the silence that falls around the camp, it might as well have been a crash of thunder.

I crack my lids, a tangle of tension wrapping around me. Logan is breathing hard, the muscles in his unshaven jaw tense. "Alastair—"

"Enough," the voice repeats, even weaker than before. "He's right. We need him."

Logan's fist is white around his gun, and the metal presses hard into my skin. Then he shoves it down and steps back, glowering at the man behind me.

I still feel the imprint between my eyes.

The groups have parted now, the brewing storm between them paused but still grumbling with threat. I follow their gazes to a man propped in a sitting position against a thick tree not too far from us. Mateo hovers over him with a grim knit to his brows.

The man is shirtless, and soggy, bloodied bandages crisscross the tattooed landscape of predatory animals and poisonous plants on his torso. He has deep brown hair and incongruously light eyes, and his right brow is struck through with a deep, old scar. He's so sickly pale, so wrapped in those ominous bandages.

Is he going to die in front of me?

Mateo bends down beside him and holds a cup to his lips, gentle and patient. Alastair takes a slow sip, and the hunters hold a bated breath, waiting for him to speak.

"We're all friends here," Alastair continues, hardly above a whisper. He doesn't move his head, but his intense eyes press upon the men and, one by one, they look away. Alastair's gaze settles on Sam. "Right, Sam?"

"Right," Sam agrees quickly. "Friends."

I stare at Sam, then examine Alastair again, a new nervousness growing. Sam was one type of threat.

Who is Alastair to command that much respect?

Logan's mouth twists to the side, and I don't like the way his finger absently caresses the hilt of his gun. My forehead throbs in response. Sam is steering me over to the camp by the cliff when I see Mateo stand, frowning.

"Why don't you share, *presidente*? You have so many women already," he calls.

By the time Sam pauses to look at him, Mateo's frown has been replaced by an innocent smile. With his angelic face, he looks like he should be asking for extra lunch money, not trading people like cattle.

Still, I would rather be with bonds-cutting don't-hurt-women

Mateo than Sam, even if Logan and his friends don't seem to share his sentiment.

"You have Akira, and besides"—Sam grabs my chin, examining my face while I refuse to look at him. His blunt fingers dig painfully into my cheeks. I keep my expression bland, even as my breathing quickens nervously—"I earned this one."

My stomach lurches. For the first time in days, I'm glad I've not had much to eat. I swallow hard around bitter bile.

"We had . . . an agreement." Alastair's wispy voice is faint, but resonant. Sam scowls. "Not while I'm around. It would hurt . . . our friendship."

Sam releases my face, pushing my chin away. "Yeah, yeah. We'll head back to the Den tomorrow, then you won't need to get your panties in a twist. We'll make sure she finds a real special job back home."

Alastair gives him a long look, then nods.

My pathetic flare of hope snuffs out. This man isn't going out of his way for me. Why should he?

Mateo's mouth pinches in worry as he looks at Alastair. He's right to be anxious—Alastair looks three days dead already. Mateo drags over a bag and peels back his friend's dressing, checking his wounds, and Alastair's eyes drift shut. It takes a moment, but his chest begins to rise and deflate in a fitful rhythm.

I work my jaw, suppressing a shudder. *Escape, escape, escape.* The word beats a drum against my skull.

"We're not going anywhere tomorrow," Mateo insists, shaking his head. He gently puts the bandage back in place. "We made litters to carry Alastair and Jorge this far, but they can't take any more. And Sayid's leg isn't looking so hot either. We're staying, *presidente.*"

Sam's voice turns coldly condescending. "All the more reason to get back to the Den where there is *medicine* and *doctors.*"

That makes me blink, then I smooth my features again. They have doctors? Plural? How big is this "den" of theirs? I've been assuming, since they targeted Bristlebrook, that they only have a small, unsecured base. But the way they're talking sends my thoughts spinning.

Or maybe it's just dehydration.

Logan leans against the tree beside Mateo and Alastair, casual as can be, but he spins his gun like he's stepped out of a Western. "If we move Alastair or Jorge, they'll die. If they die, then I don't think me and the men will be feeling so *friendly* anymore."

"If we stay here, then those dickheads from the lodge are going to find us with our asses hanging out," Sam bites out.

Mateo barks a laugh. "The Rangers? *Dios, presidente!* You don't know anything, do you?"

"You weren't there? Is that why you were so far behind us?" Logan pushes off the tree, brows lifting incredulously.

A hint of uncertainty touches Sam's features as he looks between them, apparently as confused as I am.

Logan shoots a look at Sam that promises bloodshed. "You weren't even *there*, you motherfucker? Let me guess, you were off keeping your own ass safe, as usual. God, you're even more of a piece of shit than I thought."

"Watch it," someone hisses from behind me. I glance back to see the creepy narrow-featured man crouching over something by the cliff, his attention on Logan and the others.

"Seriously? You're defending him? Jorge lost an arm in that explosion. Alastair is so full of shrapnel, he's probably going septic. Benji, Ryder and the others, all dead because of him!" Logan rages, and I see the woman step in beside him, reaching for his shoulder. He shakes her off. "Those bastards from the lodge aren't going to come after us, Sam. They blew the whole place up, themselves inside it, and took most of us out with them. They're dead too. The only reason any of us survived was that *we* hadn't cleared the trees yet. It was *luck*."

His words crack my mind with the force of an anvil. They shiver down my spine and make my knees tremble.

I misheard that. I must have. Or he's wrong. It doesn't make sense, after all, what he's saying. It's absurd.

But even as my dizzy thoughts churn, every stubborn piece of bravery and thin thread of hope turns frail.

Logan rubs his chest.

"And what was the point? There wasn't a damn woman or child in sight except for *her*. It was no easy target. And if there were supplies, we sure as hell aren't getting them now." His voice turns hoarse. "Fuck 'rebuilding society.' Fuck making a new home. Fuck the supplies. I want my friends back."

A low susurration vibrates through the men, like a discontented hive. The woman, Akira, sucks uneasily on her lower lip as she watches Logan. She's in love with him. It's in the soft knit of her brows, the hurt I see in her as she sees him hurting.

Have I ever looked like that? I was getting close, I think.

I guess I'll never know.

They blew the whole place up, themselves inside it.

Little spiderwebbed cracks fan across my fragile heart.

Mateo stands and grips Logan's arm, but his face is dark as he looks at Sam. "We're staying here until we are *all* strong enough to travel, and if any more of our friends die because of you and your vision, *cabrón*? Then you will pay for their blood with your own."

Sam is breathing hard, but I hardly notice. It's half as hard as I'm breathing. No matter how I suck in air, I can't seem to get any oxygen. Dizziness blurs my vision.

Themselves inside it.

The words don't fit inside me. They're too big, too full of implication.

"Fine." Sam clears his throat, then says more firmly, "We stay. Of course we'll stay. We want a full recovery for Alastair and Jorge."

They're dead.

Sam pushes me again toward the narrow-featured man, but I

pull back hard, shaking my head frantically. Maybe I can shake those words out of my memory.

"He wouldn't have done that," I blurt, panicked, spinning back to Mateo and Logan. I catch a few surprised, evaluating looks around me but focus on those two, on their faces. I need to see the lie there. "Dom *wouldn't* have— He was going to save them. Save all of us. He wouldn't *do* that. He—"

The grim look in Mateo's eyes cuts me off. It taps against those taut, brittle feelings inside me, and my breath catches. I open my mouth, maybe to say something—maybe to scream?—but nothing comes out. Everything strangles in my throat.

"There was no surviving. He blew the barn, and the lodge was destroyed. I saw it." He looks down at Alastair, and there's an ache in his voice as he adds, "Your man did the most damage he could on his way out."

It's only when my knees hit damp earth that I realize my legs have gone from under me, but I'm done fighting it.

They're *all* dead.

Every brittle, suppressed feeling I have erupts, splintering into a thousand shards that rupture my organs. I let my body go limp, and I crumple, curling up like a dying bug in the dirt. A low, raw keening hits my ears. It's soft, barely audible, but it whines out of my throat with grating force. My nails dig into my forehead, then into my hair, as if I can dig my grief out by the roots.

Lucky. Jaykob. Dom. Jasper. Beau.

Dead.

My keening breaks into a long, pained moan. Tears fog my eyes and then there's a boot crunching into my ribs. I wail, but reach out to the boot, wanting another one, wanting all the pain, because anything they can deliver is better than this *grief*. I've lost people before. I've never stopped losing people.

Why did it never feel like this?

Someone grips me by my hair and slaps me hard across the face. It stuns me, making me gasp. I can taste salt and snot on my lips. I laugh, and through blurry tears, I see the narrow-featured man. He slaps me again, harder, and then again as I laugh and laugh and cry, every part of me shattering.

"Crazy bitch," he mutters, but he sounds hungry, like he likes it.

I spit blood onto the ground. It might be the first time I've spat since I was four.

But who the fuck cares now?

He yanks me back, dragging me by my hair to the bank. It hurts. It's *excruciating*, and I scream, twisting. It's freeing, to let loose like that, and every part of my body screams with me. It reminds me of shattering plates and yelling at Beau, of how good that branding anger felt to be unchained.

I should have kissed him then. Kissed all of them. A thousand times, or maybe a million. It was only such a short time, but I could have kissed them more.

The narrow-featured man flips me onto my front in the dirt, then kicks me again as I cry out. He's cursing me—to be quiet, I think.

A blurry face stares back at me, pressed into the earth beside me. She's gagged, her red hair coated in filth; she gives me a fierce frown, and her eyes are full of messages I don't care to understand right now.

I press mine closed and tears squeeze between my lids as I cry, letting him hurt me. I don't care about that. I don't care about her or about any of this.

Suddenly, in the dirt, I feel thin, strong fingers clutch mine, then cling hard. It anchors me, just a little, but it's like trying to stop a sea tide with a life raft. It's hardly enough to keep me afloat.

But I don't let go.

"God damn it, Owen," Sam swears from somewhere close, his voice lowered. "Those assholes were meant to be overstretched. Where was everyone? I promised the men."

The man stops kicking me, then mutters something back to Sam.

"Fuck!" Sam swears.

I hear a muffled grunt and dully open my eyes to see him flipping the other woman onto her back. He kicks her in the side of the head, and it whips her chin around so she's staring back at me again. Blood bursts from her nose, and tears stream out the corners of her eyes, but she doesn't scream, not like me. Her head is whipped to the side until she's glaring into my eyes as Sam kicks her.

Her rage is glorious. As pretty as the pain that's shredding me.

"Fucking *bitch*," Sam shouts as he unleashes his wrath.

"God *damn* it," Owen mutters, and I feel another boot in my ribs. Then another and another. "Shut up. Shut *up*!"

But I can't. Won't. My body isn't mine right now, and I don't care what happens to it.

Let it hurt.

The woman is still staring at me, our fingers clinging together while our bodies are torn apart. She's telling me things with her eyes again, trying to keep me here.

I close my eyes, needing to shut her out, and her grip tightens painfully.

There's nothing I can do for her. Or for myself, for that matter.

My brutes are dead.

The rest of the world can burn.

Chapter 3

Jasper

How in the fuck did you lose the trail?"

My eyes sink shut, even as fear claws at my throat. Fear and fury.

But I have to work to contain my ire—if Jaykob catches sight of it, he'll undoubtedly assume it's directed at him. This time, as it happens, I'm in agreement with him. Eden has been missing for five days, but it took us two days to find her trail and leave Bristlebrook. We're behind, and we can't afford any more delays.

Too much can happen in five days.

Panic trembles through me at the thought. She's a brave, determined thing, but she's only one person. Untrained. Alone.

We've taken too long.

"Not helping, Jayk." Dominic stands from where he was examining the ground and pulls out his compass . . . but lines of tension bracket his mouth as he adjusts our direction, and I see the mountainous guilt on his shoulders. "We continue south. They've been heading directly toward Cyanide City—we just have to hope that's their goal. We might be able to pick the trail back up when we're closer."

Even frustrated as I am, it is fascinating—and somewhat alarming—to see how quickly Dominic internalizes Jaykob's criticism. I thought we'd worked through much of his fear of failing his charges, but it seems losing Eden has brought his demons to the surface.

It has certainly done so for me.

Jaykob barks a sarcastic laugh. "Great, let me know when you're ready to pull a crystal ball out of your ass. We can start scrying for her next."

I press a finger to my forehead as I fight for control. It feels frayed.

I feel frayed.

Jayk has been in an obscene mood since we discovered Eden missing. I can't blame him—though I'm doubtful he would be so fraught were any of us missing in Eden's stead. It's curious how quickly she became part of our little family.

And how quickly we lost her.

As if sensing my eyes on him, Dom gives me an impatient look.

"He's wrong, you know," I say quietly. "None of this is your fault."

The captain's return smile is bitter. "If he was wrong, Eden would be safe at Bristlebrook."

I stay quiet as Dominic scrubs a hand over his face, then squeezes the bridge of his nose. He's tired. We all are.

In the hopes of making up for lost time, we haven't stopped for more than one-hour power naps since we finally left Bristlebrook. For us not to have caught up to them by now—even with the head start they had on us—Eden and her captor can't have been stopping for very long either.

Unfortunately, I'm learning that tracking isn't an exact science

—it's hard to know how far behind we are. Each time we've found evidence that they've paused to rest, we've been too late. At least, from the size and number of the occasional footprints Dominic has scouted, we're certain Eden is alive and with only one hunter.

For now, she is.

Which makes it all the more frustrating to lose her trail. If we catch up with them after they reach Cyanide, and presumably their base, we will have more hunters to deal with. And that's *if* that's where they're heading, and *if* we can find our way there, and *if* we can find them in an enormous city when we arrive. Without the trail to follow, we introduce an array of variables.

Still, I refrain from voicing my concerns. I'm the least skilled in these matters; Jaykob and Dominic are well aware of the implications.

Darkly, I wonder if a crystal ball might not be a decent idea for tracking her after all.

"Perhaps we should rest," I venture reluctantly, noting the tired rings around their eyes, the dirt and sweat smudging their faces. Mine is no better, I'm sure.

Exhaustion is the enemy of progress. My lessons in that regard are fresh and painful; if I hadn't driven myself into the ground by arrogantly taking on too much of the surveillance work in my pathetic attempts to avoid Lucien, we might have caught the looped videos sooner. We might not be in this mess at all.

Eden might have been safe.

"Fuck. That." Jaykob shoulders past me, heading fast in the direction Dominic clocked as south.

Dominic and I exchange glances, then he shakes his head, a grim set to his shoulders. "Can you keep up?"

Humiliation bleeds through me, scalding hot.

"I'm managing," I reply stiffly, though I'm not sure it's the truth.

Dominic shakes his head. "You're slowing us down, Jasper, and we need to go faster. Can you do it? If not, you need to turn back."

His blunt words hit me with the force of a dozen blows that I am too out of practice to avoid.

Faster.

My legs are trembling, and my back is one giant ache. I'm pushing the limits of my stamina. How can I possibly go any faster? I'm already feeling my age, and the embarrassing gap between my fitness and that of the two younger men. Even Lucien's Ranger kit doesn't quite fit me, no matter how I adjust it.

In my efforts to avoid Lucien, I've skipped too many sparring sessions, missed too many workouts.

I've made myself incompetent.

Guilt and terrible fear drag at my bones. They eat me alive, and suck at my marrow. I can't fail here. Not again.

On repeat, I replay the feel of Eden's scorching, single tear splashing onto my thigh. The way she withdrew back into herself at my gentle rejection. How that glorious, delicious submission bled into scarlet cheeks and too-bright eyes that wouldn't meet mine.

My refusal wasn't meant to hurt her—but I know it did. Just as I hurt Lucien.

In all my efforts to do good, I seem only to cause harm. Every time I try to play the hero, I become the villain.

Perhaps I was wrong to come out here.

I bow my head . . . only to see Lucien's pin fastened over my heart. His silly, bright non-regulation daffodil pin that catches the light obscenely. It always seems to wink at me right when my tiredness hits hardest. My fingers press against the pin, until I feel it cut into my flesh.

Something has to change. Perhaps *I* need to.

Lucien deserves better from me, and whatever my reservations about Eden and myself being ill-matched, there is a consuming, demanding need inside me to have her back and safely nestled by my feet.

In my bed.

In my arms.

Anywhere, as long as she's safe.

My tiredness doesn't matter. My pain doesn't matter. Only Eden. If it means bringing her home, then I will run myself to expiration.

I straighten, and nod once at Dom. "I will keep up."

His eyes tighten with grim hesitation, and I raise a quelling brow.

"I don't know what Eden is going through right now, but I think we can agree that it won't be pleasant," I say before he can argue further. "When we save her, she will need someone to talk to —someone to guide her through that."

I leave unsaid that Dominic and Jaykob, in particular, distinctly lack those specific skills.

Dominic's expression breaks. His eyes close and his jaw works as he fights to contain himself.

"We both have a job to do when we find her," I murmur thickly. "I'm coming. I will keep up."

The captain's shoulders lift in a heavy breath, and he nods. "You're coming."

Without another word, he turns and stalks after Jaykob.

Ignoring my shaking legs, I push until I'm striding directly after him. Eden needs me, and Lucien needs Eden. Losing her would break his beautiful heart in a way that might never be repaired.

That cannot happen.

Whether it be by tracking skills, Ranger planning, light witchery, or the darkest blood magic, one way or another, we will bring Eden home.

CHAPTER 4

BEAU

SURVIVAL TIP #201
Living with an open wound is dangerous.
Tend it carefully, lest you rip wide open.

I *'m bringing her home, Beau, or I'm not coming home."*
"Fuck!" Tearing my eyes away from the silent trees, I
snatch my fingers back from the window frame and scowl at the
nasty slice across the pad of my index finger.

Damn it, that's the second time in the last hour.

I should give up. After a week of work, I've finally boarded
most of the windows that were shattered during the battle for
Bristlebrook, but somehow, no matter how I try to keep my hands
useful with work, my eyes keep making their way back to the still
shadows of the woods—with those last words from Dom playing
on my mind.

Rescue or vengeance. That's his plan.

There's a very good chance that most all the people I care
about are going to die out there in those woods.

Those trees might be grave markers.

And there's not a damn thing I can do about it.

Whatever words Jasper left Lucky with can't have been any kinder than Dom's words to me. Ever since they left, he's had a solemn set to his mouth and a knit to his brows that's made me check a dozen times I had his meds right. But even if, by rights, Lucky should have been giggling showtunes on that kind of high, he's barely said one word.

Maybe there's nothing to say.

I just need them to come back to me.

Sighing, I abandon the final window and pick up the empty fifteen-gallon water container. We haven't had running water since the explosion messed up our water system, and making four trips a day to the cave river to cover our basic water needs is getting old fast. And to add to the joy that is my life right now, the last three days of working outside tells me that *apparently* doctoring pipes ain't as easy as stitching up bullet wounds.

After rinsing off in the river and filling up the canister, it takes me twenty minutes to haul the damn thing back to Bristlebrook, and I'm surly and sweating again by the time I get it inside. A quick look at the clock tells me I'm overdue to give Lucky his meds, and I make my way to the med bay . . . only to grit my teeth at the head I see pushing through the door.

"If you don't get back in bed right now, you weasel, I'm going to shoot you."

Lucky teeters and has to catch himself against the doorframe to his room, then flinches in pain. Concern spikes through my gut, but when I approach, Lucky shoots me a filthy glare.

And filthy is mighty literal at this point.

His long blond hair is a knotted mess, even in the mom-bun he forced it into yesterday. His once neatly trimmed beard is now scraggly—and apparently itchy, given he's scratching at it like he has fleas.

"I'm going to get her," he says, his jaw squared stubbornly.

"You're going to get knocked on your ass in a minute," I reply, rubbing my chest, but my heart's not in the threat. No, my heart is swollen painfully, pressing against my ribcage and oozing barely contained panic, just like it's been doing all week. If I thought for one second Lucky was strong enough to handle it, I'd strap him to my back and we'd be off in minutes to help the others get our girl safely home.

"Something's wrong, Beau, I know it." His eyes are bruises in his pale face. "We have to help."

My chest squeezes more liquid panic through my veins, my lungs. His fear ignites my own.

"It's only been a week," I start, and Lucky's mouth curls in disgust, but I steamroll over the arguments I can see coming. "One week since she was taken. They left five days ago. Even going as fast as they can, they have days' worth of ground to cover—and then they have to get back. Even if everything went well, even if they got her as soon as they caught up, they couldn't be home yet. We've . . ." I falter. "We've got to trust them, Lucky."

"How can you be so *calm*?" He has a white-knuckled grip on the doorframe. "Damn it, no. I'm going. You *will* have to shoot me to keep me here."

I scrub a hand over my unshaven face. I'm too tired for this, and I'm struggling hard enough to deal with my own shit without piling his on top of it.

I get it, I do. It's a thing with soldiers, common as anything— they try to push their recovery so they can get back in the field, struggling with all that misplaced guilt for not being out there and helping their team.

But usually? It just ends up with them injuring themselves, and I am not about to let him do that—and not just because Jasper would string me up by my ankles and peel off my toenails one by one.

Lucky steps forward on wobbly legs, his mouth compressing on a wince he tries to hide, and alarm shoots through me.

"Nope. That's enough!" I swoop in, scoop him up under his legs and, gently as I can, swing him bridal style into my arms and take him back to his bed. Briefly, painfully, it reminds me of the way I carried Eden when we first met her, and the soft, gorgeous armful that she was.

Lucky isn't soft—he's bony and awkward.

And I don't find him beautiful—even though he does have real pretty hair when it's clean.

But he's in pain, same as Eden was then. *Worse* than Eden was then. I might not have my subbie here, but I do have *a* sub, and he needs me right now.

Funny enough, thinking of him as a stubborn, hurting submissive rather than a belligerent patient actually does soothe some of my frustration.

Lucky bats at me as I set him down on the bed, but in the state he's in, Eden could do more damage.

He was shot three times. He took a glancing hit across his bicep and another, deeper laceration across the trapezius that bled more than I liked. It's the third wound that worries me, though, and it isn't even technically a bullet wound—shrapnel pierced his chest, right through the apex of his lung, causing a pneumothorax.

Dom's quick work with the occlusive dressing probably saved Lucky's life, but I'd still needed to perform a needle aspiration to re-inflate his lung. And even though the bullets miraculously hadn't hit his aorta or any blood vessels that would have ended his life instantly, he's in a bad way. He lost a lot of blood and infection can kill quickly. Even all going well, he's looking at weeks, if not months, of recovery.

"All going well" does *not* include trying to take his feeble self out of bed and tearing open his stitches.

Resisting the urge to chain him to the headboard to keep his disobedient ass where it should be, I adjust Lucky's pillows.

"Back in bed. And look," I say with forced levity as I straighten, "not one single bullet needed."

He looks away, scowling.

Taking in the room, I realize his empty plate is upturned on the floor, spilling crumbs everywhere, his pillows have been tossed halfway across the room, and a book is discarded on the floor at a spine-breaking angle that would have Jasper reaching for his sharpest vampire gloves.

I sigh. I forgot how Lucky turns surly as a new-branded bull when he's sick. I've been neglecting him while I tried to get Bristle-brook back up and running. No wonder he's upset. Working so hard is the only thing that's kept me from descending into a full-blown panic.

"I need water," Lucky says as soon as I finish cleaning up the mess he made.

I glance at the half-full jug of water on his bedside. "You *have* water."

"It has a *taste*."

A throbbing starts behind my eye. Pushing aside the urge to dump it on his head, I replace it with fresh water from the canister I dumped in the hall.

Lucky ignores me, but that unhappy knit to his brows hasn't left, making me soften a little.

Until he huffs a sigh. "Did you fix the pipes yet? I need a shower."

The throbbing behind my eye intensifies. "I *tried*," I explain, full of professional, doctorly patience. *I'm a healer. I'm a healer. I'm a healer.* "It ain't that easy, Lucky. I've got no idea how to fix pipes on a good day. Them being blown apart? Not a good day."

I might as well have shit in his soup and forced him to eat it by the wretched, disgusted look he gives me.

I rub a finger over my pounding temple. It's not like I've been doing anything else, like, I don't know, saving his life, taping up shattered windows, cleaning up debris, or feeding the animals. Small things, like disposing of the ceviched corpses that decorated our front lawn.

You know, *errands*.

I try to find my patience, the way my momma would want me to. This is just panic talking. Panic and helplessness.

"They're going to bring her home, Lucky," I tell him quietly, even as my veins seize with the fear that it's a lie. There were so many men. What would so many men do with a woman alone with no rules and no one to stop them?

My throat closes over, paralyzed, and Lucky's face shuts down again.

"Leave me alone, Beau."

"Lucky—"

"Get the fuck *out*!" he shouts.

I stare at him for a moment, then go, wishing I had any kind of hope to offer.

By the time our friends reach Eden, there's a good chance there'll be nothing of her left.

CHAPTER 5

EDEN

SURVIVAL TIP #13
Embrace your pain.
It's proof you're alive.

I wake to fire. A twisted, tattooed hand blackens, wood snaps, and a blazing barn collapses in over my head. I scream and scream until smoke smothers my lungs, charring their edges like burnt parchment.

Vicious pain cracks into my too-abused ribs, cutting off my cries, and I flop into the earth. Scratchy blades of grass tickle my nose, and fine, chilly dewdrops coat my cheek. The flames suddenly bank, and I suck in sweet, aching lungfuls of air.

For a dizzy moment, I think I see a slim, feminine face staring back at me from between the trees, but when I blink again, she's gone. She is gone and so is the barn and the flames and the smoke. I may be back in the woods, but it doesn't matter.

My nightmare is real, waking or asleep.

"Shut the fuck up," the narrow-faced man snaps. Owen, I remember. His name is Owen.

Despite his vicious kick, his heart doesn't seem in it, and he returns to his blankets.

As he tucks himself in, my lip curls in low, simmering resentment. I learned to hate this week. It's as though hearing the death knell for my brutes unshackled some inner demon I've always avoided and kept leashed.

These men are the reason my brutes are dead.

Dawn creeps slowly through the trees, sluggish and unhappy. I realize there's a small pile of food beside me—burned potato and carrots. Did Owen leave these here?

A kick and a carrot. How wonderful.

I don't think I could eat anything now if my life depended on it.

I don't get up. My wrists and ankles are tied, and it's far too much effort. Instead, I savor the new bruise on my side. I'm not numb anymore. Now, I exult in my pain. The hostile, erotic nuances of the syrupy heat in my wrists, the low throb in my ribs, the bright sting of my cuts.

My brutes are *dead*.

As a budding pain connoisseur, I have to appreciate the notes of *that* particular vintage. This agony is full-bodied. Rich. Its sharpness sits on the back of my palate, and bitter tannins make my tongue cramp.

This hurt has *legs* to it.

I sip it until I'm dizzy and drunk and nauseous. It curdles in my stomach, and still, I force it down my throat until I choke and splutter.

It's been two days, and reality has sunk in. They're all dead, and I'm alone. They're dead, and I am with the hunters I have learned to hate, and if I don't figure *something* out, soon my ropes will become a noose.

Because I'll die before I let them take me back to their Den to be used. A warm corpse for them to stick themselves into.

"Are we speaking today?" a voice drawls beside me. "I really hope you're a decent conversationalist, because I am bored as fuck and this is starting to feel a little dramatic."

Irritation pricks me, but I try to ignore her.

Madison, they called her. The redhead who held my hand as I broke. As we were beaten into the earth.

I haven't spoken to her once, though she's been by my side the last two days. My silence hasn't stopped her constant tirade of insults and encouragement and attempts at conversation. But despite my best efforts to keep to myself, I can't shake that strange, oddly intimate feeling of . . . kinship.

And *that* is hard to ignore.

I wonder if it is because she's a woman, or if that's just the kind of thing that is birthed out of people bleeding together.

I wonder if it's something like what my brutes felt after they did battle together.

If I'm accessorized with my injuries, Madison is dressed to the nines. One half of her face is swollen and black, her lip is split and free bleeds every time she berates me. She has bold features, and her hair is a sweaty inferno around her head.

"You're just going to lie there?" she muses flatly. "Again? Do you *need* to be this pathetic? It's embarrassing."

Maybe it is. But it makes no difference. Being brave hasn't gotten Madison very far. It just seems to piss the hunters off more.

Then again, maybe that *is* a plan. Maybe if I piss them off enough, they'll kill me before they manage to get me back to their base. Surely death would be better than what they have planned.

And yet, I'm not the woman I was when they chased me through the woods all those weeks ago, ready to end myself with my tiny knife.

These men don't deserve my life.

In fact, they owe me theirs.

Madison groans, shifting in her ropes, but it sounds more frustrated than pained. They tied her to the tree because she tried to run twice, even though Sam said she has a bad ankle and a broken nose. They don't seem to have any qualms about injuring us. Apparently, as long as we're alive, can walk well enough, and are still . . . useable . . . we're fair game.

Madison seems to be testing the limits of their patience.

Sam wants to take it further—he keeps trying to drag her away for a "chat" to "teach her some manners"—but Alastair's men keep wandering by at convenient times.

Not that the way *they* look at us is much better.

Despite the help he's given her, Alastair frightens me.

The burned man who speaks in whispers. The burned man who, even injured, watches us with a dark, unnerving intensity.

I'm not sure if Alastair is holding Sam and Owen back because he doesn't want us to be hurt, or if he just wants us the way any powerful man wants valuable contraband.

"It hurts, right?" Madison kicks my legs with her good foot, and it sends a delicious jolt of pain up my spine. I pant into the earth. "It *all* hurts. And I'm sor—"

Her voice cracks, and I close my eyes. When she starts again, her voice is steadier. "I'm sorry for all of it. You have no idea how much. But there's no changing it. We've all lost people we shouldn't have—and it is *terrible*. It is painful as *hell*. But you can't afford this right now." Her tone hardens. "Neither of us have time for grief. Or guilt. Those feelings are useless right now. Get over it."

I ignore her again. A part of me wishes they would gag her, just to shut her up. Doesn't she see there's no point to this defiance of hers? The dead are still dead, and we're both as fucked as each other.

I don't feel *guilty* for anything. Just . . . resigned.

She kicks me again, and this time I cry out.

"Stop *lying* there. Do something, you coward. Their deaths don't give you a license to check out. You might as well spit on their cold, dead corpses doing that." She pauses, then murmurs so softly I almost don't hear her, "You're living their lives now too."

That jab hits something soft and tender. My brutes were the most vibrantly alive people I've ever met. It's wrong that they're dead. It feels perverse. Against nature. Like some vital law of the universe has been circumvented.

But Madison is wrong.

I'm not giving up. There's just nothing I can do right now. Trying to escape, or fight back, in this kind of situation is futile—it will only end up getting me hurt worse.

And yet . . .

There is no way Dom would lie here like this. He would mock me too, for being this weak. He would push me on. The backs of my eyes sting, and I trace the hard, arrogant lines of his face in my mind.

Madison *is* wrong. But maybe she's also right, in a way. My memory of my protectors is the last thing of them left. Maybe I do have a duty to carry on the best of them, to take the lessons they gave me. To be as brave as Dom, as kind as Beau. To somehow find a way to be as joyful as Lucky or as clever as Jasper. To train myself to be as full of fight as Jaykob.

But how can I do *that* when I feel like *this*? It's like all color and light has leached from my soul and everything is now cast in uninspiring shades of ash and onyx.

Aching, I roll over. It strains my arms and presses my wrists into the grass under me, but I can see Madison now.

Pretty, sickening rage rises in me like a tide.

"I want to kill them," I whisper.

She startles, her brows shooting up. "So that's a yes on the decent conversationalist thing." Then she grins. It has cruel edges. "Murder is one of my favorite topics."

And despite myself, a surprised, bemused snort escapes me. It's a terribly rude sound, but my usual manners feel far away. My body is coursing with pain—and a simmering, violent anger. The feelings are foreign. Overwhelming. There's so much to them, so many layers, and I don't know where to put them.

I've never had to find a place for feelings like this before.

I shuffle, trying to work out how to sit. It's going to hurt. With my hands tied at the base of my spine, I press off the ground and crunch my stomach. The seeping red crust on my wrists tears open, but I manage to lift myself up.

I breathe hard through the pain, embracing it, and I fight through a dizzying haze as I pull myself into a more comfortable sitting position against a thick log beside her.

She snorts when she catches me taking in her restraints.

"I'm their problem child," Madison continues, a self-depre-cating tilt to her lips. "One escape attempt gets you busted ribs. Two gets you a broken nose and wrecked ankle. The rest get you various beatings, food deprivation, and these snug little tree attachments."

I stifle a sigh, shaking my head as I look around the camp. Most of the men are still in their blankets, but two putter around a large pot suspended over a burgeoning fire. My nightmare crackles behind my eyes.

God, I hope Jayk died quickly.

"What?" Madison prompts, and my gaze swings back to her.

"What?" I ask with a tired brow raise.

"What's with this?" She shakes her head with exaggerated seri-ousness.

"Oh." I close my eyes again and rest back against the log, shoving down my grief ruthlessly. "Your escape plans sound terrible."

She scoffs, wrenching against her ropes. "You've been here two days. I've been with them for three months. Either we escape before they take us to Cyanide, or we're both worse than dead. I'm not going back there."

"Three *months*?" I whisper.

The weight of it crashes in on me. Three months of beatings. Of pain. Of cold.

I haven't been thinking that far ahead.

I haven't been thinking *at all*.

The camp is waking, rustles and restless sounds rippling over the men as they peel from their slumber.

She nods. "They captured me and a few others, including Akira." Her voice lowers. "And my Tommy."

Something about that name sounds familiar, but I can't place it. The undercurrents of savagery and sadness when she says his name tell me what I need to know about Tommy's fate.

God, there's so much grief in this camp.

My eyes drift to Alastair and Mateo's group. Alastair has been slipping in and out of consciousness—it's hard to miss, because every time he passes out, Mateo loses it. I've watched his explosions of fear and fury with interest. That's what it looks like to be on the brink of *this*. He sees my grief coming for him, knows what his impending loss will mean, and it terrifies him.

Whether or not they're lovers, like Sam implied, Mateo loves Alastair hard.

I'm not sure whether I should care. Mateo did help me . . . but I can't forget that they were at Bristlebrook. Their hands are as bloody as the rest.

Akira wanders past Alastair and curls up on the lap of one of the hunters, planting a slow kiss on his lips. And, to my surprise, that interests me too.

"I thought she was with Logan," I remark.

Madison snorts. It's not a kind sound. "Some days she is. Whore."

I grimace, and my new demon snarls at the word.

More feelings start filtering in around my pain, squeezing through gaps I didn't realize were there. The anger flares, but also a hint of shame.

Whore.

What would Madison say if she knew about the arrangement I made with my brutes?

"Don't call her that," I say coolly.

Madison raises a brow, with the hint of a smile, then glares back at Akira. "Why shouldn't I call her that? It's what she is. Gets on her fucking back for the same men who killed Tommy and a half a dozen others of our group. I hope they cut her throat when they're done with her."

"She's surviving," I reply, though a winter chill is creeping into my tone.

"She's *enjoying* it."

Madison has a compelling face, bold and uncompromising, almost handsome rather than beautiful. But there's so much thrumming energy in her, even tied to a tree, that she's hard to face down. Especially while she's glaring like that.

But Jayk had a ferocious glare on him too, and I always did better with him when I fought back.

"Good for her if she can. We all do what we have to for survival. She's being smart," I snap. "Akira isn't hurt or tied up. She's eating well and seems happy enough. Her strategy seems to be working better than yours."

Better than lying here in the dirt, drowning in grief, waiting to be carted off to a terrible fate.

Not to mention, Akira gave me a packet of tampons that the hunters actually let me use. As if getting my period isn't just adding insult to injury at this point. She didn't have to do that.

Akira is not my enemy, no matter who she's sleeping with.

"How many are there?" I ask.

I feel her eyes burning the side of my face. "Sixteen. Sam and Owen have seven, and *he* has nine. Ten if you count Akira—but no one does."

He must be Alastair. In all her ranting, Madison has always refused to say his name.

Sixteen men. Sixteen men alive when my five are dead. Sixteen reasons why I'm alone in the world again, after finally, *finally* finding a home.

That tally is . . . unacceptable.

"Why?" Madison asks.

"I'm working out how many I need to kill," I whisper, and the words shiver through me. They taste like a promise.

An oath.

I don't know how many lives it will take to make up for my five.

But sixteen feels like a good start.

When I killed the man in the woods, I hadn't thought there was anything that could bring me to take another life. But maybe I'm more built for it than I thought.

The demon in me purrs at the thought—almost frightening in its intensity—and I turn to meet Madison's eyes. And I see it in her too. Only Madison's demon is bigger and angrier than mine. She's been feeding it her rage and grief for a long time, I think.

Through the horrible, beautiful pain and anger, a sliver of my suffocating loneliness shifts back. I'm not *completely* alone. Not like Madison must have been before my sorry self was dumped beside her.

Madison's glare burns hotter, darker, her mouth twisting. Then she breaks, laughing softly.

I stare at her in consternation.

Madison smirks through bloodied lips. "It's good to know you're not completely without a spine." She considers me. "What did you say your name was?"

"Eden. It's a pleasure to meet you," I say automatically, and she snorts a laugh at the ridiculous pleasantry.

"Eden, huh? You are in the *wrong* garden, my girl." When I shoot her an irritated look, she grins. There's dried blood caked between her teeth. "*Such a pleasure*, Eden."

A blush stings my cheeks at the gentle teasing, and she laughs softly before she grows serious. "Just don't do anything stupid, okay? Having women at their base is a draw for their recruiters. Sam pushes the whole happy family, new society bullshit wherever he can, but I can read between the lines enough to know the women get passed around as a reward for whoever's made Sam the most happy. His version of a new society means a real old one." Madison shakes her head and looks at me seriously. "And even with all that, he won't hesitate to kill you."

"Won't they?" I muse. My ropes are painfully tight—there's no way I'm getting free of those without help. "They haven't killed you yet."

That seems to pull her up short. She looks away, and there's a grim cast to her profile. "I had information they needed . . . and more they might make use of."

I nod and, not wanting to think about what they might have done to get that information, I go back to taking in the camp, forcing my fizzy thoughts to take note of where they're finally stirring for the day, who leaves, who lingers, the direction one of the cooks disappears to when he mutters about using a latrine. I see a fight break out between two men that Sam breaks up quickly. Mateo watches it, tense, a short distance away.

I can't go back to Cyanide City with these men. Madison is right.

We *need* to escape.

Despite me politely not pressing her, Madison grows more and more tense beside me, stealing small glances at me and then away.

I don't want to find this woman interesting. I want to focus on myself. That's more than enough of an issue right now. But it's been so long, and she's a *she*, and *she's* in the same position as *me* right now. And despite the way I want to harden myself for what's to come, despite my hungry hate . . . I've never been particularly hard.

She gives me another tense, darted look, and I sigh. "*What?*"

Madison whips back to look at the trees. "What?"

"What's with this?" I echo her earlier words and exaggerate looking back and forth, not meeting my eye.

She huffs impatiently, like *I'm* being unreasonable.

"Aren't you going to ask?" she mutters, and her fingers tap

nervously on her lap where her hands are pinned by rope. "Whether I gave them information? What I said?"

I study her for a moment, her battered face and tangled hair. She smells like she's already decaying.

She smells like me.

"Whatever you did, it's not really my business," I say. "You did what you needed to stay alive. You don't owe anyone an explanation for that."

Her gaze is a gray tempest, and she holds my eyes for a long moment, searching them. Then her expression cracks. She blinks fast, and I watch her lips roll in and her throat work. Once. Twice. It splits the fragile flesh back open, coating her lips like glossy lipstick. She turns away, pressing her tongue to the cut.

"You're a naive idiot," she whispers fiercely.

I purse my lips but stay quiet while she pulls herself back together.

"God damn it!" Logan yells abruptly, upending the large pot they've set up for cooking over the low fire. The pot was set up between the two opposing groups and there are two more similar setups nearby, though the other two are empty and cool, the coals under them dead.

I recall the feeling of his cold, unforgiving gunmetal against my forehead and anger spikes again.

A weedy man from Sam's group skitters back. "Logan, I didn't mean to—"

"You don't like what I make, John? *You* cook, I'm done!" Logan roars.

"I can't cook!" John splutters. "All I said is just use some, like, herbs or whatever sometimes. It's bland as fuck."

"About as much flavor as your personality then," Logan says, advancing on him.

"Enough!" Sam calls, shoving his blankets back and getting up. Nights are cold, so he's still fully dressed. He rubs a hand over his face. "Someone else can cook. Get Akira to do it."

But Akira is gone and so is the hunter she was with.

"I can cook."

At first, I hardly recognize the words as my own. It only registers when Madison's head whips around, and I hear her whisper, "The fuck are you doing?"

"I can cook," I repeat, louder this time, as the kernel of an idea starts growing in my brain.

The arguing stops and several heads turn my way.

Sam examines me. "Why?"

I duck my head submissively.

"I would prefer to help, and have a chance to move a little," I say, trying to bury my nerves. I'm not sure what the best angle is here. "I'm a decent cook. And I can help tend to people too if you untie my wrists. I'm good with herbs."

Of course, I don't have any on me. Well, none except . . . a hot thrill races up my spine, then spreads through my limbs. It's an effort to not let my sudden realization show on my face.

I have the water hemlock.

When Sam captured me, he took my knife, the weapons, he rifled through my backpack, but he didn't empty it, and neither did he empty my pockets, where I'd buried the deadly water hemlock that Beau almost poisoned our dinner with.

Beau.

I wonder if his mistake might get me out of this mess. If he's still protecting me, even in death. My throat clogs.

It isn't enough to kill all the hunters . . . but it *is* enough to do some serious damage.

For the first time since I was captured, I feel the first stirrings of a plan that might actually work.

For the first time since I learned my brutes were dead, I have the urge to try.

Mateo steps forward from where he was watching us.

"You say you know herbs?" he asks, low and urgent. He

gestures at Alastair on the other side of the camp. "Can you help him?"

Alastair is slumped at the base of a massive tree, pale and still as a corpse in all his bandages, except for the tattoos that peek from every exposed swathe of skin. From here, I can't see if he's conscious or not.

I wonder if Mateo or Alastair shot at Lucky.

"Or Jorge," Mateo adds, though it's almost an afterthought.

Jorge lost an arm, they said. I can hear him, even now, babbling insensibly from Alastair's side of camp, lost to fever dreams. I don't know that anything can be done for Jorge.

And what a terrible tragedy that is.

"What herbs do you have?" I ask politely.

"What do you need?" he counters.

At least a dozen reference books spring to mind. They're all probably moldy and insect ridden now, lost in my old cave.

I start with some basics. "Do you have honey?"

Mateo shakes his head, but one of the other hunters near Alastair says, "I have some. Just for Alastair though."

"Okay." I bite my lip, trying to remember my books. "What about cranberries?" That's a no. "Turmeric?" Also no.

"Amaranth?" I ask, losing hope when I see more head shakes. "Amaranthus is local to the area and grows in wet areas. It's possible you might find it by a river or creek. You couldn't miss it; it's bright pink. Juniper berries would also be very useful."

I could make a tea, or a salve, depending on what they can find. But then I spot Sam's face, and the deepening, unhappy lines.

"These are both also very good for cooking," I say carefully. More feelings overlap the wretched agony inside me—not hiding or muting it . . . but accenting it. Adding nuance and flavor. Right now, my pain is entangled with reckless abandon.

This feeling tastes like Lucky.

My pulse pounds in my throat. Taking a risk, I murmur, as mildly as I can, "If we're staying long enough to find them, that is."

Mateo says "We are" at the same time as Sam says "We're not."

That rumbling, tense thundercloud falls over them again. Madison surreptitiously elbows me in the ribs, and the pain makes my vision haze.

I hold my breath, wondering if I'm making a mistake. If these buttons are the wrong ones to push.

The two glare at each other, then Mateo calls over his shoulder. "Ellis, Jack, go look for the amaranth and juniper berries."

Sam scowls, but only says, "Three days, then we're gone." He points at me. "You cook and you help, but then you're back in your ropes. Watch her, Mateo."

"We'll see what happens in three days, *presidente*," Mateo says lazily, turning his back on the older man. "We'll see."

I can't believe it.

My plan might actually work.

CHAPTER 6

EDEN

SURVIVAL TIP #75
*Despite literature to the contrary, not all villains are sexy.
Even if they are fantastic orators.*

Scared, angry shouts fill the air.

I lie frozen and suddenly awake, still tied against the tree, curled into Madison like the midnight hour might shade us from their eyes. It won't, of course, and our bonds are too tight to escape.

"It's okay," she whispers into my hair. "It's going to be okay."

Liar.

"Bring the girl—she can help him," one of the men shouts.

"Help *what*? He's fucking dead!" someone shouts back.

Who is dead? Alastair? The burns were bad, but he'd started looking more alert this afternoon. Or is it Jorge—the man who lost his arm at Bristlebrook? He'd been unconscious and feverish all day.

The big fire in the middle of the camp is too bright to look at but does a terrible job of illuminating anything clearly. The Sinners are furious figures in the night, their shadows looming large and ghastly against the earth as they crash together.

"This is your fault."

"You fucked this up for all of us!"

"We should have stayed at the Den."

"Jorge is *dead*, you asshole!"

A gun goes off with a reckless roar, and I flinch into the tree. Madison tucks my head into her chest, stretching her bonds as far as they'll go to soothe me like I'm an infant.

Like the frightened, pathetic coward I am.

The herbs in my pocket seem miserable. Utterly useless. There's a cry of pain, more shouts, and the shadows twist and warp nightmarishly. I squeeze my eyes shut.

I know what's coming when this falls out, when the rest of the bodies fall silent and someone wins. When their blood is high and hungry on victory, they'll come for us.

And I won't be able to do anything to stop them.

I won't be able to fight them. I won't be able to escape. I don't even think I'll have the courage to try—it will only make them hurt me more.

A tear leaks down my cheek as another gun is fired.

I will lie down, I decide. I will open my legs and let them take what they want. If I let them, maybe they won't kill me.

God, I don't want to die.

Suddenly there's a deep, angry roar, and the deafening, peppering blasts of a machine gun. Men yell, diving for cover, and everyone hits the ground at once.

"*Enough*," Sam snarls. "That's enough. Like dealing with fucking children—we are *men*!"

The silence is thunderous.

Sam climbs up onto an enormous, fallen tree. Up high above us all, his shadow is cast against the cliff, as though he's backed by a demon, stretching its blackened claws out in threat. The fire rages and burns in front of him—too much like Bristlebrook. Too wild and unkempt to be anything but unholy.

"We lost a brother tonight, and you're fighting like you want to lose another."

The sorrow that twines through the anger is convincing. Peeking up from Madison, I watch his eyes gleam in the writhing light.

"Our *brothers* died in droves for you—and for nothing!" a voice shouts back, and a few more join in.

"Is your spine that soft?" Sam snarls. "We destroyed an enemy on our doorstep. This is a *victory*."

The fire hisses and cracks.

"We are the hunters in the night. We are the last who stand against extinction. Only Sinners will live." Sam lifts his gun, his voice bouncing off the rock with an unearthly resonance. "The Final War was a *correction*. The human cattle died in their broken cities, the weak starved for what they weren't strong enough to claim, and every bloated, soft-handed prick who thought their bank accounts made them strong finally realized the lie. Because it was *us* who stole, and killed, and took. The righteous died. And the wicked won."

I watch with a frisson of dismay, and the men rise, their approving murmurs rippling like a changing tide. The starved expectation in the air is more frightening than the firefight.

Sam's teeth shine through his beard, but not in a smile. He looks like an animal, feral and mean, in command of his pack.

"Only the strong survive, my brothers—*and we are the strong*. We do not apologize. We do not moralize. This world is ours now. *We* make the rules."

Dread ekes into my marrow at the answering jeer, and Madison squeezes tighter.

"The Sinners will sprawl across this country. Banded together, who could stop us? Every one of us will live like a king. The best houses, the best food, the best medicine—and the women will get on their knees and *thank us* for our protection. The way it used to be. The way it *always* should have been."

"Oh my God." The horrified whisper escapes before I can stop it, and Madison gives me a grim look as the men cheer.

Not all of them, maybe. But more than just Sam's group.

Far, far too many.

I finally start to see it. How it happened. Sam doesn't need to be smart. Smart was a problem for suits and offices, for cutthroat business and barbed conversations. Because he's right. All he needs is men like him, who are stronger and better armed than the rest of us. The ones who were armed and ruthless and ready to begin with. All he needs to do is appeal to the thugs and thieves and rapists and promise them everything, and he'll have a horde at his feet.

Sheer, brutal numbers.

Their weapons clatter like bones clapping together, and Sam laughs, wild and raw.

"We are at war for our new life—at war against every weak, pathetic shit stain who hid in the shadows long enough to make it this far. But we are warriors, and a warrior does not fear death. He *embraces* it." Sam grins as the clattering becomes raucous, unhinged. "Have I not given you food?"

The men holler in agreement.

"Have I not given you a home?"

They shout back.

"Do you not have women sucking your cocks?"

Their cheering, sneering laughter makes me cold to the bone. I stare at them, desperate with my terrible vision and poor light to make out one kind face, one example of enraged disapproval.

But I can't find it.

I see Alastair and Mateo over by their monolithic tree, uncaught by the fire. I can hardly make them out in the dark, except to see that they are very, very still.

Horror clutches at me. Surely they can't all be like this? Surely they can't want *this*?

Logan clutches at Akira as he jeers in approval, and her face is pale as she hides under his arm.

I was wrong. This isn't Sam's men versus Alastair's. Not bad versus good. Whatever respect Alastair holds, I suddenly doubt the strength of its grasp.

Sam is offering them the world on a platter—and as long as they believe he can give it to them, Alastair can't possibly win.

Painful, heart-aching memories of *my* men tunnel through my brain. Their kindness and passion. Their respect for my boundaries. Their need to make sure I felt safe.

There were so many good men.

It's only that these men killed them.

Sam spreads his arms, and the shadows make them dragon wings against the rock.

"This is a new age, brothers. We only need to claim it."

CHAPTER 7

EDEN

SURVIVAL TIP #141
They're not friends. They're not enemies.
They're only pieces on your board.
Be ready to sacrifice them at any moment.
They will do the same to you.

My freedom is limited, supervised, and my injuries might as well be clipped wings for all I can fly away, but it's a relief each time my ropes are unraveled. My wrists need the time to breathe—and I need the time away from Madison.

Since I offered to cook and tend the injured two days ago, her incessant attempts at conversation have stopped entirely. I can see the contempt that shadows her bruised face every time I pick up my new bag of herbs, or I'm allowed to bandage up my injured wrists. I might not be sleeping with her enemies, but to Madison, attempting to make them well again might just be worse. Her displeasure coats the air around us like a bad smell.

But I find I miss her quips, and even her insults.

She's only broken her silence once, but we don't talk about the night Jorge died. She was so much braver than me then, and I'm sure she looks down on me for that too.

I've been in camp for less than a week, and she's survived with the Sinners for months. Maybe she's just used to it, but Sam's words, his plans, they frighten me to my core. That night, he spoke my fears out like a promise. The empire built on fear and intimidation, where women are used as chattel and prizes for cheap and unworthy men. How many women does he have already, even more frightened and hurt than I am now? How many more will he take in his tidal carnage?

How is *anyone* meant to stop him?

My hands are busy through the days, and I work to keep my mind active with schemes. I might not be able to fight them directly, but there's no way I can do *nothing*.

With every meal I make, and every Sinner I tend, and every moment I duck my head and don't run for freedom, they watch me less carefully.

Still, I can't act recklessly. I will only have one shot to use my water hemlock, and my vengeance needs to be effective. For myself, and for any meager hope I can offer the women back at the Den. I certainly *don't* plan on getting myself killed in my escape.

I need to find the right moment, one where I can do the most damage and not be caught. They're still watching me so closely, and their different duties mean the whole group is rarely in one place for the same meal.

But it has to be soon.

Sam's speech bought him time, but tensions were at breaking point yesterday . . . and today the camp seethes with it. With Jorge dead, all eyes are now on Alastair. Sam is pushing hard for the Sinners to leave tomorrow, and Alastair's men are growing more and more anxious.

Still, despite the pressure, my busyness is a relief, and during the days I've found some distraction from my grief, which shadows and sucks at me every moment.

But at night, when the camp falls silent and the darkness closes in around us, it's all I can think of. Corpses and emptiness and a yawning stretch of future devoid of . . . anything.

Another lifetime alone in the woods.

Years of winters that cut to the bone.

Decades of pitiless hunger.

This new era of men to live in fear of.

At night, I've craved the distraction of Madison's chattering fiercely.

This morning, Mateo gently unties my bandaged wrists and helps me to stand on my still-shaky legs. My hands are stiff, but the knots have been gentler these last few days, and the salve and bandages are slowly healing the abused flesh.

I am still far too weak.

"Okay, pretty lady?" Mateo smiles at me. He's been friendly but distant while I've been helping Alastair.

And he is the one Sinner who hasn't let me out of his annoyingly sharp sight.

I nod at him, but don't smile back. As I sling my bag over my shoulder, I dart a look at Madison. Jaw set, she doesn't look at me.

Mateo gestures for me to go ahead, but I hesitate, hating that she's disappointed in me. Hating that I care.

"You know, the silent treatment is rather childish," I burst out.

Madison's face darkens, but she doesn't say a word. She is even more busted and bruised than she was when I first saw her. As if to spite my compliance, her defiance has redoubled . . . and so have her beatings.

While I scurry about in the shadows, Madison fights back, every time. During her last outburst, Owen cracked her ribs, and she headbutted his nose. His bloodstained scream woke the whole camp, and I think he would have killed her had Alastair's men not stepped in.

Again.

"Can you at least *try* to be sensible today?" I try again. I bite my lower lip between my teeth, and then add more softly, "I'm terrified for you."

Madison turns her head away, hiding her face.

I swallow hard, and Mateo tugs at my elbow. "Come, *chica*, there's no talking to her." Mateo eyes her with a barely disguised dislike I wonder at. "Alastair spiked a fever last night. He needs you."

Suppressing a sigh, I allow Mateo to lead me away. I've only made it a few steps when I hear Madison behind me.

"Alastair killed my Tommy." Her voice isn't angry or accusatory. But it has a heavy, heavy weight. "He shot him through the head the day we were captured."

My steps falter, and I look back at her. Madison meets my eyes for the first time in two days. They're as gray and laden as storm clouds on the brink of a tempest.

My heart *aches*. Aches at how both her heart and mine were ripped in two by these men. Two bloody, broken halves of a friendship pendant, struggling to cling to life.

I'm sliced apart for her, for *me*, but Mateo pulls me away again, and I stumble after him. I sense him examining my face, and it takes every effort to keep it composed.

God. I wish I knew if I could trust her. But my *one* advantage is that water hemlock. It's the only chance we have.

And I honestly don't know what she would do if I told her about it. If she would let it slip to the Sinners in a fit of temper. If she'd demand I use it immediately—or worse, try to steal it and come up with some half-thought-through plan herself. She's impatient and hot tempered. It wouldn't surprise me in the slightest.

Madison doesn't understand. Submission isn't the same as weakness.

Jasper taught me that.

No. It's okay if she hates me for now. I'll get vengeance for us both soon enough—and I will make sure she leaves this camp with me.

"You understand, don't you? Alastair had no choice," Mateo says carefully, watching me as we walk over to him. "Her man was dangerous. A threat to the Den."

"I understand," I reply automatically, even though I don't.

Mateo feels ruthless, and though not exactly kind, he doesn't seem evil. I don't understand why he is caught up with these awful men.

As if sensing my thoughts, he catches my arm and pulls me to a stop. His voice lowers. "It would be very, very stupid to try to hurt him. I don't want to have to kill you, pretty lady."

The unspoken threat hangs in the air—*But I will.*

There's a queasy lump in my throat, but I swallow it down hard and look up at him with as much calm as I can muster.

"I don't make stupid plans, Mateo, and I have no desire for an early grave. I will do what I can for Alastair."

He stares into my eyes, and I hold his gaze steadily until, finally, he nods. Relief touches his features, and he ruffles my hair like I'm an unruly sibling. I hate that I want to like him.

But I hate the snake on his hand even more.

I step around him and make my way over to his friend.

I study Alastair's chest as I kneel beside him and hand off the slick red bandages to Mateo. He takes them away to discard them in the refuse pit south of the camp, but not before shooting a long, uneasy look at Alastair.

Mateo seems especially anxious today, and I can only assume it's because of Jorge's death.

And because we both know Alastair will likely follow him in a few days.

The two large burns on Alastair's torso are . . . not good. The edges are dark, but slick opaque liquid oozes through the cracks, and there is too much soft, puckered under-flesh exposed. The burns are raw and inflamed and make me feel grateful for my collection of injuries.

This is beyond any herbal medicine I can mix up.

Beau would know what to do, might have the skills to treat this kind of damage, but it's beyond me. It doesn't bother me much. If Alastair dies, he dies, and that's one less Sinner I need to slake my vengeance on.

Still, my freedom hangs on helping him, so I give Alastair amaranth tea and apply a honey salve. I can't tell if the tea is helping the inflammation at all—it doesn't seem any better—but at least it doesn't seem much worse than two days ago, either. And the honey should keep out bacteria and give him a chance to heal.

If he can heal.

When I've finally finished carefully applying the salve and dressed him in fresh bandages, I sit back on my heels, ignoring the stings and discomforts of my cuts and sore muscles. I haven't collected many new injuries in the last few days, at least.

"Thank you."

The murmured words have me snapping my head up. Alastair is awake—the first time he has been while I've tended him. His eyes are seafoam green, steady and inexorable as an undertide, fringed in dark lashes. They're beautiful.

I hate them.

My chest cramps, thinking of the pretty, sneaky flecks of green in Beau's hazel eyes, the mirage of colors I could have studied for hours.

Swallowing my bitterness, I begin packing away my supplies and manage to reply, "You're most welcome."

"Are you well?" he asks. His voice is low, hoarse, but it's like hearing shadows shifting in an endless cave. I can't help but strain to hear more.

But what an absurd question.

"Quite well, thank you."

His eyes drift over to the other side of camp, where Madison is refusing the water Owen is trying to feed her, clamping her jaw shut as he grabs her chin. A small line appears between Alastair's brows. I flick my gaze between the two curiously, recalling just how many times Madison has been conveniently rescued by his men.

"She's a fighter," I say.

Alastair blinks, then his features harden, and he looks back at me with a dangerous smile. "But not you. You *tend* to your enemies. The men who killed your lover."

My hands pause on the lid of the salve. *Which one?* I think bitterly. Even knowing he's trying to bait me, his words feel like needles pressing into my skin, reaching in to pierce the sticky black grief inside me.

But the reminder also prods my demon, and all of my hot, bubbling hate.

Maybe Alastair shouldn't be so quick to pick at that particular wound—I'm all too aware of the hemlock curled up beside my healing herbs.

I lift my chin and study him.

"Madison isn't very happy I'm tending to you either," I prod back.

His eyes flick to her again, and an answering flicker of satisfaction ticks through me. Like I've slotted a piece into a puzzle.

He wants her.

He wants her and he killed the man she loves.

He wants her . . . but Mateo is clearly in love with him.

"*Hmm*," I say, unable to help my knowing tone, and he drags his gaze back to mine.

We stare at one another for a moment, and then he rests his head back on the tree. "She wouldn't be."

The sourness in his tone is tart enough to curl my tongue.

I shake my head as I finish putting my small jars in the bag they gave me, wondering how I might use this new information.

"What does Mateo think about that?" I venture.

Alastair's chin tilts curiously. "What does he have to do with anything?"

"Aren't you two together?"

He smiles, but his eyes are unfathomable. "*Hmm.*"

My natural curiosity rises, but I clamp it back down. I don't care. I don't care about Alastair, or Mateo, or any of the Sinners. I don't care that he's hurt, or that he's intervened for us.

Alastair killed Madison's lover.

Alastair could have been the one who lit Jaykob's barn on fire.

My gaze drops to his chest, and his burns take on a new ugliness in my mind.

Mateo drops in beside us, looking at me with round, anxious eyes. "How is he? He's better? He seems better?"

I avoid his gaze. I hate that his desperation bothers me. It calls my own to the surface. I hate that I can't wish my grief even on my enemies.

My fingers shake as I tie my bag and rise.

"He's as good as can be without proper medicine, or supplies, or skilled care," I tell him.

"That doesn't sound good at all."

Sighing, I pull the bag over my shoulder and look up at him. "No, I'm afraid it's not."

Panic writhes in his dark eyes, and my stomach jolts. Alastair takes his hand and squeezes, but Mateo doesn't look away from me.

Stop it, stop it, Eden, I berate myself. *He doesn't deserve your pity.*

"Excuse me, I need to make lunch."

Mateo shakes Alastair off, then catches my arm and turns us away from him.

"Please, *gatita*," he begs in an undertone. "You have to save him."

"Be careful, please," I choke out as red stains my cheeks. *"And save them."*

The memory of my own frantic pleas to Dom hits me like a grenade, and I back up. Alastair is not my problem. Mateo's fear is *not* my problem. My heart pounds as memories cram in on top of one another, and I shake my head as though I can shake them loose.

All of the Sinners should have stayed back at their base. They should have left Bristlebrook *alone*.

"I— I'm doing everything I can," I stammer, stuck in the in-between of loathing and empathy. I pull back. "Please excuse me, I need to make lunch."

Mateo's hands clench like he wants to grab me again, but I sidestep him, shaking. I only make it two steps when the other side of the camp breaks out in chaos. Straggly red hair swings as Madison pivots, throwing her elbow into Sam's ribs.

With a roar, he straightens and yanks a long hunting knife from his belt. Madison pushes backwards, but her lean, muscular body is shaking as much as mine, and her injured ankle collapses under her. Sam swipes with the knife, and she flattens herself to the ground to avoid it.

I clutch my throat, taking a useless step forward. I look around for something I can do to help. For a moment, I think I see a flash of motion in the trees behind where Sam and Madison are grappling, but when I blink again, it's gone.

"Mateo," Alastair snaps in a low voice, and I whip my head around to look between the two men.

But Mateo hesitates, staring at Alastair, his jaw tight. The pinch of his mouth is unhappy, almost resigned.

"*Mateo*," the tattooed man repeats, this time in an almost gentle tone.

Madison curses in the background.

"*Mierda*," Mateo swears, unholstering his gun. "Fine, fine."

He strides over to the mini battlefield just as Sam's knife catches on Madison's shoulder, digging out a deep, scarlet gash. Mateo fires into the air, and the crack sends my ears ringing. Sam stumbles back just as Madison drops to the earth, clutching her arm and gasping in pain.

Owen, standing to the side, fingers his gun, watching Mateo over his swollen, bandaged nose.

I really wish Madison would stop trying to get herself killed.

"Come now," Mateo says lazily. "Enough for today."

"No, *I've* had enough." Sam pushes to his feet and glares down at Madison. "Rabid bitches are no use to us. She's gone too far. We can't keep her here like this—she keeps fucking getting loose."

Mateo rolls his head back like he's exhausted. "Maybe you should tie better knots, *cabrón.*"

Sam grips the holster of his gun, and I take a few more steps forward, clutching my bag of herbs as if it were any protection at all.

"You only need to hold her a short time longer," I say, willing everything in my posture, in my soul, to be soft. Compliant. *There's no threat here.* This is what he wants, right? Sweet, subservient women. "We are— we are leaving tomorrow, aren't we?"

"The fuck we are!" Mateo snarls.

Sam stares at me for a long time. Too long. I know Sam isn't particularly bright, but I wonder if he's worked out my feeble attempts at manipulation. He's still gripping his gun, and his eyes are dead and so pale a blue they might as well be chips of ice.

"I'll keep her with me until we leave. She won't be any trouble," I promise, hating the nervous edge to my words. Part of me wishes I had Madison's blatant confidence. Another part wishes Madison were more like me, and that she'd kept her mouth shut in the first place.

Having Madison with me will be bad. I have only *just* managed to become commonplace, where my movements through the camp are uninteresting and repetitive enough not to attract attention.

Madison attracts attention like a living flame in an eclipse of moths. With her with me, I'm not sure I will have the chance to slip the hemlock into a meal without anyone noticing.

"So obedient." Sam's dead eyes track over my skin like maggots looking for a feast. "You must have made a good whore for those corpses."

Mateo glances at me, shifting, but even as I choke on my revulsion, I keep my posture loose. A quick glance around the camp from under my lashes tells me the other Sinners are watching—some even appear concerned. But too many of those eyes linger on my half-exposed breasts, or Madison's bare legs as she's sprawled on the ground. They're concerned for their merchandise. For whatever they might miss out on when they get us back to the Den.

Sam strolls over to me, seeming to lose interest in Madison, who I see looking around and eyeing the trees. She's going to try to escape.

Don't do it, I silently berate her. *You can't run anywhere on that ankle.*

She shuffles forward, but as though she hears me, she glances back and sees Sam approaching me.

And she stops shifting toward the trees.

"Did those bastards at the lodge tell *you* where the women went? Or did they just like to kill them off when they got bored?" He smiles, and there's a yellowish tinge to his fat teeth. He lowers his voice to a whisper so no one else can hear. "I know I do."

Sam strokes my cheek, and I hold perfectly still, eyes averted, letting him touch me how he likes.

I learned to hate this week.

But in that moment, I learn to hate myself.

"*Presidente—*" Mateo starts.

Turning toward Mateo, Sam puts both palms in the air with a grin. "I know, I know. I'll save it for the Den."

He winks down at me.

I want to pluck out his eyeballs so he can never do it again.

Every inch of flesh he touched feels infested, like something small and insidious has nested beneath it. I cross my arms, and let my nails dig into my elbows until the pain centers me.

"We aren't going back to base," Mateo contests hotly.

Just for a moment, his gaze darts from Sam to me, then to Madison. As quietly as I can, I bend down beside her as Mateo argues with the almighty leader about leaving tomorrow. I'm not sure if it's meant as a distraction, but he and Sam both sound violent, and I see Owen and Logan and a handful of other hunters edging closer to them, like pack wolves around a fresh carcass.

"What hurts the most?" I whisper.

Madison's face is tight with pain, her gray eyes dark as a cavernous rock. They fix on me, wide and incredulous. "You *saved* me."

"As I've been trying to this whole time," I snipe, and she blinks in shock.

Ignoring it, I look her over. Her arm looks the worst. The blood isn't spurting, at least, but it is thick and flowing. Moving fast, I clean it as best I can and pull out some of the bandages they gave me from my bag, hoping they won't notice I'm using them on her.

Sam shoves Mateo hard, and Logan rushes over, swearing. Another of Sam's Sinners creeps around behind Logan, slipping his dagger into his palm.

"Move back," I mutter, wondering if this is about to turn into a bloodbath.

Madison meets my gaze, still studying me, then nods slowly.

We edge backwards, staying low, as the group descends into shouts and shoves. For just a moment, I think I see a flash of movement in the highest trees in front of us, a flare of white between the green. I focus on the spot, staring with a frown as we move closer, but it doesn't happen again. The leaves are steady and still. Shaking my head against the paranoia, I pick up my pace.

Could we escape? I can see the determination in Madison's eyes, but this feels thoughtless. Reckless. I have a plan—and this isn't it.

But I don't stop moving.

We're almost, *almost* to the trees when a shadow falls over us from behind.

"I'm sorry, *chicas*," Mateo says, and shock makes my steps stutter. "There's no escaping the boss."

A boot lands between my shoulder blade and kicks me down into the dirt. I hardly notice. I'm reeling, and though I know—I *know*—I shouldn't, I feel . . . *betrayed*.

"Fuck you," Madison spits, and I hear a hard smack before she collapses next to me, a small mark already livid on her pale temple.

He's going to hand us back to Sam. Despite all their issues, despite what Sam has planned . . . he's going to do it.

"I helped you," I say stupidly, my voice as small and hurt as I am.

"I know," he says in a voice that weighs a thousand pounds. "But you belong to us now. We're not letting you go."

CHAPTER 8

DOMINIC

SURVIVAL TIP #118
*If your feelings are beating you up,
beat on someone else instead.*

The coals are toasty, and orange shards still glow between piles of dusty ash. *Finally*. I close my eyes, taking a shuddery breath as relief crashes through me. Hard.

Jayk straightens, then starts checking the surrounds for exit tracks.

It's been over a week since Eden was taken, and we've had setback after setback—the slow start before Lucky woke up, the day it took to find the trail, the rain that washed away their tracks, and the additional day it took to find them again.

It's killing me.

We've been travelling through the night, hardly stopping, and tonight is no different. We can't stop. Not yet. Each wasted step is another spear of guilt, another gut twist of fear, another moment where any goddamned thing could be happening to her. No matter how hard we've pushed, we've been stuck behind—too far behind.

But not anymore.

This camp is *fresh*.

Jasper finally catches up and stops beside us. He's sweaty and bent at the waist, supporting himself on his knees as he breathes hard. It's odd seeing him in a Ranger kit—it looks like a costume —but I'm glad he's on our short radio comms. There are tired rings around his eyes. Probably around mine too. None of us have had more than one hour recharge naps since the battle for Bristlebrook.

"The fuck are you waiting for? Let's move," Jayk snaps at us, then stalks into the trees.

Not again.

I shove up out of my crouch. "*Stop*, Jayk. God damn it. We need a plan first."

Jayk flips me off from behind. "Fuck shit up, get the girl. Plan done."

Jasper and I exchange a long look, and he grimaces as he stands. We need to jog to catch up to Jayk.

The bastard has been on a warpath since we realized Eden was gone—the kind that has him charging ahead recklessly and taking hits at us whenever he loses his shit. The kind that will get us killed and no closer to saving Eden if he doesn't pull his damn head out of his ass. They could be anywhere in these woods.

It's probably not even an Eden thing—she's not his type and it's not like him to get attached anyway. This is probably bringing up old shit from when he lost his brother. He can't deal with losing people he feels responsible for.

I get that.

"Stop, idiot." I grab his shoulder, and he shoves me back.

"Dominic is right," Jasper says firmly. "We should take a moment to plan."

"*You* take a moment, old man. Sit your ass down if you can't keep up." Sneering, Jayk unslings his gun from around his shoulder, either not seeing or not caring how Jasper's face ices over.

Then he looks me up and down. "And you've already lost her once. Neither one of you can protect her for shit."

That one catches me under the ribs, and I take the hit hard.

I *didn't* protect her. I let Eden back out into the woods for all the wolves to find. She was my responsibility, and I failed her, just like I failed our first group of civilians. All my shitty protection got *them* was a dead kid and an attempted coup. They were right to walk out.

I remember Eden's slow, shy smile and the flick of her hair as she left to get more ammunition for us. For *me*. And I let her *go*.

Jaykob smirks, and I've had it with this shit. Before I've even stopped to think about it, my fist is crashing into his jaw, and I'm tackling him to the ground. Jayk wraps his legs through mine, then snaps me over onto my back, rolling on top of me with a hard, practiced flip as he bares his bloodied teeth. He shoves his forearm into my throat, and I punch his ribs with hard pointed knuckles until he grunts.

"You should have watched her. You had one job, and if you gave two shits about her, you would have fucking done it," he snarls at me, and he grabs my fist when I go to punch him again. It throws his balance out, and I flip us again so we're grappling in the dirt.

Jayk knees me in the thigh. "You don't deserve to *touch* her."

Out of the corner of my eye, I see Jasper sigh, then sit heavily in the grass. "Projecting," he mutters.

Ignoring him, I pull back and shove my knee into Jaykob's solar plexus. "And you do?" I snap. "You think throwing her around and tying her to your bed is going to keep her safe? Keep her *happy*? You're lucky you have us around for damage control."

Jasper takes a drink from his canteen. "*Classic* defensive aggression."

Jayk grabs the front of my shirt, then flips me over his shoulder. I hit the ground hard. *Fuck*. He's the only one who can pull moves on me like this. He fights like a cornered street rat.

"She wouldn't even be with you except for your stupid fucking deal." His next hit catches me hard on my cheekbone. "She's just traded one cage for another."

And if that doesn't piss me the fuck off.

We weren't like the hunters. Eden *always* had a choice.

So why does something about the parallel hit all fucking *wrong*?

With a low growl, I slam him backwards and Jasper pulls his legs out of the way with a hiss, getting back to his feet. Jayk and I lay into one another, cursing and grunting between hits.

And it feels good.

It feels good to hurt and burn and have a fucking tangible target for two minutes, instead of chasing ghosts. It feels *good* to bleed and feel on the outside what's been cutting me up for days.

"*Asshole.*" He hits me hard enough to make me dizzy.

"*Dick,*" I spit back, smashing an elbow into his back.

I'm just getting the edge on him—I think—when a cascade of cold-ass water crashes down over my head. Jayk reels back too, spluttering.

We both turn to glare at Jasper, who is refastening the lid on his canteen with short, clipped motions. He raises one eyebrow at us, back to his usual composure.

"You're behaving like children," Jasper says with mild disapproval. "Now, if you'd both like to rediscover your remaining brain cells, perhaps we can get back to some common ground?"

Jayk and I both flip him off, panting heavily.

Jasper gives us a withering look. "Oh yes, *hilarious*. Very amusing."

Jayk snorts, sneaking a look at me, and I feel an answering scoff of laughter. And when Jasper's disgruntled look darkens further, both of us start *laughing*.

It comes like a tide, washing up over the tension, fear, and anger of the last week—and I can't stop it ripping out of me. I catch sight of Jayk, his shoulders shaking with almost silent, snorting convulsions, an actual grin slapped across his swollen, bloodstained face.

Jasper sighs, sounding *disappointed*, and it sets me off again, until I'm bent over and gasping for air. Until it feels like the bands that have been strapping my chest tight are finally worked loose.

When I can finally control myself, I pull myself up, then stare down at Jayk.

He looks up at me, his rare, reluctant chuckles easing as he sobers. He's covered in dirt and grass and blood. He's swollen and purpling up as I watch . . . but there's the same slight looseness to his shoulders that I feel in mine. The same relief behind his eyes.

I try to think of the last time I saw Jayk laugh like that, and I can't.

I wipe my sweaty forehead with my arm, then reach out a hand. Jayk stares at it, his grin fading.

Finally, he takes it, and I help him to his feet. He moves to pull away, but I hold pressure on his arm.

"She ended the deal," I tell him. "As soon as we get her home, Eden's free to do whatever she wants."

I remember the exhilaration on her face when she told us she was ending our arrangement. Her quiet pride when she said she wanted more than just sex.

It made me want to give it to her.

Jayk goes stone faced, staring at me.

"She ended it?" Jasper asks softly. When I glance up at him, faint surprise paints his features. Then a slow, quiet approval. "Good for her."

I look back at Jayk. After a long moment, he shrugs. It looks stilted. "Whatever."

"*Whatever*?" I repeat, cocking a brow, and he scowls.

"Yeah, whatever." He turns and picks up his pack. "Not like she was ever going to stick around long anyway."

I frown. "I don't think she's going to—"

Jaykob shoulders past me, but the move lacks its usual aggression. "What are you standing around for? We're wasting time."

Considering his back, I follow him, and Jasper falls in behind me, a new energy to our steps.

We're in for another big night, and our task is still daunting. Borderline suicidal. But for the first time in days, we have a lead. For the first time in days, it feels like we're in this together.

For the first time since I saw Bristlebrook burn, I have *hope*.

We're coming, pet.

CHAPTER 9

EDEN

SURVIVAL TIP #192
*The greatest friends are those
who stand with you against the dark.
Protect them at all costs.*

The darkness is closing in around me again.

Tonight, Madison and I are both tied to the tree again, where Mateo silently secured us after our pitiful, failed escape attempt. Mercifully, that's all he did. For some reason, he didn't say a word to the other Sinners.

After exhausting herself working at her ropes and shouting insults at the men around us, Madison eventually drifted off to a restless sleep.

But, yet again, sleep doesn't have the grace to take me as well.

My hands make fists in the thin, coarse blanket, and I'm silent as I shake. I've come to dread nightfall. Every time the sun drops away, my poor vision fails—and when that unforgiving black stretches out like a starless galaxy, it begins to fill me. Drip by slow, inexorable drip.

I have ample reason to be afraid, of course, with Sinners all around me. Except they aren't why, night after night, terror takes me by the throat. I'm not frightened of what lies in the darkness.

I'm frightened of what isn't.

Because all around me, every night, is nothing. That inky wasteland is empty of feeling, of a future, of life. My brutes don't exist in this barren void of a world, and despite the breaths and rustles that tell me Sinners surround me, I can't help but feel like they don't exist either.

That I don't.

That, whether it's tonight, tomorrow, or some day weeks from now, I am going to die, and this emptiness will be all I know. Just this horrible, silent abyss that's vacant of anything that matters. Impossibly forever, beyond thought or imagination, just . . . nothing.

Or worse . . . maybe I'll live.

And I hate it, I hate myself for even thinking it, because all my life, survival has been it. The goal.

But I know what that life is like. It doesn't matter that I lived it for four years, all those days and nights by myself, clawing at the earth to give me its fruit and sinking into pages so I could pretend I wasn't alone. It doesn't matter that for all of those years, the darkness didn't frighten me.

Because back then, I didn't know.

Bristlebrook was like sinking my teeth into some kind of nectarous fruit. Like I studied sunlight and worked out how to make it slide through my veins. There, I remembered how to laugh, and fight, and bleed, and ache, and fuck, and feel.

No, I wasn't afraid of the night before. You can only be frightened of emptiness after you know what it is to be full.

No matter how careful my schemes, and how hard I fight for another day, even in the best of all scenarios where I survive, for the first time, I wonder . . . what is the point?

The night will always come for me.

And it will always be empty.

Endless.

Nothing.

And I will still be alone.

A hand grasps mine over the blanket. It's cold, like mine, but strong. Madison's long, slender fingers press between mine, and it's only then that I realize I'm crying.

Hot, silent tears squeeze out from between my pressed lids, and my shoulders shake and shake as I try to suck in air. Madison doesn't say anything, but just like that first day, she keeps me *here* like an anchor in a depthless harbor.

And I'm not *quite* alone.

I don't know how long I cry for, or how long she holds me, but by the time I finish, I'm exhausted.

Her thumb brushes soothingly over my hand, the way I imagine the right kind of mother's might.

Or a sister's.

"Tell me about them," she whispers. "What were they like with you? What were they like . . . before."

And her words are like breaking a spell. Suddenly, the sounds and smells of the camp feel real, and not like some chasmal nightmare.

"They were . . ." I take a trembling breath, the past tense sitting on my tongue like bad medicine. "They were home."

It doesn't make sense, but Madison's hand tightens on mine anyway.

"Tell me," she says.

And, in the broken silence, I do.

I tell her about stealing the bazooka and Dom chasing me. I tell her about working with Jaykob in his barn and reading with Jasper by firelight. I tell her about all the colors in Beau's eyes and the way I soaked in every second of being there.

And when I talk, she *listens* . . . and it's like she feels it too. There's a wet shine to her eyes that she tries to hide, but the slow-sliding evidence of her empathy only makes me clutch her hand tighter.

Then she tells me things too, about Tommy. About how he was always the first to listen to her, and always had her back. And how he liked to wake her up by licking her cheek, and she used to rage about how she hated it. She didn't. She tells me about how he helped her track down civilians, all the women and children and elderly that needed someone to fight for them.

She tells me how she taught them to hide in caverns and shadows, how they learned to make their own rock slings and arrows and traps. And she tells me how impossible the responsibility was, how it would have crushed her—except that Tommy would never let her be crushed. Every time she slipped, he picked her back up, and every time she broke, he helped glue her back together.

We talk for hours and hours, our whispers like ripples that keep back the shadows. And by the time I fall asleep, in the very early hours of the morning, it's with Madison beside me, and dreams of my brutes playing behind my eyes.

CHAPTER 10

DOMINIC

SURVIVAL TIP #237
He might have a big sword,
but if he doesn't know how to use it, he's no threat.
(And if he does, just shoot him.)

We travel at an even, ground-eating pace. Not fast enough to be careless about sound, but not wasting time. I don't know what miserable hour it is anymore, but it's dark except for the bright streaks of moonlight piercing the trees. Urgency bites at my heels.

We're so, so close to having her back.

About forty minutes after finding the abandoned campsite, I hear the low mutter of voices, though it's too far to make out what they're saying. Calm steals over me—the focus that always comes with an impending fight.

I gesture at Jasper to my left, and he nods, grim as a grave. Jayk is still pushing ahead, and I need to throw a pebble at the back of his head to get his attention. He whirls around, scowling, and I point at my ear, then ahead. Jayk hesitates, listening, and an eager, deadly curve twists his lips.

Using our old Ranger hand signals, I direct him to swing around and approach from the north so we can pin them between us, and he sets off instantly, picking up the pace to get in front of them. Jasper and I give him a few minutes to get into position, trailing silently.

When I'm sure Jayk's had enough time, I nod again at Jasper, and we advance quickly, converging on the sounds. I clock three figures moving between the trees, one smaller than the other two. Pushing up faster, I use the trees for cover and take out my knife. I'm about to take the largest guy out from behind when a deafening gunshot splinters the quiet, and a bullet whistles by my head.

I yank myself back behind a tree just in time and hear our targets scatter, shouting.

Jayk fired that? For fuck's sake.

This is why Beau's my guy.

One of the men bolts past my tree, and I grab him by the back of his T-shirt and yank him into me. He fights me until I slide my knife under his chin.

"Where is she?" I snap.

He goes still. "W-what? Who?"

"Dominic, I believe I've restrained one," Jasper calls, and at another time, the thread of uncertainty in his voice would make me laugh.

I pull back the knife and shove my guy forward. From this close, I can see he's a small, weedy kid. Maybe twenty. "Move. You try to run, I'll gut you."

My breaths are steady, though I can feel the pulsing excitement kicking my heart into overdrive. I'm calm, always calm in the moment, but I know the bloodlust will hit me like hard drugs as soon as we're in the clear.

This kid is lucky I take my training seriously. He'd be bleeding and in pieces right now if I didn't.

Jasper has his gun trained on a kneeling heavyset man. The

man has a round, red face and a sparse mop of brown hair. I push the kid until he's kneeling beside him.

I can't see Eden anywhere. She must have run when Jayk let off his shot.

Jasper holds the gun confidently enough—we did train him thoroughly, even if he has slacked off lately—but I can see the sweat beading at his hairline. The pale press of his knuckles. I swing my gun around and train it on the two men.

"Good work. Ease back, Jasper. I have them," I say firmly.

The last thing I need is him accidentally shooting our hostages.

He hesitates, then lifts the gun away, taking a deep breath. The sideways glance he gives me is only a touch wry. My CO voice is not all that different from my dominant voice.

"Fuck!"

Jayk's shout has both our heads snapping around. He stumbles backwards between the trees, chased by a . . .

I snap my gun around instantly. Jasper startles, then refocuses his gun on our hostages, wide-eyed.

Because barreling between the greenery is a giant wielding a fucking *sword*.

The man has thick, long hair and shoulders like cannons, and with two hands on the hilt of the monstrous blade, he swings toward Jayk's head in a swift, brutal arc, with a roar that shakes the trees.

Jayk throws himself back, then dives to the side just as I fire a warning shot at the ground by the barbarian's feet.

"Drop it. Now."

The man jumps back from the crack of sound and the sudden spray of dirt, then whirls to face me, re-angling that stupid, massive sword as his heavy shoulders heave. Taking in my rifle and the two kneeling figures beside me, he cocks his head to the side.

Then he grins. "Fair play."

He tosses the sword to the ground, and something unknots in

my shoulders, even as my pulse pounds in my ears. A *sword*? What in the Conan kind of bullshit is this?

Jayk shoves to his feet, his face filthy with fury. He storms into the forest, then comes back moments later with his rifle trained on the man.

"Fucking *move*, asshole." Jayk thrusts the barrel into his back, and I realize he's bleeding from a long, thin slice across his cheekbone. "Show me where she is or you'll be breathing through new holes in your lungs."

I examine the new man closer. Anyone who can get a hit on Jayk is trouble.

Big trouble.

"You do realize I have no idea who you're talking about," the man says in a confiding, careless tone that pisses me off instantly. He lets Jayk lead him by gunpoint, but he looks more like he's humoring a bouncer than fearing for his life.

It apparently doesn't hit Jayk in the warm and fuzzies either. His upper lip curls, and his finger twitches over the trigger.

"Stop, Jayk," I order, my mind ticking through everything and coming up with only bad news. A low, sick feeling curls in my gut. "Just get him over here."

"He fucking *cut* me with a fucking *sword*!" Jayk snaps, the end of his rifle still pressed into the man's spine.

"Longsword," the man booms heartily, his voice too damn loud for the quiet forest. He shrugs one shoulder, adjusting the leather harness across his waist. The *sheath*. "Could have gone for something smaller, but I like 'em big."

Jasper presses a long finger between his knitted brows, and bites out in a wintery tone, "Some might say you're overcompensating."

The man shoots Jasper a lazy, considering smile over his shoulder. "Want to find out?"

Jasper's return look is withering, but even though I have a

thousand questions about why this man has a goddamned *sword*, I'm already dismissing them. The sword is not important.

Only one thing matters now, and she is not in this clearing.

Apparently on the same page, Jayk gestures with his head. "Move. Go."

The man walks over to the other two and kneels beside them, taking the three of us in. He's about twice as thick and double the size of the young man next to him.

My heart compresses into a flatline. Three people. Three *men*. The small figure was the kid.

Not Eden.

"All of you, hold out your hands," I say.

They do, and I look at their dirty—but unblemished—hands. They're not hunters.

The kid glowers sullenly at me.

"Ah," Jasper says on a hard exhale, catching up.

"What?" Jayk snaps, pacing behind them like he wants to snap their necks. "That's it? Where *is* she?"

I swallow hard, but I can't respond. My jaw seems locked tight. Fucking stupid, stupid, *stupid*. How did this happen?

"We have been following . . . the wrong tracks, Jaykob," Jasper says, filling him in quietly. The strain in his voice is palpable— from Jasper, that's as close to devastation as I've ever heard.

Nausea cramps my gut as reality sinks in. *The wrong tracks*. We don't have her. How long have we been on the wrong trail? Hot bile creeps up my throat.

Jaykob stops. "No."

Jasper and I don't respond.

"Fucking *no*!" he yells, but his voice cracks on the word. Jayk throws his gun violently and it cracks against a tree.

His shout shreds me. It's hollow, echoing with the same devastated, hopeless pain that's crippling me.

Jayk turns, gripping his head, his chest heaving and eyes vacant with panic.

We've lost her. Sweet, surprising Eden.

And now we might never get her back.

Jasper leans against a tree, pinching the bridge of his nose hard. His breathing is unsteady, and it's all *I* can do to keep the gun on the three kneeling men as I try to get my focus back. My heart is racing, pounding in my chest.

I need to plan. There has to be something. If I can make a plan, I can fix this.

I have to fix it.

The men's gazes shift between us warily, curiously. The smile has died on the big man's face.

"You lost a woman?" he asks, calmer than he should be right now. As calm as *I* should be right now but somehow always fail to be when Eden is involved.

"Shut *up*," Jasper says harshly, his own composure as fucked as mine, apparently.

And the man does fall silent. For about two seconds. "Do you have albuterol?"

"What?" I snap, not in the mood for playing games.

It must have been when the rain washed the tracks away. We never found Eden's trail again, we only stumbled onto these assholes' camp, then followed their tracks.

That was *days* ago.

By the time we find her, *if* we find her, she could be dead. She could be dead now.

The thought rips at my insides. It makes the bloodlust run hot and thick. If she's dead, so is every hunter who ever so much as looked at her. If she's dead, I'll be shoulder to shoulder with Jaykob on his warpath.

Something in my chest breaks.

God, I can't go home to Beau without her.

The man regards me for a long minute with curious interest. He spreads his hands, and when I refocus my gun, he gives me a brash grin. "Look, might be I know where she is. Could be, anyway. There's a group around here that's got a thing for collecting womenfolk." His nose wrinkles. "Kind of assholes, if I'm honest."

That catches my attention, pausing my swirling, blood-soaked thoughts.

Jayk's head snaps up, eyes wild, and he stares at the man's back.

Making a reluctant decision, I lower my gun until it's ready but not overtly threatening. I stifle my desire to shout and demand, the frisson of hope just enough for me to call on my much-needed control.

"What's your name?" I ask.

"Bentley!" He claps the round, older man next to him on the back, his large hand jostling him forward, and I nearly shoot him for the sudden move alone. "These are my friends—Arthur and his son, Stephen."

"Dominic," I reply. "This is Jasper and—"

"Screw the niceties." Jaykob stalks over, all blazing eyes and dark wrath. "You know where Eden is, you tell us, or I'll paint this grass with your brains."

I don't bother arguing. Good cop, bad cop works, and Jayk's pretty reliable in his role.

And if I don't get answers fast enough, I'm switching sides.

Bentley's gaze flicks to him, then back to me. "I want to help you. I do. Anyone takes hands to a woman deserves to lose them, far as I'm concerned." He cocks a brow. "Pretty good at chopping hands off, myself, so I'd be happy to help. But I really do need to know if you have any albuterol. Inhalers. For asthma and the like."

"Oh, for fuck's—" Jayk reaches around his back for his gun, then looks over to where it's lying haplessly beside the tree. He scowls.

I roll my eyes, trying to suppress my own impatience. "We don't have inhalers," I tell Bentley, and behind the careless grin, I see his eyes cloud over.

And I don't. Beau has a stash, but I'm not about to send

anyone back to Bristlebrook. If I have my way, no other soul will set foot there ever again.

It only ever ends in disaster, and I can't be responsible for anyone else.

Whoever needs them will have to find them elsewhere.

"There are clinics," I say, as if he wouldn't have thought of this already. "Hospitals. I'm sure there are inhalers left somewhere."

The older man, Arthur, scoffs. "How much time have you spent around Cyanide City?"

Cyanide is the largest city around, and it became a war zone after the initial strikes left it half in ruins. Groups of all sizes fought it out for dominance, angling for the best resources, the best bases. Now, the signs on the roads into the city are all spray painted the same way—*Cyanide is suicide: Stay out.*

"None," I tell him.

After raiding the Ranger base, we mostly kept to the smaller towns and farms to the east of Bristlebrook for extra supplies. They're less resourced, but at least we were less likely to get our asses handed to us by a feral mob. Sometimes the path of least resistance is best.

"The Sinners own the hospital, and they cleared out every pharmacy, clinic, and high school nurse's station in twenty miles." Arthur's ruddy cheeks take on an alarming shade of red. "And they're not sharing."

"Whatever." Jayk leans in, rubbing one fist like he's getting ready to use it. "What about—"

"The Sinners?" Jasper interrupts and doesn't acknowledge the murderous glare he gets from Jayk. His head tilts, eyes assessing. "They wouldn't happen to have coiled snake tattoos on their right hands, by chance?"

"That's them." Stephen spits.

Our hunters call themselves the Sinners.

Great.

Still, having an actual, tangible lead, a destination, eases some of my choking fear.

"The hospital? That's their base?" Jayk asks, and desperate hope scores his voice. At their nod, he nods too, a hard flex to his jaw. "Looks like we're tearing up a hospital."

"Actually . . ." Bentley starts, sizing me up. He looks like a wily bear sizing up a wolf pack. "She might be closer than that."

"Bent," Arthur warns.

"What do you mean?" I ask, and I can't keep the harshness out of my voice. I'm being manipulated. I can feel it, and I can't stop it.

But I fucking *hate* it.

"So, 'bout fifty of them left Cyanide weeks ago, all geared up, and we've been on their trail for weeks, trying to find what they were up to. They set up a camp for a while, then split off in a bunch of different directions. And one of their men had an inhaler." He looks at me, as though sensing my impatience, and tilts his head meaningfully. "You keeping up? There's a theme here."

My finger touches the trigger deliberately, and Bentley snorts, catching the move. He rolls his heavy shoulders lazily anyway, like he's settling in for story time. "We followed the four of them around while they messed with a bunch of cameras, hoping they'd get sloppy and we'd get a shot at taking the meds, but they were armed up." His gaze drops to my rifle. "We didn't have the equipment to take them on."

Jayk gives me a furious, edgy look over the man's shoulder that I try to ignore. I need answers before I start firing on him for wasting our time.

"Longswords not the best for ambush attacks?" Jasper asks with biting sarcasm.

Bentley's laugh sounds like a crash of thunder. "Got him good enough."

He nods at Jayk.

Before Jayk can charge at him, I snap, "We getting around to a point here?"

Arthur breaks in quickly. "They ended up going back and setting up a camp, and we kept watch. A bit over a week ago, some of the men from the larger group started returning, all dirty, injured—in a bad way. But they started keeping a better watch, so we decided to keep our distance. We've been debating whether we should head back to Red Zone, our base in Cyanide, but we can't . . . the medicine is so close . . ."

I scrutinize him, but his desperation feels genuine. "What makes you think Eden would be there?"

"They have women, at least two in the camp. The Sinners talk big about a new world—building a community, so they *collect* women and families and take them back to the hospital," Arthur's voice is thick with distaste, "whether they want to be collected or not. It's not a community. It's a prison."

This camp must be their meet-up location for if things went south after Bristlebrook. Given we know the hunters—the *Sinners* —took Eden, it's likely that's where they were taking her. If she's not there already.

Or if they haven't broken up that camp already to head back into Cyanide.

I wonder briefly if their camp is in the same position as the one Jasper watched for days on that looped video. That was by C10. But they had to create that footage of their camp at some point so they could loop it. Would they be stupid enough to set back up in the same location?

"Where is this camp?" Jasper asks, finally walking over.

I flick him an irritated look as he takes over.

When the men don't answer fast enough, Jayk shoves Arthur. "*Where?*"

Bentley jumps up and shoves Jayk back, away from the other two.

"*Back down.*" I refix my gun on the back of Bentley's head.

Jayk and Bentley glare at each other, then Bentley glances back at me. The good humor is gone from his face, and there's an edge to it that makes me sure he has used that sword of his for more than playacting.

He glances down at Arthur and Stephen. "Let them go."

"Not happening."

Arthur swallows, glancing up at the large men looming over him as he rights himself. Then he looks back at me. His thick hands clench together in front of him. "We'll tell you where she is," he says quickly, his chin wobbling with his nerves. Then he swallows and adds, "*If* you promise to bring us the medicine from the camp."

Bentley stares down at Arthur for a long, grim second, then nods, looking at me.

But my bloodlust is spiking again. They want to keep information on Eden *hostage*?

"Want to try that again?" Apparently on the same page, Jayk moves to grab at Arthur, but Bentley blocks him again.

"*Please*," the kid, Stephen, mutters. "We wouldn't ask if it wasn't important."

He's still glowering at us with that particular brand of teenage rebellion and fear . . . but there's something in his expression that makes me pause.

He looks *desperate*.

Breathing in slow through my nose, I rein myself in. I don't really want to beat the shit out of innocent civilians, even if they are ballsy pains in the ass.

"Fine," I start.

"Oh, fuck this." Jayk grabs Bentley, curling his fists in his shirt. "Where is the goddamned camp?"

"We'll get your medicine," I grind out, and as Jayk glares at me, Bentley starts picking his fingers off his shirt, one by one.

Arthur's Adam's apple works. "Your . . . your word on it?"

"He said we'll get it," Jasper replies, and cutting savagery lurks beneath his polite tone. Silk over a guillotine. "I suggest you let that be enough, else my friend here loses the last tenuous thread on his temper."

Jayk's smile is full of teeth.

"Wonderful," Bentley says, grinning back at Jayk like he doesn't see how close he is to losing it. "Their camp is about three hours east from here. We'll come to a large cliff that looks like an apple, then we'll follow it north and go over the river. They're right there."

Jasper's brow arches. *"We?"*

"I'm all for rescuing damsels," Bentley explains. "These two can go back to Red Zone, but I'm coming for the road trip."

Without asking, he walks over and picks up the massive sword, then sheathes it at his waist. And standing there, dirt-smudged and draped in his weapon, he does look like some medieval warrior. Despite how ridiculous he is, there's a determined set to his jaw that belies his good humor.

He meets my eyes. "We don't want you getting lost on your way back to me, do we?"

My teeth press together at the insinuation. I gave my word—and that still means something to me.

"How many?" I ask instead of arguing. Bentley, at least, seems to know how to handle himself. With a camp full of men, we might need the assist.

Jayk stalks back over to his discarded gun.

"Ten? Twenty? Something like that." Arthur shrugs quickly, brow crinkled.

Jayk mutters, picking up his gun and checking it as we all get ready to leave. "Real effective watch you kept on them."

I shake my head as I sling my gun.

Because, really, it doesn't matter. Ten. Fifty. With extra hands or without. One way or another, they're all dead.

And Eden is coming home.

CHAPTER 11

EDEN

SURVIVAL TIP #89
Don't follow the herd.
Herds are born to be slaughtered.

A s I stir the pot over the low fire, I can't help but feel like a witch over an unhallowed brew. The rabbit soup is thin and watery, but I've infused it with enough flavor that its scent curls through the woods. Madison sits beside the pot, thankfully not calling too much attention to herself. She's been on her best behavior since the incident yesterday where our fates were tied together. And, after last night, we haven't left one another's side.

Despite my fears of her drawing too much attention, I'm starting to wonder if having her untied and next to me might be a blessing in disguise. In any case, it feels better to have the support. Ever since I arrived in this camp, it's felt like a thousand eyes have been watching me—from the camp . . . and from the shadows between the trees.

It's hard to banish the sneaking, seductive voice that tells me it's my brutes.

But if it is, it's from another life.

My cauldron steams and froths, and despite the bare ingredients, men keep shooting glances our way as they pack up the camp. Like the witches from those dark tales, my hair is a wild mess of dirt and twigs . . . and I'm full of thrumming, suffocating hate.

Sam is supervising the camp pack-up, deep frown lines knotting his brows. Alastair is looking more alert today, and there's color in his cheeks, but the litter of branches and blankets they've tied together hardly looks comfortable. It won't take much to undo his healing.

I'm not at all sure he'll make it far.

After the argument yesterday, Sam's side finally won out. The Sinners are to travel back to their Den.

Today.

Our time is almost up.

Sam glances back at Madison and me, and I look away meekly.

I can't see Mateo anywhere, and that makes me nervous. He's the only one missing, as far as I can tell, and I need him here for this too. Whatever conflicted feelings I had over him and Alastair died when he dragged me back to camp yesterday.

It's no matter that Madison and I likely wouldn't have made it far. And it doesn't matter that he didn't snitch on us for our escape attempt.

He brought us *back*.

There is no longer any doubt in my mind whose side he is on —it's not ours.

"They're distracted," Madison mutters from the ground.

I glance around under my lashes but see no one in earshot. Akira gives me a small wave, and I give her an equally small smile back. Behind her, I see a Sinner stare at the pot . . . and then at me. Hunger is raw in his eyes.

As I answer, nervous adrenaline skates up and down my spine.

"They're still watching us," I murmur in reply to Madison.

"They're taking us back, Eden." I look down at her and her face is stone serious. "We need a plan. Maybe I should—"

We both fall silent as a Sinner walks past, tugging on his shirt. When he's safely past us, I throw some thyme in the pot.

"I have a plan," I tell her in an undertone.

Madison snorts, then sobers again when she sees I'm serious. "What . . .?"

Casually, I reach into my herb bag and pull out the generous handful of water hemlock I carefully prepared last night. Logan looks over at me. My pulse beating a war drum in my ears, I nod to him . . . and throw the hemlock into the pot. He glances away, unconcerned.

"Hey!" Sam shouts, and I jump, but he's not looking at me. He's looking into the trees. "No! Were you born this stupid? Fuck."

He storms out of the camp, fixated on whoever has set him off again this morning.

But it's not me.

I'm not caught.

My skin feels shivery and tight. I watch Sam leave with a spike of frustration. I need him here. He should be getting the first bowl.

A light sweat has gathered along my hairline, and my stomach dances nervously.

But I don't feel guilty. I don't even feel angry, exactly.

This white-hot loathing isn't a *feeling*.

It's a state of being.

These men killed mine—and so they have to die. It's the new law of my universe.

My face feels numb, and so do my fingers, but I'm flushed with a curious, cold heat. My hate burns like a winter storm, and I walk in its eye, quivering in dread—in anticipation—of the carnage I'm about to wreak.

But I *don't* want to get caught.

I clear my throat as dawn cracks between the trees. "Breakfast is ready," I call.

My voice is steady as a stream.

As the men start wandering over, I lower my voice to a hush. "The soup is poisoned. Make sure everyone gets a bowl. And be ready to *move*."

My eyes flick to hers, which turn wide and round. "*What*—?"

"Fuck, *yes*. I thought Sam was going to make us leave without breakfast," one of the Sinners sighs to his friend, cutting Madison off, and I kick her as subtly as I can.

Her mouth snaps shut, though her eyes still bore into me.

"I thought Matty boy was going to shoot Sam and serve *him* for breakfast," his friend snorts back.

Without saying a word, I scoop a heavy ladleful of soup into their bowls, and they head back to their bags, shoving each other and laughing. I fill bowl after bowl, and Madison finally shakes herself out of her shock. She gets to her feet and, still too wide-eyed, delivers deathly meals to the men packing up the larger tents. Her steps are slow and staggering, her ankle still not able to hold her weight.

That's going to be a problem.

The line peters out until Akira stands before me with her bowl. Last, as always, but ready to take her food.

And my stomach drops. The sweet storm of hate stutters inside me, and it's like debris starts slamming into my organs.

No.

Not Akira.

But . . . I can't let on that anything's wrong. Not yet.

I feel lightheaded.

Looking around the camp, I see snake tattoos rippling on men's hands as they lift bowls and spoons to eat. I don't know how much is needed for them to die, but surely it's more than a few mouthfuls.

"Hiya," Akira says with another slight smile. "Thanks for cooking again."

My hand doesn't shift on the ladle. I think I'm frozen. Flickers of real panic begin to spark through me. No, I can't.

Not her. Not her, not her, not her.

Her smile fades, and her eyes drift to the pot. "Is everything—?"

"Mateo needs your help," Madison cuts in from behind me, cutting my spiral off in a single, neat slice.

Akira scowls, and her black hair is a pretty tangle around her face. It's much cleaner than mine or Madison's. "I'm about to eat."

Madison shrugs, leaning on me for subtle support. I see her lift her injured ankle and worry snipes at me. "Don't bitch to me about it. He's by the latrines."

With a heavy sigh, Akira gives me a rueful look—and Madison a dark one—then stalks off after Mateo. My knees turn so wobbly with relief that I need to lean on Madison for a second to gather myself.

"Thank you," I whisper. "Thank you, thank you, thank you."

Madison pulls me up, then squeezes my forearm. "I didn't do it for her." Then she looks around. "How long?"

I shake my head, following her glance. "I don't know."

The men seem fine for the moment. My throat is dry and tight. What if it's not enough? What if the timing is wrong? What if we can't get away? *What if, what if, what if?*

I feel Madison go tense beside me and follow her glance.

Alastair.

He's watching us from his spot beneath the large, throne-like tree. Staring with that same silent, unfathomable intensity. Has he caught on? Does he suspect?

He doesn't have a bowl.

My pulse starts racing again.

"I'll—" Madison starts, and I snick my tongue against my teeth in a dismissive sound.

"No. He won't believe you'd do anything to help him." I swallow. Hard. "I'll do it."

As I fill this final bowl, my hands do shake.

There's simply something *about* Alastair.

Even at his worst and most sickly, he has a frightening presence. Sitting upright, as he is today, with his eyes clearer than I've seen them, I feel suddenly sure he could have me dead at his feet in moments at the wrong provocation.

By the time I reach him, I'm trying hard to hide my trembles.

"Good morning, Eden," Alastair says, greeting me in his usual courteous whisper.

My fingers tighten on the bowl.

"Hello, Alastair," I reply, hoping he can't see the way my pulse pounds in my throat. I glance around. "Where's Mateo?"

"He's out fetching more herbs with a few of our men." Pale green eyes regard me. "You mentioned you were running low."

My stomach slithers. *Mateo is worried about Alastair*, I remind myself. He's not going out of his way for my sake, certainly. I'm not sure what Alastair and Mateo's plans are, but they've made it clear it doesn't involve my freedom, or Madison's.

And they were at Bristlebrook.

They signed their lives away the moment they threatened my men.

"Is something bothering you?" Alastair asks, and the edge of abrupt interest makes me realize I've been staring into the woods for too long. His eyes are intent on my face, and I force myself to keep still.

Despite my bowl of poison, beside this man I still feel like I'm the one in danger. Adrenaline has me tense, my veins electrified with nervous lightning.

"Apart from the obvious?" I ask, thankful my voice is only a little unsteady.

I catch sight of Madison staring at us from beside the pot. When she sees us looking, she turns away. From this angle, I can see the large, matted chunk of bloodied hair on the back of her head.

"Is it serious?" Alastair asks, and when I look at him, his eyes are on Madison too, as they so often are. There's a careful blankness to his face that says too much, but my blood is already pounding, and the abrupt flood of bitterness is too much.

"I'm not sure why you care. She and I would have been free and safe if you hadn't had Mateo bring us back." The words tumble out with a raw viciousness, and that curiosity in Alastair sharpens as he refocuses on me.

Idiot, I berate myself. The sounds of slurping are slowing. Owen dunks his bowl in the pot again without asking, taking a second helping, and that cold storm sears me with savage satisfaction.

I need to get back to Madison. I can't miss this chance.

"I'm sorry," I blurt before he can say anything, and those green eyes narrow on me in speculation. There's too much devious cleverness in them. "I shouldn't have said that. You were just following Sam."

I shove the bowl at him, as if in peace offering, then hide my shaking hands behind me when he takes it.

"Following Sam . . ." Alastair muses, stirring through the soup absently. My eyes track the motion. "Sam attracts a lot of followers. Loud, ambitious men usually do, no matter how stupid they are. With those followers comes power. He acquired a base. Weapons, medicine—"

"Women," I say quietly, wondering where he's going with this, and his head tilts like a bird of prey as he looks up at me. His stirring pauses, and I drag my eyes away before he notices the way I'm staring at it.

"No. Not women," he replies, equally as soft, but with resolute firmness. "You can't acquire something that isn't a possession."

My lips purse. "And yet here we are."

Alastair's eyes grow somber. "You might be held captive here, but Sam doesn't own you."

"Splitting hairs," I snap back. Someone groans behind me, and my muscles tense. Was that a pained groan? Or just a complaint? Time, time. I'm running out of time. "I am not free.

I am not *safe*. And that's in large part thanks to you and Mateo."

"Just how far do you think you would have gotten?" he hisses at me in an undertone, sitting forward suddenly. The soup sloshes over the rim, and I try to hide my grimace. "If you and Madison had left. You're both injured. He would have hunted you down in hours, and even I couldn't have protected you from his rage then. You need a better plan than *that*."

"Protected us?" My lips twist, caution falling away. It doesn't matter now. I only have minutes before this all falls apart. "Look at her."

I throw my head at Madison, at her knotted, bloodstained hair. At her limp. At the cascade of blues and greens and yellows and purples that make up her skin. She's going to be hard to get out of here, even with everyone poisoned.

"Does she look protected to you? Your leader did that. And there'll be worse to come when he gets us back to this Den of yours. But out of sight, out of mind then, I suppose."

I'm shaking with my anger. It's eating me. Sam won't get us back there, but only because of *me*. Alastair is a hypocrite and a coward. How *dare* he pretend to be the better man?

Alastair gives Madison a long, hard look, then his gaze comes back to me. Slowly, he shakes his head. "There are two types of followers. Some people will follow because they need something to believe in—or who just find it easier than carving their own path—and they *need* someone to take charge. They're the herd, Eden." He settles back against the tree and lifts a spoonful of soup to his lips. I hold my breath, trembling, watching the steam, but he pauses his motion to continue. "Then there's the other kind of follower."

There's something fanged and hungry skulking in his eyes now. "The other kind of follower watches the herd. He watches the leader. He listens, he obeys, he learns. And he waits for the opportunity to take the herd for his own."

My mind is racing too fast. Nerves and fear and anger and confusion are shaking me hard.

Alastair's lips part around the waiting poison.

"You want to kill Sam?" I blurt, only just remembering to quiet my tone, and he hesitates, lowering the spoon again.

I don't know if I'm disappointed or relieved.

He watches me from under his lashes, that cold, calculating light in them almost blinding. "Let's just say that I have a *different* vision for the new world. One that doesn't involve women in indentured servitude and children being used to force compliance. But these things take time." His lips compress. "And *patience*."

I stare at him as I hear someone groaning about needing some "forest time." Alastair wants to stop this. He has his own plan.

It's just coming too late to help me.

Alastair lifts his bowl, and in sudden panic, I reach out to grab it, staring at him. His eyes sharpen. The electric storm is coming to a head inside me, and my thoughts are fogged in urgent, raw adrenaline.

"Did you kill any of them?" I whisper, my voice throbbing from my throat. "Did *you* set Jaykob's barn on fire?"

Alastair stiffens, and suspicion falls over his features. "Eden," he warns. His eyes peel me open. "What did you do?"

Someone retches behind me, and the sound makes me shudder. In fear? In satisfaction? So many emotions are roiling inside me, I can't pick them out.

I lean down so our faces are close. "Answer. The. Question."

Alastair holds still for a long, tense moment, then says, "I was pinned under a burning branch by your man's blast. I wasn't close enough to hit any of them." He bites his lower lip thoughtfully, then huffs a derisive breath. "But I would have. If I'd had the opportunity. They have things we need. Things *I* need."

My grip tightens on the bowl, and my molars grind where I press them together. My hate is a violent, thorny thing. I want Alastair to bleed for even thinking it.

But if he can help the others, the women and children back at their Den . . .

"I wouldn't eat that if I were you," I grit out, choking on my loathing. I release the bowl and step back.

"Logan!" Akira screams. The sound is followed by a symphony of shouts, of vomiting. Dark, virulent satisfaction courses through me.

It sounds like freedom.

Alastair's eyes widen in alarm, the first hint of panic I've seen in him. "Eden . . ." he breathes. "What did you *do*?"

He looks down at the bowl, then drops it, staring as the soup pools in the dry dirt.

I half expect it to hiss and explode in plumes of toxic green smoke.

I take a deep breath. My stomach settles its slippery, anxious twisting. I glance back to see Owen on his hands and knees, his head pressed to the ground as his body convulses.

I lift my chin and look down at the injured man. "I killed your herd."

Then I turn and stride through the seizing, dying graveyard toward Madison. It's time for us to *leave*.

But as I start walking, the noise in the camp takes on an enraged buzz.

"Logan?" I see Akira stumble back into camp. She casts her gaze around the clearing, then lands on the solid blond man, where he's braced against a tree, choking, gagging, his face a hellish shade of purple.

"Logan!"

Her scream wedges into me, it cuts into some of my burning satisfaction.

She runs to him, her hands running all over him, and I'm caught, staring, when I hear the first crack of a gun.

Suddenly, I'm being yanked by the back of my shirt. "*Move*," Madison snaps.

I blink, then blink again, startled out of my trance. When I look around, I see a man pushing between the trees toward us, a gun in his hand. I see another kick over the pot, swearing, then spin in our direction. Another staggers to his feet, clutching for his gun. I hear an angry buzz rise above the choking and sobbing.

"Move!" Madison snaps again, as Akira lets out a bloodcurdling scream that imprints itself deep in my skull.

But this time, I *move*.

CHAPTER 12

JASPER

SURVIVAL TIP #144
*Fear the fury of a woman
who has nothing left to lose.*

This isn't a camp. It's a mausoleum.

The morning light is too bright on the repulsive, vomit-soaked corpses that lie strewn between packs and bed pallets. I count at least six. A few low groans creak like wind between heavy tree limbs. The whole place reeks like sick and unwilling defecation, and I cover my nose with my sleeve to dull the wretched stink, not caring how Jaykob might mock me for it.

One woman—distinctly *not* Eden—is hunched and wailing over a limp body with a plum-colored, eye-bulging face.

She doesn't even look up to acknowledge us.

Jaykob storms into the camp, kicking over body after body.

"Don't touch them," I caution sharply, studying their bloated, purple features. "They could be sick."

"Not sick." Dominic crouches by a large, overturned pot. "Poisoned."

Frantically, I scan the bodies, looking for silky brown hair. Glasses. Delicate hands.

I can't see her.

Relief and queasy fear spill through me. But if she's not here, then where?

Jaykob begins ripping aside half-dismantled tents and shredding apart pallets like she might be hiding under the wilted blankets, and the barbarian with the sword—pardon, the highly distinguished *ex-president of the Grande Medieval Association of America*—tears through every bag he can find. At least the thunderous buffoon is silent.

It only took two and a half hours to get here.

Dominic ignores the carnage and strides over to the sobbing woman.

"You." Dominic's voice is hard, and so emotionless I'm sure he's strangling everything inside him until it gasps. "Was there another woman here? Eden?"

She clutches more tightly at the body beneath her, her wails quieting to hushed, choked sobs.

"She's quiet. Serious." He pauses. "Beautiful."

The rasp in his tone on the last draws my attention from studying the curiously peaceful face of a man with thick bandages wrapped around his torso.

And I see the woman working something loose from beneath her dead friend.

"Dominic, watch out," I snap just as she launches herself up with a scream, a jagged dagger in her hand.

Dominic swerves back, his mouth compressing in irritation, then catches the woman's arm on the backswing. My heart staggering, I watch as he spins her and plucks the weapon from her hand. He tosses it to the side impatiently, then shoves her away from him.

As she twists around, her red, tear-streaked face crumples in anger and disbelief. She seems to be having a hard time getting air.

Dominic crosses his arms over his chest. "Eden," he repeats, as though she didn't just try to cut him to ribbons. "Was she here or not?"

I rub my forehead. "Dominic, perhaps a gentler—"

Bentley whoops behind me. "Got 'em. Got the meds, you dead bastard!"

He laughs like a cannonade, and the woman's eyes crash between him, Dom, and me, then fall to the body on the ground. Her gaze sticks.

I barely stop myself from throwing something at the obtuse human tornado.

This is not helpful. We need to get her away from here, give her a moment. She needs to be eased from this panic she's in, in a safe environment.

I sigh, then make my tone as gentle as possible as I turn to her. "I know this is impossible, but—"

The woman *snaps*. She whirls on us, tears spilling from her eyes as she screeches. It's rage-coated misery.

"I don't know where your murderous whore is," she hisses. "But I just hope you drag her back to where I can find her. I'll make her choke on her own eyeballs for this."

Jaykob freezes in his search.

"Try and threaten her again." There's a snarl in his voice that comes from some depthless hell. "*Just try it.*"

Dominic's brows slam down over his eyes, then he looks back at the pot, the discarded bowls. The dead, distended bodies that lie still in their final convulsions. He stares back at the woman.

"*Eden* did this?" There's no small amount of disbelief in his tone.

I feel the echo of it . . . as well as a rise of hope—and it's dizzying, nauseating in its intensity. If Eden did *this*, and she's not here . . .

After all of this, could she actually be free?

The woman presses her hand to her forehead and keens, half in broken, blind anger, half in hysteria.

"I don't know!" she shouts, and her voice is thick with tears. With loathing. "I don't know, I don't know, I don't *know*. She and Madison made it. It could have been Madison, I don't *know*."

Dominic looks about ready to shake some answers out of her, but at the last, he freezes. "*Madison?*"

"That bitch," she spits. She sniffs wetly and glares at us. "It doesn't matter." She lets out a bitter, small laugh that drops something heavy and cold in my gut. "It doesn't. They're both dead anyway."

"Explain." Dominic grabs the woman's arm, and he's lost any semblance of control. "*Now.*"

"God damn it!" Jaykob shouts. He pulls away from the tree he's examining. "We have gunshots. A spray."

"Shit," Bentley mutters, coming up behind him to look at the holes.

"That was half an hour ago," the woman whispers. "You can try to catch up . . ."

Dominic drops her arm and looks at me. He's pale as a gravestone.

We both turn and start running to the trees, where Jaykob has already disappeared. Behind us, the woman's voice lifts into a haunting, shadowing scream.

"But she'll be dead before you find her."

CHAPTER 13

EDEN

SURVIVAL TIP #20
You have to be the worst version of yourself to survive.
Kill the weak.
Strike from the shadows.
Run from a fight.
Leave your friends behind.

I'm going to die.

A bullet whizzes past my ear with so much speed and force I feel the rush of air. I smash through clawing brush and battering leaves, but I can't move easily, or fast, with Madison's arm slung around my shoulder.

She's slowing me down.

There's another crack of gunfire, and Madison throws us to the side as terror, fear, and the edges of blind panic start to black my vision. She urges me forward in a new direction, but I'm supporting half her weight.

Run, run, run.

It's what I do best. Run and hide. I'm not made to be a hero.

I'm not sneaking about in the shadows now. It's midmorning, and I might as well be under a spotlight.

"Give it up, whores." A voice chases us. "Only difference now is if we fuck you before or after you die."

I bite back a sob, déjà vu hitting me in a wave. Of similar trees, and similar men. Maybe the same men. It wasn't so long ago.

But I can't count on a sexy trio of men saving me this time.

This time, I can't even *run*.

Crack.

The earth sprays in front of me, and I jerk back, almost throwing Madison on her ass. She grabs my arm, yanking me behind a tree, breathing hard.

I can't do this. I can't stay. I need to leave her.

"You need to leave me," Madison says urgently, echoing my hateful, guilty thoughts. She twists her head to look around the tree, then back at me. "Go. I'm only slowing you down. I can hold them off."

Yes, part of me screams—the part of me that survived for four years in these godforsaken woods.

"No!" is what comes out of my mouth. My heart catches in my throat, stunned, overwhelmed. "I can't—"

You can! Go, go, go. Leave her behind!

Madison shoves me as another bullet slams the tree we're hiding behind with a deafening crash, and I stagger back.

Stagger *away*.

Her arm falls away from me, and I'm once again cold. Alone. *Alive*. I'm surviving. That's what I do. That's all that matters. Isn't it?

Self-hatred cripples me. Can I do this? Can I really leave her to die to save myself?

My heel crunches into the leaves behind me.

I meet her eyes, and they're filled with knowing. And somehow—incredibly—not resentful. In her hard, determined face, they're soft with understanding.

"Go," she whispers. Her stormy gray eyes are damp. "It's okay. It really is."

I step back again. And again.

Shame floods me, and tears spill over. I can't look at her now. I don't think I'll be able to look at *myself* after this.

I take another step away, turning to run, and thick, black self-loathing oozes from my pores.

But I see them as I turn—a man, tunneling through the trees toward us. There are two more, approaching from Madison's side. And more movement behind them, too.

And they see us.

It's too late.

They break into a run, and I cast around for something, anything, to defend myself. My scalp shivers with goosebumps. Madison grabs a solid, heavy rock, and I pick up a fallen branch.

Then I grab her hand, pulling her toward me until we're back to back.

"I'm sorry," I whisper, voice thick with tears and apologies.

It's not enough. It never will be.

I was going to let her *die*.

I'm sorry, I'm sorry, I'm sorry.

One man grins as he circles round, putting his gun away. He's much closer than the other two, and full of brimming, petrifying confidence.

But Madison's warmth at my back keeps me steady.

"I owe you more than my life, babe," she whispers back. "So much more."

Finally, an odd sense of calm hits me—in a way it never has while I was running and hiding.

I think . . . maybe it's better this way. For it to end here, like this.

It has to be better to die with a friend than to live a thousand lives alone.

"It was a *pleasure* to meet you, Eden," Madison says, wry and darkly amused.

And it should be impossible, but I choke out a laugh.

"And you, Madison," I reply in the same droll tone. "It's been a scream."

My hands are sweaty around the solid wood. Its bumps and grooves press into my palm. But we brace ourselves, tense and ready for death in the face of these snarling, armed men.

"You swing that thing like you're gunning for a home run, okay?" she instructs. "I hope you're good at sports."

Oh, God. We're dead.

"Hey baby," the approaching man croons to me, and I recognize him from Sam's camp. "I've been waiting for some alone time with you."

I swing the branch, but he's too far away and it just swishes pitifully in front of his face. He grins, and fear has me so tightly, pantingly, in its grip that my bladder almost releases then and there.

"Stay back," I try to snap. But the words quake in a way that makes his eyes shine.

Then he lunges, snatching the branch in one quick move. He yanks it, and I lurch forward before I release it. The man tosses it to the side and grabs me, but as soon as he does, Madison brings her rock crashing down on his head.

"The *fuck*!" another voice calls from the other direction, and I hear footsteps crackling over dry leaves. "Fucking *bitch*!"

My heart slams through my wrists, my throat, behind my eyes. The man holding me drops, letting out an unearthly cry as his forehead splits, and Madison screams back, bringing the heavy rock down again with brutal accuracy. Over and over, she crunches his face, and I watch with hands like an earthquake. Blood flicks and splats over my clothes, then in thicker chunks as his head finally fractures open.

Madison whips around to track the other two furious men as

they speed closer, her face grim. I help pull her up, and she gets to her feet with a wince.

One man leaps over a log in front of me, and I ready myself for what's about to happen, wishing for my confiscated pocketknife.

I'm just about to throw myself at him—to bite, claw, do whatever I can to do some damage as he takes me down . . . when he reels backward.

Screaming, he clutches his face as a red, liquid spurt erupts over his eye. Before I can react, something slams into his cheek, tearing it open. Rocks start flying in harsh, quick bursts—a biblical stoning.

I press back into Madison just as whistling, shouting, and catcalls light up the trees around us. I turn around just in time to see the second man falling at our feet.

There's an *arrow* protruding from his throat.

Madison pulls me backwards, barking a disbelieving laugh. My head spins as I try to take it in.

Then I see them.

Figures in the branches. Running through the trees. Slender and light, long hair, short, tall and stocky. I see a flash of a white dress, and I know, I *know* I've seen it before.

"What . . .?" I breathe.

Back the way we came, gunshots start up again, and angry male shouts—but this time, a chorus of feminine voices roar back. A storm of Valkyries.

And Madison *laughs*.

The sound rings through me like an anthem. Contagious, wild. Savage. It tangles with my fear. It makes me want to be savage too.

"Reinforcements." She whoops back to one of the calls. "The cavalry is here."

A sharp, short whistle sounds to our left, and I turn to see a slim, feminine face. A face I *recognize*.

"You were watching," I stammer, fear and abrupt excitement pumping through me. "In the trees. You were watching."

The girl salutes me. She can't be more than sixteen. "Resident stalker, at your service!"

"You shouldn't be here, Kasey. It's too dangerous," Madison snaps, sobering.

And Kasey's quick grin settles into a severe frown that ages her years. "I know. The others need help. There are more men, with weapons, and—"

"Grab their guns," Madison orders, already stripping one body of his gear.

This time, I don't hesitate. I pull the gun's strap off the man with the crushed face, avoiding looking at the cavern between his eyes.

Fear still thrums through me, but I can't run again. I *won't*.

More shots fire, and a cry rings out.

Please, God, let me be brave.

Madison quickly flicks the safety off my weapon, and I try not to think about the fact that I have no clue how to fire a gun. We take off, the girl and I pushing forward as Madison trails behind, her jaw locked tight in pain. I almost choke as I release a hard, tense breath.

The shots grow louder and louder, the calls and screams and chaos impossible to pick apart. There are people in branches, on the ground. Hiding behind trees and rocks and logs, and men whirling around, firing in gut-dropping spurts.

"*Eden!*" a frenzied voice shouts.

Mateo?

There's too much happening. Too many bodies. I can't see where he is.

Kasey and I burst around a tree, and I raise my gun shakily, trying to find a target. It's heavier and fatter than the rifles Dom and the others carried. Do I just pull the trigger?

I turn to ask Madison, but she's not behind me anymore.

Frantically, I look around to see one man grappling with a muscular, tattooed woman on the ground. I don't think I can shoot without hitting her, so I lift the gun and run in, ready to hit him with it or . . . or *something*.

Kasey screams somewhere far behind me, and I whirl around.

Only to find the barrel of Mateo's gun pressed against my forehead.

CHAPTER 14

JAYKOB

SURVIVAL TIP #21
Kill every fucker who threatens what's yours.

A girl *screams*, and it's like getting nailed in the gut with a semi-auto.

I don't do well with women screaming. Never have. But that voice ain't a woman's. It's young—too young—and it makes some locked-up part of my chest kick back hard in anger.

It takes seconds to reach the man who has her pressed into the earth, and just two more to yank him back and put a bullet through the back of his head.

Of course, the shot makes his wasted brain matter spew from his forehead, coating the kid in a fountain of blood.

Her scream cuts off, and she stares up at me with wide eyes. There are chunks in her hair, and I scowl at the sight. Stupid. Probably just bought the brat a lifetime of therapy with that move.

I expect her to flinch back, but apparently she's stupider than she looks, cause those big eyes are filled with gratitude.

It makes me itchy.

"Hide, kid," I growl, menacing as I can make it. With any luck, she'll run right back to kindergarten. "You shouldn't be out here."

"Can everyone stop saying that?" she mutters. She shakes her hair out like a dog. "I'm fourteen."

"Is that a *child*?"

Shock makes the posh prince sound scandalized. Jasper comes in from behind me and reaches out to help the kid up. The fight rages all around us, and I itch to bail.

Catching my gaze, he nods at me to move on. He seems calm enough, and he has *some* skill with that gun. More than nothing. But still, I hesitate as the kid gives Jasper's hand a suspicious look.

She glances up at me. "You know this grandpa?"

That startles a snort out of me. "He can't see or hear worth a shit, so keep an eye on him."

Jasper muffles a sigh, but the girl laughs as she takes his hand. Seeing that he has her, I turn back into the fray.

This scene in front of me is chaos. There are bodies everywhere. Men, women—I can't make out shit. Dom plugs a man through the shoulder with his dagger, and Bentley takes the Sinner's head off in one brutal swing of his sword.

Just lops a fucking *head* off.

An arrow slams into the tree beside me while I'm staring at the dismembered head, and I only glance at the arrow for half a second before I fire back in the direction it was shot.

The *fuck is this*? Swords, and now goddamned *arrows*?

The hunters—Sinners, whatever they're called—had plenty of gear. Why the hell would they be using arrows?

Feeling like we've just stepped into the middle of a shitshow, I run toward the tree where the arrow was fired from. Something hard smacks me on my bicep, and I grunt, spinning. There are people everywhere.

"You killed him!"

"*No!*"

I freeze.

"You killed all of them! Lukas said—"

"I didn't! Mateo, I didn't—"

A howl of rage cuts off that urgent, husky voice, and I don't bother going around the branches and underbrush—I go through them. The man lets out a string of Spanish, and I use it to zero in on them.

. . . and then I see her.

Five feet away, a man has a gun to Eden's temple.

Some scum-sucking, coffin-craving piece of shit is touching her. Is *threatening* her.

My vision hazes, like it's already clouded with the blood mist I'm going to make of this maggot food.

Her back is against his chest in a classic hostage position. Tears stream down the guy's face, and it's contorted in anger.

He is one twitch away from taking her away from me forever.

Careful not to make any sound that might tip him off, I train my rifle on his skull . . . but I can't take the shot.

His head is half-hidden behind hers.

And not once, not in the hundreds of deployments I've been on, not the years of brawls and beatings growing up, or even in the nights I crammed myself and Ryan into the tiny bathroom of our double-wide, shaking, as Mom screamed and shattered and shat on every single thing we owned, not *once* did I ever feel fear like this.

He's going to kill her in front of me.

My Eden.

Mine.

Moving round for a better angle on him, I hear Dom yell through the crashes and confusion. Someone runs through the trees past me, some gray-haired old woman, but she doesn't stop to fuck around, and neither do I.

The Sinner squeezes the arm around Eden's fragile neck, and I growl as she claws at it, gasping.

Wrath and pounding, agonizing panic claw at *me*.

I'm going to crush every last bone in that arm.

"Why him?" the man cries. "Why *him*? He did nothing to you. *Nothing!*"

"He didn't eat it, Mateo!" Eden yells back, her voice strangled.

Dom crashes through the bushes on the other side of the human trash heap, gunshots chasing him. A woman yells, and it's followed by whistles and whoops.

Dom stops short as he takes in the situation. Another Sinner bursts out of the trees, and Dom shoots him between the eyes with no hesitation. An arrow whizzes past his head and he throws himself to the side. Two more men leap from the trees and move toward Dom.

The man holding Eden wrenches her back, apparently not paying attention to the rest of the firefight. I'm getting close, but he has his finger hard up against his trigger. One wrong slip and she's done.

I'm done.

"He's dead. You killed him!" he sobs.

"Alastair is alive," Eden spits. "Mateo, listen to me. He's *alive.*"

"Liar!" he shouts, shoving the muzzle of the gun harder into her temple.

I'm just about to grab at him when I'm hit from the side, hard. I crash out beside Eden and the man, and in seconds, someone's knee is in my back and a wire is wrapped around my neck. The corrugated collar squeezes, crushing my windpipe, painfully jagging at the skin of my throat.

Grunting, I twist, but they got a good angle on it. I try to grab the person on my back, but I can't find a grip. Someone else pins down my legs, and the pressure between my shoulder blades intensifies, pressing me into the wire's stranglehold. Colors combust in front of my eyes.

Fuck.

But between the spackles of light, I can see heavy boots in front of me. Smaller ones in front of those.

He still has my girl.

I can't breathe. I'm losing vision. I can't *think*.

But I can do one fucking thing.

I stretch forward, and it pushes me deep, deep into the wire. I try to suck in air, but my throat only catches a deathly rattle. The pressure builds in my head until my face feels stretched, and I'm sure my brain is going to burst inside my skull like an overfilled brain balloon, but I manage to wrap both hands around that *fucking* boot . . . and I yank it hard.

The man flies backwards, and just as my vision begins to wink out, I hear him fire a single, deadly shot.

CHAPTER 15

EDEN

SURVIVAL TIP #198
Keep your feet.
Someone's always there to pull
the rug out from under you.

Mateo suddenly falls backwards and, without thinking, I throw myself forward. He fires, and I press my face into the dirt, hands over my head.

When pain *doesn't* cleave me apart, I lift up, flipping over so I can see him. He's dropped the gun between us, and two women are almost entirely covering the body of a struggling man to my left.

I lunge for the gun at the exact moment Mateo does, my heart jackhammering. My fingers close around the metal just as a large man thunders out of the forest, an enormous, bloody blade clutched in both hands. His hair falls to his shoulders, and he's covered in grime and body matter.

Scrambling back, I fight to lift the gun, not sure where to aim. Mateo claws the earth as he scrambles toward me.

The man behind him blinks as he takes everything in, then he grins and sheaths his sword. Bending down, he picks Mateo up by the back of his shirt and pants, then yanks him against his chest— an echo of the hold Mateo just had me in.

"Sorry, pretty boy, we don't hurt nice girls. You get a time out," the man chides.

My gun shakes as I stare at his hands.

Not an enemy. No serpents. Not a Sinner.

The man on the ground lets out a strangled groan as the women atop him holler gleefully.

And I realize he's in a kit. A *Ranger's* kit.

"No!" I scream, pushing up. I abandon the gun I have no idea how to use. "Get off him!"

Someone storms past me and grabs the woman bent over the man's head, throwing her to the side, and even though I know it's not possible, that even a dusting of hope could ruin me right now, I don't hesitate. I rush in and grab the other one's hair in a vicious grip.

"Get off!" I yell as I yank her by the hair, dragging her off him.

She swears at me, then kicks out my ankles. I go down hard.

An arrow spits from the trees, and I hear a muffled, "*Fuck!*"

And I . . . I *know* that voice.

My heart crashes against my ribcage as the woman climbs on top of me.

No. It's *not* possible. They're dead. They're ash and bones and they're lying together in the burned-out cavity of Bristlebrook.

"*Sir?*" I call desperately, a sob caught in my throat.

I twist to try and see. I *need* to see.

The woman on top of me slaps me hard enough that my lip splits again. It's too much. The men, and the arrows, and the shouting, and the guns. The cacophony is deafening. Movement, dizzying.

With a scream, I crunch up and wrap my hands around the woman's throat. She overbalances backwards, and I end up on top of her. She's skinny, with short blonde hair. My fingers dig into her windpipe. I see fear flash into her eyes, and it feels good. It feels *so good* not to be the victim.

Let someone be afraid of *me* for once.

A sharp, piercing whistle shudders me out of my bloodthirsty thoughts.

"Everyone *stop*!"

I pause, glancing up for just a second, and the woman underneath me twists too.

"I said stop, you fucking morons. *Enough*! The Sinners are dead."

Madison strides into view, her foot dragging, and—finally—the shouts and shots begin to die down.

"Sara, Emerson, Jessica, and Patty—you're on perimeter, set it up. Get help if you need it. I want whistles if there's movement."

I let my grip loosen on the woman's throat, but she doesn't press her advantage.

She crawls out from under me and runs over to my friend, throwing her arms around her. "Madison!"

But my eyes snap back to the Rangers' kits. To the men.

My men.

Dominic stands tall, blocking out my view of anything else. Any*one* else.

Tall and dark, angry and auric in the morning light, he looks like some unholy, sin-soaked demon. A vengeful god. Lazarus, rebirthed and blessedly, unexpectedly, *vitally* . . . alive.

But my Lazarus isn't looking at me. His eyes are glued to the tall redhead commanding everyone's attention.

An odd, distant roaring starts up in my ears.

Madison disentangles herself from the blonde woman, then looks over at Dom. Her brows lift, her lips parting. She takes a step forward, absent, like she doesn't realize she's doing it.

The roaring becomes louder. Like the blood in my veins is being whipped into a whirlwind and it's battering at my ears.

Because I know. There's no reason I should, except for the

truth on their tired faces and a sudden, nihilistic sense of foreboding.

A sense that becomes a crushing reality with Dominic's one shocked whisper.

"*Heather?*"

CHAPTER 16

EDEN

SURVIVAL TIP #206
*When you try to shoot someone,
make sure the safety is off.*

The silence stretches for a tedious eternity, until Madison
—*Heather*—shakes herself. A caustic, self-deprecating smile
blossoms on her lips.

I don't know how I didn't notice before, how soft and pillowy
those lips are.

Under all the blood anyway.

"Heya, Captain Cutie, what are you doing up and about?
Thought you were meant to be six feet under," she drawls, and my
fingers become claws. Her face softens, turns serious again. "I'm
real glad you're not."

He stares at her—at her lips, probably—and I shove to my feet.
Finally, they look away from each other.

They look at me.

Dom meets my eyes, and the sudden honey in his makes me
want to cry. How did I never realize what a heart-shattering shade

they were? Why did I keep imagining them dulled and tarnished in death, and not this melting pot of gold and amber?

"Eden," he whispers. The word is like a slow, soft caress down my spine.

"You're alive." The words spill out of me like tears, and he steps closer, like he can't help himself, and I shift into him too.

"So are you." His gaze moves over my face tentatively, like he's afraid of what he might find. In a low, rough voice, he says, "I'm sorry, Eden. I'm so fucking sor—"

Beside him, the man on the ground pulls up onto his hands and knees, coughing and cursing. Dom steps to the side, glancing down, and my heart stalls in my chest all over again.

"*Jayk?*" I choke out, and tears do spring to my eyes now.

"Fucking wire bullshit," he swears, rubbing his throat. "Who carries a *fucking* wire? Who *uses* it?"

When I laugh, there's a hysterical bite to it. "Jayk!"

I throw myself on him. Everything in me swells as he falls back onto his butt. My heart feels too painfully overwrought, too large and inflated to possibly fit inside me anymore. I bury my face in his sweaty neck, breathing him in.

"You're alive," I murmur. "You're *alive*."

He clears his throat. "Uh, yeah."

Tears spill from me, *bleed* from me, as I pepper kisses along his skin. Tenderly over his poor, abused neck, over his stubbled jaw. Bright heat lights through my veins, almost druggingly warm after how cold I've been. My nails dig into his shoulders, and I nip his chin, not even sure what I'm doing anymore except that he's *here*. He's actually here. Alive and in my arms, and not a blackened corpse who died alone and clawing for help.

His breath catches under me, and I can feel his heart battering at mine through our chests. Finally, his arms come around me, and the broken pieces of me settle. I shift up, and my lips brush over his.

That wakes him up.

If my kiss was a breath, Jayk steals it.

His mouth crashes over mine, claiming it. Owning it. He takes my split lip into the scorching wet heat of his mouth, and sucks on it hard, his tongue swiping over the blood, and I feel the sting throb in my clit. His tongue skates against mine, and then we're breathing each other's air, fighting for kisses. He growls into my mouth, and I want to drown in the way my body lights up.

My scalp tingles and head spins and everything becomes liquid and needy and drenched in the brightest, most breathtaking relief.

Jayk is *alive*. Alive, alive, alive.

Goosebumps spring to life over every inch of my skin, and when tears spill between our mouths, he licks those up too.

He grabs my ass, grinding me against him, and I gasp, clinging closer.

"Huh," I hear, very far away. "Didn't figure you for a Jayk girl."

I ignore her, kissing him deeper. My arms twine around his neck, and he sucks in a pained gasp.

I pull back, fear for him spiking. I search his face. His eyes blaze.

"Are you—?" I start.

"Good. Fine." His hand making a fist in my hair, he yanks my mouth back to his.

I let him kiss me for a minute, then pull back again, trying to ignore the heavy, insistent length of him at my core. "Wait, wait."

Breathing is hard. Unsteady. His lips are wet and rosy from kisses. *My* kisses.

I drag my eyes away, and suck in a deep breath even as I feel his eyes burning me with barely restrained patience. Tension lines every inch of his body, and I can feel his need to shred my clothes and *take* me.

I wonder if he feels my need to let him.

When I've regained a margin of control, I look back at him. Now's not our time—not when we're surrounded by strangers and coated in death. Not when I need answers, and to stare at him, at them both for hours—maybe for days—just to convince myself they're actually here and this isn't a fever dream.

I run my fingertips over his face, down his neck, drowning out everyone else until his hot, hungry gaze calms, then grows uncertain.

I linger on the angry red line that could have ended his life.

My demon howls, and hatred curls low in my gut again. Tearing my eyes from Jayk, I glare at the two women now standing near Madison. Heather.

Heather.

Maybe I was too quick to abandon Mateo's gun.

There's more going on here than I can make sense of.

"What's going on?" I ask. But rather than the sharp, demanding tone I wish it had, my voice is . . . unfortunate. Transparently lust-drunk.

Jayk grunts, then taps my ass in a "get up" motion. I edge back, and a large, warm hand takes mine, pulling me up. When I stand, I'm very close to Dom's hard body. And, God, he smells as good as Jayk. Those eyes are still poring over me, carefully guarded now, but it's only stirring the thrashing storm in me to new heights.

But *she* is here. Heather.

His Heather.

There's a crowd of people all around us. Mostly women, from young to heavily wrinkle-lined, but the crowd is dotted with men. The group is checking on one another, some tending to each other's minor wounds. Most seem to be watching us warily without trying to make it obvious that's what they're doing. I notice several still have bows and crossbows clutched in their hands.

And Mateo is still held in the giant's grip, silent and grim, his eyes red with tears.

Trying to get myself under control, I stick out a hand to Jayk to help him up.

He stares at it, then up at me, bemused. Then he bats it out of the way with a snort and gets to his feet. Jayk stares at me—at the way Dom hovers just over me—and his jaw clenches.

But before he can pull back, I catch Jayk's hand and twine our fingers together, even as I turn firmly back to Heather.

He goes entirely still.

"... Heather?" I ask uncertainly.

I look over at her, and she grimaces. "Madison is fine."

At my blank look, she shrugs. "It's Heather Madison, technically." She avoids my eyes. "Guess that should have been covered in our introductions, huh?"

She smiles, glancing up at me, but I don't smile back. All the things I told Madison, all the secrets I whispered . . . she knew them all along.

Little details come into sharp focus for me. Things I feel silly—no, downright stupid—for ignoring.

Madison is *Heather*. Heather was at Bristlebrook. Heather knew my men. Why wouldn't she have told me that? Why keep it a secret?

I hear her whisper from days ago. *"You're a naive idiot."*

I start to shake. "I'm asking now," I whisper.

No. No, no, no. She couldn't have. Not after what happened to Tommy. She wouldn't have done that to them.

To *me*.

Her brow kicks up. "Asking . . .?"

"What information did you give them, Heather?"

The wry, chagrined smile dies, and she swallows. It takes a long moment, but she meets my eyes. She's serious now, and I see the regret. I see the moment she knows I understand the weight of it.

Heather knew where the cameras were.

"How could you?" My voice breaks. Feelings batter me so hard and fast I can't recognize them.

Except one.

I let go of Jayk's hand. Unthinking, I stride forward. I scoop up the gun from the grass where I tossed it down. My pretty *rage*, the need to hurt like I hurt, it bubbles in me like my poisoned cauldron. It's overflowing, unreasonable.

But I am *done*.

She might as well have lit Bristlebrook on fire herself—right alongside our friendship.

Some shocked shouts start up, but my eyes are too blurred with tears to see them. I only see Heather, watching me, still and silent as I clumsily lift the gun. Even as I pull the trigger, I'm not sure if I want her to die or just bleed the way I'm bleeding right now.

I wait for the satisfying shock to crack out of my weapon . . . but nothing happens.

There's no scream of pain. No deserved vengeance squeezes from the cold, hard metal in my fist.

No apology.

"Get her to stop or I'll put a goddamned arrow in her," someone snaps.

With a choked, frustrated sob, I press the trigger again, and *nothing*.

"Safety's on," Jayk calls lazily. "Swipe the lever. It's over the—"

"Shut up, Jayk," Dom snaps, striding toward me.

I throw down the gun before he can reach me, and I grab Heather by her torn, filthy shirt. Right now, I don't even care that she got a good portion of those tears saving my life.

"You told them about the cameras," I spit in her face, my voice rough with fury. "You *blinded* us. Bristlebrook was your fault. You killed them. You could have killed all of them."

Heather doesn't push me off, doesn't fight at all. Her gray eyes are pained. "I did so much worse than that."

"What could be *worse*?" I shove her. Then shove her again, harder. I want to hurt her. Betrayal hits low, in places I wasn't ready to *be* hit.

I never thought Madison—

No. Madison was my friend.

Heather is a liar, a traitor, a . . . a *sneak*!

"Enough," Dom barks. His hand wraps around my bicep as he tugs me backwards.

"Get off me." I flash a glare as I shake him off. "This is between us."

"There's no *point*, Eden," he says, impatiently. Then he adds in a stern undertone, "And there are a lot of people with very sharp weapons aimed at you right now. Back. Down."

My fists curl in Heather's shirt. My demon wants *blood*. The need for it is overwhelming. Like a thirst in the most arid of deserts, desperate to be slaked.

She did this. My *friend* did this.

Lucky. Jasper. Beau.

"They trusted you." The words hurt coming out. I release her shirt and shove her. "*I* trusted you."

She stumbles back, breaking my gaze.

Dom goes to take my arm again, and I throw up my hands, needing a second. Needing to *breathe*.

Relief. Bitterness. Betrayal. Joy. Fury. It's too many things. Too many things, and all at once. My breath starts coming in short, sharp pants.

"Oh, hey!" a bright voice sing-songs. "Did we win?"

CHAPTER 17

JASPER

SURVIVAL TIP #274
Understanding the human mind may save your life.
But you won't always like what you see.

Several dozen heads whip toward us, and I suppress a sigh. The child is a curse and a demon, but at least she's finally stopped fighting to get free. She had seemed too determined by half to run into the middle of the fight with only her little rock sling.

I do have to give her some points for an excellent kick. I'm not sure I'll be able to locate my knife after she sent it flying.

"Kasey? Is that you? You'll send us all into an early grave," a woman calls, sounding harassed, but I can't make out much past Jaykob and the scrub until a face pops up next to him. The woman's eyes hone in on me. "Who is this?"

The girl rolls her eyes. "It's just Grandpa. He's too slow to hurt anyone."

My molars press together at the reminder of why I never chose to have children. She catches sight of Jaykob and bursts forward, ignoring the woman.

"Hey, can you show me how to use that gun?" she asks.

Jaykob is staring at something I can't see, but gives her an annoyed, distracted look. "No."

"Can I borrow it so I can teach myself?"

He snorts. "*Fuck* no."

"Kasey!" the woman urges again, a snap to her voice.

I ease forward, resigning myself to an awkward introduction and a lecture to Jaykob about appropriate language in front of a minor that will undoubtedly be ignored, when I finally see what has captured his anxious attention so entirely.

Eden stands in the middle of a loose flock of people who are watching her with tight expressions. She's turned away from the redheaded she-devil in the clearing. Her arms are wrapped around herself, and her hair tumbles frazzled and limp out of her braid. Her face is pale. Drawn.

She's utterly lovely.

And the sight of her *shakes* me.

I'm the vibrating tines of a fork suddenly struck against a glass for a speech. I'm hit so violently that I'm not sure if the reverberations will rip me apart. The force of my reaction stuns me. All the winding tension, the sick fear and guilt, the horror of the past eleven days whip through my insides.

She's whole.

She's *here*.

Dominic crowds her, his mouth tight with concern. He doesn't reach for her again—every inch of her body language is a scream for space.

"Move back, Captain," I say as I approach, not shifting my eyes from the beautiful, distressed librarian at his side.

Dominic's glare is frustrated but laced with worry.

It's an effort to soften my tone as I reach him, stopping a short distance away from Eden. "Back up, Dominic. I have her."

His jaw flexes, then he scrubs a hand over his short hair and nods, moving back. Not far, but enough.

My attention is already back on Eden, on the rapid rise-fall of her chest under her torn, grimy shirt. Her glasses dangle by their chain around her neck, the lenses smudged and splattered, and I can see the clamorous pulse in the almost translucent skin at her throat. She seems unbearably fragile, her bandaged wrists turned out like she's begging for mercy as she clutches at her head.

Pressing down the vicious tumult of nausea and rage, I stay several paces away from her.

"Eden? Eden, can you hear me?" I ask, my voice gentle but firm, the way I might coax a submissive from subspace. Or from a drop. "Focus on my voice, darling girl."

It takes her a moment to work it through, but I wait patiently until her chin tilts up, and she takes me in with a deep, pained gust of air that comes in several steps. Her hands slip round herself, but they get caught in the slashes of her shirt.

Her eyes are red-rimmed, but curiously dry. Her jaw is swollen on one side, her cheekbone blackened on the other. Her bottom lip is split, and dried blood is crusted under her nose.

My chest aches at how beautiful she is.

She's raw and rumpled with emotion, and when she sees me, her brow crinkles in confusion.

"Jasper? I thought—" Her voice breaks, and her breaths start coming too fast again. Her knuckles turn white as she tries to hold herself together. "I thought—"

"I know," I murmur. "I know this is a lot."

Her eyes dart to Dominic, then to the strangers fluttering all around us. They are giving us a wide berth, for the most part, but there are a good many of them talking over one another and tending each other's wounds. It's oppressively loud.

"Don't look at them," I chide her firmly. "Look at me."

Her wide eyes crash with mine, and I wonder how much she can see, and in how fine a detail, without her glasses on.

But it must be enough.

Those eyes of hers are like gravity itself. Every time she looks at me like this, the world falls away, and so thoroughly it's almost unsettling.

Her breaths slow, just a touch, as we absorb one another, and I catalog every inch of her face. Every nick of silver and indigo in the powder blue of her eyes. The noise of the crowd becomes muted, distant. Now I'm in her orbit—a planet pulled into place by a quietly burning sun.

"Very good," I murmur, and she blinks a few times, breaking our gaze. Those heavy lashes of hers cast shadows in her eyes, and I ache at the new darkness in them. The sun shouldn't be so dark. "Do me a favor now. Tell me five things you can see."

Color stings her cheeks, and she untangles her hands from her shirt. They don't remain still for long. Her fingers make quick, uneasy knots in front of her, and the pulse at her throat throbs riotously.

But she pulls back.

"I just— I'm fine," she stammers. "Please, don't trouble yourself. I'm okay. I just . . ." Her husky voice lowers further, shaky, and embarrassed. "I need a minute."

And it . . . hurts. It hurts that she doesn't trust me with her fear or her panic, or the anger I see beneath them like an underscore. It hurts that she feels the need to be strong now, when she should feel safe enough to fall apart.

But why should she trust me? I've hardly given her reason.

"I don't think you've been fine for some time, Eden," I reply gently.

Her face crumples, and I have to stop myself from taking her into my arms.

Not while she looks a moment away from flight.

Not until I'm sure of all the things that might be haunting her, and exactly how much space she might be needing right now.

"Five things, Eden." I pause, then lower my voice. "It would please me to hear them."

At that, she blinks, the color in her cheeks deepening. It's transparently manipulative. Borderline unethical. But her desire to please is so sweetly strong, even now, and the dominant in me, more than the psychologist, needs to see her steady and relaxed. Her unwilling fear scrapes on every protective instinct I have.

Her tongue darts out to touch her lower lip, then her eyes travel over my face.

"You're sweaty," she whispers. "I don't think I've ever seen you sweaty."

My lips curl up at the unflattering assessment. "It has been known to happen. Four more."

The background sounds go quiet when something kindles in her gaze. The smallest ember of humor. It sparks an answering warmth low in my chest.

"You're not hurt?" Her eyes roam more boldly over me, searching for injury. Her breaths are coming more steadily now, as she focuses on the present. On *me*. "It's hard to tell, beneath the dirt."

"I'm well, Eden, thank you. That's sweaty, dirty, and uninjured. Give me two more."

And I'm not hurt, but it slices me sweetly that her first thought is to me, to *my* well-being and not her own. This thoughtful, selfless girl whose kindness is like sandpaper against my selfishness, even after the hell she's walked through.

She tilts her head, considering me. The crinkles in her forehead soften. "You look exhausted."

I suppose dashing, brave, or handsome was too much to hope for.

I incline my head. "I'm far from at my best. It's been some days since I bathed—or slept, for that matter."

"Because you came for me."

The words are a whisper, and there's so much sudden emotion laden in her voice, in the taut lines of her face, that I feel my throat grow thick.

"Always." The word is a promise, binding as if I had scored my arm open to the bone and bled for it. I meet her eyes again. "*Always*, Eden."

Her mouth works, and the lines of her throat tense as she tries to hold herself back. As if, for some reason, my words are a surprise. Her gaze drops to my chest, to the silly, non-regulation sunshine yellow flower pin Lucky decided to affix to the front that I hadn't the heart to remove.

Her breath leaves her in a short, harsh exhale.

"Lucky." Her voice breaks. "You're wearing his uniform."

That does make a valid fifth observation.

Whatever had been holding her back, holding her *up* until that moment fails, and her face breaks too, her eyes finally flooding with tears. I step in to catch her, but she steps back.

Away from me.

Something in my chest ruptures as she presses her hand to her mouth, her head bent and shoulders bunched and shaking as she collapses into silent, full-body sobs. I feel every quiet gasp like a slap.

How badly did I defile the trust between us?

"And that quality psychology seems about on par with what I'd expect."

The edged, vicious rage that spikes through me at that snarky voice tells me who it is before I'm even able to brush off my dusty memories. I give the malicious witch a frigid glance over Eden's bent head.

"Dominic, keep that woman away from me before I do something ill advised."

It's an effort to keep my voice even, but I refuse to upset Eden further. Heather has always tested the absolute limits of my patience—and that's even without considering the ways in which she hurt Lucien.

That, I will never forgive.

Even if I have to take on hell itself, I will not allow Heather to harm anyone I love ever again. Not Lucien . . . and not Eden.

I hear the frustrated exhale behind me before Dominic pushes past. "Heat, let's get these people somewhere more secure. We need to account for all the Sinners who were in that camp. Let's check the camp for food and weapons too—minus the soup. Let's confiscate what we can."

Their voices fall away amid the bustle of the group around us, and I focus on the crying girl in front of me.

"Eden? Eden, what—?"

"The circus rat is fine," Jaykob says gruffly, and I jump at how close he is. He's leaning up on a tree, watching Eden with a tight expression on his face.

She freezes, then lifts her head. "What did you say?"

Jaykob crosses his arms over his chest and shrugs one shoulder. "That's what you're blubbering about, right? The puppy is fine. He's back at Bristlebrook on a time out. With any luck, the doc'll stitch his mouth shut next."

Guilt pricks me, and irritation at myself. Of course she didn't know. And of course she assumed the worst at their absence. It should have been the first thing out of my mouth.

And of course, Jaykob is quite sensitive to losing people.

"They're *both*—" Eden cuts herself off . . . and I watch it happen.

I see the way those shimmering eyes widen, how her expression *breaks*. I see her throw her arms around him, and how she presses her face into the crook of his neck, breathing him in like a last breath.

And there's something in Jaykob's face I've only ever caught glimpses of before, extracted deep in the most exhausted, vulnerable moments of our sessions when snippets of truth hemorrhage out of him. Something uncertain and very real.

His arms are slow to come around her—hesitant, as though he's out of practice with the motion.

He probably is.

Heat rolls over me, like the first, nauseous stirrings of a fever.

My approach is slow, and I hate that I feel like I'm intruding. I hate that I can still feel her tear scalding my thigh and hear the cool clip in her tone from our conversations after.

I hate that Jaykob is a comfort to her and I am not.

It's the one way I was meant to be useful to her.

Eden nestles into him and lets loose, soaking him to the bone with her tears, and I watch with unwilling fascination.

She is . . . not herself. Or at least, not the way she has ever been around me. Not even that first night, where she allowed Beaumont and me to ravage her. Then, she was sweetly submissive. Shocked and dazzled and achingly beautiful.

Now, her usual reserve is unshackled. Abandoned. She's an open book for him—as open as every novel I sprawled my feelings across and laid at her doorstep.

And I do feel *sick* with it.

It takes me too long to identify the emotion.

Jealousy.

My eyes drift shut, and I let out a long breath from my nose. It does nothing to settle the hot, queasy churn of my emotions.

That is . . . most inconvenient.

"Beaumont is tending to Lucien," I murmur, firmly ignoring the uncomfortable sensation. "He's receiving the best care he can. I am sure he'll be fine."

It's what I tell myself each morning. Every night.

Eden pulls back a little, until her feet touch the ground again, though she stays nestled against Jaykob. Her gaze flutters back up to mine, and she's wrecked and luminous with tears.

Why are pretty tears so perfectly designed to ruin me?

I could make her cry prettier tears than these.

Happier ones, certainly.

Jaykob's hand drops to Eden's ass, and I blink out of my trance, then glance up to find him scowling at me.

I arch a cool brow, unimpressed by the primitive mating display.

"I—" Eden shifts under his hand, darting a baffled look up at him, then looks back at me. "They're really okay? Everyone is really ... alive?"

"They're doing well, Eden," I say gently. In a cautious tone, I venture, "We were more worried about what happened to you."

And like a lantern in a gusty castle, her expression gutters out. "I'm fine. Don't trouble yourself about me."

Worry pinches at me at her avoidance, but this is no time to talk—not with her wounded and exhausted and emotions frazzled from weeks of fear. I'll find a private moment later.

"Of course." I hesitate. "Eden, I wanted to—"

She cuts me off.

"You— Well, thank you for helping me." Polite reserve steals over her features again as she turns to face me more fully. And it's only now, after seeing her intemperance with Jaykob, that I realize just how much she has been holding herself in check around me.

The thought doesn't sit well.

She clears her throat, avoiding my gaze, and shoves her hand out in front of her. "I truly am glad that you're well."

Stiffening, I stare at her outstretched palm. She might as well have slapped me with it. Jaykob doesn't bother to suppress his scoff of laughter, and my lips pinch together.

She throws herself at this savage and offers me . . . this.

Distance. Civility. I shouldn't be surprised at how it cuts.

It's my move, after all.

And no more than I have earned from her.

Smoothing my features, I wrap her hand tenderly in both of mine. Her bones are delicate, fragile as a bird's inside my own.

"And you, Eden," I murmur.

My fingertips brush over the sensitive skin at her wrist, and she shivers before she snatches her hand back.

I watch color bloom in her cheeks as she says hastily, "We should find the others."

As if summoned, there's a short whistle, then the spiteful ghoul pokes between the trees.

"Come on, babe. My people have a spot not too far from here." Heather glances between Jaykob and me with a smirk. "You can even bring your little sidekicks."

She leaves fast—infuriatingly, before I can find the words that would hamstring her on her way out. I'd forgotten that habit of hers.

I truly loathe the feeling of being left spluttering.

"You should have shot her," Jaykob mutters to Eden.

My lips quirk at that. "You tried to shoot her?"

Jaykob exchanges a rare look with me. "Safety was on."

"Ah. Shame."

Eden sighs. "I probably shouldn't have."

"I wouldn't fret." I gesture after the draconic wretch. The path of sulfur and brimstone should be easy enough to follow. "We've all imagined it."

Unfortunately, dragons are not so easy to kill.

CHAPTER 18

BEAU

SURVIVAL TIP #50
For some wounds, there's medicine.
For everything else, there's drunken bubble baths with friends.

I did it. I am Beaumont, God of doctors. Even if my patient is a blasted piece of pipe. Poor bastard had a decent chunk blown out of him during the battle for Bristlebrook, and it's taken me nearly two damn weeks to figure out how to mend the wound.

Finally, I found a dusty tub of sealant in the basement and was able to use that and metal scraps to plug the hole in a rough, field medicine kind of way. Jayk is going to have to fix it properly when he gets back because there ain't the slightest possibility that it's going to hold.

I hope Jayk can fix it. Jayk fixes everything.

Damn it, I was really hoping they'd be back by now.

Every day, every hour they don't return is like a grater peeling flesh from my spine, and I know Lucky feels it too.

Five days ago, by unspoken agreement, we stopped talking about them. Didn't seem like there was much point. We're already thinking about them, fretting over them, and it's not bringing them through these doors any faster.

We both know too well that they might never walk through them again.

And that truth has made Lucky about as charming as a rattler with a sore fang.

And I get it, I really do. But between that and the way he keeps trying to get out of bedrest to "help" me around Bristlebrook, I'm starting to hate him. Just a little bit.

We need a break. Something to lighten the tension.

So, I fixed the water, had the best shower of my life . . . and now I have a present.

I let myself into his room to find him, thankfully, in bed. As soon as I open the door, though, there's an abrupt scuffle of motion as he shoves something underneath the covers. Lucky is flushed, glittery eyed, and breathing far too hard.

Concern stabs me, followed by stinging guilt. Lucky might be a surly, miserable toddler when he's hurt, but he *is* hurt. And my responsibility.

"Are you spiking a fever?" Abandoning my package beside the door, I stride over to his bedside and pull the thermometer out of the side table. How much penicillin do I have left? Is it enough to deal with an infection? It loses so much potency over time, it's so hard to gauge.

"What? No!" Lucky smacks my hand away as I try to take his temperature.

I sigh. "Lucky, you ought to know better. You want to mess with fever about as much as a rabid badger."

I lean in again, and he twists away, making the covers fall back. The shine of white silk makes me pause. I snag it from between his sheets, and Lucky lets out a strangled yelp.

He snatches at it, but he still can't raise his right arm above his head.

"Is that one of Jasper's shirts?" I ask, dangling the fabric by my fingertips. It must be. He's the only guy I know who decided business-formal was the most appropriate attire for the apocalypse. "What are you doing with—?"

It all clicks, and this time *I* yelp, tossing the shirt back in his face. "God damn it, Lucky!"

Lucky snorts with laughter, then cackles as he pulls the shirt down. The sound of it is like sunshine breaking between clouds, and it's almost enough to make me forgive him the last few days. Almost.

Wrinkling my nose, I swipe the hand sanitizer and squirt a generous dollop into my palms. "Really?"

"Well, what was I meant to do?" Another fit of laughter overtakes him, and he winces as his chest shakes. He wipes at the amused tears under his eyes. "You've been hovering over me like a nesting hen. I thought I had a minute. Sue me!"

I eye the shirt, rubbing my now-holy-again hands together. "You're a damn klepto, you know that? A perverted one." I shudder, and now that I know he's okay—in the loosest sense of the word—I fetch the package from the door.

"My psychologist is on leave. Take it up with him." He slumps back on the pillows, all innocent eyes and overgrown beard. "Besides, he's said before I could borrow his clothes."

"To *wear*!" I shake my head, lips twitching. "You know you're messed up, right?"

"And now you're kink shaming me. Very uncool, Beau."

I roll my eyes. "Well, if you're done making Jesus cry, I have a present for you. Two, actually."

"A present? For me?" Lucky pulls himself painfully into a sitting position, eyes sparkling. Then he lifts a suspicious brow. "Is it a real one? Or is this like an I'm-giving-you-yeast-flavored-medicine-to-make-you-feel-better kind of present?"

Maybe I should take it back. Lucky doesn't deserve presents.

I lift the package, wiggling it. "It's real."

He tilts his head, his filthy blond hair flopping to the side. "Or like an I-got-you-a-new-kitchen-appliance-to-use-as-a-bedpan kind of present?"

I shove it at him, and he grins, tearing at the wrapping paper. And by wrapping paper, I mean the discarded tissue paper that comes with a box of new shoes that I found in my closet and awkwardly taped up on a whim. This was a silly idea. I don't know what I was—

"Aw, Beau." Lucky bats his lashes as he reveals the giant bottle of sherry. He sets it back on the bed. "I'll take the yeast-flavored medicine, thanks."

"Blame your boyfriend. He locked the good stuff in the wine cellar, and he still hasn't given us the passcode. This was all that was in the kitchen." I grimace. "He even locked the minibar."

At the word 'boyfriend,' Lucky gives me a sharp look . . . that he quickly buries in an easy smile. "You said two presents, right?"

"Right." I walk over to the bathroom and let the door swing open. "We have running water."

And I'm pretty sure the pest's eyes turn into hearts. He throws back the covers, and I sigh. I have seen Lucky's dick too many times in the last week.

"Why didn't you lead with that?" He pushes his legs out of bed, trying to stand, and I rush over before he collapses. He's been a little better over the last few days, but it's still going to be at least another week of healing before I'll be okay with him moving around without help.

That said, he looks like he drinks moonshine and should be missing a dozen teeth. He needs fixing.

"Would you slow down?" I grumble, supporting him carefully.

"No! This perverted klepto needs to take a massive, toilet-cracking shi—"

"Gross. *Gross*, Lucky. How you convinced two people to want to sleep with you, I don't have the slightest clue."

Lucky tenses, and I glance at him to make sure he's not in pain.

"One." He doesn't look back at me. "Just one."

Mulling that over, I settle him on the toilet. "This conversation calls for some repulsive alcohol. Do your business. I have a plan."

"Look, Beau, don't make this awkward. You're just not my type," Lucky says sympathetically. "I think it's the cleft chin. It's too wholesome."

Giving up on trying to get Lucky clean, I throw the damp sponge at him as he drinks directly from the enormous bottle. He splutters around his mouthful as it smacks him in the side of his face.

I swipe the booze and take a drink. "Please. With those manky locks? I have standards."

Lucky sinks deeper into the monstrous porcelain tub, luxuriating in the scorching hot water. His hair hangs over the edge in front of where I've pulled up a chair.

"Sure you do," he soothes, patting my hand. "This is just one friend bathing another friend under the steamy haze of candlelight. I'll ignore the fact that this seduction scene is right out of a seventies porno."

Okay, the candles might have been a step too far.

Lucky snickers, then passes the enormous bottle back to me. It's probably not responsible of me. Or great medical advice. But whatever, he's off the heavy-duty drugs now.

I take a deep drag of the cloying sherry, already well on my way to a decent buzz, then pass it back off to Lucky, eyeing the water. It's at a low enough level that it shouldn't come close to his bandages, but Lucky can't be trusted to be careful.

Balmy steam rolls around us as I test the slip-on spray attachment connected to the bath tap. "Pass the shampoo. I'll do your hair."

Lucky tilts his head back so he can see me, waggling his brows, and I roll my eyes, edging back. "Or I won't . . ."

"No, do it. Do it, please? I'll stop," he begs, laughing.

Pest. This is why Dom's my guy.

Shaking my head with a smile, I soap up his long, tangled locks. "Honestly, it's no wonder at all that Jasper is a sadist. That's the universe knowing you needed to be kept in line."

Lucky sighs, then laughs quickly in a brittle way. "Probably."

"Would you stop *doing* that? You avoid talking about him like you're a nudist at a church fair." I tug his hair, then grab the bottle with sudsy hands and drink. That swishy, giddy feeling starts to take over. I've always been a cheap drunk, but since the strikes? One snifter of port and I'm doing karaoke. "What's the deal with you two? I thought since you were getting all smooshey, y'all would be going steady now or whatever."

As intended, that startles another laugh out of my melancholic friend.

"Smooshey?" he teases. "Going steady? Well, gosh, Beau, I do think he's peachy keen, but we haven't gone out for milkshakes or anything."

I grab the brush from the bag I fetched from his room, and he twists, then yelps. I poke him. "Stay still, idiot!"

"Use the comb! You don't use the brush on wet hair. The wide-toothed comb!" Lucien insists, still wincing. He makes a grabbing motion for the sherry, then grumbles, "Honestly. It's like you want me to have split ends."

"Oh," I croon, "I'm sorry, sugar pie. You havin' a hard time gettin' pampered?" I smack the side of his head and drop the drawl. "Quit changing the subject. What's the deal with you and Jasper?"

And the deal with him and Eden—that's what I really want to know.

It's taken the most determined effort of my life not to torture myself with thoughts of what could be happening to her right now. But if I was ever going to put her life in anyone's hands, it's Dom's. I need to trust him on this.

So instead of focusing on what might be going wrong, I've been trying to think of all the things I need to do *right* when they bring her back to me. Because *when* she comes back here, I need a plan. She blew our easy-but-admittedly-stupid sex deal to shreds, so I'll really need to pull out the charm now to make sure she stays right where she belongs—between me and Dom.

If I can get Dom to play ball.

After seeing him pull back again at the riverbank, I'm starting to lose faith that he's ever going to get his shit together. His track record with women's feelings—or anyone's, if I'm honest—isn't great.

Heather was one of the few people he ever made the effort with, enough that I was willing to put my own reservations aside, and even that blew up in our faces.

I'm starting to think that while I'd be the first one to trust him with Eden's life . . . maybe I was too quick to trust him with her heart. She's had a hard life, after all. She deserves to be with people who will love her with everything.

Maybe we both do.

Eden thinks she wants all of us, and if that's what her pretty little heart wants, then I'm ready to get on board with that . . . but only if they prove they're going to treat that girl right.

I eye the back of Lucky's head. *This* infuriating bag of puppy love has a big heart, and as long as he hasn't given the whole of it to Jasper, I know he'd make her happy.

I slowly tease out the snarls in Lucky's hair, and he swirls his fingers through the scalding water.

"I don't know what's happening with us," he says finally, more seriously than I'm used to hearing from him. "I never do. He kissed me and said . . . He looked at me like—"

He breaks off and lets out a frustrated huff, then takes another big gulp of sherry. He grimaces as he pulls it away. His words begin to slur a little. "But then he didn't say a word to me after that. Didn't even visit. I know he's worried about Eden—and I'm glad he went after her, that's where he needs to be. But I just wish . . . I just wish we could have talked, I guess."

Poor Lucky. Those two have been dancing around one another for years.

Thinking, I tilt Lucky's head to the side and angle the shower head away from his bandages as I rinse the suds from his long hair. "Well, he asked about you about five times a day, if that makes you feel better. He was almost as irritating as you." I ponder that. "No, he was worse. He kept doing that scary glare thing."

Lucky hums in a way I wish he wouldn't while he's naked. "I love that glare thing."

"No boners in the tub," I order.

Clearing his throat, he moves some bubbles strategically. "He really asked about me?"

I laugh, and I'm surprised by how loud it is. Stupid sherry.

I drink some more.

"Lucky, he carried you mostly dead through a firefight and then cried at your bedside—of course he assed about you." I frown. That's not right. "Assed. *Asked*."

"Ugh!" Lucky smashes his hand in the water and it sprays bubbles everywhere. "Then *why* won't he go steady with me!"

Snickering, I pick up Lucky's fancy expired conditioner and slather it through his locks. This hair is way too much hassle. "It's the patient thing, right?"

"Yeah." He slumps miserably.

Then he brightens, turning in the tub with a little gasp of pain.

"Hey, you're a doctor!" he exclaims as I gently push him back down.

"Hope so, or you're in a lot of trouble. I stuck a needle in your lung. You know how cool that is? I don't get enough credit," I lament.

"Yeah, yeah, you're very talented," Lucky says dismissively. "But what do *you* think? About the doctor-patient thing?"

"Jasper's not a *real* doctor," I continue, stroking the conditioner through his hair. "Now if he were a *psychiatrist*, they get medical training. *That* would be impressive. Jasper just knows about psychics and stuff. Gimme another drink."

"No!" Lucky holds the bottle out of reach, trying to sit forward, but I pull him back by his hair and swipe it. "He doesn't know about psychics; he knows about *psychos*." He cracks up, then splashes me. "Pay attention!"

My head is spinning. I set Sherry beside the tub—nasty gal she is—and start rinsing Lucky's hair. "Aw, Lucky, I don't know. I'm a body doctor. It's different. Maybe he *is* in your head. Did you ever think of that? He could be right."

"I did," he admits. His cheeks are bright red. I'd be worried except they do that every time he drinks. He blows a frustrated raspberry. "But that doesn't mean I don't really love him. He hasn't even had a session with me in years; he switched me to another psychologist a year before he retired. I think it was because I told him all about that daddy sadist—what was his name?"

"Who?" I squint. "Oh, *Greg*? You bottomed for *Greg*?"

"Greg! That's it. Hairy shoulders." Lucky nods, waving Sherry around as I start to towel his locks dry. "Anyway, the point I'm making, and it's an impotent point—"

I bend over his hair, cackling.

"Impotent. *Important*, damn it. It's an important point," he lectures, but then his voice turns to a hushed whisper. "I love him. Why can't that be enough?"

"Ah, Lucky." I sigh, squeezing his good shoulder. He tilts his head back to look at me sadly again. "He just wants to protect you."

His lips tighten. "The best place to protect me is from inside me." Lucky blinks. "*Be*side me. I meant— Stop *laughing*. This is a serious conversation!"

Pressing the back of my hand over my mouth, I try to stop my sniggers, and he rolls his head loopily, scowling at me. It makes me snort harder.

I wheeze. "I'm sorry." When I can finally breathe, I repeat, "Sorry. *Sorry*. It's Sherry—she poisoned me. I'm serious. I promise."

I scrape a hand down my face, then go and take a drink from the bathroom tap. "Okay, I'm back in it." I lean on the edge of the bathtub and ask, casual as a hen in a pen, "So where does that leave Eden?"

The lonesome cast to Lucky's features breaks into daisies and rainbows. "She's so pretty."

Her big, dazed blue-gray eyes pop to mind, her hair all askew as I fucked her mouth, fitted between me and Dom like my favorite fantasy.

"Yeah." My agreement comes on a long exhale.

For all that's good, I really hope she's okay. I don't know what I'll do if she's not.

"She let me cuddle her all night. Didn't complain once. And we just talked and talked. She's so smart, like crazy smart. She knows about so many things." Lucky flicks some water between his fingers. "God, Beau, the way she smells. I just want to lick her. Like all the time."

She *is* good for licking.

No! Damn it, no. Focus. This is a reconnaissance mission.

Lucky's in love with the evil overlord. Does he love sweet, serious Eden? Or does he just want to lick her? I know better than most how she can warm a man right to the bone . . . but has he really thought this one through?

"But she's not a sadist. She's not even a domme." I shake my head. "Not even *close*."

Lucky's chin juts out. "So what?"

"Soooo," I say, waving my hands, "how's that meant to work? Are you two planning on just having boring, vanilla sex for the rest of your lives?"

He throws his head back, his eyes bruised blue and mortally offended.

"It was *not* boring." He wrinkles his nose and mimics me. "Not even *close*."

I cross my arms, then slip on the tub. I spot Sherry and decide it's time for another fling. Wrapping my lips around her neck, I drink her down like a one-night stand I plan on regretting.

I point the bottle at him. "What about Jasper?"

Lucky grabs it, looking grumpy, and some of the amber liquid sprays into the tub.

"Well, I guess I'll just have to take them *both*," he drawls.

I hum thoughtfully.

"Look, Lucks. Can I call you Lucks? I think you might just be biting off more than you can chomp on here." I muster the most sympathetic smile I can find. "Now, I don't want to sound condescending . . . but maybe you should worry about getting that whole relationship sorted before you go takin' on anyone else. Just seems sensible."

Lucky squints at me, then he smacks the water, spraying me with dirty bath juice. I shove back my chair with a shout, but the back legs catch on a tile and the chair tips, dumping me hard onto the soaking floor.

"Son of a—" I point at him, glaring. "Don't get your bandages wet!"

"Don't tell me my romantic relationships are doomed to fail!"

I pull myself up on the tub. "You're being greedy."

"Oh! OH! *No!*" he scoffs, looking at me like I just told him stars are fairy farts. He can't move much, though, so he still seems pretty pathetic. "You are *such* a hypocrite. What about you and Dom, huh? You guys get to share!"

"Well, maybe he doesn't want to anymore!" I snap back, then slump against the cold porcelain wall amid the discarded bubbles. "He doesn't want *me* anymore either."

Not our plans, not our Eden. I thought I could change his mind, but maybe I just . . . *can't*. I thought for sure he'd cave when we had her under us, submitting like she was born for it. But he didn't.

And I don't know what to do with that.

The bubbles all around me die in slow bursts.

Pop goes one dream. Oh look, there goes another. Pop, pop, *pop*.

Lucky stops trying to dump water on me with his feeble little slaps. He leans over the tub to look down at me with wide eyes.

"Oh, shit!" he says. "You're *me*!"

I lay down on the tiles, hurting in uncomfortable ways, missing the others so much my lungs ache. The booze turns sour in my gut.

"They'll be okay," Lucky whispers. "They'll get her back and everyone will be fine."

From somewhere, I work up a small smile for the blue eyes peeking over the side of the tub. "Yeah. I know they will."

Man, lies taste worse than Sherry.

CHAPTER 19

EDEN

SURVIVAL TIP #135
Appreciate the little things.
Company. Safety. Beautiful, panty-soaking men.

A nother cave. Wonderful.

We followed Heather's people through the forest to the heavy expanse of cliffs, traveling until the mid-afternoon sun tilted enough to burn back the shadows and soak us in sunlight. Finally, we reach a spot they recognized, and I watch them drop into a crawl and disappear into a low, dark rock tunnel.

I'm sweaty and exhausted, and my tired emotions are tugging me in too many directions. I know I'm obsessing. Poisoned men lying dead. Running for my life. Madison's face as I backed away from her, abandoning her like the coward I am. Madison becoming Heather. Her betrayal, my anger. Dom staring at her. Jaykob's kiss. Jasper talking me down. They rip through my mind, one after the other. I'm sick, guilty, happy, and so, so bizarrely angry.

It's all I can do to cling to Jaykob's hand, even when the path made it horribly awkward and it would have made sense to let go.

I *can't*.

His hand is warm and heavy around mine, and I've memorized the feeling of every callus against my skin. Jayk is here—alive and tangible and in my hands—and I'm not sure I can ever let him go again.

He kept glancing down at me as we walked, then away again as soon as I looked at him.

It shouldn't be possible for someone as big and tatted and bloodstained as he is, but it's almost . . . cute.

And so very, very necessary.

Eyeing off the narrow entrance of the tunnel, he reluctantly releases me from his grip, and every bit of cold and numbness and ugly despair threatens to flood back in. Like his hand on mine had been holding it at bay.

And it's ridiculous. Utterly absurd. But I'm tired, and my over-worked brain keeps dancing over my new reality—the one where every one of my brutes is still alive. Because it feels like a hallucina-tion, or some kind of black magic. Surely the colors around me are too vibrant, and those flowers smell too heady. This world is a faerie glen, ready to pull me under.

Because I am not this lucky.

Loved ones don't return from the dead . . . and they certainly don't risk themselves to save *me*.

Oblivious to my silent paralysis, Jasper lowers himself to his hands and knees and enters the tunnel. Jaykob nudges me to follow, and I breathe past my silly feelings enough to drop down, wincing as the position puts pressure on my sore wrists.

It takes an age before I finally reach the end of the tunnel, long enough for the gloom to take on specters, but when I crawl out, it's into an enormous cavern.

Jasper stands by the entrance, and he offers his hand to help me up.

Jasper. I haven't been able to look at him once the whole jour-ney. What is *wrong* with me? I tried to *shake his hand*, for heaven's sake. I might as well have asked him to a luncheon and offered my business card.

"Thank you ever so much for coming to rescue me from rape, death, and danger. Oh, you really are a sport for easing me from my meltdown like you'd hold me afloat in the most violent depths of a storm-tossed ocean. See you in November for badminton."

God, he must think I'm the most foolish woman ever to breathe air.

But even as I suck in a humiliated breath, my fingers tingle in anticipation. I lift my hand, and when my fingers slip over his palm, the tingle becomes a *sizzle*.

He doesn't help me up.

Despite my resolve to avoid his gaze, I find myself glancing up at him through my lashes.

His jaw is tight, his sharp gaze sliding over my body . . . and the way I'm kneeling before him. His hand twitches in mine, then firms, until it's almost cruel, and for a single, breathless moment, I imagine that hand wrapped around my throat, twitching just like that.

A slippery heat spills through me, shivering me awake, turning my breathing shallow and my breasts lush and abruptly oversensitive. I swallow hard . . . and feel the invisible press of his grip.

And just like it did with Jaykob, the horrible, unreasonable despair vanishes with his touch. With that gaze. It's as though kneeling for Jasper is another righting in my universe—another part of me slotted into place.

Jasper pulls me up so swiftly that I have to clutch at his shoulders for balance, and my hands flex around the warm muscles there before I steal them back. He crooks the faintest brow at me, but I'm still so close to him. Too close for speaking. Close enough that I can feel his breath fan my hair in the sweetest breeze, and my heart squeezes in my chest.

And God, I wish it would stop.

Jasper doesn't want me. He made that clear enough. My

visceral reaction to him is just cruel at this point. No matter how unexpectedly devilish he looks in Lucky's kit, disheveled and roughed up in a way that makes me want to add my own marks.

He's not mine to have.

Then Jasper tenses under my palms.

"They *live* here?"

I see Jaykob spill out of the tunnel in time to catch Jasper's shocked question. He glances over at us and scoffs, lips twisting. Shaking his head, he kneels beside the tunnel's exit and begins rummaging through his pack with a fierce scowl, not seeming to notice the people skittering away from him in startlement as they come out.

I pull back with a frown, adjusting my glasses as I turn so I can see what has Jasper so affronted.

Sun streams in from several divots in the rock, and a network of caves branches out in a dozen different directions. The setup is more organized than I expected, with caves clearly inhabited by families or small groups. There's a large hollow to my right filled with cooking equipment, and in the center of everything, several logs create a welcoming circle to gather around.

The large man with the sword is kneeling next to a listless Mateo, seemingly trying to get him to have some water, but the rest of the crowd is milling about, bustling from one makeshift setup to the next. They're slow and meandering, chatting to one another in a happy hum that floods me with nostalgia.

The wired adrenaline has mostly faded from my body, like someone has powered down the electricity that was sparking me awake, but I couldn't possibly rest now. My gaze darts from one figure to the next, from Kasey chattering to a statuesque brunette, to the two old women holding hands and whispering together. I soak in the pimple-faced young man who blushes in exasperation as a woman with gentle laugh lines tries to scrub dirt from his cheek and over to a red-haired man in his mid-twenties who talks to a bored crowd with pompous hands.

I don't know their names or their faces, but I still remember them. They're mothers, and teachers, and children, and eccentric elderly neighbors. They're all the people I thought died quick and tragic deaths during Day Death. And it's not just one or two women held in terrible captivity this time—it's *dozens* of people, free and banded together, and the weight of it finally hits me with ferocious force.

They *lived*.

I refuse, absolutely refuse to embarrass myself again by crying, but the lump in my throat and heat behind my eyes are stubbornly refusing to budge.

Every one of them is utterly beautiful.

I look back at Jasper, not understanding, wanting to share this painful joy, but there's a different kind of hurt etched into his features.

I frown, then glance back around, trying to see it as he might. To feel the damp chill in the air and the unforgiving, claustrophobic press of rock beneath and all around. The echoing sounds that somehow always become nightmarish as they repeat.

There may be icy river water somewhere, by the sound, but certainly no showers or dishwashers. There are piles of blankets and a few air mattresses, but no flickering fireplace. There's certainly nothing to keep the rain from pouring through those holes in the rock whenever the weather turns.

It's a far cry from Bristlebrook, but still . . .

"This is . . . well, it's actually quite a good setup," I tell Jasper gently, wanting to explain. "It's not so different from where I used to live."

Jasper goes very still, his lips a slash in that beautiful face, but he turns his head like he's paying attention.

I bite my lip, then gesture at the tunnel. "You see, an entrance like that makes it difficult for anyone to sneak up on you. This cave is sheltered, protected from the elements. It would be easy enough to start a fire, too, and there's fresh air from those openings that would keep it ventilated."

Tilting my head, I gesture toward the sloshing deep in the caves. "There's also water, from the sounds of it—always a plus. They would have to make sure these caves don't flood, of course. But there don't seem to be any piles of debris anywhere, at any height, that would indicate it's a common occurrence, and it seems an easy enough climb to get out through those openings up there." I shrug one shoulder. "I would hope they had a few other exit options, just in case, but all in all, it's really not so bad."

Jasper's eyes press shut, and his eyelashes are midnight against his skin.

My lips purse in confusion. "Jasper? Are you okay?"

He raises one hand for patience.

Baffled, I glance back at Jayk, only to find him staring at me with a clenched jaw and hotly intense eyes.

"I'm sorry?" I venture politely. "I think . . . I think I've missed something."

Jaykob looks down at his pack, then slings it over his shoulder and stalks over to me.

He shoves something into my hand. "Eat."

I look down at the strips of shriveled, dried jerky. My eyes slide back up to Jayk's expectant face, still confused at their odd tension.

"Um. Thank you?"

He nods once, averting his eyes, then rips off a hunk of his own jerky with his teeth.

I take a tentative bite and feel him watching me. It takes a tad too long to swallow, but I force an awkward smile. "It's very . . . chewy."

That seems to satisfy him.

It's no cheese, but I'm still grateful.

"Should we find Dominic and Mad—" I cut myself off, annoyed. "And *Heather*?"

If I'm impolite to her, is Dom going to think I'm jealous?

Of course, I *am* jealous, but I would really rather he didn't think that. I have a handle on it. I'm a mature, reasonable adult after all, even if I do feel as emotionally tossed about as a tugboat in a windstorm. Some jealousy is natural.

Besides, it isn't the real reason I want to feed *Heather* some special soup.

Jasper grimaces. "I'm sure they have their own catching up to do. Perhaps we should leave them to it."

My stomach sours. Okay. Maybe it's partly the reason.

I'm about to respond when there's a commotion by the cave's entrance.

A muscular woman backs out of the tunnel on her knees, her crossbow trained on the opening. She holds it steady as she stands, and I recognize her as the woman who tackled Jayk in the forest earlier.

A figure follows after her, crawling slowly but with his head held high and eyes trained on the arrow in his face like he's readying to catch it. With that fierce expression, I almost believe he could manage it.

Alastair.

My breath catches at seeing him alive, in a confusing mix of guilt and anger and worry. His bandages are soaked with sweat and sticking to him with fresh blood, but though he moves tenderly and his wounds are still only just starting to slowly scab over, for the first time I realize how much better he looks than the first day I saw him.

"Do you have him?" a voice calls urgently from the tunnel, alongside an ear-chilling screech.

"Yeah, I've got him," the woman calls back. "You deal with her."

"Yeah, right," the strained voice calls back. There's a loud *oof*, and the sound of a scuffle, and then two women are wriggling out of the cave—one is the short-haired blonde I half-strangled earlier . . . and the other is Akira.

Akira is struggling fiercely, and two people rush over to help the blonde with her. They lead her over to a far cave, and my stomach turns as I watch.

I hope they take care of her.

"Alastair?"

I turn in time to see Mateo pulling to his feet, pushing back the large man beside him. "*Alastair!*"

The man lets him go but trails watchfully close. Mateo staggers over to Alastair, his expression torn.

"Stay back," the woman with the crossbow snaps, but Mateo ignores her, stepping in close to the burned man.

Alastair's expression is unreadable, but I think I see his shoulders ease, just a bit. Mateo rests his forehead against his, and Alastair slips a hand to the back of his neck as they begin talking in quiet voices.

As much as I want not to care, the unrestrained emotion in Mateo's face right now, as he sees Alastair alive, hits my own tired emotions a little too hard.

I resist the childish urge to say, "I told you so."

The large man stops beside us and sighs. "The pretty ones are always taken."

Jasper gives him a reproving frown. "They're Sinners, Bentley."

"That is on the con list, for sure." He looks down at Jasper and winks. "Is that you making me a better offer?"

My brows fly up, and I examine this *Bentley* more closely. He's a bear of a man, all thick, wild long hair and shoulders the width of my old bookshelves. His chest hair peeks out from his shirt, and his nose looks as though it's been broken more than once. But I suppose he's rather attractive, in a very unpretty kind of way.

Possessiveness surges in me. I give Bentley a polite smile, though it feels tight on my lips. "Jasper isn't interested in men. Sorry."

Dear God. That wasn't what I meant to say.

And certainly not like *that*.

Goodness gracious, I might as well have peed on him!

What on earth is wrong with me? I don't do this. I'm *polite*. I've never had a jealous bone in my body, and I was *married*. I don't feel in control of myself right now. I'm frayed and tired, and realizing my men are alive only makes me want to clutch them to me and never let go.

Bentley's grin widens as his gaze slides to me, and there's a long, pointed silence beside me that makes me want to become a bat and find a new home deep in the cavernous darkness.

I wonder if Jasper is as embarrassed for me right now as I am for myself.

Jaykob slings an arm over my shoulder with a smirk. "Now, that ain't exactly—"

"Be quiet, Jaykob," Jasper hisses, pressing one finger to his temple. Then he removes it, and gives my face a tense, searching look.

He's . . . not interested in men, though. Is he? Lucky said he wasn't.

I give him the searching look back. Actually, Lucky said he thought the others were "at least mostly" straight. Whatever *that* means.

Rather than answering my unspoken question, Jasper sighs through his nose, then gives Bentley a vexed look. "I'm not interested in you."

An answer that tells me *nothing*.

"Hmm," I say, pressing into Jaykob.

Bentley raises one brow and opens his mouth like he's about to say something. Then he closes it and snorts, saying instead, "You must be the little miss they were looking for." He grins. "Serious thing, aren't you? You—"

"If you tell her to smile, I'll hit you myself," Heather says behind me.

I grit my teeth as I turn. Dom trails to a halt beside her.

"Nah, not my style," Bentley says. He lifts his chin at her in a friendly nod. "Bentley, president of the Grande Medieval Association of America."

But Heather's attention is caught on Alastair and Mateo behind him.

And when she smiles, I see their deaths.

Chapter 20

Dominic

T his is a goddamned mess.

Heather strides in front of me as we make our way back to the main cavern, pointing out the exits and the hazards like I can hear anything except this roaring in my ears. Heather. *Heat.* She's injured and filthy, and she stinks like a military gym locker room, but she's never cared about any of that. Because it's *Heather.*

Heather who saved me.

Heather who loved me.

Heather who broke me.

Heather who . . . sold me out.

We've got her group secured in this dank cave network she said they used sometimes, and I can't pretend it doesn't piss me off. There are kids here. Crotchety old folks who should be reclining on rocking chairs in Jasper's library. These people shouldn't be ducking from temporary camp to camp in these fucking woods that seethe with danger.

How much of an asshole does she really think I am that this is the better option?

I can't see Thomas loving this either.

Families pause in their business as I pass, watching me warily, and I wish I knew how to show them I'm not a damn threat. There are too many vulnerable people here, and I have no idea what to do with them.

I know that Sam wants them.

I need to get out of here. It's time to get back to Bristlebrook. We've got what we came for, and that's enough. There's no need to borrow trouble by staying.

Except Heat is here. Heat is here and Sam wants her too.

"*What?*" she prompts, looking back at me, and I realize I'm staring at her again.

"Nothing." I shake my head.

She tilts her head, and her red hair falls to the side. I used to love that hair, was obsessed with the fire of it. The fire of her.

I wait for lust to punch me in the gut, the way I remember it.

But the hit doesn't land.

Her lips curve up in a teasing tilt, but her eyes are sad. "Does that mean you don't hate me anymore, CC?"

CC. Captain Cutie. The stupid nickname that used to make me want to spank her, though that urge doesn't find me now either.

Our fight before she left was like a drone strike. It left me in ashes, and her retreating back must have caught its own burns. Memories haunt her eyes, and it's regret that comes for me now. I said a lot back then. A lot I shouldn't have.

But she's the one who walked out of Bristlebrook with Thomas, taking the rest of our civilians with her. Civilians who would rather leave a luxury damn lodge and all the protection we offered than deal with me as their leader.

And so did she.

I never hated her for it—only myself—but right now, I'm too

aware of the gaunt faces around me. Of Bristlebrook all those miles away, blown out and burned up. I'm too busy remembering Lucky lying on the floor like a ready-made ghost, blood pumping from his chest . . . and Eden, soot-stained and determined. Eden, who was sick over killing one Sinner and now apparently wiped out half a dozen. Eden, covered in bruises and her wrists sawed almost in two from too-tight bindings.

So I don't want to fucking flirt.

I want answers.

I need to know if she's the reason for this shitshow.

"We need to talk," I say, and Heather's smile fades.

She nods, and in her eyes, I see the woman who saved my life replace the one who left me. She's all business.

"Let me check on the crew and then we can go over everything."

I follow behind her, trying to work out why I feel so . . . off. I don't know what I expected to feel if I saw her again, but I thought it would be more.

I study her hair, her walk that manages to be confident even with a limp. Her ass.

Nothing.

I frown. Exhaustion, that has to be it. It's been more than two weeks, and I'm running on fumes. I've spent the last three years thinking about Heather. Hating her, wanting her, missing her so badly my lungs ached in my chest.

She saved my life the night we met, back after Day Death when we were trying to get our convoy of civilians back to Bristlebrook. We were raided on the road and took heavy losses. I would have been one of them if she hadn't come out of nowhere like a storm of fury and plugged the two guys pinning me.

After that, Heather became the best friend I ever had, besides Beau. So, I should be wanting to rip her clothes from her body. I should want to make her regret ever choosing Thomas over me. He should be here so I can punch him for leaving us without a word of goodbye.

But the urge is as absent as he is.

We spill out into the main cave, and people are milling about everywhere. So many and in such a disorganized mass that I feel instantly claustrophobic, but my gaze quickly finds Eden standing between Jaykob and Jasper, and my shoulders unknot.

Jaykob has his arm slung over her shoulder, so possessively he might as well collar her right there. Irritation pricks me. I told him she ended the deal—why the fuck is he still hanging off her? If *she* wants Jayk, then all power to her. When we talked by the river, she hadn't seemed opposed. But I swear to God, if he's giving her a hard time after everything she's been through, then—

I slam into Heather's back when she stops, and she shoves me off her.

"Dude, watch it." She gives me an incredulous look.

I steady her, and myself. Then I scrub a hand over my stubbled face with a clipped, "Sorry."

My gaze drifts back to Eden, just as Bentley eyes her off. My eyes narrow on him, but Jaykob's already yanking Eden close. Heather gives me a bemused, sideways look, and I shoot her an irritated frown.

Eden gets herself into more trouble than one soft-spoken librarian should be able to. I'm just looking out for her. It's about time I started protecting her properly.

She's just become my number one priority.

"Serious thing, aren't you," Bentley muses. "You—"

"If you tell her to smile, I'll hit you myself," Heather cuts him off, and it's my turn to eye her.

Heather's never been one to fight other people's battles. She's big on people defending themselves—especially women. The Heather I knew from three years ago would have eaten Eden for breakfast.

What the hell happened in that camp?

Heather shoves forward, ignoring Bentley's introduction, and it's only when she pushes past Jaykob that I see the tense standoff behind them. There's a crossbow trained on the two Sinners murmuring together.

"Who let the prisoners talk to each other?" I snap, and Jayk shrugs one shoulder.

"Like it matters. They're dead men anyway."

"That they are," Heather agrees, and she glances at the muscular, tattooed woman holding Alastair. "Sloane, take them to the deep cave. I'm going to have fun with this."

The man with the bandages releases the other Sinner, and tension steals over me. There's a look that some men have that says they've taken a life. This one has that look a dozen times over. He's moving slowly, and I'm sure those wounds are hurting him, but no sign of it shows on his face.

I see the SEAL tattoo on his collarbone, set in a bunch of vines and plants. He's trained, too.

And right now, he's trained on Heather.

"Cut it, Heat. We need to talk to them." I pull out my gun as a precaution—if this guy's a SEAL, then he can do plenty of damage fast with no weapon at all. But the man's eyes don't shift from her. Heather's nose wrinkles in silent, vicious hatred.

"Jayk, secure them," I order, and he releases Eden so he can get to his pack.

"You don't need to do shit," Heather says dismissively. "Go get some rest. I have this handled."

I grit my teeth. Stepping closer to her, I lower my voice. "You're emotional and not thinking straight. We need information."

Heather's eyes widen in shock, then something dangerous fires through them.

"God, you are un-fucking-believable." She bares her teeth. "*Emotional*? You want to try that again? Or are you going to suggest I'm on my period next?"

A throbbing starts up in my temple. I don't know how to talk to women—I've never been good at it, and being deployed for four tours didn't leave a huge amount of downtime to practice. Beau always smoothed that stuff over for me.

"Not emotional because you're a woman. You're emotional because you've been their captive for who the fuck knows how long. You're compromised, and we need information." Then I add with a growl, "And you look ready to murder someone."

"Because I want to murder him." She mock gasps. "Ding ding ding. We have a winner."

I grit my teeth as Heather glares at me.

"You have no idea what this man did to me, Dom. No clue what happened in that camp. You don't get a goddamn say." She lifts her voice so it carries, her jaw set. "And this? This is *my* camp. These are *my* people. They chose *me* to protect them—not you. So sit your ass down."

The Sinner's cold, pale eyes gleam as Jayk ties his wrists, and a murmuring starts up around us, but I'm caught in my own frustration. I get she wants vengeance, I do, but this is moving too fast. She's being stupid and stubborn, and she doesn't know shit about interrogation. She'll get these Sinners killed, and we *need* an inside source. But fuck if I could ever talk sense into her when she gets like this. She never *listens*.

"There is no sign of Sam anywhere. These civilians have left a storm of tracks all the way to this cave's front door. How long do you think it'll be before they come for every woman and child in here?" I snarl back. "These people are prey, and they're the predators, and you have to know that they'll be on your trail in *days*. You have no useful weapons, no fortifications, *nothing*. You!" I point at the woman restraining the Sinner. "Did you find weapons in their camp?"

She gives me a hard look, glancing at Heather for approval, then nods. "A few rifles. Some semi-auto, a few auto. A couple pistols. Jennifer's bringing them."

I shake my head, gritting my teeth, and snap my gaze back to Heather. "It's not enough. You might as well bundle them up for Cyanide now."

Wrecked with this unaccountable rage, I'm about to hit her with more when I feel a gentle hand on my forearm.

"*What?*" I snap, and my head whips around to see Eden, tense-faced and hesitant at my side.

And I instantly feel like an asshole.

"What is it?" I ask again, and it takes less effort than I thought it would to make my voice soft.

She pushes her glasses up the bridge of her nose, and she glances at the Sinners, then around the cave.

"I think it might be better if you both had this conversation in private," she says in a low, disapproving voice. "You're frightening people."

I track her glance and see the pale, anxious faces.

Shit.

Guilt and self-reproach hit my stomach like an anvil. Of course I am. Panic pricks me. I shouldn't be around people like this— they're too soft, and I'm too hard. I was made for military bases and rapid deployments. I don't know how to do this.

I look at Heather, and she grimaces.

"Back cave," she says again to Sloane, then she blows out a breath and looks at me. "You and your men come too. And we'll *talk*."

There's a warning in that, and I force a smile, hoping the civilians see it.

"Fine. We'll talk." I raise my voice pointedly, smiling as wide as I can, though it really doesn't seem to fit my cheeks. "Everything is fine. Everyone can relax."

Nobody seems to relax.

I let the smile go, my frustration ratcheting up further. Why am I so bad at this? Less than a day, and I've already scared the shit out of a bunch of innocent women. I need to get away from these civilians. Now.

Angry with myself, I nod to Jasper, Jayk, and Bentley, and we follow after Heather, the armed women, and the prisoners. After a moment, Heather turns, halting us.

I follow her look back.

Eden lingers behind, watching after us with her hands clenched in her shirt.

"You coming?" Heather calls to her.

I frown. Heather is trigger-happy at the best of times, and this is bound to be ugly. Eden isn't like her—used to violence and bloodshed. She deserves to be sheltered from the worst of this. She doesn't need Heather bullying her if she wants to rest.

Eden walks up slowly, eyeing me questioningly.

"Don't do that," Heather says. "Don't ask for permission. You have as much right as he does to be included in this."

My tongue presses against my teeth until I can control my annoyance. "She's been through enough. Stop pushing her."

Heather shakes her head. "No. You don't know what she's been through. You don't know what she can handle."

"I know better than most," I say impatiently. "She saved my life."

"She saved mine too," Heather snaps back. "Think about that. Maybe you should stop underestimating her."

"I would appreciate it if you stopped speaking for me," Eden says mildly, pausing in front of us. "*Both* of you."

I blink, then look at her. She has bruises all over her face, and her wrists look torn up. I want to clean them and wrap them up myself.

Anger hooks into my guilt.

She shouldn't look like this. I was meant to protect her.

I have to protect her. It's all that matters.

Eden takes a breath, then looks up at me, searching my face.

"You promised that I would be included in things. That you wouldn't keep secrets. Did you mean that?"

At the river. That damn river, with her between us, soaked in the blood of a man who tried to kill me. Where I washed her clean and tasted her mouth.

Where she broke our deal and forged a new one as she snuggled, naked, in my arms.

Right then, I would have promised her anything she asked.

I stare at her. "I meant it."

I remember her lips on mine after she brought me a duffle bag full of death . . . and corpses she left littering the forest with poisoned soup. Time and again, she's proved herself. Not in the hot, violent way Heather does.

Eden works quietly, steady as the gentle river we bathed in. It's different.

It's restful.

"I promised, and I meant it," I repeat in a low voice the others won't hear, and her brow furrows. "But only if you want to. You just need to—"

"Speak up," she murmurs. "Yes. I'll remember that. I would like to come."

A small, tired smile brushes her lips. They're chapped and dehydrated, and the lower one has a cut through it. But her shoulders loosen.

Heather starts talking again as we walk—slowly for her injured ankle. I ignore her, watching Eden out of the corner of my eye.

We arrive in a dark cave, and it takes a moment before one of the women lights up a dozen lanterns.

"Oh, those are nice." Bentley examines one. "You know, if the candles are too much hard work, I can show you how to make a real nice torch out of—"

"No thanks," Heather says, not looking at him.

Jayk shoves the two Sinners until they fall to their knees, and I move up to stand beside Heather. She's staring at them like her eyes could draw blood.

"Where to start?" Heather muses, walking toward them.

The bandaged man watches her with cool interest—the other man with resentful distrust.

"Perhaps with some introductions?" Jasper suggests silkily. "Who are these men, exactly?"

"Dead man one and dead man two," Heather responds, crouching in front of them. "Dom, give me your knife."

"No. Who are they, Heather?" I demand.

I need to know exactly how much use they're going to be to me. I need to know exactly what they did. As that thought hits, I check on Eden, who is watching them with a grave expression.

I need to know exactly who they did it *to*.

I shift, suddenly uncomfortable.

Heather huffs. "Dom, just give me—"

"The one who almost shot me is Mateo," Eden breaks in. "And the one with the burns is Alastair."

"Did they touch you?" Jayk says suddenly, and I realize he's still standing right behind them, his hand on his knife.

Fuck. Heather might not be my only problem here.

Heather stands, turning to stare at Eden like she's trying to communicate with her eyes. Eden glances at her, then she looks at the two Sinners.

She looks at them for a long, long time.

The burned man, Alastair, tilts his head just slightly, raising one eyebrow a fraction of an inch. The familiar look makes me want to hit him.

Finally, Eden shakes her head. "No, they didn't touch me." She glances up at Jayk. "Actually, they stopped the other Sinners from doing any serious damage. I think . . . I think the only reason I wasn't tortured, or raped, is because of them. Alastair had some weight among the Sinners, and he used it to keep us from being harmed."

Well, shit. I straighten, giving them a new look. That complicates things.

Jayk stares at Eden, then slowly removes his hand from his knife as Bentley whistles low. "And that's another one for the pro list." He looks away from the lantern he was examining and grins at Mateo. "If you ever get out of this mess, you look me up, dollface."

Jesus. Time and place.

Mateo doesn't even look in Bentley's direction.

"Why are you *defending* them?" Heather gives Eden a furious glare that could singe the hair off her head.

Rather than backing down, Eden lifts her chin with quiet dignity. "I'm not defending them, Madison. I'm just stating facts." Then she pauses, her pursed lips becoming chilly. "Heather. I'm not defending them, *Heather*."

"Same person, babe," Heather says in a hard voice. "Whether you like it or not. But they"—she points at the Sinners—"don't deserve your mercy. Or did you forget that Mateo dragged us back like pigs for a slaughter. We could have escaped then. Why are they even alive, Eden? You were meant to kill them. You had the bowl *in your hands*. He was meant to die."

Eden's hands knot in front of her, and she hesitates. There's a torn, guilty expression on her face as she looks at Heather. Something squeezes in my chest too, watching her struggle with this.

She couldn't do it. She has a soft, big heart. She never wanted to kill anyone.

I wonder what that's like.

"I—" She tucks a strand of hair over her ear, then glances at the two men. "Well, I—"

"I figured it out," Alastair breaks in smoothly. He's watching Eden again, and I'm ready to rip out his eyes, though there's nothing heated in his gaze. There's nothing in it at all. Those eyes are empty . . . and cold. "The men were dropping. It didn't take much."

Eden frowns at him, then looks at me, biting her lip. I shift closer to her.

"We can fix that right now," Heather snaps.

"Actually, I need a few things from these two first," Bentley breaks in, his voice too loud for the small cave. "Albuterol. Your little friends have a stash back at Cyanide in your 'Den,' I know you do, and I want in."

"No one cares about your damn inhalers." Heather storms up to the two Sinners, and grabs Alastair by the hair. She yanks his head back. "Tell them how much blood is on your hands. What, you're a hero because you stopped them raping us? That's the bare *fucking* minimum."

She punches him across the face, and his head whips to the side.

When he lifts it, blood coats his teeth. "Do you want to play, death wish?"

Heather hisses, then lifts her arm to hit him again. I come up behind her and catch her fist, yanking her into me.

"Enough. That's *en*—"

Heather slams her head back, and I only just pull back to avoid it, though she clips me in the solar plexus with her elbow, then wrenches herself out of my grip.

"He killed Tommy," she shouts at me, but this time, her anger is coated in tears. "Execution-style. He didn't fucking hesitate."

Her throat works, her face twisted with anger, and she shakes her head.

"Thomas is dead?" Jasper asks, his voice ringing with shock.

Her words hit me hard. Thomas. We had our share of problems, especially after Heather. He was a competitive shit, and he slacked off on basic duties more than I liked. But he was solid when he was needed, and he was in my unit for five years before we ever saw a flash of Heather's red hair. I played cards with him in dusty deserts, the sand making the cards gritty, and drank with him off duty in Eastern Europe until we were slipping off our chairs.

I hated that Heather thought he was a better man than me . . . but fuck if I ever wanted him dead.

"Tommy and me . . ." she starts, then stops, looking up and blinking. She swallows, then tries again. "We left Bristlebrook with the civs, and it was hard. Harder than we thought it would be. Eventually, we worked out some of these caves, figured out some safe places, but we knew you had cameras, and we . . . we didn't want you finding us."

Heather gives me a guilty glance, then grimaces. "We looped the feed, just through this part of the woods. We planted herbs and vegetables all through the area—wild and random, so anyone coming through the forest wouldn't know people were living around here. And we went out searching for more people."

She runs a hand over her hair. "I figured there were plenty of people who might hide from groups of armed men, so I started going out with some of our women—and we found them. Families. Older people. More women. We brought them back. When we reached fifty, we split up into different cave networks to reduce foot traffic. But we . . . struggled."

More than fifty. I try to count back in my head how many people I saw here today. There's a lot more than fifty. Maybe double that.

"Struggled how?" I ask, and I know my voice is testy. But goddamn. We were so close. We could have *helped*.

"Food," she says, and she crosses her arms over her chest. "Food was our biggest issue. We didn't have weapons, so we couldn't raid anyone, and only a few crossbows to even try to hunt. We had some snares and nets for fishing, but we had a lot of people. So we decided to try Cyanide City."

Fuck.

"Bad move, that," Bentley offers unhelpfully. "Only the worst live in Cyanide."

Jayk glares at him. "Don't you live in Cyanide, Red Zone?"

Bentley shrugs his huge shoulders. "Well, sure, that's how I know."

"Yeah, no shit," Heather says tiredly. "But we needed food. Meds. Weapons. A damn break, I don't know."

I've had enough. "Cyanide, Heat? Fucking Cyanide over Bristlebrook? Were we that bad of an option?"

She shakes her head, not looking at me. "I didn't think we'd be welcome. Not after the way we left things."

"I wouldn't have turned down *civilians*," I grit out, and it feels like I'm grinding my guts and putting them on display.

I can't bear it, the thought of being responsible for more lives. It's different with the guys—they can handle themselves. I know how to talk to them. I give them orders, and they don't get their panties in a knot about it. They just *obey*. Usually, anyway.

These people need help. Food. Housing. Women, in this world, attract predators like bees to nectar. They need to be defended. Worst, they need to trust me, and I don't know how to get them to do that.

Not when I don't even trust myself.

But I would work it out. I'd *do* it. Because what good am I if I can't protect innocent people? It was the whole reason I followed Colonel Slade—dad—into the Rangers.

Heather does look at me then, eyes like sad gray clouds. "I know, CC. I do know you wouldn't have turned us away. We just . . . we thought we had other options."

I turn away with a derisive sound. Clearly that worked out.

Finally, she sighs.

"We were trying to get into the hospital when Sam found us." She laughs bitterly. "Of all the fucking people."

Bentley sighs, leaning against the wall. "Asshole, that guy. You don't want to know the amount of booby traps we had to set up to keep the Sinners out of Red Zone."

He shudders, and while he's distracted, I eye him.

"*You* set up the snake pit?" Mateo hisses suddenly, pulling against his restraints. His brown eyes are wide and incredulous on Bentley. "That killed two of our men."

"Did it really?" Bentley's wide grin is eager, his eyes lighting up. "We knew it had been set off but didn't find any bodies. It's great to hear your work paid off. They are *not* easy to set up."

Mateo glowers at him, while Bentley seems lost to his thoughts.

Snake pits. Swords and snake pits. For fuck's sake.

I rub my head, and when I have my shit together again, I look at Heather and nod my chin at Alastair. "How does he come into it?"

Heather drags her bemused look from Bentley back to Alastair. Her face darkens.

"Tommy had made it inside, and Alastair had him pinned. He radioed Sam, and Sam told him to kill him. And he just . . . did. We heard the shot, and I saw the body afterwards." A muscle in her tight jaw flickers, and she stares at Alastair. "He didn't ask a single goddamned question."

Alastair's jaw clenches as he stares back at her.

"Did you kill him?" I ask, needing to be sure. What he says matters here.

The man meets Heather's eyes, like she's the only one in the cave. "Yes."

"Fine," I say, feeling heavy. I unstrap my gun. "I'm not making the same mistake we made with Sam. You attacked us, killed one of us, you need to die. We'll keep the other for questioning."

Alastair keeps his eyes on Heather, and I glance between them. She's burning with hatred, staring back at him, but I can't make out a single emotion on his face.

I swipe off my safety, trying to shift the sudden queasiness in my gut.

I think it's that he's on his knees. It doesn't sit right to shoot an unarmed man.

"No!" Mateo shouts as he tries to get to his feet, but Jayk

shoves him down. "*Mierda!* Get your hands off me. You touch him and I'll kill you."

"Wait." Eden's voice makes me pause for just a second, and I half-glance back at her.

"Go, little librarian. You don't need to see this."

"Give it to me," Heather insists, and when I look up at her, she's still glaring at Alastair with deep, burning hatred. But her voice isn't furious now—it's almost gentle. "I want to do it."

The uneasy feeling increases. I glance at Jasper to find him watching me intently. His head turns just slightly, and I read the question in it.

Are you sure?

This is what I have to do, right? To protect the civilians?

To protect Eden?

"No, don't you dare. I'll kill you. He doesn't deserve it. He's a good man, you asshole, don't do it," Mateo howls. His fear is infectious, almost pungent in the enclosed space.

His wide eyes snag on Alastair, and they look at each other.

For some reason, it reminds me of Beau.

It's suddenly suffocating in here. I take a step forward, lifting the gun, and the adrenaline starts pumping. It doesn't bring its usual excited flush, though. None of the sense of purpose.

It feels wrong.

"Sir, please, *don't.*"

Sir.

Heat licks up my spine, and I pause as that one word takes me out at the knees. *Sir*, she says, in that sweet little voice. *Sir*, is what she said as she counted out every time I clapped my hand against that soft, round ass of hers. My palm tingles like it wants the contact again. I want to make it jiggle. I want to hear her gasps. I want to leave every red imprint of my hand on that perfect ass like a brand.

Sir, she says.

I lower the gun, packing away the sense of relief I feel when I do, and look at her properly.

"Is this you speaking up?" I ask.

Last time, I didn't listen to the civilians, and they lost their trust in me. I need to do better. If Eden speaks . . . I'm going to listen.

Slowly, Eden drops her chin in a nod. "It is."

With her big eyes and soft lips, she looks like a determined angel perched on my right. A pretty conscience. I wonder if she ever gets tired of being so good.

"No." Heather's voice is alarmed. Almost panicked. "No, it's decided. He has to die."

I shake my head at my own thoughts. I guess that makes Heat the devil.

"I think we need him."

Eden picks over her words, and I eye her sharply. Her eyes are guarded behind her glasses but deadly serious.

"What do we need him for, Eden?" I ask, but Heather's already talking over the top of me and dragging my attention.

I watch her stalk the room, the way she does when she's frayed. Fuck, she's losing it. I need to keep an eye on her before she does something stupid.

"No! Tommy is *dead* because of him."

"And we almost died because of you," Eden snaps back, and I've never heard that tone from her before. I wouldn't have thought that tone *could* come from her.

It burns with merciless contempt.

She was at breaking point in the forest earlier. In shock. I'd put her attack on Heather down to that. But she still seems angry. I know about that kind of anger. It can be like a sickness.

Jasper's watching her too, a slight crease between his brows.

"Maybe we should be talking about what you did," Eden says harshly. "You showed them where the cameras were, you admitted that much, but it was more than that. Tommy showed you how to loop the cameras and you did that for them too, didn't you? You did everything you possibly could to send them to Bristlebrook."

"I didn't have a choice," Heather says roughly, facing off against Eden. A warrior and a librarian.

"There's always a—"

"*Don't*," Heather warns, stepping in. "Don't patronize me. We had women with us, and more here, and they wanted details. I had to give them *something*, or they would have ripped the others apart to find the rest of us."

She glances at me, then Jayk, then Jasper, then back to Eden. "Sam already had a grudge against Bristlebrook, and he thought they were there. So I just . . . encouraged that thought." Swallowing, she continues, "You have to understand, I was a spoiled brat when I left Bristlebrook—hell, maybe I still am—but when I left, I took on a responsibility for these women, and for all the ones who came after. And it was *hard*. People died, and I needed to be better. They trusted me to be better."

Her voice breaks, and she looks at me now. Jaw clenching, I nod without meeting her eyes. I know what she's saying. That kind of duty is a burden—thankless and fucking terrifying. It's why I never wanted to do it again.

"We aren't armed here. I've taught them what I could, and we've made snares and rock slings, traps, and arrows, but most of the people here aren't fighters. They're not built to defend themselves—not against armed men. But the Rangers were, Eden." Heather's voice catches. "Even with the odds stacked against them, even with low visibility, I know what Dom can do. And he and the others had a much better chance at any good outcome than we would have."

Eden shakes her head, but a tear slips down her cheek. She swipes it away angrily.

"I didn't have a choice," Heather repeats.

I nod again, throat thick. Heather is solemn and haunted, and relief trickles through me as it all finally starts to make sense. My instincts aren't broken. She did sell us out . . . and I would have done the same thing in a heartbeat.

These people had to be protected.

"Fine," Eden says abruptly, her voice husky. "I might be able to understand that. But you shouldn't have lied to me."

Some of the tension eases back as Heather raises a brow. "I didn't *lie*—"

"You lied about your name, and your intentions, and you— You befriended me under false pretenses." Eden's glasses slip down her nose, and she shoves them back up like they've personally offended her.

"Madison is what Tommy used to call me," Heather says quietly. "It stuck with this group. I'm Madison to them. I didn't lie on purpose." She takes a deep breath. "I didn't tell you I knew them because I needed a friend, and I didn't want you to hate me. Turns out, you were a good one."

Eden crosses her arms over her chest. "A better one than you, I think."

"Yeah. Probably."

I look between them, not sure how I feel about this friendship. Heather, fierce and fiery and everything I ever thought I wanted for myself. Eden, determined and thoughtful and too clever by a half.

Why does Eden want to keep Alastair alive?

"These people can't stay here," she says to Heather, then she glances at me. Her piercing blue eyes assess me. "If what Dom said is right, this place is compromised."

She swallows, then her voice becomes strained. "You know he's going to come—his men need a victory now. And Sam needs us as . . . as prizes for them. It's how he keeps them in line."

Heather and Eden exchange a long, loaded look. I hate the fear I see in their faces. This bullshit isn't something either of them should have to worry about.

Heather's shoulders drop. "No, we can't stay. We have other places. None as big, or as comfortable, but we'll manage."

And a weight attaches itself to my back. To my shoulders. To my ankles like a ball and chain.

Because I know what's coming.

It's the only right thing.

"Jasper," Eden says softly, and Jasper gives her a measured look.

His expression is tenderness itself when he says, "Of course they're welcome."

"If this place is compromised, then Bristlebrook definitely is as well." Heather frowns, glancing at me. "I don't know, maybe we should—"

"Bristlebrook is the best option," Eden says firmly. "It's defensible, further away. There are more weapons there—lots of them. Not to mention, it's far better shelter than any cave. We have stored foods, the farm. Plus, it has the added benefit of being where we defeated the Sinners last time. You *must* know it's the better option."

"Wait, weapons." Eden's brow crinkles. "If they only found guns in the Sinners' camp, then what happened to the bag of explosives I had?"

My back stiffens. "From Lucky's stash?"

She nods, and I grimace. That's bad. I look over at Alastair.

"What happened to the bag?" I demand.

Those cold, cold eyes watch me for a long moment, and when Jayk steps forward threateningly, he smiles a small, unamused smile.

"Sam was in the woods when you took off after your girl. He took the bag and some provisions and left back to Cyanide."

"He left you?" Jasper asks sharply. "Why would he do that?"

Alastair's smile could give frostbite. "Ideological differences."

"Like he would stick his neck out for anyone." Mateo mutters something in Spanish under his breath.

Jayk swears, and Jasper gives me a thoughtful look.

"All the more reason we'll need the firepower at Bristlebrook. We can watch them for an approach as well, if we move the cameras around," Jasper muses. "They can still work for surveillance as soon as they're repaired and moved to a new location."

Jayk gives him a begrudging, surprised look right as Bentley chimes in.

"You should build some fortifications too, since you know they're probably going to hit you in force. A dry moat, walls, some archery posts . . . snake-pit traps." When everyone looks at him, Bentley shrugs. "Historically, they've worked well."

Mateo scowls at the same time I do.

Great. Just what I need. Some civilian giving me advice on battle tactics.

I don't see him offering up Red Zone as a sanctuary.

"You're right. You are, it's just—" Heather exhales hard, glancing at me again. "No, you're right. Bristlebrook is the best option."

I rub my forehead as the throbbing starts back up.

Every gaunt face from the cavern flickers through my mind. Every civilian's back as they walked out of Bristlebrook. The white, limp face of the tiny eight-year-old boy who caught a bullet on my watch.

I'm not the right man for this job. Every civilian incursion to Bristlebrook has been a disaster. How am I meant to keep all of these people safe?

But I can't turn them away.

I sigh. "Then I guess we're all going back to Bristlebrook."

CHAPTER 21

EDEN

SURVIVAL TIP #26
Take what you can get.
Greed will be the end of you.

I drop my pack with a heavy sigh. We packed up for Bristlebrook early this morning, and the sun had long since crept away before Dom and Heather called a halt to our travel.

We've made it a good distance. It probably shouldn't have surprised me how quickly these people were able to gather their belongings and move as a group, but it did. Like me, they're better at running than they are at fighting.

Darkness gathers in my chest again at the thought—a niggling bleakness I can't quite shake, no matter how I try.

In my head, I back away from Madison, my *friend*, over and over. I watch myself in the camp again and again, doing anything to survive, all the time, at any cost. Sacrificing anyone. Killing anyone. But how I got here shouldn't matter, as long as I lived.

I *should* be happy. It worked. My brutes are alive, I'm free, surviving again, and I'm surrounded by a crowd of friendly faces.

So why did the night still come for me?

I try to blink past my tiredness. I didn't sleep much at all, staring at the nightmarish phantasms on the rock wall until they became my entire reality. My Plato's cave, where every unnamed doubt and fear and feeling was cast up like a specter before my eyes.

My pallet was set up by a low fire, close to Jaykob and Jasper and Dom. I thought about sneaking in beside Jaykob—just in the hopes that he might be able to make the shadows retreat again— but he was out in moments, snoring loudly enough to raise the dead, and I didn't want to disturb him. Jasper, of course, was out of the question. I don't even want to imagine what he might do if I had the audacity to try to *cuddle* him. And Dom . . . well, Dom was up having a low, serious conversation with Heather for half the night.

So I just lay there, wondering why there was still this impossible pressure on my chest.

I smile gratefully as Jennifer, a brunette with tattoos and a septum piercing, hands me some jerky and some sort of fried potato. They set up their camp for the night just as efficiently as they'd packed up, and low fires burn through the trees like tiny beacons in the dim light as dinner is cooked.

I make quick work of the food as I walk the camp, looking for my men. There are ninety-two of us in all, Dom said, and it makes for a generous sprawl through the trees.

I pass Akira, who's finally calmed down enough to sit quietly before a fire. She was given the choice to stay or go, Jasper told me, and she chose to stay. I suppose she doesn't have anywhere to go.

There are people patrolling around the camp, standing watch, and it helps relax some of my tension. I know it's unlikely that the small number of Sinners would come back for us, but I can't stop looking over my shoulder.

Toward the edges of the camp, I spot Alastair and Mateo. They're tied to a tree beside one another, and the similarities between their positions and how Heather and I were trussed in their camp can't be a coincidence.

They're both covered in blood.

The pressure on my chest increases, and I slowly make my way over. Alastair's head is tilted back against the tree trunk, and he's breathing shallowly. His bandages still haven't been changed, and Mateo seems to be unconscious.

I hesitate in front of them, my bag of herbs feeling heavy at my side.

I don't know why I have this urge to tend to them, except that I remember very distinctly how it felt to be in their position, and they did help me when I was at my most vulnerable.

But Heather is also right. They killed Thomas, captured people, went on raids with the Sinners . . . and they attacked Bristlebrook. If my instincts are right, I'd guess that Alastair was more heavily involved in the planning than he let on. Sam has the drive, certainly, and the weapons and the men. But after spending several days with him, I'm not quite confident that he has the brains to mastermind that bait and switch.

And Alastair has already revealed his scheming mind.

I tug my lower lip between my teeth. Sam is undoubtedly going back to Cyanide, and from his speech the night Jorge died, I know he doesn't plan to stay there. He and the Sinners want more of everything—territory, food, women. He's not going to stop.

Sam is a threat.

And not only to us, either. My stomach churns when I think of all the women and children he's keeping there for his bone-chilling purposes. They must be desperate and frightened, and they have *no one* fighting for them.

Except Alastair.

Alastair might be a villain, but he's a villain of a different sort —and he can't free anyone while he's tied to a tree.

Alastair's pale eyes creak open, and I'm about to start asking him my own questions when his gaze shifts to something behind me.

I whirl around, heart pounding, only to find Dom leaning against a tree, his arms crossed over his chest.

Watching me.

I press a hand to my chest. "Would you please make some noise if you're going to do that?"

Dom cocks a brow. "Pay more attention to your surroundings."

My heart rate slowly returns to a normal rhythm. "I was just..."

That brow lifts higher.

I huff, then look back down at the two men. Alastair's eyes are closed again, but I don't trust one whit that he's truly unconscious. Small hairs lift along my arms, and I'm not sure if it's the cool night or my own uneasiness.

"Did you really have to hurt them?" I ask softly. "Couldn't you just ask for whatever information you need?"

Dom snorts. "Just *ask*. Why didn't I think of that?"

My cheeks flush, and he kicks off the tree and takes my elbow, leading me a short distance away. The dry leaves crackle under our feet until we find a still-green spot littered with boulders. The air feels damper here and rich, loamy soil has a soft give under my boots. It's a smaller space . . . and an intimate one.

"We asked. They gave us bare details but nothing of use." Dom's hand lingers on my elbow for a touch too long before he releases it. "They say that Sam and his right-hand man are the only ones with the codes to enter the hospital—no one can get in without one of them authorizing it."

Surprise, then unexpected pleasure bursts in my chest. Dom is actually sharing information. *Without* being asked.

Beating down on my delight, I try to focus on his words. Something about them niggles at my memory.

"I think that must be true," I say slowly. "When they first

brought me to the camp, Sam implied that no one could hurt him
—that they needed him. He said that he could throw Alastair and
Mateo out."

Dom nods once, and I can't help but notice the strong lines of
his jaw. The pretty, healthy glow of his skin under his five-o'clock
shadow. He's had a chance to clean up . . . and clean suits him as
well as being dirty does.

"I believe it," he says in a grim tone. "But if they can't get in or
out without him, and if they can't be leveraged as hostages—"

I tuck a strand of hair behind my ear. "Sam doesn't care about
them. They cause him some trouble, I think."

And a lot more of it, if Alastair can get back to the Den.

"Right. So they're useless to us."

I glance up, and the press of his lips is terribly ominous. The
intimate night suddenly seems bleak and threatening, and the
earthy scent of decaying leaves reminds me too much of death.

"You're planning to . . . to kill them?"

The gold in his eyes isn't liquid and warm now. It's cooled
metal extinguished in a forge.

"We can't afford to keep them, Eden." He looks away from me,
leaning against a rock. If I didn't know better, I'd say he looked
conflicted. "I'm not making the same mistake with them as I did
with Sam. I'm not letting them go free only to have them turn
around and bite us on the ass down the line. They killed Thomas,
they attacked Bristlebrook—they earned their deaths."

I tilt my head, frustration rising. "Are you trying to convince
yourself or me?"

The look he shoots me then is forbidding . . . but after the
Sinners' camp and being surrounded by men who truly did want
to hurt me, Dom's glare doesn't seem quite so nerve-wracking.

"They aren't Sam," I insist. Of that much, I'm sure. "Mateo
and Alastair stepped in time and again to stop me and Heather
from being hurt."

"And from what I hear, they would have dragged you back to

the Den, and Sam would have had you anyway." Dom's eyes flash as he pushes off the rock like he can't stay still. "Come on, Eden, don't be naive. Do you really think they're good men? Why are you fighting so hard for them to live?"

"I don't think it's that simple," I argue, feeling hot. My anger is quick to spark now, too close to the surface. Too fresh from all my hate and fear and need. "Dom, I think if they go back to the Den, they'll try to stop Sam. They don't want his empire, and they don't agree with his vision."

"They signed up. They have those tattoos on their hand the same as the rest of them. They live in that base and get all the bene-fits that come with it. They've killed to protect the Sinners. They attacked us for our weapons, and for the women they thought were here." He gives me a knowing look. "Doesn't look like they're disagreeing that hard."

The yellowing leaves in the trees give a sly rustle.

I blow out a frustrated breath and adjust my glasses while I think. "No. I don't think they're good men. I think Alastair, espe-cially, is cold, and I think he only protected us because it didn't hurt his interests to do so. But I think they can be of more use free than captive." My voice turns cool. "And they're certainly of more use free than dead."

Dom studies me, his jaw tight. Then he shakes his head. "Eden, do you really think they're just going to go back and be our inside men? Help us take down Sam like we're all one big happy family?"

The silent judgment burns. I can practically feel him pitying my gullibility.

"That's not what I meant," I mutter.

What do I mean? *Should* I be fighting this hard? He's right that we can't trust them. So why do I have this irrepressible feeling that he is wrong in this?

Sam's vision *terrifies* me. And those women need a chance. Any chance.

"What's more likely is that Alastair and Mateo return to Sam, let him know just how many vulnerable people we have sitting at Bristlebrook, and they'll come back again—this time with more men. Alastair is a SEAL, Eden, and it takes about two seconds to realize he's fucking ruthless." Dom glares at me, but it doesn't feel hateful. More like he's frustrated he can't get through to me.

Which is fair, considering I'm feeling the exact same way.

Maybe if I throw one of these rocks at him, it will knock some sense into him. Or maybe it will just join the rest of the cluster that seems to be rattling about in his skull.

Dom shakes his head. "We can't risk it. We can't do anything for Sam's captives—it's just the way it is. We're outmanned and they have too many hostages. I've done enough deployments to know the odds of us coming out on top in that scenario, and they aren't good. Bentley wants more information on the meds—"

"Does *he* know how you're getting that information?" I ask tartly.

"He missed today's session." His voice turns dry. "He was busy sharpening his sword."

Sharpening his . . . oh for goodness' sake.

Dom lifts one shoulder as an owl hoots in the distance. "Heather thought we should let him be. But once Bentley has that information, we have no other need for them."

"So you *are* going to kill them." I feel sick.

How many women will never get free? How many women are being raped right now?

Dom stiffens. "That's judgmental coming from someone who left a pile of poisoned corpses in the woods just two days ago."

I flinch, then look away. I do have death on my hands. God, why won't that pressure on my chest let up? I can't even peel apart the layers of all the feelings crammed in there.

The cold wind picks up, and Dom's eyes squeeze shut. He rubs a tired hand over his face.

"Sorry," he mutters. "I shouldn't throw that back in your face."

I lift my hand dismissively. "I *did* kill them. It's only the truth."

The memories of violent retching and Akira's screams for Logan fill my ears, but rather than guilt or shame, I only feel an insistent, irksome heat spark to life.

My voice firms. "And maybe you're right and I am a hypocrite. But those men held me captive." I still feel their ties around my wrists. Their eyes under my skin. I glare at Dom. "They *threatened* me. I had to do *something* to free myself."

He's watching me closely. "Yes, you did."

But I'm caught up now. "I didn't want to be this person, Dom. I *never* did. They forced this on me."

"You feel guilty," Dom says in an even tone.

"I don't," I snap, hating how that word digs into me. Hating how it brings back Madison's face as I backed away from her. "I did what I had to do. That's what you told me back at the river, isn't it? There was a problem, and I solved it because I *had* to."

I gesture back at Alastair and Mateo, though they're out of sight now. "*Those* men, though? They don't need to die. And if they were giving you answers freely, they didn't need to be hurt and abused. They may have done terrible things, but surely we're better than that. Why aren't we allowed to be better? Why do we have to let them make us ugly? Why can't we be smart and not just *brutes*?"

I try to imagine Dom bent over the injured, bound prisoners, beating them like I was beaten, Mateo's eyes wide and panicked over his gag as Alastair took yet more damage he can't afford, and the image makes me queasy.

How many awful things are these people dragging out of us?

Dom seems caught along a similar train of thought. "You think I'm like them? Are we another cage to you, Eden?"

I take a deep breath, but it does nothing to dislodge the sick feeling in my stomach. "You're not the Sinners, Dom. Even with your ridiculous deal, I felt safe every moment I was at Bristlebrook.

But *this*? This is ugly. I think it's far too easy to slip into being a villain when there are no rules—when lives are on the line. I don't want to lose the last few good pieces of myself to this world. I've already lost too many."

The woods around us are too quiet.

Dom is, too.

I run a hand over the goosebumps on my arms. "I don't know if they deserve to live, but I think everyone's being far too quick to decide they should die. They're not a *threat* right now. They're cooperating, and I really do believe they want some of the same things we do. If we don't jump straight to torture and murder, maybe we *can* get them to switch sides."

Dom pauses, looking into the trees, but his eyes don't seem to be tracking anything. It almost feels like he's holding his breath.

Then he swallows and looks down at me.

"I'll think about it." When I tense, his eyes bore into mine as he says, "I will. I promise. I am listening, Eden."

He means it.

"I just . . ." Dom sighs, his chest pressing against his tight shirt. "I don't know that we have the luxury of moral righteousness. There are too many innocent people at risk."

He sighs and rubs a hand over his hair. Finally peering past my own chaotic feelings, I look at him. *Really* look. Dom looks exhausted . . . and worried. He just met them, and he's already invested in these people. In his own domineering way, he cares a lot.

Golden eyes flick to my face. "Just for the record, I wasn't on board with the beating they took. Heather had some things to work through—I pulled her off them before it got out of hand."

Heather.

Heather, not Dom.

Strangely, the image of her attacking Alastair doesn't bring the same sick feeling in my gut. She certainly has more cause. I remember her talking about Tommy, and about the freckle he had under his left eye that she used to kiss every morning.

I remember that stormy, endless hate I felt when I thought my men were dead.

It wasn't Dom performing a cold-blooded interrogation. It was a broken woman taking her pound of flesh.

I can't judge her for it—but we still need them.

"Alastair took a lot from her," I say finally, my unease subsiding a little.

I lean against a tree, and the scratch of the bark is strangely grounding.

"Thomas was a good man," Dom says heavily. "And Heat has always been fiery."

And that quickly, that ember sparks again in my own blood. Suddenly, rudely, I remember Dom and Beau talking about her in the woods—"fantastic in the sack," Beau said.

"Oh, I'm sure *Heat* runs scorching hot," I mutter.

What a stupid name.

Dom's eyebrow kicks up. "Aren't you two friends?"

My lips purse, and I smooth down the front of my shirt carefully. It's tattered, dirty, and bloodstained. But now it's not creased.

Am I friends with Heather? She's infuriating and reckless. I know she was cruel to Lucky, and I've seen her rough tongue with Jasper and Jaykob. She led the Sinners to Bristlebrook and nearly got my men killed.

Not to mention she's Dom's *Heat*.

But she *was* a friend to me when I desperately needed one. She poured her heart out in the dark and pulled me back into my fight to live. Yes, she gave my men up, but she did it for every person like me here who doesn't have her ferocity or skills. She fought by my side in the woods when the odds were stacked against us . . . and she didn't judge me for a moment when I decided to leave her in the dust.

When *I* betrayed *her* like the coward I am.

"It's complicated," I say primly, and Dom gives me a dry look.

Then he keeps staring at me, long enough that I start to feel self-conscious. I brush my hair over my ear, and I'm just considering making my excuses when he says, very softly, "How are you feeling, pet?"

That word paralyses me. Emotions crash in on me from every angle.

Why is he using *that* word? And why is he using it *now*?

"I'm—"

He leans in, very close, and my breathing stalls. I think I forget *how* to breathe.

"If you say 'fine,' I'm going to . . ." He trails off, frowning, as his eyes drop to my lips.

Going to . . .? I wait, expectant. Going to spank me? Heat shudders through me as I remember the bright, hot sting of his hand on my ass. Is that what he was going to say? Or something else? He's going to . . . give me a firm scolding? Kiss me senseless? Split my legs over his lap and take me hard? *What?*

With all the manners I can muster, I say casually, "Pardon, I don't think I caught that."

His eyes flick up to mine. Whatever he sees there makes the corner of his mouth curve, and his voice becomes a purr. "Tell me how you're feeling, little librarian."

I try to work some moisture into my mouth. Why is it so dry?

How can I possibly tell him how I feel when I have no idea myself? I don't know how to explain this heavy weight on me, or why even now, all around us, the night seems so crowded—just teeming with fears and thoughts I don't know how to escape. I don't know how to tell him that I want him to hold me, especially now that the woman of his dreams is here in front of him, single and sad and probably just as in need of his comfort as I am.

"It's complicated," I finally manage to say again, and before he can grill me further, I ask, "And how do *you* feel?"

Dom's wry laugh comes through his nose. I know he won't let me get away with the subject change, so I charge on before he can grill me further.

"I'm sure it's very confusing, having Heather back," I continue, and the humor in his face vanishes instantly.

Why did I say that? I don't want to talk about Heather. I don't want to hear about his feelings for her. Watching him watch her so intensely, like she's a missing relic, has been a special kind of torture, and hearing them practically finish each other's sentences makes me want to gag. They know one another. *Intimately*.

More intimately than I know him.

Dom's eyes narrow on me. "Confusing," he repeats, like he's mulling the word over.

I nod. My mouth is a desert. And it *burns*.

"Why would it be *confusing*?"

I— Is he really going to make it this difficult for me?

I lift my chin. "You were in love with her."

"Years ago." He cocks a brow, but something shutters behind his gaze. "Then she *left*."

He didn't end it. *He* wanted her to stay. He hurt his friendship with Beau for her—the thing that meant everything in the world to him.

I think about the way Dom kissed me after I delivered the bazooka. The way he looked at me then, I'd thought . . . I'd *hoped* . . .

No. Maybe if we'd had more time, this would be a different conversation.

"And now she's back," I murmur.

A muscle tics in his jaw. "She's not here for me."

But he wishes she was. My chest aches. How could he not? God, I hate it. Worse, I can see it. They're so alike. Stubborn and loyal and determined. The same qualities I admire in him, I have to admire in her.

And Dom said himself that he doesn't take on—what did he say? Soft-spoken submissives? Is that what I am?

Next to *Heat*, I suppose it's true.

Jealousy punishes my every cell, but I'm not sure what else to do here. If he doesn't want me, it's not his fault, and I can't change who I am to try.

He wants a Heather. And I'm just an Eden.

"I'm sure she's delighted for the new opportunity," I grit out.

Dom's eyes snap over my face, studying me. "What is this, Eden? Why are you pushing me at Heather?"

"I am *not*," I splutter.

"Because the last I heard, you were all over Beau's plan, ready to drag the both of us into bed with you," he taunts.

My hand flutters to my throat, just to make sure someone isn't actually cutting off the oxygen there. I stare at him.

Damn him for the images now flooding my mind. I do want to drag the both of them to bed—or let them do the dragging. Being between Beau and Dom was one of the most erotic, soul-searing experiences of my life.

"I— You—" I stammer, and his head tilts as he waits. "You didn't want me at Bristlebrook!"

Dom's brows come down. "No, I didn't."

"And you didn't want any part of the deal. You didn't want to sleep with me," I remind him, somewhat desperately. Does he really need to put me through this? We both know who he really wants.

"I didn't want in on the deal," he says with a hint of frustration. "You were a risk and a liability, and I didn't want you breaking Beau's heart."

"I told you, I'm not going to do that."

Dom's eyes swing back to mine, softening. "I know, pet."

Oh . . . My insides become warm and liquid. He *really* needs to stop with that nickname.

It makes it sound like I'm something he wants to keep.

My hand shaking, I press it against my stomach as something occurs to me. "You didn't sleep with me by the riverbank."

"From memory, we didn't get around to sleeping."

"Oh, don't be obtuse," I snip, and when his jaw flexes, I know I'm on the right track. I bite my lip, letting my mind worry over every detail of that interlude. And it looks different from this angle.

I shake my head. "You helped me out of my panic. It was very . . . kind of you."

"*Kind*," Dom repeats heavily, like he's trying to make sense of the word. He rubs his forehead. "Eden—"

"Beau was the one who asked you to help. I know you never wanted to before that. And that's okay—of course it is. I'm so thankful you . . . helped me. But he shouldn't have pushed you when you weren't interested."

Dom is still staring, only now his face is so perfectly expressionless, I can't decipher a single emotion.

"What makes you think," he finally asks, "that I didn't want you then?"

When I hesitate, he raises his brows questioningly. "Hmm? I seem to remember your hands all over my cock. Beau showed you just how I liked it." The corner of his mouth lifts humorlessly. "He's a good friend like that."

My mouth drops open, my breaths becoming shaky. Do I *remember*? The memories might incinerate me on the spot.

"I think . . ." I swallow, then clear my throat. "I may remember . . . something . . . like that."

He snorts dryly, and I blush, then sigh heavily, flustered, confused. "You didn't want me, not really. If you did you would have . . . you know."

I look at him significantly, the fire in my cheeks deepening.

Dom gives me a bland look. "No, I don't know. Why don't you tell me."

I only just suppress a growl. My God, he's infuriating. I lift my hands, one becoming a circle, then I push the index finger of my hand frantically into the hole. Then I knot my fingers together helplessly, as if to erase the ridiculous gesture.

Dom stares at my hands, incredulous. "You did not just do that."

I cringe. Okay, I'm ready to expire now. Just let me be dust and ash.

"If you don't even know how to talk about it, little librarian, you shouldn't be doing it," Dom says, sounding so dryly mocking that I bury my face in my hands.

He's smoldering dark and arrogant before me, lethal and armed in his Ranger's kit. I feel him lean in close, and goosebumps lift all over my skin.

"I didn't *fuck you*?" he says in a rough voice. "Is that what that game of charades was meant to be? Because I remember fucking you until you came dripping around my fingers. I remember you choking on Beau's cock. I remember you begging for my dick."

My whole body clenches around nothing, and I breathe him in. I'm slick and throbbing, and starting to feel very, very warm, but . . .

"You didn't give it to me," I whisper, and his lips firm, tensing. "I begged you and you didn't—because you weren't ready."

Our conversation in the river plays through my mind like a recording—a conversation largely led by Beau. I was so caught up in my own joy and pleasure-drunk state at the time that I never even noticed that Dom made me no promises. Not even the hint of one.

"You were there for me when I needed you," I continue softly. "But if you really wanted me, if you were ready for it, you would have taken it all."

"I'm so glad you're here to tell me how I feel." He's harsh, but I feel the pressure in him.

"Isn't it?" I'm not proud of the way my voice lifts. "Tell me that you wanted me, that you were certain it was the right thing.

Tell me that you want to share me with Beau, and you have no reservations. Tell me I'm the only one you think about."

Dom takes a long, deep breath, then pulls back from me and turns away. He rubs his neck, and I swallow hard.

Then Dom laughs, but it sounds almost . . . annoyed.

"You have me all worked out, is that it?" he asks as he turns back to me, dark and imposing in the night.

There's a danger in his tone, and it's wrong that it makes me flustered. It's too close to how he sounded when he chased me through the clearing and ripped my clothes from my body.

"Am I wrong?" I ask quietly, and the shadows do seem so very murky around us. They're going to haunt me again tonight, and Dom won't be there to keep them at bay.

"It's complicated, and I have bigger things to worry about right now than—" he starts tartly, throwing my earlier words back at me, but I don't let up.

"Tell me that you feel nothing for Heather."

At the mention of Heather, his eyes sharpen on mine, gleaming in the moonlight.

I push past the rough, terrifying beauty of him, and add in a whisper, "Can you really say that all that history is just . . . laid to rest?"

Dom's gaze shifts, until he's staring somewhere over my shoulder. "Heat and I . . ."

The nickname is like a scald, but he doesn't seem to see my grimace. There's a deep crease in his brows when he trails off again, and he gives another frustrated little head shake.

It's her. He can't even say it's not.

I smile sadly at him, that last spark of hope extinguishing in my chest. The shadows seem to lengthen between the trees.

His gaze refocuses on me. "Eden—"

"We can be friends, Dom." I cut him off, not wanting to hear whatever words of reassurance he's working up to. I'm so raw right now, I'm not sure how I might react. I don't know if I'm close to tears or if my chest is just going to implode from the weight on it.

He closes his eyes on a long exhale. His jaw flexes. "*Friends.*"

Does he not even want that?

"I'd like to think we're past you trying to chase me off now," I tease weakly. Then I bite my lip. "At least, I hope so."

He shakes his head again, rubbing a hand over his mouth. When he looks at me, his eyes are filled with things I don't understand.

"I don't want to chase you off, Eden."

I shiver. Does he have to sound like that? Like every word is a caress? Some kind of intimate promise?

"Good." Tears prick the back of my eyes, even as I force my smile wider. "We'll be . . . we'll be good friends then."

Dom lets out a sound similar to a growl, but I turn and stride away. I need to. I'm moments away from doing something silly— like falling to my knees and begging him to love me.

As I walk away, I make a promise to myself. I *will* be his friend. And Heather's, too, if I can bear it. I *will* bear it.

I'm not in a position to turn down friends. I've lived too long alone, and I know, better than most, how unendurable loneliness can be. Friends are more special than so many people appreciate.

Especially ones who would fight and die for you.

I make my way through the camp, with no intention of anything except escaping as far as I can from that conversation without leaving the safety of people.

I can do it. I *will* learn to be a better friend. One who doesn't leave people to die to save their own skin. One who doesn't let a tiny little bump of jealousy get in the way of two people who have cared about one another for years. Surely, I'm not so petty as that.

Okay, so it might be a gigantic, unbearable, bone-aching *gorge* of jealousy, but the point stands.

I can do it.

I've spent most of my life being polite and courteous no matter what was roiling about inside me. I can do it again now, for a good cause.

The night presses in around me.

Because with the way I'm feeling now, I think I'm going to need some friends very soon.

CHAPTER 22

JAYKOB

SURVIVAL TIP #310
Don't share your things.
You'll never get them back.

I'm pinned.

Adrenaline spikes, and I bare my teeth as I look for an escape, but they have me surrounded, three on one, backed up against a boulder. Normally, I'd come out swinging anyway, but here? I don't stand a damn chance. Sweat gathers at the nape of my neck.

I need to get free. Now.

"So I was on the ground, and *three* of them were attacking me," the annoying kid chatters excitedly, waving her hands like she's doing charades. "He fought them off with his bare hands."

Three?

I scowl at her. The girl is parked in front of me, talking at a mile-a-damn-minute to two gray-haired old bats who look like they must have been around for the fall of Rome. They have me boxed. I consider shoving past them, but that seems like an asshole move. They'd probably break a hip.

"Oh my!" one of the broads exclaims. She has a dozen eye-bleedingly colorful necklaces around her neck and flowers tied in her hair. Must be a hippie. "Did you hear that, Ida?"

"Oh yes, so very brave!" The fancy-looking Black woman next to the hippie pats my arm like I'm some stray mutt looking for approval, and not a six-three tatted soldier still stained with yesterday's bloodbath.

I glare at her too, but she's beaming at the brat, so I glower at the kid instead.

"There was *one* guy attacking you, not three, and I *shot* him—and then I left your ass behind!"

That part's important. They're making out like I did something special, when all I did was dispose of some trash. Of course I was going to take him out—he was the damn enemy.

The kid just happened to be there.

But instead of giving me that disgusted look I'm used to, the woman is still *petting* me. I shouldn't have stopped when they said they needed help setting up their camp. Should have known it was a trap.

"Such a hero," the hippie murmurs.

The sweaty feeling increases. What is *wrong* with these people?

The moonlight glints off something behind them, and I realize it's Eden's glasses. Her face is tense and white, and I frown, distracted. She looks like she's being chased, but a quick glance around tells me there's nothing behind her.

Who the hell scared off Miss Manners?

Just then, she looks up, her big eyes getting all wide as she takes it all in.

And fuck if this isn't embarrassing. Pinned to a boulder by an infant and two geriatric hippies.

The girl—Kasey or whatever—rocks back on her heels excitedly. "I think he used kung fu! That's how he killed all five of them. He's probably a master."

The hippie nods seriously. "And thank God for that. It's been too long since I trained."

I stare at her. Are they *high*? "It wasn't kung—"

The fancy one, Ida, starts stretching, and I'm so fucking done. Fuck dignity.

"*I don't know kung fu!*" I snap as the hippie joins in, dropping into a deep lunge.

I shoot Eden a panicked look over their heads, to find her anxious frown gone. She looks like she's trying not to smile—so I scowl at her too.

Eden presses her fingers to her mouth, then walks over. "Jayk, could you help me find something to eat?"

Relief breaks through my chest. As the flock of hens in front of me turn to look at her, a gap opens, and I start edging between them.

And I'm not *fleeing*. This was just a stacked fight.

"Did you hear?" the kid asks Eden in an innocent voice that makes my hackles rise. "He's a total superhero. He killed *ten* of those jerks with a Pez dispenser and then carried me out of the battle by his pinkie."

I pause my retreat as it finally hits me. "Are you all *fucking* with me?"

Kasey snorts first, then the women next to her, then suddenly they're all breaking into peals of laughter.

The hippie howls. "*Kung fu!* At my age! Could you imagine it?"

"Ethel, my God." Ida slings an arm around her shoulders and laughs into her hair. "I'm going to imagine it daily."

I stare at them, teeth grinding, then stalk over to Eden. And so what if I end up just behind her shoulder? These biddies are ruthless.

"Ahhh." Ethel, the hippie, finally straightens with a giggle, wiping away her tears. "Oh, goodness me."

Ida steadies herself, then helps Ethel adjust her necklaces.

"You'll have to forgive us, dear, your man here was easy sport," she says to Eden, her dark, wrinkled cheeks still flushed with amused color.

Your man.

I feel my own cheeks burn, that odd panic returning.

I glare at Ida. "I'm not her man."

Eden won't think I told her that, will she? I steal a glance at her from under my brows.

Ethel snickers, and I start wondering how many of her teeth might fall out if I shove a gag in her mouth.

Eden twists, looking up at me, and I pull away before she catches me staring.

"I—" I feel her searching my face. "Aren't you?"

My heart pounds in my ears as I slowly turn to stare back at her. She called off the deal. That's meant to be us done. It was the only reason I had to drag her into my bed. What does she mean, *"Aren't I?"*

Is this another joke? They all going to laugh at this one too? 'Cause it's not fucking funny.

But she doesn't look like she's laughing. If anything, she looks nervous.

My chest thumps hard, my mind racing. She did hold my hand yesterday . . . and she kissed me. Not Dom or Jasper.

Me.

My own stomach twisting, I ask gruffly, "Am I?"

Her lashes fall down in a pretty kind of flutter, and it pisses me off because I instantly stop being able to read her.

"But we did want to say thank you," Ethel chimes in before Eden can answer me, and I almost growl at her.

Does this woman not know when to shut up? She definitely doesn't need all her teeth. The gag is going to happen. I have the duct tape in my go bag.

Eden turns so she's standing beside me just as Ida slips her hand into Ethel's. They're both watching me now, with Kasey peeking up at me from beside them, and something in their expressions makes me edgy.

They're all soft and gooey, and I've got to get out of here before this goes from uncomfortable to them trying to pinch my cheeks. Or worse, they start *crying*. I take a step back, but a firm hand takes my elbow to hold me in place.

Eden's bones are like twigs, and she has the strength of a gnat. I could shake her off without breaking a sweat.

But I don't feel like it.

So Old Ida keeps giving me *that look*. "Kasey here is my goddaughter, and she has more recklessness than good sense. When we lost her in that mess . . ."

She trails off, and Ethel takes her hand quietly and murmurs, "Well, we're just very glad you were there."

I shift, uncomfortable. I hate this. I killed someone. I splattered their brains all over their precious goddaughter. "Yeah, well, I'm not her babysitter. Keep a better eye on her if you don't want her to become a—"

"Jayk is happy she's safe too," Eden says, and I glower down at her. "If you don't mind, I'm quite tired. Would it be okay if we . . .?"

"Oh no, of course not, dear." Ida waves her hand with a smile. "You two have fun."

"She said she was *tired*, Ida," Ethel scolds, but her eyes are too bright. "They're going to bed."

Ida snorts, then puts her hands over the kid's ears. "She'll be a lot more tired if she does get that one into bed, I'd wager."

Damn right.

Eden starts tugging at my arm, and when I look down at her, I see her face is as cherry red as my old pick-up. I smirk at her, then let her drag me away, finally feeling a bit better about the whole humiliating experience.

Your man.

I stare at the librarian as she leads me away. She's cleaned up since the fight yesterday—she got rid of the blood at least—but she's still mussed up and sweaty and smudged with dirt from travel. Same as me. Same as most people here. That cave water was cold as shit. No one was doing more than a splash wash this morning unless they wanted to freeze their nips off.

At least her wrists are properly bandaged now. Won't surprise me if those cuts scar.

We stop in a quieter part of the woods. The camp is near enough to hear and smell, but far enough that not every Ethel and Ida is going to stumble all over us. We're well within the boundaries of the patrol, and they're not even doing too shit of a job.

I look at her curiously, wondering what her plan is here.

Good girls don't take bad boys out into the deep dark woods.

Not unless they're planning on being bad too.

But after a few minutes of watching her awkwardly examine every star-lit tree around us like it's even more fascinating than the one before it, I snort. This girl is so in her own head, she has no clue how to get out.

"I'm going back to camp."

She snaps up, finally looking at me. "No, wait. Don't."

"Don't?" I stroll toward her, and she flattens herself against her favorite tree. Nervously, she pushes her glasses back up her nose—and damn if that move doesn't get me every time.

I smirk as I close in on her. It's so much more fun being the hunter.

"You want to let me in on why you dragged me out here, Miss Manners?"

This close, I can smell her. And without all the fancy shampoos and expired perfumes, I know it's just her. Raw and real as it gets. She swallows, her nostrils flaring gently, and my cock stirs. I want to fist my hand around that throat. I want to feel that swallow.

"I—" Her gaze drops to my mouth, but then she drags it away.

And whatever she's looking at in the night-time brings back that harried look on her face.

She takes my hand again, and it's so . . . innocent. I stare down at it, baffled, but my fingers are wrapping around hers before I can think twice about it.

The princess is holding my hand.

"I just . . . don't want to be alone tonight," she whispers. "Please don't leave me alone."

And my skin prickles all the way up my back.

Because she doesn't sound like she's trying to ride my dick— she sounds *scared*.

"Why? What happened?" My voice comes out about five times harsher than I mean it to, and when she flinches, I scowl.

The gentle coddling thing ain't my style.

At all.

"Nothing happened," she says, and at my huff, she scowls back. "It didn't!"

"Yeah, sure thing, sweetheart. You just suddenly developed a fear of the sandman, and now you need me to run him off for you."

I swear to God, I'll rip apart whoever put that look on her face. She's been through enough. She's meant to be okay now.

She hides those big eyes from me again, stiffening, and I realize I'm making it worse.

"I think this was a mistake." Eden pulls her hand out of mine, and I want to snatch it back. "I should go."

But I catch her arm before she can run off, and she wheels around.

"Not happening." Color is high in her cheeks, and her chest lifts in a quick rise-fall. "You've got your panties in a wad about something, and I want to know what it is."

That's sensitive, right?

"Charming," she mutters, but I ignore her.

Crowding her, I press her back against the tree. "What's the deal, Miss Manners? What's got you afraid of the dark?"

That seems to trigger something.

Eden tries to shove me off, but I stay put. I want my answers, and she wouldn't have dragged me out here if she didn't want to give them to me.

She leaves her hands on my chest, the nails digging in above my kit, and I try not to think about how fucking good they feel there. I can still feel the imprint of where she dragged them down my shoulders the last time she let me between her thighs.

"Why am I *afraid*?" she hisses, and her nails dig in harder, drawing a grunt from me. "How could I *not* be? This world is horrible. You're either left alone, or you're surrounded by people who want to hurt you. There are no rules, no safe places. It's all a lie. There's just awful people doing awful things, and the only way to stop them is by making yourself awful too."

Yeah. No shit.

"The world is a fucked-up place. It always has been. People are just more honest about it now." I study her for a minute. Her eyes are wet, and she's breathing hard, and those nails of hers are about to leave me with a brand-new scar.

"You're angry." Fuck. I like angry.

"Ugh. Why does everyone keep *saying* that?"

Everyone? I frown. Who's *everyone*?

Before I can ask, a bloodcurdling howl rips through the night. We both freeze, listening, as it rises in pitch and volume.

"That's Mateo." Her face goes tight, her breaths coming even faster. "Heather's at Alastair again. God, this isn't right."

I tense. The prisoners are bad news—we should have killed them on sight, like all the others. Having enemies in the camp, captive or not, makes me itchy.

"What do you care?"

She gives me that frigid pursed-lip disapproval. "She's *torturing* them. They don't have any more information. It's just sport for her. I understand she's angry, I do, but they are of more use to us as allies."

Another shout shatters the night, and I glare at her. "One of them had a gun to your head in that firefight, Miss Manners. You think it was shooting daisies?"

"No, but—"

"He was going to blow you to pieces," I growl. "*In front of me.* He was dead the minute he picked up that gun."

She shoves at me again, and I press her into the tree until her breasts are flattened against my chest and her hair rubs against the bark. It's back in its bun, and just looking at how tight it is gives me a migraine.

Eden glares back at me over the rim of her glasses, all prim and indignant and accidentally hot as fuck. It makes me want to shock her over and over again.

I want her to try and scold me with my cock up her ass.

"You seeing yourself right now? You're angry as shit. But if you want to pretend like you're not choking on it, you go ahead. I'm not your daddy. But I got all the pretty red flags in my file, sugar. I *know* angry."

Her glare drops to my lips, and she's breathing hard against me. I feel every press of her breasts, every shift of her stomach against my dick.

"I don't *want* to be angry," she snipes.

I scoff, keeping my eyes on hers. I like how they snap at me. "Bullshit. As if that didn't keep you alive." I bring my face close to hers. "Not a very *polite* feeling though, is it? Does it make you uncomfortable, princess? Feeling all the messy shit?"

Her eyes widen, and she laughs—and she sounds fucking insane.

"You think I care about being *polite* right now?" Eden shoves at my shoulders, then lifts her hand to hit me. I catch her below her bandaged wrist with no effort at all.

With a frustrated screech, she squirms in my grip, and it rubs her body all over mine. It's soft and giving everywhere. She's the softest thing I ever felt. Maybe the softest thing I ever want to feel.

I groan, and she freezes as I rock my hips against her. Her breath catches.

"*Jayk.*"

My name is half a snarl, half a moan. It's my new favorite sound. I bury my face in her neck, and her scent makes me shudder in need.

I really thought we were going to find her in pieces.

"You want to hide away from every piece of shit out there instead of fighting, then I'll build you a damn fortress." I grab her thigh and hitch it over my hip so I can line myself up with her pretty cunt properly. I fuck her against the tree through our clothes, and she gasps.

"You need a monster to protect you from the monsters, then I'll do the dirty work. My hands are already filthy with it." Her white little canines dig into her lower lip like a pincushion, and there's furious color in her cheeks, like she's already on the brink of need. She was like this last time. Hungry and so fucking responsive.

"But if you want to learn how to rip out their throats yourself, sugar, then I'll show you how to fucking *bite*." Burying my other hand in her hair, I pull her head to the side and lick down her neck with the flat of my tongue, tasting her sweat. I could eat her whole right now. She arches up into me with a tiny mewl, and I bite down hard on her neck.

I'm dining on princess tonight.

"Jayk! God—" She finds a grip in my short hair and holds me to her while she grinds on my dick, and I'm glad she's not playing coy right now because I am not in the mood.

Breathing hard, I pull my teeth from her and look up.

"You should be angry," I growl at her. "Every bit of this situation is fucked."

She shakes her head, and I tighten my grip on her hair to stop the denial. Scraped against the tree, it's starting to tumble from its prissy bun, but I wait until her dazed eyes meet mine. Then I smirk.

"You don't need to fake it with me, Miss Manners. I'm not scared of your fight."

Her eyes flare, like the hottest, bluest part of a flame—and it lights me up too.

"Show me, sugar," I taunt as I rub my dick against her again. "Show me how much damage a polite little princess can do."

Her nails become cutting. "Shut up, Jayk."

I snort. "Sticks and stones may—"

Her mouth crashes against mine. She savages my lower lip with her teeth, and I growl as she draws blood. I lick into her mouth, drinking in her need, and she claims my tongue. She sucks on it, rubs it with hers, free and so fucking wild that my dick presses against my zipper, desperate to be the next thing in that wet mouth of hers.

I shove her back by her throat, and I feel the column of it working against my palm as she swallows and gasps for air. I release her only long enough to grip the back of her shirt and pull it over her head, stripping her in one move. Then she's clawing at my kit —without success.

She wrenches at my shoulder straps, and I take over, snapping off buckles and Velcro and zippers to unload my kit and unstrap my belt in seconds, until I'm down to my shirt and my cock is finally freed from my unzipped pants. Eden's pants drop, and I'm just about to go back to roughing her mouth with my tongue when I look down.

And goddamn, I have to take a long, hard second to rein myself back in.

Because though her nipples are tight and her body is quivering with restless need . . . she's also covered in deep, ugly bruises.

And I just slammed her against a tree.

"Did they touch you?"

At my growl, her face grows grim, and it sets off a bomb under my skin. I'm beyond being sensitive. She said those captive Sinners stopped Sam from fucking around with the women, but those bruises . . .

"Did they—"

"They didn't rape me," she cuts me off, her tone almost as harsh as mine. "They just beat me. Kicked me. Threatened me." Her mouth twists. "They just tied me down and pushed me around for sport."

Just.

She already killed them, and right now, I hate her for it. I stare at every mark on her skin, memorizing them.

"Don't," she warns, and when I meet her eyes, she pulls her hair free of her bun, and it tumbles all around her like a waterfall. "I don't need your pity."

Look at her, throwing my words back at me. I grit my teeth and shake my head, coming back in close to her mouth.

"I don't pity you, sugar. Just pity any survivors you left. They're going to beg for your poison."

Eden shivers, her gaze growing hooded. Whatever she says, there's a part of her that likes it. Deep down, happy about it or not, she liked making them hurt for what they did. It turns her on to think of me hurting them too.

Her eyes skim down my body, and they darken, lingering on my bared cock, and she might as well have sucked it into her mouth for the way my balls tighten.

I'm already dripping precum for her, and I coat my palm in it, then give myself a stroke. She watches the whole thing, and I grip my dick hard at the base, trying to strangle the urge to put her on her ass and shove myself into that soaking pussy.

"You want this?"

She nods, her tongue teasing her lower lip. The sight of the pink, wet drag of it wrenches another growl out of me.

"Well, I'm not going to serve it up to you, princess." My blood is pounding with the need to do just that—to take her to the ground and bury myself in her throat until she gags on it—but I want to see her do it. I want to see her *fight*. "You want to swallow my dick, then come and get it."

"Why are you such a jerk all of the time?" she snaps, and I give her a lazy smirk as I crowd her against the tree. My glossy crown rubs against her silky soft stomach, painting her in me.

"Just how I'm wired, sugar. Just like you're wired to pant for it." I bend down and she yanks her head back. I chase her, nipping at her neck. "Come get it, Miss Manners. Show me how you burn."

She buries her hands in my hair, yanking me against her throat, even as she pulls down hard. It fucking hurts, and I laugh before I bite her again, harder than before, then suck on her like she's candy. Crying out, she rakes her nails brutally down the back of my neck, over my shoulders, all the way down my back to my ass.

Then she shoves me back, and I grab her chin in a rough grip, forcing her mouth to mine. I lick at her lips, then bite down. Impatient, I tilt her head back by her chin for a deeper angle on her mouth. Pressing my cock into her, I hold her to the tree with my body weight, though I make sure she has enough room to wriggle free if she really wants to.

She struggles, clawing at my sides, and I stop fucking her mouth with my tongue long enough to press my blunt, dirty fingertips hard into her pretty cheeks. Her lips part in an obscene promise, and I bring my other hand up and press two fingers inside, over her protesting tongue and deep into her tight throat. It's scorching hot and so fucking wet I send up a prayer that I don't blow before I even get inside her.

Her throat constricts as she chokes, and saliva pools around my fingers. I pull them out a little, letting her breathe, then shove them back in again until she gags, almost drowning in my own need.

She glares, bucking against me, but I'm living for the feel of her throat strangling my fingers. She's staying put. Her glasses are on a ridiculous tilt on her nose, that old-lady chain she has attached to them bouncing against her cheeks, and it's one of the hottest things I've ever seen.

Then she wrenches hard out of my grip and pushes forward, sucking my fingers even deeper down her throat, until her saliva coats my palm and drips down my wrist and my dick is demanding to replace them. Her eyes water as she takes me, but as I curse, they fill with satisfaction.

Then she fucking bites me.

With a growl, I yank my throbbing fingers out of her mouth, and she gasps for air, then slaps me across the cheek. My head whips to the side, and I laugh.

When I look back at her, she's staring at my cheek, horrified, but her eyes are drunk with lust.

"Come on, sugar, I can take it," I taunt. "Give me more. Show me all that pretty rage."

The horror fades. "Take off your shirt," she demands.

I cock a brow, but yank it over my head. "That make you happy, princess?" I grasp my dick and give it another rough stroke. "You want to inspect the merchandise before you claim it?"

Eden steps into me, then scratches me viciously down my chest until I hiss. "Don't be an ass, Jayk. You're already mine."

My smirk fades as I stare at her, but she's already dropping to her knees. She slaps at my hand until I release my cock, and her hand replaces mine. It's slim, her skin so much softer than my calloused disasters, but her grip is punishing.

She looks up at me as her mouth parts, and she draws me onto her tongue. Need and naked fury seethe in the depths of her eyes. She's not a princess right now, or a librarian.

She's letting her monster out.

Mine.

Eden takes me deep into her mouth, and the heat is incinerating. It's slippery, and she's sucking me down like she needs my cock to live, and I feel myself slicking her mouth, seconds away from losing it. Shuddering, I groan.

I can't take my eyes off her.

Grabbing her hair, I pull her off my dick, needing something else more.

"Say it again," I order.

She blinks, dazed, her lips glistening. "You're mine," she whispers.

With a growl, I come down hard on top of her, taking her mouth. I cup her breasts, tugging roughly at her nipples, then shove her legs apart with my knee. Eden sobs a moan and reaches down to take my dick in her fist. She writhes against me to get herself to where she wants to be, then blatantly rubs the fat crown of me against her soaking, slick clit.

"Fuck," I grit out, bracing myself above her. I widen my stance and lean forward so she can use me how she likes, flicking and rubbing and grinding my dick all over herself until her head is arching back and her mouth is dropping open with her little pant-cries.

Sweat pricks down my spine as the pressure in my balls builds. I told her to take me and she fucking is—using my body to take her pleasure, demanding everything, angry, and sweet, and hungry, and *mine*.

"Jayk, please."

She notches my cock against her slick hole, and I feel my head push inside as she wraps her legs around my waist. Her heat is sucking me in as surely as her mouth did, and I bite her neck again, trying to stop myself from blowing right now when it hits me.

"Fuck," I swear against her sweat-damp skin. "Fuck, *fuck*."

I try to pull back, but her legs are like a vice, and I groan.

"Don't stop," she begs, her voice husky. Demanding. "Not now, Jayk, don't you dare."

"Condom," I growl, almost panicked. If she doesn't let me out of her right this second, it's going to be a meaningless discussion. I shove a hand against her hip, but the soft flesh there feels so good, all I can do is squeeze it.

"Wha—?"

"Condom, Eden. I don't have a fucking condom." Her hips shift, and it presses me another inch inside her. Another scorching, tight, perfect fucking inch. I groan into her hair.

Her heels dig into the base of my spine, right where all the pressure is building. "I don't care."

It's exactly what I want to hear right now, but I hesitate, trying to fight past my hindbrain that tells me to fuck, and fuck *now*.

"But—"

Eden grasps my hair in both of her hands and yanks my head back until she's looking me in the eyes. Her face is flushed dark and rosy, her eyes overbright and heavy-lidded. Her dark hair is mussed and tangled around us both.

"Jayk, I need you to fuck me. Right now. Fill me up. Soak me in your cum. I need you to—"

I slam into her, then shut her up with a kiss before her words snap the last thread of my control. But it might be a mistake, because now she's all around me. Her cunt is clutching at me, squeezing and pulsing, and she's sobbing into my mouth. Her taste, her heat, her need, her perfect fucking body all around me, raw and all over me, as I punish her pussy.

I take her ass in one hand, angling her so I can ram my entire thick length in deep, and her breast with another, plucking at her peachy pink nipple until I know it hurts. Eden erupts under me, coming in brutal, desperate waves as she grinds her soft body against me. Her hands are everywhere, but finally find my ass, and her nails dig in as she pulls me home and comes all over my dick.

My vision hazes over, and everything narrows to those perfect pulses. Her wetness is everywhere, over my cock, my thighs.

In her ear, I pant, "Say it again."

I can feel her nipples like pebbles against my chest, and her shocked, gasping moans are in my ear. Her arms wrap around my shoulders, and she turns to look at me.

And it's too close, like this, with her eyes all soft and serious.

But I can't look away.

"Mine," she whispers fiercely.

And the word is dynamite. I groan, slamming into her once, twice, and I'm done. Pleasure explodes in my spine, all over my skin like shrapnel, and I unload everything into her, soaking her pussy with my cum, branding her with it, like I've never done with another woman.

I'm pretty sure I black out for a second, because when I come to, Eden's dropping slow, lingering kisses over my damp face, her hands brushing against my skin soothingly. I wait for the instinct to shove free to kick in, but it doesn't. Watching her intensely, I let it happen.

Hesitantly, I brush a strand of hair off her face, then let my fingertips trace the curve of her lower lip. It curves further at my touch.

She's so fucking pretty.

And . . . mine. Apparently.

What's a guy like me even meant to do with someone like her?

Her hand trails to my cheek, where she slapped me. "Did I hurt you?"

"One of these days, I'm going to show you how to hit me properly." I smirk.

It would be good for her anyway. She should know how to protect herself.

"Are you a masochist too?" she asks, tilting her head.

That makes me snort. "No, sugar, I just think fucking has to be the one time where you should be able to run on instinct and get all the shit out that's been riding you. If you need to take a swing at me for that to happen, then good for you."

Her fingers pause on my skin. "I don't want you to hit me. Just to be perfectly clear."

"You sure about that?" I slap her ass. It jostles her against me, and she yelps, shifting.

When she moves, I slip out of her, and the loss of her warmth makes me scowl.

"Oh." Eden makes a strangled sound, freezing.

"What?" I look around, but we're still alone between the trees.

"Um." Her eyes are wide, and she presses her legs together. "Nothing."

I inspect her. Her voice is doing that squeaky thing.

I move closer, and she shifts back, then squirms. Her cheeks are flushing a deep pink again. When her thighs clench again, I catch on.

A slow smirk rolls over my face. "Lie back, sugar."

Her hand presses to her throat. "Oh, no. I think that's quite all right. Would you have a, um, tissue? Or—"

I grab her ankles, then yank them toward me, and she falls back onto her elbows. Taking a knee in each hand, I force her legs apart. She resists me for a second, then sighs, and they fall to the side.

Her pretty pussy is a dripping mess, slick and glistening with our cum, and I growl at the sight of it, mesmerized. Leaning over her, I run my fingers through it, mixing us together. I rub it up over her clit, and she must still be sensitive, because she flinches with a gasp. I rub it in, watching her face as she squirms.

"I— Jayk. I don't have anything to clean up with."

That makes me want to grin. "Too bad, I guess."

"Don't you have anythi—?"

"Nope." Probably a dozen cloths, towels, and bandages. "Nothing."

I lift my glossy fingers and I'm already getting hard again when I bring them to her mouth. She doesn't even protest as she licks them clean.

But before I can go back for another swipe, she grabs my wrist and pulls me over her again, leaning up for another kiss.

When she pulls back, I stare down at her. "You ended the

deal," I say, wanting answers but not knowing how to ask for them.

She nods, watching me back. "I didn't want to be with anyone only because I had to. I only want it to happen if it's real. Because we both want it."

"You and me?" I ask, and it feels like the million-dollar question. Did she really end that deal so she could choose . . . me?

Eden sits up, and I need to lean back to let her, so we're on a more even field. Her gaze becomes uncertain. "Me and . . . whichever of you still wanted me."

Right.

Bitterness crashes in, though I know it shouldn't. It's nothing different to what I expected, not really.

"Anyone will do, huh?" I want it to be a sneer, I try to make it a sneer, but for some reason it comes out as hurt as I feel.

My cheeks burn.

I pull back, and Eden grabs my arm again, not letting me up.

"You're making me reconsider slapping you again," she says huffily, and I scowl at her. "Jayk, you all brought me in under this 'deal.' And maybe I'm just too inexperienced, or too soft, or inconstant, or *something*, but I developed feelings. For *all* of you. And I can't turn them off."

All of us. My lip curls.

She shifts up onto her knees. "Now, I don't know what's going to happen with anyone else. Frankly, most of you are terrible at expressing your feelings, and I'm starting to realize I'm not much better. But I do have them. For you. A lot of them." Eden's throat works. "I thought you died, Jayk, and it wrecked me. All I wanted was to have you back. And now you're here."

My heart thunders, like it doesn't know whether to race to her, or away. I have this urge, this familiar one, to shove her away, say some asshole thing and leave her ass in the dust. Sex is one thing, but my belongings are *mine*. Sharing your shit is how it gets mishandled. Broken.

Taken.

If she's mine, Eden is *mine*.

But I have this other urge. Because she's right in front of me and her skin is glowing like crushed pearls, looking like some violated wood nymph, sticky with my cum and covered in my marks, saying she wants all of me.

And I don't want to shove her away.

"Tell the others to fuck off," I tell her in a low voice.

Eden's eyes widen. "I can't do that, Jayk."

"Why not?" I snort. "Like they've been so good to you? Dom hanging off his ex and Jasper scared to even shake your hand? You think—?"

Her lips flatten. "Stop it. That's between us. You can decide for yourself, but not for me. And not for them." She looks away, and her eyes look all shiny. "They might not care, I don't know. But right now, I just . . . I just want to know if you do."

Her eyes drop to her hands, like she's afraid to look at me.

What the hell am I meant to do with this?

I shake my head to myself. I'm going to tell her to shove it. I am. This is bullshit, and—

Is her *lip quivering*?

I grab her chin, and yank her to me, sucking that shaking lip into my mouth until her hands are clutching at my shoulders and she's trembling for a different reason.

"Mine," I snap, and then kiss her again as her eyes fill with tears.

But my mind is racing.

One way or another, she's going to have to make a choice.

Because I will *never* fucking share.

CHAPTER 23

EDEN

SURVIVAL TIP #59
Avoid people at all costs.
Apart from being dangerous,
it's usually just terribly awkward.

When I wake, it's slow and warm and floating in Jayk's scent. We made it back to camp after our soul-shattering sex in the woods, half-clothed and disheveled, and I didn't even have to ask for the company—he hauled me into his pallet with him and wouldn't let me go. I rub my cheek into him, dreamy and romantic after the first full night's sleep I've had in weeks.

Mine, he said. He dragged so many things out of me last night, feelings I didn't even know were there. I unleashed on him—and he not only took it, he urged me on. Like all my messy, ugly feelings were just some heavy load he wanted to help me shuck.

I can't say they're gone. Outside of this contented bubble, trouble awaits, and all my dark thoughts lurk.

But I do feel lighter.

My whole life, I've solved my problems myself. Worked

through my feelings privately, so they wouldn't be a burden to anyone . . . or an annoyance.

Jayk doesn't find my feelings annoying. He's hungry for them.

Stretching against him, I smile, slowly taking in the gentle sounds of the camp being packed away. He's delightfully warm. Deliciously so. I drink in his closeness like the sweetest dream. Snuggle into him like—

A rough hand claps against my ass, then gives it a coarse squeeze.

My starry haze disappears with the *snap*, and I yelp, lifting my head from his lap. Jayk is sitting up, bare-chested in the cool morning air, smirking at me.

In the dim morning light, I see every red mark, every bruise, every scratch I left on him last night. I run my finger over one of them wonderingly, and he watches me, a hint of uncertainty flickering over his face.

I hear someone shift, and I whip around to see Dom and Jasper sitting beside one another on a log next to our low fire, both holding steaming mugs in almost exactly the same way.

Both staring at us.

My cheeks flame, and I pull back, but Jayk grasps me around my neck and yanks me until I fall over him, then plants a long, deep, impossibly thorough kiss on my mouth. I'm panting into him by the time he releases me, and he pats my cheek.

I'm still blinking, dazed, when he gets to his feet, and his arousal is thick and insistent against his zipper beside my head. Proud—and blatantly obvious. Jayk doesn't seem to care, though Dom's and Jasper's eyes follow him as he very slowly pulls on his shirt, then his kit.

Then their gazes switch back to me.

Well, this is just . . . I work up a tense, uncomfortable smile.

Damn it, Jayk.

I smooth some of my hair back, becoming conscious of just how . . . sticky I am.

I did what I could last night with a canteen of water and some obligingly large leaves, but what I really need is a vat of boiling water and a scrubbing brush.

"Good morning," I manage. "Did you both, um, have a good night?"

And I'm impressed with how polite I sound right up until Dom lifts an eyebrow.

"Not as good as Jayk's," he says dryly, and I cringe.

Jayk checks his pistol at his hip, then shrugs. "I need to piss a storm. Watch her for me."

Jasper pauses his cup before it reaches his lips, then throws an arch look my way as Jayk strolls off.

"He has a . . . surprising charm," I say awkwardly.

Jasper takes a sip from his tea. "His appeal is boundless, I'm sure."

They both watch me silently, and my ears grow hot. I begin packing up, trying not to make it obvious that I'm rushing. But between Jasper watching me with clinical concern since they found me and my tense conversation with Dominic last night, I don't particularly feel like lingering to see what new wave of awkwardness they plan on bringing.

"Eden, I wanted to—"

"Oh, I'm just about packed now," I say with forced cheer, slinging my pack hurriedly over my back. I don't want to have another talk about my *feelings*. Not with anyone. Especially not with Jasper. The last time I spoke to him about my feelings, I ended up crying at his feet. "We'd best be on our way, shouldn't we? Don't want to . . . lose the light."

As if in mockery, the sun sleepily peeks between the trees, barely risen.

Jasper sets his cup to the side, and then stands, lifting a small black bag from beside him. He comes very close, close enough that I can smell toothpaste and chamomile, then places it in my hands.

"I wanted," he repeats evenly, a quiet reproach in his gaze, "to provide you with some toiletries. So you might clean up, if you wished."

Oh.

"Thank you," I mutter, and then back up, retreating more quickly than grace would call for as I decide once and for all that it's not them.

I am the reason my life is so painfully awkward.

"You all almost ready to clear out? We're gone in ten."

I turn to see Heather walking toward us, a small, cheerful smile on her face. She's wiping her bloody hands on a rag, and some of my nausea returns.

If Alastair and Mateo die, what *will* happen to those captive women and children?

She bumps my shoulder, and Jasper moves to the far end of the log, his lips quirking in a moue of distaste. I don't even want to see Dom's reaction to her presence.

"You good?" Heather asks. Then she blinks, wrinkling her nose. "Girl, you reek of sex."

Oh, *God*. Mortification floods me—again—but I drop a pointed look at her hands. "Was that really necessary?"

Heather examines her nails, then digs some blood out from one of them.

"Better than sex, honestly." She sighs. "He bleeds so pretty. I haven't been able to make him scream yet, but I'm working on it. I'm going to break him—he doesn't understand yet that I'm in control, but he will. Just need to make sure I don't accidentally kill him before I do."

I stare at her, remembering my own rage, my own desire to kill. But my demon is tucked away now, sick and overfull on the deaths it demanded. Now I know my men are alive, I can think again— can push past any immediate, cheap satisfaction in vengeance.

But Heather's demon is still raging.

How does one reason with a demon?

"I think this is getting out of hand," I say hesitantly, glancing at Dom, who gives me a long look back. "Surely we can use them. Heather, there are so many people back at the Den. Maybe they can help."

Heather's face hardens. "If they were going to *help*, they would have. They wouldn't have shot Tommy in the head and taken our group captive."

"But—"

"No. Stop being naive, Eden," she snaps, and her hair is a living flame around her. "You got your fun, now let me have mine."

Fun? It was necessary, even satisfying, to poison those men. I chose a path and took it, knowing what it would mean—but it wasn't *fun*. I was a storm that day, and those men weren't the only casualties.

It razed me to the ground as well.

I give her a reproving look and am about to try again when she steps away.

She glances at Dom, effectively ending the conversation with me, and I try not to sniff in irritation.

"Bentley's leaving back to Red Zone today—the prisoners aren't giving him anything more on the meds, so he's taking off with what he has. If you need anything from him, get it now." She looks up at the sun, then around at all of us. "We're out in five minutes."

Heather moves to walk away, then hesitates. I watch her tensely as she takes a deep breath, then glances at me. She gives me a tentative smile. "You should use them to wash. You really do smell like a barnyard."

I blush, and she grins. After a moment, I relent and give her a wry smile back.

Then her gaze moves over my shoulder, and she rolls her eyes. "Oh, God. No wonder. That's what happens when you roll around with animals."

I glance up to see Jayk, who's scowling at her like he's planning her early death. I step a little closer to him and frown at Heather.

Heather leaves with a little finger wave, and Jayk growls beside me.

"I'm going to kill her." He glares at Dom. "She's been on me since day one. I'm going to do it."

"Make sure you pack both stakes and silver bullets," Jasper mutters into his tea. "We haven't yet pinpointed her exact species."

Rather than defending her, Dom gives Jayk a tight look. "I'll get her to knock it off."

Both Jayk and Jasper pause. Jasper lowers his cup, examining Dom with minutely raised brows.

Dom's gaze finds me next. "I'm keeping her from killing them. That's the best I can do for now."

It's my turn for my brows to lift, and I stare at him too.

Dom ignores us, standing. "All of you, move it. We're not going to be the ones holding up the camp."

We all watch him go.

"Do you think . . ." Jasper muses as he gets to his feet, readying his things.

Jayk snorts beside me like he's breaking out of a trance. "Don't froth over it. He still thinks she shits diamonds."

My heart squeezes, my eyes still on Dom's large, retreating back.

"Perhaps," Jasper concedes.

But as he brushes past me, he murmurs, "But maybe not for long."

THE PANICKED SCREAMS start up again that night, causing an answering hush to fall over the camp. I had wondered, with Bentley gone and no reason to keep pushing for information on the Sinners' medical reserves, whether Heather might finally decide to kill her captives.

But it seems she really is determined to make Alastair scream.

And he seems just as determined not to.

For the next four nights, Jaykob tries to drag me far enough away that I don't have to hear Mateo's panicked, furious cries. But they chase me anyway.

For the next four nights, Heather and Dom disappear for hours and return late, and I dread the new state I see Alastair in every day. Though she carefully rebandages him after every *session*, feeding him antibiotics and painkillers like he's her pet, nothing can hide the swollen, blackening flesh, or the evidence of fresh cuts and burns.

Her hate is eating her alive . . . and it's going to swallow Alastair as well.

And with him dead, so is any chance of rescuing the women and children under Sam's control.

CHAPTER 24

EDEN

SURVIVAL TIP #102
Every choice might shatter your life.
Choose wisely.

"No! No, you fucking bitch. Not the—"

Mateo's raw terrified shout cuts off. Or *is* cut off.

It lingers in the brisk night air for a moment, then the people around me start moving again, like they never heard it in the first place. There's a deep brook by our latest campground and many of us are taking the opportunity to clean up as best we can while we can.

"How many rooms are there at Bristlebrook again?" Kasey asks. She scoops water in her palms, then rubs her whole face, messy and inefficient. We're still two days from Bristlebrook at the rate we're traveling, but I'm being asked about every detail.

"Twelve bedrooms," I answer absently, straining to hear any more yells.

Are they getting worse? It sounds like they're getting worse.

"Huh. I wonder which one I'll get," Kasey remarks. "Which one's the best one? Can I call dibs?"

Ava, the blonde woman I strangled in the firefight, splashes her. "No way are you getting a room, twerp."

"Yeah—you'll have to fight me for one." Sloane grins, adjusting her crossbow across her muscular thighs as she keeps watch on the trees.

I apologized to Ava days ago for the whole almost accidentally choking her to death thing, and she was quite good-humored about it. Sloane also apologized to Jayk for strangling him with the wire.

He was not quite so good-humored about it.

"You should all make a list," a self-important voice pipes up behind me, and Ava rolls her eyes at me where he can't see. "I'll talk to Dominic about who stays where and let you know what you should do when we get to Bristlebrook."

"Yeah, sure, we'll do that," Sloane says unenthusiastically, and I bite back a smile.

Aaron is a red-haired young man in his mid-twenties, and he apparently designated himself interim leader while Heather and Tommy were captured.

Apparently, no one else agreed with his appointment.

"What do you think, Akira dear? What are you most excited about?" Ida asks as she wrings out an enormous pair of panties into the creek. "I, for one, cannot *wait* for a shower."

Akira moves slowly, cleaning her arms and wrists with a damp cloth. She glances at me, her face hardening for a moment, then turns back to Ida, murmuring something I can't hear. She started speaking again two days ago, but not to me.

She's kept as far from me as possible, which keeps my guilt at a steady prickle. Not over Logan—the memory of his gun to my head banishes remorse over him quickly enough—but I do feel for her grief. The memory of my own is fresh enough that my empathy is more difficult to quash.

"Do you and Jaykob normally stay together?" Ethel asks me slyly. "Or is this a new development?"

I blink, refocusing, and realize a few of them are looking at me. "Oh, I—" I clear my throat. "It's new."

Why is it just now occurring to me that anything I do is now going to have an audience? I grimace as I pack up my toothbrush.

"Well, no wonder you look so tired!" Ida exclaims. "But you tell that boy to let you get some rest. It's a marathon, not a sprint, and I'm sure your poor—"

"Kasey, Ida. Remember Kasey's here," Ethel chides with twinkling eyes.

"What? No, I can hear," Kasey insists, looking between them. "What is it? I want to hear."

Ida coughs, then says delicately, "Even a good kitty needs rest, that's all I'm saying."

I strangle on air as the women snicker. Good lord. I'm too private for this. Not that there's much privacy where Jaykob's concerned. I don't think I've ever met a man so utterly uncaring of what he's doing or who he is doing it around.

"I like him," Ava says, laughing. "He's a terrible fucking sport about everything."

My lips twitch reluctantly.

After he saved Kasey, it's clear the women have taken to him. It's equally clear that he has no clue what to do with that. They tease the poor man incessantly.

"Hey, Jayk, did you see that bird earlier?"

"Jayk, my man, you need to borrow some sugar?"

"Jayky, up for cribbage later?"

Watching him scowl suspiciously at every gently teasing wave and wink has become the new highlight of my day.

Well, one of them.

As we've traveled, Jayk has been stealing me away incessantly—ravaging me quickly against the forest floor, barely bothering to hide us from the crowds, or more thoroughly at night, owning and marking me like he's branding himself on my body.

I'm not exactly complaining. The bruises that now decorate my skin are far more enjoyable than those I had even a week ago.

But the possessiveness has been . . . interesting.

He's been quick to drag me away from Dom and Jasper whenever they wander close, and while it is a touch irritating, it's also somewhat welcome. For days, Dom has been tethered to Heather, discussing patrols and logistics and plans to guard against Sam returning, and I'm still working out how to talk to either one of them without choking on my own jealousy.

And Jasper has been watching me. Every time I search for him, I find his eyes on me—silent and unbearably intent. I can see his questions lying beneath the surface. All the things he wants to ask about and pick apart and examine. He means well, I'm sure he does, but the thought of peeling myself open for him to inspect makes my palms clammy. I can't read him, and I'm worried if I let him under my skin again, I'll never be able to get him out.

So Jayk's unexpected greed has been a relief.

He's kept me close at night, too . . . but while at first the sheer shock of him seemed to shine a light on every dark shadow in my mind, it hasn't lasted.

Every night, I wake covered in sweat and drowning in my thoughts.

Every night, I hold myself still in his arms and watch the gloom creep toward me as my pulse thunders in my throat.

Every night, it gets *worse*.

Ethel and Ida are right—I am exhausted. But it's not from Jaykob's attentions.

Or not just from that, anyway.

I squeeze out my washcloth beside the little pebbly creek and stand as the others chatter around me. I'm clean but still feel somehow not. With my men alive, Jayk keeping me sated and close, and all of us returning to Bristlebrook with dozens of new friends, things are more hopeful than they've been for me in years.

But I can't shake it.

This feeling like I'm just waiting for the next bad thing to happen—or like it's already on its way. It's *always* on its way. Things are never okay for long.

And I can't shake these thoughts that tell me the next time we won't be so lucky, that we've only borrowed time, that my men were meant to be dead, and all the lives I took will have a price.

When the time comes, will I even have the courage to pay it?

I step back from the creek, the others fading away, and in my mind, it becomes the woods after the poisoning, and I'm stepping away from Heather as men converge on her. I'm abandoning my friend to die. I'm saving my own skin. I couldn't skulk in the shadows, or hide in tree branches, then, and in the light, I'm a coward. Now the shadows are punishing me. They're—

Another hoarse yell cracks through the night, followed by a string of Spanish and a burst of birds fleeing the trees.

I flinch, turning toward the sound, my chest heavy.

"I'm going to head back to camp," I murmur to Ava, and she waves me off, though she also darts a look toward the trees as I move away.

When I broached the subject of the captives with her yesterday, she just shrugged. She trusts Heather with her life.

They all do.

Mateo's sickening shouts dwindle, but I find myself moving toward the chilling absence of sound, veering away from the straight route back to our sleeping pallets that Jaykob growled at me to take.

Yet it's still almost a surprise when I find myself in the shaded nook in front of where Alastair and Mateo are tied. Alastair's face is swollen and bloodied, his breathing shallow, his head resting on Mateo's shoulder.

I pause in front of them, feeling nauseous.

Wrong, wrong, wrong.

Even a clean death would be better than this.

Mateo glares at me, his eyes like coals in the night.

Before I even know what I'm doing, I'm kneeling in front of Alastair. I pull a fresh cloth from my bag and soak it in the antiseptic Jasper gave me from his med kit, then dab at a particularly vicious cut on Alastair's forehead. His eyelids part, and he watches me like an injured dragon.

"Why bother?" Mateo brushes his cheek against Alastair's hair. "Your friend will only make him hurt again tomorrow."

My hand pauses in its treatment. I know he's right.

"I'm sorry," I whisper.

Mateo leans forward. "Don't be sorry, *gatita*. *Stop this*."

"I *can't*," I hiss back, helpless. "I'm sorry, Mateo, but I can't. They won't listen to me."

"So make them listen."

My chest tightens, and it becomes hard to breathe.

When I had words with Dom about it, he shrugged me off uncomfortably, muttering something about how this was Heather's fight.

Only it's no kind of fight at all.

And while Heather has been trying to talk to me about anything and everything else under the sun, insistently trying to draw me back into our friendship, if I bring up Alastair, she stalks off like I singed her tail.

Every. Single. Time.

She won't hear it.

I fall back onto my heels. "I shouldn't have come. I'm sorry."

A tattooed hand snatches my wrist, faster than my breath can strangle in my throat. Alastair's grip is surprisingly strong, despite his weakened state—and fear turns me to ice.

Rope binds his wrists, and they strain against his grasp on me.

"Free us."

His voice is a rasp. A whisper.

It chills me to the bone.

"No."

The grip tightens. "One hundred and twenty-four."

"*What?*" I resist the urge to yank my wrist out of his hand. It's punishingly strong.

"One hundred and twenty-four women and children are being held at the Den," he says softly, and so slowly. His cunning curls through the words. "Three hundred and twelve men keep them there. Using them. Treating them as slaves. Trading them. They use the children to keep the women in line, you know."

"Stop talking." I do try to yank back now, but his grip tightens over my hardly healed skin, and I whimper.

"Eighty of those men are mine. Many more are on the verge of joining me." He's calm and steady, but there are eddies and under-currents in his voice. So many dangerous things, just beneath the surface. "It all falls apart if we die here. Those children will never be saved."

I squeeze my eyes closed, Sam's speech back at the camp ringing in my ears. My pulse is rampaging—he must feel it at my wrist.

He's right. I know he's right.

"Dominic will save them," I blurt. "They all will."

Alastair tsks. "Your Ranger didn't even want these civilians. Do you think he'd risk his men to take on more burdens?"

He really does listen to everything. How much did he note that day in the cave—staying silent while we all bickered? Even as it makes my skin crawl, though . . . maybe that kind of shrewd crafti-ness is what they need.

Do I believe that Dom would risk his men for those strangers? I remember what he said a few days ago—*"We can't do anything for Sam's captives—it's just the way it is."*

Do *I* even want him to?

I just got my men back. The thought of anyone being held captive crushes me . . . but I don't think I could take losing them again. I won't risk myself, and I won't risk them.

Coward, coward, coward.

"No," I whisper, but not in refusal this time. "No, he won't risk it."

Alastair's grasp on my wrist gentles. "Free us, clever girl. Free us, and I'll free them."

I bend my head, panic and adrenaline seizing me. If I do this, I'm betraying them. Heather would never forgive me. Dom was so clear in his orders—he's made it no secret that he expects me to obey them. He listened to me, let me reason with him, and made his decision. I told him I would trust him.

But I *don't*.

Not in this.

He's making the wrong call.

Shaking violently, I nod to Alastair, and he releases my wrists. I scramble for the little multi-tool Jayk slipped into my belt, and it takes two tries for my trembling fingers to peel out the knife.

I press them to his ropes, and then pause.

"I need your word," I say.

Alastair tilts his head. One eye is almost swollen shut. "I told you I would free them."

I shake my head slowly. "Not that. I need you to swear that you won't ever return to Bristlebrook." I shift the knife until it's against his throat, and take a deep, steadying breath. "And that you will never, ever cause harm to one of my men ever again."

"Get that blade away from his throat." Mateo's voice is a flame kissing a Molotov cocktail, one lick away from exploding.

I press the blade deeper into Alastair's skin, until even in the darkness, the blood drop glows. "Your word on it."

"I give it," Alastair says in his hushed, husky voice. "On one condition."

I wait, expectant.

"If your men ever enter Cyanide, my promise is void." He shoves forward, so quickly that I need to snatch my knife back before I cut his throat. "Cyanide is *mine*."

Fear and dislike shiver over me, but I bring my blade to his ropes and slice through them quickly, then the ones around his waist, and finally Mateo's.

I stand, glancing around as Mateo helps Alastair to his feet. The forest gloom stands in silent judgment, but nothing moves.

Keeping them to be tortured and killed felt wrong, but so does this.

Dom has a sore, vulnerable spot where leading civilians is concerned. If he finds out I broke his trust . . .

Guilt is already eating into my veins when Alastair turns to me. He's still supremely injured. He might not make it back to the city anyway.

"This is as much as I can help you. If they find you, I can't do anything."

"They won't find us," Mateo says firmly.

I believe him. He'll do everything he can to get Alastair to Cyanide City alive.

As they depart, I do too, hurrying through the shadows. Me again, sneaking about in the night. Lying. Killing. Betraying.

I don't know when I started becoming this person, but I don't think I like her.

I don't think I like her at all.

CHAPTER 25

EDEN

SURVIVAL TIP #188
*The darkest place in the world is your own head.
Don't lose yourself to it.*

The campfire crackles and burns before my eyes. I've been staring at it for so long, I'm starting to see shapes between the embers.

"They're going to come for Bristlebrook, Dom, I'm telling you. *He* will tell Sam, and there's no way Sam will leave this many of us be. How many fortifications are we going to need to keep hundreds of men out?" Heather argues across the fire in a low voice.

Dom rubs his palm into his forehead. He's exhausted, I can see it from here.

"He knows, too." Dom sighs. "He was in that cave when we were talking. He knows we're planning to move the cameras, to fortify, all of it. He heard. They'll plan for it. He's a fucking SEAL —he'll know how to counter most of what we can set up."

Sick, sludgy guilt clogs my veins at the worry scoring his tone, and I breathe out slowly. I didn't . . . think of that.

If I'm wrong, I might have killed us all.

I think of how crushed Dom would be if he discovered my lie. He listened to me. He tried to help.

God, even if I'm right, I'm wrong. So, so wrong.

Heather's breath is shaky too. "We should find a base some-where else—farmland, maybe? Drones don't seem to be a problem anymore."

Dom throws another log onto the fire. "Head out to farmland and we're going to run right into Reaper territory. Jayk nearly lost a foot when we stole the pigs." He shakes his head. "Everywhere worth having is already claimed, Heat. Throw yourself on their mercy if you want—you might have better luck than we did." He shrugs. "Or they could be just like Sam."

"Reapers?" Heather sighs, then lowers her voice further until I almost can't hear. "Dom, how fucked are we here?"

Dom pauses. "We'll fortify. Move the cameras. We'll make it work."

"Yeah, and when they descend on us with more than three hundred men?" She curses. "They should never have gotten free. Sam wouldn't have the balls or the brains to come after us again without Alastair making his plans for him. He's smart, Dom."

"They should never have been held that long." Dom's voice is hard. "They had time to think of an escape plan."

My eyes flick over to him, startled, and through the fire our eyes catch. It finally starts to feel warm, just for a moment.

He really did argue for me.

"Don't even start with me . . ."

As Heather starts bickering, Dom's attention is drawn back into their conversation, and I refocus on the flames. The two of them haven't stopped arguing since they found Alastair and Mateo missing. Dom was livid. Heather, devastated. Then *furious*. She came down like the thunder of heaven on their tracks, only to lose them in the cave networks. They were clever in their escape, and if Heather had had the capacity to bring down the entire mountain on their heads, I know she would have lit the fuse.

Since then, she's been edgy and short, and I sense a kind of bleak desperation in her, one that calls out to my own. She *needed* that hate. As much as I believe Alastair needed to be freed, I know I just stole her crutch out from under her . . . and now she's limping.

Dom seems to have decided that they managed their own escape, but I heard Heather go so far as to accuse *him* of letting them loose—though I have no clue where she'd get that idea from.

Neither of them accused me, though. It's as though it didn't even occur to them.

Because they *trust* me.

Jaykob is out on his patrol duty again, and Jasper was cursing over taking his turn to cook.

And so, I stare. In the flames, I see myself tearfully confessing to Dom. I see him and Heather, furious and betrayed, casting me from Bristlebrook. I see Jasper's disappointment, and Beau's conflict over who to side with . . . only for him to choose Dom. He'll always choose Dom. I see Lucky being torn up, but ultimately backing down—deferring to the others as he tends to do.

I think Jaykob might follow me, but who knows? For all that he takes me like he never wants to leave my arms, he's hardly bared his soul. In fact, he actively avoids having a conversation with me whenever possible. And whether he's willing to admit it to himself or not, Bristlebrook is his home, and these men are his family.

It's incredible how guilt can take you in little nibbles. Bite after tiny bite, you just . . . disappear.

I haven't slept in two days, and I'm utterly fried. We'll arrive at Bristlebrook tomorrow, and I'm just hoping that being back home is enough to fix this. I need to see Beau and Lucky again. I miss them like air.

"It's a beautiful fire."

Jasper sits down beside me, but I don't take my eyes from the flames. He's had a chance to wash, and he smells like the tea he's drinking. He offers me a tin cup rippling with more of the same, and I take it. It feels overly hot in my chilled fingers.

The fire flickers and writhes. "Is it beautiful?" I ask. "One wrong flare and everything around us goes up. Just like Bristlebrook."

"Hmm."

Jasper stretches his legs out in front of us, toward the fire. "We take our precautions, of course. Build it sensibly. But there's always that risk, yes."

A log falls in the fire—and it looks like Jaykob's barn collapsing. My fingers press into my cup until my knuckles whiten.

"On the other hand, without fire, we couldn't cook our food, would struggle to keep warm . . . and we wouldn't have this delicious tea." He leans in close to me, and his hand cups mine under the metal and lifts it gently. "Drink, Eden."

Something in the implicit order wakes me up, and I blink away from the fire. After a moment, I take a deep sip, and Jasper settles back beside me.

I can't get used to him like this. He's groomed as well as possible under the circumstances, but he's still in Ranger's clothes, and far less formal than I've ever seen him. That bothersome, intriguing strand of sable hair falls over his forehead.

"People have been known to write down their thoughts, their hopes, and then burn them in flames like these. A kind of cleansing." His eyes are intent, but I don't have the energy to try and retreat from him tonight.

I glance toward the raging heat.

"We'd need a bigger fire," I mutter.

"I have a pen and paper, if you'd like to try it," he offers. "I can't speak to the spiritual aspect, but writing things down can be cathartic in itself—if you don't want to talk."

"I don't." It's a little too sharp, like the edges of brittle honeycomb waiting to be snapped.

Jasper doesn't seem to take offense, just inclines his head.

I let out a long breath. "I don't want to write either. I just want to get back to Bristlebrook. Things will be better there."

He watches me, lying back on his elbows, and the light trips over his face, turning him one minute infernal, the next, angelic.

"Hmm."

He's beautiful enough to make my breath catch, but that little sound has me shooting him an edged look. It's his "too polite to disagree" sound, and I've heard it often of late.

"I'm sure you'll be pleased to see Beaumont," he says. "And Lucien."

At the change of subject, I survey him under my glasses. Even when we're not playing chess, it always feels as though we are.

I'm not sure if this is him not wanting me on defense, or if it's a new kind of attack.

"I can't wait."

Jasper's eyebrows twitch just slightly at my tone, and I relent. "I need to see for myself that they're okay."

"They're fine, Eden," Dom says, cutting off his conversation with Heather. "We wouldn't have told you they were if they weren't."

He shifts around from the other side of the fire. It takes Heather a moment to follow.

"No, I know. I just saw Lucky take that shot, and Jayk didn't even really know what had happened or what Beau was doing about it. Just that he was 'fixing him.'" I blow out a breath. "I only want to see him for myself, that's all."

Dom nods, his eyes lingering on me. "Beau knows what he's doing."

"Lucien took shrapnel to the apex of his lung, which caused a pneumothorax," Jasper interrupts smoothly. "Dominic field treated him, but Beaumont was required for a needle aspiration to reinflate his lung. Lucien also received two gunshot wounds, but neither were life threatening, outside of the risk of infection. Beaumont is treating him with appropriate drugs, and though there was some concern about their efficacy after so many years, he was quite firm in his belief that if Lucien was sensible and adhered to his bed rest, he would be well enough." Jasper purses his lips. "Infection was the largest cause for concern, I believe."

His words have the rhythm of recitation.

"Very . . . thorough," Heather chokes out, and when I glance at her, her tongue is pressed into her cheek.

Dom gives her an impatient look, then lowers his voice as he says something to her, drawing her attention. The tea turns bitter in my mouth, but I return my attention to Jasper.

His cheeks are pink.

Something from the other day flits into my mind, and I frown. I try to banish it . . . but the thought persists.

"You're very attentive to his care," I whisper.

Jasper sighs, then pulls himself up until he's sitting. "I've been trying to work out how to tell you. Since your comment to Bentley . . . I wasn't sure just how much you know."

My eyes widen. "You're *gay*? Is that why you—"

Dom and Heather look over at my exclamation, a perfect, synchronized pair, as my mouth clicks shut. I don't want to go back to his rejection of me. The door is *closed* on that particular conversation.

But Jasper doesn't seem to get the silent message.

"That's not why I refused you," he says gently, and our chess game plays in his eyes too. He's cast in amber by the firelight, and it makes his dark hair, dark eyes, look dipped in gold. "My sadism is not what you need, Eden, and that reasoning holds now. But to clarify, I don't hold a preference for gender. My attraction is more fluid, based more on the person and their . . . interests. I had thought Lucien might have said something." His voice lowers to a mutter. "He can't keep his mouth shut about anything else."

"Lucky?" I swallow, feeling like the ground is crumbling under my feet faster than I can find steady earth. "Why . . . why would Lucky know?"

But I know.

Even as I ask, things are starting to slip into place. Lucky's lingering looks, the blushing, the way he dropped plates at dinner and how he stole me away on Jasper's day. It's incredible how one piece of context puts a new light on everything.

He wasn't doing those things to spend time with me.

It was to keep me away from Jasper.

But Lucky *said. "We aren't interested in each other that way."* He said those exact words. *He* implied Jasper was straight.

He lied to me. He *used* me.

My emotions are a dark spiral, and violent, shameful betrayal slams through it.

My tea sloshes over the rim of my cup, and I realize I've been strangling it. The burning liquid scalds my fingers, and I drop the cup with a curse. Jasper moves to take my hands, but I pull them sharply away, standing.

Dom. Jasper.

Now Lucky, too.

God. How delusional can I possibly be? Am I so attention starved that I invented these romances so entirely in my head? Silly, silly Eden. They brought me to Bristlebrook for sex, and apparently I just took them not being blatantly awful as interest.

I have to admit, though. This makes more sense. I'd taken for granted that being the only woman around gave me a certain advantage—that one fact helped significantly to put years of insecurity to the side. Even so far as to believe that five men, these five incredible men, could truly want me.

How naive of me.

I'm not experienced enough for this. One sheltered, lonely marriage and a life devoted to work and study haven't prepared me to read a room, it seems.

I told Lucky I didn't know how to play his games.

I press a hand to my chest, sure I might feel my heart rip even between the bone and sinew, and Jasper follows me to my feet.

"Girl, how many of these guys are you juggling?" Heather snorts. "You missed a few things from your run-down."

"Are there not villagers somewhere for you to feast on?" Jasper bites out, though I feel his eyes hovering over me.

Heather snaps her teeth with a wink as Dom stands, frowning. "You didn't know about Jasper and Lucky?"

Jasper and Lucky, he says, like they fit together. Like the duo is something discussed often and casually.

Jasper pinches the bridge of his nose. "Up until very recently there was nothing between me and Lucien."

Heather stretches from her place on the ground. "Except for all those times you dragged him off to your secret room and played out every one of his submissive, masochistic little fantasies." She tilts her head. "Except for that, right?"

My lips part.

"He's a sadist, and he occasionally needs to work out his shit on someone who likes to take it. Which I do. So, you know . . . it makes sense."

I close my eyes, mortified. Stupid, stupid, *stupid*.

"Leave us *be*, you abhorrent harpy," Jasper snaps. "Dominic, could you please . . .?"

"This abhorrent harpy is good on her perch." I open my eyes to see Heather settling back into a more comfortable position. "But you go ahead."

Jasper's shoulders rise sharply, silently, then he says gently, "Eden, I promise you that there is nothing between me and Lucien. There can't be. I was his psychologist—it would be unethical in the extreme. It is better, far better for everyone, that he be with you. Yes, on a handful of regrettable occasions, I gave in to my shameful impulses and we performed a scene, but he never touched me, we never kissed, we never did anything until just before the attack on Bristlebrook. I . . . I slipped."

He cuts off, and he looks *agonized*.

He looks how I feel.

"He's in love with you." The words feel true as soon as I say them. "And you're in love with him."

Jasper's mouth is still open, and his chest falls fast. His dark eyes glitter. "It doesn't matter."

Lucky. Sweet, funny, gorgeous Lucky . . . is in love with someone else. Tears burn the back of my eyes. "Of course it matters."

Jasper is perfect for Lucky. He needs Lucky's joy and light, and Lucky craves his darkness.

Jasper's need to fulfill his sadism with someone who matched him was exactly why things failed with his wife, and here in front of him, *always in front of him,* is his perfect fit. Sexually, and apparently emotionally too.

He said he slipped, but that's not right at all.

He already fell.

Jasper shakes his head once, in a sharp, panicked gesture. "No. I can't."

"Jasper," Dom cuts in, his voice heavy with warning, and Jasper stops, swallowing.

Jasper runs a hand over his face, turning away. "A slip. It was—"

"No." My lips are numb. "He loves you, Jasper."

"He *can't.*"

"He does," I snap. Everything falls before me in sharp detail— finally, the full, beautifully painful picture. It was all for him. Every touch and kiss, every moment he pulled me away, all of it was for Jasper.

I'm sure Lucky likes me, I doubt he could fake that much, but I never had a chance to talk to him after I broke the deal. As far as he was concerned, I was there for sex. What a brilliant opportunity that must have been to make Jasper jealous.

The worst part is, I can't even blame him. He wasn't cruel to me. He didn't do anything wrong. It was all fair, under our arrangement.

I just had to go and get my stupid heart involved.

So I push down my own broken heart and glare at Jasper. "Lucky loves you and you love him and you're *rejecting* him? How many years, Jasper? How many years have you been doing this to one another?"

His shoulders hunch in Lucky's uniform.

"You're very, very good at pushing people away, and I'm sure you have every reason. You're very clever, so I'm sure you've built a brilliant case against yourself. But it doesn't matter, because you're hurting him. God, it all makes sense now. I never understood why he was so deeply lonely. It's this."

Jasper turns back around, stricken. "He's not. Lucien is strong. He's so fond of you, you'll be happy."

Fond. It's a slice to my hamstrings. A crippling blow.

"He will never love me while he's craving you. Stop hurting him, Jasper. You're being selfish."

"*Selfish*?" Jasper stiffens, and this time fury suffuses his forbidding features. "Careful, dear girl, you go too far. Everything I've done is to keep Lucien from harm."

I know he's right. This is not my place. But everything is bursting inside of me, organs imploding, one by one. I'm already too tired, too on edge. They're foolish, all of them. Can none of them appreciate what it is to be loved like that? To *love* like that?

My mother, my grandmother, my father—whoever he was—or even my husband, Henry, none of them ever loved me so well. I want it. Badly. I wanted it to be mine.

This is a repulsive waste. Discarding uneaten banquets in the trash, instead of giving them to the starving.

"Well, you're failing miserably," I tell him, unable to keep the harshness from my voice. How is it that Lucky lied to me more intimately, and yet I still understand him more than I do Jasper? I know what it is to want. To *crave*. "Lucky deserves better. This is your hang-up, *your* issue. If you truly loved him, you'd get over yourself. You'd give him *everything*, instead of teasing him over and again with this awful push and pull. You slipped? How many times? How many times have you broken his heart through the years, Jasper? God, I don't understand—"

"Enough, Eden." Dom touches my arm, and I snap my head to look at him. My control is gone, shattered, the way it was when I drew the gun on Heather, and when I unleashed on Jaykob. My control used to be the one thing I had, and now I can find it exactly nowhere.

"You've said enough," he repeats.

Something in his voice makes me glance at Jasper, who is white to his lips, staring at me. After a moment, he spins on his heel and walks off.

"I need to talk to him. Are you okay here?" Dom asks, distracted, and at my shaky nod, he picks up his pack and leaves after Jasper.

As he does, the guilt from the last two days returns with inhuman force. It pumps through this aching, shredded thing in my chest like poison. Lucky and Jasper. Dom and Heather. Myself and my terrible secrets.

A low whistle pulls me from my thoughts. "Now that was a show."

I press a hand to my mouth. "Not now, Heather."

"Hey," she says, and she waits until I look down at her. When I do, her expression is surprisingly compassionate. "Do you know what you're doing there?"

She tilts her head after Dom and Jasper.

I laugh humorlessly. "Does it seem like I know what I'm doing there?"

Heather leans forward and hooks her arms around her knees, looking up at me. "Look. A bit of unsolicited advice?" Her gray eyes are grim now. "Choose."

"Choose?" The word has a vile taste.

Her shoulders lift. "As someone who has been caught between multiple guys before, it seems like a fun place to be . . . right up until it isn't. Don't be that person. She's not a fun person to be."

Hesitantly, I sit down beside her. Choose. Lucky is in love with Jasper. Jasper with him. Dom with her. The loss of each of them hollows me, like three gaping wounds, all still fresh and bloody. That was *their* choice.

I can't carve out another one by choosing between Jayk and Beau. I *can't*.

"I've made such a mess of things, Madison." Tears fill my eyes, and the panic catches me with harsh, hitching breaths. "I don't know what I'm doing anymore. The things I've done. Who I *am* . . ."

Her hand finds mine and squeezes.

"You and me both," she whispers back, her voice suspiciously thick. "We'll figure it out."

I squeeze her hand back, then pull my knees in to my chest.

Tomorrow we'll be back at Bristlebrook. All of us. Me, Jayk, Jasper, Lucky, Beau, Dom, and Heather.

One big happy family.

CHAPTER 26

JASPER

SURVIVAL TIP #31
*If you refuse to bend,
you'll break.*

I flee the fireside like it was hit by a drone strike—I need to outrun the carnage. I'm shaking all over, and I stop to lean against a tree, trying to work air into my compressed lungs.

If you truly loved him, you'd get over yourself and do what will truly make him happy.

Nausea hits me. What am I doing?

What have I *done*?

"Give me a number." Dominic is a weighty presence behind me, one I would recognize anywhere.

A number from one to five, he means. It's a technique I've used often to gauge how much pain a submissive is in during a scene. One Dominic, on occasion, uses also.

"Five," I breathe, breaking apart.

If I could safeword on life, at this moment, I would. I feel unwell—the guilt I have been battling for years is defeating me, finally.

Deservedly.

Dominic's hand finds my shoulder, and he turns me so my back is against the trunk of the tree. In front of him, I let some of my mask disappear. I let him see the worry, the fear . . . and the unbearable guilt. He knows. If anyone understands the weight of responsibility, it is him—not only as captain, but as a dominant as well.

"Have a drink."

A canteen presses against my other hand, and I push it away.

"No, thank you. I—"

"I said *drink*, Jasper."

At that tone, I look up at him, momentarily off guard. He used his dominant voice.

On *me*.

Giving him a sardonic look from under my lashes, I take his canteen and drink. The cool water, the need to pause and breathe through my nose, does help. I wipe the lip of the flask and return it to him.

"Thank you."

Dominic nods, then crosses his arms, waiting.

I arch a brow at him as he uses my own techniques against me once more. I would be impressed . . . if it weren't so irritating.

Particularly since they work.

I sigh, shaking my head. I am feeling too many things right now to pick them apart myself.

"Do you agree with her?" I ask quietly.

Dominic tilts his head, golden eyes sharp on me as he thinks it over.

"Look, I agree whatever dynamic you've had going on doesn't seem to be working for either of you. But she's also coming at it from one angle." Dominic grimaces. "Eden's a submissive, and she's close to Lucky. She's going to be seeing it from that side. A lot of people will—it's easy to be sympathetic with a love-sick subbie."

I flinch. I don't want Lucien to be sick over me. I never wanted it. I craved it—the sinful, terrible parts of me did—the way an addict craves a hit. But never in my heart.

There, I only ever wished him whole.

"Submissives forget sometimes, I think, how heavy this responsibility can be for a dom. It's your job, your whole job, to look out for him. To make sure you're not doing any harm. As our shrink, you get that twofold. The weight of that can crush a person, if they're not careful." Something dark and unhappy flickers over Dominic's face, then he blows out a breath. "You're a smart guy, Jasper, and you're not a masochist. I don't think you'd push him away if you didn't really believe you were crossing a line, even if I don't understand it."

I look up at him, taken aback by his observation. I'm moved by it, too. I know the others don't approve of my resistance. That has been clear enough in Beaumont's disappointed glances through the years. In Jaykob's eye rolls.

It means more than Dominic can know that he understands.

The nod he gives in return is brief. Matter of fact, even. "I'm going to go against popular opinion about Lucky here and say that you're allowed to have boundaries too. If this is one of them, then you're entitled to it—and Lucky shouldn't be pushing you on it, no matter how he feels."

I rub the tension over my eye. "I haven't communicated particularly well with him. That's my failing. I've given him too many mixed signals for him to be able to understand. He had . . . plenty of his own thoughts on my reasoning."

The fall air is rich with decaying leaves, and it swirls around us lightly. His words have haunted me this entire trip, every brief moment I wasn't worrying over Eden—*"How dare you stand here and tell me I don't know my own mind?"*

What if he's right?

What if he isn't?

Dominic's mouth flattens. "Any reasoning is good enough for a boundary, Jasper. You know that."

"I do," I say quietly, unsettled. Then I push off the tree, my hand fisting around my hair like it's around Lucien's throat. "It's not that simple. It was perfect, Dominic. Utterly perfect. His mouth, his touch, his *love*."

I break off, my throat raw, and swallow. I turn to face the other man, willing him to understand what I cannot. How can something so criminally terrible feel celestial? Why is it that I want to knot him and Eden and myself together, even though I know I'd be taking advantage of him, and that my sadism would only hurt her further? Why must everything be so complicated?

"He almost gave his life to save mine—and for what? What have I given him to earn that? There's nothing in the world worth that price, least of all me. How can he feel that strongly if it's all a lie? How can *I*?"

I breathe hard, every word hurting as it leaves me, and Dominic walks over and pulls me into a hug. I'm so stunned, I freeze.

I don't think he has ever hugged me before.

It takes a long moment before I sigh and rest my forehead on his shoulder.

"It feels like my head and my heart are at war, and I don't know how to reconcile them," I whisper.

Dominic sighs, then says, "What is it that you're most worried about? Being with him, I mean? What do you think will happen?"

Happen?

I pull back, frowning. "I don't believe I'm following. Being with Lucien is wrong—"

Dominic raises a hand. "I know. I know. But what's the consequence?"

"I— He needs to be free to form healthy relationships. He trusted me to provide his care, Dominic. Not to be lusting after him like a teenager," I snap.

I turn, that ill feeling returning to my stomach.

"He is free to do that, isn't he? You don't seem against him and Eden. It doesn't seem to be holding him back in any of his relationships, does it?" Dom asks in a reasonable tone, and I glare at him. "And let's rewind there too. It's not like he was seeking out your professional help because of childhood trauma or abuse. He was only in your office by mandate."

"He still had things to work through, as we all do," I retort. "Lucien has a beautiful and rare ability to see the good and positive light in the world, even when terrible things happen. But he still had questions, concerns, worries that we worked through together."

"Can I take a stab and say they centered around his romantic life?" Dominic asks dryly.

My gaze lifts in puzzlement. Lucien's sessions are none of Dominic's business—but many of them did gravitate toward sex and romance. Submission. Masochism.

Talking him through it was almost the death of me.

Dominic snorts, and I narrow my gaze on him.

He quirks a brow. "Did you ever think that he was just in love with you from day one and spent every session trying to seduce you?"

I swallow hard.

"All I know is he came out of your first session into the barracks and spent three damn hours talking about you. Jayk nearly threw him through the window." Dom rolls his eyes, and in spite of myself, my lips twitch. "You did right by him, Jasper. You talked to your supervisor. You had him moved to another shrink. You resigned. And you both still have these feelings."

I rub my hands over my face. I tried. I do know that. Weakness and all, I have truly tried to resist him.

"I'm not a shrink, Jasper. I don't know the ins and outs, but be honest—do you really think you'd cause more harm if you were together? Because Eden is right about that. Being apart is killing both of you." His eyes are soft and unbearably understanding, and I have to look down as mine sting.

Lucien's yellow flower pin gleams in the moonlight, and I squeeze my eyes shut at the sight. Several tears squeeze out too.

Ever since Eden arrived at Bristlebrook, I've begun to question this very thing. Question *everything*. I'd worried that Lucien's love for me was more an obsession. That, almost, was easier to dismiss as false. But the fact that he could feel easily and so naturally for Eden, and still have feelings for me, tells me something different.

Lucien is a secure, emotionally stable, highly intelligent man with an infinite capacity for love.

He's expressed his informed opinion now, with all the facts, and he still wants me. *Loves* me. Would my love in return truly do him harm?

Or is it, as Eden said, the thing that could free us both from our misery?

Perhaps I need a new vow for myself. One devoted to only bringing Lucien joy. Surely that can't be sinful? My lust may be depraved—but my love is only pure.

Finally, I pull my handkerchief from my pocket and wipe my eyes, then return it. I look at Dominic and nod.

"Thank you," I murmur, putting as much gratitude into the words as will fit. Dominic and I have talked over the years—as equals and comrades of a sort. Brothers, perhaps, after so long in this home together.

But this may be the first time I've truly thought of him as a friend.

"I will speak with Lucien when I return." I quirk a smile, a low buzz of anticipation working its way through my veins. "I think I have some groveling to do."

Dominic studies me hard, like he might be able to pinpoint any reservations with his gaze alone.

Then he shakes his head, a wry laugh falling out of him. "I don't have any advice for that one."

I watch him thoughtfully. There's been a heaviness to his steps ever since we left Bristlebrook, but rather than easing when we found Eden, it seems to have grown more burdensome.

"Dominic, was I wrong to invite the civilians back to Bristlebrook?"

It's a carefully asked question. Bristlebrook is my home, after all. Still, Dominic has led us faithfully for years, and I know his concerns about newcomers—and I just placed ninety-two right under his nose.

His laugh fades, and his gaze becomes introspective. Sightless. Every line of his face grows grim.

"You weren't wrong," he says finally. "It was the only right thing to do."

"You have reservations." It's not a question.

Dominic blows out a long, hard breath. When he looks at me, I see every shade of fear in his eyes.

"How am I meant to provide for that many people, Jasper? How the fuck am I meant to keep them safe and fed when there's an army coming for us? Heather said they have another three hundred-plus men back in their Den."

I consider him. I'm not insensible to how dire our outlook is, but Dominic is repeating problematic patterns here.

"Try to examine the language you just used," I urge. "Can you identify any concerns we've discussed in the past?"

The mulish look he gives me in return belongs on a toddler.

"I'm not talking to you as my head doctor, Jasper."

He's asking . . . as a friend. How novel.

I incline my head. "Fine. You said 'how am *I* meant to provide' and 'how do *I* keep them safe.' Why do you insist on shouldering sole responsibility for these problems? We have a community of people here with a fantastic range of skills."

His brows lower, and he stares at me hard. "I'm captain. They're coming back to Bristlebrook, where *I* lead. I have the most training—the best chance of keeping them safe."

We've had variations of this argument over the years, and while it was only myself and the Ranger squad at Bristlebrook, there seemed little reason to push the point. But it's different now. These civilians change everything.

When we first left for Bristlebrook over four years ago, amid all the chaos and strikes and panic, we gathered everyone we could who needed our help. Too many for just four Rangers. When we were attacked by those raiders and that child died, it hit us all hard. But I think part of Dominic died then too.

He already had a habit of shouldering too much blame, but after that incident, it became problematic. Sam's attempted coup, the civilians leaving, Heather leaving, all of the following events only confirmed his own bias—that he needs to do more, be better . . . and that if anything fails, it's his fault. Never mind how many of us are here, ready to share the burden.

Enough is enough.

"Dominic, you wanted me to be frank with you and so I will be. You are not the civilians' leader—Heather is. They chose her, and while I question their taste, it is their decision to make."

He crosses his arms, the trenchant set to his jaw digging in.

I continue in the same firm tone. "You may be best positioned to organize our defense, but that doesn't provide you with the skills or qualifications to lead a community."

"There has to be someone ultimately in charge, Jasper. I can't have them second guessing when to follow me or when to follow Heather, especially with an attack coming," Dominic argues— though I notice a moment's hesitation.

Like, for once, he might be thinking twice about my words.

"That is a very . . . militaristic . . . point of view," I say delicately.

His eyes flash, like gold in a pan. "We're living in a militaristic world."

"Hmm." I give him a long look, then murmur, "Is that the world you want?"

He falls quiet, staring at me. Tension brackets his mouth, and I feel for him. It would be nice if I could unburden him the way he helped unburden me. At least a little.

This will take a while to sink in, I think.

"You grew up in a very particular environment, Dominic. One that was centered around duty and responsibility. You take too much on. Consider whether another option might be possible here."

Military base after military base. Two dedicated military parents, each taking years-long tours during his childhood. It's hardly a wonder that he and Beaumont latched onto one another like long-lost soul brothers, meeting when they did.

"Eden said something to me before everything went down at Bristlebrook." Dominic frowns. "She said that I needed to stop treating her like a soldier."

He looks perplexed enough that I stifle my amused smile. Brave submissive.

"She may enjoy being treated as a person. You might find that many of us do," I say instead, as mildly as I can, but his acerbic look tells me he caught the undertone anyway. I try again. "Talk to her like you would Beaumont. You're quite open with him. Relaxed. Perhaps try asking *before* ordering."

"Asking," he repeats heavily.

I can't stop my amusement showing now. "It does marvelous things."

"Were we always this much of a mess? Or is it all just going to hell? I feel like we're all at breaking point lately."

I turn back toward camp, and he follows my lead for a change. A small start.

"I think it's how these things often are. Breaking point isn't always a bad place to be. These weak points have always been there, Dominic, undermining us. Perhaps if we fall apart now, we can become something stronger later," I say, thinking of my kintsugi, and all of the beautiful gold-mended lines. Thinking of Eden asking whether I believed my flaws could ever become something beautiful.

It might be that I'm beginning to.

The air on the way back to camp smells richer, clearer, and my lips turn up.

Dominic examines me sideways, then ahead, frowning in thought. We walk back into camp together in silence.

Thinking on what we might become.

CHAPTER 27

EDEN

SURVIVAL TIP #46
Watch out for trees.
They may appear out of nowhere.

My hand finds my hair for the third time in as many minutes, smoothing back the strands I already know are neatly contained. We're nearing Bristlebrook, and I'm fluttering. I don't know if nerves, dread, excitement, or misery has me more firmly in its grip, but whichever it is, I'm ready for it to be done. I'm so close to seeing Beau again. And Lucky . . .

Lucky and I need to talk.

"You know, I can just find you a mirror," Dom says in an undertone, and I glance up at him. His lips are suspiciously quirked, like he's fighting a smile.

I snatch my hand from my hair. He's been walking silently beside me for nearly an hour, but for some reason *this* is the first thing he's decided to comment on.

In my politest tone, I reply, "That won't be necessary, thank you."

Oh, he's *definitely* fighting a smile. "And here I thought you didn't have a vain streak."

I huff an exasperated sigh, trying not to squirm. "Doesn't everyone?"

I'm not quite sure about this side of Dom. I've seen glimpses of it, with Beau and Lucky, but he's usually so serious—especially lately.

Dom shrugs, then says dryly, "I couldn't give two shits."

He's lethal like this. Dark and a little disheveled, as confident in this terrain as if he were born to it.

"Like you need to," I mutter.

His smile breaks free, stealing away the stern planes of his face. I lift my gaze to stare at the greenery, the people walking beside us, *anything* that's not that unfairly gorgeous grin.

No, thank you. If I look at him for any longer, I'm likely to walk into a tree.

Dom nudges me with his elbow, and I half tilt my face his way. Maybe it will be like being blasted with only half a furnace.

"You don't need to worry, Eden. You're beautiful. They're not going to take their eyes off you."

Did he just . . . compliment me?

He says it casually, like it's nothing, like my pulse doesn't immediately trip over itself in the exultant thrill of it. God, he really is gorgeous. Thrumming with power and careless confidence, the dark, formidable strength in his hard body, those fiery golden eyes that are almost too intense for me to—

His arm flings out and his hand buries itself in the front of my shirt, then he's yanking me hard in front of him. I catch onto his arms with a muffled cry . . . and it takes a second to see his bemused raised brow, just inches from my face.

"Tree."

"What?"

He nods his head to the enormous oak—the one looming massively, painfully obvious just an inch from where I'd been walking. That suppressed little smirk twitches his lips again. "*Tree.*"

My cheeks *burn*.

"My eyes," I say weakly. *Eden, you're officially an obvious, oblivious disaster*. "Bad eyesight. Terrible."

That smile becomes dry and too knowing.

"Sure, your eyes." He leans in closer. Half an inch more and we'd be kissing. "Here's some old Army advice—it helps if you watch where you're going."

Is he saying words? I'm sure there are words. Embarrassing ones. It's just . . . his eyes are molten. My brain stalls as I shiver, melting a little, caught up in memories of riverbanks and bright, stinging spanks.

Dom cocks one brow at me. He releases my shirt and steps around me, continuing on like he didn't just sexy grenade my brain.

Cringing, I hurry up beside him again. "Why are you walking with me, anyway? Don't you need to plan?"

With Heather.

I look around for her and find her gritting her teeth as Aaron walks beside her, telling her something with a pompous wave of his hands. She catches my eye and shoots me a pained look. Then her gaze flicks to Dom, then back to me, and her brow lifts slightly.

Biting my lip, I look away.

"Plans are done. We deliberately tripped one of the motion cameras—Beau should have seen the notification." He nods at Sloane as she walks past. "Besides, we're *friends*." He gives me a dry look under sinfully dark lashes. "Friends walk together."

My cheeks heat. Just one friend casually walking into a tree while staring at another friend.

Bristling, I mutter, "Well you haven't been terribly *friendly* since our last conversation. I wasn't sure we still were."

Not that he's been unfriendly. He's just been . . . busy.

With Heather.

"I'm ready for a pillow fight when you are," he says, utterly deadpan, and this time I'm the one who has to fight back a reluctant smile. Then he shrugs. "And you can blame your boyfriend for the rest. He throws you over his shoulder every time I get close."

There's more than a thread of irritation in his voice, and I examine him closer. "Is that why you sent him ahead to Bristlebrook this morning?"

"That would be an abuse of my authority," Dom says mildly.

"And you wouldn't do that, of course."

"Send a soldier on ahead so I could spend time with his girl?"

I press a hand to my stomach and nod faintly.

"I wouldn't do all that just for a friend," he says, and his brow kicks up as he gives me a long look. My body reacts much too viscerally to the light flirting. Just as my cheeks start to heat, he seems to sober a bit. "Do you have a plan for that?"

At my questioning look, he shakes his head. "Jayk doesn't play well with others. He knows the score with Beau?"

I stare at him, then stare at the ground, stepping over a gnarled, fallen branch as I collect my thoughts. Of all the things I was worried about having to confront while I was at Bristlebrook— Heather and Dom falling back in love, someone discovering I let our prisoners escape, Lucky leaving me for Jasper, Lucky *not* leaving me and always pining for more—Beau and Jaykob not being okay with us was not on my list.

"I told him. How I feel, I mean. About"—*everyone*—"about Beau. He knows."

I did tell him, I know I did, though I was kind of bliss-drunk at the time. Did he agree? I can't remember. He certainly didn't argue.

But he has been terribly possessive the last few days . . .

"I'm not choosing," I say defensively, Heather's words from last night ringing in my ears. "They both want me, and I want them. We'll figure it out. I can do this."

"Sure, you're nailing it." Dom looks, too casually, over at Jasper, who is walking beside us, serious and silent as he has been since our argument last night. "Sharing is easy, don't let me tell you different."

As I look at Jasper, he pauses, his attention caught by a bush of yellow flowers.

I purse my lips as I glance back at Dom, my dread and guilt creeping back in. Is this just going to be another way I hurt people?

With Dom and I not talking much the last few days, I haven't had to look him in the eye. It's hard to hear him talk and walk with me so casually, knowing that I went behind his back. I'm not a good liar. If he asks me outright if I let the captives go, I'm not sure I could do it.

Dom bumps his arm against my shoulder again. "Just talk to them. A lot. Then keep talking."

I nod, drawing a shaky breath. It's hard to look at him for an altogether different reason right this moment. Guilt swirls inside me.

"Are you excited to see Beau?" I ask, needing the distraction.

His smile warms, and it's like seeing light glimmer in an ocean cave, an unexpected beauty in its dark and deadly home. It's so disarming, so close to boyish happiness, that my worries vanish, just for a moment.

"There's a bottle of whiskey with our names on it. As soon as we get the civs set up, we're pulling an action flick marathon—because apparently that's all Jasper's parents ever used to watch apart from the K-dramas, and *that's* not happening." He rolls his eyes, but the glint in them tells me he knows just how many nights I stayed up watching them.

"Sounds like you have him all booked up," I say, laughing.

With him smiling like that, I can't find it in me to be put out. I rarely see Dom as anything less than serious and laden with responsibility. He clearly needs to see Beau as much as I do.

I'm the one to bump his shoulder this time.

"Just let me say hello before you cart him off." Just the thought of getting a hug from him is enough to thicken my throat with longing. "I've missed him."

His smile fades a little. "You need to see him." He shakes his head. "The marathon can wait. I have a lot to do anyway."

"No, Dom, no." I lay my hand on his arm. It's large and solid as steel under my gentle fingers. "It's fine. You need a break."

A break is the least I can give him. Between getting kidnapped and setting his prisoners free, it's a wonder I haven't turned his hair snow white.

He falls silent for a moment, looking at me sideways. Slowly, he says, "You could join us. If you wanted."

I almost skip another step. "Join your marathon?"

Dom lifts one shoulder, and that droll smile begins to curl his lips again. "I'll remove the 'No girls allowed' sign just for you."

I laugh, enjoying this side of him more and more. We walk in companionable silence for a while, until I pause to gather some cuttings of wild lemon balm. I should be able to replant those when we arrive, and it's a handy plant to have around.

"You haven't been sleeping," Dom remarks as he watches me, and I tense.

Standing, I tuck the cuttings in my borrowed pack. "How much farther to Bristlebrook?"

Dom is quiet for a long minute as we walk, then he sighs. "Above a *friend's* paygrade?"

I bite my lip, peeking up at him, not quite able to make out his tone. I just don't want to get into this. Not now and maybe not ever.

He meets my gaze, brooding and intense. "You don't have to talk to me, pet, but you do have to talk to someone. And that *is* an order."

That look. That name. That *tone*.

My brain short-circuits, and it's only when I'm staring at his back that I realize he stopped me in my tracks. And it's the strangest thing, but for some reason, the idea that he might take this—all the decisions about this awful, confused way I'm feeling —out of my hands . . . is a relief.

With a sudden surge of lightness, I call to his back, "Or what?"

My pulse strikes against my throat when he pauses and throws me a heated look over his shoulder.

"Or I'm giving myself a promotion—and I won't be *friendly* about it."

It takes me a moment to restart my steps, and another half an hour trailing along behind him, trying to pull apart every hidden meaning in his words before the solid thump of music starts to register.

Dom's radio clicks on with a static buzz, and a blare of background music. "Dom? You in range? Acknowledge, over."

Beau. I hurry up closer, in time to see some of the subtle tension in Dom bleed out. He pushes a button on his kit radio.

"Roger, Beau. Reading loud and clear." He pauses. "It's good to hear your voice. Over."

His radio clicks on again, and the music in the background is deafening. "I'd like to say the same, but I can't hear shit. Can you get her up here any faster? Lucky won't turn off the—"

There's the sound of a scuffle, and the radio sounds like it's thumped a few times.

"Captain, this is Steel Rain. I've commandeered this radio for an important broadcast. You're being too slow, and I want to see Eden. Over."

Dom gives me an amused look as my cheeks heat—and my heart aches. Why is Lucky being adorable now? He's in love with Jasper. I don't want my heart to fill like this. Not when it's only going to burst as soon as Jasper finally admits to his feelings.

And he *will* admit to them. I know what I said last night shook something in him.

Lucky is a masochist. Jasper, a sadist. To use Lucky's words . . . it just makes sense.

He and I don't. Not really. Lucky needs more than I can ever give him—Jasper's caution about me not fitting him because I'm not a masochist fits just as neatly to my situation with Lucky. I'm not a dominant or a sadist. And now that I know he loves Jasper, it seems absurd to even try to compete. It's *Jasper*. Wickedly beautiful, heartbreakingly cruel, sadistic, clever, thoughtful Jasper. It's impossible to miss the appeal.

They'll be beautiful together, as soon as Jasper extracts his head from his behind. Lucky has been lonely—it's no wonder he wanted someone to pass the time with. Particularly under the bonds of our deal, and no emotional risk needing to be taken.

But God. Does he have to be so *sweet*?

The music is getting louder, thrumming with a rock rhythm I'm sure I've heard before.

Dom's eyes lift skyward, and he clicks his radio back on. "For the last time, we're not calling you Steel Rain, Lucky. We're almost there, over."

Dom's radio clicks on again to a loud *thump*. "Please hurry, would you? He's been playing this song on repeat for the last hour, and I'm ready to strangle him. Over and out."

The trees in front of us start to change, turning from green and into burned-out husks. The massive front lawn is charcoal black, but sprouting with greenery between the death, and the apple tree's bare boughs seem like the frail limbs of an injured patient. There's a massive pile of debris sitting like a grave marker where Jaykob's barn used to tower.

At least the bodies have been cleared away.

Bristlebrook looms behind all of it, set deep into the cliff. Windows are taped and boarded shut, and there are new marks and imperfections scarring its face . . . but it's still beautiful. Still strong and safe and the most special place I've ever lived.

Best of all, on the porch, I see Beau and Lucky standing in wait.

It's only then, finally, as our people pool out of the trees, that the song hits me.

Garden of Eden.

I laugh, and tears spill out of my eyes.

I'm *home*.

CHAPTER 28

EDEN

SURVIVAL TIP #264
Cuddle the pretty men.
It might be your last chance.

I take off at a run, tears streaming down my face, and they jump down from the porch, running to meet me.

We're just about to converge, and it looks like Lucky is bracing for a tackle, when Beau grabs his collar at the last minute, jerking him back hard.

Lucky chokes, and Beau pats his back as he stops beside him. Adrenaline and relief flood my body, and I hungrily take in every feature. They look good. Clean. There's healthy color in their cheeks and nothing obviously, critically wrong.

"Lucky, cool it. You gotta ask first," Beau says, all exasperation. His eyes lift, then run over me, so thoroughly I feel it everywhere.

We stare at one another for a long moment, his gaze pulling me in like a lasso.

"Hey there, darlin'." His voice is a soft, low croon. "You up for a cuddle?"

That voice from him is like someone bringing a glass of hot, steaming water to the nape of my neck, and then pouring it down my spine.

He takes in my reaction, and a slow, warm smile works its way over his face.

"No!" Lucky coughs, then glares indignantly as he points at Beau. "You are not playing that card. Injured beats Southern."

Injured. I scan Lucky again, worry nipping at me. He shouldn't have run over here if he's hurt.

He sags against Beau, pressing a hand to his chest. "Can you check my stitches, doc?" He groans pitifully. "I think you tore them open."

Beau shoves Lucky off him. "You don't have any stitches, you filthy liar; don't you even try it. Don't listen to him, Eden."

Lucky flips him off, a grin breaking through his pouty expression, and relief crowds me again. The two of them are gorgeous in the sunshine, teasing and relaxed and that absurd song is playing for the fifth time, and my throat starts to feel thick and hot again.

We've come out a little battered, but they're really okay.

Lucky must see something of what I'm feeling, because his face softens, and he reaches out for me—then hesitates just before contact. My heart squeezes at the consideration, knowing he's worried, that both of them are, about what happened to me.

"I'm sorry. I am, I just—" The smile I work up feels agonized, my eyes tortured as I drink them in, and Lucky's hand drops. "I'm so glad you're okay. So, so glad."

Relief avalanches over his face, his eyes lightening to the crisp blue of ice-tipped skies. He cares for me, I know he does, but even that care hurts to see. It's always been Jasper for him. It always will be, no matter our new, sweet closeness.

Beau's shoulders come down slowly with his long exhale.

"I'll take that cuddle now, if it's still on offer?" I whisper tremulously, suddenly needing it, craving their arms around me more than anything.

Beau beats Lucky to it by a half second, bending down and

wrapping his arms around my waist until he's lifting me in a gentle, enveloping hug. He only has me to himself for a moment before Lucky throws his arms around both of us at a terribly awkward angle.

Beau catches on quickly, turning and lowering me with the practice of someone who has done more than a little sharing so that Lucky can hug me from behind.

Lucky presses his face into my neck, and I realize he's shaking. "I was so scared," he whispers into my skin. "I've never been so scared. I'm so glad you're safe."

I'm enclosed in them, and it's like being infused with warmth. It sinks into my skin and deep into my core, and I could be buried in them happily. Their familiar sounds and delicious smells and easy kindness.

"Ah, you've found one another," Jasper murmurs behind us, barely audible above the blasting music.

Abruptly, reality comes crashing in. He'll be wanting Lucky now. He might as well rip him from my arms.

Resentment takes a solid swipe at my joy, and jealous hurt returns to nibble at the rest of it. Stiffening, I pull back, and they let me go reluctantly. I lift my glasses to swipe at my tears, only to have a square of silken cloth pressed into my palm.

I glance up, and Jasper meets my eyes. His face is a careful mask, but his eyes are tentative on mine. Flushing and confused, I look away and use the cloth to dab at my eyes.

Am I jealous that he will take Lucky?

Or that Lucky will have Jasper?

Jaykob strides from the other side of the tree line. I reach out my hand as he nears us, missing him already, though it's only been a few hours.

"Oh, hey, Jayk. Was Henrietta okay?" Lucky grins. "And thanks for bringing—"

He shoves past us without stopping, ignoring my outstretched hand.

"—Eden home." Lucky frowns at his back as he stalks into Bristlebrook. "Is he hungry or something?"

Dom's warning about Jayk rings in my ears, and I take a deep breath, trying to push aside my worry. He agreed to the deal, didn't he? Surely that shows at least some capacity or willingness to share.

Before he cared, a voice taunts me. I push that away too.

Talk, Dom said. If only getting Jayk to talk about his feelings didn't leave me feeling like Androcles trying to pull the thorn from the lion's paw.

The music abruptly cuts off inside.

Beau sighs. "Thank god."

"Everyone, come through," Dom barks, and I turn to see the crowd staring up at Bristlebrook with a mixture of trepidation and awe. Firm and elegant against the natural rock, it does make a sight, even battle weary as it is.

"Scratch that," Heather yells back to her people, ignoring Dom's sharp look. "Everyone, set up out here for the moment. We know you're all tired and want to get clean, but we'll be taking turns. Five oldest first, come through—you get first shot at showers."

"Seriously? So ageist," Kasey calls back, rolling her eyes, and a brunette in her forties I don't know too well tugs her hair good-naturedly.

Heather directs her people easily, and I feel the tension in Beau and Lucky wind tighter and tighter. With another frustrated look at Heather, Dom helps Ida up onto the porch since the stairs are half-destroyed, and then Ethel after her. Three others in their fifties follow quickly—one couple, Beth and David, and a woman named Leanne—and he directs them all up the stairs, then jerks his head at us to follow him in.

When we reach the porch, I squeak as Beau lifts me up from behind, though it's only a short step, and his fingers linger on my waist afterwards. But when I glance up at him, his mouth is set in a deep scowl.

As soon as the door shuts behind us, he directs his glare at Dom. "You brought her back here?"

Jayk is leaning against the wall next to the kitchen, flicking his knife, which I'm coming to realize is his favorite defensive move. Dom shifts, his stance widening just slightly like he's planning for an attack.

"Good to see you too," he says dryly.

But Beau isn't having it. "Never again, Dom. I thought we were done with this."

"These people needed a safe place."

"Are you fucking her?" Beau snaps, and I don't think I've ever seen him this angry. His face is lit with anger, his body a tornado of riotous energy.

At his question, though, I can't help but steal a glance at Dom. *Are* they sleeping together? I haven't seen them so much as hold hands. Does someone like Dom even hold hands?

Dom's face hardens. "Is that really the first thing you're asking me?"

I wrap my arms around my waist at the non-answer.

Beau pulls back like Dom swung at him. His face settles into cynical lines that don't suit it at all. "Not any of my business, I suppose. Hasn't been for a long while."

Hating that look on his face, I touch his elbow, and Beau tenses again, looking down at me. There's so much sorrow in the unhappy set of his mouth. He cups my face, then draws me into his side.

"Did you even talk to Eden before you jumped into someone else's bed?" Beau asks bitterly, and I wince as I hear Lucky shift uncomfortably next to me. "Or I suppose you didn't bother. You were never invested in this in the first place, right?"

The confirmation from Beau, that Dom really wasn't ever interested in me, burns cold in my chest. It becomes an ice fire, its frost burning through my veins.

I feel Dom's eyes on me, but I don't look at him. Instead, I tug on Beau's shirt. "Stop, Beau. Please. It's okay. Dom and I talked. We're . . ."

I glance at Dom uncertainly, and he lifts a brow back at me, looking like a pissed-off panther.

"We're pals." His golden eyes flare like a lashing tail. "Aren't we, *buddy*?"

I lift my chin quellingly. Does he have to make it sound so ridiculous? Maybe it's because of how transparently, humiliatingly into him I am.

If he *is* with Heather, I'll really need to fix that.

"Yes. We're friends." I lay my hand on Beau's chest. "Everything with Heather is complicated. But these people trust her . . . and so do I."

The words come easier than I expected them to. Between Dom, Jasper, and Lucky, this may just be the origin story of my transformation into a literal green-eyed monster, but I *do* trust Heather—with my life, at least, and certainly with her people's safety.

"She saved my life," I tell him firmly as the front door swings open.

"Only after you saved mine." Heather walks in, slowing as she glances between us all. She looks at Beau and crosses her arms. "Hey there, Doctor Delicious, trying to kick me out already?"

"Don't call him that," I mutter at the same time Beau snaps, "Don't call me that."

Heather's brows fly up, looking between us. "Him too?" She laughs, deep and throaty, then her eyes bounce around the room. "Wait, all of them?"

Jayk pushes off the wall with a scowl, though he's staring at me and Beau, not at her. I smile at him, wishing he'd come over, but he doesn't seem to see it.

Jasper's return look to Heather is chillingly cool. He angles himself in front of Lucky casually, but so deliberately that the warning is unmistakable. Behind him, Lucky blinks in surprise, color touching his cheeks.

My heart lurches again, along with no small amount of embarrassment. Was he always this obvious? Was I really that *oblivious*? Lucky doesn't wear his heart on his sleeve. It's in his eyes—and they're glued on Jasper.

Heather points a thumb at Dom, though she tilts her head at me. "Him too?"

When I don't answer, she looks at Dom. "You too?"

"Heather stays," he says, ignoring her. "Now if you can all stop gossiping, can we sort out how we're going to house everyone? Let's clear out the gym, the music room, the games room, and the spare sitting room. On top of that, we have seven spare rooms—ten if we all buddy up." He shakes his head. "That's still only going to get a bit over half of them inside."

Heather shrugs. "So we give priority to the old and injured. Get the young ones in too. My people are used to sleeping rough. They can rotate around if they want, and we can get started building some more permanent structures."

Beau gives her a look caustic enough to strip skin. "Are you staying here that long? Doesn't seem like your style."

Dom, Jasper, and Lucky stay silent, and I frown at them. "Yes, of course. We all agreed that this was going to be a new home for them, right?"

Dom nods once, but he looks resigned more than enthusiastic, that heavy tension returning to his shoulders like he's trying to keep the world balanced there.

I look at Jasper, who is still watching Heather with frigid wariness. I remember what I overheard Dom and Beau saying, all those weeks ago, how Heather told Lucky to stay back with the women and children because he wasn't man enough to protect anyone. Just the memory of it is enough to raise my hackles too. It reminds me of how she sneered at Akira. I don't know how to reconcile that with the woman who coaxed me out of my numbness and helped me set fire to my rage. It's like she doesn't know how to stop fighting, even when she should.

"Jasper," I prompt, and though it hurts me to look at him right now, I keep my gaze steady as he meets my eyes.

And his eyes say a great many things. In our exchanged glance, I see his displeasure melt. I see him remember the cave, and the state of the people when they were there. His horror at the cold and the lack of amenities. We have a whole conversation. In this one thing, we're agreed.

He inclines his head. "They may stay as long as they wish, Eden."

"Greeeaaat. Thanks for permission to use the trees you don't own in woods that don't belong to you for people you have no say over." Heather rolls her shoulders, looking bored.

Beau's hand tightens on my waist.

"Madison," I urge, wincing as the sinful angles of Jasper's face sharpen to razors again. "Could you please . . .?"

She waves her hand. "Fine, fine. Playing nice."

"Who's buddying together?" Dom asks. "Then we'll tell the rest and get the rooms cleared out." He glances at Beau. "We should—"

"How about it, darlin'?" Beau cuts Dom off smoothly. He runs his hand up my back and leans in, the green in his gaze dancing. "You ready to go steady with me?"

I try—unsuccessfully—to bite down on a bashful smile at his blatant flirting. His eyes drop to my lips.

"Hey!" Lucky pipes up indignantly. "You can't just take her! You know I'm just going to break in, right? Get ready to snuggle."

I close my eyes briefly at his words, my amusement fading. Jasper. He's in love with *Jasper*. And as soon as he has him, there'll be no need for snuggles with me.

I hope I kept his heart warm enough for its new owner.

"Fuck this shit."

That growl is not amused, and I turn to see Jaykob storming

toward the door. My already ripping heart drops into my stomach with a queasy splash.

"Jayk, wait!" I pull out of Beau's arms to run after him, and I catch him just as he pushes through the door.

He throws my hand off and crowds me against the door. It slams closed as I'm pressed back against it.

"Wait for *what*?" He's huge in front of me, rough and big and mean. He slams a hand above my head and his heavy, tatted biceps are lined with strain. "From what I see, there ain't nothing for me to wait for."

Something slams against the door behind me. "Get off her, asshole. You hurt her and I'll plug you so full of bullets, your corpse will give the maggots lead poisoning," Heather yells through it.

"He won't hurt her, Heat. Lay off," Dom snaps.

My guilt comes flying back in full force. I've only been back for *minutes*. How am I already messing this up?

"Jayk, I told you. I'm yours—but I'm also his. I—"

"I. Don't. Share." His eyes are full of midnight hurt and anger swirls through them like clouds. "And you already made your choice. Wasn't like I didn't know how this would go."

I tangle my hands in the front of his shirt before he can storm off. I know my nails are cutting into his chest, but I don't care. It's practically his love language.

"Don't you *dare*." I press up against him, and when he pulls back, I yank at his shirt to pull him back down. It doesn't move him, but the fabric strains. "There *is* no choice, Jayk. I need you."

He stares into me, fierce and hard, but with his eyes so deep on mine, I see the tiny moment of hesitation. I feel that second where he presses back into my touch, the way he does each time we come together. Like a finger-brush is never enough for him. He needs a press, a claw, a *demand*.

And so I dig in.

I need to get through to him. I *have* to. He's finally started to talk to me. In those sweet, vulnerable moments after he punishes my body, when he touches me like I'm the wing of a butterfly he's afraid to crush, I've felt him wanting to share. Wanting to believe in it.

And it's such a perfect mirror for me, for the way my heart aches and tears and transforms into something new, something bigger and stronger every time we're together, that I just can't let him reject it. He has to understand.

I've lost Jasper, Dom, and Lucky—I can't lose him too. I *need* him.

I'm breathless, waiting, and watching closely enough that I see the exact moment I lose him.

His eyes shutter, and my heart cries out.

"You go back in and play house with your *Beau*." He sneers. "I don't play make believe."

He grasps my wrists, firm but so gentle around where he knows I'm still healing, and pulls my hands off his chest.

"I'll be out with the rest of the plebs." The sneer drops, and he looks away. Something soft and raw touches his features, and when he speaks again, it's full of quiet hurt. "Just leave me alone, Eden. I don't want to see you anymore."

He strides off toward the trees, and I press a hand to my mouth to stop it trembling. I'm not sure it helps, because my hand is shaking like a leaf itself.

But without Jayk blocking the view . . . I finally realize that every single person camped out on the front lawn just had a front-row ticket to see that particular showdown.

I stare down at them, and they stare back at me. Ava, and Sloane, and Aaron, Judith and Carol and Danielle and more, all looking up at me with a varying mix of amusement, disapproval, shock, disappointment, and dismay.

"Oh, damn," Kasey remarks into the silence.

And as if that's a prompt, almost eighty-five heads turn away in a flurry of movement, as if they all simultaneously found something else to do.

My eyes sink shut as I try to collect myself. *Jayk*. My heart jerks, ripping further. It's as though someone has tied invisible strings to it, attached to each one of these men, and they keep being yanked in different directions—or just slicing through the tender muscle.

There's nothing I can do now. He won't talk to me and doesn't want to hear it.

But I'm not letting this go. I can't.

I turn. My hand quavering on the doorknob, I return inside, almost bumping into Heather, who is hovering in front of the door.

Only to find more eyes on me.

Beau pulls me back in for a hug and presses a kiss to my hair. "I'm sorry, pet. That wasn't the most tactful of me. I'll help you talk to him tomorrow."

I bury my face in his chest for a moment, just breathing him in until the hot, stinging urge to cry recedes. In that moment, I love him. I love him for his first instinct not being relief, or to take the opportunity to push Jayk away. He's going to help me bring him back in. To us.

I nod, then turn to face everyone else. Jasper's dark eyes glitter with concern, and I avoid them desperately.

"What else has been decided?" I ask quietly.

There's an awkward silence.

Lucky rubs the back of his head. His hair is half out today, and the movement makes the strands shiver prettily. "Look, I'm going to be honest—we were totally eavesdropping the whole time."

Of course they were.

"We're almost done." Heather's still looking at me like I'm someone entirely new to her. "They just need to buddy rooms. CC, should you and I take one? Might make planning easier since we're up all night anyway." Then she looks at Jasper. "Then you two get to cuddle up. Win-win."

I don't know who goes more rigid, me or Beau. My tender heart takes the lash, bloody and rough. I just . . . can't. Not right now. I can't think of Dom and Heather *up all night* together, or even Jasper and Lucky falling into one another, finally.

Beau draws me against his chest as I start to waver.

Don't cry, don't cry, don't cry. You didn't cry when you killed a half-dozen men, you will not start in front of a room full of your exes.

"No," Jasper says abruptly, and I flinch, glancing up. "No, Heather and I will share a room. Dominic and Lucky can share."

"What?" Lucky chokes out, staring at him, and the hurt is naked on his face.

Every single thing he does is oriented around Jasper. I'm the worst kind of fool to have missed it.

"Yeah, I'm going with *what*, too." Heather wrinkles her nose at Jasper. "I am not sleeping with the silent serial killer."

"Ah, but shtriga can only be killed while feeding." Jasper adjusts his cuff neatly. "So don't prey on any children and you should have no cause for concern."

"Not. Happen—"

"I have a spare, hidden room in my quarters. I will reside there, and you may take the master suite. We will only need to see one another on entry and exit, so do try to remain clothed. I suffer nightmares enough without the additional fuel." Jasper gives her a severe look. "Or you may claim one of the other rooms and displace some of your people. The choice is yours."

Heather rolls her eyes. "Fine. I'll sleep in the creepy lair."

Dom sighs, looking at Lucky. "The first prank, you're out on your ass. I mean it."

But Lucky's still staring at Jasper, his mouth tight. It takes him a moment to look at Dom, and another to find a smile. "Got it, Cap."

Dom moves toward the door, brushing past Beau and I, and I

feel him briefly squeeze my arm as he walks past. Heather follows quickly.

In the commotion, I study Jasper—and as if sensing my gaze, he meets my eyes.

Why wouldn't he choose to stay with Lucky? I'm sure he wants to. Is he continuing with his stubbornness? Why would he willingly keep Heather with him?

His face gentles, just a fraction. And the compassion there is what makes it finally click.

He wasn't keeping Heather with him. He was keeping her away from Dom. And perhaps, giving me some breathing room about Lucky.

He's been watching me for days, silent and clever, the concern in his eyes deepening by the hour. This is his way of helping.

He's giving me a reprieve.

I take a deep breath, and mouth "thank you" at him.

The corner of his mouth lifts just a fraction, and he inclines his head.

You're welcome.

CHAPTER 29

DOMINIC

SURVIVAL TIP #222
*If you can't band together,
then you'll fall apart.*

The meeting breaks up quickly as civilians start filtering inside. Heather hangs back to get them settled, and several women flock over to Lucky as Jasper leads Eden upstairs, talking to her in a low voice.

I only watch them for a second before Beau draws my attention, heading up the opposite staircase. Target acquired. This is the longest we've gone without seeing each other since before Day Death, and it's stupid that the first thing we've done is fight. I have a movie marathon, a bottle of whiskey, and his girlfriend all planned out for a date—just need to get the civs settled in first.

I find him in his room, throwing clothes onto his bed.

Leaning against the doorframe, I cross my arms. "Don't be mad, honey. Just give me a chance to explain."

Beau throws a boot behind him, and I need to swerve to stop it hitting me. I stare at it, then stifle a sigh. It's going to be one of *those* fights.

I debate whether to go fix myself a coffee and come back to it later—coaxing Beau out of a stink like this is a long, painful process, and I'm already up to my ears in shit.

Sam only had two days of travel to get back to Cyanide from that camp. With all these civilians loading us down, it took us over a week to arrive at Bristlebrook. I don't know how long it'll take Sam to mobilize a force against us, but it's possible he already has —and with the cameras compromised, we're flying blind.

Coming off the gut-rip of losing Eden, tracking her, discovering Heather, and all my fucked-up civ baggage, I'm sapped. I might as well be a hollowed-out tree, and at this point, a strong wind is going to knock me over.

Maybe Jasper's right and I need to give up more control.

But there's only one person I've ever been able to do that with . . . and he's throwing fucking shoes at me.

Beau turns abruptly, gathering up his clothes in a pile high enough to hide his face and walking past me to the door.

I follow, snagging up a sock as it drops.

"I'm not sleeping with her," I tell him lazily.

Beau doesn't like to fight. I need to approach this carefully or he's going to slam down a silent treatment like a tank hatch.

I try to push down my exhaustion.

It's harder to push down my disappointment.

I really just needed to see my best friend today.

He stops outside of Eden's door, and I see the moment he realizes he'll need to drop his clothes to open it . . . or ask me for help.

I lean against the wall beside the door, waiting. He stares at me, then dumps the clothes on the floor at his feet without dropping eye contact. Then he swings the door open with deliberate care, gathers up the clothes again, and brings them inside.

I roll my eyes to the ceiling, my teeth on edge. Patience. Find some damn patience.

As he comes back out, I grab his arm. "Are you listening? I'm not fucking Heather. Untwist your panties, would you?"

He wrenches it out of my grip, and gives me a hard-eyed, stubborn-as-shit look that tells me I can kiss any kind of reprieve from the swamp-ass last few weeks goodbye.

He comes back out of his room a minute later with his favorite pillow under his arm, the one that's sucked in enough of his night-drool that it can probably be used for DNA tests two hundred years from now.

I rub at the tension building between my eyes. It hasn't strayed far since I agreed to take on the civilians.

Since *we* took them on, I correct myself sourly, thinking of Jasper.

Damn it, if it's *we*, why do I still feel like I'm the only one who gets how quickly they could all die here? There's this weight tied around my neck, and it's just getting heavier and heavier.

The only time it's eased at all has been around Eden. Finally seeing her safe, talking to her in the woods, watching her nearly walk into a tree because she was checking me out. Just the idea of watching stupid movies with her and Beau tonight had turned my whole mood around.

I decide to try another tactic and follow Beau back into his room for his next trip. He moves around to his musty green armchair. He bends, trying to lift it from behind, but it's too big. At this rate, he's going to give himself a hernia.

I walk around to the front of it and lift it up. Just for a moment, with both of us working together, it's perfectly balanced.

Then he drops it.

My breath leaves me with an *oof* as the heavy weight slams down, and I reel back.

Passive. Aggressive. Asshole.

Slamming my hands on the top of the armchair, I lean over it to glare at him. "What the hell was that?"

Beau shrugs a dismissive shoulder. "I don't want the chair anymore. It can stay here."

"You do want the damn chair. It's your favorite chair."

I try to un-grit my teeth. Beau has a favorite chair. He has a favorite everything. He falls hard and obsessively at the drop of a hat.

He hesitates, looking down at the wide, velvet-coated monstrosity.

I tap it, nodding. "Good. I've got this end now, just pick it up."

Beau's eyes lift to me, and then he gives me a slow shake of his head.

"No, Dom, I don't think you do have your end. In fact, I don't think you ever had it. I always, *always* pick it up first, and some-times you come round to chip in when it suits you. But you'll let your end drop—you always do. Hell, you've dropped more chairs than I can even keep track of. I don't know that I trust you to put your hands on my chair."

I don't think we're talking about the chair anymore.

Trying to parcel out what he's *actually* trying to say is giving me a migraine. "Beau, I haven't slept. I'm tired. And stressed. I haven't showered in two weeks, and I smell worse than the barracks bathroom after curry night. Can you just tell me what the problem is so I can fix it?"

If he tells me *I should just know*, I'm going to set his chair on fire.

Beau's face clouds over, like a storm is setting in, and then he leans over the chair.

And something *beeps* at his waist. Beau looks down, checking the receiver he has attached to his belt. If the radio or any of the cameras are set off, the receiver sends an alert.

He looks up at me, then heads for the door without a word. I catch up quickly, falling in beside him as we make for the study. We cross the inner balcony, and as we pass the music room, I hear Eden and Jasper talking through the cracked door.

Beau must hear it too, because his steps slow for a moment, before he glances at me and picks the pace back up.

I can feel the build in him now. His steps are too clipped, his mouth too tight. He's like clockwork, and he's right on track to be beating down his wrath like it really is a sin he needs to strangle.

We pass through the secret bookcase, and by the time we make it into the study, he looks ready to burst.

Ready to wait him out, I look up at the cameras, but most of them are dormant. The only motion camera activated is way out west, where a new Reapers banner is flapping across the main road out of the forest.

Great. They've rebranded.

I glance back at our HAM radio. "Has Bentley been trying to reach us?"

I walk over to it and open our transmission, fixing the dials and tuning in to the Cyanide repeater group. I gave him our call sign and took his down, but he said he wouldn't talk to anyone until he heard my voice.

"There have been some messages. Nothing that made a lick of sense." Beau crosses his arms over his chest. "Do you still love her?"

Eden pops into my mind, biting back a smile as she pushes up her glasses.

For some reason, panic licks through my chest.

"Why is it always zero to one hundred with you? No, I don't love her. I didn't love her before she was taken either. I've had less than a dozen conversations with her." Jesus fucking Christ. Love? "Why would you even ask that, Beau? I told you I wasn't ready, and you just keep pushing. If she had any expectations for us that I let down, it's because you set her up to fail."

Beau tilts his head, his brows dropping.

I scowl. "No, you don't get to be mad. She's brave, I'll give you that. Clever as hell, and she's got a ruthless streak too. You wait till you hear how she got out from under them, Beau—because we did jack shit. It was all her."

What was I saying?

Right. I'm not in love with Eden.

"I was asking about Heather," Beau says, letting out a disbelieving huff like *I'm* too much for him. "Are you still in love with *Heather*?"

"Heather?" I repeat, confused.

"Yes, Dom, *Heather*. You know, the woman you ditched me for because you were so head-over-heels. The one whose name you couldn't bear to hear. You show up with her out of nowhere, and whether you're fucking her or not, the question stands—do you love her?" Beau asks, and he might be breathing steadily through his nose, but it might as well be steam.

Why would I love Heather? Respect her, fine, but my memories are fresh. I remember every bit of the chest-shredding pain, the shame of her walking out with my civilians, the shock of losing her to Thomas . . . and realizing that I'd just shot my closest friendship to hell for someone who never really cared. Point blank, execution-style.

Back then, I was so sure that the only way any of our relationships would survive was if they were separate. Because me, Heather, and Beau all together? It wasn't working.

Turns out, we didn't work without him anyway.

"I'm not in love with Heather," I say, meeting his eyes. "She made sense to me back then—she still does. She's honest. She's up front with her shit, good or bad. She's smart, good in a fight—"

"Do you want a partner or a soldier?" Beau scoffs.

The derisive sound feels like shit when I'm trying to explain.

"Fuck off, Beau. I don't know anything *but* soldiers." He should know this. He does know this. He just never understood it, not really. "Bristlebrook is the first time I've lived off a military base in my entire life. I went to military schools. My mother was military. My father was military. The only women I've ever even spoken to who weren't military were submissives that *you* hooked us up with—and you and I both know how that worked out."

Beau's lips twist at that. Like I need the reminder that I messed things up for both of us, over and over.

But it's not like he helped. He was always so quick to dive in and kiss every bruise better. Wipe every tear. If I stuck my foot in it, he apologized for me. The only time he ever let me do anything myself was when *he* was mad or if they pissed *him* off. Then I was flown in to be the big bad wolf again.

It's no fucking wonder they never trusted me.

"Heather was different. She wasn't there for you, for once. It was easier for me. She is a damn soldier—we didn't do all that messy emotional stuff."

I've always had Beau for that. He's the only one I know how to talk to like this.

Beau uncrosses his arms, shaking his head. He looks like he's thinking. "Eden deserves the messy emotional stuff. She needs it."

"Yeah, no shit, Beau. This is my problem. I'm learning a foreign fucking language here," I snap, getting frustrated.

Eden needs it. The civilians need it. Everyone needs me to be better. Softer. Or I'm going to lose all of them, all over again.

The panic isn't an ember anymore. It's a full, fiery blaze.

I want to be better. I still remember her reaching out her hand to me after I spanked her by the river. She was already cuddling with Beau. He was handling the aftercare, as usual, so she shouldn't have needed me too.

But she still invited me in.

Every time she looks at me, she keeps inviting me in.

Beau matches my frustration, and it always looks strange on his face. Like they aren't muscles he ever exercises.

"So learn the damn language, Dom. It's not that hard. You just need to get over your shit and actually open up for once." He stops, then breathes in, and it's the labored kind of breath someone takes after catching a bullet. When he continues, he's forced the calm back into his voice, "You need to make up your mind. Either you're all in, or you're all out."

My muscles lock up as I realize what this is. "An ultimatum? You're really giving me a fucking ultimatum?"

Hasn't he been listening? We need to do things differently this time. Not just throw ourselves in headfirst and miraculously expect a different outcome. Just *get over it*?

Fucking. How?

If I knew what I was doing, this wouldn't be a problem in the first place. And trying to figure it out now, with all the rest of the shit we're dealing with, seems impossible.

I don't want to hurt her, and going all in now before I've worked out what the hell I'm doing seems like the quickest way for me to fuck everything up again. It was good talking to her today. Flirting. The pressure was off, and I just got to enjoy it. She even talked to me about the others—about her *feelings*.

Why can't I just start here? Why can't we just find our own way to this?

Why is it always Beau's way or the highway?

And why can't I say any of that without him shutting down and walking out, every fucking time?

Finally, Beau sighs. He walks over to me slowly, and then he grips my arm. There's a sad, bitter set to his mouth now. The anger has simmered down behind his eyes.

It's worse than anger.

He looks resigned.

"You know, I never got it before. How you could back away from The Plan like you did—that something ever felt more important than that. But I get it now." He smiles, but it's full of glass and it's sharp enough to cut. "I love her, Dom. Eden deserves everything. She deserves to feel safe and loved. I can't keep being your emotional crutch, and I don't want you hurting her. Or me when you mess it up."

Beau squeezes my arm. It feels like he's got my heart in his fist instead.

I wonder if he can feel the blood leaking between his fingers.

"I think we need to take a break. You do whatever you have to with Heather. I need to focus on Eden. Figure out how to do this properly, without you."

Without me.

I watch Beau leave without a word and sink into Jasper's chair, my head in my hands. My mind swings to movie night.

There's not going to *be* a movie night. No whiskey. No shy smiles. No overinflated action sequences we can pick over, trying to work out the best way to actually shoot a helicopter out of the sky.

There's no reprieve. Just more problems.

"Uhhhhhhh. So! Bad timing, sounds like, but I do have news." Bentley's booming voice crackles over the HAM radio, and my head snaps up.

The red light is on, and it suddenly registers that I opened the transmission *before* that fucked-up little heart-to-heart. It's not a secure line. Anyone could have heard that. *Sam* could have heard that.

"Let me know if you need another minute," he prompts. "Heavy, that. I've been known as *quite* the romantic, though. *Great* at giving advice. All you really need to get someone to fall in love with you is one starry night, a tarp, three eggs, a violinist, and a *lot* of lube—works every time."

I grab the mic. "You said you had news?"

I sound clipped and rude as fuck, but right now, I couldn't care less.

"That I do." There's a shuffle on the other end, and there's a distorted whine before it settles. "First up, we have people watching the Den. Thought it might interest you that Alastair and the pretty one, Mateo, walked back through their gates two days ago."

I only just stop myself from smacking the mic against my forehead.

I expected it, but the confirmation is still brutal. Two Navy fucking SEALs helping the enemy tanks our already shitty odds badly.

Bentley clears his throat. "You sound like you've had a rough day, so I won't call you a brainless moron for letting them escape."

"Thanks," I mutter under my breath.

"Look, the Sinners are running a recruitment drive—you keep playing around on channels and you'll hear them. They're making promises, and reading between the lines, they're promising land, resources, and women. We've seen about forty new men come back with their raiding parties, Alastair and Mateo right at the head of their trucks." There's a pause, and then his voice turns harsh. "And we were attacked last night."

I sit up, worry spiking. I don't know much about Bentley, or their Red Zone, but he seems like good people. There are few enough like that now that losing them would be devastating.

Not to mention, as brutally selfish as it is to admit, they're best situated right now to give us intel—and we desperately need it.

"Are your people okay?" I ask.

"For now. Our snake pit got blown to shreds—it looks like they're testing out their new firepower. Thanks for that too, by the way. We're lucky they didn't hit our base. We have . . . people here. Our base can't take a hit like that."

"Fuck," I swear.

Recruitment drives and weapons tests only mean one thing.

They're ramping up for something big.

And if they're already promising women, they must be pretty confident they're about to come into a windfall of them.

"You catch all that?" Bentley asks, when the silence starts to stretch on too long.

I realize I've been staring off into the distance, looking toward a short, bleak and bloody future. They have over three hundred men, SEALs, weapons . . . what chance do we possibly have against all of that? Training and experience tells me the answer.

We're very, very fucked.

"Caught it," I say shortly. I press my hands over my eyes. "Thanks for the update. Keep in touch when you have more news. Stay safe."

"Yeah, sure. You—"

I cut the line off and let myself take a minute—just one—to just be sick to my stomach.

Somehow, against all odds, I have to keep these people safe. Somehow, I need to gain their trust and keep it, because even our slimmest odds rely on all of us being able to mobilize and defend Bristlebrook together.

The heavy chain around my neck winds tighter and tighter.

It feels like a noose.

If Bristlebrook's safety relies on getting civilians to trust me, then we're already dead.

CHAPTER 30

LUCKY

SURVIVAL TIP #175
When a gorgeous sadist brings you flowers,
watch out for hidden thorns.

Damn *it.* How did I lose her again already? She disappeared
so fast after that delightful disaster of a meeting, and I *need*
to see her.

Two women give me wary looks as we pass in the hall, and I
know my tense smile isn't enough to reassure them. Normally, I'd
be doing everything I could to help them feel at home—and I will,
later—but right now, I just can't.

I push around a corner toward the gym, where a mass of
people are rearranging furniture. Dom looks up as I stick my head
in the room and, even though it's unchivalrous as hell not to help
these tired women, I pivot on my heel and hightail it away before
he can order me to stay.

Eden needs me more.

She looked fragile in that meeting. Like she was being held
together with bubblegum and dollar-store tape.

She needs a hug at least as badly as I need to give her one.

This last month has been the hardest, most brutal month of my life. I might have recovered from my physical wounds, more or less, but sitting in this lodge, unable to do anything except torture myself with every way she could be hurt—knowing I could do *nothing* for her—was like being hit with the most insidious infection. Purely toxic. Borderline fatal.

What good is all this training if I can't protect the people I love? What good am I *at all* if she's killed while I'm wrapped up in bed? They had her for *days*—I don't have the details, but Dom told me that much. A week, he said. She must have been so scared.

Just the thought of it makes my throat hot, and that helpless anger burns again.

She deserves so much more. All I want to do is erase every line of strain on her face, banish every shadow that haunts her eyes. They should never have been there in the first place.

I just . . . need her to smile again.

She's had such a sorry life, and it's *wrong*, so fundamentally against nature, that someone so sweet and wickedly clever should be so sad. Every cell in my body demands a balance to it. I didn't protect her. I was fucking *useless* to everyone.

So I have to make this right. Somehow, I have to fix it.

A quick check of her room tells me she's not there, though there's already a pile of Beau's things on her bed. He's not wasting any time—not that I can blame him. I'm big enough to admit that I'm impressed by how fast he called dibs. Not that it matters. Beau better get used to sharing with someone other than Dom, because I'm about to be Eden's new favorite stalker.

I cross the inner balcony and hear low voices coming from the music room.

"Please, don't apologize, Eden. You were right. My methods have led me nowhere—it's past time for change."

I pause outside the door. I'd recognize that silky voice anywhere. And right now, it's soft. Much softer than I'm used to hearing.

Jasper and Eden.

Before everything went down, things were tense between them, and Eden's pain and embarrassment was like an open wound. She's proud, she hid it, but he might as well have left a brand in her flesh. He's given me a brand just like it, and I know its shape, its feel. I know how he can hurt. I just don't know if he hurt her ego or her heart.

But the way they're talking now . . . have things changed?

I can't help the images, the guilty fantasies that keep creeping up on me. Him laying her low, making her crawl across his library floor in nothing but her glasses. Her rubbing her cheek against his thigh as he necklaces her throat with his hand.

Her cheeks stained red and her eyes sparkling with tears as he ties her legs apart and paddles her pussy. Him making me lick that paddle clean. Him dragging me by the hair until I'm tonguing her ass, her pussy, everywhere she's wet and soaking for us.

I adjust my hardening cock in my pants.

I . . . hope they've made up.

"So you're going to tell him?" Eden asks politely. *Too* politely.

Him? *Me* him? Tell me what? Why are they talking about me without me? I frown at the door. It's probably arrogant to assume they're talking about me.

I still think it's me they're talking about though.

"Yes, I will." Jasper makes a small sound, like he's clearing his throat. "If you'd prefer I waited, Eden, I can. We don't need to rush this. If it would be easier for you—"

"No." Her voice is too high. Too high and still so polite. "No, you've both waited long enough. Please don't wait. I can't . . . I'd rather get this over with."

"Eden." He sounds *pained*. "It doesn't have to be this way—so black and white. You deserve your happiness too. I wouldn't ask you to choose."

"He already has."

Nope. No. This isn't sexy. This isn't a how-do-we-orchestratea-sweaty-threesome conversation. Or a how-exactly-do-we-tell-Lucky-we-both-adore-him conversation. This sounds bad.

I push into the room. I don't know what I expect to find, but the sight of them hurts. They're standing three feet apart—an extremely *polite* distance—and they both look wrong. Jasper's shoulders are stiff, and he's holding himself with none of his usual detached sophistication. He's looking at her like he's been flayed, and she's salting his wounds.

Eden's even worse. Her tired, beautiful face is rigid . . . and her head is ducked in a submissiveness that seems closer to defeat.

I *hate* it.

"Hey, beautiful. I've been looking for you everywhere. No more running off on me, okay? I don't think I can take it." I mean it as a tease, but it comes out upset and too stressed.

I wonder if I can steal a pair of Jasper's handcuffs and just fix us together for a while. Like a few years. It might be long enough to get my anxiety under control.

Eden's lips press together, and she swallows, fretful lines appearing in her forehead. She glances at Jasper but doesn't quite meet his gaze.

"Do you mind—?" She cuts off, then bites her lip. Are those *tears*? "May I say goodbye?"

Goodbye? I give Jasper a sharp look.

Jasper closes his eyes, and when he opens them again, they're soft as a raven's wing. "Of course, Eden."

Eden turns, then walks over to me like each step is agony. Dread sinks into me. It sticks around my organs like sludge, making it hard to breathe. When she reaches me, she still doesn't look up, but wraps her arms around my waist. I'm quick to wrap mine around her too, firm enough that she can't get away easily, though my body is already starting to panic. What is this? My heart pounds.

"You're scaring me," I whisper to her. I can feel the press of her forehead against my chest. The rims of her glasses. She's lost weight again in the last few weeks. She's delicate and fucking precious in my arms.

She shakes her head and looks up, and her eyes are red-rimmed with the tears she's trying not to shed. I don't like this. Whatever it is, I'm pretty sure I *hate* it.

Her hand finds my cheek, and her fingers gently stroke my beard. She has nice fingers, deft and graceful.

"This is for the best, Lucky. It really is," she whispers back.

Panic spikes. "*What* is?"

The hollow of her throat goes taut. "It never should have been me. It was never meant to be. I've been so blind, but I see it now."

Her lips roll in, and a tear spills over. I catch it with the backs of my fingers, and watch the glistening drop melt against my skin. No. This doesn't make sense. Why is she crying? What is she *saying*? Why is it suddenly so hard to breathe?

"I don't—" I start.

"He loves you, Lucky," she says, so quietly even I can hardly hear it. "He loves you so much. I think he's finally ready to admit it. You don't have to be lonely for him anymore. You can be happy together—and I really . . ." Her voice catches. "I really want you to be happy, Lucky."

Every muscle in my body locks up, my brain caught on that one phrase.

He loves you.
He loves you.
He loves you.
He loves you.
He loves you.

I feel the barest brush of soft, warm lips against mine—the dream of a kiss. And then they're gone. Eden steps back, and all the warmth is sucked away in a puff of icy air.

"Be happy, Lucky."

I'm still paralyzed as she walks to the door. As she leaves. As her footsteps retreat.

It never should have been me.

"No," I say into the silence. The loss of her, the panic, it cracks like lightning, and I move toward the door, though I know she's already gone. *Again.* "*No, no, no.*"

What does she *mean* it never should have been her? It was *always* meant to be her. Her reluctant smiles and secret mischief. The way she looks covered in kimchi. The warmth and friendship she drowned me in when I was gasping from the loneliness of it. Her scandalized pleasure and quiet vulnerability. Her selfless fucking bravery.

"No!" I shout at the empty hall, my hand a fist in my hair.

This isn't right. This isn't how this is meant to be.

Should I go after her? What was this?

The door swings shut in front of me, and then Jasper is standing in front of it. In front of me.

"Hello, Lucien."

"Don't. *Don't* Lucien me." I'm going to throw up. She won't go far, right? She's still in the house. She wouldn't leave Bristlebrook, would she? "What the hell was that, Jasper?"

I'm breathing too fast. I *just* got her back. I stare at the door.

She was *crying*.

I actually feel it—the moment my heart ruptures. It physically, truly hurts. I press my hand against my chest, like I should feel blood spilling out of it, a more fatal blow than my bullet wounds.

I only wanted to make her smile.

"Did you have something to do with that? What did you say to her?" Anger rises to meet my panic. I search his face, suddenly furious. It's one thing for him to hurt me; it's another thing entirely for him to hurt Eden. "Fix it. Fix it *now.*"

Jasper studies my face right back, a slight frown marring the smooth marble of his own. "Eden made her own decision."

"About *what*?"

Shockingly, Jasper looks hesitant. "About this."

He pulls something from his pocket. It's a small yellow flower,

I realize, rumpled and a little wilted from its confines. He twirls it between his fingers and looks up at me from beneath those sinful lashes. His eyes are fathomless. Beautiful.

Tentatively, he reaches up and tucks it behind my ear, into my hair, and I freeze at the touch. His fingers stroke my hair the whole way back down to my chest. My scalp tingles, and my whole body lights up with gooseflesh.

I've forgotten how to breathe. Just *poof*. Gone.

He studies the flower, and the curve of his lips is almost . . . affectionate.

Why is he looking at me like that? Since he left, I've braced for everything on his return. For coldness. Distance. Another few years of half-caught glances and jacking myself off to thoughts of him.

I wasn't prepared for a flower and a smile.

"Every day I was out there, I was in a panic," he says softly. "I couldn't bear the thought of Eden being hurt, and I was acutely aware that we might be too late. Or worse, that we might be so because I was too slow. Too inept." Jasper's eyes close for a moment on a tired exhale.

His usual elegance is disturbed, his beauty especially raw today. There are weary lines at the corners of his eyes, and his inky hair is uncharacteristically mussed. For the first time, I spot a few silver hairs flecking the obsidian at his temples. He's exhausted, I realize, and battling the same guilt I am.

That we all are.

"There were several moments when I thought I physically couldn't do it. I reached my utter limit. And then I would see your pin." Jasper absently touches the bright daffodil pin on my uniform, the one my mom gave me but I was never allowed to wear while I was officially in service.

He's still in my uniform.

Despite my alarm, my mind trips over itself, seeing him in it. Unlike when he left, it seems to fit him better. A little better, anyway.

Jasper's eyes lift back to mine, and they're naked with emotion. He's looking at me . . . differently. The stilted, agonized expression he wore with Eden is gone, and in its place is something my body recognizes but my memories don't. It's intimate and so dangerous that the small hairs on the nape of my neck stand on end, and my panicked heart starts racing for a different reason.

"This pin of yours reminded me of you. Cheerful. Almost absurd. But hopeful. You never give up, Lucien. Your tenacity is one of your most beautiful and admirable qualities," he says softly.

He steps in, and I step back, not in rejection but just . . . confused. He's being charming. Eden was crying. I don't know how I'm feeling, but I know I'm feeling so much of it, whatever it is. He continues, unperturbed, stepping forward again and tracking me with those perilous eyes.

"I saw the flower on the way here, and it again reminded me of you. So I plucked it." His smile turns self-deprecating. "If only I could have decided to keep you so quickly."

I step back again, and my thighs hit the raised arm of the couch. He stops close enough that we're sharing the same breath. His fingers brush the flower again.

"I've hurt it, I can see that now. Perhaps I should have left it alone." The tips of his fingers trail over my cheekbone, my brow, down my nose, pausing on my lips.

"But you and I both know I don't have the willpower for that," Jasper confides, and his voice roughens with emotion. "I'm unspeakably sorry, Lucien, for all the harm I've caused you. In everything I've done to keep you safe, I've only crushed you further. And still, somehow, you're all the more beautiful for your bruises."

His thumb smears over my lip, anointing itself in my mouth, and I see him swallow. I think . . . I'm starting to catch on to what this is. My heart seizes, torn. I've waited for it for so long, imagined it so many ways, it feels like an impossibility. Like some genie has plucked my deepest wish from the depths of my dreams and made it flesh.

Only . . . I don't know if this is my deepest wish anymore.

Eden isn't here too.

"I love you, Lucien," Jasper says, looking me straight in the eye. "I think I loved you the moment you first walked into my office and gave me the most thorough eye fuck of my life. I've loved you during every session, for every smile, and with every tear you spilled at my feet. I'm done hurting you, dear boy, in every way bar the ones that bring you joy."

I stare at him, my lips parting. Both of him? There are two of him.

Am I going to faint?

I sit down hard on the arm of the couch, and amusement sparks in Jasper's eyes. With his leg, he kicks my knees open and steps into the new space.

"Speak, Lucien," he says in his Sir voice.

Speak? My head is *spinning*.

"I—"

A midnight brow lifts. "If I'd known it was so easy to silence you, I might have confessed my feelings sooner."

"You love me?" I whisper.

Love. He can't mean this. He'll take it away again. He's tired, he'll rethink it, like he rethinks our scenes every time they end.

"Obsessively." He tilts my chin up further, and his grip tightens as if he can press the words into my skin. "Incomprehensibly."

My eyes narrow on him. "Kiss me, then. Kiss me like you—"

His mouth is on mine. Silken heat. Wet perfection. His tongue licks into my mouth, and I feel it along my cock. Again and again, he teases me in the most perfect, erotic assault. Suddenly, there's a searing pain in my lip, and I realize he's bit down. I taste bitter copper, and the sharp sting turns me to liquid need. I groan into his mouth, and his kiss turns gentle. Tender. He presses his lips against my new cut with heartbreaking care, cradling my chin in his face, and tears spring to my eyes.

"I love you," I tell him between kisses. "I love you so much. I always have."

He sighs on a groan and takes my mouth deeply again.

The beginnings of joy start sparking in my chest. This is real. It's really real. It's finally happened.

When he finally pulls back, we're both hard and panting and I'm wondering if I'm going to be stripped down and fucked raw over this couch.

He must see the question in my eyes, because he releases the front of my shirt and pulls back further, a small smile on his lips. "Not today."

"Why not?" That sounds pouty. It should probably embarrass me, but it doesn't. I feel pouty.

His smile deepens, and I stare. It's rare—unbelievably rare—to see such bare happiness on Jasper's face. It transforms him, like he somehow transcends from a black-winged devil and into some achingly beautiful angel, bursting with light.

My throat closes over at the sight.

"Because I'm not here for a quick fuck, Lucien. I have seven years of courting to make up for." He kisses my cheek. "Seven years of romance." He nips my earlobe. "Seven years of apologies."

He wants to *romance* me? My heart melts—just liquefies in my chest into a pink, candy-scented puddle.

He rests his forehead against mine. "I plan on seducing you, Lucien. Thoroughly."

Breathlessly, I laugh at the absurdity of needing to be seduced. As if he couldn't have me groveling for him to take me any way he wanted. My cock throbs in need, and I reach down to rub my dick through my pants, needing relief, not caring how undignified it is. Jasper has seen me a lot less dignified.

Hopefully, he'll be seeing it again soon.

Jasper grips my wrist. Hard. "Your cock belongs only to me,

brat. You touch yourself without permission again and there will be consequences."

The casual cruelty of him almost has me coming in my pants, so it takes a moment for his meaning to filter through.

Only to me, he said.

Eden.

Through the maelstrom of emotions of the last half hour, my brain finally catches up.

"What do you mean *only*?"

Jasper takes one look at my face and sobers, pulling back enough that I can stand again. It's hard to look at him now, especially rumpled and in my uniform. I ache for him—I always ache for him. But I ache for her now too, and I can't separate them.

"It was Eden's decision, Lucien," he says quietly.

"What was? I need you to explain that part. Because it sounds like I get you only if I lose her, is that right?"

No. No! She doesn't get to make decisions about me. *For* me. I've had enough of that already. I can't do this again.

Jasper gives a single shake of his head. "I wouldn't make you choose, Lucien. I told you—I don't want to cause you any more hurt, and the two of you are more overdue for happiness than anyone I've met. But once she figured out how we felt, Eden thought it best to give us space."

"Permanent space?" I demand.

He remains silent, and I know it's true. That's it. That's what she was saying, that she's leaving me.

"Breathe, Lucien." Jasper touches my shoulder, but I shake him off. I shake him off because I need to think, and I can't damn well do it with him *touching* me.

"I can't do it, Jasper. I love her," I say.

"I know you're fond of her, but—"

I turn, my hand in my hair. "No, I'm not fond of her. I love her. It might have taken you seven years to work that out, but I got there faster."

I don't miss his almost imperceptible flinch. I know it's an asshole thing to say, but it's also true.

"I'll talk to her. I'll make her understand. It can't just be one, Jasper. I need you both."

Should I go after her now? Or is it better to give her some time to rest? I can't mess this up.

I can't lose her again.

Jasper regards me with a somber expression. "You might want to prepare yourself, Lucien. She seemed quite set in her decision."

"Why are you speaking about her like you don't want her too?" I snap. Fear and worry snarl through me, knotting me up. "You might fool the rest of them, but not me. If anyone knows what it looks like when you're holding yourself back from someone, it's me. And I *know* she wants you."

He always has his mask on around her. He's always careful, always polite. With Dom and Beau, even Jaykob, he's elegant but relaxed, and I can read him fine—his annoyance, his amusement. With me, he was always marble, and it was impossible to chip away at the facade. For years I thought he didn't like me, just for that reason. I know better now. He controls himself so tightly when he's closest to losing it.

He looks at her the same way.

A chill ices over his features. "I won't explain this again to you. If you can convince her to be with you also, then I wish you the best, but even if I were sure she wanted me—and I am certainly *not* —I would destroy that girl. Particularly now, after what she has been through. She is hanging by a thread, and the last thing she needs is a sadist unleashing violence she does not want against her."

That takes the hot air out of me.

"Jayk has been fucking her," I argue helplessly. "You know what he's like. He probably hunted her, roughed her up. If she's fine with that, then why not you?"

"Please." Jasper rubs his temple with one long finger. "Do not compare my methods to Jaykob's. You might as well compare a butcher's yard to an operating table."

"But—"

"It is another thing entirely, Lucien." His eyes flash. "Indelicate as it may be, there is a benefit to his approach with her. She has freedom, agency—the ability to fight back. She can reclaim her control with him. With me? I will take it from her."

"You don't have to be like that with her," I mumble after a moment. "You can be . . . nice."

He arches a very unimpressed eyebrow. "No. I can't." He takes a breath, then releases a sigh. When he looks at me, his eyes are dangerous—a slow burn of heat. "I want to hurt her, Lucien. I want to hurt her so badly I can taste it."

I shiver, intrigued and frightened by that look.

"She's a sweet thing. Still so innocent."

His tongue slides over his lower lip, like he is tasting it. Like his want for her is on his mouth. In his skin. He's turned on, I realize. Painfully so. He usually takes care to make sure I don't see it, but he's not even trying now.

He's making a point.

Those dark eyes envelop me again. "If you put her in my hands, dear boy, I will break her . . . and I will enjoy every moment of it."

I believe him.

Something happens in me then—a violent kind of arousal, followed by an equally urgent surge of protectiveness. *Could* Eden enjoy Jasper's brand of pain?

I think of her bandaged wrists and her exhausted, haunted eyes.

And I stay quiet, silently acknowledging the warning.

"She knows why I refused her," Jasper continues softly. "If she ever desires to truly try, then I would be willing, but not before." The heat extinguishes in his eyes, leaving them cold and lonely and touched with longing. "Eden is . . . an uncommon woman. I want to see her thrive."

My own longing throbs through my body, and I nod unhappily. "Fine. Fine. But I have to try for myself. I'll romance her or talk to her. I'll do whatever I need to, but I'm going to get through to her."

Jasper walks over to me, then adjusts the flower in my hair. "Then, my love, it seems we have similar quests."

And then he kisses me.

For a long, long time, he *kisses me*.

CHAPTER 31

EDEN

SURVIVAL TIP #328
Move in with the gorgeous man.
For protection and stuff.

I explode into my room, my eyes blurry with tears, and as soon as the door shuts, I press my back against it, letting the sobs take me. I'm here, I'm back at Bristlebrook.

And everything is still falling apart.

"Hey, hey now."

I snap my head up, scrambling to my feet in alarm, only for the slow, coaxing words to register. Beau is in the middle of a messy pile of his things in the sitting area, holding a table lamp. Through my tears, I give it a puzzled look. He sets it on the coffee table and comes toward me.

"That's the best lamp in this whole lodge. Perfect for night reading. I'll share a lot with the new folks, but we're keeping the lamp."

We're. He's moving in with me. We're going to *live together*.

I feel my lip quivering again and look down, sniffling. It's repulsive. Damn it. This is getting absurd. I can't keep crying. What a pointless exercise.

Why does my freedom seem to have come at the expense of my self-control?

"I'm so sorry. I thought I was alone."

Beau's hand finds my face, his fingers firm and strong against my skin as he tilts my chin up. His woodland eyes are full of safe glens. "Not if I have anything to say about it."

My tears spill over.

"No, damn it. Not again!" I wail, swiping at them. Useless, miserable things they are. I glare up at his bewildered expression and pull my trembling chin free. The kindness in his face nearly sets me off again, and I point at him. "*No!* Don't be nice to me."

Beau eyes my tears, a bemused cant to his head. "Just talk to me, darlin'. Tell me what's wrong."

Why is his voice so *soothing*? A raw, broken sob escapes, and I retreat toward the bathroom. "*Stop it!*"

Is he incapable of following simple instructions? Is this a dominant thing?

"I'm not doing anything. Hey." He catches my arm and turns me around, then raises his hands at my tearful scowl. A worried crease appears between his brows. "Do you want me to make you some tea? Is it something else? Who do I need to beat up?"

Tea?!

I stare at him as my battered, broken heart swells.

"You are *such* an asshole," I whisper. His eyes widen incredulously, and I storm into the bathroom and slam the door behind me. "Go away!"

Beautiful, considerate, wonderful *jerk*.

The tears are running freely now, and I clumsily take off my glasses, my breaths coming in enormous, quaking gasps as I bend over the sink. I can't make them stop.

No. No *more crying*, I glare at my rumpled, red-faced reflection. *Stop it, Eden. You're a rock. You're a blade.*

I'm safe at Bristlebrook—it's ridiculous to cry *now*. And, God, crying about *feelings* of all things. I should know better than that. I never used to be a crier.

Why do these men seem to have direct access to my tear ducts?

Fat drops flood over my cheeks in defiance of my glare.

The door opens and closes behind me, and I spin to see Beau leaning against the door, one leg kicked over the other. He gives me a patient look.

"Darlin', I don't usually think of myself as a slow man, but you're going to have to catch me up here. Is this about Jayk?"

Jayk. And Dom, Jasper, Lucky . . .

I bury my forehead in my hands as my heart rips, and another sound escapes me, like a wounded animal.

"For the love of God, Beau, *stop*," I beg on a hitching sob. Is that snot coming out of my nose? Why is being sad so disgusting? "I can't get this"—*sniff, sob*—"under control"—*sob, wail, cry*—"while you're being nice."

His pretty eyes roll up in exasperation. "You want me to be *mean* to you?"

I wipe uselessly at my traitorous eyes again. "If it wouldn't be too much trouble."

Beau scrubs a long-suffering hand over his too-tempting face, then he scowls. "Your hair is a mess and your breath smells like something died in your throat. Happy now?"

I stare at him.

"Why would you *say* that?" I keen, as a raw, hacking sob shakes my whole body.

Beau straightens off the door, looking nothing short of panicked. "No—*no, no, no*. I was just doing what you said!"

"I said be mean, not *cruel*." I touch my hair, unable to stop the way my whole body is wracked with tears. My lip trembles. "What's wrong with my hair? Dom said it was nice."

"It *is* nice. Eden— Don't cry, darlin'. I— No, okay. That's enough of this."

Beau stalks over and scoops me up, face set in utter exasperation. He wrenches open the shower door, then dumps me inside. A moment later, the shower springs to life, dousing me in shockingly cold water from three angles.

I squeal, then gasp as the frigid water makes the air explode from my lungs. My clothes quickly soak through, and I twist, screeching, trying to get out of the water. Beau pushes me back in carelessly. It feels like actual snow is pelting my exposed skin. I push out again, only to have Beau shove me back in.

My fists clench, and I shriek in pure frustration.

"Get it out. I've got time," he drawls, that panic now vanished, transformed into something that almost resembles . . .

"Are you *laughing* at me right now?" I hiss.

It's hard to remain dignified mid-meltdown while snot-stained, soaked to the bone in a shower, and with your nipples pebbling faster than a high-speed train. Soon I won't need him to let me out the shower door—I'll be able to carve my way free.

"You wretched, awful—"

"Ah, ah." Beau's mouth curls up on one side. "You're pretty disrespectful for a subbie standing in icy water. You find yourself some manners and maybe we can have a civilized conversation."

Somehow, to my annoyance, the cold water *has* shocked the hysteria out of me.

And even more annoyingly, that dangerous glint in his eye *does* have me rethinking my insults.

"Might you . . . please turn on the warm water?" I lift my chin.

My teeth are chattering.

That half-smile widens into a full one. "I might."

But he doesn't move.

"Please, oh mighty and generous sir," I grit out as politely as I can—and when Beau throws his head back and laughs, I bite down on my molars.

It's Beau's turn to wipe the corners of his eyes. "Very cute, darlin', but you can stick to calling me Beau. Politely."

He turns one of the knobs under his hand, and I'm blessed with an instant cascade of heat. I close my eyes, breathing out hard in relief as the scalding warmth seeps into my chilly skin.

I feel hands tugging at the waist of my shirt, and after a moment of hesitation, I let him strip it off me, quickly followed by my bra. He's half-stepped into the water now, and it soaks him too. I move to unbuckle my belt, but he gently removes my hands.

"Let me," he says softly. "Let me take over now, darlin'."

Those pretty woodland eyes meet mine, and I whisper, "Yes, Beau."

His jaw clenches, and my head drops back against the wall as I watch him strip me of my belt, my shoes, my socks, my pants. Finally, he reaches for my underwear and hesitates, his eyes flicking over my face. When I don't stop him, he pulls them down gently, and I feel his breath against my thighs.

It's instinct, all nature, for me to part them while he's on one knee before me, and I hold my breath. His gaze lingers on my parted legs, the cleft in between, and a different kind of heat ripples through me.

When he stands, my breath leaves me in a disappointed rush.

Beau throws the sodden clothes into the bathroom, then unwinds the bandages from around my wrists. His jaw flexes at the rent flesh, though it's now well on its way to healing, but he doesn't say a word.

He wraps his large hand around the back of my neck, pulling me off the wall. Then his hands are in my hair, plucking it free of its tie until it tumbles around my shoulders.

I shiver under the water, his touch, and he pinches my chin. His eyes don't dip down once.

"Now, I want you to stay in here for as long as you need to," he tells me. "I don't want you worrying about what anyone else is doing in this house. You have no jobs to do and nowhere else to be. Just enjoy the shower. Use every product that makes you feel good. Pamper yourself."

He raises a stern brow, and my thighs press together at the sight of it. I think stern Beau might be a problem for me. But it's the tenderness in his eyes that makes my heart soften all over again.

"If taking care of yourself involves crying, then you do that too." His thumb runs along my jaw. "There's no shame in tears, pet—you don't need to earn them and there's no limit on how many you're allowed to cry. It so happens that I like a good cry myself. You put on a sappy movie, and I will wreck an entire box of tissues."

At my faint smile, he chucks me under the chin. "And if you'd rather cuddle up and cry on me, then my shoulders are good for it too. You come out when you're ready, and I'll be waiting."

Water is raining down on us both, tangling in my lashes, coating his clothes, and still . . . he's perfect right now. Gorgeous and warm, calm and steady. Clean lines and sneaky sensuality. He's everything I need in this moment. Everything I wish I *was* in this moment.

I wonder if he loans out that kind of control.

Beau leans forward and presses a swift, firm kiss on my lips, and my fingers fly up to trace the imprint as he backs up.

Biting back a smile, I say sweetly, "I'm surprised you braved that kiss." My smile is cherry syrup, saccharine and tart. "You know, considering my breath smells like carrion."

Beau smirks back. "Toothpaste is on the shelf. I'd recommend it."

He pulls his saturated shirt over his head, then tosses it down on the pile.

My smile dies, and my tongue sticks to the roof of my mouth as he turns toward the door with a wink, every golden muscle gleaming under the lights.

"See you soon, darlin'."

I SPEND a sinful amount of time in the shower. Truly sinful. Pray to God for using up half the lakes in the forest sinful.

While I appreciated Beau's sweet invitation to continue my breakdown in the shower, I decide to ignore it. My tears before are the last ones I'll shed over this whole ordeal.

They have to be.

I'm back at Bristlebrook, and despite all the uncertainty and plans that need to be made, I'm safe, and I have a beautiful, wonderful man who has moved into my room. It's more than I've had most of my life, and I need to remember how lucky I really am. There's no point in dwelling on this. On my guilt, or my anger, or my heartbreak.

None of it helps me, and it's only making me feel worse to think on it.

And so I won't.

Instead, I brush my teeth. With *toothpaste*. I scrub every inch of my skin. Shave. Wash my hair. I even scatter scented shower salts over the floor only to realize they lost their scent long ago. I breathe in the steamy cloud.

In the mirror after my shower, I moisturize, then I dry my hair and catalog all the ways that I'm exactly the same as when I left.

By the time I'm done, I feel steadier. Determined. A little more myself.

Glancing around the room, I realize I didn't bring any clothes in with me, so I wrap a towel around me and open the door . . . to a sight.

The fireplace is crackling, bathing the room in a cozy, amber light. There's a wedge of cheese on the low table, cut up into small pieces, along with dried meat and some vegetables. A bottle of wine sits beside the platter, with a glass that glimmers in the light.

Beau's things have been packed away, and Beau himself is sprawled on the bed, shirtless and resting against the sweeping wooden headboard, a glass of wine in his hand.

Curiously, his medical bag is beside him.

His eyes light on me.

"Well, now," he murmurs. "Aren't you enough to break a man's heart."

I stare at his chest. In the firelight, he's soaked in gold. It highlights every dip and hollow of his abdominals, the planes of his pecs, the brown discs of his nipples. Heat flushes through me. He takes a slow sip of his wine, then gets off the bed.

"Come on, let's get you fed."

I'm torn between agreeing and wanting to dive straight into that bed with him, but at the hollow ache in my stomach, I follow him to the couch. I need to adjust the short towel over my thighs, but it hardly covers them.

Beau sits beside me, pours me a glass of wine, then he plucks up a wedge of cheese. I move to get my own, but he catches my hand.

"Let me."

He leans over me, coaxing me back into the couch, and I take a deep, shaky breath. He smells good. His eyes are intent, fixed on my mouth, and my legs part just a little, already feeling warm and slick.

Beau brings the cheese to my lips. "Eat."

I blink up at him, confused heat stinging my cheeks. "I'm perfectly capable of feeding myself."

"I know you are." He drags the cheese across my lips, and I snatch a small bite with my teeth, melting at how it crumbles softly in my mouth. His eyes are warm, the gold in them snug around the green. "Does it bother you?"

Hesitating, I shake my head, eyes tracking the rest of the cheese. He feeds it to me, then brushes his fingers softly over my lips.

"Then let me take care of you, pet. I need to see for myself that you're okay. It's been . . . a long month."

The signs of strain are there. He's let his stubble go longer than I've seen before, and worry lines bracket his mouth and the laugh lines don't crinkle at me so freely. Mostly, it's in his eyes. In the way they linger on me, like I might vanish in a puff of air at any moment.

My breath catches, and I kiss his fingertips gently, thanking him with my eyes. Thanking him for so much more than the food.

At my compliance, the tense lines in his forehead ease, and he slowly provides me morsel after morsel. I relax into the soft cushions and let him gift me with a few sips of wine and plenty of delicious food, and I let my body unclench from the weeks of tension. I'm in Beau's safe, clever hands.

I watch the light kiss his skin and the casual tense and release of his muscles as he moves between me and the platter. I smile at the way he frowns as he chooses which pieces to give me, feeding me only the choicest pieces and eating the rest himself. And I eat until I'm full and heart-warm and deeply languorous.

When the food is done, Beau feeds me my last sip of wine, catching a drop at the corner of my mouth with his thumb. My breath catches.

Watching him, my heart pounding, I gently suck his thumb into my mouth and drag my tongue over the drop, licking it clean.

Something dark and hot moves in his eyes. Rather than withdrawing his thumb, he presses down on my tongue until my mouth opens, and he watches as saliva pools around the digit. He dips his head and licks into my mouth, kissing me druggingly deep until I whimper, rubbing my thighs together.

"Would you like anything else?" he asks when he pulls back, his words rough against my lips. His fingers toy with the flimsy edge of my towel.

Dazed, I meet his eyes. "Not . . . to eat."

Beau places the wine glass on the table then lifts me, and I wrap my legs around him instinctively, my arms going about his neck. His hands cup my ass as he walks me to the bed, and I arch into the touch with a shudder. The flimsy front knot on my towel begins to fall open, and as he drops me on the bed, it loses its valiant battle.

His eyes drop to my breasts, and he curses, staring.

"You're bruised," he says in a low, tense voice, and I glance down.

My breasts are decorated in finger-shaped kisses of purple, blue, and yellow.

"Jaykob," I explain gently. "They're almost all from Jayk now." I even manage a rueful smile. "They're everywhere."

God, I hope he'll make more of them. He was upset, but I'll make him understand.

I have to make him understand.

Beau's eyes trail down to my wrists. "Those aren't from Jayk."

I don't need to look to know. "No, they're not." I touch the left one, slightly more ravaged than the right. "Do you think they'll scar?"

It's a petty, vain question, but I still want the answer. I want to know if I'll bear the marks of that time in my flesh for the rest of my life.

He shakes his head.

"I don't know, pet." His gaze rests on mine. "Eden, you don't have to talk about it if you don't want, but I need to know. Is there anything I should do, or not do, around you right now? Anything at all that you might find triggering or you might not want at all?"

Oh. I draw my knees up to my chest as my mind flickers over the past few weeks, the question pulling me out of the moment, even while I appreciate the care behind asking.

"I don't want to be tied up," I whisper. "No bindings, or blindfolds."

Beau nods easily, and I'm thankful there's not one ounce of pity on his face. "Anything else, any way you don't want to be . . . touched?"

My face softens. "They didn't assault me, Beau. Not sexually. And I wasn't raped. They hurt me and frightened me, but they didn't do that. I can . . . tell you more about the details later. If you like."

Beau's hand comes up to rub against his jaw as he blinks hard, and I realize he's getting emotional. Kneeling up, I touch his hand against his face.

"I'm okay, Beau." I kiss his cheek. "I really am."

"I thought—" His voice is choked. "I thought there was no way. I thought for sure . . ."

"I was very, very lucky," I murmur. "Mostly thanks to some men in the camp who were against the idea. Also thanks to Madison."

Beau stiffens a little. "Heather?"

"She drew their attention a lot. I thought at the time that she was just being reckless, angry. But I can't help but wonder if she was trying to keep the attention on her."

The thought has niggled at me for days. I know she couldn't control her anger around them, but there were times it felt too pointed. Too well timed.

"She is brave—I'll give her that much," he says grudgingly.

It shouldn't sting, but it does. One more example of Heather's strength, where I skulked in the shadows and ran when it counted.

"Do you—?" I bite my lip. "I know with Dom it was complicated, but are you and Heather . . .? Do you still have feelings for her?"

Startled, Beau snorts. "No. I'd sooner put my dick in a bear trap before I let it anywhere near her again." His mouth forms an unhappy line. "And Dom is stupider and more careless than I ever thought to go back to her."

My throat sticks. "He loves her."

"He was meant to love *us*," Beau snaps, then he stops, wincing. "I'm sorry, Eden. I don't want to talk about those two right now."

He runs his eyes over me, and a slow release of tension rolls through his shoulders.

"Not when I have the most beautiful woman I've ever seen

naked and in my bed." Beau brushes a kiss against my lips, then pulls back. "Do you want to sleep, Eden?"

He's serious, but I see the dark mischief behind his eyes—the male *need*. My body responds quickly, almost violently, to that look.

"No, Beau. I don't want to sleep."

After a beat, as if to make sure I'm serious, that slow, devastating smile sprawls across his face. "What's your safeword, Eden?" he asks.

I swallow. "Bristlebrook."

It's more true now than it ever has been. My haven. My sanctuary. The safest place I know.

Maybe it shouldn't be, considering what happened here—except that they didn't win.

There's warm approval in his budding smile. "We can work on traffic lights here too, okay? If I ask, and you're feeling good, you say green. You need me to slow down, say yellow. Red works in place of your safeword too. These are used all the time in the kink community, Eden, so you can say them with any of the guys and they'll know what it means too."

Traffic lights. I smile at him too. I like the idea of being able to slow things down without stopping.

I *really* like that he thinks I still have a chance with any of the others.

Beau pulls a chair over to the side of the low bed and sits in front of me, then reaches for his medical bag.

"Darlin', as your doctor, I feel it is my duty to give you a *very* thorough check-up."

CHAPTER 32

EDEN

A check-up?

There's wicked intent in the curve of Beau's lips as he opens his medical bag. He slings his stethoscope around his neck with easy confidence.

"Now, what brings you in today, miss?"

I stare at him uncertainly. "To my . . . room?"

His lips twitch but he gives me a patient look. "To my surgery."

Beau reaches out a large hand for me to shake, and I drop my stare. He has lovely hands, with neat, trimmed nails and well-kept cuticles. So different from Jayk's, rough and heavily calloused and demanding.

I slip my hand into Beau's, and he shakes it.

"Doctor Beaumont Bennett, I'll be performing your examination today. And you are?" His fingers brush over my pulse, and I shiver, my body sparking to life with awareness.

"Oh." I bite my lip. "Is this a . . . role-play thing?"

My cheeks heat. I haven't done that. *Can* I do that? I work the lip between my teeth, staring at Beau's stethoscope, glancing at his medical bag.

At his chest.

This can't be too difficult, surely. Beau can check my pulse and make me drink some water and then he'll . . . okay, I have no idea what he'll do. I'm not at all sure what Beau is like when he's not shattering my soul on a riverbank with his best friend. Still, he's been feeding me cheese and wine and compliments all night.

I'm sure he'll be very sweet.

Maybe he'll give me a lollipop after.

Beau raises one brow, waiting, his palm warm in mine.

"I'm Eden," I whisper hesitantly. "Eden Anderson."

Releasing my hand, he smiles in approval, and I can't tell if it's Beau's pleasure that I'm playing his game—or if Doctor Bennett is pleased to meet his new patient.

"It's real nice to meet you, Miss Anderson. It's not every day I get a patient as pretty as you walk through my door."

My door, he means. My lips twitch at the silly charade.

But, if he were my doctor . . .

I arch my brows primly, and I tease, "I don't think that's very appropriate to say, Doctor Bennett."

At the word "doctor," he pauses, his eyes flaring dark and hot.

"Now, now, Miss Anderson, let's not throw around accusations," he scolds. His gaze travels lasciviously over my bared breasts, my stomach, my pussy—I feel it like he ran his hands all over me. "A girl like you should trust her doctor, don't you think?"

Some of my amusement fades, and my tongue runs over my lip as I shiver, something about his tone hitting differently.

Okay. Okay, this is fine.

Beau might be sweet . . . but I don't think Doctor Bennett is going to be handing out lollipops.

As if reading my thoughts, my doctor raises one firm brow. "You are going to put yourself in my hands, aren't you?"

I breathe out shakily, wondering where this sudden, violent arousal has come from.

"Yes, Doctor Bennett."

"That's a good girl." He reaches into his bag and pulls out a small, black device. "We're rather short-staffed here today. Do you mind if I take a recording—for my notes? It will be held in strictest confidence, of course, unless you choose to share it."

My eyes widen, my breathing coming faster. An audio recording? Why does he want to do that? I eye the recorder. Does it matter? It's not like it can be spread around on the internet.

"Yes, that's fine," I agree nervously.

Doctor Bennett gives a kindly nod, flicking the device on and resting it on the side table. He pulls a box of gloves from his bag.

"Tell me, do you have any allergies? Any concerns with latex?"

When I give a minute shake of my head, he removes the thin black material from the packaging.

My lips part as I watch him pull on the gloves. My eyes linger on them, oddly fascinated—so impersonal, so clinical. It should be ridiculous, while he's bare chested and blatantly aroused in front of me.

It's not ridiculous.

I'm already wet, but I feel a sudden rush of slickness between my thighs and shift.

He places the bag on the bed beside me. "Do you have any conditions? Are you on any medications? Is there any family history I should be aware of?"

My nipples are pebbled and painfully sensitive, and every time his kindly, not-quite-impartial glance sweeps over them, they tighten further. I shiver.

Maybe I'll go along with this. Just for a while more.

"I don't have any conditions that I know of—apart from failing eyesight, but I'm not entirely sure of my family history," I say meekly, my fingers worrying in front of me. "I'm not on any medications, either."

Doctor Bennett nods seriously. "And are you sexually active?"

The flush in my cheeks deepens. "Yes."

"Of course you are. Pretty girl like you must be taking dick from all the boys," he says indulgently, and my breath stalls, even as heat rolls over me.

"Doctor Bennett!" My hand flies to my throat, my uncertain, scandalized body clenching around nothing.

His eyes flare again, and he leans forward, patting my knee soothingly. "It's okay, Miss Anderson. Just let me take over. It's all part of the examination."

I stare at him, stunned by my arousal.

It's . . . sick. *Manipulative.*

So why am I so, so wet for it?

I feel my brow knit anxiously, and heat creeps down my chest, making it bloom a soft pink. And my doctor is tracking every shift, assessing each reaction, testing my responses.

This does feel like an examination—a kind of exploratory inspection—but the medical reasoning feels questionable.

Doctor Bennett's hand curls under my right knee, and he wraps his other hand around my left, then he drags my naked body to the edge of the bed.

I feel myself leave a humiliatingly wet trail along the bedspread.

"Open your legs," he instructs, and I realize they're clamped shut against the evidence of my interest. When I hesitate for a moment, he flicks his gaze up, and his latex-covered fingers stroke encouragingly at the sensitive skin behind my knees. "I need to see, Miss Anderson. It won't be much of an examination if I can't see, now, will it?"

Swallowing a moan, I part my legs slowly in front of him, spreading them wide. His eyes drop to my glistening pussy.

I wonder if he might touch me, but apart from a brief flare of his nostrils, he doesn't respond, just takes me in with unprofessional interest.

He stands and steps to the side, then places my feet on each arm of the large chair so they're propped up and stretched wide. From this angle, with my ass just barely on the edge of the bed, I have the sudden worry that I'm so wet, I might drip onto the floor.

"Lie back now. It's time for me to examine you."

Doctor Bennett's latex-covered palm presses against my breastbone, and he pushes me backwards until I'm lying against the mattress. His easy control, the casual confidence, makes my eyes hood as I watch him stand over me.

He pulls off his stethoscope, his eyes gleaming as he looks over my body lying bare for him. "I'm going to check your heart rate. Lie still for me."

Placing the buds in his ears, he takes the metal chest piece and rests it against my chest. I gasp at the sudden burst of cold against my heated skin, and he gives me a disapproving frown.

"Please, Miss Anderson. If you're not going to cooperate . . ."

"No," I say quickly, shakily. "I'll be good. I'm sorry. I'll stay still."

The frown melts away. "Ah, I knew you would be a good patient for me. So cooperative."

He pauses for a moment, cocking his head as he listens to my heart, as *I* try to work out why his words flood my skin with fiery heat.

Then Doctor Bennett raises a brow at me and murmurs, "My, my. Your heart is *racing*, Miss Anderson."

That is . . . unsurprising.

I blush, trying not to dislodge his stethoscope with my rapid breaths.

"Am I making you uncomfortable?" he questions innocently. "Give me a color."

A color? Is this his traffic lights? I wish I could clamp my legs together to control how wet I'm getting. Instead, I can only briefly press my eyes closed as I feel moisture spill from my pussy, dripping down into the crease of my ass.

"No, Doctor Bennett," I murmur huskily. "I'm green, thank you."

"Very good."

He moves the stethoscope a few times, until my skin ripples from gooseflesh and the cool metal finally starts to warm. Then he leans over and pulls out several devices, unwrapping them from their new packages. I pay no attention to those, too caught watching the flex and arch of his golden arms and abdominals as he hovers over me.

Doctor Bennett places one knee on the bed, bending close to my face. "Let me check your eyes."

He removes my glasses, then holds my lids open as he flashes a bright light into each eye, dazzling me.

"Pupils are dilated," he murmurs to the recording. He puts my glasses back on carefully as I blink owlishly, disoriented. His hand takes my cheeks, puckering my mouth, and it's just this side of painful. "Temperature now. In your mouth. Under your tongue, that's right."

Doctor Bennett inserts a thermometer into my mouth, and I close my lips around it. He pulls the thermometer free and looks at the reading impassively.

"Temperature is elevated." My doctor's eyes are too bright as he tsks. "Well, now. That's not good at all." His fingers brush over my lips. "Open your mouth again. Wider. I said *wider*, Miss Anderson."

I stretch my mouth open as wide as it will go, my jaw straining, and he shakes his head. With two gloved fingers, he rubs my tongue, pressing down on it until it flattens. The medical smell of them floods my nose, and at first the latex tastes rubbery and dry, but it quickly slicks up.

Doctor Bennett shines a light into my mouth, bending down to get a better look, then his fingers work over my tongue, deeper into my throat.

I whimper, then gag around his dispassionate fingers, helpless as he pushes himself into me. More moisture slips from my pussy, trailing down until it kisses wetly into my clenching rosebud, then drips onto the floor.

It's . . . obscene.

"Remain still," my doctor chides. "I need to assess your throat."

His fingers slide back for a moment as I catch a breath, then he rubs them back in, deeper than before, until my throat closes around them and I gag again, and again, choking on him. My saliva covers his glove, and he lets out a small grunt before wrenching his fingers back out.

I gasp for air, squirming on the bed, my pussy clenching, my nipples hard and needy for attention.

"Doctor Bennett," I manage shakily. "Please."

His eyes sweep over me again, and my doctor can't hide the pleased satisfaction in the set of his mouth, even as he gives me a serious look.

"It's worse than I expected, I'm afraid. Rapid heartbeat, elevated temperature, dilated pupils, tight, hot throat. I'm going to need to perform an internal inspection, Miss Anderson." He pauses, then murmurs, "It can be quite . . . invasive."

"I-invasive?"

His wet, gloved hand brushes against my nipple. *Accidentally*, I'm sure.

"It's medically necessary, Miss Anderson. It brings me no pleasure." I almost choke at that, and he adds, "You do want me to make you feel better, don't you? A poor, sick girl like you needs someone to help her."

I bite my lip against a whimper as my pussy *throbs*. I need to end this. I can't take any more. Maybe I *am* sick. My body is trembling, aching, full of unwholesome need. I've become used to Jaykob's quick, brutal pleasure.

This? This is *torture*.

But the way my doctor is looking at me, his abdominals

clenched, his erection thick and straining against his pants, the high color in his cheeks, tells me he's getting off on this as much as I am.

So I let out a tremulous breath.

"Please help me, Doctor Bennett," I beg huskily, letting him see my need. As if it weren't absolutely transparent already. "I'm suddenly feeling . . . very unwell."

That warm, indulgent smile returns, and he brushes over my wet lips again as he meets my eyes. "Such a good little patient, letting her doctor take care of all her needs."

I'm not proud of the unwilling, deprived sound I make at his words, but they act like a tongue around my clit. Is it possible to come from words alone?

"I need to perform a breast exam, Miss Anderson. Please hold still."

His hand trails from my mouth, down my collarbone, to my breasts. He takes one in his hand, testing the weight, plucking the nipple until I arch, a small cry escaping me. Watching my reactions, he does the same to the other.

"Nipples are responsive. Intense reactions to breast stimulation. May require further examination," he addresses the recording device. He grips one breast harder in his hand, massaging it, until a pained breath escapes. It's mixed with a moan. "Evidence of some bruising and bite marks. It appears the patient enjoys rough handling. Possibly incurable."

The chair moves beneath my feet as I squirm, and Doctor Bennett slaps my breast.

"I'm disappointed, Miss Anderson. I thought you were going to behave."

Behave? I'm on *fire*. I try to still my shaking legs, and my toes press into the wooden arms.

"I'm sorry, doctor," I choke out. "I seem to be having . . . some difficulty."

My doctor pauses, then gives me a sympathetic smile, though his jaw is tight with restraint of his own.

"Yes, you do seem overcome." His hand flattens against my stomach, and the heat of him is scalding. I stare at it, fixated on it, desperate for it to move down to where I need it. "Tell me, Miss Anderson, when was your last sexual encounter?"

"Wh-what?" His finger taps impatiently on my stomach, then swirls around on the skin like a promise, and I almost sob. "Yesterday. It was yesterday."

Heat glints in his eyes. "Interesting. I wouldn't expect a patient who was so recently active to be such a desperate, squirming, needy little slut."

Oh, my . . . God.

My whole body *shudders*. I feel a coil of bright burning tension take up deep and low in my abdomen, and I pant out another whimper. That word on that kindly, patient face is *wrong*.

I want him to say it again.

As he takes in my reaction, a small smile blooms on his lips, and he shakes his head.

"Note that Miss Anderson seems to respond to all manner of disgusting stimuli," he tells the recorder, sounding amused, and I don't even have it in me to glare.

I arch up into his hand on my stomach, and he shoves me back down carelessly. Then Doctor Bennett gets off the bed and walks around until he's beside my legs. He touches my knee beside him, encouraging it to fall open further.

I let it, and I feel my pussy part. It's unbearably hot. Soaking wet. And as I peel open, my moisture drips onto the floor, and I gasp, embarrassed.

"Ah, now, we can't have that," he says, watching it disapprovingly. Reaching into the bag, he pulls out a large specimen jar, and places it at my entrance. "Such a waste. I have to take a sample— for testing, you understand."

With the heel of his palm, he presses down just above my pubic bone, into my abdomen, and I yelp, stunned at the sudden, violent, pleasurable pressure that lights up my whole core with heat. It ignites an urge to come, almost inseparable from the need to pee, and I let out a strangled, high-pitched sound as the pressure makes moisture gush out of me.

Then Beau removes his hand, takes two fingers, and slowly drags them through my pussy, on either side of my clit, and more slickness dribbles down.

I lift my hips into his delicious, insufficient touch, desperate tears squeezing from the corners of my eyes.

"Beau." I sob. "*Please.*"

He ignores me, lifting the jar and examining the contents. Dipping one finger in, then out, he rubs my slick between his fingers.

"Pleasing consistency. Delightful scent." Looking me in the eye, he sucks his finger into his mouth. "Tastes like fucking heaven."

My hands make fists in the sheets to stop myself from reaching down and touching myself as I breathe in little gasping pants. It would take nothing. A rub or two, that's all, and I would come so hard. I didn't know it was possible to be so turned on with someone barely even touching me.

"Now, I'm thinking a second opinion is required," Doctor Bennett says to the recorder.

He dips his fingers into the specimen jar, scooping up the moisture, then bends over my head again. Without waiting to be asked, I open my mouth, and he gives me a surprised look. Then he smiles.

"Very nice, Miss Anderson." I suck his fingers into my mouth, letting the flavor of myself mix with the latex, letting it become one of the most arousing things I've ever tasted.

He watches me swallow with hot, dangerous eyes, his tongue resting against his bottom lip. The look is a little feral, more animal than doctor, and it takes a moment for him to take a breath and withdraw. It makes something warm surge in my chest, mixing with my arousal, my embarrassment, the confusing degradation of it all.

He *loves* this.

Doctor Bennett's hand wraps around my thigh as he stares hungrily down at my pussy.

"Describe the encounter, please," he orders pleasantly.

I blink fast, confused, trying to get my fogged brain to catch up. The . . . encounter? The encounter with Jayk? He wants to know about Jayk?

Biting my lip, I glance at the recording device.

"Is that medically necessary, doctor?" I ask uncertainly.

He raises a brow. "Of course. Your cunt looks recently used, Miss Anderson. I need to properly assess the damage. Now, if you would please . . ."

God, the way he speaks to me. He did it by the river too, so it shouldn't shock me.

He's just usually such a gentleman.

My wide eyes stay fixed on him, and my breathing becomes choppy as I recall my *recent activity*. "I— It was after we stopped for lunch yesterday. He put his hand over my mouth and pulled me away into the woods nearby."

I saw Jayk coming, of course, prowling around me as I ate. He pounced on me as soon as I finished. I lick my lips, glancing quickly at my doctor's professionally interested face.

"Jayk made me fight him again, poking at me until I did." Jaykob's encouraging smirks and taunts are infuriating—it doesn't take much now for him to provoke me. "It's pointless, of course. I could never beat him, but he makes me try. He wrestles me to the ground, pins me, strips off our clothes, makes me fight back. He shows me where to hit him, even though I'm not very strong. But I finally got on top this time."

I trail off huskily. Okay, he definitely *let* me get on top after I got one hit in that was not quite as terrible as the rest. It still felt good. I was hot and hungry and annoyed and aroused when it finally happened, and when he gave me this rough smirk, I could swear it was almost . . . proud.

Beau hums like he's listening, bending to inspect my pussy. His gloved fingers spread my lips apart as he looks, and my cheeks burn at the humiliation of it.

"Continue, Miss Anderson," he prompts absently.

"He—he dragged me up his body until I was kneeling . . . over his face." I falter, remembering his mouth on me there, his hands biting into my thighs as he ate me out messily. Roughly. His lips and nose and teeth and tongue *devoured* me. "He used his mouth on me," I whisper quickly. "And I came."

Hard. And fast.

A lot faster than *this*.

Doctor Bennett gives me another stern look, then I feel one latex finger from his other hand press into my clutching hole to the first knuckle. He wiggles it, and I sob out a moan, arching. It's everything. It's not enough.

"Now Miss Anderson, do you really expect me to believe this cunt is all torn up because you rode a man's face and soaked him in your cum?" He shakes his head, dissatisfied. "It is not advised that you lie to your doctor, my girl."

He begins to remove his finger, and I cry out, "No, that's—that's not all. Please, Doctor Bennett, there's more. I'll tell you. Don't stop . . . helping me. Please."

His finger pauses in its retreat, and he raises a brow at me, waiting.

Flushed, almost panicked, I blurt, "After I . . . did what you said, he pushed me over. He pinned me to the ground, Doctor Bennett, on my stomach, and he spread my legs wide open. Then he . . ."

"Say it, Miss Anderson."

I squirm as his finger sinks in to the second knuckle, then withdraws. When he pushes back in, it's with two, and they curl up, rubbing my slick, hot walls, and I sob in relief.

"He fucked me. He fucked me hard, from behind, like an animal. He grabbed my hips and didn't touch me. He just used me until he came. He made me all wet, Doctor Bennett. I was so wet."

I'm so wet now, painting the floor, drenching his hand.

Doctor Bennett's eyes sharpen on me. "He didn't use a condom?"

I clench around his fingers, the pleasure of it making my eyes roll, and I shake my head.

"N-no. We decided not to. I don't want to anymore." I look up at him pleadingly. "You said you're as sure as you can be that you're all clean, right? And I am too? Please, I don't want to use them anymore. I want your cum, Doctor Bennett. I want—"

He plunges his fingers into me, then brings his thumb up to circle over my clit, once, twice, and then my orgasm is ripping through me with brutal, gasping force, and I come sweating and twisting into the mattress.

"No condoms," Doctor Bennett agrees hoarsely. He breathes hard for a moment, then flips me over on the bed, pushing me deeper into the center of it. "Kneel, face in the mattress, arms crossed and above your head—comfortable, but so you're extended. Do *not* put pressure on those wrists, you hearin' me?"

My body is limp, shaking, obliterated, and coasting in the after-shocks of that mind-altering orgasm, but I try to obey him. He kneels up on the bed beside me, correcting me with deliberate, quick moves.

"Legs further apart." He presses down between my shoulder blades until my face and chest are pressed into the soft bedspread. "Arch your back."

Still shivering, I do, and as my brain slowly starts to de-fog, I realize how exposed I am in this position. I hear the crinkle of fabric as Beau quickly strips out of his remaining clothes, and I pant into the mattress.

"This is called humble, or slaver's kiss. If we ask for it, this is the position you should take."

There are names? Is he still Doctor Bennett now, or is he Beau?

"Yes, Doctor Bennett," I reply, not sure why except that I still want to.

It's still turning me on.

He runs his hand down my back, then up the backs of my thighs as he settles in behind me. I feel the heat of him, the heaviness of his cock between my legs, the searing heat of him bobbing against my clit.

"Tell me, is this the position you were in yesterday, Miss Anderson?" he asks, his voice hungry with need.

He must be gripping himself, because the way the fat head of his dick rubs through my wetness, stroking over my sensitive clit, is too firm, too deliberate, and my mouth parts on a breathless moan.

"Use your words, Miss Anderson. I am trying to do an accurate assessment of how the damage occurred."

"Yes, Doctor, it was like this. He had me like this," I whine, my arousal re-cresting almost immediately. I'm too worked up, too exposed and used and desperate to please him.

He fits his head against my entrance, notching in, and I bite my lip hard against the urge to push back. His hands grasp my hips, his thumb rubbing over my skin.

"Yes, now, I can see how these bruises came up. I can't see any others." He pauses. "Are you injured anywhere else, Miss Anderson?"

"No, Doctor Bennett," I tell him desperately. "But I ache."

"Where do you ache, Miss Anderson?" he purrs, and self-satisfaction melts through his voice, but I'm too focused on his cock teasing my entrance.

"In my . . . pussy," I whimper, clenching around his crown. "Please, Doctor Bennett, help me. It hurts."

I feel his dick twitch and sink in another inch, feel the stretch of it. But despite the greedy, scorching heat of him and the way my body tries greedily to clutch and draw him in, he just strokes me soothingly.

"Don't you worry, Miss Anderson. I told you that you were my favorite patient. I take good care of my special patients."

He sinks in one more inch, and I'm quaking with the control of just taking it—of just letting him use me and take and say these perfect, vile things.

"My methods are somewhat unorthodox," my evil doctor says in that same soothing, slightly amused tone. "But I assure you, you will feel so good when I'm done. Just let it happen, Miss Anderson."

His cock is perfect. Absolutely perfect. I need more of it. All of it. All of *him*.

"I trust you, Doctor Bennett," I whisper . . . and that makes him pause.

He lets out a soft warning growl, and my pussy pulses in response.

"Have you had anal intercourse yet, Miss Anderson?" he asks in a too-casual tone, and I freeze, breathless.

And suddenly hyper aware that my doctor must have an obscene view of my open, exposed cheeks. I immediately want to close, to hide, but there's no way. Not in this position.

"N-no," I stutter as his hands leave me.

"No?" I hear a squirt, and cold liquid is trickling between my cheeks, then a thumb circles my back hole, pressing the liquid around it. Into it. I twitch away, just for a second, only for him to grasp my hips and yank me back, impaling me on his thick cock.

I cry out, my body frantically trying to adjust to the full length and width of him. My inner walls squeeze, meeting incredible, delicious pressure, and the almost painful feeling quickly rewrites itself as pleasure.

I shudder in relief, shaking with coarse, desperate desire.

"He didn't take you here?" He sounds surprised.

"We didn't . . . no lube," I gasp out as his thumb presses in further, invading the first ring. If I thought his cock was pressure, this is already more. Or a strange, different kind, at least.

I know Jayk wanted to do it that way—he seems quite possessive about my ass, actually—but he held back, muttering something about "doing it right."

"Hmm," Doctor Bennett says, and it's half a growl. "No, of course this ass hasn't swallowed a dick."

His thumb pops through the second ring of muscle, and I can't help it this time—my body arches into his finger. It impales his cock further in me, until I'm grinding against the base, my moisture soaking the coarse hairs.

"This is tight, sweet virgin ass, right here." His voice is rough now, tight with tension. He pulls his thumb back, then pushes in again, and I shudder. "We need to stretch this out before it can take one of our cocks. You will take our cocks here, won't you, Miss Anderson? You're going to let your doctor fuck every one of your greedy holes as a thank you for taking such good care of you, aren't you?"

He fucks my ass with his thumb again, and my brain is spiraling, lost in the pressure everywhere, the tug against my forbidden inner muscles, the mindless carnality of it all.

"Yes." The word is a moan, a plea. Pure need.

"Yes, who?"

My forehead rolls in the blanket, the game slipping away. "Yes, shi— Ah! *Beau*. You can do anything to me. Take me, use me, make me—"

"Fuck," he swears, and in seconds, he uses his knee to push mine out, widening my stance unbearably. I might have fallen, but he grips my hip with his free hand.

Then he pulls his cock out of me.

"The doctor will make you feel good now, pet. Take your medicine like a good girl."

His words make my mind blank with lust, but he's already slamming home, his cock pounding into me with short, powerful punches that I feel everywhere. He hits every magic place inside me, lighting me up, and I can't move, can't do much in this position except take his dick however he wants to give it to me. Hard. Hungry. His body controls mine with sinful, practiced confidence, even as I hear him groan with strain.

This stretched out, I feel his pumping cock in flawless detail, I feel him swell, the heat of him. I can smell his body mixing with mine in viscerally perfect ways.

Then his thumb drags in and out of my back hole, and the torturously sensitive nerve endings leap to life, blending, mixing with the punishment in my pussy. My nipples rub against the bedspread, my mouth cries into it until I'm almost suffocated, and still, he fucks into me, harder, faster.

"Beau," I cry, and I'm not sure if it's a plea or a prayer. "*Beau, Beau, Beau.*"

"Fuck, fuck, you feel so fucking good, darlin'. You're soaking my dick. So hot, so fucking wet."

He gasps, his thrusts becoming reckless, almost painful. His hands leave my ass, my hip, and one gets planted in my back, holding me down as he leans over me, while the other wrenches my hair back. The angle is so deep, I sob at the sheer, agonizing perfection of it.

"Milk my cock, pet. Take it all. I'm going to coat your pretty cunt."

I explode. The words, his smell, his dick, the ecstatic pleasure tearing through my body from my earlier orgasm, all of it collides in an eclipse so intense that my vision blackens and my body is seared through, clear of any other thought but *Beau.*

Somewhere, I know he's using me for his own final, hungry thrusts, but I'm already crashed out and floating among perfect, dazzling stars.

CHAPTER 33

EDEN

SURVIVAL TIP #239
When you hit a high,
ride it.

I don't know if it's seconds, minutes, or hours later when I hear his raw, hungry sounds as he releases. I feel him fill me, coat me with his cum, like he promised. The sensations blend, push this tingling, buoyant euphoria to new heights.

The bed feels good, his hot, wet cum between my legs feels good, my body feels *so good*. I wait to come down from my high, but it doesn't seem to be going anywhere—only settling into something floaty and delicious.

I feel Beau turn my head to the side, and suddenly my lungs are full of sweet, clear air, and I'm not breathing in the hot, rumpled blankets. I giggle helplessly as the air tickles my lungs. And when gooseflesh erupts giddily over my scalp and skin, I giggle at that too. It all feels wonderful, like the room is sparkling with some invisible, happy magic.

"Oh, so it's like that, is it?" He sounds like himself again now, amused and roughed with pleasure.

His voice makes me happy too, and I rub my cheek into the blankets with a sigh. A warm, wet cloth slides up my thighs. Between my legs. It disappears, then comes back again to towel clean the cleft of my ass.

"'Sgood," I mumble, all of it shivering over me with sweet, blissed-out tingles.

"I bet," Beau murmurs with a soft laugh. He gathers my hair, then pulls it all to one side. "I love your hair out like this, pet. It's so pretty wrapped all around you."

"Hmm," I hum contentedly, and he kisses my shoulder.

"Drink this." He makes me drink water, then more water, like I'm a fish. And the thought of me being his *pet*, his pet fish, makes me giggle so hard I can't drink anymore and he takes the water away.

And I don't know why it's striking me like this. Vaguely, I know this isn't usual.

I just don't really care.

I hear something snap open, then a cool liquid dribbles over my back, quickly chased by wide, warm hands. He pushes the liquid over my skin, then squeezes with his palms, his fingers, rubbing it over my back until I'm moaning softly, helpless and delirious. He rubs over my shoulders, digging into tense muscles and working loose every knot, then down over my arms, my legs.

He flips over my limp body, and I think I'm still smiling, my eyes heavy-lidded as he does my front. I can still see his own soft smile and the glow in his eyes. He's not stoking me higher with his touch, though everything feels unbearably good. He's soothing me. Loving me with his hands, his eyes, and suddenly all the emotions in me crest, hard, in a totally unexpected way.

My breath hitches as it crashes in on me, too good, too beautiful and right and safe and—

I burst into tears.

"There we go." He drags me into his arms as I cry into his

chest. Despite my promise of *no more* mere pitiful hours before, I'm sobbing hard. "I've got you, darlin'. It's okay."

But it's not. The only thing that's okay is him, this room, this moment.

With his arms around me, I cry for all my apathy, then my terror, and for my anger. As he strokes my hair, I cry for all the blood on my hands and the person I became to win my freedom. He presses kisses to my temple as I cry for the women and children at the Den who aren't free, and who might never be, and all the others who might be caught and used if Sam goes unchecked.

He strokes my skin as I cry for my cowardice as I retreated, ready to leave Heather in the dirt. I cry for my brutes dying, for the shock of them being alive, for Heather being Heather after all, and the way Dom is always around her as Beau gently wipes my face. He whispers sweet nothings as I cry for my disgusting, awful lies and the way I've sneaked around Dom's back and disobeyed his orders.

And he wipes my face as I cry for hurting Jayk—for not realizing his expectations were so different from my own. For Lucky and how happy he's going to be, and how much it's going to hurt to watch it. For Jasper and what we never were and now certainly will never be.

Mostly, I cry because I still feel dark and sticky and cowardly and full of so much *residue*. My anger is like ashy coals that still sometimes find their old spark, though there's no place for fire like that at Bristlebrook.

Never again.

And I cry because, despite all of those terrible things, this was wonderful. I feel filled up, then emptied out, then filled again. His care, and Bristlebrook, and his words and his touch, all of it is just . . .

"I love you," I whisper against Beau's neck, the words falling out of me. Inevitable. Too true and right in this moment for them to possibly be stopped. They've been coming since the moment I met him and he defied Dom and soothed my fear so he could tend my ankle.

My perfect, wonderful doctor.

Beau stops breathing, his hands halting on my back.

I'm not sure what I'm expecting—some kindly misdirection. A gentle explanation of why I couldn't possibly feel this way. It feels like that happens so often, whenever my feelings are involved.

I don't expect him to tilt my head back.

And I don't expect it when he says, "I love you too, Eden." His eyes gleam with emotion. "I love you so hard it breaks my heart."

I release a hard, painful breath. My heart fills, overflows. He loves me? *Beau loves me.*

We stare at each other for a long, charged moment before I huff a damp laugh.

"You're a really terrible doctor, you know," I tell him.

Beau blinks, surprised, then snorts, a cheeky grin crashing over his face.

I'm laughing when I tease, "Really awful. That is *not* standard medical practice. Do they let you get away with that? They should take your license."

He laughs too, his eyes sparkling wickedly. "I'll have you know, darlin', my patients always leave satisfied."

I widen my eyes at him. "All of them? Jayk never mentioned . . ."

"Not all of them, brat." He pinches my butt, and I squeak through my giggles. His forehead rests on mine as he sobers. "Only my favorite patient."

My throat feels thick. I haven't had this before. Not like this. I remember telling my husband I loved him. I even remember meaning it.

I don't think I knew what it meant.

It never felt like this.

I touch his cheek lightly, enjoying the graze of his stubble against my fingertips. "You don't think this is too soon?"

How soon is too soon to fall in love?

Beau gives me a tender half-smile, and I can feel the raised crease of it like the sweetest kiss. "I've been waiting my whole life to fall in love with you."

My eyes sting again, and I blink hard. "Ohhh," I growl in frustration. "Don't. I—"

"Don't be nice to you?" He rolls his eyes, though he's still smiling. "You need to stop fretting, darlin'. I'm not afraid of your tears."

Fortunate for him, considering I just drowned his chest in them. Funny, how similar his words are to Jayk's—*I'm not scared of your fight*.

I swallow hard, thinking, tracing through the drying, salty tears I've dampened him with. Whatever he says, this is enough. I've cried *enough*.

Beau loves me.

He's here with me, and he *loves* me. I just want to float here, for now, where I'm safe.

The mess outside that door will come for me soon enough.

So we sip lazily at our wine, and he makes me blushingly recount what I liked about the scene—almost everything—and what I didn't like—the way he held off my orgasm, an answer which makes him laugh far too hard for some reason, before he promises that next time, I will have as many orgasms as I can handle, with no edging involved. A promise that sounds good in theory but for some reason, when paired with that hyper-amused smile, makes me nervous.

We talk about—God—*anal stretching*. Or Beau talks, at least. I listen while staring politely at the bedsheets, trying to look like discussions about enemas, and potential tearing, and proper lubricants, and *training kits* doesn't make me want to hide under them.

Beau as an *actual* doctor is much more embarrassing than Doctor Bennett.

We edge around discussing the others, though I think he

gathers enough from what I don't say to know none of it is going well. Those are a problem for tomorrow. Not for now. Not for here.

When we're drowsy and not making sense anymore, Beau settles me against him, murmuring his I love yous that I whisper back to him in the sweetest, loveliest loop.

And that's how I sleep—locked safe and untouchable in his arms.

When I open my eyes, it's with sweating palms and my heart pounding in my throat. It's dark. So dark. Everywhere and on all sides. There's a tight, anxious crush around my chest that has nothing to do with the arm banded loosely around my belly.

Beau. Beau is here. I'm at Bristlebrook. I'm safe.

I repeat the mantra over and over, paralyzed in my bed. My bed that was meant to be *safe*. But this bed, Beau's arms, they can't lock out the night any better than Jaykob's did.

You can't run from shadows.

There are no thoughts to the familiar crash and tumble of feelings anymore. Just the dread, the fear. The *guilt*.

Beau snores lightly, peacefully behind me, and I'm struck violently with fear for him. All the things that could happen *to* him.

Trembling, I finally manage to unlock my limbs. The door feels like a horrible vulnerability. And the room is too large—too many things could be hiding in it.

As quietly as I can, I move my heavy bedside table and shift it until it's wedged against the closed door. It doesn't make me feel better, not really, but at least we'll hear if someone tries to come in.

I return to bed and stare at it, infected by the night.

Nowhere is safe.

Too many people like me survived.

CHAPTER 34

JASPER

SURVIVAL TIP #299
Don't murder your roommate.
Bodies make such a terrible mess.

We stumble down the hall until we reach Dominic's room —stumble because the brat won't stop *touching* me. I press Lucien against the closed door, my mouth on his throat. His frantic heartbeat pulses against my tongue, and electrified pressure zaps my spine—to push, to punish, to please.

I move my mouth back to his again, luxuriating in the give of it, the heat, the way his tongue battles mine. Wrapping my hand around his throat, I press my fingers into the sides of his neck with enough warning pressure to make him groan helplessly, but not enough to cut off his airway.

I fight with my own restraint. I want Lucien on his knees. I want to choke him, suspend him, tie him into positions so tense he begs for release. I want to drip hot wax down his spine until he burns the way I burn. I want to test every whip and cane and flogger I own against that pretty skin. I want to cut him, freeze him, electrify him. I want to know every pressure point on his body so I can make him hurt with a single squeeze of my hand. I want to know what makes him cry, how far I can take him until he touches the clouds, and which pain is his favorite.

The possibilities are thrilling, *drugging*. The endless fantasies I've had have never been enough for the few times I've slipped, and now I can have them all.

And yet, I know . . . none will beat this one.

"Say it again," I demand against his mouth.

He tries to kiss me again, the greedy brat, and I tighten my grip until he whimpers. He's still wearing the sad, wilted yellow flower in his hair, and he won't let me replace it with one better.

"I love you," Lucien says, his eyes glued transparently to my lips. His dimple kisses his cheek. "Now you."

My heart tears and tangles in my throat at the deprived neediness in his tone. My Lucien hurts. I push down my guilt and run my nose lightly down his, until he shivers. Until my lips brush over his again in a delicious tease for us both.

"I love you, Lucien."

I'm just about to slip my tongue into his mouth when the door opens, and Lucien falls back with a yelp. Dominic catches him, his face marked with impatience. I realize there's an action movie playing on his TV in the background, its volume turned down low.

"I'm not listening to you fuck him against my door. You have a bed. Use it."

Lucien laughs, straightening. He pats Dom's cheek. "You know, Jasper, he's right. We should just . . ."

I step back out of Lucien's grip, but I can't help the odd curl of my lips. This giddy nectar that has replaced my blood is washing against all my worries.

He's dazzling.

"I will see you tomorrow, Lucien. And all the days after that."

Lucien's laughter fades as he stares at me.

"You promise?" he asks. He forces a smile to soften the question, but his furrowed brow is disquieted. "I kind of feel like my clothes are about to turn into rags and I'll have to bitch out the fairy godmother to give me another night."

"I promise." The words, the need for them, hurt.

My heart shreds a little more when he gives me a relieved smile, and self-loathing slithers in to plug the slices.

I've been hurting him so badly for so long.

Eden, that clever, beautiful girl, was right about that. Of all the people I might have expected to confront me about it, I hadn't considered it might be her. It takes enormous bravery, and deep selflessness, to do so. Especially at the cost of her own relationship.

Yet another thing that doesn't sit right.

Giving me one last thorough and completely unsubtle eye-fuck, he turns to Dominic. "So which side of the bed is yours? Are you a cuddler? I always thought you'd be a cuddler."

Dominic delivers me a flat look, then drops it to Lucien.

"You get the couch." He raises one dry brow. "You don't annoy me for three days straight and we'll talk cuddles."

Lucien grins and winks at me. "Okay, I'm going to shower." He backs up toward the bathroom. "Extra hot. Steamy. Lots of bubbles."

My eyes narrow on the wretched tease as perverse, soapy images pour through my thoughts. My already throbbing cock aches.

He'll pay for that.

"That looks like it went well."

I tear my eyes from Lucien's disappearing figure to find Dominic leaning against the doorframe, his arms crossed and a slight smile on his face.

The knowing look almost makes me want to blush.

"It did," I agree softly. It went better than I deserved. I look at the closed door of the bathroom as the shower clicks on. It hurts me that he and Eden are at odds when I can see how deeply they both care. I want them both to be happy. "And you? Did you resolve things with Beaumont?"

I glance back in time to see Dominic grimace.

Distracted by Lucien, I'm only just now seeing the deepening cracks in Dom. The strain and stress. He's been up too, it's clear. It's also clear it wasn't for as enjoyable a reason. Stubble sits rough and heavy on his jaw, and there are tense lines in his forehead.

I had thought returning to Bristlebrook would lighten his stress—not increase it.

Dominic looks across the hall to Eden's room. To *Beaumont* and Eden's room.

"No."

One word. My concern deepens.

"Dominic, I'm sure it can be resolved."

He scrubs a hand down his face and shakes his head. "Look, if you're heading back to your room, can you just tell Heather to meet me in the library? We need to go over the plan for tomorrow."

"Now? It's past three in the morning."

After weeks of traveling, I should have long since been in bed myself.

But Lucien is difficult to refuse.

"There's never enough time." Dominic sighs. "Jayk and I only finished setting up the civilians with tents and bedding an hour ago. I've been making a start on inventory lists too."

Ah. I'd shirked that duty. As had Lucien. And Beaumont too, if the sounds from behind Eden's door could be believed.

I shouldn't have done that. Not while Dominic is already teetering under the weight on his shoulders.

"I see." I grimace. "Well, if you insist on meeting with the medusa, do remember not to look her in the eye."

He catches my arm, and I can see the moment he loses his patience. "Stop this. We have enough shit to deal with without you two at each other's throats. Our generator can't handle this many people. We have no defenses readied. We have no vegetable garden. All our dried meat is gone. We have a minimal stock of long-life supplies, and we only have a tenth of the animals needed to feed more than ninety. Not to mention the fact that Bentley's confirmed that Sam is recruiting more men. The Sinners are chomping for revenge and desperate to lock these women down."

Dread creeps over me, and I look at him seriously. "How long until the food runs out?"

The grim set to his jaw is not reassuring.

"We start rations tomorrow. Replanting. Hunting." Dominic shakes his head. "With all that? Weeks at most. We can't be put under siege or we're fucked. So yeah, Jasper. I need Heather—to *plan*."

His words settle uneasily over me.

Sobered, I nod once. "I'll fetch her."

He nods and leaves, and it takes me a long moment before I can bring myself to turn away from the comforting, torturous sound of Lucien's shower and head back to my room.

Weeks.

I knew our situation was bad, but not how dire. How long before these people balk against food rations? How long until a new militia descends? Fear grips my stomach. Lucien has only just recovered from his wounds. Eden is *just now* safe.

We can't afford another attack. *I* can't afford it.

I knock before entering my room, though the need to do so feels deeply irritating.

"Midlife crisis trauma center, only middle-aged washouts may enter," Heather snipes behind the door.

How am I meant to maintain my own composure when she insists on antagonizing me?

Breathing through my nose, I enter.

The pestilent poltergeist is sitting in my armchair, flicking through one of my books.

"Oh look, the lackluster lackey himself. Looks like you're A-OK to come in."

"Get your filthy feet off my coffee table," I snap, my fingers twitching against the urge to remove them myself.

Heather's dark red brow lifts. "These feet?"

She flattens her toes on the table and rubs her feet over the dark wood.

Infuriating, repulsive, adversarial *child*. Biting down hard against an outpouring of vitriol, I move to my cupboards and begin pointedly pulling out cleaning supplies.

"You know, these comments are pretty suggestive. Your boyfriend know how much you book-flirt with Eden?"

I freeze, one hand on the disinfectant as she continues lazily, "*Woman's power lies in man's passion, and she knows how to use it, if man doesn't understand himself. He has only one choice: to be the tyrant over or the slave of woman*—to which you write, 'Let me be both. Your tyrant and your slave. In allowing me to own you, you own me.'" Heather whistles low. "Spicy. Pretty scandalous stuff."

Spinning, I see she has my copy of *Venus in Furs*, stolen from my bedside. Raw panic flutters over the things I wrote in that forsaken book.

"Give that back to me, you thieving demon. Don't you read another word."

Heather flicks through the pages and pauses. "*A slap in the face is more effective than ten lectures. It makes you understand very quickly*—and you say, 'You must tell me if Jaykob agrees.' Huh. She slapped the caveman. Nice."

I bolt over to her, abandoning dignity, and she stands on my armchair, holding it out of reach.

"*I want to go on whipping without pity until you beg for mercy, until you lose your senses.* You just say, '*Beg me.*' Honestly? A little threatening."

I leap up onto the armchair and tear the book from her hand. She elbows me in the gut, and I grunt as I get off the chair.

Smoothing my hair back, I hold the book to my chest. Did she rumple the pages? No matter what Dominic said, if she rumpled my pages, I will murder her on the spot.

"Dominic would like to see you in the library," I grit out. "So please—get out."

Heather grins, then steps onto my coffee table, walking to the end of it. "Touchy, touchy." She jumps down and heads to the door. "Just let me know if you want me to give her the book. I'll even put a restraining order on top—make it nice and easy for her."

The door closes behind her, and I stare at her pack, contemplating emptying the contents into the fire.

There's a brief knock, and I turn toward it to snarl, "I will salt your sinuses while you sleep if you do not give me a moment's peace."

The door opens on Beaumont's bemused face, and he glances around the room warily. "So room sharing is starting off mighty swell over here, I see."

I massage my temple with one finger, my fatigue truly making itself known. Beaumont, however, looks disgustingly refreshed for —I glance at my grandfather clock—half-past three in the morning.

"Not all of us have such charming companions," I mutter. I contemplate how to rid myself of Beaumont. My bed is calling me. "Speaking of which, why are you here and not with her?"

He shrugs, stretching. "Woke up early. Too wired."

I hardly need to wonder why. I do wonder what she looks like, though, all sleepy and sated and tangled in her bedsheets. I watched her more than I'm proud of—more than I can brush away—while we traveled home. Eden doesn't sleep easily. Even resting against Jaykob, the firelight flickering over her face, her dreams always seemed to trouble her.

It took all my strength, each night I watched, not to lean over and kiss the tense lines in her forehead.

Jaykob might have murdered me if I tried.

Beaumont hesitates, then frowns, a shadow passing over his face. "Look, I wanted to talk to you about something. Eden moved her bedside table in front of the door. Do you know why she'd do that?"

That gets my attention. I lift my head, watching him.

Eden is concerning me. She's hardly sleeping. Eating minimally. She's struggling to maintain her composure—displaying classic signs of emotional dysregulation, hypervigilance, hyperarousal, as well as bouts of listlessness and aggression. Classic symptoms of post-traumatic stress, and hardly surprising, all things considered.

I only wish she might be willing to discuss it.

I've been patient, giving her space, but it only seems to be worsening.

"You know why," I murmur, meeting his eyes.

Beaumont's face darkens. "She should never have had to deal with this."

Sadness drenches me. "No, she shouldn't. But she has—what matters now is how she deals with it. Many of the civilians are dealing with trauma. Some have already come to talk with me about it during our travels."

"But she hasn't," he says. He knows his submissive.

"No, she hasn't."

Beaumont seems to struggle with that for a moment, his jaw working as he thinks. "Well, that's fine. I'll just make her. She doesn't get a choice, and you can help her."

I raise a brow. "You know that's not how this works, Beaumont."

"*Our* therapy was mandatory," he says mulishly, and I fight a sigh. He's impossibly stubborn sometimes.

"You willingly agreed to that condition as part of your service. Eden is free to do as she wishes. Her autonomy is important, Beaumont. Especially now. Surely you understand that." I give him a severe look, and glance down at my book.

I need to hide this in my private room.

Where *no one* will ever see it again.

I stride toward my walk-in, and Beaumont follows me through my hidden door.

"I do understand that, but she's only hurting herself here. As her dominant, I—"

"Did she agree to a total power exchange?" I ask sharply, cutting off that insufferably smug sentence. "Or any dynamic in which you have control over that kind of decision-making?"

"No, but . . . Oh, shoot."

My private room is perhaps my favorite in this house. It's decadent, all dark woods and burnished gold, lit in subtle warm light. The length of one wall is taken up by a set of low cabinets. Above them hang dozens upon dozens of tools. Whips and canes, paddles and blindfolds, all manner of ropes, clamps, wands, and restraints, vampire gloves and masks, and much, much more.

Beaumont stops behind me, and I turn to see him staring, stunned, around the room. He knew about it, of course, but he's never been invited inside. Only Lucien has seen it.

"Mary, mother of God," he breathes, amused.

He looks around at the St Andrew's cross, my adjustable paddling bench, the enormous area cleared for suspension or whipping, depending on my mood. He stares at my sex lounge, the stockade, and my king-sized, four-poster bed with the cage beneath it—noting the dozens of loops and hooks around it for bondage.

His eyes linger longest on the gynecologist's chair, of course.

"Are you open to sharing this?" he blurts.

The thought of him taking Eden here, to *my* place, and fucking her. Dominating her. Touching those gloriously soft thighs. Perhaps even bringing tears to those heart-wrenching eyes . . .

It chokes me with something hot and snarled. It chokes me to senselessness.

"*No,*" I hiss.

I'm shaking, I realize. I force myself to breathe in deeply, shocked again at my reaction. It's as vicious, as absent of prudence, as my obsession with Lucien.

How I want to hurt her.

"You know that's a damned shame, don't you?" Beaumont pouts.

Pouts like he hasn't had his mouth on her breasts. Pouts like he doesn't know how easy he has it, when his only kinks involve dirty talk and sharing and roleplay that makes a mockery of his profession.

He doesn't know this kind of conflict.

"You cannot compel her into therapy," I say curtly, turning to face him and not caring if I look as cold as I feel. "Suggest, fine. Support her, certainly. But the choice is hers, Beaumont. You're crossing a line, and she's not stupid. She'll seek help when she's ready."

Beaumont doesn't miss my tone, and his easy expression vanishes. "If you hadn't got her feelings all in a twist over you, then maybe she'd be more willing to get that help. She doesn't trust you, you know?"

His words scrape over every wound.

"The books, the nights you spent reading with her, you went halfway to seducing her and then dumped her on her ass. I hope you know that if you have any more intentions toward my girl, you'll have to go through me first?"

"Do you think I'm unaware?" I bite back, furious. It's too late. Too early. I'm too heartsick. "Do you think I miss the wariness in her eyes every time I speak to her? You think I don't notice how much more comfortable she is with any one of you than she is with me?"

Beaumont's mouth clicks shut, his expression turning hesitant.

"Look around, doctor. You know what I am. Must I keep explaining this to everyone? You talk about her vulnerability, her anxiety, her *captivity*?" My lip curls up, and I point to the cage under my bed. "All I can think of is how prettily she would cry as I slept above her."

I look at the ropes and chains and silks and cuffs. "Would you have me tie her up and spread her out? Do you know it makes me hard, to think of how those delicate limbs would *strain* at the joints? Perhaps I can wrap my ropes around her slashed wrists? Would you prefer that?"

He stiffens, tensing.

"Shall I tease her pretty clit with my knife? Flog her bruised back? Maybe if I—"

"*Stop*," Beaumont snaps, and I fall silent, exhausted, aching.

"I cannot be different." I swallow, sad and hollow. "I tried for Soomin, I truly did, and it hurt us to the bone. I had some early hope with Eden. After she was with Jaykob, I thought, *perhaps*. But during that chess game, I was only honest with her. I told her the lightest part of my darkness—and it *frightened* her." I settle against the cabinets and murmur, "I can only imagine how much worse it would be now."

I stay there, thinking, until finally, Beaumont comes to lean against the cabinets beside me. "I'm sorry. I didn't think."

I sigh. "You're a naturally caring person, Beaumont, but you lack empathy, and you overstep boundaries. This is one of them."

"I lack *empathy*?"

"What did you say to Dominic earlier today?" I ask, and his mouth snaps shut, his jaw settling into a willful line. "You did damage, whatever it was. I hope you realize that. Losing Eden terrified him. Gaining the civilians has done almost as much. He is trying very, very hard right now to grow into who he needs to be for her and for them—and to finally share the load he carries. You've carried bitterness about Heather with you for years, but be careful not to let your anger about the past destroy the happiness you might find in the present."

With every word, Beaumont grows stiffer and stiffer. "Oh, and I'm the one crossing boundaries? This is none of your business, Jasper."

"Perhaps not. But he is my friend, too."

It's past time we started acting like it. We've all spent far too long ignoring our problems for the sake of keeping the peace.

There won't be true peace until they're resolved.

Beaumont is perhaps the most stubborn patient I've ever dealt with. He's charming about it, usually, but where Dominic is quick to highlight and attempt to quash any real or imagined flaw in himself, Beaumont often refuses to see his own at all.

"I told him I didn't want him with Eden," he says finally. Defensively. "Our relationships keep failing, time and again, because he never connects with them—not past surface level. He's doing the same thing with her. Just holding back, never giving her anything to work with. I'm done."

"Ah." I try to think how to word this delicately. "Your bond is important, Beaumont. The two of you work seamlessly as partners, and it's beautiful to see . . . but while compensating for one another's weaknesses has made you a strong unit, it's perhaps also meant that you haven't invested time into working on improving them. It might be time to start."

His jaw sets stubbornly. "Tell *him* that."

I rub the growing tension between my eyes and decide to let it go. Beaumont does usually get there in the end. He has too kind of a heart not to try. It will likely just be a long and bumpy journey.

We stay there in silence together for a long time, lost in thought.

Until Beaumont rubs the back of his neck. "Now, honestly, this might be an awkward time to ask, considering this conversation and all . . . but you wouldn't have an anal training kit at hand, would you?"

Slowly, I turn my head to stare at him.

He raises his hands at whatever devil he sees in my gaze, standing up quickly as he chuckles. "Okay, it's a bad time. I can understand that."

He's going to open her up, every part of her. He'll rub lubrication into her sweet pussy, between those pale cheeks. He'll rub his fingers inside her tight little rosebud and prepare to split her with his cock.

She'll almost definitely cry a little, the first time.

I close my eyes and breathe out. "I loathe you."

"Yeah, that's right and fair," he says agreeably.

Standing, I open one of the cabinets and a light flicks on. I pick over the three boxes I see and take the one from the bottom.

"This one." I hand the box to Beaumont. "They're all unopened, of course."

His eyes drop to the cabinet. "Can I see the others?"

"No." I can't control how possessive the word is. It has a mind of its own.

But it has to be these. Weighted and heavy, cold and metallic, with those delicious balls inside that will have her shuddering and clenching with every step.

I can only imagine the way they will stretch her hole. How pretty they'll be nestled in her cheeks. I plan on spending a good amount of time imagining it, in fact.

Beaumont rolls his eyes. "Fine. Thank you."

"You're the luckiest degenerate in the world," I mutter. "I do hope you know that."

He winks, his whole body loose and enviously happy. "I know. I promise you, I know."

CHAPTER 35

EDEN

SURVIVAL TIP #126
Feeling overwhelmed?
Put a plug in it.

I wake grainy-eyed and exhausted the next morning, with the bedside table no longer wedged against the door, but returned to its spot beside me. There's a wooden box sitting atop it, beside a short note.

You'd better believe we're talking about that later.

I stop after the first line and sigh. Wonderful.

Now, I've left you a training kit. Follow the instructions I left and insert the smallest plug. Leave it in for two hours, then take a break. Put it back in this afternoon. I want to see it in your ass tonight.
Rest up. Eat up.
I love you.
—Beau

I stare at the wooden box beside me nervously. He wants me to stretch myself out for him. So that he can put his cock in my ass. Chewing at my lip, I open it and see a series of metal plugs with flared ends—there's three of them, increasing in size. I eye the largest one nervously. It looks . . . far bigger than Beau's thumb.

It also doesn't look as large as Beau's cock—or Jaykob's. I hope that's a concern I still need to have. I need to speak with him as soon as possible.

I nibble at the food Beau left for me and shower in cold water when the heat doesn't click on. And then I spend twenty minutes mortifyingly working my way through *Doctor Bennett's* cleaning and insertion instructions before I leave my room with the smallest plug snug between my cheeks and a small bottle of lubricant in my pocket, in case it needs . . . adjusting.

It didn't go in easily, even with the lube, and I'm hyperaware of how deeply the plug is nestled, cold and wide, inside me. It bobs and rubs against my puckered hole with each step, shifting inside me like a scandalous facsimile of Beau's finger. To make matters worse, it seems there's some kind of weighted ball inside the toy. It rolls with my every step, striking my forbidden inner walls with teeth-chattering smacks I feel everywhere.

This accursed plug makes my whole body, already used and humming from Beau's attention last night, vibrate with lewd tension.

How on God's green earth am I meant to talk to Jaykob sensibly with this *thing* in me?

People teem through the halls, carrying linen and packs. I nod to them and keep moving, trying not to make it obvious that I'm waddling. Sweat is beading on my brow. Can they see the sweat? Will they *know*? Do people assume these kinds of things?

A few of their glances seem disapproving, and it almost sends me running back to my room. I try to walk more naturally as I make my way downstairs.

I don't think I succeed.

They've set up camp on the lawn. Several large, unfamiliar tents occupy the grass, nestled around the apple tree, and I can only assume they must have been pulled out of storage from somewhere. A little guiltily, I realize a lot of work must have been done last night. I'll have to be more useful today.

As useful as one can be with a plug in one's butt.

As I wander through the tents, I can see that the lawn is alive with activity despite the early hour. I hear a chainsaw and some shouting as a slender shortleaf pine is felled. There are half a dozen people digging a hole before the rim of the tree line, keeping clear of the massive pile of debris from Jaykob's barn.

Heather, Dom, and Aaron are clustered in front of a wide tent, and it looks like there are nearly a dozen people sparring behind it, practicing under Beau's watchful eye.

I can't see Jaykob anywhere, so I reluctantly make my way over, weaving through people as they carry on with their business.

"Stop!" Dom barks at Mary Beth, an apple-cheeked woman carrying an axe.

Behind him, I jump at the same time she freezes. Mary Beth looks at him with trepidatious eyes.

"Do you know how to use that?" Dom crosses his arms over his chest, looming like an unimpressed king.

I trail to a halt before they see me.

"Would you stop doing that?" Heather snaps at Dom, stepping in front of Mary Beth. "She's on the felling team for a reason. This has already been organized—stop terrorizing my people."

Dominic grimaces, looking surprisingly contrite, but Mary Beth takes one glance at his ominous presence and scurries away.

Aaron crosses his arms over his chest, mimicking Dom's stance but managing none of the forceful presence. His red hair is a few shades closer to blond than Heather's dark copper, and it blazes in the morning light.

He gives her a patronizing look. "Dominic is right, Madison. They could use some supervision. I'll take charge of—"

Heather rolls her eyes. "Aaron, you don't know your head from your asshole, so can you please shut up and find something else to do?"

His face turns a mottled red, and he looks to Dom in outrage, but Dom just rolls his eyes.

My gaze flits between Dom and Heather as Aaron stalks off. Is this how they flirt? Bickering and bickering until they explode?

Heather catches sight of me and hurries over with a relieved expression, and I tuck my hands into my pockets so I don't claw at her. We are friends, after all. Or close enough to friends, anyway. All of us.

Friendly, friendly friends.

"Thank God. Save me from men who think they know better." She links arms with me, turning me back toward Dom, and I need to bite my lips together to stop a whimper as the plug presses deep inside my ass.

Taking a shivery breath, I search for a distraction and glance at Aaron's disappearing back desperately. "That was a little bit harsh, don't you think? He's only very young."

Heather snorts. "Yeah, trust me, babe. These men will walk all over you if you let them. Take it from someone who grew up with five brothers and was on the force for ten years—you need to be tough, or they'll snatch any bit of control out of your hands they can."

I glance at her sideways—at her low dark red ponytail, her striking, strong face. Her words hit me in an odd way. I wish I had half Heather's fearlessness, her capability. *Any* of that toughness.

But is that what I need to do to become strong? Push back like everything is a fight I need to win? It seems . . . exhausting.

Is it so wrong to lose some control to the right person?

Like a magnet, my gaze is drawn back to Dom, who looks like a war hero in front of his battle tent. He's already watching me approach, standing like a dark pillar in the early sunlight, a beacon of strength and confidence.

And control.

Each step kisses the toy in and out of me, and it feels wrong, too sinful, to think of him, to talk to him, knowing that I'm being penetrated. That I'm full and my tender tissues are swollen and straining against the invasion.

We stop in front of Dom, and I adjust my weight as my uneasiness grows.

The ball in the metal plug rolls around inside my ass.

"You here to spar?" Dom asks as I bite back a squeak.

I shift again to get comfortable, and it rolls heavily again, internally spanking my nerve endings.

"Ah . . . *hmm*?" I say desperately.

Dom is talking. *Focus, Eden.*

He's talking to me, and it needs to make sense. My eyes fall to his chest. His broad, muscular, perfect chest. I clench against the invading plug. It presses back, unyielding, shooting spine-tingling ripples through me.

It's just . . . rude.

"Sparring." He looks over my pants and boots, and nods in approval. "I'll get you started. You should learn some self-defense."

"*Absolutely* not."

Good lord. I can't even imagine what that would do to those infernal weighted beads.

His gaze sharpens on me. "Come on, pet. We have women in their seventies with more grunt than you're showing."

That stings, hitting just a little too close to home, but I stay silent as he gestures to the scene behind him. Reluctantly, I step around the tent to see two dozen people sparring in pairs behind him, including Ethel and Ida at the end. The civilians look . . . better than I expected. They move rhythmically as Beau looks on, calling out instructions, moving arms and adjusting hands as he walks along the line.

Surprisingly, he seems to be getting a few cold looks too, like the ones I received as I walked over. I *knew* it wasn't my imagination.

But why on earth would they be cold to *Beau*?

"Are things this serious?" I ask quietly.

This camp is a storm of activity. They're wasting no time, and I know why. It's not hard for me to imagine Sam up on that rock, talking about their new era. Their *war*.

That's what this is.

We're preparing for war.

"Yes." The answer is like a pill, no sugarcoating. "We start rationing as of today. Any food approvals go through Lucky."

I bite back my grimace. Guess I won't be looking for extra food. I've been hungry before. I would rather face that than having to sit through Lucky apologizing to me for falling for Jasper.

"All the more reason," Dom continues, "for you to start out here. I'd feel better if you knew how to defend yourself."

I stare at him for a moment, trying to pinpoint how many times his words actually made my stomach flip.

But finally, I shake my head. "Actually, I was looking for Jayk. Have you seen him? I need to talk to him."

Dom pauses, and something like regret passes over his face.

"Right." Dom runs a hand over his hair. The motion shoots his biceps right into my field of vision. "Look, Jayk's not here. He left early this morning with Sloane, Ava, Akira, and Kasey to start fixing and relocating the cameras. We need to get this place defensible and functioning as soon as possible. He volunteered."

Despite the commanding nonchalance of his words, the sympathy in his eyes is enough to send my heart tumbling sickeningly to my feet.

"Jayk is *gone*?" Panic—and a flare of anger—lights my chest. "No. No, no. He can't be gone. He wouldn't just leave without talking to me."

I stare imploringly at Dom as my words become shaky, waiting for him to agree. When he doesn't, I flick my gaze to Heather, who gives me a pitying look.

"I don't think you want my opinion on that."

My throat becomes hot. "Why would he just *go*? I was right here. I've been with him for *days*, and he didn't say a word to me. I don't understand this at all. How could he just . . . leave me behind?"

They don't answer—there's no point. Because I do know why. Jayk is throwing up his defenses again, and I am being shut *out*.

I take a deep breath, trying to get a handle on myself, but it pushes the plug deep inside, and I gasp as the uncomfortable pressure rips through my anger. I don't think I like it right at this moment. It's not rewriting as pleasure.

Stressed, strung out, I press a hand to my too-tight chest.

"Darlin'? You okay?"

Beau shoulders past Dom, not even glancing at him. He examines my face, and I can only hope it's not as flushed red as it feels. I'm hurting, and angry, and unwillingly aroused and this damn plug is only making everything so much worse.

"Did you hear that Jayk left?" I demand. "Just *left*, without saying a word. I know he was angry, but it's hardly as though this was a surprise. I told him I had feelings for you as well. Several times. After *everything*, how can he just—"

Walk away.

Just like that, my anger bleeds into something soft and aching. Understanding clicks into place. People have never had a problem walking away from me. My mother, my father, even Henry joined the Army without a glance backwards. I don't know why this one should surprise me, but for some reason it does.

I was too difficult. I made it too hard for him to stay.

Of course he left.

Dom's eyes, heavy and serious, travel over my face. "Jayk just needs some time to cool off, pet. Give him a few days and try again."

"She's not yours to take care of, Dom. Back off," Beau says curtly, so cold and clipped that I recoil.

Something menacing charges across Dom's face. "Then do a better job."

No, this is wrong. Beau and Dom are a team. Their anger, Lucky's panic, Jaykob's pride. I'm in the middle of this whole mess and every single one of them is hurting because of me.

"Ugh, the testosterone," Heather groans, and two sets of irritated gazes fly her way. "You need to get out of here, Eden? Just say the word and we can run away together. We'll have a wonderful life."

"Heather bailing out on us, how on-brand," Beau mutters.

God, *all of us* need to stop. Dom is right—the Sinners are still out there. That is the real threat. Women are still being kidnapped, and there are dozens more captive. Hurting. Afraid.

They're going to come for us. Bristlebrook will be razed again —and at this rate, we'll be too focused on our own drama to be properly prepared.

How am I meant to face them again? When it comes down to it, I know I'm not like Lucky, ready to take a bullet. I already know what I am.

I run. I hide. I poison in secret. I let prisoners run free. I lie about it.

But God, I can't be alone again. I can't go out into those woods, and . . .

Jayk is out in those woods. The Sinners are going to be marching right through there. Anything could happen to them out there.

My ribs tighten like bands around my panicked heartbeat. I stare up at Dom. "I'm sorry, but did you say *Kasey* went with Jaykob? With *Akira*? Why on earth would you send Kasey out there? She's just a child. It's *dangerous* out there."

Dom's brows lift slightly, but he keeps his calm, still watching me. "There's no way the Sinners could get back here this fast. We have a few days at the earliest before they attack. The risk is minimal, and she insisted on joining them—she's following him around like a puppy, ripped up her shirt to look just like him." Dom snorts. "She idolizes him."

I shake my head. Then I shake it again, not understanding. Kasey has been at his heels all week—of course she hero-worships him. But that's all the more reason she should stay here. She *is* a puppy. A kid. Weak and vulnerable.

My throat feels tight. "That was a mistake, Dom. She shouldn't be out there. I cannot *believe* you approved that."

"If we didn't let her go, she would have trailed after them anyway." Dom pauses, then looks at me dryly. "Much like someone else I know."

"It's still a *risk*," I snap. "You should have kept her here."

"Eden, do you really think Jayk would let anything happen to her?"

I lift a hand to my head. My heart is pounding, pounding, and I can't slow it down. I can feel them all watching me, their eyes picking me apart.

Akira's out with them. Akira who loathes me for killing Logan. Akira who can't look at me without looking like she wants to peel the skin from my body.

She wouldn't do something to Jayk to get back at me, would she?

"Jayk can't protect Kasey. No one can. It doesn't matter how many people she has around her, she's in danger. Don't you see that?"

"Akira doesn't have a problem with anyone but you and Heather. She's been good with the other civilians. Some time away from the two of you might do her some good. Jayk's keeping an eye on her." Dom lowers his voice. "Eden, is this really about Kasey? Or are you afraid for yourself?"

My chest is constricting, and I'm struggling for air.

My eyes flick from face to face—Dom, Heather, Beau—every one of them brave and steady and so much stronger than me.

"I'm not afraid. I'm not a coward," I whisper.

Beau's gaze digs in like a grave. "This doesn't have anything to do with cowardice, darlin'. I think you need to have a talk with Jasper. He can help. You don't need to be feeling like this."

Jasper. God. I *know* what he can help with. With drawing me in, talking me down, with making me feel like we're the only two people in the world.

Only to crush me in his fist.

Jasper breaks my heart every time I talk to him. And I don't have enough glue right now to keep putting it back together.

"No. No. I need to go." I step away from all of them. The grass is a blur under me. "Just give me some space. All of you, just leave me *alone*."

CHAPTER 36

EDEN

I storm back into Bristlebrook, only to find half a dozen people in the living room. Breathing hard, I look around at them, catching more than a few frowns.

Jennifer pushes past me, and I grab her arm. This isn't in my head.

"Why is everyone mad at me?" I ask, my voice catching.

"*Why?*" She tongues her lip piercing with a disbelieving scoff. "You trade Jayk in the second you get back here? That boy is sick over you. God knows why. Maybe the next person he chooses will know something about loyalty."

"*What?*"

Jennifer pulls out of my grip, stalking off, and when I look around, the women avoid my eyes. The frantic battering in my chest increases. Of course. What else are they going to think? They like Jayk. They saw us fight.

They know I'm the villain.

My eyes burn, and I push into the kitchen, hoping for some peace. Some silence. *Something*.

Of course, I'm not that fortunate.

I freeze, wide-eyed, as I take in Jasper and Lucky atop the breakfast bar, and the sharp stop makes the ball clatter inside me heavily enough to make me pant out a silent gasp.

Jasper has him pinned by the throat, shirtless and stretched out like a carnal banquet. Over him, Jasper's silk shirt is unbuttoned to the waist, displaying his chest to full advantage.

I . . . I have never seen Jasper with so few clothes.

He isn't heavily muscled or crisply defined, not like the others, but there's an understated strength and grace to his body, like it was put together as art as well as for function. He's ivory and onyx. Coiled intensity and elegant confidence. It feels decadent to see him like this—like a rare and unexpected treasure that renders me speechless.

Underneath him, Lucky is lean and cut, lightly tanned and shivering with lust. He's decorated with new scars—on his chest, in the crest of muscle between his neck and shoulder, on his arm. They're shiny and still pink.

They're too lost, too caught up in one another to have spotted me yet. Lucky arches up, squirming, and Jasper gives Lucky a look so heated and intense that Lucky stills entirely under him. His hair is messily falling out of its loose ties, like he hasn't bothered to put it up properly.

There are bright yellow flowers knotted through his tiny braids. Flowers. There's something so dizzily romantic about it that my heart throbs painfully, fluttering for a different reason. Or maybe it is the same panic, just in a different flavor.

He has *flowers* in his hair.

In seconds, the sight of them has reshaped my brain. My burning, unbearable jealousy wars with crippling, painful desire. And I don't understand it. I don't know why seeing them together, these two that *I* want, should make me hurt so gorgeously.

Jasper moves his hand from Lucky's throat to grasp his wrists, and he presses them down on either side of Lucky's head. He lowers himself until their chests are pressed together, hard and slick, and Jasper's wicked mouth begins its hedonic descent.

"That is *not* hygienic," I blurt, quivering with something like panic but not.

Jasper's head tilts to look at me, an inch from Lucky's face. The danger, the warning, the need in his face remind me forcefully of a vampire being kept from its prey.

I take one step backwards, and the plug shifts, rubbing against my sensitive, slick flesh, lighting up my every nerve ending with breathless pressure.

"This is a *kitchen*. And as far as I'm aware, we haven't yet resorted to cannibalism. So you should just—" I look at the ceiling. I think my hands are shaking. "Just put your clothes back on, for goodness' sake."

For *my* sake.

"Or you could come over here and give me a kiss too," Lucky teases, his voice thick and husky.

I whip my head to stare at him, the offer like the crack of a cane against my tender heart. Jasper is buttoning his shirt unhurriedly, his predatory expression gone and replaced with something cruelly kind.

What am I *doing* here?

I back toward the door, suddenly mortified. They can do whatever they like. They're together. They're in love.

I am the intruder here.

"I'm sorry. I shouldn't have—" I shake my head, and my glasses slip down. I push them back up, scrambling to find the door handle behind me. "This is none of my business."

Jasper dismounts the breakfast bar with the ease of an equestrian and strides toward me, just as Lucky sits up, a different kind of heat glinting in his eye.

"Of course it's your business."

I look behind me and realize I'm not even standing in front of the door. Jasper reaches me before I can move the foot and a half left to escape.

He pauses in front of me. Even under the bright lights, he's all Hadean darkness and impious angles. Watching him top Lucky was intoxicating. *Distressing.* I can't help but wonder what they would look like together, truly naked and twined together. Lucky's sunshine and Jasper's glowing moon.

I'm sure it's glorious.

I'm sure I'll never have the chance to see it.

"Talk with him, Eden. He's hurting for you." Jasper touches my chin gently, turning my face as he examines it. "And when you're ready, please come talk to me. It hurts *me* to see you so lost."

Lost.

How does he always see me so clearly? I think it's what frightens me most about him.

I tear my chin out of his hands, hating how I feel instantly vulnerable in them. My lips tremble, and I need to press them together to make them stop.

Jasper inclines his head with a gentle, dissatisfied sigh, then leaves. The door clicks shut behind him.

Lucky is watching me. I can feel it, even if I can't look at him. My fingers knot in front of me.

"Lucky, if you'll excuse me, I have to . . ." I trail off, biting down on my lower lip as I try to think of a reason that would allow me to politely run as far and fast from this conversation as possible.

I would rather stick rusty nails in my palms than hear Lucky apologize to me for falling in love with Jasper.

"Have to leave just so you don't have to talk to me?" Hurt and bitterness bleeds through the question. "Yeah, Jasper used to do that to me too. You two can be more alike than you think."

At this moment, I don't believe he means it as a compliment.

My hands pause in their anxious knots, and I lift my chin a

fraction. What more does he want from me? I've been graceful. I've been as kind as I can.

Do I really need to have my face rubbed in this?

"There's really no point to this, Lucky. You certainly don't need to apologize for your feelings for Jasper." My breath snags, and I can't help the resentment. I want to bury it. I *should* bury it. But I need him to leave me be. My voice lifts. "Surely you can understand why this is difficult for me. Is it so hard for you to give me some time?"

Lucky slides off the breakfast bar, his expression hardening in a way I'm not used to seeing from him, and it's like watching someone put on some kind of . . . of illicit pornography. His muscles are so tightly defined, so beautifully carved, that they beg to be traced.

I *have* traced them. He watched me giggle like a fool as I touched him.

My fingers curl into fists as loss steals the air from my lungs.

Only Jasper will know their patterns now. He's Jasper's to touch. Jasper's to love. Jasper's to giggle with.

Damn it. I'm going to cry again. I blink hard.

"You think I'm trying to . . . apologize?" he prompts, and I realize he's angry.

Why should *he* be angry? Lucky got what he wanted.

But his eyes flash like blue lightning. "Why the hell should *I* apologize? *You* handed me over to Jasper like I was a brood mare. *You* apologize!"

And it's as if that lightning zaps straight up my spine, with ferocious, electric fury. I stare down my nose at him, sizzling with incredulity.

"Why should you apologize? You *cannot* be serious. No, you are—I can see you are. *Oh.*" I laugh, and it's an angry, disbelieving laugh that I have no hope of containing. Then my eyes snap to his. "Why should you *apologize*? How dare you. I've been trying to be the bigger person here."

I stalk up to him and poke him in his beautiful, obnoxiously firm chest. "You lied to my face. You and Jasper don't *feel that way* about one another? Do you recall telling me that? Perhaps I should have asked for clarification. Because when *I* heard that, I thought you meant that you weren't in love with him."

I laugh again, and this time it's teary—and more than a little unhinged. "*I* thought you meant you didn't want to kiss him, and sleep with him, and let him touch you everywhere. I thought you meant you were free to love—"

Me.

The word hangs in the air as I press a hand against my mouth. But it's too late. The words have already escaped. Why can't he let this be?

Am I not allowed to save any piece of dignity here?

Lucky's eyes drip with angry hurt. An answering flush of heavy heat builds in my throat. I'm angry, and his pain fuels mine.

"I *was* loving you," he tells me fiercely. "Jasper told me a thousand times, in a thousand ways that he didn't want me. I was alone, Eden. When you came here—" It's his turn to break off, sounding choked. "You were as lonely as me."

"Oh." I nod tearily, blinking up at the ceiling as that awful laugh escapes me again. "Wonderful. Please tell me more about how you *pitied* me."

"You were so sad. All I wanted to do was make you smile. It's still all I want to do." He swallows, and I hear his bitterness when he continues in a rush. "You *gave me away*, just like that. You didn't fight for me at all. The second Jayk walked out the door, you ran after him, but I've been right here, and you couldn't wait to shove me into Jasper's arms."

Shove him? He *threw himself* into them. As if he wasn't desperate for Jasper, wasn't watching him every day, hanging on his every sentence. Every little glance in my memories has tortured me, mocked me for my sheer gullibility.

"You're in love with him," I shout, and my tears spill over.

Again. I let out a high-pitched frustrated screech as I swat at them. "Why does this keep happening?"

"Because you're fucking miserable," he shouts back, and I turn and glare at him. His face is alive with his anger. "You've been back for less than a day, and I can already see it."

I flinch a little at that, and my shoulders curl in. "I'm surprised you noticed with your tongue crammed down Jasper's throat."

I know it's unfair. Petty. But it *hurts*. I saw us together, I really did. I saw food fights in the kitchen and fooling around in every room. I saw myself waking up to teasing kisses and learning how to *play*.

Lucky lets out a short, angry growl. He grips my shirt and yanks me into him. It startles me, completely, to have Lucky grab me this way, and I can only stare through my glasses as he brings his face close to mine.

"You do not get to wrap me up like a present for him and then be mad when he opens it," he grinds out.

"You think I wanted to? What was I meant to do, Lucky? How am I meant to win here? Because I can't see a single way." My words are hushed, haunted. Because I really *can't*. "You *love* one another—you're perfect. The two of you are both . . . so perfect. And I'm not."

How am I meant to compete with Jasper? How am I meant to compete with *Lucky*?

More tears spill over. "I'm just the sad little girl you wanted to cheer up."

Lucky's eyes run over my face, his anger filtering into sadness.

"You still need cheering up," he whispers. "Look at you, you're a mess."

I choke on a laugh that's immediately chased by agony. Because he's right.

Lucky releases my shirt and wraps his arms around me, and I let myself crumple into him like a used tissue. I bury my face in his chest, breathing him in. Maybe if I breathe in deeply enough, I can trap him inside me and never let him go.

He rests his cheek in my hair. "It doesn't have to be like this. Why didn't you talk to me?"

His heart pounds against my skin. How else could it be? All those days we were together, he was thinking of Jasper. In the games room the first day, he was watching Jasper. When he stole me away and we made kimchi, it was to keep me away from Jasper. After my chess game, he couldn't wait to quiz me *about Jasper.*

The only time it seemed like it was just the two of us was . . .

Something oily and cold slithers under my skin as I ask, "When we played Twister, I asked you to . . . to fuck me. Why didn't you?"

Pressed this close against him, I feel every inch of his sudden tension.

"Eden . . ."

That too. Even that moment between us was somehow about *him.*

I sigh, all the frustration and anger in me releasing in this slow, inexorable exhale, like the inevitable wilt of a pierced tire.

I step out of Lucky's arms, smoothing down my shirt. I just feel sad.

Sad and empty.

"I didn't give you to Jasper, Lucky." My eyes feel bright and wet when I look up at him. I smile, and taste tears on my lips. "You were already his. I just . . . borrowed you. For a little while."

His shoulders lift in a sharp, short breath, and he shakes his head.

"*No.* Eden, I panicked. That's all." He grasps my upper arms, so lightly, like he's not ready to let me go, and bends down to look me in the eyes. "Beautiful, if you want me to prove how much I want you, I'll do it right now. We can go upstairs, and I'll prove it to you in every position you can think of." He laughs, a little wild. "Or that I can think of—I'll show you every way."

The images come in a deluge—his strong, flexible body taking

me in a hundred obscene ways. A thousand. I turn away, needing
him to stop touching me.

I get so confused when he touches me.

And it's all hurting too much.

I brush my fingers over the breakfast bar where Jasper had him
spread out, and the marble is icy under my fingertips. My mouth
twists in self-deprecation.

"Now that he gave you permission?" I ask softly.

The lines of his throat go taut, and his eyes glisten. God. I
don't want him to cry. I don't want this for either of us.

But how can he not see?

I stare at him, anguished. "He'll always be your dominant.
Your sadist. I can't give you any of that. It hurts too much to come
in as less, Lucky. I've done it all my life, and I just . . . can't."

And just like that, I see his temper flare again.

I didn't even know Lucky had a temper.

"I'm not exactly jumping to dominate anyone lately either,
Eden." His tight expression isn't particularly kind, but his eyes are
full of pain. "Does that mean you'll always love Beau better
than me?"

My lips part in shock, but he's not done.

"Or what about Jayk? Do you have a tiered system? Which one
of us is your favorite then? Or is that why Jayk walked out?" he
snaps.

How *dare* he bring up Jayk now?

"No, of course not," I fire back, furious. And oddly defensive.
"This is different. I *told* Jaykob that I had feelings for all of you—
including him. *You* all made this stupid deal. You all made me love
you, and now what?" My brow crumples. I think my heart does
too. "It's awful, and I *hate* it. Heather was right. This whole idea
that we all might work was too ambitious. It's all too much."

And it hurts to realize it. It might kill me. Because how *am* I
meant to choose?

Surely, they'll have to do it. I can't. It would break me.

At Heather's name, Lucky rolls his eyes. "Sure, trust the woman who skewered half of our hearts and the rest of our egos. Great plan."

"Don't be facetious."

"You're a hypocrite." At the word, my back stiffens, and he smiles sourly. "How can you think it's possible for you to love multiple people just the same amount, but that I can't do the same? We're crazy complex people, Eden. Not everyone can be everything for someone. You and me, we can't be each other's dominants—but is that really the only thing you need from a partner?"

"Lucky, stop," I whisper.

He's pressing at my hopes, the things I'd started to believe. But I'm not the girl I was even a few weeks ago. I'm not one woman among five men.

I'm a wreck. A mess. And they have dozens of wonderful opportunities now at their doorstep. How can I keep all of them? How terribly selfish can I be?

Lucky lifts his hands, like he's begging me to see. His face is heartbreakingly earnest.

"No, I won't stop. You know I'm right. You need me too, Eden. The doms are heavy on their rules and orders. You need someone to be on *your* team, even when it doesn't make sense. You need someone to help you keep them in line—they always think it's the other way around, but us subbies know better. You need me to make you laugh, and someone to just play with, and someone to fuck sometimes with zero expectations. Because whatever they think, vanilla doesn't mean boring. Not always. Not when it's us."

I step back, and my back hits the breakfast bar. The plug is a mockery, a cruelty now. Because suddenly I'm thinking that Lucky would *know* what it feels like. And if things were different, maybe I could talk to him about it. If things were different, maybe he'd tease me about it. Maybe he'd want to see. Maybe he could explain the things I'm too embarrassed to ask Beau, but I know he would understand—like why the pressure is sometimes good and sometimes bad, and if it feels different when it's a cock and not a plug, and what to do when they're putting it in.

And I do want to spend hours and days making kimchi and laughing and learning new games. I want Jaykob to chase me and Lucky to hide me, Beau to comfort me and Dom to own me, and Jasper to shelter me at his feet.

I bury my face in my hands, my tears coming fast now. It's cruel of them to make me want it when it's not mine to have. Why is Lucky confusing me like this?

He stops in front of me, and I can feel his urgency.

"I need it too, Eden. I need *you*." His voice aches. "Jasper is one part of me, and he always will be. But I need you, Eden. Because he'll always be cold sometimes, and you're everything that's warm. He hurts me in ways that make me sing, but you always make me feel *good*. It's not about better, or more. You both make me dizzy. You both make me ache. And if I could spend the rest of my life loving both of you, I couldn't imagine one better spent."

I'm sobbing now, hopelessly confused.

Blurrily, I see him catch a teary breath, then wipe at his own cheeks.

Finally, he whispers, "I can't make decisions for you, sweetheart. This is your battle. But think about how you're going to have this same conversation with Jayk. How are you going to make him believe it if you don't believe it yourself?"

It might be my battle, but he's the one landing the blows. Each one devastating. Perfectly placed to kill.

I shake my head, holding it like I can keep it together with my hands alone. I'm straining at the seams.

"God, Eden," he chokes. "Your problem is that you don't think anyone would choose you—so you don't even let yourself believe that it could be real. Fuck Heather. Fight for yourself. Be brave." Lucky's voice softens. "I hate that anyone ever told you that you couldn't have it all."

I curl into myself at that, raw, pained sounds emptying out of me.

A hundred moments play in my head—all the times my hand was beaten for reaching, and wanting was called grasping, all the moments I was told to lower my eyes instead of lifting my chin. How they somehow made me less, and never more.

"I'm not going to sleep with Jasper, Eden. Not until you make a decision—because whatever you think, he's not first, and I need both of you to understand that before anything happens. It's both of you for me. It always will be."

I hear Lucky's deep breath.

"And one final thing," he rasps. "I know you don't want to see Jasper at the moment, either. But this way you're feeling? Angry, and out of control, and anxious, and all out of sorts? All the thoughts that are messing you up about whatever happened? It's called PTSD, and you need to see him about it. Think of it as a combat-given gunshot wound to your mental health. See a professional before you bleed the hell out in front of us."

My sobs cut off, and I pause. I lift my head, staring at him tensely.

How could he possibly know all of that?

I know PTSD exists, of course. But that has nothing to do with my guilt. Being a weak and terrible person is not a disorder. That's what this is, not . . . that.

Isn't it?

His sad, serious eyes meet mine, as if making sure I heard him. Then he nods.

As I watch him go, I wonder . . . how am I possibly meant to go to war for them, when I don't even have the courage to fight for myself?

CHAPTER 37

EVERYONE

SURVIVAL TIP #10
One week changed the world.
In one week, you can start changing yourself.

EDEN

I join the morning sparring sessions.

I'm weak and far behind the others—my playful sex-sparring with Jayk apparently didn't help me all that much with this. My mind is in chaos, my stomach pangs with hunger from the slim rations, I'm not sleeping, and my shame and anger might be eating me alive, but it feels . . . surprisingly good to take control of something again. To *fight*.

I feel good enough that I can laugh when Ethel plants me on my ass. I even feel good enough that I can ignore the snide jabs of the women about "musical beds" and "poor Jaykob." I ignore the washing soap going missing when it's time to clean my own clothes in the river, since we're still short a washing machine. I also ignore the card games and wine nights I'm not invited to.

It's harder to ignore Beau, Lucky, and Jasper as they all *happen to* stop by while I train—each of them offering their own words of encouragement. Or teasing, in Lucky's case.

And if I get flustered every time Dominic smiles at me, or corrects my stance, or brings me terrible coffee and walks with me afterwards, I'm managing it. He's still fighting with Beau, so it feels like the least I can do is sit with him for a while and listen to his worries—particularly since I'm the cause of half of them. I even try not to spend the whole time staring at him, though he's sinfully gorgeous when he lets his guard down.

Slowly, the idea of us being friends starts to feel less and less absurd.

It's Dom's grim tone when he talks about the food supplies that drives me to start replanting our garden. We don't have many seeds left, and they'll take a while to grow, but I need to do my part. As it always has, working with the earth soothes me in its own way.

Every time the shadows between the trees loom too large, or my mind begins conjuring men pouring from between them, or my guilt and shame starts a new spiral, I dig my hands deep into the earth and wait for the anxious sweat to stop soaking my spine.

Bristlebrook writhes with worry and expectation. The air is breathless, frenetic, and like Bristlebrook, I feel on the brink of *something*.

Change is coming.

Rather than the prospect frightening me, I feel almost . . . relieved. There is too much tension, lately. Too much uncertainty.

I'm ready for it to break.

Two days after I start sparring, I arrive back at my room to a thick textbook at my door. The words "PTSD" and "Workbook" leap out at me like an accusation, and it takes me a long muscle-screaming minute to convince my body to bend down to retrieve it.

Hesitantly, I open the cover, and a beautifully appointed letter falls out.

Dearest Eden,

I do hope you will forgive my presumption and take my gift as intended—as a gesture of care and deep affection. You've chosen to strengthen your body and arm it with new skills, and my greatest hope is that you will do the same with your mind.

Your curiosity is a beautiful strength, Eden. I know you believe in the power of knowledge—so let this be your first step. This textbook has a wealth of information, strategies, and exercises. I've left notes and tabs on sections I believe may be of particular use to you.

Please read, Eden. Learn. Question yourself. Know that your own thoughts can be your worst enemy, and above all, be kind to yourself.

That, as it happens, can be the hardest battle of all.

When you're ready, please come and talk to me. You're not alone. I am always here for you—at any hour and for any concern.
—Jasper

My fingers tremble as they run over his words. Then I flick through pages riddled with Jasper's notes. His secret language to me.

Jasper.

Rather than forcing me open like a clamshell and plundering my insides, he's put the control back in my hands. With a book and his notes, he's helping me in a way I can't refuse.

You're not alone.

I know I'm not.

I think of Jayk, so quick to help me with my anger. Dom, recognizing my guilt. Beau saw my need for safety, and Lucky my stress and sleeplessness. And now Jasper, delicately handling my confusion and fear.

My mind has been a bog I'm struggling to break free of—but I'm not caught in a camp of threats anymore. My brutes aren't dead. They're here with me, alive and waiting.

And all of them have been telling me the same thing.

It's time I started listening.

I settle back into bed, and flick on Beau's terribly ugly lamp—and I turn the first page.

JASPER

I turn a page of my book, soaking in the quiet peace of the library. Most of the civilians have settled into their beds for the night, and I have the room to myself.

Almost to myself.

"You're fidgeting," I murmur. I don't say it, but I know we both hear the silent, "*Again*."

Out of the corner of my eye, I see Lucien bite back a grimace and settle back into the Nadu position. He's on his knees, legs spread, his hands resting on his thighs, and his bare chest teases me.

It should be relaxing for us both—a deep balm after a long day. But despite the cushion I've allowed him to kneel upon, he looks like I've stuck him atop pine cones.

Lucien's gaze drifts up to me, and I raise a cool eyebrow at the impertinence.

He looks down quickly.

I close my book with a sigh. "Speak freely, Lucien."

His shoulders slump in relief and those blue eyes fly up to mine. "On a scale of one to ten, how much does this get you off?"

Get me . . .

I regard him dourly. "Right now, that would be a *one*."

The brat doesn't even have the grace to look bashful. "I'm bored. Wouldn't you rather go for a walk? Or I can show you how to do a cartwheel. That could be funny."

Lucien dimples, and I resist the urge to lick into the teasing divot. It's been four days since I returned to Bristlebrook and being with him—without sex—has been an education.

Infuriating. Delightful. Agonizing. Heart-aching.

But definitely infuriating.

"It's been five minutes." I regard him under my lashes. Even now, he fidgets. "You can't manage high protocol for *five minutes*?"

Lucien's head tilts. His dark blond hair spills over his shoulders in a way that calls for my fist.

"You could punish me for it?" His dimple deepens, and he pulls himself up toward me so slowly that it can be nothing but deliberate. "That could make this game more fun."

I watch with a raised, curious brow. Over the last few days, he's been testing me—and I suppose I have been doing the same. Our sadomasochistic dynamic has always come naturally and easily—and within a scene, our dominant-submissive dynamic has as well.

Outside of a scene, however, is another matter.

"This is not meant to be a game, Lucien," I chide gently, and he studies my face.

"Right. Sorry. I know. I can try—"

I cup his chin and smear the words against his lips, hard enough that his eyes widen, and he shudders, then licks my fingertips.

"Do not apologize for discussing boundaries," I say mildly. I sit back and rest my hand on my chin. "You've enjoyed high protocol during a scene—is that the extent of it, then? You derive no pleasure from it outside of the S&M dynamic?"

After a moment, he rests his chin on the arm of the chair and looks up at me ruefully. "When I say I would rather walk on hot coals for you than sit still at your feet for hours, I mean it with every bit of sincerity."

My lips curl reluctantly, and I hope I manage to withhold the slight sting of disappointment. I deeply enjoy those lovely, quiet moments with a submissive—when the world falls away and we can lose ourselves to the simplest, most stripped-back form of the dynamic. Care and control. Not for pain or need or force. Just for the pleasure of being together in a way that serves us both.

But the pleasure only comes from mutual enjoyment.

I can do without this.

"Perhaps I could have guessed that this wouldn't be your forte." I stroke his hair back off his forehead to show him I'm teasing, and his dimples test me again.

A mischievous light infects his smile. "You know, it takes a pretty self-involved dom to think any sub finds them interesting enough to stare at their toes for three hours."

With his fear of rejection ebbing, his hesitance and stammering have ebbed too. And unleashed, Lucien's confidence is deadly. I'm almost helpless to resist him like this. His relentless flirting is an assault against my self-control, and he seems to now delight in surprising me—and in *pushing* me.

The brattiness is getting out of hand. He's taunting me now, all but begging for a punishment that would leave him shattered and coated in his own cum—or in mine.

But though we both crave the delicious, chilling tension of an S&M scene, I'm not willing to tempt fate. I am as determined as he is to make sure he keeps his promise to Eden.

"Perhaps I am self-involved. Or perhaps this just takes a submissive who has an attention span longer than thirty seconds." I lean down toward him. "You could use the opportunity to think on grander things, Lucien. Philosophy. Poetry. Or if you don't have the patience for that, then perhaps you could spend a few hours thinking of all the ways you could spread yourself out so that you can get fucked like the rapacious little brat you are."

Heat steals over Lucien's face, the color searing his cheeks—but he laughs softly as he looks at me. "Well, my homework is done, professor. I've already spent years thinking of every single way I want you to fuck—"

Need slices through me, and I kiss the confession from his mouth.

When he sighs, I tighten my hand in his silky, playful hair and ravage him deeper, harder, until he softens under me. Until that sigh becomes a groan. Answering heat curls in my abdomen. My cock hardens so quickly it's almost painful.

Apart from fucking Lucien's mouth to orgasm last month, I haven't come into anything but my own hand in almost six years—long before Day Death was even on the horizon.

And I *need*.

Still, when Lucien's hand begins to slide up my thigh, I catch his wrist and wrench my mouth away. I stare at his glistening lips and tighten my grip until he gasps. His eyes brighten at the small hurt, becoming luminous as streaking stars.

It's impossible not to think of how that hot, greedy mouth felt around my cock, but I force myself to push the thoughts away.

I meet his gaze, and she hangs there between us—the answer to *why*, and *stop*, and *no more*.

"Do you think she'd like this?" Lucien whispers into the heavy silence. "Seeing us like this?"

That gives me pause. Neither of us missed her arousal when she saw us in the kitchen. I've never been particularly prone to public displays, but that day Lucien had tempted me past bearing, rubbing up against me, teasing me, and I'd snapped, pinning him where anyone could walk in.

But the idea of Eden's nervous eyes on us has an almost brutal appeal.

"I think," I say, with a last tenuous thread of control, "if she saw us right now, she might claw my eyes out."

That gets a reaction.

Lucien pulls back with a groan, and I release him. He reaches down and adjusts his hard, desperate length in his pants. I watch the move avidly.

"This is going to kill me. I'm going to be so backed up, cum is going to explode from my eyeballs and that's how I'll die."

If I'm to draw no satisfaction from my palm, it hardly feels fair he should be able to from his.

I stroke a finger along his jaw. "As long as you don't ruin the upholstery, darling."

He smirks for a moment, but then it fades.

I watch it disappear with a low throb in my chest, then stand. He takes my hand, and when he stands, I pull him against my chest. I wish Eden were here too—that I could hold them both close, and safe, and beautifully together.

But it's up to her now. I've done all I can for her until she comes to see me. And she will. I have to believe it.

She's been incredible this week.

I may be too emotionally compromised to be an impartial psychologist for her, but I can help her as a friend. I will help her however I can.

"It will work out, Lucien. She'll come back to . . ." *Us.* I swallow down the hazardous word. "To you."

Lucky sighs, then nods against me.

"Come now," I murmur. "Let's get you to bed."

I lead him to Dominic's room and let him go reluctantly, with lingering kisses—and extra, always extra, for all the years I missed.

I close the door behind him, thinking of the day I'll be bringing him to my own bed instead.

LUCKY

The door swings open in front of me, but it's the wrong face.

Beau's eyes drop to the cheese in my hands, then he lifts them back up to my face. He steps out of the room and presses his back against the closed door, barring the way in.

"Darn it, Lucky. Aren't you meant to be in charge of rations?" he says in exasperation. "How do you think things are going to go for her if the others catch on that you're sneaking her cheese? They're already on her ass about Jayk."

All the more reason Eden could use some cheese. Damn it, I know I shouldn't be here. I've been trying to give her space. But it's been days, and all I've had from her are these long, thoughtful looks from a distance.

The waiting is killing me.

Beau raises his brows, and I give him my most winning smile.

"Well, who says this is for Eden? Maybe I brought it for you, buddy. You've been working hard lately." I assume. I actually have no clue what Beau has been up to. I wave my hand, taking a stab. "Doctoring . . . and things."

His lips curl up as he nods knowingly. "Now, you're right. I have been working hard."

"It's what I've been telling everyone." I shrug.

Beau plucks the folded cloth from my hands and unwraps the cheese. Watching me, he picks it up and takes a bite. An *enormous* bite.

I bite my tongue to strangle my protest, my foot starting to tap anxiously.

Still watching me, he raises the cheese to his lips again, and I can't take it. I snatch it out of his hands.

"What is *wrong* with you?" I scold, as I inspect the damage. Jesus. Has he always had such gigantic beaver teeth? I glare at him. "Don't you want her to be happy? You'll just eat all of it? Just gobble all of her joy away, bite by bite. That's the last bit, you know!"

Beau pokes my chest. "Stop trying to manipulate our girlfriend with cheese!"

"*Our?*" Hope crashes through me. I grab his poking hand. "Has she said something?"

"Give her some time, Lucky. She's working through a lot right now."

The haunted look on his face only worries me more.

"We might not have time," I say softly.

I know what the eve of battle feels like. It might be days, or even weeks, but all this planning, all this energy, is building toward the break. Sooner or later, this tension will burst.

And who knows who will survive it.

BEAU

We're not going to survive this.

I've been going over our inventory list of med supplies, and what seemed like a lot for six people is not much of anything for over ninety. The good stuff will be locked away, and we have enough bandages and over-the-counter items to last for a little while, but if we're hit hard, we're going to need to start making some tough decisions on where resources go.

For the last week, I've been treating person after person for lumps and bruises, rotten teeth and hangnails, mis-healed bones, malnutrition, you name it. For what they've been through, they're in good shape.

It's just not fighting shape.

Someone pounds again on the door to our room, and I grit my teeth. I know who it is. Only one person pounds on a door like that at eleven at night.

"Open up, Beau. It's been four days; this is getting ridiculous."

I re-roll a long strip of cloth, not looking at the door.

On the bed, Eden looks up from her book and rests her pencil and pad of paper on her knee. She looks at me, her big eyes damp and red-rimmed, like they often are when she works through Jasper's book.

I shake my head at her, and she sighs.

"I need to talk to you—as captain. At the very least, respect that."

Like pulling the captain card has ever worked on me outside of combat.

My lips thin, and I refocus on the bandage. If Dom really needs anything medical sorted, he can talk to Clare or Leanne—the two nurses of the group—or Deanna, the ex-primary care physician. They know every person in this camp better than I do, and they've all been working with me day in and day out.

There's a soft *thunk* against the door, then a heavy sigh. "Beau, please . . . I need you."

My throat grows thick, and I look at the door. He *doesn't* need me. He proved that when he decided to nuke The Plan.

At the end of the day, it's not even about Heather.

Dom didn't choose Eden. Not after she saved our lives, not after the river, not after the battle for Bristlebrook. He didn't even choose her after running after her for weeks, knowing what almost happened. Not one of her amazing qualities are enough for him, not even knowing that I'm head over ass in love with her, and that all three of us could have had it all.

We're not enough for him.

And I've finally realized, he's not enough for us.

I feel Eden's eyes on me, then she throws the covers back and walks to the door.

"Eden," I say warningly, but she gives me a tight, unhappy look.

"You're being unfair."

Ignoring my scowl, she opens the door and steps into the frame to talk to him.

Their voices are too low for me to hear, but I can see them. She's holding her nightgown closed at the neck to hide the deep cleavage. Dom leans against the doorframe above her, looking huge and imposing above her delicate figure.

They look good together.

They could have been great.

After a moment, he drops his arm and straightens, then squeezes her shoulder before he leaves.

Eden steps back inside and looks at me.

I throw down the bandage and pick up another one. "Leave it be, darlin'."

She comes to settle in beside me, and she stops my hand on the half-rolled fabric. Her hair is loose and tumbling all about her, and it smells like jasmine. She leaves it out for me, even though it takes her twice as long to care for in the morning.

"He's your best friend, Beau."

I look at her hand on mine, sweet and soft. "I'm tired of being a better friend to him than he is to me. I'm tired of wanting it more than he does."

"Beau." The hand squeezes. "He keeps coming right back to that door because he *does* want it."

Not enough.

"He told me about your 'Plan,'" she says. "How you both wanted to find someone together? I'm . . . sorry. That I couldn't be the one."

Myocardial infarction. My heart stalls painfully in my chest.

Turning, I look her in the eyes. "This is why, Eden. You *are* the one. You're everything. And if he can't see that, he's stupider than I realized. He doesn't deserve you."

Pink touches her cheeks in a gentle caress. I see her throat work as she swallows, looking away.

"He's allowed to want other things. He's been a good friend to me since the rescue." Her thumb strokes my hand. "Don't lose him over me, Beau. You two can be friends without me between you."

The pink in her cheeks darkens to a deep flush—the shade it gets only when she's embarrassed . . . or squirming with need.

"You know, I don't think I can remember even having a relationship without him," I confess. "Sometimes I wonder if that's why we always failed. Neither one of us knew how to be a whole person for someone, and I think we always knew, if it came down to it, we'd choose each other. No one was ever more important than us. Jasper called us codependent."

A small frown appears between her brows, and she looks up again to watch my face.

I run a knuckle over the lines.

"I think it's time he and I had a break. We've been trying and failing for so long, and I can't afford to fail this time. Because it's you." She looks like a tired angel, so beautiful it wrecks my heart. As I touch her, the lines soften. Smooth out. "I'm going to love you right, darlin'—even if it takes a lifetime to work out how. I'm not having him wreck it."

I lean down and brush my lips against hers.

Eden sighs into my kiss. I can tell she wants to say more, that she doesn't agree, but I can't hear it right now. We kiss for long enough that she grows soft and needy underneath me, and I take her slow right there on the couch.

After I tuck her into bed, I go and stand at the window to watch the half-moon in the sky—and I waste hours wishing it were whole.

DOMINIC

The half-moon casts its sad beams over our defenses.

The tents rustle in the night, buffeted by a slow wind. Around Bristlebrook, the dry moat is hollow and unfinished, and the wooden spears piled beside it are dull and uncarved. There are two wooden vantages half-built on either side of the lodge—placed so we can fire on an invading force if they try to make it past the moat. That is, if they're finished in time.

We have pit-traps and explosives on trips—all exposed and deactivated for now.

But it's not going to matter.

If the Sinners descend on us in force, we might be able to hold them off. Maybe. But a lot of these people are going to die. Sam has the duffel of explosives that Eden took from Lucky's stash. And with SEAL-trained Alastair and Mateo giving advice on strategy, those are going to do some damage no matter how I slice it.

If they're really smart, the Sinners will just wait us out—we don't have enough food to keep these people from starving under a siege.

In the shadow of the porch, where no one can see me, I grip my head in my hands as the dread takes over.

These people are going to die . . . and I don't know how to save them.

I sit there for a long time, until finally, movement catches my eye. Heather walks from tent to tent, checking on the inhabitants one by one. Some are silent, but she stops and talks to others. Laughing with them. Reassuring them.

In an odd way, it reassures me too.

I think of Jasper telling me I take on too much responsibility. He understands better than most how hard it is for me to give up control, but maybe I haven't been trying hard enough . . . because he was right.

These people aren't military, but they are good at what they do. Heather drew these people together and kept them there, and she's doing a damn good job.

Better than I ever did.

I look around Bristlebrook again, and rather than seeing everything unfinished, I see everything that *has* been done. It's been one week, and they've accomplished so much. They're organized. We have hunting teams and fishing teams, the medical team, the supply team. We have maintenance teams and rations teams. After I mentioned my concern over food, Eden started working on a new vegetable garden, too.

Somehow, despite the rations, despite the danger, despite their unhappiness, these civilians are holding together . . . and it has nothing to do with me.

The night breeze teases over me. It's crisp and free, and charged with the turn of a new season. Mary Beth grins up at Heather as she moves on, in a proud, easy way no civilian has ever looked at me, and it finally hits me.

Maybe I'm *not* the king.

Maybe I never was.

Maybe I'm just general to the queen.

Heather is the one holding the community together. She's working on their problems—on the lack of food and shelter, on their fears and feelings.

Maybe I just need to focus on my one job.

I need to figure out a way to save us from Sam.

JAYKOB

"Will this be enough to save them?" Kasey asks, her hands buried in the back of the camera.

Ava shines the flashlight over the machinery as I cross my arms.

"Just screw the cap back on," I mutter.

We've been gone for five days, and the distance is starting to itch at me. I don't like thinking of anything happening while I'm not there.

The kid's face screws up in concentration until the cap clicks into place. Then she turns it, spotting the pivoting lens that says the camera is active.

"Nailed it!" She stands, handing it over to me with a smirk. "Told you I could do it myself."

I shrug off my dark mood.

"What do you want? A trophy?" I secure the camera high on

the tree we agreed on as Ava and Sloane nudge the girl in congratulations.

Akira hangs back, stone-faced and disengaged as she has been since we left. I know the look, and she's too fucked with grief to be much good to anyone right now. Been there. She's moving at least, which is something.

I look the camera over before I step back. It was tight work—Kasey handled the tools well. For someone who only saw it done twice before, she picked it up fast.

Ava and Sloane stand protectively over Kasey, giving me identical, expectant looks over her head. I scowl at them. Sloane cracks her tattooed knuckles.

The kid looks up at me, then shrugs. "Yeah, whatever. It doesn't matter. Can we get the next one tonight? You said it's south, right?"

She looks down at the compass I gave her. The one I *only* gave her because she kept asking me every other minute which way we were fucking going.

"You did a good job," I mutter. "For a rookie."

Her excited eyes fly up to me, and I hate that they make me panic, every time. Ryan used to get that look whenever Mom came back in after one of her episodes with an armful of candy she couldn't afford. His eyes would shine as he ate, and hers would be tight and anxious as she checked the trailer for damage. Damage she never found because I always cleaned up before she got there.

Mom had shit hard enough without worrying about that too.

My family has always been a clusterfuck and a half. I don't know why this kid has attached itself to me like a baby koala, but if she wants a big brother, she'd be better off clinging onto Lucky.

Or *Beau*.

Kasey grins at me. "It's cool. I'll take your rations as payment." She saunters south. "You know, since I'm doing your job for you and all."

Ava laughs and winks as she passes me, then Akira follows. Sloane falls in beside me, and I give her an irritated sideways look.

"Home stretch now," she muses.

I grunt noncommittally. Maybe the biggest surprise of this trip has been that I don't actually hate Ava and Sloane. They can handle themselves. They get shit done with minimal fuss, and they talk around me easily—looping me in or not without missing a beat. The only thing they ride my ass about is coddling the tweeny-bopper's feelings.

It's made for a low-key trip, but now Sloane's wrecking it— giving me those long, you-should-talk-to-me glances.

"I don't do girl talk," I tell her, and scowl at how defensive it sounds.

"Jesus fucking Christ, dude." She scowls back. "Girl talk? Get the fuck out of here with that."

We walk together for ten more minutes before I start to wonder if I pissed her off.

"If you need to girl talk, you can do it," I mutter. "But don't expect me to hug you or anything."

I only just catch her elbow before it hits my ribs, and she snorts. "Not me, idiot. *You*."

I shove her away, but her muscles are solid, and she doesn't shift far. Her thighs are like steel weights, and I wonder for a moment how much she can lift.

I stalk around her, and she follows.

"You have a plan for how to deal with your pretty librarian when you finally stop running away from home?" she asks, then huffs a sigh when I stiffen. "Yeah, yeah, I know. Not my business— except that you aired your shit in front of everyone, so now you have to deal with people taking sides."

"What sides?" I snap a branch in front of me with too much force.

"You know, you versus Eden versus this doctor guy," Sloane

scoffs. "I, for one, say fuck the doctor off. Biggest, most fragile egos on the goddamned planet."

Me *versus* Eden?

My stomach sours at the idea. She's been fun to tussle with and throw around. She gets this determined little scrunch to her face when she comes after me, and her fists still feel like eggshells cracking against my abs, but there's nothing cute about her fury. That comes from the cold deep, and it's easy as hell to see it's been on a slow burn for a long time. It's the fury that killed half a camp of men—and I *know* she didn't just kill them to get herself free, whatever she told the others.

She killed them for us.

For *me*.

Fighting with her feels like shit. She should be chained to my fucking side and happy to be there.

She fits there.

I wonder if the *doctor* has made her scream yet. She comes like a freight train for me. There's no way he can fuck her better than I can. Girl is primal as shit. She *needs* what I give her.

Sloane doesn't seem to care that I haven't said anything. She adds casually, "For what it's worth, any girl who cheats is a piece of shit. I liked her, I did, but if you—"

"She didn't cheat." I want to suck the words back in—I'm not plaiting daisy chains here, and Sloane should mind her own business.

But I don't want this shit getting around about Eden.

Sloane looks puzzled, teasing her lip piercing with her tongue. "She didn't? Did you guys break up then?"

"She was with all of us," I mutter.

"Wait, she . . .? *All* of you?" Sloane stares at me, her mouth dropping open as she processes that. Finally, she snorts, shaking her head. "Well, damn. Okay. Get it."

Her amusement pisses me off. I stop and glower at her. "You even think of crawling up her ass about that, I'll shoot you."

She flips me off. "Not my style. But shit, Jayk. If you knew she was with him, then what the hell is up *your* ass?"

I shrug, watching her warily. Is this girl talk? It's got more cussing than I thought.

Then Sloane groans.

"Fuck," she curses, rubbing the back of her neck. "I thought she was the asshole. But it's you. You're the asshole."

I scowl. "I ain't the asshole—*she* shacked up with *him*."

"The old takebacksies rule. Gotcha." Sloane rolls her eyes. "Come on, man. You can't agree to share and then get mad when she does."

"What's keeping you guys? It's already late. Can we keep it moving?" Ava appears between the trees, then looks between us. "Well, he looks like he's trying to shit a brick sideways, so this is clearly going well."

"What's going well?" Kasey wanders out behind her, then Akira, who doesn't look my way.

My shoulders hunch more and more with every glance.

"Turns out, Eden didn't cheat. She's with both of them, and he's backing out and getting mad at her for still being into her other partner," Sloane just blurts in front of everyone.

I glare at all of them. This is why I don't talk about shit.

Ava winces, then gives me a disappointed look. "That's rough, Jayk."

"She's *mine*," I snap.

Ava and Sloane exchange sympathetic glances that make me want to punch a tree.

"It's not just about fucking around anymore. She has to choose." My mouth twists. "And it's not going to be me."

There's always been this hard, bitter ball that lives in my chest. Right now it feels cracked open, leaking acid through my insides.

I really thought she might do it for a minute there. I thought it might be us.

But it only took two minutes back at Bristlebrook to remember I'm bottom of the damn pack.

"You're way better than that other guy," Kasey says, crossing her arms over her chest. "Just tell her you like her. It's all about the confidence, you know?"

"They tell you that on Sesame Street?" I ask, matching her stance, and she makes a face at me.

"She's kind of right, though." Ava looks me up and down. "The pity party? Not hot."

I glare at her too, even though I know she's right. It's part of why I came out in the damn woods—so I could wallow in peace.

"If you want her to give up multiple dudes just for you, you're going to have to put *up*," Sloane says dubiously from my other side.

"Fix the hair," Ava agrees.

"The clothes." Sloane nods.

"The *face*," Kasey chimes in with a shudder.

"What's wrong with my *face*?" I rub my jaw. They were never going to slap me on a magazine cover, but I haven't broken any mirrors lately either.

"You really should wash it," Kasey whispers.

Fourteen-year-olds are assholes.

"We'll help you," Sloane says, like she's doing me some big-ass favor.

"I didn't ask you to," I growl.

"Someone has to," Ava mutters. Then she claps her hands. "You have skills, my man. You're smart. You're not atrocious looking. You're a decent as fuck human. You just need some . . . sprucing."

Sloane walks over and claps my shoulder, hard enough that I grunt.

"Operation: Jayk Gets the Girl is a go."

CHAPTER 38

DOMINIC

SURVIVAL TIP #174
Stepping up sometimes means stepping down.

My door slams open, and I have my gun up and pointed at Heather's head before her face registers. When it does, I cock the pistol back, raising a brow at her appearance.

Her hair is wild and damp around her—and the top half of it is a screaming, vivid blue. It streaks down in marred, uneven lines through the rest of her red hair.

I step back with a sigh, holstering my pistol. "Lucky, it's for you."

"Huh?" Lucky steps out of the bathroom, pinning his hair up with more flowers. When he sees Heather, he staggers to a halt.

"*You.*" Her eyes spit fire.

Lucky pastes a wide, innocent smile on his face.

"*Moi?*" He frowns up at her hair, clicking his tongue. "Blue is not your color, is it?"

I catch Heather as she launches for him, then settle her back on her feet. As much as I've decided to back off her on the alpha pissing contest, I'm getting really fucking sick of playing interference between her and the guys. Honestly, I'm not sure who's worse, and I'm exhausted enough right now.

I've spent all day poring over maps and our inventory lists, trying to work out how to gain an edge, looking at potential escape routes if we're put under siege, organizing lists of who will be on direct ground combat, resupply and support, or remote engagement.

But on the upside, this is the first time I've seen Lucky brighten up without Jasper in the room. His conversation with Eden left him wrecked. As his roommate, I heard all about it.

And not by choice.

Eden herself hasn't said a word.

"I'm not going to kill him, Dom." Heather tries to wrestle out of my hold. "I'll just take an arm. Or maybe his hair. See how he likes *that*."

She catches me with a sharp elbow to the kidney, and I grunt, then throw her back.

"Lay off, Heather." Then I glare at Lucky. "One more move like this, and I'll move you out onto the lawn—and you'll lose shower access."

He crosses his arms over his chest, and his smile is punchably smug. "Jasper won't let that happen. Jasper *likes* me showered."

"I'll shower you myself, if necessary."

My eyes cut to Jasper as he appears in my door, leaning against the frame with studied elegance. I point to him, exasperated. "You, control your subbie."

Jasper arches one cool brow at me, then looks Heather over. A small, vicious smile lights his lips as his gaze lingers on her blue hair. He spreads his hands. "He *is* a brat. Alas. What *am* I to do?"

For fuck's sake.

Heather glares at them, but at least she's stopped trying to attack Lucky.

My headache returns with a vengeance. Funny enough, it seems to come back every time these three are in proximity.

"Are you here for a reason?" I ask him tiredly. Five days of hard labor to get Bristlebrook in shape after two weeks of relentless foot travel will do that.

Jasper nods. "It appears Jaykob has the last camera we agreed upon online. He and the others should be back here in about two days. They looked well."

"Good." I rub a hand over my head. That's one less thing to worry about at least.

"Two days?" Lucky glances around at us, and the light fades from his blue eyes. "That's the anniversary of Day Death. It's been five years."

We all fall still.

Day Death.

The night of the strikes was the worst night of my life. Not that I'm special—it was the worst night of most people's lives.

The guys and I were all at Darkside, the kink club we used to frequent. All of us . . . except for Beau, who was out of town visiting his family.

That night, I was on monitoring duty—I was watching over a primal hunt in the gardens while everything went down. When the hunt was done, I came back in to a nightmare. The usually dim club was lit up in fluorescents and the emergency broadcast was blaring over the speakers, reciting every city and town and military base that had been hit by the initial ICBMs.

That list included Beau's hometown.

For a full ten minutes, I thought my whole life was over. We were getting dozens of messages from my father, Colonel Slade, to return to base, the civilians at the club were in hysterics, Jasper and Lucky were trying to call their families—and I couldn't focus on any of it.

Not until Beau just waltzed his oblivious ass right into the club.

By pure fucking luck, he'd left home early that morning and drove through the day to get back to town, listening to some stupid-ass unsolved mysteries podcast so intently that he hadn't turned on his goddamned radio.

My soul left my body when I realized he was okay.

And part of his died when he realized his family wasn't.

The rest of that night is a blur of fighting and fire and returning to base only to find it already destroyed . . . the Colonel and my mother with it.

I try not to think about it—the whole thing was a shit storm anyway—but every year on the anniversary of Day Death, we always do something.

I didn't realize it had come up so fast.

Lucky swallows hard. He shifts toward Jasper, then hesitates, glancing at him.

Jasper gives him a look under his lashes, and Lucky relaxes. Jasper hooks a finger in his belt loop and draws him close.

"We should hold a bond-fire," Lucky suggests as he settles in.

Bond-fire?

"You mean a bonfire?" I give Lucky a flat look. "Don't you think we have enough to do without adding a party to it?"

"That's exactly why we should do it," Lucky argues, and the red creeps up his cheeks as Jasper keeps watching him in that same heavy-lidded way. "Everyone needs to blow off some steam. Things are too tense. We should shake it up—give them something to *bond* over, beyond all the shitty memories. And I don't know a quicker way to bond people than drunken fireside shenanigans. So, a *bond*-fire."

Sounds like a quick way to overload the med bay.

"I think Bristlebrook has seen enough fire." I turn to Heather. "Did you get a list of med supplies from Beau?"

At this point, he's more likely to talk to her than he is to me. After our argument the first day, he hasn't spoken to me once.

I brought Eden home, safe and sound, and all Beau can do is knot himself up over Heather. Without even talking to me, he decided I left him again. He doesn't care enough to even hear me out. Doesn't give a shit that between Sam and the civilians and all this crushing responsibility, I feel like I'm choking on my own panic. He hasn't thought for one second about anything but his damn self and what he *thinks* is happening between me and Heather. I don't move fast enough on Eden, and apparently, I'm done.

Like I have the luxury to sit down and think about anything but keeping these people alive. We *need* to be worrying about the camp. The civilians. Working as a damn team to get the job done.

At least Heather seems on board with that plan—even if we do keep slamming our heads against one another like rams fighting for top spot. I can't remember if it always felt like this with her, or if fucking her used to make it better.

But I don't feel like fucking her, that's for damn sure.

Instead of answering me, Heather is looking thoughtfully at Lucky.

"He might not have the worst idea," she says begrudgingly. She looks up at me. "Everyone needs to de-stress. Morale is down, and that's always a hard day. This could help a lot. Plus, there's the whole Eden thing . . ."

"What Eden thing?" I frown.

The look Heather gives me is dry enough for tumbleweed. "The civilians hating her thing."

"Oh that. I've been trying to get them to stop." Lucky sighs.

Jasper grimaces as he plays with the ends of Lucky's hair. "As have I. They're quite stubborn about it."

At my confusion, Heather gives me a pitying look. "How have you not noticed? You really are oblivious to anything but barricades and inventory." Heather's lips curve in a sly smile. "Well. That and a certain librarian. You know she prefers you in the red shirt, by the way."

Like I care.

I give her an irritated look as I think back to my conversations with Eden. At some point every day since she's been back, we've wound up having coffee together.

We've mostly talked about logistics. The people giving me trouble. Whether I've eaten that day. Come to think of it, I've done most of the talking. She's been the only thing keeping me sane.

But she hasn't said a thing about anyone hating her.

I glare at all of them. "*What* Eden thing? Who the hell doesn't like *Eden*?"

I shove away the memories of me ready to drag her out of Bristlebrook. That was different. I didn't know her then. Eden's quiet about all the ways she's special—she keeps the focus on everyone else. Drawing them together. Building them up.

Who the fuck is trying to tear her down?

Heather pats my chest. "Pitchforks away, CC. They're just mad she chose Beau over Jayk. They'll get over it."

I bat her hand away and look at my blue shirt. Come to think of it, this one is a little tight.

"She didn't choose Beau over Jayk," I point out as I go to find a new shirt. What is this high school bullshit? "Tell them to pull their heads out of their asses and mind their own business."

"I'm sure that'll work a treat." Heather leans back against an armchair, rolling her eyes. "I don't know what to tell you. They like Jayk. They have fun teasing him. He lets Kasey trail around after him. He's been helping people pack up and put down their camps. Apparently, him being a crabby-ass loose cannon doesn't bother them. I can only imagine it's because they're hard up for some di—"

"I helped them too," I mutter.

I've done nothing *but* help them. Doesn't seem to matter. They either seem scared of me or they annoy the shit out of me about a thousand different things.

Lucky laughs, pulling away from Jasper. He slings his gun around his chest—he's out on hunting duty today.

"Jayk helps. You . . . organize," Lucky says diplomatically, then adds with a grin. "Loudly."

I hesitate as I pull on my last red shirt.

That really is how they see me.

I sigh. "Fine, set it up. Whatever. Let people get drunk and fall into a firepit. A few less civilians for me to deal with." Pausing again, I look at Heather and grimace. "For *us* to deal with. If that works for you?"

Heather's brows couldn't creep up any higher short of flying off her face. "Yeah. That works for me."

I stalk toward the door, and Heather follows. We have a lot to go over today.

"Oh, and Heather?" Lucky calls.

Heather glances back at Lucky as she reaches the door. He dimples sweetly, looking up at her hair. "You call my boyfriend a middle-aged washout again, and your hair won't be blue. It will be gone."

She leans back, smiling back just as sweetly. Her hair really is fucked. "You touch my hair again, and I'll snip off the end of every flogger, break every cane, and burn every rope in your smutty little cock cave."

Heather finger waves at Lucky's horrified stare, then drags me out. We make our way out to the lawn where the teams should be gathering to get their instructions for the day. I find myself glaring at the civilians as we leave the house, wondering if they're the ones giving Eden a hard time.

"What?" Heather prompts as we make it into the crisp air.

I look down at her. "What?"

She scoffs, then walks us over to the coffee table that gets set up every day. We don't have enough goat's milk to waste on coffee, or any sugar, so it's just black instant sludge. I don't feel like lining my stomach with battery acid today, so I watch her have at it.

"I've been talking to you for five minutes about shooting practice and who is ready, and you haven't listened to a single word."

She has? I grimace, eyeing her. Finally, I blurt, "Why is everyone so invested in Eden's relationships? She's had a hard enough time already. She doesn't need this shit."

Her twitching lips are instantly annoying. "Dom, I'm guessing things were a bit . . . intense . . . when Eden got here, right? The first time, I mean."

I cross my arms as she pours herself a tepid cup. "Why would you say that?"

She gives me an amused look, her brows quirked pityingly in a way that usually means she thinks I'm being dense.

"Five men with too much testosterone who hadn't seen a woman in over three years?" Her voice becomes droll. "Just a guess."

I roll my eyes. "It was civilized."

Sort of. There was only one brawl over it.

Heather snorts into her cup, grimacing as she tastes it. We start making our way through the tents when she continues. "Look, there are eighty-five women here and only seven men—and all of those men are already taken. Except Aaron, and *ugh*. Even excluding the ones who don't give a shit about you one way or another, there's some interest in your availability."

That almost stops me short. I stare at her as we walk. "*What?*" I shake my head. "You're off base. No one has approached me."

Heather laughs, and a few heads turn to look at us. "Yeah, okay, CC. Except they *have* been approaching you. Didn't you wonder why Mila kept asking you about the moat? How to hold the shovel, how deep she should dig, my God, you're so clever for thinking of it . . ."

She makes a face.

Mila . . . The name doesn't shake anything free, but I do remember being interrupted half a dozen times yesterday.

"I thought she was just stupid," I mutter. Who asks three times if their hole is to my liking?

Oh. Right. Maybe she *was* flirting.

"What does that have to do with Eden?"

She shrugs. "Jayk and Beau, that's two out of five into her—people think it's a little greedy. Jasper and Lucky seem off limits to them, for obvious reasons. That only leaves you, who terrifies half of them, unless they can convince Jayk to give them a comfort fuck."

"Jesus fucking Christ."

Why are people even thinking about this when they have their lives to worry about? Getting laid isn't *that* good.

For some reason, the image of Eden on Beau's lap pops into my mind. An image of the river follows, her hands all over me, her little squeaks as I laid my hand against her ass.

I shake my head, then look at Heather as we draw to a halt. Her eyes scan the lawn, cataloging the half-dug dry moat, the half-built barricades, the people hurrying around.

"You haven't come on to me once." I'm not really sure why I say it. Or why I'm saying it *now*. I don't even know how I feel about it.

It should make me feel something, right?

Heather shoots me a sideways look, studying my face. I study hers back.

She's still beautiful. Not in a model way or a cute way. Her gray eyes are sharp as a hawk's, her mouth is a little too large. Her cheekbones are pointed, and her jaw is a touch too strong to be too feminine. It's all a bit out of balance, but it works. It's striking. Strong.

It's doing absolutely nothing for me.

"You haven't come on to me either," she says. Her mouth curves up on one side, then she turns back to the lawn and sips her coffee. She sighs quietly. "I loved him, Dom. So much it hurt to breathe around him. Even though he's dead, I just . . . I still choose him."

Thomas. I look at her profile—her expression is dark, turbulent. Of course she's still cut up over him. It's only been a few months, and Heather loves hard.

I wait for the jealousy, but that doesn't come either. I only feel sad for her. I nudge her shoulder with mine. I'm not good at comforting people, but she smiles up at me anyway, like she's trying to shake it off.

"Now, I might not have been opposed to a sympathy fuck." Heather grins mischievously. "But I wouldn't do my girl dirty like that."

Her girl?

I give her a puzzled look. "Is this about that Mila chick? Because I don't—"

Heather laughs, cutting me off. "You seriously need to get out of battle mode." She turns me to face the other direction, toward the trees. "I'll give you a minute, but you'll spot her."

I'm about to cut this conversation off, seeing the teams starting to gather on the lawn, when I see her. Eden is trying to balance three shovels over her shoulder, and two duffels. At least three people walk past without helping her. I frown as she drops one of the shovels, looking frazzled.

She still has those tired rings under her eyes. Jasper tells me she still hasn't been to see him. Stubborn little brat.

"She's kind of great, Dom. I don't even know if she likes me that much, but you should have seen her in the camp, keeping her head down, playing it smart. She was patient—and then she was fucking ruthless. She saved my life more than once out there." Heather's voice is quiet, a little wondering. "She wants you, you know. I feel the need to point that out, since you apparently have the self-awareness of a hamster on a wheel."

I give Heather a sharp look, but my gaze drifts back to Eden. I know she's attracted to me—even I'm not that oblivious. But she was the one to declare us *friends*. Is she just waiting for me to make a move? Or does it end at wanting me to fuck her?

That's usually how it goes with the nice ones Beau and I have tried to share. They fall for him, and they just put up with me for the sex.

I don't think she'd do that though. The more I talk to her, the more I like her.

She doesn't ever act like she wants to bail on me to find Beau.

"Lock her down, Dom. She'll choose you over Jayk or Beau if you play it right. You're the better choice."

Stiffening, I give her a hard look. "Can it. She wants them both, and they want her. I know sharing never worked for you, Heather, and that's fine, but it's her choice."

Her blue-tinged copper hair swings as she shakes her head and tuts. "If she ends up with three of you, you'll be lucky if these women don't napalm her pussy just to get some action. This is the end of days, CC. These people are great, but they're horny as hell." Her snort is derisive. "Look, do what you want. Share or don't share—it's your life. But lock. Her. Down."

Heather touches my arm, and Eden looks over right at that moment. The other shovels tumble, and she has to drop the duffels to avoid them whacking her in the face.

I stifle a smile.

Turning, I pluck Heather's coffee out of her hands, and start walking toward Eden.

"Wait! I didn't mean *now*. We have a meeting!" she calls after me, exasperated.

I turn around, walking backwards.

"You don't need me," I call back, loud enough that several heads turn our way. I chuck her a salute, then add, "Boss."

Heather stares at me, stunned, and I grin as I turn back around.

Right in time to see Eden, looking up from amid her pile of fallen things. Her eyes widen as she sees me coming toward her.

Heather has the meeting handled.

Right now, my *friend* needs help.

CHAPTER 39

EDEN

E den, Eden. You're okay, darlin'. Just breathe."

My hands strangle the sheets. It takes me too long to realize I'm awake and staring at the ceiling, at the dark. I still see Logan holding a gun to my head, Sam's specter cast against a cliff as he roused his men into a fury . . . men stalking toward Heather as I left her to die.

Hot tears leak from the corners of my eyes, spilling onto the bed.

"Breathe, Eden. That's it—in and out. Look at me, pet."

I force my gaze to Beau, and he smiles for me. It's tight, and there are unhappy lines at the corners of his eyes, but I can see how hard he's trying to keep it there.

"Good girl, just like that."

I pull in a long, slow breath, then another. The shadows are gathered all around Beau like a cloak, but he's warm and real and beautiful beside me. He smells delicious, he smells like *us*, in this intangible way. Like by living together, our scents are permanently mixed, slightly altered, to always carry one another.

The thought of that helps steady me too.

Slowly, I sit up, and he passes me a glass of cool water from my bedside, kissing my forehead as I sip it.

Beau strokes my thigh under his shirt that I'm wearing as a nightshirt. "Eden, I've been patient, I truly have, but you need to talk about this with someone. Whatever this is . . . it's eating you up."

"I've been working on it," I say, a little defensively.

Every night, I've been going through Jasper's workbook, and it isn't as though that has been easy. Some of it goes even further back beyond the last few weeks—it would be an understatement to say it hasn't been dredging some things up.

Beau nods. "I know you have, darlin'. But at the end of the day, that is just one book. It's not much better than googling your symptoms and then self-treating at home. You need direction."

Swallowing, I look at the workbook as cold sweat cools on my skin.

Beau is right. Working in the garden, sparring, the workbook, it's all helped, but it's not enough. It's only been a week, of course, and my reading tells me that these things can take time. But I'm struggling, and I do have resources in front of me that I haven't had the courage to use.

Perhaps it's unfair of me. Jasper has been nothing but thoughtful and considerate—with me, with the other civilians . . . and about Lucky. He wants to help, and I don't want to feel like this. It's logical. Simple, even.

But it's *hard*.

Jasper is beautiful. Wickedly intelligent. Cultured. How am I meant to show him all the ugly parts of myself, when I want so desperately for him to see me as beautiful too? I know the burn of his rejection, and I'm terrified to face it again.

Not to mention . . . I know his reservations about his patients.

If I talk to him, will that close the door once and for all on this tension between us? Where *is* the line between talking to him as a friend and confidant and as a psychologist?

I stifle a sigh and put the thought from my mind. He isn't my lover, and I doubt he'll ever be. It's vain of me to hold out for such an insubstantial reason—just another example of my fear holding me back.

I'm too aware now of the momentum at Bristlebrook. In myself. Jaykob arrives back tomorrow. Lucky is awaiting an answer. The "bond-fire" is almost set up. And at any moment, we could find ourselves at war.

I should take the time now, while there still *is* time.

With shaking hands, I peel back the covers. I put on my glasses like they're armor, gather my workbook and notepad, then stand.

Beau runs his eyes over me, then smiles faintly as he shakes his head. "You're going to make Jasper's night."

I frown at him, but he continues before I can ask what he means. "You want me to come? Moral support?"

My heart melts a little, but I squeeze his hand. "I need to do this myself."

He nods in understanding, and I make my way quickly to Jasper's room, only for a sleepily disgruntled Heather to tell me he isn't there.

But at the end of the hall, light peers up at me from under the library door like a will-o'-the-wisp beckoning me on. Not wanting to wake anyone else, I pad softly toward the promising light and slip through the door.

Jasper is draped over an enormous armchair by the fireplace, a book open on his lap. His white silk shirt is unbuttoned at the collar, and his inky hair is ever so slightly mussed, the silvers at his temple more pronounced. He's kissed all over by the warm light, haloed by the fire like some righteous angel.

He glances up as I enter. Under his gaze, I pause by the door, feeling weighed and measured for entrance into his space.

"Eden." Without looking away from me, he closes his book. "Are you well?"

The hard edges of his workbook press into the skin of my arms. It's incredible how difficult it is to bite back my usual instinct to smile demurely and murmur something reassuring.

Instead, I press my trembling lips together and shake my head.

The heart-cutting angles of his face soften. "Come here."

When he calls, I come.

Moving toward Jasper never feels like mechanical motions. There is no one foot in front of the other, no notion of distance. It feels like floating through space, planets tightening an orbit. I'm a riverboat on the Styx, drifting toward fate.

He watches me as I'm pulled closer, knowing and calm, like a benevolent god accepting a supplicant. When I stop in front of him, I see the faintest brush of approval grace his lips, and my whole body glows with it.

But then his gaze drops. Travels down my body. Jasper pauses, and his expression empties entirely. As he turns his head, the light glances away from his face, casting it in cool shadows.

"Ah. You brought the workbook," he says politely, his voice as glossy and smooth as ice spheres. "May I see it?"

I freeze, staring at him.

It happened so quickly, a blink could miss it. Warm to cold, caring to polite. Like he can just flick a switch and power himself down.

Uneasily, I search his face, looking for something in it to lean on—but it's like he's disappeared.

Jasper waits patiently, and new anxiety churns in my stomach as I pry my arms from around the book. There's so much in there. So many private thoughts, so many fears. The workbook didn't mince words, asking for recounts of events, associated feelings. It pushed for information about my past and childhood.

I look down at the book, my notepad on top, clutched between my sweaty palms, and I step back. Then again. I step back until my legs hit the armchair opposite him, and I sit down, watching him warily.

I *can't*. Not like this.

Jasper leans against the arm of the chair as he regards me, his fingers brushing his lips thoughtfully. "You don't trust me."

There's no accusation in his words, but it's not a question either. My fingers rub against the workbook. There's a charge in the air, this low buzz of awareness that always lives in the quiet spaces between us.

Jasper and I spend so much time talking without words—as we measure, as we test.

But I'm not here to play chess with him today.

"Why do you do that? You turn so cold." Something like surprise flickers over his face—a moment and it's gone. So I press. "I don't know what to expect from you, Jasper. How am I supposed to trust you when I have no idea what you're thinking?"

The firelight flares in his dark eyes, then his eyelashes curtain the flames.

"What I'm thinking doesn't matter." He inclines his head. "We're here for you."

"Right," I breathe, looking down at my lap. The churn in my stomach worsens. I don't know if I can do this—sit here while he picks at my wounds with clinical eyes.

After a moment, I hear Jasper sigh, and glance up to see him settling back in his chair as he regards me.

"Eden, are you here for my help?" He pauses, and his voice lowers. "Or for another reason?"

What other reason could there be?

I become aware of just how much collarbone his unbuttoned shirt reveals, the strong, elegant wrists exposed by his pushed-back cuffs. How he is always so covered and elegant, and yet somehow always manages to look carnal.

"Another reason?" I ask uncertainly.

"What is it you want from me, Eden?" His question is a gentle lure, his eyes intense. "Do you want my help? My friendship?" His brows lift, and his voice becomes a purr. "My *cock*?"

My eyes widen in shock, a breathless sound escaping me. A smile touches his lips as he waits.

I stare at those lips, his pretty, refined lips that I'm somehow stunned can form a word like that. Such a round, ripe word, with a hard smack on the end that he takes in the back of his throat.

Jasper's *cock*.

I came here with my workbook. Why on earth would he think *that*?

I clear my throat to calmly explain that he's mistaken, but—to my horror—a panicked laugh escapes me instead. It comes out high-pitched and a tad hysterical.

"N-no. I would *never* try to . . ." My eyes drop to his lap, where his legs are crossed, then I rip them away to stare over at the book-shelves. "I'm not here for . . . for that. Not that— I'm sure it's very nice. Lucky seems fond of it."

Eden! Stop. My mouth opens again, and I swing my horrified eyes back to him.

"*Not* that I'm thinking about that. That is *your* business. I've never imagined it. I've never even thought about . . . My God. I am so sorry. I don't know what I—"

Jasper's dark, rich laugh cuts me off, and my horror swirls down a drain.

That *sound*.

Jasper's laugh is like a fresh swirl of cream over the bitterest chocolate torte. The sweetness is classic, but unexpectedly debauched.

I stare at him as his chuckles fade, and he regards me with undisguised amusement. He absently traces his lips with a fingertip.

"Do tell me more about how you are *not* thinking about me," he murmurs, wicked enjoyment painting his voice.

I want to respond, but my brain has been seared clear of words.

My eyes track his every feature, fascinated by how such small changes in his muscles somehow transform his whole face. The lush give of his mouth, the savage angle of his jaw, the hollows and the light of his face and throat.

Jasper is more than beautiful—he's biblical.

"I didn't know you could do that," I whisper.

It's an absurd thing to say, and possibly offensive, but Jasper just arches one brow.

"You thought I fell for a man like Lucien and didn't have a sense of humor?"

Jealousy stings, but so does my own flutter of affection. "He's determined to help me discover mine."

His eyes warm. "I know."

The air kindles between us, but still, I hesitate. I can't help but watch him, waiting for the moment he'll close off again.

Jasper takes it in, seeing through me as he always does. His finger taps thoughtfully against the leather arm of his chair.

"How can I make you comfortable, Eden? What is it you wish to know?"

Everything.

I look him over, the cool silk hugging the lines of his body, the gleaming loafers on his feet. He's so lovely . . . and so very far away.

Before my pitiful, tattered courage fails, I whisper, "How can I stop you from shutting down?"

Watching so closely, I *do* recognize the minute knit in his brow. The almost imperceptible pause in the rhythm of his tapping fingers.

Unable to look at him, I stare at the half-organized bookshelves —the complicated job just started, only to be left wholly unfinished.

I try to explain.

"My whole life, I've relied on being able to read people. I've become quite good at it, and it's one of my few skills that has kept me safe." I swallow hard and look back at Jasper. "I can't read you at all when you're like this. I can't tell if you're mildly curious or horrified, if you hate me, if you're judging me . . ."

"I'm not." Jasper's eyes flick over my face. "Eden, this is what I do. It's my job."

I bite my lip against a hurt huff, but I don't entirely stifle it. My chin lifts in a nod that feels only a touch shy of sarcastic. "Well. That's very professional of you."

The tension between us becomes thorny.

His lashes veil his eyes. "Why does it matter so much to you what I think?"

My incredulous gaze swings to meet his, the question sitting heavily between us. My chest squeezes until it bleeds.

Finally, in a low voice, I manage, "You *know* why."

Jasper's tapping stalls entirely. His eyes bore into mine, unwavering and intense in their silent question. I stare back at him until his brow creases, and finally, he sits back in his chair. He turns to look sightlessly into the flames, his fingers perched broodingly over his lips.

It's my turn to frown at him. "You had to know."

I can't help the way I watch him. Constantly. Obsessively. Perhaps he's so used to drawing eyes he never noticed. It's in the fluid, deliberate way he moves. How every light and shadow clings to his face. He's the worst form of addiction. A high I could chase but never have.

Jasper lets out a disdainful breath through his nose.

"You aren't exactly transparent yourself, Eden." His furrowed brow deepens pensively. "I saw how you were with Jaykob—with Lucien and Beaumont. You don't approach me like that."

The unfairness of it stings my throat.

"I know where I stand with them, Jasper. *You* rejected *me*, don't forget. Lucky might continue to beg for your affection after something like that, but I will not."

His dark eyes fly back to mine, then, limned in fiery light. "That's what you want? My affection? Eden, you have it. But be careful what you push for, dear girl—you know why I refused you."

My toes curl into the rug at my feet.

There's too much silky threat in his voice, and it should make me nervous. It *does* make me nervous. But not in the cold, anxious way. This way whispers over my skin with unspoken promises.

I'm both tempted and afraid to push him further.

"You don't want me. Not like that." The breathless words are unsteady, unsure.

Something in his posture shifts, becomes a little more sinuous. I have the sudden feeling that I have offended him now. A slight, dangerous smile curves his lips as one brow slashes a bold question.

"Do I not?" He tsks, and his eyes drift down over me in an excruciating, deliberate caress.

I pause, a shiver of heat and horror slipping up my spine. *You're going to make Jasper's night*, Beau said.

As I look down at myself, I realize why.

Beau's T-shirt is sheer and clings to me hopelessly—it outlines my breasts in sharp relief, presses against my stomach, and hovers around my upper thighs with breathy little flutters. I'm not wearing a bra, or underwear, and both of those facts are painfully obvious.

It's no wonder he asked what I was here for.

"Would you like to know why I shut down? You come in here and parade yourself half-naked in front of me, your nipples begging for my clamps—and in another man's shirt, no less. You've re-crossed your legs twice without a care, though I can see every single inch between your pretty thighs. It was either take control of myself, my girl . . . or take control of you."

I clamp my legs together, mortified. Jasper leans forward, and the sharp motion dislodges a single, rogue lock of his sable hair. The one that always escapes his control.

"It's too late for that. When it comes to you, Eden, I see everything." His voice becomes a hiss. "Did you think I wouldn't look?

That I wouldn't *care*? The things that I imagine of you would curl your hair. You are *oblivious* to the threat of me, and that alone tells me you have no understanding of the things I would do to you."

We stare at one another for a long moment, perilous promises whirling between us.

Jasper's eyes have been on me constantly since they found me outside the Sinners' camp. Looking at him now, the severe edges of him for once barely contained by his restraint, I wonder whether it wasn't just out of professional interest or cursory friendship. Was he wishing he were in Jaykob's place, fucking me between the trees?

He's right that I still don't entirely know what it means to be with a sadist. But he's wrong about the rest.

I do see the danger of him.

In many ways, Jasper is the most dangerous man in this house.

"You decided *for* me that I would never find out," I remind him. My body is tingling, alive with tension. Shakily, I add, "I was willing to try."

Jasper's return stare is intense. Settling back in his chair, he looks like a prince weighing the price of a crime.

"I won't hurt you any more than you've already been hurt, Eden," he says finally. "Not now, while everything is so fresh. And that is no reflection on how much I care about or am attracted to you."

I fight with his words. Despite his suggestion, I'm not oblivious. I know he's trying to protect me—but if he wants me like he says he does, and I'm willing, why won't he give it a chance? In that moment, I sympathize with the years of frustration Lucky had to go through.

But *not now* has possibilities. *Not now* is not a "no."

Not now makes my heart race.

"Do we understand one another now?" he asks.

Jasper wears no mask now, his expression haunted and lovely, kind, and hungry. I see the same restlessness in him I feel. The same frustration.

I sigh. "Yes. I think we do."

I look down at the workbook in my lap thoughtfully.

"If you didn't come here to see me as a professional, Eden, and if you didn't come here to seduce me"—he smiles faintly, and I return the look wryly—"why did you come?"

I wish I had an easy answer for that.

"I came to see *you*, Jasper." I sigh heavily, willing him to understand what I don't understand myself. "I'm just . . . lost. And I needed you tonight. Not you, the faraway psychologist. I need the person who talked me down when I panicked. The one who made me feel like I might actually be able to make a home here."

His forehead twitches then—a hint of surprise, just for an instant.

The tension in the room thickens again, spreading between us like a gently tugging chain.

Jasper tilts his head, and that single lock of hair sways. "You want my help, but no professional distance between us—is that right?"

No distance. There are so many things I want from him, things that my mind continues to push down, but my body silently begs for.

No distance is the barest start of that.

Pushing my glasses back up my nose, I nod.

Jasper nods back. "Then come here."

CHAPTER 40

EDEN

SURVIVAL TIP #20
You have to be the ~~worst~~ best version of yourself to ~~survive~~ live.
~~Kill~~ Protect the weak.
~~Strike from~~ Kiss in the shadows.
~~Run from a~~ Stand and fight.
~~Leave your friends behind.~~ Protect your friends at all costs.

For a moment, I'm caught off guard. Physical distance, he meant.

Then slowly, I stand, hugging my workbook and notepad to my chest. On trembling legs, I walk over to him. My skin feels sensitive, hot, the fabric of my shirt scraping over it provocatively.

I stop in front of him, and despite the fact that I am standing and he's sitting, he still seems to loom before me with the quiet confidence of an indolent king.

His eyes on mine, Jasper spreads his thighs wide.

I think I stop breathing.

My scandalized eyes drop helplessly.

I don't know why that one shift to separate his legs should feel as indecent as his mouth around the word *cock*. Perhaps because it feels like an invitation. A beckoning into some private, privileged alcove—one where very few may be allowed.

He watches me with those dark, dark eyes, and fiendish flames dance around us.

"*Kneel.*"

The word shudders through me like a prayer, a call for reverence.

Not taking my eyes off him, I lower myself to my knees. It's a delicious space. His thighs are firm and hot beside me, sheathed in his black slacks. I'm utterly surrounded by him.

The tips of Jasper's fingers tease the strands of hair at my temple until I look up at him. He's so salaciously close, and yet from down here, he looks so far above me.

On instinct, I nestle into his fingers, and he strokes my temple with his thumb. Jasper looks down at my kneeling form—and looks and looks. His hand tightens painfully in my hair, and I don't even have time to suck in a surprised breath before it smooths out reassuringly.

My heart trips a beat.

"You flower as a submissive, Eden." Jasper's eyes travel over my face, and he murmurs, "If you need to talk, I suspect this might be easiest for us both."

In this nook, I can smell him, feel him. I'm conscious of every whisper of fabric, every shift, every breath. I'm aware of the fact that he truly isn't unaffected by me right now.

I rest my head against his inner thigh, and he watches me curve into him. It's so intimate, this place where only lovers usually dwell. It feels even more intimate, somehow, *without* the flurry of movement. To just rest here, soaking in the feeling of his strength under my cheek.

Maybe he's right. I do feel closer to him like this, in ways that have nothing to do with proximity.

Hesitantly, his finger tracks over my hairline. "I can't approach you as a professional, Eden. I'm already too compromised, and you, too close. But if you need to talk, come to me like this—share your concerns with me as a dominant . . . and I will care for my submissive."

His delicate touch sends shivers all over me. It seems a tenuous, uncomfortable line for him to walk, but here, I finally feel my tension starting to fall away.

"Your submissive?" I meet his gaze. It lingers.

Jasper hesitates, then says in a cautious tone, "Not all dominant-submissive relationships are sexual, Eden. Perhaps we can try this."

My eyes slip toward his erection, standing in not-at-all subtle defiance of his words. It's a breathless, tense kind of look. I'm attracted to Jasper—almost violently so—and he's clearly not unmoved by me.

Just for a moment, I wonder if I *could* seduce him.

"Okay. But I'm okay with it being sexual," I venture, holding my breath. "Just so we're clear."

Jasper's thigh twitches under my cheek, and his voice lowers. "Behave, my girl. You don't want my brand of pain."

Sharp and dangerous things lurk in his eyes. Yet they're such unfairly gorgeous eyes. It's the characteristic cruelty of nature that he should be so unsafe, like the luring bloom of my water hemlock hiding its poisoned and deadly roots.

I've had so much pain the last few weeks—and part of me wonders what it might be like to make that pain pretty.

But now is not the time.

Instead, I give him something I guard even more closely than my body.

I lift the workbook and my notepad. They're suddenly heavy, but I pass them to him silently. It occurs to me that it's the first time I've given him scribbles of *my* secret thoughts.

It feels like handing over part of my soul.

"Very brave," he murmurs, and I press my face into his thigh at the instant sting in my eyes.

He hasn't read a word, yet somehow pierces the heart of it.

My shame. My cowardice. My pathetic, unhelpful weakness.

But I stay, curled at his feet, as Jasper begins working his way through my notes. He refers to the notepad when needed, asking questions on occasion, but mostly he seems to drink it in with deep thought. His hand often drifts back to my hair, petting me softly, until I gradually begin to relax, allowing myself to steal the comfort he offers.

Jasper is calm as he reads, and not a flicker of surprise crosses his face. I wonder then what it would take to shock him. Working with soldiers who have been deployed under extreme conditions, surely he's heard terrible things. I wonder if my problems seem small to him, or insignificant.

I'm not sure if that would make me feel better or worse.

"There is a lot to unpack here," he says finally, then he looks down at me softly. "But there are two things that keep coming up. There's one that I can't find any specific details about—you call it A and M. There seems to be an enormous amount of shame attached to this event. Can you explain what happened?"

One by one, I feel my muscles turn to stone.

Alastair and Mateo.

I can't tell Jasper about that. Nothing will change it now anyway, but if Dom finds out how I lied, it will crush him. Bile rises in my throat. I'm too horrifically aware of the news out of Cyanide City. Bentley and the people in Red Zone are in as dreadful a position as we are. Worse, in some ways, because of proximity alone.

The Sinners' sweeps of the city. Weapons testing. Training regimes for their new recruits.

New women captured.

And worst of all, it's as Dom suspected. Alastair and Mateo rejoined Sam. They manipulated me. Dom warned me, and I still let it happen.

They *did* manipulate me, didn't they? Could they still be

working against him in secret? It seems too much to hope for now, when I'm not frightened and facing them in the secret, dark shadows of the woods.

"We don't have to talk about that one right now," Jasper says, and I pull in air, realizing I've been sitting frozen at his feet for too long.

"Perhaps this one. You say here that there was an incident during your escape, and you were going to abandon Heather? Those are your words, mind."

Despite how mildly he says it, I flinch, dropping my gaze.

"You've listed your associated emotion as guilt." His long, elegant fingers smooth my hair back from my forehead. "Can you walk me through that?"

As if called, the emotions creep through me.

I press my cheek more firmly against his thigh, like I might be able to take his strength by osmosis.

"It's not complicated, Jasper," I tell him bitterly. "I left her. If the others hadn't arrived, she would have died for me, and I would have let her. I didn't have her back. I didn't protect her. I did what I always do. Run. Hide. Skulk in the shadows and only come out of them when there's no danger."

Shame burns through me like a fever, and my heart picks up in agitation. I hate that he knows it now too. I hate everything that he can see. I close my eyes, like it might stop me from seeing it too.

"I'm so weak, Jasper. Everyone around me, all of these people —*kids*, Jasper, Kasey is *fourteen*—they're all so brave. They're fierce and capable, and God, I'm not. I'm afraid *all of the time*. And that makes me angry, because how dare the Sinners do that to me? How dare they take so much? What gives them the right to make me feel like this? To put me in these situations and become this person. I just want it all to stop."

I bite my lip as it all fills my throat. "But it won't. It never will. I know I have to be better, and braver, but I don't know if I can.

I'm not like Heather, or you, or the Rangers. I'm just a librarian. I was never meant for this."

Jasper's hand cups my cheek, and it's only then I realize it's wet. I open my eyes, and he's watching me patiently. Steadily. Just holding the space while I get it all out.

When I have myself back under control, he nods.

"To begin, while we're talking—and I know it's difficult—but try to avoid using words like *always*, and *all the time*." His voice is at once delicate and firm. "Superlatives and generalizations are rarely helpful, Eden. It can start to conflate a single action with an entire personality. No one, or two, or five actions define a person's being. Being able to separate what happened from who you are as a person is important. Does that make sense?"

His words paralyze me, and I stare at his thigh. The heat and press of it against me. Finally, I nod.

"We will go through this together, but I do want to make a few things clear. What you're describing, the person you're painting yourself as—this image doesn't align with my experience of you, Eden." His gaze has the gentle weight of soft-falling snow.

"You saved Dominic and Beaumont. You navigated a firefight to bring Dominic weapons. Within a week of being captured, you gained a modicum of trust from your captors, put yourself in a position to take action, and you had the courage to follow through on it despite the incredible risk. You managed to free both yourself *and* Heather." Jasper raises his brows. "And that's not to mention years of survival on your own. All of those actions require resilience and bravery—and also the extremely rare ability to think and act intelligently when your life is in danger."

I shake my head, throat clogging at the pretty scene he's drawing. The one-sided coin that hides the horror on the other side.

He catches my chin and turns it up. "You are here as my submissive and not as my patient. If you have something to say, you may ask me for permission to talk—but if you shake your head like that at me again when I am telling you a truth, I will spank you raw."

His dark gaze tunnels into mine, and my mouth drops open. I'm full of sickness, of guilt and dread and shame.

How can he make me shiver amid all that?

I eye him. Would he really do it?

Jasper releases me and sits back. Something in the calm surety of his face tells me that *yes*. He really would.

"Yes, Jasper," I say, and I'm sure it sounds as stunned as I feel.

He smiles faintly at my expression. "Then listen to me carefully, Eden. We are all made up of decisions and experiences, both good and bad. We are flawed people who triumph and fail daily. It is not a crime to be human." Jasper grimaces, glancing away for a moment, then back. "It's something even I have to remind myself of often."

I run my hand lightly up his calf in an instinctual reassurance —like he's given me so often tonight. I feel his thigh flex under my cheek again, but he doesn't otherwise react.

"If your issues stem from a false self-perception, then we can work on changing that. If they stem from problematic patterns of behavior, then we can help break those habits. But choice is everything, Eden. You can choose to do the work. You can choose to fight, to learn new skills, to grow and change in whichever ways will make you proud moving forward." His voice grows unbearably kind. "We can't change the things that happen to us—only change what they help us to become."

I stare at him, thinking. Choice. It always comes back to choice.

Who *do* I want to be?

Put so simply, it seems clear. I've been on the verge of it for days—fueled by Jayk and Lucky and Beau and Dom. Even Heather, and her urge for me to *pick one*.

I do know what I want.

I want to act in ways that make me proud. I want to be strong enough to protect the people I care about. I want to be brave enough to tell them how I feel. I don't want to choose between the people I love—and I don't want them to have to choose for me, either. I want them to have every happiness, because it's too rare in this world, and they deserve all of it. I want to be better than jealousy and pettiness.

I want what Jasper promised the first day I arrived at Bristlebrook—a family and a safe home.

I can fight for that, I think.

In fact, I think I have a lot of people around me who are rooting for me to do just that.

I look up to find Jasper watching me, that thoughtful, almost unreadable expression on his face again. But this time I see the pride.

"Shall we begin?" he asks, and I nod.

Right now, fighting for that future means fighting for myself . . . so that's what I do.

For hours, we go through everything I wrote down in the last week. Sitting at his feet feels like sitting on battlements and facing down an enemy. Jasper challenges me and comforts me in turns, bringing tears to my eyes only to wipe them away.

We talk until I grow too drowsy to continue, and I fall asleep in the cradle of his legs with the first stirring of hope that maybe this feeling isn't forever. Maybe this is just now.

And maybe I really can have it all.

CHAPTER 41

EDEN

SURVIVAL TIP #331
*Remember the dead,
so you remember to live.*

The music thrums through the forest, so thick with bass that I feel the reverberation in my feet. It pours through the shattered remains of the music room's windows, still unfixed after they were destroyed in the battle for Bristlebrook.

I pause at the edge of the porch, the short drop feeling like the precipice of some great cliff.

It's only just dark, but there are flashlights and solar lights strung up between the trees, and long planks spanning the dry moat to allow people to cross it easily. Drunken giggles and shouts tinkle from nearby tables laden with booze, sounding more relaxed than I can remember anyone being in a long time.

The apple tree glows like a soft, nebulous beacon in the dimming light. At least two dozen votive candles dangle from its darkened branches, in remembrance of our dead. Several people sit underneath the boughs, talking quietly to one another. And in the center of the lawn, the tents have been cleared away to make room for the enormous, raging bonfire. It flickers and charges, its smoky scent puffing along on the light breeze.

I'd worried the fire might bring up bad memories, but instead, the passionate lick and churn of the flames makes me want to dance and rage. It's as though the tension coiling inside me this week has finally crested, broken apart into something terrifyingly free.

I've finally made a choice—tonight, I'm going after what I want.

I hear a low whistle. "Well, now, darlin'. I'm going to have to declare martial law—you're putting my heart and health into civil unrest in that dress."

Turning, I bite down on an amused smile, and Beau takes my hand.

"Spin, let me see you."

I re-adjust my glasses and try not to squirm as I spin for him.

The dress isn't anything scandalous, but it's the most feminine thing I've worn since before I was captured. It's floral and flows around my legs, with a fitted bodice that ties over my breasts that I'm trying very hard not to yank up to my throat. It even has *pockets*.

But Beau looks gorgeous. His hair is still wet from the shower, and his long-sleeved shirt clings to his chest and arms.

"Martial law?" I arch my brows primly, then tease as he tugs me into his arms, "So I suppose I'm under military control now?"

Beau's laugh is tinged in surprise, and I blush as my smile grows. It's getting easier to flirt with Beau. Especially when he's constantly flirting with me. It's getting easier to do *everything* with Beau.

The music kicks up into a fast, playful tempo, and several women hoot around the fire. I catch sight of Heather as she pulls someone back from the fire. She glances up right as Beau runs his hands down my back and makes a face at me.

"You are most definitely under my control, civilian." I shiver as he teases me with a kiss. His hands curve over my ass, squeezing, and my breath strangles in my throat. "Are you still wearing it?"

It is heavy and delicious inside me. Over the last few days, I've grown used to the plugs, the sensation and increasing sizes, the care and cleaning. Beau has been teasing me with them, working me over until I've begged for him just to take me there.

But he hasn't. Not yet.

I'm finally on the last and largest training plug, and just having it inside is so intense, my eyes practically cross with every step. I even have a small bottle of lube in my pocket, as Beau instructed, even though it drags my dress down a little on one side.

"Just in case," he said.

Rather than giving him the answer he wants, though, I give him a narrow-eyed look through my glasses. "What. Does. It. Say?"

Beau's smile turns sly.

We talked a few hours ago, and he insisted on me wearing the plug tonight. I know it's going to be a distraction, but he swears it will help with my plan to talk with Lucky and Jayk. Worse, after we talked, he bent me over and wrote *something* on my ass in black marker—then had the audacity to order me not to look or else I would be in "big trouble."

I spent the whole time I was getting ready wondering what "big trouble" actually meant. Then telling myself I was a grown woman, and no man can really tell me not to look at my own body, and who is he to give me sexy threats anyway?

I didn't look, though.

"I wasn't writing to you, little notepad," Beau tells me with an affectionate smile. His hands tighten over my soft dress, and I gasp lightly, grasping his biceps for support. "Now tell me—are you *wearing* it?"

I bite my lip as I shiver. "I'm wearing it."

"Wearing what?" Dom asks behind me, and I jump, catching Beau's wrist and awkwardly pushing his hand off my ass.

But that doesn't go down well.

Beau yanks me against him with his free hand, then spanks my ass hard, twice. The thick plug, slick with lube, presses deep inside me as I clench, and the metal ball inside it jangles hard with the motion. It's not like the first day I tried it. Now, the sensation is quick to rewrite to brutal pleasure, and the sharp sting of Beau's palm licks into the throbbing ache of the plug.

Instantly wet, I press my head into Beau's firm chest and whimper needily.

He tunnels his hand into my hair. "Good civilians let their protectors touch them however they want."

I draw in a shaky breath and nod. This was one of many things we talked about—*negotiated*—over the last week. Putting it into practice is just a little . . . different.

"So you've discovered Beau's love of roleplay." Dom's voice is dryly amused, and I twist to stare at him.

He's leaning against one of the porch posts, lusciously imposing in his red Henley. My tongue sticks to the roof of my mouth. There's something wicked about the scarlet against his dark coloring, something vibrant and raw that demands attention. Admiration.

I haven't quite found the courage to ask where Dom used to fit into Beau's elaborate fantasies, though I'm desperately curious.

Mentioning Dom in front of Beau at the moment is the quickest way to end a conversation.

Dom's eyes travel down my body. "As your *friend*, let me know if you want some tips."

My cheeks flush.

The idea of him coaching me on how to please Beau has my body clenching helplessly again. The dual emptiness of my pussy and the obscene pressure in my ass is still confusing. What would it feel like to be filled everywhere?

I glance between Dom and Beau, one dark and dangerous, the other golden tanned and patient.

I'm busy picturing being impaled between them when Beau's

hand tightens on my ass. "She doesn't need any tips. She's not your friend. Eden doesn't need you at all."

The improper image bursts.

"Eden and I are BFFs now," Dom deadpans, then his expression sours. "My last one bailed on me, so I had an opening."

Beau's muscles become rocky under my palm. "Seemed to me like you found a replacement for both of us with no trouble at all. Just how long *was* it before you told Eden she didn't measure up to your ex and dumped her on her ass?"

Dom's brows drop like a heavy falling tree, and my heart aches for him.

I lift my chin. "Beau, enough. I told you that's not what happened. Don't use me as an excuse for your fight, because he and I are getting along just fine."

Beau continues to glare at Dom as if I didn't speak at all.

"Have either of you seen Lucky or Jayk?" I ask firmly before he can start in again.

Beau has been utterly unreasonable—he won't hear that Dom didn't "break up" with me. He won't even hear that there was nothing to break up. It's not like Dom and I ever really started in the first place.

As I look over the sea of women, desperate for a distraction, the music changes, slipping into something dark and vibrating with suspense. The easy energy of the crowd shifts, and people begin looking around.

Beau pauses his argument, looking over as the crowd behind the bonfire parts, then his muscles relax slightly.

"Hurry on, darlin'. You're not going to want to miss this."

"What's *this*?" I stand on my tiptoes, straining to see.

"A mating dance," Dom mutters under his breath. "He's going to cause a riot."

Beau ignores him.

"*This* is your entertainment." He drops me a grin. "Your new boyfriend is giving you a show."

CHAPTER 42

EDEN

ucky?
    The music pulses like a heartbeat, intense and expectant. Beau jumps off the porch, and I clamber down after him, my plug pressing in and out of me in an intimate kiss.

We pass the bonfire to find the crowd has swollen on the lawn, forming a large circle. There, I see Jayk for the first time in a week. He's cleaned up, looking freshly shaven and unfairly beddable as he sprawls over one of the raised wooden vantages the building team has been working on. He's . . . is he in a button-up? Where on earth did he get that?

He's also surrounded by women.

As my eyes land on him, his gaze jerks away. Sloane leans in close, whispering something, and he stiffens, then, slowly, his arm slings around her shoulders.

I stare at it, and rage bursts to life inside me, storming like it did when I had hemlock in my pocket and a camp to kill. Sloane has the unexpected beauty of a Valkyrie—gorgeously strong and with rippling confidence, she and Jayk look like a warrior queen and king beside one another. Worse, I *like* Sloane.

My glasses slip down my nose, and I shove them back up furiously.

"Easy, killer," Dom murmurs beside me, and my lips tighten.

Beau steps in behind me. "He didn't sleep with her, pet."

Oh, I know *that*. Jaykob is as transparent as Beau about his feelings, albeit in a very different way. A man like Jayk doesn't say "mine" unless he means it.

"He's playing games," I bite out, cataloguing every inch of tattooed skin that's touching hers. Jayk is trying to make me jealous.

Of all the petty, stupid, *ridiculous* things.

Beau squeezes my upper arms. "Just remember the plan."

The plan. Right. Of course.

If Jayk doesn't stop touching her, I am nuking the plan, and I might take him with it.

Even as I think it, Lucky's voice comes back to haunt me, calling me a hypocrite, and I force my hands to unclench. I'm being a better person today.

The tension in the crowd ratchets higher, and the music takes on a breathless edge. I find myself waiting as anxiously as everyone else, craning my head to see what's coming.

Then Jasper walks into the center of the clearing, a small pile of cards firmly in hand.

In the darkening night, he seems soaked in moonlight. His arresting beauty draws every eye, silences every squeal and chatter —a prince awaiting proper deference for his address.

The thrumming beat strikes a sharp rhythm in my throat.

"Five years ago, nightmares walked free of dreams and through our streets."

Tension ripples through the crowd. My eyes are riveted on Jasper.

"In one night, our cities burned. Order perished. And

unkindest of all . . . we saw what humanity was capable of. Our neighbors murdered. Our friends rioted. Our authorities stole. Good people transformed, and this new world warped many of them in mere *hours*."

A chill steals over my skin as a low breeze stirs. Jasper glows like a beacon, silvered by starlight, and his dark eyes travel the crowd.

"But not you," he says softly. "Many of us here have done things we aren't proud of to survive in this new world—but with every choice, we learn. And by standing here, on the anniversary of that deathful day, and not with men like the Sinners, we show we are making new choices. We choose to build, rather than to destroy. We choose friendship over fearmongering. Community before coercion. We choose each other, and we choose to be better than our worst choices."

Solemn agreement whispers over the crowd. I cast my eyes around, shocked at the number of people nodding. Ava has her head bowed, like Jasper's words are hard to hear, and Ida has Ethel's hand pressed to her lips as she listens.

My throat thickens, and something shifts for me, then, moved by the music and moonlight and Jasper's words. *This* was what he was trying to say last night. This isn't just my fight. Every one of us has been through this. Day Death demanded sacrifice, and it didn't just claim the lives of our loved ones. It claimed pieces of our souls.

And it's not just me who wants more.

I can see the want in their faces. It's in the way they've thrown themselves into making Bristlebrook a home. We all want a life that is more than survival. We all want a way to thrive without carving out everything about ourselves that makes us *good*.

Jasper inclines his head, and for a moment, I feel his eyes on me. Without a single lash in hand, he's cut me to my core.

"I cannot pretend our suffering is over. But none of us made it this far without discovering our strength. We will draw on every ounce of it in the days and weeks ahead—and when our own strength fails, we will lean on those around us. Together, we are strong." Jasper pauses, then smiles gently. "Welcome, my new friends, to Bristlebrook. Our home."

A cheer goes up, and my eyes sting as I laugh, carried away by the crowd. Beau's lips press against my hair, and I nestle back into him.

Jasper waits, that smile still shining from his face, until the noise begins to die down. As it does, the music changes again, slipping into something slick and sexy, with a heavy, fast-pumping beat.

"In honor of our new home, and in the spirit of our new friendship, we have thrown this"—he looks down at the card in his hand and sighs—"*bond*-fire."

I have to stifle another laugh. This is Lucky, if I ever heard it.

"Light a candle and hang it on our tree in remembrance of those you loved, and please enjoy the music, the fire, and the vast selection of alcohol." Jasper's expression is a little pained at that —I know he's quite fond of his collection. Or he was. "We have also arranged for a pig to be roasted as a special break to our rations."

The cheer from the crowd is even louder this time. Akira is in charge of Team Bacon, as they've been anointed, and they're the unofficial heroes of the night.

"Finally," Jasper calls over the excited jeers, "we have some entertainment for you tonight."

He looks down, skimming his notes again, and frowns. He turns toward the lodge and calls, "Lucien, I refuse to read this."

There's no answer—except the song abruptly cuts off, then starts again, playing that slick, introductory beat.

Jasper presses an index finger against his forehead and rubs it, sighing again as he turns back around.

In a flat, unimpressed voice, he reads, "He simmers with sex. He's more scorching than sin. He's the hottest man in this house. Yes, hotter than Jayk. He'll set your panties on fire. He sizzles with . . . untamed masculine energy."

Jasper closes his eyes, shaking his head minutely, and I can't stop my giggles anymore. The crowd is hollering, riotous.

Jasper gives them a scathing look, then finishes hurriedly. "Please give a warm welcome to the smoldering smokeshow himself—Lucien."

As soon as the last word leaves his lips, he shoves down his cards and stalks over to us.

He ends up next to me, shoving the cards in his pocket. "I don't know how I let him talk me into this."

"I do," Dom says under his breath. "And he really could have done it in *your* room."

The usual spike of jealousy, curiosity, and lust hits me, but right then I see a shirtless, gleaming Lucky appear at the head of the circle, a long, thick staff in one hand.

The music pauses for a beat—and then Lucky winks.

He whips the staff into the air, and it catches fire on both ends in a wicked bloom that has the crowd roaring back as the playful, sexy music crashes back in. Grinning, Lucky throws himself into a series of rapid flips and turns, the staff spinning and flaring around his arching body as he hits every beat of the music, and the thumping music starts a rhythm inside me that demands an answer.

He slides to his knees in the middle of the crowd, in front of me and Jasper, spinning the fiery staff faster and faster over his head, around his neck, above his chest. And in the middle of it all, his body *undulates*, thrusting up from the earth in an erotic, unholy dance.

My mouth goes dry, and my clammy hand finds Jasper's silk sleeve. Lucky's abs glisten under the firelight, like he's oiled himself to show every muscle, every tattoo, every inch of himself in carnal perfection.

Jasper breathes in an unsteady breath beside me.

At the surge of a wild guitar, Lucky punches up with a laugh, then moves into a series of fast, tight backflips the length of the crowd, his staff turning with him. He flirts with the women as he dances and slices through the air, throwing dimples and flames like kisses into the crowd.

And they're losing it. Whistles and screams tear through the night.

I can't even blame them.

Lucky moves like his body is made for sex.

Sliding back into the middle of the circle, Lucky cracks the staff against his hand over his head until everyone starts clapping. Then he *moves*—it's one part dance, one part war, and at least two parts pure temptation. Faster and faster, the fire arcs around his rippling body like a hellish halo. Strands of his hair are escaping his bun, clinging around his damp face in a teasing caress.

Then the music begins its final rise.

Lucky throws the staff, its end piercing the earth in a fierce gust.

The flames catch on the grass, ripping over the earth in a perfect heart around him. The crowd *oohs*.

Lucky launches forward, grasping the still-vibrating staff under the flaming tip, swinging himself around it, his body twisting in perfect control. Every muscle in his biceps, his forearms, is tensed and glimmering with sweat.

Every turn proudly showcases his body. His strength. His passion.

His . . . untamed masculine energy.

When he finally turns to a halt on the grass, it's on his knees, in the middle of the flaming heart, looking at me and Jasper. The music ends and the women are laughing, screaming, but I can only stare at him.

I'm wet, slippery, my body thrumming and tense and pressing into the plug in my ass. Jasper's breaths are short and hard beside me.

"Fucking mating dance," Dom mutters. "I'm going to put the fire out. Make sure nobody molests Lucky."

Jasper hisses, and I glare at the women who are creeping in toward him.

Without a word, both Jasper and I lurch forward, making our way to Lucky before any of the scavengers get too bold. The plug is an insistent thrust inside me, playing havoc with my already over-stimulated body. It makes walking an awkward, thrilling experience, and it's an effort to maintain the semblance of composure.

I'm not sure I quite manage it.

Lucky is sitting back on his heels when we stop in front of him. His hair is damp around the edges, and he *is* oiled up, his chest and arms slick and shiny. The tips of my fingers prickle with the urge to touch him—to smear that oil all over his skin.

It's odd seeing him kneeling, but a quick look at the color high on Jasper's cheekbones tells me it's not for my benefit.

I pause again, glancing between them. I'm not sure how this etiquette works. I need to talk to Lucky, but he's already with Jasper . . . Does he get priority? Is there a ticket system for this?

Lucky grins lazily. "Have fun?"

"Watching you put on a strip show for almost a hundred women?" I can feel Jasper's barely contained tension.

The crowd of women press closer, their eyes on Lucky's tattoos, on his arms and chest and gorgeous face. I wish I had a spray bottle. I'd squirt them like overzealous puppies.

Lucky shakes his head slowly. "The show wasn't for them." His dimple kisses his cheek. "It was for the two of you."

Jasper *and* me.

Relief relaxes my shoulders, and I let my smile slip free.

"You were incredible," I tell him huskily, and his eyes brighten.

"Yeah? Even though master and commander over here ruined my intro?"

Jasper gives Lucky a withering look, but I laugh. Oddly, my nerves seem to have vanished. Here in front of him, with him smiling at me, I'm only filled with bright, bright happiness. Lucky *is* happiness.

I glance at Jasper. "Would you mind terribly if I spoke with Lucky in private for a moment?"

Jasper's dark eyes flick up, searching mine. His lips curve just slightly, and I read the approval. He inclines his head.

"By all means."

Lucky looks between us, a touch warily—an animal who has been flicked on the nose too many times before. I hold out my hand.

"Come with me, Lucky. I have your answer."

CHAPTER 43

LUCKY

SURVIVAL TIP #160
Don't make promises on behalf of your poor, neglected dick.

I have your answer.

There are whistles and catcalls coming from every angle, but I ignore them all as Eden's words send my stomach tumbling. In that sweet, church-girl dress, she looks carnally innocent. She doesn't *look* like she's about to grind my heart under her heel.

She'd look more upset if she was going to break me, wouldn't she?

Please be good news. Please be good news.

I leap to my feet and take her wrist, and her pulse flutters against my fingertips. I'm about to drag her off when Jasper adjusts his cufflinks casually.

"Say goodbye, Lucien."

Hesitating, I glance at Eden, remembering her jealousy in the kitchen. The last thing I want to do is make it worse before we get a chance to talk.

She doesn't look jealous, though. Or not only that.

Her eyes are wide and curious as they dart between us, and

even under the skirts of her dress, I can see the way she shifts her thighs together. Her prurient interest sends lust knotting low in my stomach—and gives me another boost of hope.

Still, she's run away from me too many times already, so I keep hold of her wrist and tug her with me as I step into Jasper. Careful not to touch his silk shirt with my oiled skin—because I'm a brat, not suicidal—I lean in slowly.

Eden's breaths become unsteady beside me. I can feel the heat of her, the heat of him, both of them closing me in, surrounding me deliciously. Damn it, I'm too needy for this, and I have too many fantasies that involve the three of us being even closer than this flashing through my mind. I hover over his lips, my head all light and dizzy. It's almost too tense.

Can't have that.

Mischief makes me grin. "Bye, Jasper!"

Before his eyes have even started to widen, I'm pivoting to bolt away with Eden in hand—only Jasper's reflexes are faster than I gave him credit for.

Grabbing the front of my waistband, he yanks me back toward him, and I drag in a surprised breath. His eyes are dark-burning coals, sparking with warning.

That look always makes my knees soft and my cock instantly hard.

"You're pushing me again, Lucien," Jasper says silkily.

"I said goodbye." *Danger. Danger!* I give him a sweet smile. "Like you asked."

I shouldn't keep teasing him, not when he's only holding back because I asked. It's just that Jasper's scary glare is pretty much my favorite kind of foreplay at this point.

"Very literal," Jasper purrs.

The back of his fingers brush over my abdomen like a brand, and I shudder, my skin flinching at the unexpected contact. I'm so touch-starved that if his fingers dipped any further to find my cock, I'd probably come in his hand.

Eden shifts again beside me, breathing fast, and knowing she's getting turned on by me, *by me and Jasper*, makes my balls throb harder.

I've kept my promise to her, and I haven't touched myself after I promised Jasper I wouldn't. And with Jasper around me, willing and available, it is *hard*. The whole experience has made me decide that I really should stop making promises on behalf of my poor, neglected dick.

Jasper leans in, hovering over my mouth the way I did to his moments before.

"If you don't want to kiss me, dear boy, that's quite all right. Never say I'm an unobservant dominant. I'll be sure to remember how little you enjoy my mouth."

I freeze, then quickly lean in, chasing his mouth, but he releases my sweatpants and steps back.

"No. *No, no.*" I laugh nervously. My cock is stiff and begging for attention, and that cruel shine in his eyes tells me he'll follow through on his word. I've been imagining Jasper sucking my dick since the day I met him. He can't deprive me of that *now*, not when it's finally a real possibility.

"I love your mouth," I assure him. "I want it on me. A lot. All the time. I didn't mean it. You know I didn't mean it, right?"

Jasper just gives me a slight smile and turns to Eden. The delicate tendons in her throat stand out in stark relief as her gaze travels over his face. His smile takes on a lick of satisfaction I could read a mile away.

He *loves* that she's turned on by him.

A fact I would also appreciate more if I wasn't fixated on a starving future without kisses, or without Jasper's hot mouth around my cock.

"Jasper, I didn't mean it," I say again, a little frantically.

He ignores me. "Enjoy your night, Eden. If you have some time later, it would be lovely to take a walk with you."

Some of the foggy lust fades from her eyes, and she smiles shyly up at him. Her skirts swish about her calves.

"I'd like that," she says. She touches his arm gracefully. "Thank you for your speech. You can't know what it means to finally feel a part of something."

I expect some sort of elegant dismissal, but he stares down at her hand. Artless spots of color appear on his cheekbones.

"You inspired me," he tells her, and Eden ducks her head to hide her smile.

My selfish panic fades as I take them in.

No way. My eyes slide between them. No *way*.

My heart stutters.

They're looking at each other. *Really* looking. Not reserved or polite. Not even in simple lust. They're looking at each other the way they look at me.

Only with about sixty percent less exasperation.

I caught Jasper brooding over his speech in his study this morning, apparently not even registering the Reapers' recruitment call for more farmhands that was blaring on repeat over our HAM radio.

He said that he and Eden had finally talked. That they'd "cleared the air."

This air is *not* clear. It's frothing with heart-shaped bubbles and heady pheromones. This air is full of possibility.

A smile teases my lips, yearning aching in my chest. If this is what I think it is . . . if Eden *isn't* turning me down, and if they're looking at one another like *that* . . .

I rock up onto my toes in excitement, and they startle out of their adorable little bubble. Eden adjusts her glasses, and Jasper straightens his shirt.

This ache might actually crack my chest open.

"I love you," I whisper as I watch them both, and their stunned eyes snap up to mine.

Eden's gaze slips to Jasper, uncertainty falling over her expression, and I wince, realizing she thinks I'm talking about him.

Jasper gives me a look of silent reproach under his dark lashes.

Right. Tell her first. Got it.

Whoops.

Eden tugs at her wrist in my grip as she tries to back up, but that is *not* happening. No more running. I yank her close to me, grasping her other wrist and holding her an inch from my body. An inch before I stain and coat and wreck that virtuous little dress with the slipperiness on my skin.

She gasps, staring at me through her glasses with prettily shocked eyes. Her forearms flex in my grip, and as her gaze drops, rolling over my chest with reluctant, indecent interest, her tongue comes out to tease her lower lip.

Relieved smugness rolls through my chest. She's not turning me down.

I'm about sixty percent sure.

"You had something to say to me, beautiful?" I prompt.

I want this conversation to happen. I want it to be over.

I want to kiss her.

Her throat works as she swallows, then she nods. "Could we go somewhere?"

I glance at Jasper, and he gives me a slight smile. With a final nervous grin at him, I tug her toward the trees.

Women are still crowded around us, staring at me as lasciviously as Eden is, but with none of her pitiful attempts to hide it.

One of the women, Corinne, whoops as she passes us, drink in hand. "Looking good, sweet cheeks!"

Her friend wolf whistles, and I grin, then whistle back.

Eden glares in their direction, so ferociously that it startles a laugh out of me.

"Jealous?" I tease, and she lets out a harsh, exasperated sound.

"Just a little tired of people trying to *make* me jealous," she snipes, with a glance to her right.

I follow it to see Jayk sitting up on one of the raised platforms. A half-dozen women are clustered around them, and one woman I haven't met yet is sitting stiffly on his lap.

Hmm. Eden's not wrong. It *does* look like a classic afternoon special move. Poor guy has it bad if he's resorting to the cheap tricks.

Jayk's eyes are locked on us, and I give him a friendly little wave.

He flicks his pocketknife open.

The cutie.

"Want to make *him* jealous?" I ask, and Eden's steps slow.

"That would be immature," she says, glancing up at me.

"Childish, even," I agree.

Something sparkles in her eyes, and she begins to turn back to him. I catch her chin, angling it back toward me.

"No, no, no. You can't *look* at him." I roll my eyes, and a confused crinkle appears between her brows.

"I can't?"

Her lips are rosy, parted, and my dick strains. I know how good she feels.

I lower my head, and her breathing falters.

"You have to make it look like you aren't thinking about anyone but me." I trace the line of her bodice where it ties over her breasts, barely holding them in. Goosebumps lift under my fingertips, a barely raised texture on her painfully soft skin. "Make it look like he's the furthest thing from your mind."

"Um . . ."

"You need to look like you want to taste me." I brush a kiss over her chilly cheek, and she shivers. "Like you want me naked."

Her chest lifts as she breathes in sharply, and color rides her cheekbones. My skin feels tight and too sensitive. I trail my hand up to wrap around her throat, over her frantic heartbeat.

I feel her hot little breaths against my cheek as I move my mouth to whisper in her ear. "Look at me like you love me."

The words slip out of me too needily, too close to a demand, and I flush with embarrassment. Not waiting to see her reaction, I lean down to her throat and suck her panicky pulse into my mouth. My beard scratches against her skin, and she tips her head back, letting out a sharp, stunned moan.

Eden tastes delicious, like her want for me is dusted on her skin. Her heartbeat throbs against my tongue, and my balls ache in response. Suddenly, I understand vampires. The desire to sink into someone and suck and suck and suck.

I lick the column of her throat, wanting more of her. I remember burying my face between her thighs. How slippery wet she gets. How she soaked my beard, and I ate her until I tasted her all the way down my throat.

Which is sounding like a really good option right now.

Eden's hands find my shoulders, then slip down over the oil, and she squeaks.

I wrench myself back before I lose it and hike her dress up in front of everyone, my chest heaving harder than it did after my entire fire routine. We stare at each other, and it takes me a second to come back to myself enough to look up at Jayk.

When I do, he's not on the platform.

Eden, trembling and pink-cheeked, looks over too, and some of the shine in her eyes dies.

It's a travesty.

Eden's eyes should always shine.

"He was jealous . . ." I attempt, and her lips roll in.

"He left. Again." She shakes her head. "That was stupid of me . . . and not very kind."

She suddenly looks small, the fragile hope, the openness I saw in her before closing up like an old wound I want to tend.

"Come on, beautiful." I lead her the final few steps over the bridge we created for the dry moat, and she follows me into the woods without a word.

There are solar lights throughout the forest, still dusty from storage. The old boxes of Jasper's mother's wedding decorations were well and truly raided for this party. I lead Eden a short way away, to a mossy glade that bursts with wildflowers. They're dizzyingly fragrant, and their scent twists with the gentle smoke of the bonfire. From here, the music is only a dull beat in the distance.

Eden walks around the space, her fingers brushing the petals. She's moving slowly, a little awkwardly, but she doesn't seem injured. She might have pushed herself too hard sparring.

She's been hustling hard—Dom even said, "She's been doing great."

So he's been gushing, obviously.

"You've been wearing these in your hair," she says to herself, examining the yellow flowers.

Every time I think of that half-crushed, wilted thing Jasper pulled from his pocket, my spine turns to liquid.

I rub the back of my neck with a smile. "You noticed that?"

Those large, pretty eyes roll.

"As if anyone can keep their eyes off you." Then she adds in a wry mutter, "And as tonight's performance shows, you know it."

Flirting. She's flirting. My heart lifts with my smile.

"You liked the show? I wanted to do aerials, but Beau nixed it until I have another month or two of healing under my belt."

Spoilsport.

Eden doesn't smile though; her eyes are snagged back on my chest. I watch as they slip down and down, and my smile becomes wicked. I wonder if she knows how transparent she is when she's turned on.

I hook a thumb into the waistband of my sweatpants, and it dips precariously. Her lower lip vanishes into her mouth as her eyes widen.

"The show was . . ." She takes a breath, then swallows. "Good."

"Good?" I roll my shoulders back, and she follows the movement, her eyes running all over my chest. "Just good?"

"I—" Eden tears her gaze away. "It made me feel things."

"Things, huh?" My grin deepens, and I step closer. "Show me."

Her gaze darts back, and I watch her measure the distance between us like I might pounce. She's been playing with Jayk too much.

I don't want to wrestle her to the ground. I just want proof she wants this.

"Show you what?" she asks breathlessly.

One more step, and I'm almost in touching distance. "Lift your dress and show me how it made you feel."

Eden's cheeks are pink, eyes a bit too bright, and in her floral dress with her thick hair all about her, she looks too innocent for the things I want to do to her. But I know she's not. She'd let all five of us stuff her full of our cocks if we asked her to.

Or if we told her to.

"I didn't bring you here for this." Her voice sounds like sex. "We should . . . talk."

Enjoying the way she's responding to me, I run my hand down my oiled abdomen. Her eyes track it religiously. "You brought me out here to give me an answer, right? Whether you want me?"

More than that. I need to know if she's okay with me and Jasper—by the way she looked at us earlier, I'm hoping it's a yes, but it will break me if it's not.

Hesitant, Eden nods. It makes her hair ripple prettily, and I watch the ends dance around her waist.

My breathing loses its rhythm. "So do it like this," I coax. "If you want me, if you want everything that comes along with that . . . lift your dress."

Her hands tighten in the fabric, and I wait, every muscle tense.

Then her skirts begin to lift. I see her ankles, her taut calves, one slow inch after another. I feel every one like a pulse through my cock.

Then she stops.

"Wait. I can't."

My heart thunders as I try to process the rejection.

"No. I mean, I do want you, Lucky. I want everything with you. It's just . . . Beau made me wear . . ." She huffs, distressed. "I have a . . . *thing*."

Beau? What?

I stare at her—and at the way she's easing from foot to foot. Her stiffness, the way she keeps rubbing her thighs together . . .

It clicks.

"Eden." I stick my tongue in my cheek. I can't be this lucky. *No one* can. "What are you wearing under that pretty dress?"

She lowers her head, looking up at me over her glasses pleadingly. It's adorable.

Still not taking it easy on her though.

"Show me, beautiful. Show me how the mean doctor has been teasing you."

Her lids flutter shut.

She starts lifting the skirts again, up and up until I see her thighs, lean from weeks of walking. The soft skin begging for my tongue. Her heavy-lidded eyes open as she lifts the dress higher still, watching my face intently.

Eden's panties are a soft pink that match the flowers on her dress, with a little bow at the top. They're wholesome and cute . . . and her soaking pussy has made a dark, lewd stain on the sweet fabric.

Her hands tremble on her dress as I stare.

And stare and stare.

I sink to my knees in front of her, and her inner thigh twitches. Fuck, I can smell her here. My mouth waters.

"So pretty," I say hoarsely.

I can't see a vibrator or any type of wearable. Whatever Beau's toy is, it must be internal.

Better investigate.

Leaning up, I press my tongue against the stain, and she gasps, flinching. The first taste of her kills my amusement. I thought I remembered how good she tastes, but I was dead wrong. She's sweet and tangy, and the scent of her fills me.

Not wanting her to move, I grasp her thighs as I lick the damp fabric, grinding her down into my mouth. Eden cries out, and I shudder in response. The dress dips over my head as she loses her grip, but I ignore it, focused on the taste of her on my tongue. I can't get enough through the fabric.

I need more.

Torn between impatience and wanting to take my time, I roll her panties down fast, lifting her ankles one at a time to get them all the way off, and her hands tuck back her dress so she can lean on my slick shoulders to keep her balance.

Dazed, I look up, remembering how oiled I am when her fingers rub over me.

"It'll wreck your dress," I warn.

Eden's pupils are blown dark and starved. "I don't care about the dress, Lucky."

Thank God.

I move my hands up, parting her sweet pussy with my fingers. She's dripping wet and blushing pink, and I bring my mouth back over her, not wanting to waste any of it. I groan into her as she coats me. She whimpers, but I don't look up. I'm busy, lost exploring every silky, slippery contour of her with my tongue.

She's balanced awkwardly over me, and one of her hands moves to my hair for a better grip as she rubs herself against my face. My beard scrapes her thighs, her pussy until I'm covered in her. Marked by her. Her frantic, panting cries spur me on like a whip.

I circle her clit with my tongue, and her hand tightens brutally in my hair.

"More." Her voice is broken with need.

My stiff cock leaks precum. More, she says.

Short of a safeword, I'm not stopping for anything.

Laying my tongue flat against her clit, I rub and suckle until I get the right rhythm and her cries pick up pace and volume, until her thighs quake under my hands. Her hands clutch at my hair and the pain of it makes my whole body sing.

I run a finger to her tight, hot hole, and breach her entrance. Her inner muscles crush my finger in scorching, satin heat, and I freeze, feeling the resistance.

I think I found her toy.

Swallowing hard, I add a second finger, rubbing and slowly pumping until she falls apart with a raw, shattered cry.

Her knees give out, and I have to move quickly to catch her before she falls. She lets out a strangled sound—half a squeal, half a moan—and clamps her legs together as she comes down on top of me.

Eden leans against me, panting, her face in my neck. My breathing is just as wrecked. Every part of my body is demanding to be inside her.

Now.

I grasp her chin and pull her mouth to mine, kissing her roughly. Her soft, curious hands slip over my chest, and I eat her stunned moan. I want her to taste herself.

She should know how fucking good she tastes.

Gripping her around the waist, I lower her backwards, and she makes that same squeal again.

I pull back long enough to stare at her flushed, greedy face. "Are you okay?"

"Toy," she pants out.

I rest my forehead against hers and swallow hard. "Are you wearing a plug?"

Eden nods against me.

Fuck. Fuck. Fuckity fuck.

Something feral takes hold. "I need to see it."

She squeaks as I flip her over. I rapidly arrange her to where I want her—to where I *need* her—and soon she's bent over in front of me, her face buried in wildflowers. Her legs are split, kneeling on either side of mine, and her ass is in my lap like a present, my erection digging into her abdomen.

And like a present, I get to unwrap her.

Shaking with excitement, I lift her filmy skirts over her head, exposing her ass.

Her ass that is decorated in thick black writing.

Prepared this for you, buddy.

Startled, my laugh fires out of me like a shot.

"What does it say?" she asks anxiously.

"Wait, you don't *know*?" I look at it again—and bend over her ass, laughing so hard tears come to my eyes. Beau gets me the best presents.

Huffing, she moves to get up, but I coax her back down.

And finally see past the writing.

Spread as she is over my lap, her pale cheeks are parted, and the silver base of the plug winks at me where it's buried inside of her. She's applied plenty of lube, and her whole cleft glistens with it.

It's a wide one too, big and thick. I give it a soft, experimental tug and watch the tight, creased skin stretch and strain. As it moves, Eden arches her back with a gasp, and I feel something roll around inside the plug. It has weighted balls.

My hands shake on the toy.

"Beau made you put it in?" I ask, twisting it a little.

Her thighs clamp around me at the same time her hole sucks slickly at the toy, and she lets out another hoarse sob. Pressure builds in the base of my spine, rampant lust tearing through me. Her tender body quivers at the invasion, and everything in me is demanding I invade her more.

"Y-yes. He said . . . he wanted me to wear it while I spoke to you and Jayk. To get a r-reaction. What does it say?" She squirms on my lap, and I pump the toy inside her until she pushes back against my hand like she can't get enough. Like she *needs* to be fucked.

"It's a private message," I tell her, mimicking her prim tone—but the effect is ruined by how my voice shakes. "I'm sure it's none of your business."

Pressing down against her back, I thrust my cock up into her—it's imperfect, the sensation blunted by too many clothes and the angle almost painful, but I need some friction. I need more. The sight of the plug disappearing in her is straight up depraved.

Beau wanted a reaction.

Fucking. Granted.

"It's so big," she whimpers.

The end of the plug is flared enough that it hides where they're joined, so I tilt it to the side. Her hands tear up the grass at the change of angle, crushing several heady flowers as the plug stretches and pushes under the taut skin. She's puckered tightly around the base of it, and I feel the phantom grip around my dick.

"I know, beautiful. The pressure's a lot, huh? You're taking it so good." I tweak it inside her again, and the balls clatter. "It's fun being on the other side of this. How fast do you think I can make them move?"

I jiggle the end of the plug and Eden squeals, back arching. "Stop, stop. Ah."

I pause my fascinated jiggling. "Too much?"

Eden tosses me a furious look over her shoulder. "My derriere is *not* a pinball machine."

Laughing, I squeeze her ass. God, she looks so good filled up like this.

In a low voice, I ask, "Do you like it?"

I know the answer, I can feel it in the way her pussy is soaking. I can see it in the flush of her skin and how she arches into my touch, silently begging for more.

But hearing her soft, ashamed, "Yes" still makes me groan.

"Has he taken it? Have you had a cock in this ass yet?" I ask, and she shakes her head. I knead both cheeks in my hands, pressing them together, pulling them apart, knowing the balls are rolling around inside her like wrecking balls.

She squirms, breathing in stutters, and I spank her hard. "Oh, baby, you don't know what you're missing out on. It feels so fucking good."

Eden shudders, pushing her ass into my hands. "Have you . . . With Jasper . . .? *Ah.*"

"Has Jasper fucked me? Only my mouth. Only once." In reality, anyway. In my dreams he's done it every night since we met. Mesmerized by her hungry, wanton body, I can't help myself. "You curious, beautiful? You want to see what I look like with his dick in my ass?"

Her greedy movements grow more frantic. "Yes," she moans.

The thought of her there with us, watching him break me, *take* me, makes my whole body flush with want.

Rubbing my cock into her again, I work the plug completely out of her, watching her pretty, slick hole gape. I tease it with the end of the plug, drunkenly watching her rosebud kiss the metal. The urge to take it, to fuck into her hard, pounds into me.

Is that what Beau wanted? He has to know he's playing with fire sending her out like this. I shove the plug back in hard and she gasps, arching her back.

I can't fuck her ass for the first time in the middle of the woods. She deserves a bed. She deserves a bed, right? Something romantic.

I have to shove down hard on the voice insisting that anal annihilation *is* romantic.

And that's *me.*

If Jayk sees that message, he's going to rearrange her insides.

I run my hands up and down her back, not sure if I'm soothing her or myself. "Fuck, Eden. I need to fuck you. I have a condom. Let me fuck you, beautiful. Have mercy on me."

"Don't any of you talk?" She groans, rubbing her hips down over my cock. "No condoms. Burn them. Done with them."

Yes, ma'am.

I shove back so I'm kneeling behind her, enough to free my cock, then I hesitate.

"Eden, sweetheart, turn over. I want to see your face the first time I'm inside you."

She turns around quickly until she's lying on her back, hooking her knees over my waist with a practice that tells me Beau's been coaching her. I'll give him a drink for it later, because it means my dick is already notched against her entrance as I settle between her legs and lean over her.

Her curious hands find my chest, glancing up at me with searching heat.

"Touch me all you like, beautiful, you don't need to ask when you're with me."

She smiles like I just offered myself on a platter. Her fingers trail over my muscles, sliding through the oil, and she shivers.

"Your body is incredible," she whispers, looking delighted enough that I feel myself preen.

Needing to taste her, I brush a kiss across her lips. Then another, deeper and wetter, taking her mouth as I sink into her.

God. Damn.

She's so hot—scalding—and the pressure of the plug in her ass compresses the already tight space into nothing. Her pussy is slick and snug and so perfect, I'm gritting my teeth so I don't come apart before I'm all the way in.

Her lips part, her head tilting back as I fill her. The pressure is so intense, her body is almost pushing me out as I invade her, and I see tears gather at the corners of her eyes.

Seeing them, I stop, shaking, a sheen of sweat on my face. "You okay, beautiful?"

Her pretty dress is already stained by dirt and oil.

Eden's nods rub her dark hair against the ground. "Don't stop. Please don't. I've been empty all day. God, it's so much. You're so much."

My control snaps.

I slam home, and she bucks against me. Her heels press into the base of my spine, and she kisses me desperately. I kiss her back hard, fucking into her. The searing, silken rub of her cunt against my bare cock is obscene. It's too much. I'm too wound up from years of deprivation, from days of Jasper's taunting touches.

"Eden, fuck." I gasp against her mouth.

Then with a groan I flip her so she's on top, her breasts flattened against my chest as she kneels astride me. Her glasses slip, landing askew over her nose, and her hair is a tangled curtain around us. With her lips rosy red and her blue-gray eyes darkened and dazed, she looks like a ravished librarian.

Fuck, she *is* a ravished librarian.

"I don't know how to . . ." she starts, looking down at me.

I kiss her. "Just hold on, gorgeous."

I wrap one arm around her waist to hold her in place and plant my feet on the ground between her legs.

I roll my hips up hard, impaling her in one stroke, and she cries out, her glasses jostling. Her moisture coats my cock on the backslide, slicking my balls in her warmth.

Eden leans down to lick at my lips, at herself *on* my lips, and my free hand finds the end of the plug. As I thrust into her again, I pull the plug until it almost pops out, then push it back in as I pull out.

She sobs into my mouth, clinging to my shoulders as I pound up into her, harder and harder. Sweat beads on my forehead at the effort not to flood her with my cum.

"You feel so good," I groan against her lips, as her pussy squeezes me with heat. "So good, beautiful. I love you so much. Don't leave me again."

The words are falling out of me, and I can't make them stop. It's like her perfect body won't hold a secret, and it all has to come out if I'm inside her. There's no space for holding back between our pressed bodies. She's too good, and I've missed her too much, and after I'm through fucking her, I want to spend hours talking to her—just being *with* her—before I get to be inside her again.

Eden's eyes fly open over her slipping glasses, and they're a battleground of pleasure. "I won't leave. I promise."

She kisses me clumsily, and again, and again. Then she sobs on a moan as I twist the plug, making sure it rolls against the sensitive inner rim. I can feel it move against my cock—can even feel the heartbeat of the balls striking her internally.

"I love you so much, Lucky. I'm sorry I made you wait. No choosing. Either of us. We get—" She gasps as I thrust into her wildly, losing my rhythm as she says everything I've ever wanted her to say. "We get all of it."

"Fuck." Her cunt is swollen and so, so hot. "All of it. You want us both to fill you up? Me and Jasper? Just like this?"

At Jasper's name, her breath catches.

I press my dick in to the hilt, then grind against her, swirling my pelvis over her clit at the same time I pump the toy in her ass.

"Lucky, God. You shouldn't." Despite her husky protest, her head drops back as she rubs her hips over me, writhing like her whole body is as overworked as mine.

"Why not?" The teasing words are an effort to get out, and she's probably right, but I can't shake this kernel of worry that she's still too jealous. That this will be too much.

She's not just jealous, though. I saw the way she looked at us— in the kitchen and earlier tonight. It turns her on as much as it hurts her. But hurting just adds spice to the good things.

"I don't . . ." Eden presses her head into my chest as I drag out of her, then start rocking up in sharp, short punches.

"It'll feel even better, you know," I say against her hair. "A nice, hot cock in your ass instead of this toy. Jasper pressed up behind you. Both our dicks filling you up."

The fantasy is too real for me. Too vivid. The toy works against me inside her, separated by only one thin, sensitive strip of flesh.

He could fuck both of us like this, into her, against me, all three of us together the way we should be, needy, reckless, sweaty. Perfect.

"Shit, fuck. I need you to come now, beautiful. I can't— I'm going to . . ."

Eden cries out, her hips jerking over mine as her inner muscles clench and grip my dick. Unable to hold back anymore, I wrap both arms around her waist and bury myself deep, my orgasm tearing out of me. Cataclysmic. Perfect. I spill everything into her wet heat, making her wetter, covering us both.

She becomes limp over me, draping me like a blanket as she nestles on my chest to recover, but her pussy still milks every drop of my cum with insistent, shattering pulses.

I try to remember how to breathe.

Then a twig crunches, and I realize we're not alone.

"Lucien, must you always make such a mess."

CHAPTER 44

EDEN

SURVIVAL TIP #263
Two is company. Three's a crowd.
Four's a party.

Jasper's voice has me shoving up on Lucky's chest, which knocks him back against the ground with an *oof* as he tries to lift. I scramble to my feet, yanking down my dress.

Lucky's cum trickles out of me, and I halt, feeling it slide down my thigh.

Even after days of Jayk filling me at every opportunity, I'm still not used to the sensation. Particularly not while Jasper, pristine and elegant, watches intently from several feet away.

Jasper.

Oh, God.

Did he hear all those filthy things Lucky was saying about him? Did he see my reaction?

I thought he was going to let us be alone together.

Did he change his mind?

"May I help you?" I ask, my voice husky and edged in panic.

Jasper is like a fox slinking in to observe two hares, his interest sharp-toothed. He examines me thoughtfully, then his gaze falls to Lucky, who has rolled lazily onto his side.

In the starlight, his golden hair turns almost silver, and it twists messily around his face in glinting strands. His cock is still out, glistening and spent, and he seems to have a complete lack of self-consciousness about it. On his side like this, he's all colorful fiendish tattoos and lean muscles. I can even see the flexed indent in the side of his ass.

He said I can touch him as much as I want, and it feels like a luxury. Beau thoroughly controls our scenes, so until we're cuddling afterwards, tired and sated, I don't have free rein. Jaykob encourages me to take what I want—but he also takes what *he* wants. Given his size, aggression, and general impatience, it tends to mean I don't get much time to explore.

I want to touch Lucky. I want to touch him much, much more than I already have.

Jasper's gaze lingers over him the same way as mine does.

"This 'Team Bacon' is apparently having a drama of some sort or another. I believe they require your assistance, Lucien. I thought it best I fetch you myself." Jasper glances pointedly over Lucky's disheveled state. "You've put on quite enough of a show already."

Lucky's dimple makes a reappearance, teasing me. "It would have been a good one though. Did you know that Eden's wearing a—?"

"Lucky!" I exclaim, my hand flying to my throat. I dart an embarrassed look at an amused Jasper.

"Darling girl, I'm not so easily shocked as that." His eyes gleam —the fox about to take its kill. "Where did you suppose Beaumont sourced those plugs so quickly? I picked them out myself."

He *what*?

"You *know*?" I stare at him, horrified. "You know I'm wearing a . . . ?"

Beau. I am going to murder him. He'll *wish* for water hemlock. How on earth did he even ask for that?

Now, hi there, Jasper, I would really like to stretch my girl-friend's ass out as far as I can. Be a doll and help me out?

Did they discuss this over tea? How is that appropriate information to share?

"Yes, Eden," Jasper says. "I am *vividly* aware."

Lucky just laughs, rolling up in a quick, seamless motion to his feet.

I'm still staring at Jasper.

He knows. He knows the exact size, and shape, and material, and weight of what's inside me. God, he might as well have put it inside me himself.

I swallow, but my throat and mouth are suddenly arid, and I swallow again, trying to work up some moisture. I'm still tingling and languid from my orgasms, from having Lucky's scandalously perfect mouth worshipping me. He devours me like I'm his last meal and his blatant, vocal enjoyment is one of the most erotic things I've ever experienced.

Jasper knows it too.

Jasper is standing there, knowing I have his boyfriend's cum running down my legs and a plug throbbing in my ass.

It makes me cringe. It also makes me wet.

Jasper meets my gaze, and his brow arches higher. Surely he can't tell that this turns me on. I've become quite good at hiding it, I think.

Lucky finally tugs up his sweatpants, covering himself with a long-suffering sigh. "Fine, I guess I better go see what the issue is. Eden, can we cuddle tonight? I'll join you and Beau, I don't care."

Jasper shoots him a sharp frown. "No. You will stay with me tonight, Lucien. If you wish to cuddle with Eden, then she can come to us."

It takes several moments for me to realize I stopped breathing, and I suck air back in on a wheeze. Cuddle with Lucky in the same bed as *Jasper*? Jasper watching us. In bed. Together. Me, in bed, with Jasper.

What does Jasper even wear to bed? More silk? Bunny slippers? Nothing?

I might faint.

Lucky's beard bristling over my cheek jolts me out of my dazed imagining.

"You going to see Jayk now?" he asks, and I bite my lip as I worry over my plan.

I hadn't counted on having sex tonight—in hindsight, that seems naive, but going to see Jayk directly after sleeping with Lucky is possibly the quickest way to put him on defense, and I need him to hear me out.

"I should probably . . . clean up first," I manage. As I speak, more cum leaks out of me in a warm, wet gush.

"Nah. You definitely should *not* do that," Lucky says, running his hand up my arm.

Jasper shakes his head, then walks over, pulling a thin gossamer soft swathe of fabric from his pants.

But he doesn't hand it to me.

He hands it to Lucky.

"Clean her, Lucien," Jasper instructs, and his dark eyes find mine again.

They glitter like blood diamonds.

My heart batters against my breastbone, my hand covering the tie of my bodice over my dress. I suddenly feel exposed. He knows about the plug. He knows the state Lucky left me in. Those eyes are seeing everything—and it's far, far too much.

Is this a dominant-submissive relationship without sex?

Because it feels *incredibly* sexual.

I glance at Lucky, waiting for a quip or some sassy backtalk, but he's gripping the silk handkerchief in a white-knuckled fist.

Then he drops to his knees behind me, so smoothly, so easily, I realize it's a motion he's made many, many times before.

He lifts my dress from behind, and I tense. From this angle, Jasper can't see much, but it's so . . . indecorous. Apart from that first night at Bristlebrook, Jasper and I have met over books and dinner, tea and chess and conversation that seduces and confuses me by turn. We've been clothed and mannered.

Standing in the woods before him, dirty and tangled and soaked in cum, my ass exposed to the air, I feel positively heathen. Like he's some seraphic being, stepping down from clouds and deigning to amuse himself with filthy mortals.

"Hold your dress for our Lucien, darling girl."

I lower my hands from my bodice to hold my dress over my hips.

Lucky tugs at my ankle, and I let him drag it out, widening my stance. I glance down at him, and he looks up at me, something heated and vulnerable in his eyes.

"He can behave, with the right motivation." Jasper is looking at Lucky too, his posture loose, but face tight with searing intensity. "He looks exquisite down there, don't you agree?"

Lucky sucks in a short, harsh breath, his cheeks coloring. It's odd, talking about him like this, like he's an object or a pleasing pet. But I feel myself growing wetter, and I don't think I can blame Lucky's cum for all of it.

To my surprise, Lucky avoids my eyes, and I suddenly wonder if he feels it too. Despite all his laughing confidence, I wonder if he feels as chipped open and exposed when he's on his knees as I do.

"He does," I say softly. A breeze stirs, sliding over my damp, swollen flesh, and I breathe out through my teeth. "Lucky always looks exquisite."

Lucky's eyes close briefly, relief touching his features. Then he looks back between my legs. The silk handkerchief slides up my inner thigh, smearing through the slick mess, then up over my soaked pussy. He works silently, cleaning me like I'm helpless to do it myself. His motions are trembling, imperfect, and every swipe leaves a streaked, sticky residue on my skin. The delicious, shameful humiliation of it makes me look up at the canopy.

Jasper's eyes watch and watch and watch.

Then Lucky holds up the handkerchief like an offering. "This can't take anymore."

His hoarse voice shakes, and I hear the silent meaning—*I can't take anymore.*

Jasper takes the handkerchief, folding it with a neat motion and placing it in his pocket. "You didn't tend her cunt, Lucien. Be a good boy and lick her clean."

I stare at Jasper's pocket.

Is he *keeping* that?

Did he really just say the word *cunt*?

Lucky's grip on my calf grows painful, and his forehead falls against my leg for a moment as he groans. But Jasper is still so cool and collected, so utterly unhurried. In his silk and slacks, he looks artfully dissolute.

I feel Lucky's beard against my inner thighs. The hot, wet press of his mouth.

My body is feverish. Shaking. I've already come twice, but anticipation prickles my skin. Lucky is too good with his tongue.

"Are you quite all right, my dear?" Jasper asks pleasantly.

Cum and my own desire pools between my legs, and Lucky swipes through my lips, gathering it on his tongue. I can't stifle my whimper, and I nod wildly.

It's warm as summer out here, I'm sure of it. Or perhaps the bonfire got out of hand, and the woods are on fire all around us.

I don't think I would stop, regardless.

Lucky takes another leisurely swipe, and I flinch as he brushes my oversensitive clit.

Jasper glances down at his watch. "Do hurry up, Lucien. You have somewhere to be."

Lucky makes a muffled sound against my pussy, then grabs my ass in both hands, anchoring me against his mouth. He doesn't stop to tease this time—he's truly licking me clean, seeking out every bit of himself on me. He buries his tongue inside me, making me kick up on my toes at the sensation, but he yanks me back down and licks out my slick entrance until I'm a shaking wreck.

Despite trying to avoid Jasper's eyes, I get caught in them. They measure me thoughtfully, and I feel my orgasm build.

"That should be enough. Thank you, Lucien."

"No, *please*," I gasp. "Please don't stop."

Lucky gives my thigh a sympathetic squeeze as he stands.

Jasper looks at Lucky, then smiles slightly. "Ah, you have a gift. Kiss me, then, my wretched boy."

I'm lost, utterly confused, until Lucky gives me a mischievous wink. Jasper grasps the short, wet bristles of his beard, then pulls him in for a kiss. As Lucky's mouth splits open, I see the moisture, the white, slick, too-glossy tangle of their tongues. Jasper kisses him luxuriantly, tasting my orgasm, Lucky's cum, with as much fervor as Lucky had while licking me.

Jasper is tasting my pussy.

The moan that escapes me is needy, almost a whine.

Non-sexual. He's my *non-sexual* dominant.

Dear God. No. I know I'm out of touch, but surely this doesn't count as *non-sexual*.

Jasper strokes Lucky's cheek with the back of his fingers. "I do appreciate a creative apology. Consider yourself forgiven."

Forgiven? For Lucky teasing him about the kiss earlier? I glance between them, dizzy with need. The fusing of their mouths is seared on the back of my eyelids, burning into me every time I blink.

I need more.

"You had best hurry on," Jasper murmurs, glancing down at his watch again.

"In a second," Lucky says in a thick voice. "Do you have a pen?"

Jasper purses his lips and looks up at him with mild bemusement. "Do I look as though I'm the type of person who carries a pen with them at all times?"

Lucky grins.

Jasper sighs, then pulls a pen from his pocket. "Take it."

Lucky slides me a wicked look. "I'm writing a note on the other side."

The other . . .? I barely stop myself from stomping my foot. "No!"

"Other side?" Jasper frowns.

Lucky laughs, then moves back around behind me. I scowl.

"Only if you tell me what Beau wrote," I bargain.

"Just bend over and let it happen." He flips my skirts again and pauses. "Which, incidentally, you might need to do with Jayk."

These *men*. Honestly.

I don't move, though, as the pen slides over my skin.

I feel Jasper's curiosity boring into me.

"If I don't get to know, you don't get to know," I say tartly, and he gives me an amused look.

It's probably something like *Lucky waz here*. Or *High five*.

Demeaning.

"In your professional opinion, what does it mean when someone is turned on by being embarrassed?" I ask abruptly, and the pen swerves on my butt.

Jasper's slight smile grows more pronounced. "Perhaps a degradation kink." He looks me over, then nods. "Be careful with that one. I think you may be quite particular about the ways in which you enjoy it."

Lucky pinches my cheek as he stands again, and I look at him warily. "Are you going to get me murdered?"

"I wouldn't do that." He hands the pen back to Jasper with an impish smile. "But for legal reasons, I can't claim responsibility for anything that happens to you because of the things that may or may not be written on your body."

I am so dead.

"Just don't let him see, surely that's the easiest solution,"

Jasper suggests, taking in my consternation with an amused smile as he strolls over to me.

He sounds like he could be discussing scores in billiards rather than advising me on how to avoid handing my rear end—perhaps literally—to a cranky, emotionally inhibited primal dom.

Instead of leaving, Lucky pauses, watching us.

"Right," I breathe. "Of course. Very logical."

Jasper's gentle hand touches my elbow, and I glance up.

He's . . . very close. He's very close and his lips are still lustrous from Lucky's filthy kiss. He knows what I taste like.

It suddenly seems catastrophic that I don't have the same privilege.

"Are you okay with what happened here, Eden?" Jasper asks softly, catching my mood shift.

I can't look away from his lips. The ache to kiss him is enough to take my breath. I want the three of us on my tongue like a Eucharist.

"Yes." I rub the gooseflesh on my arm, and realize I've shifted close to him. "Why did you stop him from making me . . .? Why wouldn't you let me . . .?"

"Come?" His dark brow curves up like a drawn bow. "What makes you think you've earned the privilege, sweet Eden? You'll need to work much harder than that with me, I'm afraid."

"I can work hard." The words leave me in a needy rush before I can stop them, and I bite down on my lip before I humiliate myself further.

But I can't help it. My swollen pussy throbs at his words. Despite my two earlier orgasms, the one Lucky left me on taunts me cruelly.

Jasper only gives me a slight, affectionate smile.

He reaches up toward my hair, pausing until I nod permission, then sweeps it over my shoulders. "There is something tragically lovely in an unsatisfied woman."

He gently pulls a leaf from my hair, plucking the strands of my hair like a harpsichord. I feel the prickle in my scalp, and all the way down my spine. Then he pulls another free.

"You're quivering right now, do you know? So full of unspent need. It's a siren call for men like us. To taste it. To spend it. To waste all that gorgeous lust on our vile perversions." He finger-combs lightly through my tangles, holding my hair, and patiently working through each one. "There's a flush in your skin, over your breasts and cheeks. It begs to be darkened."

Jasper twists a long strand of my hair and lays it over my chest.

"And I imagine right now, your cunt is desperate to be fucked."

My breath leaves me in a hard rush. He's stunning and so care-lessly relaxed as he tidies me, except that I can see the hard length of him pressing against his slacks. Tension is thick as smoke between us.

Jasper examines me, then his gaze catches on my cheekbone. He brings his thumb to his mouth, and he licks it. The flash of wet, pink tongue has my nipples tightening, hard and desperate against my bra. He rubs his thumb over my cheek, almost cupping the whole left side of my face.

I nestle my cheek into his palm, and he pauses. The next sweep of his thumb is softer. Quietly affectionate. It doesn't quite soothe the scorching frustration inside me, but it soothes some-thing else.

"There," he murmurs. "Jaykob couldn't ask for a more lovely woman."

My heart freedives.

I don't have words for him. I don't know what I could say. But he did once tell me that some things are best said without words.

Twisting, I press my lips into his palm, keeping my eyes on his sharp, beautiful face.

"Careful, my girl."

His eyes are a warning . . . but I'm rather tired of his warnings. My curiosity is stronger. My body is still shivering with need, and

Jasper smells wonderful, like books and man and something that silently screams sex.

My gaze drops to his lips.

"Hey, darlin', have you seen—?"

Beau spills from between the trees, and I almost shove my dress down before I remember the way he spanked me earlier for removing his hand. I keep it hiked up around my waist. Maybe if he sees what a desperate mess I am right now, he'll take pity on me and let me come.

I take a step toward Beau, and Lucky uses the opportunity to swoop in and steal a kiss from Jasper.

"Lucky," Beau finishes, his brows lifting in amusement as he takes us in. "Well, well. What do we have here?"

Lucky turns in Jasper's grip. "Is this about Team Bacon? If it is, Jasper already told me."

He doesn't seem in a hurry to go anywhere. His eyes settle back on me, a startlingly possessive glow in them. I bite my lip, watching as Jasper's hands track down over Lucky's ass, and Lucky smirks at me.

"Forget them. They'll live." Beau's eyes linger on me. "You look like you're having fun."

Feeling daring and too worked up for sense, I give him a pleading look under my lashes. "I need some help, Doctor Bennett."

Beau's eyes widen, then he laughs, deep and loud. "Aren't you just a little flirt now?"

He strolls over to me, a wide, amused smile painting his face. I don't even have it in me to be embarrassed right now, not if it means he'll ease this awful ache.

Jasper tsks. "Lucien said she was on her way to Jaykob. You know how he neglects foreplay—better to send her to him squirming."

Lucky turns back to him, kissing his neck, and I watch them avidly. His sunshine against Jasper's moonlight and shadows.

Jasper tunnels his hand through Lucky's hair, holding him to him.

Beau's hand runs up the back of my thigh, and I shiver. "Aw, but look how sad she is."

Jasper arches a dry brow. "You and I are very different types of dominants."

His eyes flare as Beau slips his fingers lazily between my legs, sliding through the new gush of wetness. I arch my back more deeply, the way he likes, pushing myself into his hand.

Jasper's gaze slides up to examine my face, and with acute regret, he adds, "She's not nearly sad enough."

Beau tuts. "Once again, the sadist thinks he's so much more scary because he works with pain. That just sounds like the easy way out to me."

Lucky laughs nervously, then edges away from Jasper, but Jasper tightens his grip on Lucky's hair, yanking it back against his shoulder so Lucky is chained against him. Jasper gives him a look so coldly amused that my whole body clenches. At the same time, Beau brushes against my swollen clit, and I sigh in relief.

There's something happening here, and I'm not certain what it is, but a meteor could strike our forest and I wouldn't care, so long as Beau keeps *touching* me.

Jasper looks at Beau with mild condescension.

"I'm sure you're quite good at what you do, Beaumont. But you are missing your other half, and you do so rely on one another. I have no doubt you have the ability to throw the poor girl an orgasm or two." Jasper strokes over Lucky's vulnerable throat. "But without Dominic, I don't believe you have the discipline to truly wreck your submissive with pain *or* pleasure."

Oh.

Oh, dear.

At the mention of Dominic, the good-humored smile around Beau's mouth flatlines. His hand pauses on my clit, and I bite down on my lip to stop from begging.

"Now that's a bit rich, considering you're too afraid of yourself to even touch her," he bites out.

Jasper gives him a sharp look. "Careful, Beaumont. I warned you about this."

Lucky seems to be holding his breath. He glances at Jasper, then Beau. I find myself doing the same thing.

Jasper warned Beau? About . . . touching me?

Beau slaps my pussy lightly, and I flinch at the shocking, sudden sting. Jasper lets out an equally sudden hiss. He straightens, his fingers tightening on Lucky's throat.

Lucky arches into the touch, his lashes fluttering closed.

"You have a mighty big mouth, Jasper. I think it's about time you backed it up." Beau comes around and smiles down at me. Lifting his glistening fingers, he paints Lucky's cum over my lips like war paint. "Funnily enough, I'm feeling the need to expand my horizons. How about a lesson—sadism 101?"

Beau leans down and teases my mouth with a slow, silken kiss. It's the kind of kiss that loosens my mind and un-tenses every muscle. Drugging. Endlessly delicious. His shirt abrades my nipples, and the scent of him invades me.

When he pulls back, his breath fans against my lips and the golden-brown glints in his eyes have been swallowed by want, and I'm trembling with the need to rub myself all over him.

"Beaumont . . ." Jasper breathes, staring at us.

Color crests in his savagely beautiful cheeks. I vividly remember writhing on Beau's lap, my legs split wide around Jasper as he bared me to the room. It's the only time he's touched me, *kissed* me, and I'd been too lost to sensation at the time to watch him.

I *need* to watch him.

"I heard your concerns," Beau says. "But it looks to me like you have a perfectly willing submissive right there. I'm sure he'd be happy to give our girl a demonstration on how to be a good little pain slut."

"You persist in putting her within my reach."

A muscle tics in Jasper's jaw as he finally looks up at Beau. His displeasure curls between them like black smoke, and Lucky shivers in his grip, watching Jasper with a heavy-lidded expression.

Beau slides him a wry look. "I heard your warnings, Jasper. We've all heard them. But I think our girl needs to see a demonstration—let her decide for herself what she wants to get herself in for moving forward."

Jasper's eyes flick down to watch Beau play with me, indecision flickering over his face . . . along with devious hunger.

My heart twists as I realize what Beau's doing. He helped me build the courage to talk to Lucky. Dom was completely off the table, of course, but he even helped me plan for Jayk. I didn't talk to him about Jasper, though. It felt too out of reach, given Jasper's reservations, and I didn't know how to broach it.

Apparently, Beau does.

Lucky's hand trembles on Jasper's chest. "The pain slut is in."

Jasper looks down at him, his face all vengeful angles, and his Adam's apple bobs.

Beau's voice becomes soothing. "There isn't a thing to fret about here, Jasper. I have our girl. She might be more interested in what you have to offer than you give her credit for."

Jasper's eyes sink closed, his lashes an inky veil. With Lucky clutched in his grip, the both of them breathlessly still, they look like some ancient mosaic—a press of light and dark that belongs to the reverence of a church.

I feel overfull, needy. This is too good to be true.

"I'll throw in a sweetener," Beau muses. "You turn your submissive into a crying, squirming wreck, and I'll make sure she is one, too. Then we can send her to Jaykob covered in cum and desperate for a good fuck, just like you wanted."

My excitement comes to a screeching halt.

Too good to be true, indeed.

Beau's hand necklaces my throat in a gentle mimicry of Jasper's hold on Lucky. He pulls me up by it, directing me with slow, easy confidence until I'm standing in front of him. Then higher still, until I'm on my tip-toes and struggling to balance.

"Is that fair, darlin'? You want to make Jasper happy, don't you? He's going to be working so hard. You're going to behave no matter what I do to you, isn't that right? The least you can do is take what I'm going to give you like a good, grateful girl."

My whole body feels like weeping, and it's a fight to keep the despair out of my face when I nod. "Yes, Beau."

Beau kisses my lips sweetly again, right as his hand tightens on my neck, and the dual, overwhelming sensations make me shudder. My calves start to ache, but even a small drop of my heels makes my neck strain against his grip.

Jasper's eyes watch and watch and watch, until the uncertainty in his expression has vanished entirely. He's Lucifer, banished of doubts and the desire for purity. Only degenerate, ungodly intent lines his face now.

Danger makes the air barbed and spicy, but desire makes me crave the bite.

"Very well, then, Beaumont. You get your wish," Jasper surveys me with open lust, and I can see his cock, hard and pressing against his slacks. "Welcome to the show."

CHAPTER 45

JASPER

SURVIVAL TIP #152
*The reward for giving in
may be worth the torment of holding back.*

It's almost too much want, all at once.

Eden is lovely in her misery. Her mouth is a soft, pouty moue of sadness, and her breaths are already coming in nervous little pants. It's *obscene*. Her curiosity might wreck me, but here, Beaumont is giving me a soft place to land.

Lucien hasn't stopped pressing those soft, bristly kisses to my throat—an indulgent liberty I'd usually stop him taking without permission, but it feels so unforgivably decadent that I can't bring myself to do it. His entire body is pressed against me. His cock is hard and heavy against my hip, and almost entirely visible in the pathetic excuse for clothing that is his sweatpants.

I pull him off my neck and up to my mouth, kissing him fiercely. Deeply. He's quivering with the need to be fucked, just as Eden is, and since they so messily indulged in one another, we're now free to do the same.

His mouth sears me, too decadent and delicious to enjoy for

long if I want this to last. I tear his hair tie free of his bun, so his hair tumbles out wildly around him, then push him away from me.

"Remove your sweatpants, Lucien. Let our submissive admire all of you."

He salutes teasingly, shoots a wink at Eden, and he rids himself of his clothes in an instant.

As he turns, I admire every glorious inch of him. His body is breathtaking, and *finally*, I have reign over it. *My* body—to touch, and fuck, and break.

My cock is painful, trapped in my slacks, but I ignore it. I will enjoy fucking him, intensely, but this part is the real joy for me.

Their submission.

Their *need*.

"Is there anything you would like to add to your usual limits?" I ask, snapping the hair tie around my wrist. "Any concerns?"

Lucien's dimple plays with me, and with his hair out like this, he's enough to steal my breath.

But I can see the brat in him before the words are even out of his mouth.

"No concerns at all. All your toys are in the house." Lucien's eyes twinkle. "But don't worry. I'm down for a spanking. It'll be cute."

Eden makes a strangled sound, and I raise a slow, deliberate brow, filing that particular insult away for later. I don't want to take today too far. I'm wary of frightening Eden, and Lucien and I are still finding our way.

But it doesn't give him carte blanche.

"Dangerous, dangerous games," I murmur and watch the nerves and excitement spark in his eyes.

For many long, long years, I didn't think I could ever enjoy a brat. There's an elegance to the dance between submissive and dominant. I find pleasure in the willing, graceful fall into compliance. Beauty in the silent micro-gestures, and the anticipation of needs on both sides. It's gorgeous work, where each person strives to ensure the other is fulfilled.

Lucien is another challenge altogether. I don't know all the steps to this dance, but it's full of bright music and quick, dizzying turns that keep me on my toes.

In all the reverence of my craft, I never thought I could want to laugh.

"Be careful of his left shoulder," Beaumont advises. "No strain on it at all—and no impact."

I nod as I circle Lucien, my fingers tracing those awful scars that nearly cost me my life. I'm already cautious of his wounds, but I appreciate Beaumont's concern. He took good care of my Lucien.

"Beaumont, I'm curious. How well does your submissive choke on a cock? Because mine needs a lesson in the value of silence."

He gives me an amused look, then he tilts Eden's head back further, his hand under her chin. "You remember your non-verbals?"

"Y-yes?" There's an enjoyable edge to her voice now.

His other hand drifts around her, and he squeezes her pussy through her dress. She gasps, her eyes flying around between us, but his hand at her throat holds her fast.

"Get on your knees, pet, and open your mouth. Show them how pretty you look with my dick in your throat."

Beside me, Lucien lets out a small groan, his eyes riveted on Eden as she sinks to her knees. In her pretty dress, she looks like a descending cloud.

I move around behind Lucien, and as she opens her mouth wide, that pink tongue invitingly lewd, I drop heavy, sucking kisses to the side of his neck. He shudders against me, and I run my hand down his oil-slick chest until I grasp his cock.

I press my eyes closed and breathe in through my nose, trying to control myself, but Lucien's scent is all around me. He's hard and hot in my hand, silken steel curved into my grasp. I've touched him before, of course—in the study when he humbled me, in passing during our rare scenes—but I've never allowed myself the pleasure of truly *savoring* it.

I give him a slow, firm stroke, overcome by the feel of him. His twitches, the catch of his breath, the slide of him against my sensitive palm. I do it again, and his breath turns ragged. He presses his ass against my cock, and I squeeze him painfully hard in warning.

Lucien gasps, arching into the cruel grip like it's a tender kiss.

"Poor, predictable Lucien," I murmur against his neck, and he swallows, trying to catch his breath, his eyes still on Eden.

Beaumont has freed his cock and is filling her lovely mouth carelessly. Her lips are split wide around him as she tries valiantly to take him. His hands grip her hair tightly, and he fucks into her once, jostling her glasses. She chokes a little as he bottoms out, but he doesn't spend time getting her comfortable. Beaumont starts punching his hips forward, fucking her wet mouth with a groan of enjoyment.

He looks over and gives us a lazy grin, his hips never pausing. "Eden has hard limits on bondage and any kind of closed fist beatings."

He says it lightly, brushing past the information so quickly, I know better than to comment.

He yanks her face tight against his abdomen and buries himself deep. He grinds against her slick, dripping lips, and my own cock throbs jealously.

I'm sure she feels like magic.

Strained tears spill from Eden's dazed eyes, but her skin is luminous with gorgeous, wanton color. Her hips are restless, shifting like she can't get pressure where she needs it.

I'm not used to seeing her so undone, so stripped of her composure. My pulse pounds at me to take, take, take.

The sight of her like this is ruining me.

Holding her head in place, Beaumont tilts her slightly to the side so she can see Lucien and me, and she blinks her glittering tears away as she stares appreciatively at Lucien's hungry cock. I start stroking him just the way I know he likes it—the way I've made him touch himself in front of me before. I want her lost in need we won't satisfy.

I want it to *hurt*.

Beaumont starts fucking her mouth hard and continues easily. "She's good with degradation and humiliation, but don't touch her past or any body shaming—except for her filthy little pussy. Her hot, tight, slutty mouth is fair game too. She has no problem with those, do you, pet?"

He taps the tip of her nose.

She looks up at him with grateful, wet eyes as he rides her face, and his composure breaks, his head tipping back as he groans. Lucien is fighting to stay still, but it's a tragically losing battle. His cock is swollen in my hand, the tip dewing with precum.

"Oh, fuck," he swears under his breath, and he sounds as though he's already being tortured. "She's so fucking pretty. Look at her take him."

He's right.

Eden is gorgeous on her knees, and I'm stunned by her sheer determination. Beaumont isn't small, and her cheeks are red from the effort already, yet she's taking him incredibly deep, sucking on him like she prefers him to air. Her loving enthusiasm is enthralling.

My cock presses against my slacks, desperate for the same devoted attention.

"She does swallow his dick so well, doesn't she?" I croon in Lucien's ear, and Eden's gaze soars back to mine at the compliment.

She pierces me through with those eyes of hers.

I lower my hand to cup Lucien's balls, then squeeze brutally. "Polite, respectful submissives get all the cock."

With my other hand, I pull his hair tie from around my wrist, and twist it heartlessly tight around his sac.

"Oh, *fuck*," Lucien swears again, and a hypnotic shudder wracks him head to toe.

Eden makes a quick squeak of shock in the back of her throat. A tiny one. *Adorable.*

I fight the uncivilized urge to rub my cock through my clothes. There are many things I enjoy about my work, but the evolution of sounds—the sordid symphony of it—is one of the best. Turning those sweet squeaks into raw screams is a delight. Breaking a submissive until tears flow and I can taste that unfiltered, fractured need? *That* is a calling.

I run a finger under the bind to ensure it's painful but not cutting off blood flow, then tug his florid cock teasingly. Pulling it harder, I press his length tight against his abdomen. It smears the slick head of him over his skin in a beautiful mess.

My heart pumps wicked lust through my veins. "How does that feel, hm?"

Lucien shifts, gasping. "Hurts. Fuck. It hurts."

That shaky, husky tone sends savage satisfaction singing through me. "Everything can be a tool when used creatively, dear boy. I don't need my room to make you beg for me." I twist his tender, tied sac and kiss his cheek as he cries out. "Tell me if you experience any tingling or numbness."

There's a breathy moan, and I look up from my handiwork to see Beaumont pulling Eden off him and kneeling behind her, hitching her skirts high enough for us to see that perfect pussy. He spreads her knees wide, and the view is debauched. She's puffy and flushed a dark pink, already used and sopping wet from Lucien, despite his attempted cleaning.

Beaumont runs his hands over the gleaming wetness along her thighs, then dips his fingers through her pussy, spreading her and coating himself in the moisture. He avoids her clit, languorously touching her everywhere else.

"God damn, pet, you really love having my cock in your mouth, don't you?" His voice is rough with lust.

My own cock strains for freedom. To sink into that plush, used hole and claim it for myself. Lucien already left her soaking. Fucking her would mean sheathing myself in both of them.

Lucien groans beside me, his eyes stuck on Beaumont's hand, and I'm distracted by the tiny shifts of his hips as he tries to ease the pressure on his balls. Standing as he is, I can't enjoy the full sight of my efforts.

"Dancer pose, Lucien, and clasp your ankles. Legs apart. Let's see how long you can last."

I haven't done this with him before, but I have seen him move through yoga poses before. Watched obsessively as each position showcased his body in a new, intricately beautiful way. Held long enough, it will become a stress position, and another subtle, delightful layer of discomfort for my masochist.

Lucien blinks, then lets out a shaky laugh. I smile. I suspected he might enjoy this.

He *is* a show off, after all.

He bends, hinging from the hips and leaning forward. He gracefully kicks one leg up and angles his toes toward his head, then reaches back with both hands to grasp his ankle. He's balanced on one leg, his back in a deep, perfect arch, and I let out an appreciative sigh.

I run my nails up his inner thigh until he shivers. "Gorgeous."

The position engages his chest, abdominals, hips, thighs, hamstrings, and calves, and they're all locked tight to keep his balance. Still oiled and glistening, he looks like an obscene sculpture.

He's on perfect display.

I hear the slick slide of Beaumont teasing Eden, and her breaths start coming in high, desperate pants.

"Don't you dare come, darlin'. I can feel you wriggling. Don't you make a liar out of me in front of the mean sadist, now."

Eden's eyes are glassy, her back arched, and she nods. Her pitiable expression could make me come in my pants.

"Focus on me, sweet girl," I instruct, and she looks at me and Lucien.

She swallows tearily, her mouth parting in need.

"This is a stress position." As I lecture her, I trace Lucien's tensed abdominals, smearing my finger through the glossy precum he's wasted on his stomach. "For someone as flexible as Lucien, it's reasonably difficult to hold, but certainly doable. At first. The strain will increase the longer he stays in position, becoming more and more excruciating as his muscles begin to tire—and as I make it difficult for him. It's a test he's designed to fail. Fortunately for us both, Lucien loves to lose to me."

I use one hand to spread his cheeks, admiring his hole, and a tremble runs through my lovely sculpture. I run my nails up his inner thighs with my other hand, then tug his balls viciously.

"*Ah.*" Lucien wobbles as he jerks.

That pain will be a lance through his spine. Enough to make him feel nauseous.

It makes me victorious.

"Oh my *God*," Eden cries out on a sob. "Beau, *please*, I can't."

Gritting my teeth, I close my eyes for a moment. I can't take it anymore. I need to know.

"How does she feel?" I ask, turning to stare back at her. At her lost, helpless face, red with strain and need.

Beaumont gives me a knowing look, his own eyes lit with feral need and his fingers buried in her pussy. "Feel for yourself."

Want grips me as tightly as I've tied Lucien. Touch her. Touch *Eden*.

I've been so well behaved around her. Polite enough that she's taken me at face value.

But the things I want from her are depraved.

She knelt for me so sweetly yesterday. So trustingly. Dancing through my doors in fabric so thin and soft I could see every detail of her nipples in sharp relief. Nestled at my feet, untethered from her fears, she was unspeakably lovely.

When she left, I didn't even make it back to my room. My cock was aching—in *agony*. I fucked my fist in the middle of the library to the fleeting glances of pussy she unthinkingly graced me with. To the remembered feel of her cheek against my thigh. And I brought myself off to her lingering scent in the air.

Perhaps I should be ashamed of it, but for once, I'm not.

We were marvelous together.

"Hold this position, Lucien. Don't move."

He grimaces, his face tight with beautiful discomfort.

With a final, affectionate squeeze of Lucien's cock, I walk over to the others and kneel in front of Eden.

"Do you still want to come, Eden?" I ask, brushing her hair back. Even tangled, it's lovely. I'd love to see it knotted with Lucien's. They would make a striking swirl.

This time, she hesitates, looking at me with wary, tear-stained eyes that only delight me further. She knows it's a trick question.

"Only if it pleases you, Jasper," she whispers, and a startled smile lifts my mouth.

Pretty, pretty words.

I glance up at Beaumont, who smiles smugly back at me. I know he couldn't care less about things like this—the elegant nuances or formal training. Which means . . . he's been teaching her for my benefit, and she's clever enough to know when to employ the respectful phrasing.

"It would please me to see your breasts, Eden. It would please me to make you cry in earnest." I examine her. "Are you sure you still want that?"

"Y-yes." Her eyes dart behind me to Lucien, and I hear his hiss of discomfort.

Lucien enjoys a great many aspects of masochism, but he prefers an active target. The anticipation of wax, or a shock, or a strike. Enduring slow, steadily increasing pain is more of a struggle. Patience is not his strong suit.

Eden, on the other hand, looks fascinated.

Clamping a hand around her throat, I squeeze the sides very lightly, feeling her swallow. I push her up and backwards until she's pressed against Beaumont's chest.

"Now that's a pretty necklace," he says, kissing her cheek.

I brush a kiss across her lips, tasting her little gasp. "Make her another one."

Beaumont replaces my hand at her throat, and his other hand begins working her needy little clit in practiced motions, easing off when her breaths start getting too gaspy.

It's difficult to tear my eyes away, but while she's distracted, I twine the tie at the front of her dress around my finger and pull it free. The front of her dress falls open, revealing her filmy white lace bra, and pretty as it is, I yank that down too. Her breasts spill brazenly over the underwire, and it props them up in profane ways.

I swallow hard. I touched her that first night, until she was writhing and wanton on Beaumont's lap, but I can't remember the last time before that I saw a naked woman. It's been a very, very long time.

She's unholy.

I bring my face close to hers and slide my hands over her breasts. Cupping them, testing their weight and softness, enjoying the hard pebbles her nipples make against my palms. She pants against my mouth, but she has the sense not to try and kiss me without permission.

She moans, and I'm not sure if it's in response to what I'm doing, or what Beaumont is doing to her clit.

I wrap my fingers around one nipple, flicking it gently and watching her flinch.

"Hmm, very sensitive. That's not good for you," I murmur.

I pinch her cruelly, then tug her nipple down hard. She

squeals, trying to escape, and Beaumont tightens his grip on her throat. It forces her back to arch and grinds her ass against him.

"Easy, now, pet. You let him do what he wants to you. We want to make new friends, remember?" Beaumont croons to her.

Her eyes are big and fill with licentious shock at his words.

"Color?" I ask sharply, my lust clamorous and demanding *more*. If Beaumont's been coaching her, he's surely familiarized her with traffic lights.

She pauses just long enough to assure me she's taking stock of herself, then bites her lip. "Green. I'm still green."

I lean down and suck the nipple into my mouth as a reward for us both, and she cries out. She's divine in my mouth, and I can see every inch of her squirming distress. I soothe my tongue over the abused flesh, waiting until her choked sounds rise in pitch, then I nip her hard, twisting her other nipple at the same time.

Eden yelps.

"That's perfect, darlin'. You like how he hurts you, don't you? Look how pretty you are when you cry," Beaumont soothes as I make her suffer.

I swap sides, giving her other breast as much attention as the first. I nip all over her skin in a careful pattern, then give her slick, soothing kisses. Rewarding strokes. Kind and cruel in turn. It's mild pain, but it's a start. She's responding to it.

To *me*.

All the while, Beaumont works under her dress, touching her in ways that keep her pleasure stoked high, but never enough to bring her over.

I have to admire it. He is right, in many ways. It's one thing to torture someone with pain, and it's another kind entirely to torture them with pleasure. It's a delicate, difficult edge to keep someone balanced on without losing them.

"Are you enjoying the show, Lucien?" I call back.

His laugh is hoarse and desperately edged. "Five stars. Ten. Instant classic."

I smile.

Eden is too lost to join in his amusement. She arches and wriggles, but she has nowhere to go, and by the time I'm done biting and ravaging her soft skin, there are red flowers blooming all over her chest. Some of them will come up in gorgeous shades of blue and purple, others will quickly yellow. Her breasts will be a beautiful bouquet for days.

Her breaths are hitching now, on the verge of bigger tears than the ones that already track down her face. She's poignantly aroused.

I am murderously hard.

I lay a tender hand on her cheek. "Gorgeous girl."

Leaning in, I lick the tears from her cheek, and she shudders.

"You did so well. You're so lovely when you hurt for me." I kiss her vulnerable, tear-stained mouth. "Still green?"

She nods, and I feel a spike of relief. This is only introductory pain. She wears it beautifully, but I'm glad we're not at her limit.

Beaumont squeezes her ass with a groan. "Bend over, pet. Eyes on Lucky. I need to fuck this pussy."

His words send more tears falling from her eyes, this time, in gratitude. She's shaking, wrecked from Beaumont's edging.

She shouldn't be too grateful. She's still not going to come.

I stand and turn to Lucien, who is quaking with the effort of staying upright. As I watch, he shifts, trying to ease the pressure on his restrained balls. His face is a mask of pain now.

Beneath me, Eden falls onto her hands and knees, her breasts swinging forward, and my gaze slips to her ass.

To the writing there.

I come around to glance at the message and sigh. "Eden, do *not* let Jaykob see that message."

Beaumont snorts, and Lucky bursts out laughing. His raised ankle slips in his hands, and he collapses hard onto his knees, groaning and laughing as he rolls onto his back, curling up protectively. I purse my lips in displeasure.

This is why I don't play with others.

Beaumont wrecked my sculpture.

I walk back over to Lucien and shove his legs down. I straddle his waist, rubbing my ass over his throbbing, swollen cock. Reaching back, I fondle his tied sac and his laugher cuts off on a choked moan. He feels so good. Taut and tender and terribly sensitive.

Having him under me quickly assuages my annoyance.

"Do you want to play with Beaumont, or do you want to play with me?" I ask silkily.

I squeeze his already strangled flesh, and he arches, the muscles in his neck cording with the agony of it.

"You," he gasps. "You. Always you."

There's a squeal and a gasp, followed by a loud smack, and I look over to see Beaumont's smile fading. There's a feral flare in his eyes. He grips Eden's hips with both hands and pushes his cock into her sweet cunt. Her high-pitched moan cuts the air like a whip.

He ignores it and starts fucking into her. I can hear the wet slide from here, and she starts crying out on each brutal thrust. Her glasses fall off her face with the force but catch about her neck by their chain, bouncing against her breasts.

She's approaching anguish.

Lucien rubs his hand against my cock through my slacks, and I snarl as I snatch his wrist, that brief touch almost enough to end me.

"You know better." I pin it to the ground next to his head.

He smiles at me, that dimple a villainous tease. "You looked uncomfortable. What kind of good submissive wouldn't try to ease their great and powerful lord and master's discomfort?"

Undisciplined brat.

I kiss him greedily, painfully, tasting every inch of his mouth, and he sighs into me. I hear Eden's sobs start to crest, sounding hopelessly hoarse.

"Bend over. Match our girl. Hands and knees."

I move off him so he can comply, and he settles in close to Eden, so they're face to face. He reaches out and wipes a tear off her cheek, and she rubs her face into his hand.

My heart wrenches against my ribcage.

Her tears. His sweetness. My need to hurt, and punish, and wreck is too strong.

I unbuckle my belt with one hand, and as though it's an alarm blaring, he stops moving. Only the slick smack of Beaumont pounding into Eden breaks the silence.

"Lucien will be getting a belting," I explain to her, though I'm not sure how coherent she is right now. "My belt is wide enough for him to experience some thud, but it's largely a stinging pain. Although pain is subjective, I believe it's fair to say this is much more painful than a spank. Would you agree, Lucien?"

There's an uneasy silence, then he says in a hoarse voice, "It's definitely more painful."

His nerves are like a high for me. The anticipation is luscious, curling between all of us.

Except perhaps Beaumont, who seems understandably lost in Eden's pussy.

Sliding the belt out of its loops, I bend it into a strap. I wish I had a cane, but this will do. Lucien's always had a love-hate relationship with the belt.

"This won't be kind, Lucien," I warn.

"I like you cruel," he whispers.

He soothes the jagged, unhappy scars in me. God, to be wanted like this—to be wanted *for* this—is such a gift.

Swallowing back grateful emotion of my own, I run the belt over the back of his thighs, over his ass, letting the tension grow thick and heavy as he waits. I pull the belt back, and when he grows taut with tension, I gently touch back down until he curses under his breath.

I can't help my delighted grin at his consternation, and I send a mischievous look at Eden, and her breath catches.

Beaumont's breath whistles from between his gritted teeth, his face set in strain. "This pussy is trying so hard to come."

He laughs, but this one sounds pained. Suddenly, he changes his rhythm, and Eden cries out in panic.

"*No, no, no,*" she begs on a broken sob.

Beaumont starts thrusting more slowly, languorously into her, stroking her soothingly as she tries to grind herself back on his dick.

I see Lucien staring at her and take the opportunity to land a swift, warning clap across his ass. It's only a warm up, but he flinches in surprise anyway.

I land three more, varying where I hit, enjoying the soft pink that starts smothering his skin. He quivers, but not enough. He's sore, but not broken.

Without warning, I land a brutal blow across his taut flesh, one hard enough to welt, and he grunts. More. *More, more, more.* I swing again and it lands violently against his other cheek with a loud, cock-stroking *clap.*

Eden yelps at the sound, her eyes wide, and Beaumont smiles.

"Jealous, darlin'? You want a hand on your ass, all you have to do is ask."

Beaumont smacks her cheek, then the other, and then starts thrusting more slowly, languorously, and she starts to cry, like gently falling rain. Her hands fall out from under her, and she drops to her elbows, her cheek pressing into the grass.

"Green," she whispers between her sweet little sniffles. "Green. I'm green."

Fuck.

I take in a deep, shuddery breath, heat chasing through my body. My balls throb, as that gorgeous, careful focus begins to slide over me. Every twitch, every sound becomes hyperreal.

I start up a rhythm, and the music begins to play in earnest.

The smacks and the cries, Eden's sobs and Lucky's pained groans, the wet slap of Beaumont's thrusts. Lucien begins to shake, his sounds losing restraint, becoming tearfully edged, and I finally pause, my arm aching.

I rub a hand over Lucien's perfect, glowing ass, feeling the welts already rising on his hot skin. He lets out a choked, needy sound.

Beaumont stops playing with Eden. He stops grinding and toying with her clit. He stops teasing. He grasps her hips again in both hands and uses her cunt to ease himself.

"You should feel this pussy, Jasper. She feels like a fucking satin vice around my cock." He swears, then groans, his thrusts punishing. "You don't even need to touch her, really. She has such a needy little hole, just feed it a dick and it begs to come."

Eden moans on a long shudder, and Lucien clutches her hand, squeezing.

They're holding hands.

My heart shatters and reforms in an instant.

I don't know why it hits me just now, and with such violent force, but that simple knit of hands feels momentous. My two submissives, one crying in gentle, graceful sobs, the other crying freely, still filled with a honed, restless energy. Opposites, in many ways, but joined together in this.

For me.

Please let her want this too.

"Last one, Lucien. Where do you want it?" I ask, my throat thick with need.

It takes him a minute, but in a small, shaky voice, he says, "Left side."

Nodding, I pull back, and looking over both of them, I smile as I bring the belt down savagely against his right.

He howls— tormented, achingly beautiful—and I drop to my knees behind him, wrapping an arm around his lower back so I can kiss the aching flesh.

"You did so well, dear boy. So good to take all that for me."

Beaumont lets out a low, long groan as he comes, and I yank Lucien back by his hair so I can kiss his mouth. His lips are salty with tears, and I moan, grinding against his ass.

I pull back roughly.

"Beaumont, get her on her back and spread her out for Lucien." I press another kiss to Lucien's lips. "You've earned a present."

Beaumont gives me a ragged look where he pants over Eden, then he pulls out and coaxes her onto her back. He rests the back of her head on his thigh and runs his hands over her cheeks.

At my tap, Lucien crawls to Eden.

She's splayed out over the grass. Her dress is around her waist, her legs spread wide, and her scarlet, abused breasts are on display. Cum leaks out of her defiled pussy, and her face is a masterpiece of inconsolable desire.

Lucien trembles on all fours over her.

I tremble, too.

"Are you okay?" he asks, and I rub my hand over his ass in approval of the question.

Eden nods, her throat working. "I just r-really need to come."

"Do you want to?" I try not to betray how much the answer means to me.

Her cunt is soaking wet, used and likely very sore, particularly with that plug still in her ass. Even her thighs gleam with moisture.

These are unkind, nasty games, and I can understand if she wants no part of them.

Of me.

Her eyes fill with tears, and she shakes her head. "No."

The pitiful word, with that broken expression, has my cock leaking precum.

"No," I agree, and this time, I don't bother to keep the thick lust out of my voice. Relief lives along beside it.

Lucien's face is a mix of need and sympathy.

"That pussy is for you, sweet boy," I offer him generously. "You've been so good, so patient for her, and even more so for me." I tuck his hair over his ear and kiss his cheek as he stares at her, his eyes soft and undefended. "You don't need to wait anymore, Lucien. Have us both, now. You've more than earned it."

I look down at my beautiful, tragically unsatisfied Eden. Beaumont pets her hair, and sweat has beaded at her temples.

"Don't you agree, sweet girl? You'll let him use that pussy, won't you?"

Her eyes soften on Lucien, some of the devastation easing from her features. Her thighs widen even further.

"Please, Lucky. Use me. I— I won't try to come." Her face fills with determination. "I won't come."

My heart squeezes. She so easily finds her bravery for others.

If only she could see it.

Lucky kneels between her legs, staring at her, his hands hovering over her like he doesn't know where to start.

"Fuck her, Lucien. Take what you want. She's your reward. Enjoy her how you please," I order.

The tether snaps, and he shoves her thighs painfully wide, then fucks into her in one thrust. He bends his head into the crook of her neck for a moment as he gasps at the relief of her sweet cunt squeezing him.

I kneel.

Before Lucien can get too comfortable, I reach between his legs and untie the hair band from around his balls. Crying out, he presses in deep into Eden's pussy, as if the soft, soaking pliancy might ease the hurt as the blood rushes back in.

"Fuck, fuck," he swears, his voice teary and vulnerable.

His hands start traveling everywhere, all over her, grasping and pinching and stroking.

"You feel so good," he groans to her. "I'm sorry, beautiful. I can't be gentle. I need it. I'm sorry but I need it."

He grabs her hips and starts fucking her hard, and Eden sobs, writhes, but between the two of them, she has nowhere to go.

Settled behind Lucien, my eyes are locked on his ass as it flexes with his efforts. My blood roars in my ears, and my body beats a war drum, demanding its need to finally, violently stake my claim. This won't last long.

Beau leans down and tugs at her dress, then tosses me a bottle.

I'm so caught up in fighting my own lust that I almost miss the catch. But I'm grateful for it. There may be some flavors of sadist who enjoy that brand of pain, but I am not one of them. It's too indelicate, too hazard prone. There are better kinds of pain than that.

"I love you," Lucky sobs against Eden's neck, and she shudders under him, releasing a sharp cry that's full of inconsolable pain and brutal desire.

My hands shake on the bottle as Lucien's thrusts grow frantic.

"Don't you come now, darlin'. You've been doing so well. You can hold on just a little bit longer." Beau catches her hands, twining her fingers in his and holding her steady. His hooded eyes are tender on her strained, red face.

Tears stream down her cheeks, and my cock swells. She's so helpless right now. So perfectly at our mercy. She's been broken in, slaved to pleasure, and the cruel, vicious part of me that usually wants to hurt and hurt badly, is oddly contented.

I coat myself in the slippery, cold lube, anticipation hitting me hard and hot and low in my abdomen.

Lucien's reddened, abused ass and her tortured face are more than satisfying. They thrill me. The sight of them all together fills me viscerally. My Lucien and my Eden and my dear friend, lost in a wonderful storm of aching love and sweet pain.

After squirting another generous dollop of lube into my hand, I drop the bottle. Leaning over Lucien, I plant a hand on his back, pressing him tight against Eden. When I'm sure he'll stay, I pull back and bring my lubed fingers to the shadowed cleft of his ass, coating him in it. Consecrating him.

"Jasper . . . God. *Please*. I can't wait anymore."

Lucien is shaking now, and I lean down, kissing my way up his spine. "I know, love."

I breach his taut hole with my finger, and we both groan. His ring clamps tight against me in a hungry promise, and inside is satin steel.

"Wh-what does it feel like?"

Eden's voice is almost unrecognizable, hitching with tears, but she's watching Lucky's face with a pained, wondering expression.

Lucky shudders as I add a second finger, then turns his head to look at her. His face is as ruined with tears as hers. "It— *Fuck*. He's using his . . . his fingers, beautiful. It's so fucking good. You know how good."

I roll my forehead against his back, gritting my teeth as precum coats my cock. It's beyond any attempt of strangling now. I need to come.

This is all the preparation my Lucien gets.

Fumbling, shaking, I line myself up with his slick, clutching hole. I watch the join, unable to miss the moment I'm finally inside him for anything.

My crown presses into him, and the searing heat, the steady resistance has me gritting my teeth and praying. I'm so close, and he's a vice.

Eden's breath catches, her eyes darting between him and me, her pupils blown. Beaumont strokes his fingers over her kindly, sweetly, murmuring calming praise as she holds herself back. Her fingers are white-knuckled in his hands.

She's been through an unbearable amount tonight. Her obedience, her discipline, are glorious. I don't think I've ever seen a submissive so committed to upholding her promise.

Lucien pants, staring at her. "He's . . . he's working his way in. It's different to your plug. He's so *hot*. It's a different, *ah*."

I watch myself push into him, *disappear* into him, and his toes curl beside me as he takes my cock like he was made for it. Delicate tears fall from his eyes, and Eden leans in to press a kiss against his mouth.

Lucien quakes, and when their mouths break apart, he finishes shakily, "It's a different kind of hard. It's better. It hurts, but you'll like it. Jayk will help you. It'll be good."

There's an intense pressure over every inch of me. Over my skin. My cock. My *heart*. The sight of them pressed together, helping each other, is too much.

I grip Lucien hard, not being gentle over his belted flesh. "This is it, Lucien. Whatever wicked spell you cast on me has worked. You win. I'm yours. I hope it hurts."

I shove inside of him in one brutal, violent thrust.

Lucien's velvet ass encases my cock, and I feel him throb around me. Lucien holds Eden to him like a lifeline, still buried between her thighs. Her legs are split around us both, and ungraceful, base possessiveness floods me.

"Eden," I snap, and her eyes flick to me. "Eyes on me as I fuck you both."

Lucien's words are jumbled now. A mix of *please*, and *thank you*, and *I love you*. I don't know if he's saying it to me or her, but it doesn't matter.

It's all of us now.

I break. I fuck into them roughly, my own unsatisfied need rising in me like a tide. He's unbearably hot, and her awed, desperate eyes cling to my face as I lose all semblance of control. Lucien's body trembles as I fuck him into her, and in my mind, I'm buried in her too.

I *will* be.

I won't have distance like this between us again before I've claimed her raw.

Lucien sobs, then he pushes back into me, his ass clamping brutally around my cock as he comes. My own orgasm rips out of me, forceful and decadent, painful after holding back for so, so long.

It rips *me*. Suddenly, I'm sure this night has left all of us in tiny, shattered pieces.

Pieces that might fit better together than I had ever hoped.

CHAPTER 46

EDEN

SURVIVAL TIP #214
Don't poke the bear.

Beau leads me back to the party, and I adjust my dirtied dress. It took over an hour of cuddles and makeshift water bottle clean ups before either Lucky or I could walk . . . and I don't think Jasper or Beau were much better.

My body has gone past need now. I am in the worst-best pain I have ever experienced.

Worst, because I still haven't come, and it should be positively illegal to be edged for so long and by so many gorgeous men.

Best, because it was one of the most beautiful things I've ever seen. Watching Jasper and Lucky together is like gospel, or like some holy reckoning that I didn't know existed. I know Jasper took it easy on the pain demonstration . . . but didn't with anything else.

Jasper looked shaken to his core.

He was still struggling to find his composure when I left, and as much as I would have liked to stay and comfort him, I still have one more dangerous beast to hunt tonight.

One major problem, however, is that I have no clue where Jaykob is right now.

The bonfire is still a fiery typhoon in the middle of the lawn—Dom and Jada are circling the fire. They're both urging people back from the flames, keeping an eye on the burn. The music is pumping in beat-heavy dance music, and the lawn is littered with dancing women, drinking women, women grouped together and chatting atop blankets.

But no Jaykob.

Sloane, Ava, Jennifer, Ida, Ethel, and Kasey are still on the raised platform he was on earlier, though. Maybe they know where he is.

Nerves swirl through my stomach.

Jennifer hasn't spoken to me again all week after she ripped into me like a protective jackal for betraying Jayk—and I have no idea what he might have said while he was out with Sloane and the others.

It doesn't matter. I have to try.

"Good luck, darlin'. I'll be right here if you need me," Beau says, and I nod briskly.

Bracing myself, I walk up to the platform only to find that there's a ladder to get up. I sigh, then carefully climb up. It wrecks terrible havoc on the thick plug inside me, which has become almost painful in my overused body. I grit my teeth until I finally reach the top.

"Eden!" Ava calls cheerfully, and I give her an uncertain look.

A warm chorus of welcomes follows. *Too* welcome.

This is suspicious. It is suspicious, isn't it?

"Hello everyone." I smile stiffly, hoping against hope I don't look as sweaty and . . . sticky . . . as I'm starting to feel. I should be scalded in cleansing fire before talking to *anyone*, but I can't bring myself to waste any more time. "Would you happen to know where Jaykob went?"

Sloane hoots and slaps Jennifer. "Yes! Pay up, half your rations. The plan worked. She's jealous and desperate for his di—"

"*D*elightful company!" Jennifer interrupts, looking meaningfully at Kasey, who rolls her eyes. "And I'm not paying up yet. Eden, tell me—are you going for smooches or to yell at him?"

She gives me a tipsy, evaluating look.

I stare at them from the top of the ladder, flummoxed. Why are they all being nice to me? The moonlight is silver-white over Bristlebrook, like the heavens hung a chandelier just for this night. The women are sprawled over the barricade, loose and relaxed. There's a deck of cards strewn between them, and Ida drops her hand with a sigh.

"I—" I stammer. "I haven't decided yet. Possibly both?"

Ava frowns, her short hair ruffling in the breeze. "Who gets rations for both? Did anyone bet on that?"

Ethel lifts a wrinkled hand from where she's lying back, watching the stars. "That would be me."

Ida grumbles, adjusting her shawl over her shoulders.

"He's out checking people aren't getting close to the pit traps. He wouldn't let me come," Kasey says with a sour look. Then she frowns at me worriedly. "Be nice to him, okay? He showered and shaved and dressed up for you and everything. He just wants you to like him best."

Her serious features tell me that she wants that too.

Wait, what does she mean *best*?

At my hesitant look, Sloane nods at me. "He told us that you were with all of them." She shrugs. "Honestly explained a lot."

They *know*?

Startled, I blink. "Jayk told you that? He had an actual, real conversation with you?"

"Sure, we're friends." Sloane shrugs, like it's nothing.

Friends.

I'm stung and touched all at once. Jayk has *friends*. Of course the men should count . . . but while I think Jayk would go to war for them, I'm not sure he would talk to them. Talking with Sloane and Ava is huge for him, and I'm glad they have his back.

But it brings my own relationship with him into sharp relief. In all the times we've slept together, and for all that I feel like I understand him better than I do any of my men, we've hardly talked.

We're long overdue.

"Sorry for being a dick and all," Jennifer says with a grimace. "You should have said something! I thought you did him dirty, and he was so cute over you. Watching you all the time when you weren't looking." She frowns thoughtfully and takes a drink. "Maybe that's creepy, actually. Is that creepy?"

Jayk watched me?

Ava laughs, then shrugs at me. "We're spreading the important details around the group, just, you know, so they know you're not a cheating scumbag. You shouldn't have a problem with anyone anymore. I mean, there might be some side-eye . . ."

"But they should keep it together," Sloane finishes, then she breaks into a rueful smile. "Could really do with some more men around here though. We keep telling Madison, but I'm pretty sure she's worried they're going to snatch away her crown."

"As if we'd let that happen," Jennifer scoffs.

Reeling and caught off-guard by their turnaround on me, I jump when Ava nudges me.

"I saw him last over by the western pits," she says. "When you've had enough male posturing for the night, come find us. We're breaking out the drinking games as soon as Team Bacon gets their act together and crack out porky. Madison should be off monitoring duty by then, too."

Sloane whistles sharply at that, and Ida lifts her whiskey into the air with a laugh. A small smile finds me. Drinking games sound like a terrible idea.

"I'll consider it," I laugh. I'm about to start descending the ladder again when I catch sight of Kasey, still not chattering with the others.

She's still worried about him.

"Hey," I say, and when she looks at me, I give her back a look just as serious. "I love him—I'm just trying to make him believe it."

Kasey gives me a half-smile.

With their chatter re-starting behind me, I descend the ladder again and make my way to the western edge of the forest. It's darker on this side, and I pluck one of the large solar lanterns off a tree and head toward the pit traps.

My body is slippery and tingling, the frustrated echoes of my thwarted orgasm still edging me. Being with Jayk is always a wild ride—and one that usually ends with me being ridden wildly. We can't have a relationship based only on sex, though. Not the one I want with him.

As I get closer to the traps, I examine the ground, and in between the smaller footprints, I note several larger ones with at least three different shaped boot treads between them.

Uneasiness stirs in the pit of my stomach as a chilly breeze kicks up. They said the woods are safe, and no alarm has been tripped. These footprints are probably just from my men doing rounds over the course of the day.

Right?

I still don't move. In the dim light, I strain to hear something, anything. Music throbs from back at the party, and I tune it out. There's something up ahead. Some*one*.

They're coming toward me.

My pulse skitters, and I quickly drag myself behind a heavy bush. The scratchy leaves scrape at my skin. Picking up a rock at my feet, I break open the lantern as quietly as possible and with a sharp smack, I crack the bulb inside.

The light dies.

I make myself as still as possible, the rock still clenched in one hand.

A large figure appears a moment later, holding a flashlight, but they're hard to make out through the greenery and my terrible vision. He turns, looking down at the ground.

"Come out, subbie," Jayk says, and all the tension drains out of me.

I step out from behind the bush and frown. "What gave me away?"

I can't help but feel miffed. I'd thought I hid quite quickly.

He nods down at the dirt, then brushes his foot over it. "Smear it next time. Dead giveaway."

Even with my glasses, in this light, I can hardly even see his foot.

My brows lift. "You can *see* that?"

Ugh. I am so overdue for an optometrist appointment.

"You should go back to the party," he mutters, looking down at me.

"No, we need to *talk*."

Jayk goes rigid, then nudges me back toward Bristlebrook. "I told you I don't want to talk to you, Eden."

He's not sneering at me, or taunting. There's no smirk or belligerence in his voice. It encourages me to turn back to him.

The night air swirls around us, laden with smoke and pine. I lay a hand on his chest, over the buttons of the fancy shirt that doesn't suit him at all.

"Yes, you do. Why else would you get all dressed up like this? Shave?" I reach up to touch his cheek—his smooth, shaved cheek—and he flinches back when my fingertips make contact. I let them curl as I lower my hand and hold in my aching sigh. "You look incredible, Jayk, but you don't need to do any of that for me."

His eyes catch the light for a moment, then he looks away.

"Go back to Lucky. He's *fun*." Even in the dark, I can see his mouth twist. "Just go. I mean it. You don't want to talk to me right now."

I think, for some reason, of Dom, telling me to use my voice. Of Jasper sending me on my hunt. Of Heather, sighing over me not standing up for myself.

Bond-fire or not, for me, tonight is a claiming—but not just of my men. It's a claiming of the person I want to be. After Jayk walking away from me without a word, after a week of his silence, I've had enough.

"If not now, then when?" I ask him. "It's never a good time to talk with you, Jayk. You're either trying to get in my pants, or marking your territory, or storming off. There's no in between."

Jayk grabs me around my waist so quickly I gasp. He yanks me against him and grinds his dick against me, all rough hands and sneering hurt.

"You're one to talk, princess. It ain't like you've been inviting me for tea and biscuits."

The balls clatter inside me, and the reminder is sharp and brutal.

"I-I *am*," I insist, though it comes out a touch breathy. "We can have tea and biscuits."

Jayk lowers his rough-hewn face to mine. "I'm not doing shit with you right now. You don't think I know what you look like after you've been fucked?" His grip tightens. "You fucking smell like sex, Eden."

I can smell Jayk too, for the first time in days—because for days, he was gone. Hurt and frustration swell in me like a blizzard.

Lifting my chin, I give him a frosty look. "Yes, I do, and I love it. It could have been you, too, but you *left*. You just walked out."

Jayk wrenches back and darkness slams in around him again, until only his eyes shine with an ungodly light. His wounded anger clouds the space between us.

"You took two seconds to run back to Beau!" he growls.

"I *told* you I loved him too."

His angry scoff blisters the air. "You don't get to have everything, princess. That's not how this world works. You might have been brought up different, but it's about time you got a reality check."

He stalks around me, staring at me, and he's so untethered right now, so raw and predatory that I find myself holding taut. Still. It's a struggle to hold my ground.

His voice is a lashing snarl. "You're owed *nothing*. There's no sharing. There's no smorgasbord of options you get to pick at when you're hungry. The only things you get are what you steal and will kill to protect. You pick *one* person—and *maybe* they pick you back."

Jayk's glare bites in the night. "Go pick them, princess—and leave me the hell alone."

Rage settles over my lust like a sheen of oil. God, I am *so sick* of him being wrong about me.

I push my glasses up my nose and fight not to shout. "I am no *princess*, Jayk. I didn't *grow up with everything*. I survived, and that's all I did—until I came here. You all gave me more, and now I want it. I'm keeping it. So yes, I pick you. *And* I pick them."

Jayk snorts derisively, flashing me a hateful glare.

"Choosing them doesn't mean I love you any less, Jayk," I insist heatedly. "When you've been told you're worth nothing for long enough, you start feeling like that's all you deserve—but I want more than that. I want all of it. I want all of you."

He comes around behind me like a stalking wolf. "I'm nothing now, is that it? You get to run around here and treat me like a sex toy and fuck everyone here, and I—"

"I have *never* treated you like that. If anything, it's the other way around. *Your* stupid deal made me into a sex toy. That's *all* I would have been to you if I hadn't put an end to it."

The night is dark and blankets us through the trees, and I wish my frustration could burn bright enough to beat it back. I'm going to scream with it. He's too angry. Too ready to hear the worst and refusing to accept the best.

"I didn't come here to fight with you, Jayk, but don't you dare put any kind of moral judgment on me for sleeping with all of you when that was the entire reason you all wanted me here in the first place. Or was I only meant to like it with you?" I ask, voice harsh, and his teeth glint in the moonlight as he sneers.

I step back into his space, and he grips my arms hard enough for me to feel every warning callous, but I lean up anyway.

"I *love* being at Jasper's feet as he strokes my hair. I adored when Dom spanked me while I choked on Beau's dick. It turns me on that Lucky and Beau fucked me and then sent me on to see you, and that Beau has been filling me with these ridiculous plugs to get me ready for him." I end on a hiss, but I think I've gone too far when Jayk's face goes unnaturally still.

He shoves my arms down, spins me around, and yanks up my dress. There's no *please* or *maybe* about his touch—there never is—he moves me like I'm a doll for him to undress, his coarse hands scraping over my skin.

His hand slides between my ass cheeks and finds the plug.

"You let him put this in you?" he growls. "This was *mine*. You . . . what the fuck is this?"

My dress is yanked higher again, and I can tell the moment he reads the writing on my ass. The skirts fall back down, and I turn, looking at Jayk nervously. He's almost monstrous in the dark. My heart is beating too fast, and my body has been used and teased beyond bearing. I should be extinguished of lust. Done. Maxed out.

But I'm not.

After Beau's edging, my body is dancing with hot, squirming need. I want Jayk. I want everything he can give me.

"Say your safeword, Eden." The words are ground out, raw as teeth through flesh. "Say it. Right. Now."

My stomach flips in apprehension, and I edge back half a step.

Jayk tracks it, trembling with restraint.

He's angry. He's *really* angry. Angry enough that I should probably listen to him. But every bit of trepidation is married to shivery, decadent lust. There's something wrong with me, probably, but I can't make myself ashamed of it. Jayk makes my fear safe.

Though he doesn't seem very safe right now.

"I don't want to say it." My body quakes, edgy with tension. "I'm not ending this until we talk."

Jayk leans forward, his legs spreading into an attack position I recognize from sparring practice.

"Then *run*, princess." He's made of shadows now, of the fanged and hungry predators that live in the night. "Run as fast as you can."

CHAPTER 47

EDEN

SURVIVAL TIP #325
Sometimes, to catch your prey,
you need to become the prey.

I run.

Jayk doesn't follow immediately, and I'm quickly swallowed by trees. I lift my skirts, holding them so they won't trip me up, and my pulse roars in my ears.

There's only one path through here—a wide, clear cut between the greenery that is far too easy to follow. Jayk is faster than me. If I stay on the path, he'll find me in no time.

I run ahead, and when I find the right spot, I turn left toward Bristlebrook. Then I pick up a leafy branch and run it behind me to obscure my tracks as I double back in a wide loop. My heart is racing, but my mind is still alert, pumping adrenaline but not the throat-closing fear I felt while being chased by the Sinners.

I won't be easy prey.

I won't panic.

My light, floral dress works against me in the dark, so I keep low behind a log, watching the path. Jayk appears moments later, prowling quickly, his eyes scanning the ground, then the trees. I hold my breath as he passes and watch him take my bait trail toward Bristlebrook.

When I'm sure he's gone, I pick my way over the path, careful to only place my feet in my previous tracks, then push through the thick, springy brush on the other side. My hands shake as it bounces back into place behind me, concealing me without any of its tough leaves bending to alert Jayk to my passage.

Then I sprint away from Bristlebrook, off all safe paths, watching my feet enough so I don't trip. The plug is thick and tight and resonant inside me, beating like a countdown. I bounce off rocks where possible, knowing they won't mark my movements, but there's so many dry, crunchy fall leaves everywhere.

Worried, I veer toward the distant stream. It runs at a trickle, and its rocky bed is a blessing. I slip my shoes off and step into it until the brisk water bites at my ankles. The trees are sparser through here, exposing me, but it also allows the dappled moonlight to light my way. It silvers the water until I'm stepping through liquid metal.

I look over my shoulder but can't see anything. I can't hear anything either. I walk quickly, letting the stream hide my tracks . . . and it hits me that I'm enjoying myself. It's been over twenty minutes, and he still hasn't caught me.

There's no smoke this deep in the woods, just earthy growth and piney trees.

Home.

My toes are beginning to go numb, and I decide I've gone far enough. It's still night and there are plenty of predators in these woods—of the animal variety, if not the human.

I'm just stepping out of the water when I hear a crack to my right. I freeze, looking toward the sound, wishing I didn't feel quite so much like a fragile-limbed deer testing the air.

Nothing moves.

I take a slow, ginger step from the water, listening closely.

"*Run*, princess."

His voice is on my left—and *close*.

In pure startled reflex, I scream, bolting away from the sound. He's right behind me, big and huge and lit with starry anger. I dart around a tree, skidding in the loose foliage.

He appears on the other side of the trunk, right in my face, and I fall on my ass as I jolt back. The plug wedges deep inside me, and I cry out, heart thundering in my throat. At my temple.

In my core.

"You think this is a game?" he snaps. He stands with a foot on either side of my waist, looming over me like a devil over hell. Every broad, muscular inch of him pulses with hurt. "Is it *funny*, watching me fall for you and then just moving on to someone better?"

I scramble back, not taking my eyes off him. He's all danger. Unreasonable anger.

I might have pushed this too far. This isn't a game. He's hurting and upset.

Still, it takes every effort not to run.

Staring up at him from the ground, quivering, I whisper, "There is no one better than you, Jayk."

"Don't *lie*." He drops to his knees over me, straddling my waist. His hand wraps around my neck, gripping me tight, and he drags my chest off the ground. I draw in a quick breath, just to assure myself I can, and wrap my fingers around his steely wrist.

But I don't pull him away. Something about his hand on my throat, him holding me at his mercy while I squirm under him, blanks my mind of thought. My quick swallows have the tendons in my neck pressing against his palms, and I find myself pressing into the mindlessly carnal grip.

His fingertips pinch and nip the sides of my throat. "Why aren't you *running*?"

"I don't want . . . to run from you," I manage to get out

between slightly panicked pants, tied up and torn between nervousness and indecent lust.

My fearful body begs me to hit back, kiss him, fuck, fight, *run*, like I do every time we come together. Jayk has a way of turning cowardly instincts into something animal, something cardinal—something crudely, lustfully essential. But tonight's not a night for running. Not for myself, and not for Jayk.

My heart tells me we need to try something else.

It takes everything in me to pry my fingers from around his wrist and lower them submissively to my side.

"I don't need to run from you."

Jayk flashes me his teeth in a terrifying caricature of a smile. "Yes, sugar. You do."

He slams me onto my back by my throat, and begins tearing at his belt, then his zipper. I squirm under his hand as he yanks out his thick, heavy cock. This close, I see the fat vein running up the side—every swollen, florid, angry inch of him.

"You take everyone else's dick tonight, you're taking mine too."

Jayk moves up to straddle my chest, then his grip moves from my throat to my hair, grabbing a fistful at the roots. He lifts my head by my hair and drags it to his cock at a painful angle. Holding himself steady at the root with his other hand, he shoves into my mouth, so hard and deep that tears come to my eyes and my glasses slip down my nose.

In one adrenal part of my brain, I am terrified by him. My heart pounds and skids, and my palms sweat as he punches his hips forward, riding my face. My tongue pushes against his filling, scorching cock, and he only groans. It's almost too much.

Almost.

Because the other part of me is stormed with need. That craves every punishing slide into my mouth and the scent of him all around me. Being overwhelmed, being made helpless by Jayk, is like being conquered by a divine adversary. I'm a reward I always want him to win.

Jayk hits my gag reflex again, and my tears spill over as I look up at him. He doesn't stop for my tears. It's not like Jasper, who savors their creation—Jayk just doesn't seem to care. With both hands, he holds my head still as he fucks my throat the way he wants, using me even as I choke and writhe under him.

"Fuck, that's good."

Adrenaline rises in time with my desire. He's taken my mouth before, of course, but not this roughly. I know I could slap his legs, and he'd stop right now, but I haven't made *my* point yet. He can't scare me away. He's not too much, or too awful, or too base, or any of the things he's convinced himself of.

If I have to go through a trial for that, then so be it.

Particularly if *this* is the trial.

If I stopped him, I wouldn't have the throbbing weight of him in my mouth. The taste of his precum spilling over my tongue and consecrating my throat. I wouldn't have freeing tears dripping off my chin or his scent filling my nose.

"Fuck," he groans as I look up at him through blurry tears. "Your mouth is mine. Your throat is mine. All of this. *Mine.*"

He buries himself to the hilt, holding my head close to him, and I choke, my nails finding the firm skin of his abdomen as dark spots haze my vision.

Then he pulls himself free, his cock drenched in my saliva, and I cough hoarsely, trying to breathe. With harsh, angry motions, he turns me over and yanks my dress up.

Fear pricks me now. I can't see him, and he's dead silent except for his rough, fast breaths. His demanding hand reaches for the plug, and instinct takes over.

I lunge forward, trying to crawl out from under him.

"No," he snaps.

He grabs my hips and pulls me backwards in a short, careless move, then plants a forearm across my shoulders. He shoves me down with it, holding me forcefully against the brittle, cracking leaves with his weight.

"I'm done being the good guy here, Eden. It doesn't suit me anyway. You come to me soaked in another man's cum, fucking taunting me with it, you're going to get fucked. I'm going to erase them from your fucking skin. They're not giving me your ass, sugar. It's already *mine*."

I'm shuddering with need, and my throat is tight with anxiety. I try to move free, but he's pinned me too securely. All it does is rub the back of my thighs against his rough jeans.

His hand finds the crevice of my ass, then tugs at the plug, yanking it free with little ceremony until it pops out and he throws it to the side. I gasp at the sudden release of pressure. My clit aches, begging for attention it's not receiving, but so overwhelmed from its earlier attention, I'm not sure it could handle it if it did get it.

He spreads my ass wide and makes a crude, dark sound of satisfaction. "Whatever they fucking prepared you for, sugar, it sure as shit wasn't this."

Rough and crude, he spits against my gaping, puckered hole, and I feel the wet saliva dripping into me and all around the cleft of my ass. His unforgiving fingers return quickly, working his spit into me with fast, invasive pumps.

I shake hard at the abrupt assault. It's not quite slick. Not the slippery ease of when I had the plug. Each pump has resistance, a little tug to it that both frightens and exhilarates me.

I whimper, caught, unable to do anything but let him work me savagely, and the fear in me increases. Starts to surpass my neediness, just a little.

The plug was huge. A lot. And *that* was mostly stationary inside me. Jaykob is bigger, and definitely not stationary. This is going to hurt. He wants to fuck me hard, after all. He's made that clear.

This is a punishment, and he's going to split me open.

Jayk pulls his fingers out, then smears them on my ass. My face pressed into the earth, I squeeze my eyes shut against the dirt as his wide, hot crown kisses the sensitive ring of muscle. I brace myself for him to shove in, to tear me open, and I tremble in rigid, fearful anticipation.

And then suddenly, he's gone.

CHAPTER 48

EDEN

SURVIVAL TIP #41
Being torn open hurts.
Bring lube.

The pressure on my back vanishes, and his cock is no longer pushing against me. I flip over, searching for him, and find him a short distance away.

"*Fuck*," he swears like a punch. He's dead white . . . and he's shaking worse than me.

"Jayk?" I venture in a low voice.

At my voice, he flinches back, then kicks a tree so sharply and violently that I squeak.

He whirls to face me, his eyes tempest-tossed and thalassic. He grips the back of his head like he might crack it open between his hands.

"Are you okay?"

I've never heard him sound like that—so hushed, so ripe with fear.

I rub my arms. "Yes, of course, Jayk. I'm fine. What are you—?"

"Why didn't you safeword?" he snarls, then his jaw snaps shut, and he cringes, giving me an agonized, apologetic look. "Fuck. *Fuck*, I'm sorry. I can't— I don't know how to . . ."

He steps back, like he wants to run away, then stops. My stomach dips at how upset he is, and the night's bitter air digs its teeth into my exposed skin.

Safeword?

I stare at him. "Jayk, I'm okay. I didn't need to use it. I was fine. Mostly fine. I can take it, I promise."

He runs a hand over his face, looking sick. "You were *afraid* of me. Fuck, Eden. You don't take a damn thing you don't want to. Not ever."

"I did want to," I insist. I don't think I've ever seen him like this.

He's *panicking*.

I get to my feet and step toward him, and he backs up.

"Jayk," I say soothingly, "I got nervous for a minute. I haven't done that part before. But I know you would never take it too far. I trust you."

He retreats again, and his back hits the tree.

"You shouldn't." He shakes his head again, his voice low and rough. "I was going to fuck your virgin ass into the ground. You shouldn't trust me for shit."

They shouldn't, it's sick and wrong, especially while he's upset, but his words stoke my lust again. Now I'm not actually faced with the immediate threat of his sizeable cock ripping me open, the idea goes back to being thoroughly intriguing.

Jasper is going to have to work overtime on my therapy.

"You didn't . . . do that. You stopped. You stopped, and I'm fine. And even if you didn't, I would have been fine—because it's you, and as messed up as it is, I like it when you use me. I love it when you claim me. I love all of this as much as you do." I bite my lip. "And I should have told you when I started getting worried. Beau told me a hundred times about the traffic lights."

Green for good, red for stop—and yellow to slow down.

I should have said yellow.

Jayk looks away, his throat working, the hard lines of his face for once looking soft.

"Fuck, Eden, stop. It's not your fault. *I* should have told you about all of that shit. I should have noticed you were . . . I was too angry. I never should have touched you." He runs a hand over his mouth. "I fucked up."

"You *did* notice. You *did* stop," I assure him. I close the last bit of space between us, touching his arm, needing him to be okay.

"Stop comforting me." Jayk closes his eyes on a sick grimace. "You shouldn't be the one comforting me right now."

I stroke his skin lightly, his muscles are rocks under my fingertips. Even wrecked with worry, he's gorgeous. Somehow more gorgeous for that worry. His eyes are darker than midnight, tormented and lonely. His smooth, shaved face is still throwing me, and so is that lovely button-up shirt. All the ways he's trying to smooth himself out for me when he shouldn't.

I love him rough.

"So comfort *me*, then," I suggest, wondering if this is the right way to go.

His eyes open, then search mine with more hesitance than I've ever seen from him. It looks strange on his gruff face.

"How?" He asks it low, like he's ashamed, and my stomach flips. "Sit down."

Silent and guilt-stricken, he slides to sit at the base of the tree. I straddle his wide lap, the way he did to me earlier, and sit. His jeans abrade my sensitive inner thighs, and I shiver.

"Now hug me," I whisper.

He stares at me for a moment, then he slowly brings his large, solid arms around me. One slides around my waist, and his fingers wind into my hair, only this time he's gentle, so painfully careful as he holds me. I nestle into him, working into the right spot. It's a different fit to Beau—Jayk is bulkier and a touch shorter—but I find my nook.

His heart is racing. We stay there, silent, until the rough hand in my hair starts to move in soft, reverent little strokes and his pulse finally starts to slow.

All these misunderstandings between us need to stop. I've been naked with him more than anyone except possibly Beau, but we haven't really stripped ourselves bare. Jayk is right that it's not just him. I've never pushed him to talk to me, even when we had days of nakedly wrestling in every glen we could find on our way back to Bristlebrook. I hadn't wanted to talk then—I was so lost in my own head.

But I'm starting to see a path out now.

"I grew up in a trailer park," I whisper against his neck, and his hand falters in its strokes. "I know you keep calling me a princess, Jayk, but I'm really not. I lived in a single-wide with my grand-mother after my mother took off to chase drugs. Again. And it was the best thing she could have done. At least the trailer was safe and clean. My grandmother fed me and clothed me and put me through school. It wasn't so bad."

"Bullshit. You don't talk like—"

I pull back a little and give him a tart look.

"Not everyone who grew up like us speaks like a bruiser, Jayk. You have to admit, you lean into it. My grandmother was quite firm about presenting well—and what she didn't catch, my husband trained out of me." I run my fingers over his smooth jaw, memories escaping me. "All this is to say, we're not as different as you think. I do know what it's like to have nothing. I know what it's like to feel like . . . less."

There's a long beat of silence as he stares at me, darkness swirling in his gaze. The breeze is brisk around us, but between us, a soft-curling warmth starts to draw us together. He releases a hard breath and shakes his head slowly.

"You're not less." He catches my hand against his jaw, and his swallows mine whole. "You're everything, Eden."

As if realizing what he just said, he tears his eyes from mine and drops our hands, his jaw flexing, and my heart pools in my chest.

Staring at our joined hands, I twine our fingers together. "When you storm off . . . like when you left the other day . . . you can't do that. It kills me."

It hurts to say—this part especially feels like I'm handing him a tool to destroy me.

Only I know he won't. If anyone would understand this, it's him.

"So many people have walked out on me, and I never knew if that was it. I spent so many nights just wondering, watching the door, waiting and waiting. For my mother, for my husband . . . I don't count on people easily, Jayk. I never have. I thought I'd stopped watching doors for people—but I'm watching yours." My words finish small and vulnerable, and I'm not sure how he'll take them.

I know Jayk can handle my fight.

I just don't know if he can handle my heart.

"I need space to think sometimes," he mutters, a look in his eye like he's expecting me to attack. "I'm not good with sudden decisions."

I hate it . . . but I can understand it.

"Just tell me when you're going?" I swallow hard. "And when you're coming back?"

He looks down at me nestled against him, and something surprised and soft moves in the depths of his eyes. Slowly, he nods, then settles me more tightly into his chest. I lay my head into the cradle of his neck.

Jayk is warm and big against me, but his heartbeat is fast and scattered.

I wonder if he's ever talked like this before.

I wonder if he knows how much it means to me.

"We didn't grow up alike," he says after a minute. His jaw clenches, and then he breathes out like it hurts him. "My mom was the best mom in the world. We had shit all, and she worked three jobs to keep us afloat for years when my piece of shit sperm donor wouldn't pay child support. He practically shit gold, but wouldn't acknowledge his bastard spawn—and my mom was too love-fucked to even try to go after him for the money."

Jayk scoffs bitterly, and I keep touching him in slow, even strokes. I think of the picture I saw of him on the trailer with his mom and his brother, the one I hid in his toolbox for safe-keeping. They looked happy then.

Love-fucked.

Is that how he thinks of it? Love as a thing that fucks you over?

Jaykob's jaw works, and I touch the flex with the gentle tip of my finger.

"She was the best mom until she wasn't." He flashes me a defensive, moonlit look. "She got sick. It wasn't her fault."

My heart feels like it's being unthreaded. "How old were you?"

"Ten? Eleven? Ryan was younger. He didn't get it." He shrugs one shoulder. "She just started losing time. Forgetting things. Talking to herself. She lost job after job. I wanted to get her help, but we just had no fucking money. I picked up odd jobs where I could, but no one wanted to hire a punk-ass kid. I started in with some shit I'm not proud of—a lot of petty, dangerous things that could have landed my ass in serious water, but it covered rent for a while, and it kept Ryan fed."

Oh, God. I saw enough growing up to know the kind of things he might be talking about. Thievery. Car jackings.

And that's on the easy end.

Jaykob's voice becomes gravel, painful enough to strip skin.

"It started getting worse, though. She'd have these episodes. She got real paranoid, and she'd see things. You couldn't reason with her. It got so bad I'd just lock myself in the bathroom with Ryan and wait until she finished screaming." Jayk blinks hard, and

I realize his eyes are wet. I press my palm against his cheek, and he swallows with a shrug. "It wasn't her fault, you know? She was sick. She didn't mean to."

Oh, Jayk.

I stroke his cheekbone with my thumb. "I know. You did everything you could have. You kept your brother safe."

It's too much. Far too much responsibility for a boy. For anyone.

"How did you get out?"

Please, let him have gotten out.

"She had a brother a few towns over. My uncle. They hadn't talked since she took up with my old man, but he was a decent guy." The guilt on his face deepens. "I called him after Ryan started following me to jobs. Little shit was going to get himself killed."

I have to press my lips together to hold back my tears. *Thank you, Ryan*, I send up silently.

Jayk looks back at me, a little steadier now. "My uncle owned his own shop, and he took us all in. Even got her on some meds, and they helped her a lot. Ryan and I worked for him for a few years, but my uncle couldn't really afford it. So when Ryan enlisted, I followed his ass to keep him out of trouble."

His expression goes black. I know Ryan didn't make it. I think he's going to talk about that, but he surprises me.

"You know my old man wouldn't even help her out?" he says with a familiar bitter twist to his mouth. "I went to see him, and he kicked me on my ass. All he cared about was making sure I didn't disturb his *real* family. Guess I wasn't good enough for him either."

My heart splits wide open.

"Jayk, you have to stop thinking like you're not enough. You're so talented and so smart. You've kept Bristlebrook running, the cameras working, you've defended your home and the other men and *me*. That's not even to mention how you've been helping all of these civilians—can't you see how fast you won them over?"

As I ask, he shifts uncomfortably under me, and I press myself closer. I'm sitting over his zipper now, where he locked himself away. He's still half-hard, and I do my best to ignore that.

He needs to hear this, and I'll do everything I can to make him believe it.

Not all wars are won with fists—I need to win this with words.

"Jayk, they adore you. I've been shunned all week because they thought I broke your heart," I say in exasperation, and his brows slam down.

"They *what*?" He scowls. "I'll fix it. They won't bother you again."

I press a kiss against his cheek with a soft laugh, and it brushes away some of the darkness of the last few minutes. Jayk can go from threatening to wreck me with his cock to protective mother hen in ten minutes.

It's rather . . . endearing.

If you look at it from a certain angle.

"My point is, they like you. They need you. So do the other men." His ears turn pink, and I touch the tips. "And so do I."

He sighs, dropping his head back against the tree, sounding so defeated my throat aches.

"Yeah, well, I'm still not enough for you, am I? If I was, you wouldn't need the others."

"Oh, Jayk," I breathe, hurting everywhere. I press a kiss to his mouth, and he lets me, so I kiss him again and again, my eyes prickling with tears. "It has nothing to do with need—or being enough. I can survive without all of you. I think I've proven that. This has everything to do with love."

Jayk's arm becomes a hard band around my waist, and I ignore my nerves. He's all defense now, and I need to push my advantage.

The roots of the trees press into my knees, and it's too brisk for real comfort, but I'm still glad this is happening out here. Jayk has always felt like the outdoors to me. Wild and windswept.

"I fell for them, Jayk. The same way I fell in love with you." Slowly, so slowly, he meets my eyes, his gaze guarded as heavily as Bristlebrook, and I stroke my fingers along his hairline. "I love every brash, rude, loyal, hard-working, careful, passionate part of you. I just love them too, for all the things that make them who they are. You're more than enough, but I can't help how I feel— not for any of you. And I'm not going to try anymore."

He's raw, broken open, but forever with Jayk, there's a touch of belligerence.

"And what if I asked you to choose?"

"I won't do it," I say instantly. "I just won't. I *can't*. Jayk, you don't want that either. You don't want me with you and constantly thinking about them. And I couldn't be with them without thinking about you. I love all of you too much."

The silence between us is heavy, broken only by distant rustles and the soft gush of the river. His eyes search my face, all that belligerence bleeding into something confused and vulnerable.

How many times has he let himself be soft with someone? Has he ever felt safe enough to try?

I think of all my years pasting on polite smiles against the cruel words people whispered behind their hands. I think of him, swinging fists against those same words.

Finally, in a gruff, tentative voice, he asks, "You love me?"

"Beyond reason. I love you so much, Jayk."

His hand touches my face like he might break me. He doesn't look like my hunter right now. He looks like I have him pinned and at his mercy.

"I don't know how to do this."

I kiss him, aching with the need to soothe and fix. He reminds me of myself, when I first met them, injured and on the run. I was so lost, so *uncertain* then. It was Beau who showed me how it might be different. Beau, so quick and certain of his feelings, right from the start, and Lucky right on his heels.

I'm grateful that they led the way. It's the only reason I know how to give this to Jayk.

He and I didn't learn how to love safely. Love came turbulent and unpredictable—always with the threat of it being snatched away.

It still does.

I *know* Jaykob loves me, even if he can't say it yet . . . but this arrangement may be too much for him. He might leave me, really leave me, over this.

The thought of losing him terrifies me, and I kiss him again, harder, until his tongue slips out to battle with mine and hot, honeyed desire starts to wind through my cold fear.

"You don't need to decide right now," I murmur against his lips. "Just think about it. Please. Really think about it. I love you so much, Jayk."

His hand smooths along my face until he's cupping it. Startled, my eyes fly open, and I see him watching me.

The kiss changes.

His aggression eases back, and for the first time ever, he kisses me slow. It turns deep. Languorous. His lids hood, and mine slide shut as I sink into him.

I'm drunk on it.

I didn't know Jayk could kiss like this—so full of unselfish desire. In it, I hear all the things he can't find the words for.

I love you. I need you. I'm fucking terrified.

My hands rub over his chest as I pant into his mouth.

I kiss him back.

I know. I have you. I love you.

His cock is hot and hard again under me, and I can't ignore it anymore. He's kissing me like he loves me, and even unspoken, I'm filled with desperate need for him to mark it on my body. I reach down to fumble with his zipper. He helps me, pulling the unsatisfied length free again.

"Are you sure? We don't have to do anything," he says, with more sweet awkwardness than I'm used to from him.

My lips hover a breath from his.

"I want you to take me." His hands are resting lightly on my waist, and I hold them, dragging them under my skirts. Breathing raggedly, he lets me move him further, until I've dragged his hands to my ass. "I want you to take me *here*."

As if he can't help himself, his hands squeeze hard, and he scowls. "What is wrong with you? Don't you want some fucking romance?"

I swallow a moan as his hands tighten further, enough to bite. Enough to bruise. After Beau's coaxing touches, it feels especially crude.

I tremble, growing wet and pliant on top of him.

"It's yours, Jayk. The first time, anyway. Make it good for me. Make me like it."

At 'first time,' his eyes flare jealously, and a thrill runs through me.

I lean in and lick his lips, tasting him. "Please, Jayk. Show me how you wanted to do it. I want it to be you."

Jayk lets out a rumble of warning, deep in his chest, and I shiver. His fingers travel over my soft skin until his fingertip grazes over my puckered hole.

"Fuck," he swears against my lips. He kisses me, harder this time. "I don't have anything out here. I don't even have lube."

Oh. I lift up my dress, feeling around for the little bottle and draw it out. He stares at it.

"Anything else?" I ask breathlessly.

He yanks me against his chest, and I feel his cock throbbing against my stomach.

"You had that this whole fucking time?" His hand claps against my ass in a brutal slap, and I cry out, squirming against him until my clit is pressed against his rigid cock. The sting quickly mellows into my favorite flush of heat, and I can't help the immediate, restless grind of my hips.

"Don't let *anyone* fuck your ass without lube. Do you have any fucking clue how much that will hurt? I almost tore you open. I—"

"I love you." My open, needy words cut him off mid-tirade, and he takes a shuddery breath, that uncertain look coming over his face again.

"I love you." I kiss his lips, his jaw, anywhere I can reach. "I lo—"

He captures my mouth, swallowing the sound. He kisses me again in that slow, vulnerable, deeply un-Jayk way.

He begins to lift my dress up, tugging it up over my breasts until they fall free and he's lifted it over my head. Suddenly, I'm naked on his lap in the middle of the forest. He stares at me like he's never seen my body before. Like he doesn't know every curve and dip and taste by now. He stares at me like he's praying.

My nipples harden further in the cool air, but he's so scorching hot that I hardly feel it.

He eases me off him, then stands, not taking his eyes off me as his hands move to the buttons on his shirt. His unpracticed fingers fumble over them, and he scowls.

Shivering with need and smiling at his consternation, I come over to help. When my hands come over his, he pauses, swallowing, then lets them fall. I unfasten each button without a word, and he watches me undress him with intense eyes and unsteady breaths.

When his shirt falls open, I step into his warmth and press a biting kiss to his chest.

His breath hisses out, his cock twitching at the contact, and with more urgency, he tugs off his shirt.

To my surprise, he studiously lays it on the ground, growling in irritation when the arms don't fall flat. He gives up and looks over at me.

"Lie back on that."

I bite the inside of my lip hard to stop from smiling at him as my chest fills with sweet, laughing amusement. On a normal day, Jayk pulls my hair, bites me, slaps my cheeks, calls me name after name, he throws me where he wants me. But he still gives me pillows to kneel on. Shirts to lie on.

I must not hide my laughter well enough, because his eyes narrow on me anyway, and quicker than I can blink, he's grabbed me and is swinging me up over his shoulder. He stalks back over to the nest he's made, and in seconds he has me dumped on my back.

Jayk comes down over the top of me, and his next kiss has more bite to it.

He pulls back just enough to murmur against my lips, his eyes deliciously warning. "Laugh at me again, sugar, and we'll revisit me playing nice."

His chest brushes over my nipples, and I arch up into him, running my hands greedily up his arms.

But I can't stop my smile. "I love yo—"

Jayk claims my mouth for another one of those strange, lovely kisses. Then he's yanking my legs up, pressing my knees to my shoulders. I'm folded in two like this, everything wide open and exposed, and I feel the breeze brushing over my wet pussy.

He breaks the kiss, and his eyes linger on mine, full of things I don't think he really understands. "Keep your legs open."

Jayk drops a sucking kiss against my chest, between my breasts, then works his way down my body. When he sees the mess Beau and Lucky made of my pussy, he pulls back and slaps it, sneering a little.

I jerk hard, a shocked moan escaping me at his roughness after all the gentle touches, but he doesn't linger. His mouth moves to my thigh, more punishing now, and then those sucking, biting kisses move over my ass cheek.

I start to shake as his hands pull me open again.

Oh, God. He's staring directly at me. I don't know how I

ended up here, naked and spread wide, anointed by two men's cum and praying for a third, but I'm so glad I did. I wait for his fingers to spear me, but that's not what I'm given.

Jaykob's hot, wet mouth closes over my tight hole with that same sucking kiss. I gasp, squealing and shocked to my core, as he clamps his mouth over me and *licks*. He savors the sensitive, forbidden crease, exploring me, getting me thoroughly wet.

This is more than any plug. More, even, than his cock. I only thought he'd tasted me everywhere before.

Apparently, I was very, very wrong.

When he buries his face deeper between my cheeks and begins to tongue me in earnest, my squeal becomes a raw, unfiltered moan. It feels too good. Unexpected and obscene. He's soaking me in his spit, and it drips all around my ass. Jayk works his tongue around, and then into my now-slick hole like it's his mission, grunting at the breach, and I'm shaking hard with sharp, unholy need.

"Jayk. Oh, Jayk, Jayk, Jayk."

With one hand, he begins to rub my clit, and it's sensitive to the point of pain, and his mouth is so overwhelming, so illicit and perfect that it only makes me cry out, that desperate urge to come rising sharply again. His hands disappear for a moment, and I hear the click of the lube bottle, and then a slick, wet squirt.

He fucks me with his tongue for a moment more, then he pulls back a few inches. He swipes at his chin with his forearm, licking his mouth, and his gaze finds mine. His midnight blue eyes have turned almost wholly black with raw, savage need. His cheeks are bright with color and his chest heaves . . . but his expression is devout.

"Could make a whole meal out of that ass of yours," he growls.

Jayk eases his slippery fingers over the wet mess he left, and this time, when he presses a fingertip against my rosebud, it eases in with little resistance.

"So fucking tight." It's somewhere between a prayer and a curse.

He bites my thigh, then kisses the sting.

I arch into the bite, wanting his finger in me, but he braces himself and stays gentle, worshipful as he pushes past the inner ring. My legs are strained in this position, but I wouldn't move for anything.

Jayk pulls out, then starts working two slick fingers into my ass, making sure I'm wet and slippery, until every stroke becomes a glide, and I'm gasping and wriggling for more of that pretty pressure.

He squeezes my thigh, then kneels up. Grabbing the bottle of lube, he opens it with one hand, the other still working my hole, with three fingers now. He squirts the cold liquid directly onto his cock, then throws the bottle down.

The lube slides down his straining, ruddy length, and the sight is almost enough to set off my orgasm.

His fingers still buried in my ass, he presses his palm against me so his hand cups my pussy, and his thumb begins circling my slippery, aching clit. Slowly, the fingers in my ass start to stretch, testing the give, and I cry out.

"You're going to take this dick, sugar, and you better fucking say thank you." His taunting words lack their usual bite.

I'm shaking hard, my pussy aching. My nipples are pebbled tight, and all of me throbs with the need to be filled.

My words start tripping out in a broken jumble. "I love it, Jayk. I love everything. All of it. *You*. Please, give it to me."

His cock is taut with need, begging for attention, and Jayk's hand comes up to coat himself in the lube, slicking himself up thoroughly as he fucks his fist. At the same time, his fingers work deeper into my ass.

"Shit. Fuck. I can feel your ass sucking my fingers." Jayk's jaw tightens with restrained violence, but his eyes keep watching mine. "Tell me if it hurts."

I can only nod as he starts pulling his fingers out. Then the blunt, flared head of his dick is nudging against my wet, stretched hole. Jaykob grips himself, grips me, and forces his way inside. My toes curl at the shock of his crown popping past the resisting ring, and my body rushes to adjust to the sudden invasion—to the massive, wide girth of him.

It's like the plug and not. With the plug there was a give. That pressure that settles as you close around the small end, tucking it inside you.

Jaykob's cock doesn't have a small end.

I squeeze against the pressure, like it's possible to push him out, and he lets out a string of curses, his grip on me becoming brutal as he holds himself still. He's shaking with the effort of it, I realize, and I'm shaking too, with the strain of him. Sweat pops up along my skin, and I can feel every pulse of blood pounding through my ass around where he's wedged inside.

"Are you . . . okay?" he grits out.

My reply is a garbled, distressed moan, and his eyes squeeze shut as he swears again. He begins pulling out.

"*No.*" That comes out clear enough, and he meets my eyes. I shake my head, panting hard. "Just one . . . give me a minute. You're so much, I just . . . I need a minute."

I squeeze against him again, and his head drops back, every muscle in his chest and neck straining. Then he breathes out, and his jaw set hard and his eyes a tempest, he starts circling my clit again. It's just this side of painful, but shivers begin racking through me.

Slowly, my body does begin to adjust, getting used to the wild, wicked pressure of his spearing cock. I begin making tiny, minute rocking motions, easing over half an inch of him. It lights the delicious nerve endings back up, turning the pressure-pain into something good again. Something more familiar.

I'm suddenly very, very grateful for my training.

As I start moving, Jayk pushes my thighs further apart then

spits onto where we're joined. I should be past blushing, but I squirm in dissolute embarrassment at the vulgar move. He rubs the slick all over us, then grabs my waist again.

"H-how much more?" I ask shakily, and he snorts.

"More." Jayk watches my face as he starts pushing his cock in deeper, and my toes curl. "Much, much more."

It doesn't go in easily. Even with the lube, we fight and press and he starts pumping his hips forward and claiming every inch, until I can feel him everywhere. He's under my skin. He's in me and on me and all around. And that incredible, unbearable pressure becomes more and more erotic.

I feel impaled by him, owned, like he really is staking a claim on my body that he won't give up. That he *can't*.

How could he give this up?

Finally, the coarse hair of his thighs is pressing against my ass, and he's fully seated inside me. We're both breathing hard, and he grinds his hips against me in a rough, torturous swirl.

I get ready for him to start moving properly now. To fuck me. But he surprises me.

Jayk leans over me, resting his forehead against mine. His face is turbulent, and his eyes are agonized. So, so softly, he brushes my hair back.

Tentatively, I lift my hands and run them over his back, holding him to me, and he starts kissing my cheek, my neck, my jaw. As he does, he rocks his hips, slowly at first, easing the way, and when I moan sharply, the strokes start coming longer, harder, each one quivering with restrained power.

Jayk grunts against my neck, and the sounds that are escaping me are unintelligible. Hardly human. It feels like my whole body is awake, like he's lit every nerve ending on fire and I'm sizzling on a wire toward something beautiful and explosive.

My heart is running on a parallel line.

Because every calloused stroke against my skin is reverent. His every kiss is a gift, and every thrust a prayer.

Jayk isn't punishing me anymore.

This is an apology. A liturgy.

A mating.

It's too much. Jayk looking at me like this, touching me like my skin is too soft for his hands, is bringing me to a sweet, breathless peak. It's a different kind of orgasm to the one he usually delivers me. Those are merciless and brutal, detonating in me like a bomb and demolishing my body.

This orgasm is from the soul.

Jayk thrusts harder, punching into me as he groans, and every part of my body breaks apart. My orgasm is tender as it rips me apart, and I curve up so I'm clinging around Jayk's neck as it moves through me.

As I whimper, he starts to shake . . . and as he comes too, I hear him whisper desperately, "I've never had anything for myself before, Eden. I can't share you."

My breath catches as he fills me in hot jerks.

And desperately pray that he's wrong.

Chapter 49

Eden

Survival tip #343
*Fisticuffs isn't an appropriate method
of conflict resolution.*

Jayk and I stop briefly by the stream to clean up before we head back to Bristlebrook. We're quiet, lost in our thoughts, and Jayk seems to be moving as if on autopilot, a deep frown on his face.

"I can't share you."

I try not to let the words curdle in my stomach. He shared his past with me. It was the most raw and real and vulnerable we've ever been together. It wasn't a goodbye, was it? He wouldn't tell me all of that, open up like that, only to let me go, would he? Is this how Lucky felt, all those days ago? He was right. I have been a hypocrite.

I need to be better.

Suddenly, his hand finds mine, rough and calloused. I glance over to find him looking at me, his expression serious . . . but still open. I smile softly at him, and his hand tightens around mine like a weighted blanket.

Breathing deeply, I let the night air fill me, cool and rich and scented with flowers.

I've done what I came to do tonight. Things between me and Lucky are wonderful, and I've said what I came to say to Jaykob. I don't know if it's enough, but if this relationship doesn't work, it won't be because he doesn't know how much I love him. I've been as clear as I can be about what I want and how I feel.

It's his choice.

The sounds of the party grow louder, more drunken, the music cranked up as loud as it will go. When we make it out from between the trees, I see a large group gathered around a smaller fire where a large pig is being spit-roasted.

Jaykob and I make it back onto the lawn and hover beside one another awkwardly. He releases my hand slowly, and it's hard not to snatch it back to me.

"What . . . now?" I ask.

That frown returns to his face. "I need time." His hand finds his pocketknife, his thumb smoothing over it. "I need to think."

More time. Is he going to run off again? I force a smile and nod.

He steps closer and tentatively reaches up. Feather soft, he touches the corner of my stiff smile, and I let it fall away.

"Three days," he says in a low, gruff voice. "Three, and I'll come back."

A hard, hot lump fills my throat. His eyes are like the midnight sky, dark and endless navy, filled with deep, secret stars.

He *listened*.

I breathe out, and this time, my smile comes more naturally. "I can do three days."

We're staring at each other, neither of us making an effort to be the first to leave, when Beau almost storms past us. He stops mid-stride and turns, looking between us.

A warm, amused smile tugs his lips up on one side. "Well, hi there, darlin'—don't you look ridden hard and put away wet. Good night?"

Jaykob keeps staring at me for a moment, then he spins and plants a hard, heavy fist in Beau's solar plexus. My hand flies to my mouth as I yelp.

"Jayk!" I squeak. "Stop! What are you *doing*?"

Beau's hand finds Jayk's muscular shoulder to steady himself as he gasps for air.

"Write me a message like that again and see what happens," Jayk growls into Beau's ear. "I nearly ripped her apart. Next time, I'm coming after you."

He stands, releasing him, and Beau straightens stiffly, groaning a laugh.

"She had her safeword. I know she's safe with you," he says good-naturedly, and Jayk's return look is so violent, it might as well be a second punch.

"She might be if she'd use it," Jayk grits out. "Or if I wasn't such a blind, dumb fuck."

Uh-oh.

He doesn't even have the grace to look at me as he outs me shamelessly, and Beau's smile withers. He gives me a surprised, concerned look that twists my stomach, and I give him a reassuring head shake.

Jayk's jaw works like he's fighting words, then he adds in a low voice, "If you're fucking her then you watch out for that. She wants to prove she can *take* it."

Finally, he darts a hard look back at me—but even as I scowl at him, I can see it's laced in worry.

But for goodness' sake, I *could* have taken it.

Maybe.

Probably, anyway.

"I'll take care of it," Beau says in a curt voice, disappointed eyes on me, and I shift, then back up.

Right into Jasper's chest.

He looks down at me with a curious expression, and I step to the side, away from all of them.

"Take care of what, pray tell?" he asks, and I glance at Beau and Jayk.

Surely this doesn't need to be common knowledge. It was *barely* an issue. It was a misunderstanding, really, and for just a moment. No harm, no foul and all that.

"Eden didn't use her safeword when she needed to," Beau explains, a grim set to his square jaw, and I gape in affront.

Seriously? Is this a military thing? A dominant thing? Is there some kind of code I'm not aware of here?

Nothing is sacred.

"*Need* is a rather strong word," I reason, twisting my fingers together, and Jaykob glowers at me.

"Ah. That is a problem." Jasper's brows lower, just a shade. His eyes scan me, then Jaykob. "Are you both okay?"

My eyes widen a little, startled that he thought to include Jaykob in that. He's right to, of course. Of the two of us, Jayk was more upset. For some reason, I'd always thought that Jayk probably wouldn't have shared much with Jasper, despite him being their psychologist, but I wonder if I'm wrong. Jasper does have him pegged.

Jayk tenses like a cornered wolf, but his eyes are still on me.

"You needed it, and I fucked up," Jayk snaps. He turns to Beau, his jaw set, and he plants his feet like he's bracing himself. "Hit me."

Jasper sighs, short and hard, as Beau gives Jayk an exasperated look. "I'm not hitting you."

Jayk's brows slam down. "Just hit me. I'll give you two." He glances at me, then his lips twist. "Three. I'll give you three."

"Jaykob, we need to have another discussion about how you resolve your conflicts," Jasper says, rubbing his forehead.

Jayk ignores him, staring hard at Beau, who rolls his eyes.

"Do you have any idea how much these hands are worth?"

Beau looks down at them. "I'm not hitting you, you damn fool. If you're feeling guilty, you make it up to her, not to me."

"I'm *fine*," I insist again when Jayk scowls. "I had the barest moment of hesitation."

I spot Lucky coming up behind Jayk, and my heart lifts at the chance of an ally.

"Just hit me," Jayk growls out.

Lucky shrugs, then drops low to deliver an uppercut to Jayk's kidney. Jayk flinches back with a grunt, and Lucky slaps him lightly on the back with a grin.

"So why are we hitting Jayk?" Lucky asks, and I throw up my hands.

These men are too much.

"Oh, Lucky, there you are," Beau says as Jayk straightens with a grimace. "Did you find Akira?"

Worry prickles. "Akira's missing?"

Lucky shakes his head. He's fixed his hair since I last saw it, and it's now half up, the rest blond and loose over his shoulders.

"Nah, not exactly. Some of the others said she was upset, so she's probably just avoiding the party. There are a few people looking just in case she needs a hug. Hammy Porker is ready now anyway—if *that* hadn't been sorted, we would have had a mob on our hands. You're welcome, by the way." He looks down at my dress and raises both brows. "How are *you*? I mean, you're walking straight. That's a surprise."

"Eden didn't use her safeword with Jaykob," Jasper fills him in absently, and I glare at him in affront.

This is a *cabal*.

Lucky sucks in a breath and winces at me. "Oh man, did you freeze? I did that during my first big electrical play scene."

Okay, this is quite enough.

"I didn't freeze," I explain firmly. "I was just slightly nervous. For a *moment*. I would have gotten past it, I'm sure, but Jayk noticed and stopped. We talked. Everything is fine. This is honestly a non-issue."

Lucky laughs, but it sounds panicked. I'm trying to puzzle out why when I look around the three very still, very dark faces of Beau, Jasper, and Jayk.

"Really, I think you're all being a little drama—"

Lucky's hand suddenly wraps around my mouth from behind, and he drags me back.

"She doesn't know what she's talking about. She's very sorry and will definitely be vocal whenever she's scared or uncomfortable. She absolutely, one hundred percent, has learned her lesson, and as her self-designated sub tutor, I'm going to take her away to talk to her about this. Right now." He keeps dragging me away from them and whispers in my ear. "Over a lot of alcohol."

"Stop, Lucien." Jasper's voice is a whip crack, and my bewildered gaze finds my stern sadist. The air crackles around him.

Lucky sighs, giving me a squeeze. "Please stop glaring at them. You're making me nervous."

Over my shoulder, I give him a bemused look. Must they all be so dramatic?

Jasper glances at Beau and Jayk.

"Jaykob, would you like to handle this?" he asks, and Jayk looks like a forbidding boulder.

"No one needs to handle shit. She and I squared up." He levels brutal glares on each of the others. "Let's be real fucking clear. I don't want you touching her. I don't want you *breathing* on her. But if you're going to keep fucking her, then just watch out for that shit."

His glare swings to me . . . and it loses its heat.

"Three days," he says.

My heart swells painfully. I understand his jealousy, I really do. But he's still looking out for me.

"Three days," I confirm, then I add quietly, "I love you."

Dark color rolls into his cheeks, and he gives me a final, long look before stalking off.

I'm staring after him when Lucky shatters my thoughts. "Three days? What's in three days?"

Beau shakes his head, looking at me with a gentle expression. "I love you? Good for you, darlin'."

"I'm pleased you had a chance to speak with Jaykob, Eden, but this conversation isn't over." Jasper steps in closer to me and takes my hand, and the cool, silky touch makes me shiver. His expression is subdued. "I wouldn't presume to arrange a punishment for an incident between yourself and another dominant, but I must be sure you understand the importance of communication and safe-words—particularly during a scene. I'm assuming Beaumont has had a discussion with you about this?"

Some of my exasperation with them fades and guilt stings me. Beau raises both brows expectantly, disappointment etched in the gold-green of his eyes.

"He has, yes," I agree, shifting.

Jasper nods. "So you do understand that continuing while you are uncomfortable is both dangerous and detrimental to yourself —that we are complicated creatures and kink can press on a variety of expected and unexpected triggers, and that discomfort is our body's way of protecting itself from trauma. I'm sure you know by now that slowing down or stopping a scene is always, *always* preferred to that alternative."

Unsettled, I nod. Beau had talked about it, of course, but I hadn't truly considered it with any particular depth.

"Yes, Jasper," I say, shamefaced, and I feel Lucky shift closer to me from behind.

"And so you do understand that your dominant's only interest is in your pleasure, and not in being the cause of any suffering, do you not? How terrifying the concept is that we might miss an unspoken signal from a submissive?" At my stricken look, Jasper lets out a sigh, patting my hand. "I understand the impulse, Eden, I do, but pushing on because you want to please us will only do harm on both sides. It's something I'm particularly conscious of, and I imagine Jaykob is as well, given the nature of our interests."

My stomach churns. Yes, Jaykob was certainly conscious of it. He was downright mortified. The guilt deepens.

"I'm sorry," I whisper. "I wasn't thinking. I promise I'll speak up if it happens again."

Jasper's eyes move over my face, and finally, he nods. "Yes. I believe you will. Clever as you are, I'm sure you would like to read up on the matter further. I'll provide you with some kink education books. I'm sure you'll find them illuminating, and I'd dearly love to hear your thoughts. An essay on safety in dominant-submissive relationships should do it, don't you agree?"

Lucky lets out a strangled laugh behind me, and I step back so my heel digs into his foot, and he yelps, backing up. My eyes narrow on Jasper as I study his mild expression.

Wouldn't presume to punish me, my rear end.

I don't have to agree to this. I know I don't.

And yet, I know this is motivated by worry. Jasper is a sadist— one who continually insists I have no understanding of what that means. If I'm ever to get the chance to find out, he needs to trust me as much as I do him.

"Would two thousand words be sufficient?" I ask politely.

Approval adds a gracious glow to his features. "Quite. I'll provide you with a limits list to fill out also." His lips tilt. "I believe we'll be needing it."

Needing it? We will? Me and the other men? Or me and Jasper?

Excitement sparks like raw dynamite in my veins.

"Ah, now that would be helpful." Beau grins, giving me and Jasper an amused look.

Lucky bounds forward again, slinging an arm about my shoulder. "Eden, are you opposed to threesomes? Four can be a crowd, and I feel like we should wind it back. No offense, Beau. That will be on the sheet, but I think I need to know now. I humbly volunteer to be part of your first threesome. I humbly volunteer Jasper as well."

Jasper arches a brow at Lucky just as the music jumps back into something bright and bouncy that provokes a chorus of drunken cheers.

I can't tell if it's a *no* brow or a *careful sassing me* brow.

"She isn't opposed, and you're too late." Beau directs his slow smirk at Lucky, but his eyes find mine, filled with riverbanks and spankings.

My cheeks heat, and I bite my lip as I smile back.

"What kind of threesome, though?" Lucky asks shamelessly. "Are we talking taking turns? DP? DVP? DAP? Wait, no, scratch that last one. We can tackle that later."

Beau snorts, and I look suspiciously between them. "I don't know what that means, but I'm sure it's not appropriate to discuss in public."

I brush some dirt off my dress, then give it up as a hopeless cause. I'm okay with being a little filthy.

With these men, I'm okay with being very filthy.

I take a deep, full breath of the wild woods—in this moment, feeling wonderfully, completely settled.

I look between the three men before me and grin. "Shall we join the party? I think it's past time I participated in this bond-fire."

CHAPTER 50

EDEN

SURVIVAL TIP #168
Wine.

I shake the long skirts of my dress from side to side, popping my hips to the bright, mindless beat. Lucky cackles—again—even though I'm *sure* I got the right rhythm this time. Jasper shuffles, swaying just a bit, clicking his fingers to the music.

He is definitely off beat.

I've never been to a nightclub before, but I know I'm doing it right. I wish Beau was here to mediate, but he had to return to his monitoring duties.

His sad, boring, dance-free monitoring duties.

Lucky swipes a tear from under his eye. "You two . . . so bad. How are you *so* . . . so, so, so bad?"

He snorts another laugh, and Jasper stops dancing, pink-cheeked. "This is *not* my kind of dancing, Lucien."

I don't stop. I was tired before—when I came out of the woods, I was ready to keel over from exhaustion. But that went away after drink six.

The music is *in me* now.

Mary Beth is hanging off a grinning Sloane again, her lipstick smeared and streaked over Sloane's neck. Beside me, Jennifer whoops, then bumps her hip with mine. I laugh, then we bump hips again, and her sticky drink sprays out of her cup.

Some lands on my dress in a damp, pungent splash—but at this point, what does it matter?

"Show me your kind of dancing then."

Lucky slides his hands up Jasper's chest, and my perfect rhythm falters as I stare.

And Jennifer's next hip bump sends me flying.

I collide into them with a squeal. We're a human knot. A tangle of limbs and scorching hot skin—and far too many clothes.

"Oh hello," I say brightly, my head swimming.

Swimming quite a lot, actually.

I've only had three or five drinks.

"Hello, beautiful girl," Jasper purrs, and I feel the shuddering vibration through my whole body. He shifts to put his arm around me, so I'm more included in the cuddle.

It's hot—very, very hot—in the cuddle.

"You're beautiful," I tell him, very seriously. It seems important that he knows that.

"He really is, isn't he?" Lucky sighs, looking at him with pretty, dazed blue eyes.

Jasper regards us both with an affectionate smile that makes me feel far more wobbly than the booze does. I glance at Lucky, at the dimple that winks from his cheek, and I lean over and kiss it. He freezes in surprise for a second, then laughs and drags his mouth around so he's kissing me.

His mouth tastes like vodka and mint leaves, and I enjoy it for a long, delicious moment before he's pulled away and Jasper kisses him.

Jasper's grip is firm on Lucky's cheeks and Lucky shivers. I stare at the join of their mouths and spot a hint of their tongues. Lucky's hands move down Jasper's chest, and my eyes drop to follow them, fascinated.

My heart pounds a reckless rhythm. Right now, I don't feel jealous at all.

I just want to see more.

I rest my hand against Jasper's chest for balance as I peer down at his belt, and he tenses—and grasps Lucky's hands before they find their target.

Lucky and I both sigh in disappointment.

Jasper pulls back, and his lips glisten. I lean in, desperate to find out what his mouth tastes like, too. It seems only fair to go around the circle.

But Jasper backs up, wrenching free of our huddle.

"You've been drinking." He wipes his mouth, but his fingers linger on his lips, red from Lucky's kisses. His eyes glitter like obsidian as he looks between us. "Enough of that. We can continue to dance—that's all."

Lucky tugs me into his side, and I look up as his smile turns sly and a little too big. "All I want is to dance, oh terrifying lord and master." He leans down to whisper to me, "Eden, how good are you at twerking?"

I'm saved from answering by a loud screech behind me.

"Eden!"

A tornado of red and blue hair slams into my side, dousing me with the scent of boozy figs, and my glasses slip down my nose.

It takes me a moment to realize that it's Heather hugging me, a dark, long-necked bottle in one hand.

I pat her arm awkwardly, laughing. "Hello! Are you done monitoring?"

She makes a face. "Finally. Aaron took ages to relieve me. Come dance with me—Ava and the others are on the other side."

I already danced with Ava and the others. Ethel was the one

who showed me my hip-popping move. I want to keep flirting with Jasper and Lucky.

Heather follows my gaze to the couple, who are dancing. This time slow and pressed together . . . and watching me.

We're only a foot away, but—for some godforsaken reason—I wave at them.

Lucky breaks into another round of laughter, pressing his head into Jasper's chest.

"Oh, girl, look, if you want to rail the whole squad, good for you, but you're leaving someone out. How about you go find Dom? He's sitting over . . . there." Heather turns me toward the apple tree, where Dom is standing, surveying the party. "He's looking extra hot tonight. Stupid hot. Rip-his-clothes-off-with-your-teeth hot."

Irritation rips through me, spoiling some of my happy glow.

"I know how good he looks." It comes out tight. My teeth feel glued together.

Heather nudges me toward the lit-up tree, shooting me a taunting, gray-eyed wink. "Just go for him. You know he can fuck like a—"

I shove out of her grip. "I *will* slap you."

She laughs, and I pluck her bottle from her hand.

"I'm taking this as an asshole tax," I tell her primly, then turn back toward Lucky and Jasper, my fluttery skirts swishing about my legs.

This is a happy night. I'm going to spend it doing happy things with happy people.

"Eden, wait. Hey!" Heather laughs again. "I'm not into him, if that's what's been holding you back. He's very thoroughly over me too. Just let me play matchmaker—I owe it to both of you."

I stagger to a stop, then turn around in surprise.

They're . . . *not* into each other?

My mind races as I look her over, flipping through images of her and Dom over the last two weeks. Talking. Laughing. Bickering. Staying up late together . . . but no hand-holding. No long, lingering looks.

Does Dom even hold hands?

I chew on my lower lip. Bold. Tonight, I am *bold*.

"You don't want him?" I ask. Heather's head tilts, and suddenly, boldness turns to panic. "Isn't that—? I mean, don't you . . . You're very pretty. And he's very pretty. And you know what he looks like naked. God. I hate that you know what he looks like naked. It makes it very hard to like you. You're also very rude. That also makes it hard to like you. You really should be nicer to people." I rub my forehead, flustered. "Except Dom. You don't have to be nicer to him. How nice *are* you to him? Just so I know."

Heather crosses her arms, her brows raised, and I tug at the bodice of my dress.

"Is it warm out here? It's *hot*." I eye the bonfire, but it's still where I left it. Chugging along like it's dancing to the music.

Heather shakes her head. "I didn't pick Dom, Eden. He deserves to be picked."

Dom is . . . single. Totally free and available. Unattached. He's also been talking to me every day.

My happy feelings start flooding back, and I grin.

Needing to swish the taste of verbal diarrhea out of my mouth, I take a quick swig of the bottle.

And immediately choke.

The foul sweet-sour taste burns my tongue and I splutter, spraying ruby liquid everywhere.

Heather snatches the bottle from my hands, laughing as she gathers my hair and holds it out of the way. "To the side, rookie. You're going to wreck your dress if you spit it all up like that."

I gag again.

She whacks my back. "Girl, I really thought with five guys on the run, you would have at least worked out how to swallow."

She raises her arm again, and I grab her hand before she makes contact, glaring at her with teary eyes as I suck in air.

"That is repulsive," I gasp. "What on earth *is* that?"

Heather looks at the bottle and shrugs. "Port? The creepy vampire didn't put it out with the rest of the bottles, so I figured it was probably good."

I shake my head. "Not good. Bad. *Awful.*"

"Like me," Heather adds.

My cheeks heat. "I just think you should be nicer to people. These things have a way of coming back around." I slide her a sideways look. "And you *did* just call Jasper a creepy vampire. Jasper is lovely."

"Of course *you* think that. You should see the things he writes in his book about you." Her shoulders shake with her shudder. "Definitely creepy."

"Book?" I ask, but Heather waves me off.

"Look, I'm sorry I've been an ass. Dom chewed me out for it the other day too. I'll try to go easier on the guys." She gives me a half-smile. "I don't know how you do it, honestly—you have the patience of a saint. I've never been like that. I wish I was."

Heather wishes she was like . . . me?

I blink in surprise. "Because you take action. You're brave. You pulled me back together in that camp. You were the one to stay and fight. I wish I was more like *you*."

Heather's already shaking her head. I realize she's staring at the apple tree, at the candles hanging like fruit from its dead boughs.

She scoffs bitterly. "What the hell did it get me? I led my people into danger, I got Tommy killed, got a dozen of us imprisoned, I almost got all of *you* killed, and I spent three months in that camp without anything changing. You kept your head. You got them to trust you, and *you* got us out."

Oh no, I'm too drunk for this.

I throw my arms around her and squeeze. It was one of the first things I saw in Madison—her rage, her grief . . . her shame. Like recognizes like. For all that we have almost nothing else in common, we share that.

Blood and pain and beatings in the mud.

"We did it together," I whisper into her hair. In this moment, just this one, I even believe it. Maybe she couldn't have escaped without me and my poison plan, and I couldn't have escaped without her and her people fighting for me.

Heather hugs me too. I feel her chest hitch against mine, hear the catch in her breath, and I rub her back.

Neither one of us escaped the Sinners without scars—but I was lucky. I got my men back. I get a second chance, and I'm finally feeling strong enough to make use of it.

Heather will never get Thomas back, and the civilians that the Sinners captured may never be freed.

I wonder where she gets her strength from.

"Eden, a full moon is approaching. I do hope you're being cautious," Jasper calls in a lazy, elegant voice over the music.

Heather pulls out of my arms and gives him a bored look. Before she can say anything, I point at Jasper.

"You be nice. We're *all* going to be nice." I raise a chastising brow and look between him, Lucky, and Heather. "We have enemies enough outside Bristlebrook without having them in here too."

Lucky grins roguishly. "Deal. But only if you scold me like that again."

His smile is too impossibly sweet to resist. I poke out my tongue at him, and his eyes drop to it, his smile slipping.

Jasper and Heather stand across from one another, like it's a Western and they're preparing to duel.

Finally, Heather huffs. "What do you think? Can werebitches and vamp-daddies be friends?"

Jasper's dark hair stirs in the breeze, and he looks her over speculatively. "Perhaps we can call a truce." He lowers his chin, and his voice turns grim. "If you show respect to the things that belong to me."

"People or possessions?" she shoots back. "Because if you're talking about your kinky diary, then—"

"Both," he says curtly. Warningly.

Heather snorts a laugh.

"Fine. Consider it a truce." She looks between all three of us, and a devious, dangerous smile spreads across her lips. "And I know *just* how to celebrate our new arrangement."

CHAPTER 51

DOMINIC

SURVIVAL TIP #186
Some candles burn brighter.
Don't let them go out.

I settle back, leaning against the trunk of the apple tree. It's a good place to wait between rounds—I have a clear line of sight to the moat, the food and alcohol tables, and the bonfire, and the candles hanging from the branches around me are quiet company.

A tall brunette by the fire gives me a quiet nod, letting me know everything's under control. Shelby has a good head on her shoulders—she handled one bout of tears, sent two people who were well past drunk to their beds, and carted off Mila to see Beau after she twisted her ankle. I know because we *talked*.

I *also* talked to Valerie and Patrick, a couple in their early fifties who are monitoring the surrounding woods, and Isabel—but she only stuttered that she was twenty-one, then scurried away, clutching her bourbon.

Still, it wasn't terrible.

I'm watching the dry moat, contemplating how we might be

able to use our remaining explosives to best advantage, when I hear Eden.

When I hear Eden *squeal*.

I look over to find Heather dragging my disheveled librarian toward me—though she's stumbling almost as badly. Eden's pulling back against Heather's hand, shaking her head. Her cheeks are flushed a brilliant pink, her glasses dangle around her neck by their chain, and her eyes are sparkling in the starlight.

"No, no, no, I can't. Don't make me do it." Eden laughs. "Let go!"

Heather's hair swings around her as she smirks. "Fine."

She releases Eden's hand, and Eden tumbles backwards with a screech, landing on her ass in the middle of the lawn. She laughs.

And I stare.

All week, we've been talking. She's a good listener, attentive, thoughtful. She doesn't rush to fill silences . . . unless she gets flustered. I've seen her stutter, frown, smile, rage, and cry.

I haven't seen her laugh like this. Uninhibited. *Happy*.

It looks good on her.

A smile tugs across my face. I start walking over as Heather reaches down and tries to pull Eden up with both hands, without much luck.

They've hardly registered my presence before I'm hooking my arms under Eden's and pulling her to her feet. When she stands, she . . . doesn't.

Eden leans heavily against my chest, her head rolling back to look at me like it's made of rubber. There are leaves all through her hair, and her breath smells like alcohol.

"Dom!" Heather exclaims. "Good timing. Eden has something to say to you."

Eden's nails dig into my chest, and her eyes widen. "I don't!"

Bemused, I study her, then Heather, who grins at me. She doesn't seem anywhere near as tipsy as Eden.

She starts backing up, then pauses, her eyes lighting on the tree . . . and her grin falls away. She stares up at the candles for a long, shadowed moment.

"Heather? You okay?" I ask quietly.

The moment breaks, and she lifts a dismissive hand, then turns and walks away. There have been more than a few people who have had a hard time looking at that tree tonight.

I glance back down at Eden. She's staring up at me with wide, nervous eyes.

"Something to say?" I ask, settling her closer against me.

"No," she says quickly.

Too quickly.

I raise a dry brow. "Uh-huh." When she keeps staring at me, I snort. "Okay, pet, come with me."

Arm around her waist, I help her over to the tree where I left my bag. She sits down under the roots as I kneel and flip it open, pushing past the first aid kit and whistle to get to the water bottle.

She takes it and sips the water without complaint, staring up at the candles. There's a raw kind of beauty about the tree this way, burned and stark and slowly healing, lit with a hazy glow.

"Did you light one?" she asks softly. "Is that too personal to ask?"

I sit beside her, looking up at the reminders of our dead.

"I lit one for my parents." It seemed only right. We weren't close—they were distant, job-driven people—but I still loved them. "And I lit one for the Bennetts."

Eden's head rolls sideways to look at me. "For Beau's family?"

I give her bottle a stern look, and she huffs, smiling. When she takes another drink, I look back up at the candle I lit for them.

"They were great. His dad was a crafty old ass. He quoted the Bible too much, but he had a soft heart. Brought Beau a pride flag when he turned eighteen along with a whole speech about how he'd support our lifestyle, how happy he was that Beau found a man like me." I snort. "I let Beau figure out how to explain that one to him, but it was cute."

Eden laughs softly, nestling in closer. She rests her chin on my shoulder.

"Mama Bennett's pies were a slice of heaven. She used to bring them every time we got back from a deployment—spoiled the whole squad." I smile, remembering. "His sisters were menaces. Beth almost blew up their town marrying Coby Colson—the Colsons and the Bennetts had rival ranches, you see. Then there was Brooke, she was the business head. She got her peach farm up and running and turning a profit in just a few years. And Bailey. Man, Bailey was trouble. Beau and I tried to keep her out of it, but we didn't know half of what she got up to. The half we did know was enough to curl my damn hair. She was sweet, though."

They were almost at the center of the first strikes. They would have been dead before they even knew what happened.

Beau doesn't bring them up often—he grieved them hard and talking about them is like taking a bullet spray to the gut. But it's also nice. They were good people. They should be remembered.

I twist my neck to look down at Eden, who blinks at me with gentle compassion.

"Did you light any?" I ask.

I don't know when I started getting curious about her—about her opinions, who she misses, what keeps her up at night—but I can't turn it off. I don't even want to anymore.

"One," she whispers, and her eyes unfocus like a rippling pond. "I lit it for the women Sam has captive. I don't . . . I don't want to forget them."

Her regal features turn haunted, and grim understanding adds another weight around my shoulders. It doesn't surprise me that Eden thinks about them. She almost *was* them.

The thought sits like a pile of rancid shit.

"We won't," I promise. "It won't be easy, Eden, not with the amount of men he has—especially not with Alastair and Mateo backing him up—but if we're ever in a position to try, I swear we'll get them out."

Eden flinches, ducking her head, and the acid in my gut etches away at me further. It's not enough. Not for her, and not for the women kept at the Den.

But this isn't a problem I can fix. Not right now.

Instead, I shift so I can put my arm around her shoulders, and her head flops onto my chest. Slowly, the tight, worn expression on her face eases.

She yawns like a tired kitten, and her eyes start to wander.

"Pretty shirt." She nestles her cheek against me. "Soft."

My heart does strange, unsteady things as I watch her. If she can hear it, she doesn't let on. I let my fingers sink into the soft ends of her hair. She sighs at the gentle tugs, and the unselfconscious sound cuts me off at the knees.

"What the hell did you get up to tonight?" I ask.

I haven't even seen her tipsy before. She usually stops at a drink or two.

"The sex part or the drinking part?" she mumbles, and I tense.

My gaze rakes over her filthy dress. That explains that then.

The need to know everything she's done tonight—*every* night—grips me, and I have to remind myself that she's been drinking. It wouldn't be right to drag every detail out of her now.

I'll wait until she's sober.

Picking a stubborn leaf out of her hair, I say, "The drinking part."

She hums, and I feel the vibration over every inch of my skin. "Heather and Lucky and the other women played Never Have I Ever with me. Have you played it?" Her proud smile curves against my chest. "I've done more things than I thought." She frowns. "That also means I had to drink a lot, you understand."

She yawns again, and I run a hand over my face. This is going to kill me.

Trying not to think about all the *things* she might have done—all the things *I* could do with her—I tap her back to urge her to get up. "Come on, let's get you to bed."

Eden's startled eyes swing up to mine, and I smirk.

"Back to *your* bed," I clarify.

Her sigh is audible . . . and disappointed. Not the kind of sigh a *friend* might make when she's told she's not getting any.

I help her to her feet, and she wobbles.

"Did you know that Lucky has had sex on the back of a horse? How do you even *do* that?" she asks.

"I don't know, pet," I say, amused.

"He won the whole game, you know. He was very drunk," she says disapprovingly, then almost trips over her own feet as she steps toward the house. I catch her silently as she continues without missing a beat. "It was very irresponsible of him."

She slaps my chest. "Oh!"

I raise an eyebrow. "Oh?"

"Can you tell me what this says?" she asks.

Then she turns around and pulls her dress up to her waist.

In the middle of the goddamned lawn.

My smile crashes and burns as I stare at her bare ass. It's pale and round and a little dirt smudged. Fingerprint-sized bruises are already blooming on her hips.

Fuck.

A scalding shudder shoots down my spine. The urge to throw her over my shoulder and lock her to my bed is harder than it should be to shut down.

"What does it say?" she asks again. "They wouldn't tell me."

Say?

I drag my fuck-fogged thoughts out of the gutter and focus on the writing—and my snort escapes like a gunshot.

"What makes you think I'll tell you?" I ask.

Beau wrote the left side, I'd bet rations on it. Which meant Lucky wrote the right. Jayk can't take a joke, and it's obviously not Jasper's style.

Eden throws a disgruntled frown over her shoulder. "You're supposed to be my friend, remember?"

I step up to her and place my hands over hers. Mine shake at the effort not to grab and slap the silky, exposed skin.

Her breath catches, and the frown falls away. After a moment, she tilts her head back, and the ends of her hair tease her hips.

She watches me as I tug her dress back down.

"What if I don't want to be friends anymore?" I taunt.

Eden's lips part, ripe and ready, and her tongue dips out to tease the lower lip. "Because you don't like me?"

I shake my head slowly. "I like you."

Like. It doesn't fit in my mouth right. It's too mild. It doesn't fit the way my eyes track her across a room. It doesn't fit the way I fuck my fist every morning thinking about her. It doesn't fit how talking to her is the highlight of my whole day.

Her lips form an "o."

Very, very lightly, I brush the right side of her ass through her dress. "This one says 'Prepared this for you, buddy.'" I brush the left side, smiling wryly. "This one says, 'Tag, you're it.'"

Her eyes widen. "That's *terrible*."

But her lips twitch, then roll in, and then suddenly she's giggling.

"Poor Jayk," she gasps.

She clutches me for support, and I start laughing too.

"Okay, pet, come on. You need to sleep." I swing her into my arms bridal style, and she doesn't protest as I start walking us toward the house.

She fits in my arms like she was made to be there. Finally, she stops laughing, but her cheeks are still rosy and her nose a bit red from drinking. She rests her head back against me with a happy sigh, watching me.

"What does DAP mean?" she asks.

I miss a step, stumbling slightly, then correct myself. I stare down at her for a second, then put my eyes back on where I'm going.

"Jesus fucking Christ," I mutter.

She shakes her head, frowning thoughtfully. "No, I don't think that's it."

Why does she need to know? There's no way in hell this is on the table yet.

My dick doesn't seem to care about that kind of detail.

"Double anal penetration," I tell her. "It means double anal penetration."

"Oh." Her voice is faint. Then her frown deepens. "That seems impractical."

"Double vaginal is easier," I agree, and she looks up at me with interest.

On a different day, with her completely sober and Beau back on my side, I would spend hours easing her into just that. It wouldn't even be that difficult. She comes hard and easily—it wouldn't take much to get her limp and relaxed and soaking wet. Just imagining her broken expression, how good her pussy would feel stuffed with our cocks, makes me grip her to my chest harder.

"Have you done it with Beau before?" she asks in a hushed, curious voice.

Like she's trying not to let anyone hear.

Like she didn't just expose her ass to half the party.

I round the bonfire.

"Yep." I don't want to think about the other times. The way we're going, I don't even know if there will be more times with Beau.

Her fingers brush along the stubble at my jaw. "He misses you too."

I hope it's true. I doubt it's enough. He and I both know that I need him more than he needs me.

Her touch starts soft. Hesitant. When I don't stop her, she gets bolder. Her fingertips trail up to my lips, tracing the outline. It brings a smile back to them.

I step up the porch stairs, avoiding tripping over a collection of empty bottles.

"What are you doing, pet?" I ask in a low voice, glancing down at her.

She's very focused on my mouth.

"Touching you," she says absently. "Stop me if you need me to."

Damn it. She's too cute like this. Intent and wondering and dreamy. I never want her to stop.

I slow down as I make my way up the imperial staircase as that thought hits me hard.

I *don't* ever want her to stop.

I want her touches and her giggles and her soft, serious frowns. I want to talk to her and listen to her and be around her. I want her on her knees and in my bed and following my orders on how to take my cock.

I want to love her.

"You're so pretty," she murmurs.

"Pretty?" Startled, I look down at her again.

I've been called a lot of things, but *pretty* isn't usually on the list.

"Mmm." Her fingers slide over my throat, over my rampaging pulse. "I think about your face a lot. I think about you naked a *lot*."

We're almost at her room, but I slow to a glacial pace as I stare at her. She's perfectly snuggled in my arms, the fabric of her dress flirting with my skin in hungry little brushes.

My gaze lingers on her mouth, remembering the way it looked wrapped around Beau's cock. "Not very platonic of you."

Whatever it is that's coursing through me is running hot and sweet.

This is the kind of thing I always missed out on. The moment they would roll out of my arms and into Beau's. It never used to interest me much.

It interests me a hell of a lot now.

I wonder how bad it would be if I shirked my responsibilities just to watch her sleep.

Eden sighs heavily.

"I don't want to be just your friend anymore," she confesses. Her hands tease along my collarbone. "Heather and Lucky and Jasper said I should tell you something."

"Oh?"

"Yes." She nods seriously, then takes a deep breath. "I like you. A lot. In fact, I really, truly, maybe think that I—"

"Wait," I say, my heart pounding. She stops. Even her hand pauses on my skin. Her eyes find mine, and I try to smooth my tone. "Can we talk about this tomorrow? I want to hear it. But I want to hear it when you're sober."

My control is just a burning thread to lit dynamite at this point. She's soft and pliant and looking up at me with these sweet little take-me eyes.

If she tells me that she wants me now, I don't think I'll be able to stop myself.

"Okay," she says, whispering her promise. "I won't forget."

So diligent.

My lips twitch, and I match her tone. "I trust you."

For some reason, she flinches at that, and she rests her cheek against my chest. The soft weight is like a lingering kiss.

We're outside her door now, but I'm not ready for this to end. I don't want to hand her over to Beau yet.

I lower her legs to the floor, then let her lean her back against the wall beside her door. Her hands are buried in my shirt, and I keep mine around her waist to hold her up. She's lost the few extra pounds she gained while she was with us before. Her captivity and the strict rations are starting to show on her, and I hate it, just because I know what it means. She's hungry. We're not getting her enough food.

No one is getting enough food—and unless we change something soon, we're starting a slow, inexorable starvation game.

Her face mirrors the dark turn my thoughts have taken.

"What is it, pet?"

She stares at my chest, mouth tight and flat. She looks ready for the gallows.

It takes her a long time before she whispers, and it's so low I have to strain to hear her.

"Do you think if someone did something really, truly wrong, but their intentions were good, that you might be able to forgive them for it?" She swallows, then pushes her hair back off her face and into the messy tangle behind her ears. Her teeth bite deeply into her lower lip, then she releases it to add, "Especially if they were so, so sorry."

A chill slithers through my chest. Is she talking about something that happened in the camp? She has to know I don't judge her for the poison.

"Eden, we've all done things we're not proud of. All we can do is own our shit and do better moving forward. You don't need to be sorry for anything you did out there," I tell her.

Eden still doesn't meet my eyes, and her fingers tighten in my shirt. All I can see is the dark waterfall of her hair as she finally nods.

"Dom, I need to tell you something." She takes a deep breath. "When we were all coming back from the camp, I—"

Her bedroom door swings open, cutting her off, and we both look up to see Beau stagger out, wide-eyed and pale.

His hands are covered in blood.

CHAPTER 52

BEAU

SURVIVAL TIP #37
*If an infection risks the whole system,
then make the hard call.
Amputate.*

The room is scarlet and rust. Blood splatters the walls like paint—heavy and slowly dripping in some places, and light and drying in others. It's smeared on the windows, and it scars the curtains. The bed is gorged with it, dripping on the floor, and the large, heavy mound of blankets in its center makes my brain go blank with fear.

This amount of blood means death.

"Eden!" My voice is sharp with panic. I'm at our bedside in seconds. The bed I woke up in this morning, with my Eden wrapped in my arms.

My hands shake as they hover over the blankets, my vision narrowing on the gentle protrusion underneath.

It can't be her. She was at the party. She was with Jasper and Lucky—they had her.

It can't, it can't, it can't.

I can't make my fingers grip the blanket; visions of this very day five years ago are locking down my muscles. Of walking into Darkside, our kink club, to everyone watching the emergency broadcast. Of realizing that my mama and dad and Beth, Brooke, and Bailey couldn't have made it out. They'd been heading home for Sunday dinner, smack square in the middle of the blast radius.

You don't recover from a loss like that.

I can't lose my family again.

Gritting my teeth, I rip back the drenched blankets . . . only to find a heap of red-stained pillows.

My breath swings out of me. I lower my head, shaking harder as I try to catch my breath. I'm perilously close to tears.

It's not her. It's not her blood.

Relief is more than a feeling. It's a prayer, and it takes me a full minute before I can breathe well enough to look around again. So much blood. It might not be Eden's, but it's someone's.

My eyes track back over the violent splatters. The malicious destruction. Whoever did this meant harm—and they're inside Bristlebrook.

I need to find Eden. Now.

Nothing is touching her ever again.

I don't trust my legs beneath me as I leave the room. My knees feel like loose hay, and my bloody hands slip over the door handle as I leave.

Somehow, Eden's right there, and so is Dom.

She's leaning against the wall, pretty and mussed and tangled. But whole. Uninjured.

I can't stop myself. I grab her to me and squeeze her against my chest. She makes a small sound of surprise, but then she wraps her arms around me and squeezes me back. Her hair smells faintly of smoke, but her heart is beating a reassuring rhythm against my chest.

"What happened?" Dom demands beside us. "Beau, talk to me."

I suddenly catch sight of the red on my hands and release her, realizing I've left a bloody smear on her arm that she doesn't even glance at.

Dom catches my shoulder in a firm grip, turning me to face him.

"It's not yours?" He looks me over with hard eyes. When I don't answer him immediately, he shakes me. "Beau, tell me you're not hurt?"

I tear my eyes from Eden as her hands bunch nervously in her dress. "It's not mine. The room is a bloodbath, though."

Seeing Eden lets me breathe—and having Dom here settles the rest of the anxiety wracking my gut. However broken things are between us, he's still my family too.

It steadies me enough for my brain to kick back in.

I meet his eyes. "It's a lot of blood, Dom. This was a statement. There's someone here."

Dom's brows lower, and I know the look. He's running through the possibilities.

Then he makes an abrupt, dissatisfied sound and presses his hand against the door so it swings open. He moves into the room, and Eden shuffles closer to me.

She's blinking fast, but her eyes are foggy, and from the alcohol on her breath, I'd say she's more than tipsy right now.

Hell of a way to try and sober up.

"Fuck," Dom swears. "Beau, did you see this?"

I follow him inside, with Eden right on my heels. He's in the bathroom, staring at the mirror. Written in large, bloody letters is the word, "KILLER."

I turn to see Eden's cheeks whiten . . . right as Dom's turn dark.

His eyes are molten, savage rage. "The civilians have pushed this jealousy shit too far. Put the bond-fire out. I'm investigating this *now*."

"Jealousy? Dom, it says 'killer.' In *blood*. This is beyond hurt feelings. Someone died for this," I argue, trying to work out how much blood there actually is. A lot of it is splatter, which looks more dramatic than high volume—there's liters on the bed though.

Liters means death.

"Not someone. Some*thing*," Eden says in a hushed voice.

She leans into Dom, not even seeming to realize she's doing it, and he takes her weight just as unconsciously, moving his arm to make room for her.

Eden's eyes are glued to the smeared accusation.

"Did you ever find Akira, Beau?"

Akira.

"No, I got distracted dealing with a sprained ankle. Aaron was still looking, but . . ." I close my eyes as it hits me. "She hates you."

The whole camp knows it at this point. Akira's lover died in the Sinners' camp, and she refuses to be anywhere near Eden. I know Eden's been giving her a wide berth, but while Bristlebrook is hardly a shoebox, it doesn't exactly absorb nearly a hundred people without a hitch either.

Eden hugs herself, and Dom's hand squeezes the nape of her neck, his thumb sweeping soothingly over her skin. My eyes snag on the motion.

What *were* they doing in the hall?

Eden nods once, stealing my attention. She looks ill. The tip of her nose is too red and shiny, the rest of her too pale.

"She was on Team Bacon tonight, too." She frowns up at Dom. "They would have gutted and bled the pig, wouldn't they?"

"It was meant to be cooked to extend rations." Dom's mouth takes on a grim press as he catches on. "We need to be sure that's what this is. Let's organize a head count and then get everyone sober enough to sweep the woods."

My shoulders unknot some. One woman wielding pig's blood is a damned sight different to a pile of Sinners sneaking through our ranks. Is that all this is? Bitterness and too much alcohol?

"Teams of three?" I ask Dom.

"No less—and let's arm them up, just in case. I'm done taking chances."

I quickly wash my hands, then move toward the wardrobe where I store my rifle. I've had my pistol on me all night, but as Dom said, we need to be sure, and I'm not getting caught with my ass out.

But when I look, my rifle's nowhere to be found.

"She's swiped it," I tell him, and Dom's breath leaves him in an annoyed *snick*.

"Fine. We'll get you another and warn the crews she may be hostile," he says.

We're both filing out of the room when I realize that Eden is still hovering in the bathroom, staring at the mirror with a wan expression.

Killer.

Damn it, she doesn't need this.

"Hey now, darlin'. You here with me?" I call gently, and she startles, then with one last look at the mirror, she picks her way over to us, a little uneasy on her feet.

I'm about to take her hand when Dom scoops her up in his arms and starts walking across the inner balcony to the other side of the house.

I stare after them. No. After *everything*, he does not get to spend two weeks hanging off his ex, picking over options like fruits in a basket and deciding if Eden and I are good enough for him. He rejected me for her once already. He rejected Eden, too.

He doesn't get to just waltz back over here with a shrug after all that and say, "Oh, maybe I will give her a try. Serve her up for me, Beau."

No, sir. He does not.

I swallow down my anger, reminding myself that we have a bigger issue at hand . . . but it goes down like a slow and bitter poison.

When I catch up to him, he's knocking on Jasper's door. Eden clinging to his neck and looking up at him in a trusting way that would have had me in a thrill just a month ago.

Now I just want to shake her and tell her not to do it. He's no good with people's hearts. That's why the civilians don't like him.

Heather opens the door, her blue-tinged red hair all kinked up on one side, and an ill expression on her face. "What?"

Charming as ever.

Sometimes I wonder what I ever saw in her, but I know it's just one more example of me bending over to try and make something work for Dom in a way he would never do for me.

"We need to talk—Jasper and Lucky, too." Dom adjusts his grip on Eden, and Heather widens the door open.

Aaron turns into the hall with Mila giggling under his arm. Just walking by, casual as anything, like he didn't have duties tonight that he's shirking right in front of us.

My jaw flexes, but Dom beats me to it.

"You're meant to be out looking for Akira," he snaps, his black brows like low-hanging thunderclouds. "If you're here, you better have found her."

Aaron looks Dom up and down with enough belligerence that if Eden wasn't in his arms, I'm sure Dom would have slugged him.

"Look, you get to have your fun, let me have mine. She's probably just sulking off somewhere. No reason I should have to ruin my night over it." Aaron shrugs. His cheeks are a bright enough red that they match his hair. He's been drinking, too.

Dom's eyes flash like lightning. "You're given orders for a reason, you little shit. Consider your night ruined. Go outside and get Jayk—tell him we have a civilian MIA and that we're dealing with an emergency. Then round up every person you can find and get them to come to the lodge for a head count."

Aaron stares at him, his smug expression vanishing into something satisfyingly uncertain. Mila steps away from him, rubbing her arm.

"Move," Dom barks, and Aaron jumps into action, spinning and hurrying toward the staircase.

Dom narrows his eyes on Mila, and she edges backward, but Heather steps forward before he can start in on her too.

"Mila, cut the music. That will get people moving. When they come back, get them to wait on the lawn. Someone will be out soon," she says.

Mila nods, then scampers toward the music room without a glance back.

"You're not very diplomatic," Eden mumbles into Dom's chest with a sigh. "They won't like you if you keep being mean."

"I don't need them to like me. I just need them to do as they're told." He walks into the room, and Heather points at Jasper's enormous walk-in wardrobe.

The walk-in that I now know hides his secret sex room. We all filter into the moody space, and I try not to get distracted by the kinky candy store that surrounds us.

"Holyyyy shit," Heather says, turning to take in every dimly lit inch. "And I thought I was freaky."

Eden's head lifts as she looks around, her eyes enormous in her face. They bounce from the toys to the paddling bench, over to the bed with the cage and the chains dangling from the ceiling, over the gynecologist's chair and St Andrew's Cross and the other furniture that decorates the room. Her eyes linger on the whips, then on the chains.

"*I knew it,*" she whispers.

Jasper and Lucky are nowhere to be found, but after a moment, the sound of retching registers from behind a far door.

Given that I have never once seen Jasper drunk, I'm going to take a wild stab and say that *Mr Smokeshow* is not feeling so hot right now.

Eden's gaze finds the door, and she winces. "He really was too good at Never Have I Ever."

I walk over to her, and Dom hands her to me absently, like it's the most natural thing in the world. Like it used to be.

Nothing is sitting right. I set Eden down on her feet, and she sways against me, then rubs a hand down her face.

Dom stalks over to the bathroom and pounds on the door. "Come out, Jasper. We have shit going down."

"Dom," Eden scolds tiredly, "you're going to give them a heart attack."

Heather runs her finger along the cabinet with the cuffs and ropes. "At his advanced age, that could be fatal."

Jasper opens the bathroom door, his shirt hanging open. Through it, I can see Lucky draped over the toilet, his head tilted to look at us. He lifts his hand in acknowledgement, and I nod at him. Then he rolls, noisily heaving his guts into the toilet.

"*Oh.*"

I look down at Eden. She's staring at Lucky, her face turning green around the edges. She swallows hard. His back heaves as he vomits again.

Jasper leans against the doorframe, running a hand over his unkempt hair. "What is it, Dominic? I'm assuming it can't wait until morning?"

"It can't. Akira trashed Eden's room with pig's blood, stole Beau's rifle, and has been missing for . . ." Dom looks at me.

"Six or seven hours, best I can tell," I finish, stroking Eden's knotted hair gingerly.

"You think she's gone back to the Den?" Heather asks. Any hint of teasing has been wiped from her face, and her strong face is set in battle-axed lines.

"She knows where the cameras were moved to," Dom says in a low voice, and the pieces start falling in together.

If Akira's planning to sell us out, she has all the tools to do it. The cameras we could move again if we really had to, but the pit traps and the defenses? Not to mention she knows our exact numbers and the weapons we've been testing, our food inventory and where we access our water. . .

"Can we catch her before she reaches Cyanide?" Jasper asks, and my stomach sinks at the thought of it.

It's like Sam all over again, only I doubt she'll stop and make camp long enough to let us gain on her.

"We've had people all through the woods for the last week. I wouldn't even know where to start picking out her tracks." Dom rubs a hand over his chin. "We can ask Bentley to post some men to watch the main roads into the city, maybe they can catch her there—but they're playing conservatively right now, and the Sinners will be watching who enters their turf. I don't know if Red Zone will risk a direct conflict with them over her, not when the Sinners are apparently on a rampage."

"So what do we do?" Heather asks. "Just let her take the intel back and take the hit? We're already fucked enough without losing that edge."

Eden presses her fingers against her lips, breathing through her nose, and I rub circles on her back as the full gravity of the situation hits me.

My eyes find Dom.

There are heavy shadows under his eyes, and now that I'm looking, I'm thinking that stubble is more than one day old. I've been focused on my new patients, all the daily hurts and issues that come up, and all the long-suffered problems we can start finding treatments for. I've been worrying about Eden, and prepping Deanna and the nurses on the best way to treat the kind of trauma injuries we might see in an attack.

It's not like I've been oblivious to the fortifications, or the rations, or how serious our situation is.

But fucked?

They've been putting on a good face. The teams have been organized and efficient, and while people are grumbling over empty bellies, talk has been far from defeatist. If not exactly sunshine and daisies, it's seemed under control.

I should have known better.

Dom's always been hard and unyielding, a fortress to the world. He's always come to me to bounce ideas—or to ease his doubts. It's strange being on the outside.

I try to shake the sudden guilt that I've been letting him down, but the tension in him is hard to see. Maybe I shouldn't have shut him out that completely. I might have taken it too far.

Dom sighs. "We should—"

There's a whistle from the outer room—one of our Ranger calls. I whistle back. A moment later, Jayk walks in through the open door, slowing as he glances around the room. He rolls his eyes at the wall of toys.

"What?" he asks Dom.

He glances at Eden, then away again just as fast, like it's not transparent as a wet T-shirt contest what he's doing.

In the bathroom, Lucky makes an awful, guttural retch, and it's chased by a chunky sounding splash. I grimace, but Eden lets out a low groan.

"Darlin', are you feeling okay?"

She pushes off me and bolts for the bathroom. Jasper flattens himself against the doorframe, and Lucky dives to the side just in time for her to hurl her guts up into the toilet. Then again.

And again.

"Oh look. Two submissives on their knees, Jasper. Is it everything you imagined?" Heather teases, though there's none of the snarky undertone that usually comes with her jibes.

Despite the gravity of the situation—or maybe because of it—I find myself biting back a snort at Jasper's heavy sigh.

"Dear baby Jesus, how much did you drink?" I grimace as Eden gags again, and I'm about to go help her when Jasper turns and kneels beside her. He holds her hair back gently, his expression softening into open tenderness.

Well, I'll be.

She really is quietly lassoing all of us right to her.

"Nowhere near as much as me," Lucky groans, slumped against the vanity, a dramatic hand against his clammy forehead. "Eden, I love you, but you need to move. I have dibs on the toilet."

Dom turns away from them to face Jayk, none of the brief levity touching him. He's too in the problem, in the puzzle of a solution, and he won't come out until he's found it.

"Let's start on what we can handle," he says. Dom fills Jayk in quickly, then, pausing, he glances at Jasper. After a long moment, he drags his gaze over all of us. "Does anyone have any opinions? Ideas?"

He could have declared a cow-tipping expedition and it would have surprised me less.

Dom orders—he doesn't consult.

"I can handle the head count and sweep of the forest," Heather offers with a nod. "I'll make sure she's the only one missing and that she hasn't left any other delightful surprises for us."

"Are you sober?" Dom asks with a frown.

Heather shrugs one shoulder. "Sober enough."

Jayk is staring at Dom like he might be able to identify a sudden personality-altering brain tumor just by looking at him.

Apparently not able to spot one, he just leans back against the wall and flicks out his pocketknife. "I can help with the sweep."

Dom nods and glances back at Jasper, who's helping Eden over to sit in the shower. "You stay and take care of these two. Beau and I will call Bentley and meet back here."

I don't argue. Everyone disperses, and I walk beside Dom as we make our way to Jasper's study. He's dark and brooding, his mind clearly tackling the world.

"If you need to talk it through . . . we can talk," I say in an undertone.

Dom glances at me, then blows a disbelieving breath out his

nose. "*Now* you'll talk? That's great, Beau, but the world didn't stop this week while you were sulking. I could have used it then."

I follow him into the library, hard on his heels. "I didn't realize things were this bad. I've had plenty enough on my own plate to think about."

"Right. Sharing a bed with Eden every night was an ordeal, I'm sure," he deadpans.

"Don't bring her into this," I growl, my boots muddying Jasper's stately rug. "You could have been there too. It could have been all three of us dealing with all of it together—you were the one who couldn't make up your mind. Clearly, that's worked out a treat for you. Now I'm graciously offering to help you anyway, because whatever you think, you can't do this by yourself."

We pause outside the enormous bookcase that hides the secret passage, and Dom flicks the hidden latch.

He looks over at me with hard eyes. "Fuck you, and fuck your ultimatum, Beau."

He yanks the bookcase open and stalks through like a raging bull. Grinding my teeth, I push after him, pulling the bookcase closed behind us.

He's already punching in the door code and entering the surveillance room when I reach him.

Aniyah swings around to look at us, her brown eyes curious but unsurprised. Behind her, the display screens show forest scene after forest scene, while the small laptop on the desk shows the feed from the camera in the hall. She saw us coming.

"Heather's doing a headcount on the lawn. Akira's missing," Dom tells her, then he lifts his chin at the screens. "Did you see anything?"

Aniyah stands, her brows lifting in surprise. "No, nothing."

He nods. "Fine. Head down for the count. We'll take over here until you get back."

We watch her leave, then I turn to face Dom. Neither of us says anything for a long moment, and I can feel the bitterness hanging between us.

It makes it hard to be the first person to talk. "All I'm saying is that I might have taken it too far. I'm not a total asshole, Dom. I might be done with the idea of you, me, and Eden, but I'm still here for the team. I can help with planning."

Dom crosses his arms, his eyes narrowing on me. I see the vein at his temple that tells me I'm pissing him off. "Very Christian of you."

My temper rises too at his flippancy. "I don't trust you with her, Dom, and I don't trust you with me. I saw how you were with her tonight, and I might not be able to stop it, not if that's what she wants, but I won't be a part of it."

I hold his eyes so I know he's hearing me on this. "I won't top with you. I won't talk about her with you. All I'm going to do is get myself ready to pick up the pieces when you eventually break her heart—because that's what's going to happen. Only this time, I'm making sure mine isn't in the crossfire too. When you get over it and you're ready to move on, I won't go with you next time. I'm staying with her."

He's so very still across from me, like a wolf facing down a rival pack. It doesn't feel good, standing against him. It feels like a false split on a timeline—a low-likelihood reality we wound up in but never should have been spun into existence.

"It's not like that," he says finally, in a tight, unhappy voice. "You always rush in and push things too fast, way before we're ready for them. I was making sure it was right, Beau, and this time, it actually is. Whether you like it or not, she wants me, and I want her too. I'm going all in with her."

I raise my brows, but it says enough that I don't even feel a blip of hope at his words. "You love her then?"

Dom hesitates, and the sound that escapes me is cynical. "See, this is what *you* do, Dom, every time we do this. You never care as much as you should—it makes it too easy to change your mind.

Then I end up having to leave someone I care about, and it doesn't even matter to you."

"Bullshit." His eyes blaze. "You never *had* to leave anyone. That was your choice, and you made it because, for all your words, you never loved any of them either. You were just nicer about it. Heather ripped my heart out, Beau. I never planned on doing any of this ever again—I swore I wouldn't. But Eden is something else. So yeah, I've been playing defensively here. I don't want to break her heart or mine."

Like he can help himself.

I don't think I ever realized before just how much bitterness I was holding in. How much it hurt me every time I had to say goodbye to someone new. Every relationship, I felt like I had to work doubly as hard, doing all the emotional heavy lifting that Dom avoided on top of my own.

"Yeah, well, defensive doesn't suit you." I turn toward the HAM radio so we can call Bentley. We won't be able to say much —these communications are always open to anyone listening—but we can give him a heads up. I run my finger over the short list of known call signs beside the radio, skipping past our own and the Reapers' and going straight to Red Zone.

My lips compress bitterly as I add, "You're a Ranger, through and through. Rapid offensive deployments are your specialty. You're quick in and just as quick to get out before you get hurt. It's a real shame you never look back to see the destruction you leave behind you."

I flick the switch on the radio. I'm adjusting the dials to start transmitting when Dom sucks in an audible breath behind me.

"What did you just say?"

I turn warily. Dom and I haven't brawled since military school —not outside of practice—but I know he's on the edge.

He doesn't look angry, though. There's a look like a dawning sky breaking across his face.

"We're *Rangers*," he repeats. He runs a hand over his hair.

Quirking a bemused eyebrow at him, I nod, but I'm not sure he sees it.

Then he looks up at me, his eyes refocusing—and he *grins*.

"We're Rangers, Beau. Why the fuck are we sitting here planning for a battle we can't win or a siege we can't outlast? We need to change the game. Play to our strengths. I've been too focused on the civilians. I haven't been looking at the big picture." Dom shakes his dark head, relief stark in his eyes, and I struggle to catch up, because if he's saying what I think he is, then . . .

"You want to take the fight to them?" I ask in shock.

His grin becomes a slow, confident smirk. "We need to get the team ready. We're going to Cyanide."

CHAPTER 53

EDEN

SURVIVAL TIP #309
Friends don't give friends orders.
(Unless they like it.)

It takes surprisingly little time to get a team mobilized. Before I've even recovered from my hangover, the sun still squinting blearily over the trees, Dom and Heather have the Rangers and a handful of the best civilian fighters packed and almost ready to go. Akira was nowhere to be found, but we can't afford to lose any more time looking for her. Our team needs to move.

I quietly pack my own bags, wincing at the awful state of my room that I don't have time to clean.

They don't know it yet, but I'm coming with them.

Bristlebrook teems with restless energy. As I walk through the halls, I feel the change in the air, hear whispers about how things are finally taking a turn. I hear them chattering about the food and medicine we'll bring home, and the freedom of their friends who were captured alongside Heather all those months ago.

Out on the lawn, Dom and Heather are busy directing people.

Taking this, leaving that. But I can see their confidence. Their excitement.

They're trained for this. The Rangers specialize in raids. Location seizures. Target extraction. They have the training and the arms, and they've even enlisted Bentley and his men to join their attack in exchange for Bristlebrook's supply of inhalers. And of all things, the Sinners aren't expecting an attack.

This is the best edge we'll ever have.

But that same anticipation is a guillotine over my neck.

All I can think about is Sam up on that rock, whipping his men into a ferocious, bloodthirsty fury. He has an army of killers, a grudge against Bristlebrook, my bag of confiscated explosives, and when I freed the SEALs, I handed him two very effective strategic weapons . . . and my men are planning to walk right into his Den.

I can't spend any more weeks agonizing over what happened to them, wondering if they're dead, wondering if I'm going to end up exactly where I was when I was in the Sinners' camp. Alone in the dark.

No, I can't sit here, safe at Bristlebrook, while they go to fight. This won't be another Heather situation, where I let someone put themselves in danger while I hide.

I'm *going* to Cyanide.

I walk across the grass toward Dom, bracing myself for a fight . . . but someone's beaten me to it.

Jayk has his arms crossed, facing off with Dom. "I don't do babysitting duty, fucker. They're Heather's minions—let her be queen of the castle."

I slow, watching him, and my fingers itch to smooth the defensive sneer coating his face.

Heather looks up from the bags of rations she's setting out for people to pack, her eyes turbulent. "Alastair owes me a life. I'm going."

Sloane is so focused on checking her gun, it couldn't be more obvious that she's eavesdropping. Then I catch sight of Aaron, blatantly staring as he picks up a rations pack.

Apparently, it can be more obvious.

"I'm half the reason you all don't get blown to shit every mission. Why the hell am I the one getting benched?" Jaykob's eyes are bitterly dark today as they sweep over the gathered team. "Did I forget to make you a fucking friendship bracelet or something?"

Lucky looks up from where he's sprawled in the grass, dimpling. "Thank God you were the one to bring it up. I expected mine on Tuesday, bud. What's the deal?"

Beau shakes his head, biting back a smile, and walks up beside Jayk. He clasps his shoulder. "Come on now, Jayk, don't be like that. We're all friends here. Maybe when we get back we can all do something nice. You, me, and Eden. I reckon she'd—"

Jayk grabs Beau's wrist so fast and hard I squeak, my heart leaping into my throat.

"The only thing I'm going to do with you and Eden is show her how I can beat someone unconscious with their own dismembered limbs." He drops Beau's hand violently. "Touch me again, and I'll start with your arm."

Sloane snorts, and when Beau gives her an irritated look, she turns it into a cough.

"Is that possible? I feel like it would be too floppy." Lucky nudges Jasper who hushes him.

Dom glances around at the avid crowd, and steps in toward Jayk, lowering his voice. "Staying isn't a punishment, Jaykob. We need someone here to defend Bristlebrook if things go to hell, and the civilians trust you better than any of us. They can keep things running, but they need you to watch out for them. We can't leave without protecting the people here."

They stare one another down for a long moment, and I worry my lower lip between my teeth, shifting. Jayk's gaze slides to me, and the stiff anger in his face slips, indecision warring in his eyes.

"Get Jasper to stay. It's his house," he says, but the fight has left his voice.

Dom's shoulders relax. He's back in his Ranger kit today—they all are—and it's even better than his red shirts. He looks like he did the day I met him, dangerously competent and starkly attractive.

"Jasper isn't as versed on the explosives, or how to set the trip wires." Dom's lips curve into a dry smile. "Besides, I think if you left, Kasey would do an Eden and follow you into battle with a bazooka."

At the mention of Kasey, Jayk's head tips back in defeat.

"She's a little shit." He doesn't wait for a response before he straightens and turns back to the house. "Fine. Whatever. You're fucking welcome. Try not to fucking die."

"Thank you," Lucky singsongs after him.

"No, wait." I'm hurrying over to him before I've even decided to move.

He might be staying, but I'm leaving.

I catch Jayk's wrist, and he flinches as though the contact sizzles.

"I need more time, Eden," he says, quietly enough that I don't think anyone else can hear.

"I just need to tell you—"

"Hey, Jayk!" Kasey calls from the porch, a big grin on her freckled face. "Come show me how to fix the tap!"

Jayk scowls over at her in exasperation. "Do you not know how to say please, you little shit?"

She makes a bored face at him, and he mutters under his breath.

He gives me a brief, distracted glance. "Two days."

Jayk tugs his wrist free of my grip, then leaves before I can say anything else. Why does it feel like I'm always staring after him?

Sighing, I turn back to the others, and several heads quickly snap back around to look at their packs.

Subtle.

Lucky winks at me, though, before looking around at the Rangers. "Should we get *him* a friendship bracelet? He's feeling left out again."

"He *is* being left out again. You guys are shitty friends," Ava mutters, swiping a round of ammo. "None of you even came to say hi when he got back. You take him for granted."

Lucky, Beau, and Jasper turn to look at her, identical frowns on their faces.

Dom keeps his gaze on me, though. "Eden, you don't have to be here for this. The next few weeks will be busy around here. We need to keep getting Bristlebrook ready to handle this many people —your garden could make a big difference to a lot of people here."

Ah. Of course *he's* not focused on the romantic interplay.

Though I do have some frustratingly foggy memories of being in his arms. I remember him smiling under the apple tree, his eyes like warm honey.

I remember almost telling him about freeing Alastair and Mateo.

I tell him gently, "I'm not staying at Bristlebrook. I'm coming with you."

Next to him, Beau stiffens, and he scoffs a disbelieving laugh. "No, darlin', you're not. We only just got you safe. Your pretty little behind is staying here."

"I'm afraid I must agree with Beaumont." Jasper's eyes are serious as he buckles his pack. He's in a set of Lucky's Ranger kit again, but he looks more comfortable in it now. "You've only just started training, Eden, and distractions in the field can be deadly."

I lift my chin. "Respectfully, I'm not asking. I'm informing you of my decision."

Lucky assesses me—far more seriously than I'm used to. Heather keeps handing out the ration bags to the armed civilians, but she slides me an amused smile.

My eyes find Dom's, and I tense, ready for an argument from him, too.

Bonfire smoke still lingers in the air, and it smells like Jaykob's barn. My ears won't stop ringing with Jasper's scream when Lucky was pummeled by bullets. Things are just starting to come together. I can't lose them again.

I can't lose *myself* again.

I hold his pensive stare, my stomach bubbling, but to my surprise, his chin dips.

"I'd feel better having you where I can see you anyway." He gives me a wry look. "You get in too much fucking trouble when you're left alone."

He agreed.

Dom agreed.

I braced for the leader . . . and got my friend instead. He knows how much I need this.

"No. Don't do this," Beau says, standing. His face pulls taut with worry. "You're doing so much good here. Just stay back with Jayk—it'll give you two a chance to smooth things over."

"This is her fight too, Beau. She has as much right as Heather to come," Dom argues mildly, not bothering to stand. Every inch of him is calm, careless confidence. "She can handle herself for the trip, we've seen that. And she'll follow my orders."

He doesn't look at me as he says the last, but I know it's directed at me.

"I'll do anything you ask," I agree easily.

Dom does look at me then, his eyes glinting in the morning light. "Will you?"

Lucky snorts, and what I said registers. My cheeks heat as I shoot Lucky a scowl, and he winks at me.

Jasper, on the other hand, looks as grim as Beau. Like I've announced some calamitous desire to end it all and they're readying for a final death march.

I try to soften my expression as I look between them. "I don't want to get in the way. I just can't spend weeks here waiting, not knowing if you're going to come home or not." Just the thought of it has my palms sweating and my throat closing over. "I already thought you were all dead once, and it nearly broke me. I can't do it again."

"The waiting was . . . really shitty," Lucky mutters. He's not quite looking at anyone, but his sallow cheeks tell their own story. The weeks I was captured weren't easy for him.

Beau sighs, turning away from all of us, his hands knitting over the back of his head.

I understand his worry. I feel it just as much.

But this isn't a decision I'll let him make for me.

"We leave in an hour," Dom tells me, and I nod, dropping my pack beside his.

Jayk is going to lose it when he realizes I'm leaving, but I'm not sure what to do if he won't talk to me.

My eyes drift to the wreckage of Jayk's barn. People have slowly been clearing away the debris, but it hasn't been a priority, and there's still a lot there. Something sparks in my memory, and I frown, thinking. I wonder . . .

Maybe this is for the best. Jaykob doesn't want to see me right now, and I don't particularly feel up for an argument. He's made it clear enough that he wants time to think.

Time I can give him.

And maybe I can leave him with something else, too.

CHAPTER 54

JAYKOB

SURVIVAL TIP #259
Don't let them die on your watch.
The couch time with Jasper ain't worth it.

Sweat rolls down my forehead, and I swipe it away with my forearm. I stand back in the muddy ditch, staring at the finally un-fucked pipes.

"Try it now," I shout out, and Jada ducks off to go turn the water back on at the valve.

Whatever the doc did to "fix" the water line should be used in engineering manuals—*How to Be Totally Fucking Inept: A Step-by-Step Guide to Shitting on Jaykob's Day.* How the hell is he a doctor? If his brain was half the size of his ego, I might not have had to spend six damn hours refitting every inch of pipe *he* destroyed beyond repair. The thing was spraying water like a sprinkler, just hours away from bursting and taking out our water supply for good.

Eden wants him, and he can't even solve a basic household problem.

Eden can't live in a leaky house.

She doesn't have a clue what's good for her. I've lived with those assholes for years, and they're selfish, ungrateful, whiney dicks. I know I'm no prince, but I ain't blind—Miss Manners likes that. She likes *me*, and who the fuck am I to say she shouldn't?

I want to keep her.

Wanting her has gone past need and right into obsession. I'm obsessed with her soft little mouth, and her plush tits, and the way she quivers under me like my perfect prey. I'm obsessed with how she talks, and fights, and how she listens with her whole attention —like what I'm saying matters, and she doesn't care I don't say it fancy. I'm obsessed with all the steel under her prim politeness. She clawed her way to surviving, just like me.

She just had prettier nails doing it.

My rough-ass hands have no business being near her, but she wants to hold them. She wants them on her, *in* her.

But she doesn't want to be in my bed every night.

She doesn't want to be by my side all the damn time.

She only wants me when she's not wanting *them*.

Those fuckheads are ruining everything for me again. I won't share a house with them, let alone my woman.

I can't do this sharing shit. I have to walk. I *should* walk.

But why should they get to keep her? They can't even keep a pipe intact.

Kasey takes my tools, then jumps up to sit on the ledge, wiping them off with actual care this time instead of shoving them right back in the toolbox. She turned up with it two days ago—the only one of the civilians who didn't turn up to cheer the *heroes* out like it was a middle grade pop concert.

The kid stayed with me, and we got some real work done.

The pipes creak and groan, spluttering on. I'm soaked to my knees and covered in mud from the trial-and-error, but it finally looks like it's going to hold.

Kasey whoops, and I roll my eyes.

"I'm doing the next one. I'm calling it." Her grin splits her freckled face, and she adjusts her makeshift toolbelt.

I let her keep a few basics. I'll give her some more if she doesn't trash what I gave her.

I pull myself out of the ditch. "There won't be a next one. That was quality work—that'll hold for years."

"In *years*, then." She gives me a bored look, then mutters, "Not like I'm going to be going anywhere else."

"Where the hell else do you want to be?" I eye her. She's annoying, sure, but I didn't think she was stupid. Bristlebrook is the safest place for her.

Kasey shrugs awkwardly, turning back to the tools. "I don't know. You're cool for a dinosaur, but it'd be nice to hang out with someone my age. If there is anyone still alive."

I stare at her short, shaggy hair. She cut it yesterday, saying something about how she was sick of it getting in her eyes when she worked—which just makes sense. She usually makes sense, even when she's driving me up the wall. She just doesn't usually *say* things.

I ease from foot to foot, uncomfortable. "Friends are overrated."

Kasey snorts, then looks up at me pityingly. "*That's* your advice?"

"What the hell are you asking *me* advice for? You're worried every pimple-nosed teenager is dead and they probably are." I scowl, and she scowls back.

"You suck at this. I'm confiding in you, asshole. How am I ever going to get a boyfriend if everyone is like seventy?" She slams down the lid on the toolbox. "I'm going to die friendless and alone."

I cross my arms over my chest, narrowing my eyes on her. She's like five-foot-nothing and skinny as hell, but she still has all that baby plumpness in her face. When do they even shed that for their grown-up skin?

"What the fuck do you need a boyfriend for? I'm teaching you how to do shit. So you miss out on crusty socks and BO, big whoop."

Kasey mutters something under her breath I can't hear, and I look around. Isn't there someone else who can do this with her?

The two old bats are nearby and seem conveniently deaf right about now. They're almost as coated in crap as I am as they muck around in the garden.

Eden's garden.

Where the hell is she? She wasn't out here yesterday either. I said I needed time, not *space*. It's not like I can't look at her while I think.

I suddenly realize it's been three days. It's time to give her an answer, but I've got nothing.

Only my damn hindbrain growling *mine, mine, mine.*

Kasey huffs, getting to her feet. "You are useless at this. Forget it. Tell me more about the pipes."

Jada comes back around from the side of the house with a questioning look, and I nod back to her. She looks down at the giant hole in the lawn and gives me a rueful smile.

"Thanks, Jayk. Put me in the roof if you need to, but I'm way too sparky to be around water."

I grunt, shrugging. She was an electrician back before it all went to shit, and she's been taking most of the wire work off my hands with about twice as much skill.

"Did you say he got it?" Ethel calls out, finally bothering to tune the hell in.

Jada grins at her. "Water's officially fixed!"

Ida rips off her glove and whistles while Ethel laughs. They all do this, get all worked up over me doing the simplest shit—the shit I *always* do—and I don't know how to turn it off.

"So I'm going to get started on fixing the dishwasher. It's been fritzing, but I had a look yesterday and it shouldn't take too long," Jada says, and I give her a blank look.

"Yeah, fine, whatever," I mutter. They do know I'm not in charge, right?

She lowers her voice. "The rations team also said they've run out of protein. It's getting rough. They're trying to come up with ways to stretch the reserves until the others come back. Do you think we could use another pig? We're struggling to feed them anyway."

Kasey steps in closer to me, looking anxiously between us. I hope she doesn't expect me to solve all her problems for her. That ain't my job.

My shoulders bunch. "I don't got a clue what to do with rations. Isn't this their whole job? What are you asking me for? I'm just here to make sure you don't get your asses blown to kingdom come while the battle brigade is off playing hero."

Jada's forehead scrunches. "O-okay. I'll tell them."

"Do we have many left? What do we do after we run out of pigs?" Kasey asks. "We're not catching anywhere near enough game, right?"

Fuck if I know. Maybe we can kill off the ones who bat their eyelashes too much and eat them. It's not my problem. I'm not going back out to gun-happy Reaper central to pick up any more, neither.

Kasey's arms come around herself, and they're the size of twigs. I grit my teeth.

Jada's face gets all soft and patronizing like the kid can't handle a bit of reality—which is just bullshit. She's had nothing but reality.

Jada winks. "Don't worry, Kasey. They'll be back before then with supplies. Eden said she'd keep an eye out for honey, too, and I will hand over my left ovary for a piece of that action."

Eden?

Sudden panic needles every inch of my skin. I whip my head around again, searching for her, but I know she's not here. My body isn't prickling with that charged awareness she always zaps me with without even trying. I could find her in a room, blind and deaf, by the feel of the fucking air.

The air is flat. Dead. It has been for two days.

She's not being *polite*—she left.

They're taking her into a war zone.

"Ah, crap. Damn it, Jada. I was going to break it to him gently."

"Jayk, are you good?"

Adrenaline is thumping through my blood. I storm toward the house, where I've stored my kit and my gun. She's not leaving with them. She's sure as fuck not getting within grabbing length of the Sinners. I told her I'd protect her.

My vision's a red haze, and the next thing I know, my gun is in my hands. Forget my kit. Bag, rations packs, ammo, and I'm out.

She wants to be prey?

This hunt will be more than she bargained for.

"Jayk, wait. Stop." A small hand yanks at my shirt.

"Get off me, kid." I move toward the kitchen, but she digs her heels in, and it just means I'm dragging her along the polished floorboards.

I stop and glare down at her, and her puppy face is scrunched and defiant. I try to shake her off, and her one-handed grip tightens.

Then she thrusts something toward my face.

"Just read this first. She gave it to me, and I was meant to give it to you today—or whenever you realized she'd left." Kasey rolls her eyes. "Seriously, you're kind of a shitty boyfriend, you know that? Who doesn't realize their girlfriend is missing for two days?"

I stare at her, taking that hit below the belt.

I didn't realize she left last time, either. I was hiding out in my barn and hoping she'd come to me like some corsage-wearing teenager waiting for a prom date.

I snatch the envelope out of her hand and tear through the

stationery—*Jasper's* fancy stationery. Inside, there's a letter . . . and a photograph.

The photo is familiar and strange all at once. Familiar, because it's mine. That's my trailer, my face, my mother, and my little brother, back when that was my whole tiny world. Back with my imperfect family who loved me like hell, and I loved them even while we descended into it.

But it's strange because this picture was in my barn, and that went up in flames. I thought they were gone.

The photo starts to shake, and then I realize it's me.

I look up at Kasey, and she gives me a half-smile and shrugs. "Eden found it. She said she put it in your toolbox so it wouldn't get lost, and I guess it survived the fire. Pretty lucky, huh?"

Ida and Ethel come through the front doors, all worried looking, but I ignore them.

Eden did this. Something soft and aching settles in my chest, but it's too big for the cramped, dank space. It stretches out my rib cage, needing somewhere to go.

I open the letter.

Jayk,

I think both of us understand, in our own way, how precious family truly is. The right family is worth killing for. Even worth dying for.

You, Dom, Beau, Lucky, and Jasper are my family now, and it's taken me twenty-eight years, but because of you, I've finally found something that means more to me than survival. There is so, so much more to living than that.

Please don't come after me. Use this time to think, instead, and protect the civilians. They're counting on you.

Whatever your decision about us, you will still be my family.

I love you, Jayk, with all my heart and never only a part of it.

—Eden

P.S. Kasey needs you more than I do right now. I know a sister wasn't what you bargained for, but you've landed one, so be nice to her. I already know you're the best big brother she could have.

"If you're going, then I'm coming with you," Kasey says. "Just let me pack. I'll be quick, okay? I won't slow you down."

Sister. I drag my eyes up from the page.

No. She's just a little bug, and she's latched on to me. "You're not going."

I try to shake her off, but she just glowers at me.

"You're not going by yourself, asshole. It could be dangerous."

"Don't call me an asshole, you little shit. It's rude." I glare at her.

Kasey rubs her nose slowly with her middle finger, and I scowl. It's kind of . . . sweet. The pipsqueak means it, too.

The paper crumples in my hand, and I look back down at it, my chest squeezing. Ryan's face grins up at me.

"Are you going?" Ethel asks, and the bells on her top ring out. "Is there a problem?"

Bells. For fuck's sake. If an enemy did make it to Bristlebrook, she'd be their first target. Might as well wear a neon hat that just says "KILL ME."

It's not like it hasn't happened before, either. I was caught with my pants around my ankles in my own barn when the Sinners came for us, and it took every one of us not to die that day.

Shit.

"I'm staying." I yank out of Kasey's grip without a word and stalk back down the hall to return my gun.

Eden was right about one thing. Family is worth dying for.

They're also worth sacrificing for.

I would sacrifice every one of those jackasses to keep her safe, because they are not my family—she is. *She* fought for me. *She* helped me.

She loves me.

They've been ignoring me and taking me for granted and thinking the worst of me for years. They can go rot for all I care.

So if Eden wants to fight? She'll get her fight. But every last one of the others better be ready to throw themselves on a fucking frag before she gets so much as a scratch, or I'll rip them apart myself.

Because I've had enough.

Eden started me wondering if I could ever be worth more than my shitty past. The civilians have me thinking that maybe I *am* worth more. They trust me. Respect me. I help them out, and I actually get some god damned gratitude.

I'm the one who solves their problems. Pipes, and cameras, and . . .

Food.

A wild thought hits me. Risky. But it's worth a shot.

I change direction, taking the stairs up toward Jasper's study. At the top, I stop and look down at Ida and Ethel, who are watching me like I've lost half my brain.

I lean over the balcony. "There's no problem, okay? I have an idea."

Kasey crosses her arms, looking at me warily, like I might try to bail on her again and she needs to guard the door like a bull terrier.

"You coming or not, kid?" I ask, and her scowl melts away. She hurries up the stairs behind me.

This is it. Time for a change. I'm done with the servants' quarters. I'm done with them stealing away my girl. I'm done with all of them. It's time for a new pecking order, and I'm stepping up.

My decision is made.

They made me the king of the castle.

And only the king gets the queen.

CHAPTER 55

EDEN

SURVIVAL TIP #317
The fairytales lied.
The ancient forests are safe.
Cities are where people go to die.

The city is a ruin.

Overcast clouds cling to the skeletal remains of towering buildings, rubble sits in tumbled, blackened piles, and I've seen two signs with the old city name graffitied out. That city doesn't exist anymore.

It's Cyanide now.

It took eight days of travel, but we're here, and we've been stalking behind the tree line in the cold morning air for over an hour now. Dom and Beau went ahead to scout the path that Bentley directed us to take—despite the uncomfortable distance between them, they were quick to buddy up for the dangerous job.

"We're good to move," Dom says right beside me, and I yelp.

He cocks a brow at me, and Lucky laughs, ruffling my hair. "Beautiful, I know he's a bit rough on the eyes, but screaming in his face is just rude."

Dom gives Lucky a dry look as I press a palm over my racing heart and huff. "Dom isn't rough on anything except my behind."

Both of them pause, glancing at me, Dom's eyes glinting with memories and Lucky's twinkling with humor. Color starts creeping into my cheeks as my brain catches up to my treacherous mouth.

"I-I mean . . ."

Beau strides in behind Dom, and I beam at him, flustered. "Beau!"

He cocks a brow the exact same way Dom did moments before, and my racing heart twists at the gesture. These two shouldn't be fighting. They've been friends for so long that it's like they're slowly sawing away a limb—one they might be able to limp through without, but the loss would change them irrevocably.

Beau reaches over to nudge my glasses back up, stroking my cheek absently as his hand falls away. "You okay here?"

"Can we move now? We're wasting time." Heather shoulders between us. Her hair is bound, her face hard.

Dom nods, whistling, and our group gathers—Beau, Lucky, Jasper, Heather, Aaron, Ava, Sloane, Jennifer, Katherine, Jo, and Sara.

But I keep my eyes on Heather.

Since the decision was made to attack the Den, it's like Heather's hatred woke back up. It writhes, alive and vibrant and in need of its target. It reminds me too much of her furious reckless-ness in the camp, with Sam, and with Alastair and Mateo . . . and it frightens me. She may have given up leadership for this mission in favor of Dom's experience, but I don't know what that will be worth if she's confronted by Alastair.

Dom brings his rifle around, holding it ready.

"Move out. Keep quiet and low, in pairs, ten paces apart. Watch for signals. Just because we didn't spot something on scout doesn't mean nothing will crop up to bite us on the ass." Dom looks around at everyone one by one, as if to assure himself we're receiving the message. "We're meant to wait by the pharmacy. Bentley said he regularly has people on watch there, so we should get picked up soon. Anyone spots anything, blow your whistle. You *hear* a whistle, you stop like your life depends on it—because it might."

I touch the whistle that's dangling by a makeshift chain around my neck. It presses against my skin with chilly reassurance. I'm packed carefully. My bag is efficient and as small as it can be outside our traveling supplies, food, and sleeping necessities. I have a pistol at my hip, that I'm only starting to learn how to use, and I have a new knife at my ankle. I'm packed to survive.

At Dom's signal, we move. I step in beside Heather, claiming her as the other half of my paired team. She held my hand in the dark when I needed it . . . and I'm starting to think she might be drowning in it.

We started this fight against the Sinners together, and that's how we'll end it.

Heather looks down at me, and I push my glasses up my nose, giving her a stubborn, determined look that dares her to pick someone else. The quiet fury on her face eases, and she gives me a half-smile, then pushes forward. There's an assured confidence in her quick steps, like she's on her way to a board meeting and not into a dead city for a mission that might turn us into its new victims.

I have to beat back my rising anxiety again, wiping my palms surreptitiously on my pants as I hurry to match her pace.

We enter the city through an encroaching wave of trees at a very particular point that Dom checks fastidiously. As we enter into the streets, an awful, slithering feeling of danger writhes under my skin. Our footsteps are too loud on the pavement, every whispered brush seeming to echo and bounce off the cavernous buildings. Debris fills the streets, and I try not to look too closely at the flutters of cloth and the discolored white sticks that lie in awkward heaps.

We shouldn't be here.

The forest is my new home. Cities are graveyards, and the evidence of the killing blows are everywhere. In the dismembered buildings. In the shrapnel gouges through the asphalt. In the blackened stains that cloud the alleys. Between machines and marauders, cities haven't been safe for years, if they ever were.

As we walk, however, I start to appreciate the slow press of nature. Grass and flowers spurt from cracks in the pavement, almost carpeting some spaces. Lichen claws along walls. After five years, the forest is swallowing the city whole.

We pick our way carefully, our weapons drawn and our partners close. Heather is sharp-eyed and serious as she watches our surroundings—a battle queen taking in the field and watching my back.

As her partner, I also need to watch hers.

We follow Dom and Beau, pausing when they indicate to pause, continuing when they move, and I watch Heather's blind spots. Dom moves confidently, and I watch him curiously out of the corner of my eye, wondering how he seems to know every turn. It takes me about ten minutes to spot the red swords spray painted on the buildings in subtle locations—by a low drainpipe, on a car, on the frame of a window. Each sword points us forward.

I slow down to look at a large pinned-up piece of paper on the wall of a building that looks newer than the rest.

THE SINNERS OFFER SANCTUARY
TO THOSE IN NEED

FOOD, SHELTER, AND SAFETY AVAILABLE

GO TO THE HOSPITAL ON THE SOUTH SIDE
OF THE CITY FOR YOUR NEW HOME

There's an abrupt, loud clatter to my right, and I shove

Heather into an alley, swinging around to lift my gun toward the sound as my blood roars in my ears.

Only to see a large rat leap off a car and skitter away down the street.

My hand trembles on the gun as I lower it and switch the safety back on. I don't even remember turning it off. I turn awkwardly.

"Sorry, that was . . ."

Foolish? Embarrassing? Over-dramatic? I squirm, noticing that Dom and the others have paused to wait for us.

"Exactly what you should do," Heather finishes for me. She clasps my upper arm and squeezes it, her eyes soft. "Come on. Keep moving."

Heather pushes off the wall and leads us back out of the alley, nodding to Dom. My heart races with adrenaline as we keep moving. I didn't run. I protected her—from a rat that she didn't need protecting from. It's an insignificant thing, but I did it. I can do this.

Why is it so much more terrifying looking out for others than it is just looking out for yourself?

It takes nearly an hour to reach the meet location, only to find the pharmacy we're meant to wait in is hollowed out. The front windows are shattered, and glass litters the ground like sharp, glinting judgment. Empty shelves lie where they were overturned and packages lie in discarded heaps.

I wonder, absently, if Akira will come through this city—or if she has already. We didn't see any sign of her along the route, but there are others she could have taken. I would not have wanted to go through this city by myself.

Dom grimaces at seeing the location, looking around the exposed streets.

Lucky ducks into a larger building behind us and whistles a moment later. We filter in behind him. It's large, with its darkened windows still intact, and the dust-laden office furniture gives us plenty of things to hide behind while still having a view of the pharmacy and surrounding streets—a much more advantageous spot to wait.

I sit with my back to a desk and pull out my water for a quick sip and swallow hard when Heather comes to sit beside me. She takes a swig from her own water bottle and rests her arms on her bent knees, seeming lost to miasmic thoughts.

"Heather, are you okay?" I ask her in an undertone.

She squeezes a hand over her eyes. "What the fuck are we doing here, Eden?"

I assume that's rhetorical, so I stay silent and wait for her to get out whatever she needs to say. Toward the back of the room, Jasper settles in, watching us with serious, thoughtful eyes.

Heather shakes her head.

"No. I know what *I'm* doing here. This is payback. I'm here to make this right." Her hand falls away, and she nods, looking at me expectantly, like she wants me to confirm it for her.

I raise my brows. "Which is it? Payback? Or are you here to get your friends free? I only ask because they seem like very different agendas."

Wherein lies the crux of my concern. If Heather compromises this mission because of her need for revenge, I don't think she'll ever forgive herself.

Heather stares at me hard, then her breath swings out of her. She tilts her head back, and in the mid-morning light, her hair is russet, caught through with strands of fire. There's still the barest hint of blue from Lucky's dye.

"I'll follow the plan, Eden." She's grim and serious, and her demon lurks in her voice. "I just want them dead. The captives come first, I know they do, but if I get a chance at Sam, or Mateo, or . . . *him* . . . then I need to take it. I had them right where I wanted them, and I got sloppy. I should have taken the fucking kill."

Heather breaks off, her voice turning ragged, and she swallows hard.

I swallow too, and I can taste her rage. My guilt. All of it mixes together until it goes down bitter and lumpy.

She didn't get sloppy. *I* did.

I didn't make sure Sam got his soup. I let Alastair and Mateo free. We had the opportunity to carve off three heads of the hydra, and I let my feelings get the best of me.

Never again.

I'm not the best person for this fight. I know I'm not. But Dom didn't even argue to keep me out of it this time, just said I have to keep behind him. I've been debating whether I should sit this one out—I want to help, not be a liability—but Heather's face decides me.

She deserves her revenge. If someone had taken mine from me when I thought my brutes were dead, I would have killed them. She's owed Alastair's life, and I returned it to him twice over.

I need to fix it. I need to be the one to fight by someone's side for once . . . rather than stabbing them in the back.

I look up at her, determined. "We'll take the kill tonight, Heather. I'll do whatever I can to help make that happen."

Heather's eyes shine. Then she blinks hard, nodding. I take her hand, and she squeezes it.

"You're a good friend, Eden."

I close my eyes against the roll of self-hatred and squeeze back, knowing that I am anything but.

"Heather, I—"

With a sudden, blinding punch, an arrow spears through the door beside us, landing with a hard thud against a faded "Hang in there" poster. I flinch back at the abrupt burst of activity, right as Dom fires off a quick flurry of bullets, shattering the windows to our building in an ear-splitting crash, and Heather releases my hand, shouting at our group to stay down.

It's chaotic, frenetic, and I'm tensed to move, to *act*, when a voice booms from outside.

"Stop! Stop, you assholes! It's us! We come in peace!"

Dom curses and stops firing, swinging the end of his gun up to the ceiling, and I move my finger away from my Beretta's trigger.

In the resounding silence, a white swathe of fabric unfurls dramatically from around the vibrating arrow.

Dom's head slowly ticks around to stare at it, then he lets out a long, hard breath.

"Bentley?" he snaps.

Moments later, Bentley and two bow-wielding men peek into the building, then move in, their footsteps crunching on the broken glass. Bentley towers over the others, a colossal monolith with a giant sword sheathed at his hip and a scowl on his face. His dark brown hair flies free, turning him especially wild.

Half a dozen guns are trained on the newcomers, but Bentley ignores the threat, pointing at the white fabric. "White flag means *don't* shoot!"

Dom squeezes the bridge of his nose, and Heather gestures for everyone to relax. Mutters ripple over the group, and Aaron glares at Bentley, his face turning as red as his hair.

"Nothing says peace like a sudden, rapid assault on your allies," Jasper mutters, neatly slinging his gun.

"You *shot* your peace flag at us?" Lucky jumps up to go and examine the arrow, and he snorts a laugh. "You're officially my new hero."

Bentley's gaze swings round to Lucky, and the scowl fades into an appraising smirk. "I could be."

Lucky glances back at him with a startled grin.

Jasper strolls up behind him. He grasps the back of Lucky's neck in a cruel grip and brings his mouth to his ear. "I'm going to need to get you a collar."

Lucky's dimples make a slow, bright appearance.

A collar? Like a . . . dog?

I'm trying to puzzle that out—and why it might make Lucky smile like that—when Dom stands, snapping the safety back on his gun, his jaw tight.

"Remind me again why we're trusting you with a sneak attack?"

Bentley wipes the resigned look off his face at Jasper and Lucky's flirting, and he gives Dom a long look. "Because I know how to get into their Den."

Dom's eyes harden on him for a moment, as if assessing the truth of that. Finally, he nods.

Bentley nods back. "You have the inhalers?"

Beau steps out from behind Dom, where he'd been covering him watchfully. He swings his pack—much larger and heavier than mine—and pulls out a carefully packed bag. The half a dozen inhalers are clearly visible.

He holds up a bottle. "I also brought some oral corticosteroids. I'm assuming if you want the inhalers this badly, the asthma has to be acute."

"Thank God," one of the men breathes.

Bentley claps the man on the back, but he's staring at the bottle like it's the elixir of life.

"Thank you," he says, his voice thick, and quieter than I've heard him speak before, and Beau gives him a half-smile, his eyes soft with understanding.

Breaking the moment, Bentley glances around at all of us. A wily grin eases across his face.

"Follow me, little ducklings. Make sure you stay nice and close to Mommy. One wrong turn and the Sinners will make confetti out of your brains—and that's not even counting all of *my* fun surprises." Bentley winks, then turns back to the city. "Welcome to Cyanide. Try not to die."

CHAPTER 56

EDEN

SURVIVAL TIP #121
Loud ≠ right

Red Zone base is a fortress. They're set up in the once-grand City Hall building—because their medieval society's head-quarters was apparently too close to the Sinners' Den for comfort —and it is three glorious stories of wounded elegance and history. There's a gaping hole in its roof where a strike decimated part of the building, but somehow it looks hardier for it. A building that has seen battle and survived.

I adore it instantly.

I adore it slightly less when Bentley has to disable the "gas bomb" from his secret underground entrance—the one that would save us from having to navigate the two hundred yards of wire fences, landmines, pit traps, trip wires, and leg-hold traps that surround the building on all sides.

They might have fewer explosives than we do, but Bentley's creativity leaves Bristlebrook in the dust.

As soon as we arrive inside, Bentley directs us over to a small basin, ordering us to remove our dusty shoes and wash up before he allows us any deeper into the building.

I quickly see why. It's pristine. There are no carpets or rugs to be found, and the hardwood gleams like it's brand new. I spot at least three air purifiers purring away—they're not plugged in, so I can only assume they're battery operated.

Odder still, we're the ones who stand out here.

Every other person we see is carrying some form of sword or bow or strange dagger. They nod to us, friendly enough, clearly having been given word of our coming, but they continue on with their business. Red Zone is as restless as Bristlebrook, and they're clearly readying for a fight.

But the strangest thing about this place is a simple yet special one.

There are teenagers here.

Perhaps two dozen of them litter the halls and rooms, all about fifteen or sixteen years old. They sit and walk together in small clusters, laughing and chattering carelessly. They must have only been ten or eleven when the strikes hit, and Bentley quietly explains that they'd been on an overnight field trip for their history class to visit the medieval society and the museum.

Most of them never saw their families again.

As Bentley walks around his "war room," I find myself looking at him differently. Despite his air of ridiculousness, he stayed. He stayed and risked his life to keep a class full of terrified children safe from an apocalypse. For five years, he and his society have made their own history. I have to admire them for that.

Even if they do spend twenty minutes begging Dom to let them use a battering ram on the hospital's front gates.

The room is bustling, with people coming in and out as they go to rest or refuel or pick up final supplies for our attack tonight. But in all the commotion, my eyes keep drifting to the lonely teenager standing still and silent by the darkened window. A slim shadow with curious eyes.

The table is layered with two dozen maps from different years. This city used to be a hub of rail activity, and for over two hundred years it's been built up, layer by layer. The original street level is far below what is used today.

Bentley found several maps that indicated a way up inside the hospital grounds through those tunnels. Apparently, the runner he sent confirmed it—they're useable.

The plan expanded from there.

The idea is to move in the middle of the night. The decoy group will create a diversion to spur the guards into raising an alert, drawing as many as possible away from the women and children and out into the street.

The rooftop group will be watching from above and will rain hell down on the exposed Sinners, and then the underground group will pour out of the ground and into the hospital to covertly infiltrate the Den, handle any remaining Sinners, and rescue the women and children.

For hours, they've argued over every detail, and night started its creep over the sky hours ago. It won't be long until we leave, and nervousness is growing in me with every minute.

We're actually doing it. We're going to attack the Den, the Sinners' base. We're outnumbered, and likely outgunned, and the only edges we have are surprise and an experienced team of Rangers. I'm trying not to underestimate the value of that, but this rock of dread in my stomach refuses to budge.

Dom nods at something Jasper said. "We need a Ranger with each group on radio comms to direct the assault. I'll take the underground group with our stealthiest—and as many women as we can. Heather, Ava, Sloane, Jennifer, and Eden, that's you with me, and whoever else you have for me, Bentley. We don't want to frighten these captive civs any more than we have to, and friendly faces won't go astray. Beau, you're on the roof with Red Zone, and Lucky, you're running the decoy with Jasper and Aaron."

"No, no, *no*." Aaron's frustration is palpable, and he punches his index finger against the map. "I should lead the decoy force. The Rangers should take the underground pass, Red Zone can take the rooftops, and I am the next most senior. I led our people when Thomas left. Give me some men and some of those explosives. I'll run the decoy."

"For fuck's sake, Aaron, enough," Heather snaps. She's rubbing her forehead with an index finger, and she looks more exhausted than she should, given our comparatively easy day. "Tommy was never in charge, I was—and you sure as hell didn't *take over* anything. You wouldn't even be here if you weren't a crack shot."

I bite my tongue, grimacing as Aaron's face turns a mottled red.

Aaron has been an uncomfortable addition to our trip—largely because of his own irrepressible urge to talk down to everyone, and partially because Heather has had the temper of a wounded hyena.

Bentley whistles low, then holds up a map in front of his face. His warm-faced right-hand man beside him, Arthur, ducks behind it as well.

Lucky's foot plays with mine under the table, like it has for the last twenty minutes, though he appears to remain studiously attentive to the group. I nudge him back, and his foot taps on the top of mine like a little spank.

And the shadow in the corner only tilts his head, watching and watching.

Aaron's bruised ego flashes in his eyes, and he leans over the table toward Heather. "Why are *you* here, Madison? Your last mission into Cyanide was a fucking disaster. I can't believe any of them want to follow you after you got Thomas killed."

"Hey!" Sloane snaps at him, pushing up from her chair.

Faster than I can suck in a breath, Heather has thrown her dagger. It pierces the wood right in front of his crotch.

Aaron wheels back with a shout. "Fucking *bitch*!"

"For fuck's sake." Dom points at Aaron, then at Heather. "Both of you, get out. Come back when you've cooled off. We don't have time for this."

Aaron gives him a dark, sullen glare and stalks out of the room, but Heather stands, breathing heavily, seeming lost in herself. Jasper watches her with a concerned crease to his brow that I recognize.

I stand, but before I can go over to her, she shakes herself. "I'll take five, but you're not benching me just because some twenty-two-year-old testosterone factory can't see past his own unimpressive dick."

Heather leaves a heavy tension in her wake. I debate following her, but I finally decide to give her some space. I know she won't be satisfied until Alastair's head is rolling between her feet.

"She's right," Ava says loyally, leaning against the wall. "Aaron keeps trying to push her buttons."

"She's making them too easy to push." Beau looks up from the map and runs a hand down his face. "No-one's arguing that Aaron is prince charming—the boy doesn't have two brain cells to rub together—but Heather is burning hot right now. We all best watch she doesn't get herself into trouble out there."

My doctor doesn't look at Dom as he agrees with him, but Dom gives him a grudging look of gratitude anyway.

Bentley crumples the map so he can look at the room again. "How do we feel about pouring molten oil on their heads? They used it in the Hundred Years' War's Siege of Orléans and it sounded like a party to me."

"We're not bringing . . ." Dom cuts himself off and sighs again.

They begin arguing again, back and forth over the same things they've been discussing for the last hour, so instead of taking my seat, I find myself drifting over to the window.

The teenage boy stands amid the curtains, just outside of the glare—a ghost who only exists in shadows. His hair is black as night and a shade too long, and he watches out the window with a quiet yearning.

He's vampirically pale, but when he glances up at me, his large, beautiful eyes transform his whole face into something tragic and lovely. They're the dappled brown of a pebbled riverbed, rippling with emotion.

"Hello," he says in a soft, airy kind of voice.

"Hi." I give him a little, awkward wave. "My name is Eden— I'm with the Bristlebrook group."

Ugh. Obviously. He's been watching us for the last six hours.

He nods, smiling softly. "I know. You brought me my medicine. I'm Soren."

I blink, looking at him, then glance about, noting the air purifiers placed strategically around this room as well. He's the boy who has asthma.

Severe asthma, it would seem.

I step closer, looking out the window down to a small patio outside where a group of teenagers are happily sprawled under the moonlight. I glance back at him, and he shakes his head at the silent question.

"It's better if I stay inside. The city air is hard on my lungs. There's too much rubble, and the Sinners keep stirring it up. It's not worth wasting the medicine." He smiles ruefully. He looks ethereally sad in the dim lights—and much, much older than fifteen.

My heart is just starting to shred up at the melancholy in him when he waves a dismissive hand, looking back at the table blanketed in maps.

"Besides, this is fascinating. It's like a modern Sack of Rome. I hope you don't mind me staying to listen. My uncle said it was fine."

Soren glances at Bentley, and realization hits me. "You're Bentley's nephew?"

No wonder Bentley was so desperate for medicine. The voices by the table rise.

"We can't bring a fucking cauldron with us. How would we even heat it? No hot oil. No battering ram. We have explosives. Rifles. Jesus Christ." Dom sounds almost ready to flip the table, and I suppress a smile.

At Soren's nod, I lean against the windowsill. "Your uncle is a wonderful man. He came to help rescue me, you know."

Soren's smile grows into a grin. "He said you didn't need it."

Well. I'm not sure that's entirely true, but I'm flattered enough that I grin too.

Dom straightens from the table. "Okay, enough. There's such a thing as overplanning. Anyone who doesn't need to be here should go and get something to eat, do whatever you need to do. We leave in an hour."

Soren turns and coughs into his elbow. "I should go say goodbye to my uncle."

I nod at him kindly and turn to see the room quickly empty of people. Dom lingers at the head of the table, staring down at the map. He's never looked more kingly to me than he does now, imposing and gorgeous and towering over his strategy papers, the weight of responsibility balancing solidly on his shoulders.

But under that, I see the man whose dry humor keeps catching me off guard and whose eyes melt over me like a pot of gold. He's also the man who has spent week on week now sharing his worries.

I should go now and get ready with the rest of them. I'm hungry and I need some water . . . but this may be the last time we're alone together. It's the first time we've been truly alone since the night of the bond-fire.

And I still owe him some truths.

CHAPTER 57

EDEN

SURVIVAL TIP #243
Check your entrances and exits are secure against invaders.

When the last person leaves, I clear my throat, and he tilts his head my way, listening and unsurprised, like he's been waiting for me to signal him. Inexplicable goosebumps lift on my arms.

"Do you need anything?" I ask, and his eyes travel over me.

"Doing the rounds? First Heather, now me . . . Are you worrying about me, little librarian?"

His gaze meets mine, and it sears me through—a flash of lightning through my core that leaves me hollowed out, burning, and so, so empty. I dampen my lips as I swallow. I thought he might be tired, on edge like he had been for days and days when we arrived at Bristlebrook, but he's not.

Dom is charged, zinging with electric energy that he's clearly trying to keep banked. He's too still. Every movement is deliberate and heavy, except for that flash-fire sweep of his eyes over my face, my breasts, my lips.

This is his element. The offense and attack of it. The strategy and fight. Away from the civilians he doesn't understand and their frustrating, daily little issues. *This* is what he loves.

He's breathtaking.

I take a slow, nervous step toward him. "I always worry about you. I worry about all of you."

Dom tracks my step, and the next, his muscles coiling tight. His forearms flex where he's leaning on the table, and I can't help but stare at them. He's pushed up his sleeves and I can see the dark hair on his arms and the corded strength in his massive hands. Gorgeous hands. Hands that have held me. Hands that have touched me.

"And what if I do need something? You plan on doing something about it, pet?"

His voice is a deep, taunting rumble, and my body is helpless under it. I feel overfull—a fruit that's grown too ripe, too swollen with sweet, sticky need. He hasn't even touched me, and I'm ready to fall at his feet.

Step.

My voice lowers huskily. "I suppose . . . I would offer to serve you."

At the word 'serve,' Dom's eyes snap to mine, and there's no mistaking it anymore. I don't know when I got so bold, but I'm not the same woman he met in the woods all those weeks ago. Now, I know that turbulent look doesn't mean he's mad.

I know what a man looks like when he wants me.

When I'm only a foot from him, Dom straightens slowly, towering over me. His size is deliciously intimidating, his expression dark and intent. I tremble.

"Before a battle, adrenaline starts kicking in. Some soldiers like to blow off the tension. Some fight. Some like to fuck." Dom's eyes are a challenge.

As casually as I can, I sit on the table in front of him, on top of his war maps . . . and I let my legs fall slightly open. The effect is spoiled by the fact I'm in sensible pants and not a skirt, but it doesn't seem to matter.

Dom watches every move I make like he's planning a different kind of strategy. I can see his mind working, teasing at the new problem, sharp and precise. My pulse is rioting in my veins, my nipples hard and tight in my bra. It feels dangerous to tease a man like Dom.

"Oh?" I squeak.

Apparently, my new boldness has no effect on my ability to speak like a human instead of a chewable dog toy.

Dom places his hands back on the table and leans over me. His knuckles are white with pressure, and his mouth is inches from mine.

"Friends don't offer to service fuck their friends, Eden," he says, cocking a dry, mocking brow.

My mind detonates. I stare at his lips, right at the seam where they turn wet. It's an effort to lift my eyes to his, and my nerves jump back to life. I need to do this now. I'm not leaving anything until *after* anymore. I know how quickly things can change.

Now *matters*. It might be the only thing that does.

"You're not just a friend to me, sir," I murmur.

Dom's breath rushes out of his mouth and over mine. The raging tension in his eyes burns brighter. "So you *didn't* forget."

I shake my head. The end of the bond-fire is patchy—a flicker of dizzy drinks and hazy candles and Dom's eyes drowning out the sky. But I remember talking to him. I remember trying to confess how I felt.

"Tell me," he orders, and the firm demand has an immediate effect on me.

"I want you, Dom," I whisper. I'm so nervous, I shake. I don't have Beau coaxing me through this one. This is just me and Dom, and I don't want to mess it up. "I need you, as much as any of them. I tried to give you space, because I thought you wanted Heather, but it turns out you don't. You don't, right? She said you don't."

Dom opens his mouth, but I barge on. "I want to be with you, if you want me too. I think you're brilliant. I think you're so incredibly smart, and capable, and you have this beautiful ability to look at your own actions and just decide to change them when you don't like what you see. Do you know how rare that is? To be willing to look at your own flaws and fix them. You're a fantastic leader, and a great friend—even though you tease me *far* too much—and of course it doesn't hurt that you're utterly gorgeous and every time I'm around you, I think about you bending me over and spanking me, and what it might feel like to—"

Dom yanks my hips into his and slams his mouth over mine.

When our lips collide, he groans. His mouth commands a response, and I sigh into it, softening for him. It's like the harder he is, the more I need to give. The rougher his hands, the more my body molds into them. I feel myself growing lush and wet, my pussy throbbing in time with the pounding in my temple.

There's a thrilling urgency to the way he touches me. He grips my ass and squeezes my breasts, and his tongue is in my mouth like an invading force. His breath is hot over my skin as my hands fumble at the belt of his uniform.

It's an all-out assault on my senses.

His spicy scent, his sumptuous taste, the brutal strength of him—I can't breathe anything but him, and I don't know if I can survive on it, but I know I can die happily *for* it.

Dom rips my shirt up and over my head. "You don't know what you're getting into with me, Eden. You let yourself into my bed and you're going to be fucked hard. There are *rules*."

My head swims, and I finally get his belt free and sob at the relief of it. My clit aches fiercely, begging to be touched. Dom is so vitally masculine, and it calls to something ancient and fundamentally feminine in me, something that is already preparing my body to take him, that wants to be filled and stretched to its limits.

"I can deal with rules," I mumble against his lips.

I reach inside his pants, only to get the barest touch of heat before he tears my hand away. He pins it to the table, squeezing it in a silent command to keep it there, and then grabs me by the neck, laying me down until I'm sprawled over the hardwood with confident, commanding force.

In seconds, his hands have freed the button at my waist, and he strips my pants off and over my boots in a harsh, sudden motion. My breath hisses out at the sudden chill against my heated flesh.

Dom gives me a molten, carnal look, then leans over me again. "Rules one through five. Don't touch me unless I tell you to. Address me as 'sir.' Stay where I put you. Don't speak unless you're moaning my fucking name, answering a question, or safeing out."

Dom tugs his cock free of his pants, and the thick, heavy length of him begs for my mouth. He gives me a hard, knowing look. "And when I ask for a hole to use, you better present one to me. Fast."

Jesus Christ. My skin feels too tight and hot for my body, my breasts too sensitive and full for my bra. I want to trace the vein with my tongue and suck him until he spills in my mouth. I want him to fuck me so hard that my body screams at the effort.

I arch my back off the table toward him in offering, my breathing shivery, and he takes it. Dom's mouth comes down against my neck in a hot, wet press, biting me and then sucking the abused flesh hard enough to mark.

I cry out as he claims me. It's been so hard, dancing around him for weeks. Admiring him and talking to him and laughing at his biting humor. All I've wanted is for him to touch me like this, to *want* me like this, and he *does*.

I pant as my nails scratch against the table, trying to find purchase. Some leverage. Anything that would help bring me closer into contact with Dom without breaking a rule. Dom is owning me with his mouth like I belong to him, and it feels so unbearably good, I could come from just the relief.

His mouth travels over my breasts, restlessly, hungrily, like he can't taste enough of me, then he captures my mouth again, licking into it. Then he pulls back—but only far enough to see me. We're still breathing the same sex-soaked air.

"Fuck, Eden. You need to know something. Beau will be the first one to tell you I fuck up every relationship I get into. After everything that went down with him and . . ." Dom cuts off, and I'm glad. I don't want another woman's name on his mouth right now.

Dom shakes his head, bleeding dark memories and a tumult of feelings. "After everything, I wasn't going to do this again. I was *done* with this shit. It cost me too fucking much, and it wasn't worth it. And then *you* showed up with your big, prim fucking eyes, and you just keep looking out for all of us, even when you shouldn't. Even when we don't deserve it."

He kisses me again, almost angrily, and I shudder under the onslaught.

"Give me a hole, pet. Now." His cock throbs against my thigh, and he squeezes my ass in his hands, yanking me to the end of the table and crumpling several maps in the process.

A hole. My heart hammers at his coarseness.

I part my legs eagerly, propping my boots up on the table edge on either side of my ass and letting my knees fall wide. I don't have it in me to be embarrassed. I *want* him to use me. He makes me feel coarse and lewd in the most decadent, shameful way.

In a second, Dom's hand finds my panties and yanks them to one side, and he sinks two fingers into my swollen, wet cunt with no prep. They go in embarrassingly easily. I can feel myself encasing his fingers, the way I'm dripping around his hand, and I grind myself over him. His fingers crook, rubbing over the sensitive satin flesh, and I cry out, clamping down on him, needing *more*. More pressure, more friction, more fast, furious *fucking*.

Dom grips his flushed cock with his free hand, looking down at me with angry, tender ferocity. "You've become my new best friend, pet, and I don't know how it happened. I'm too fucking hard for you."

I'm riding his thick fingers and watching him pump his dick, mesmerized by the fat drop of liquid squeezing over his crown. I'm panting now. Squirming. It's hard to focus on what he's saying, especially when his thumb begins working over my clit. I arch again at the violent pleasure that rocks through me, suddenly terrified that I'm going to come before he gets inside me.

"You're soft, Eden. I always thought that meant weak. How I grew up, that's what it meant." Dom's eyes lock on mine, gorgeously gilded in regret. "It's not. You're soft so you don't break. You mold. You bend. You give and take, and I still think you need to be harder, because you take too much from everyone. But *fuck*, you take it beautifully."

Dom groans, and I don't know if he's talking about me or what we're doing anymore, because color is riding his cheeks into battle. His jaw flexes and his eyes are locked on my pussy as he toys with my clit.

I vaguely remember him giving me rules, so I stop myself from begging him to fuck me. Just. I'm writhing on his hand, and he keeps fucking me with it as he watches me with hooded, hungry eyes.

"Dom," I beg urgently instead, my voice filled with transparent desperation. "*Sir.*"

Dom curses, and he yanks his fingers out of me, then roughly fits the thick, flared head of his cock to my entrance. We both shudder at the contact.

Dom squeezes my ass, and I force my eyes open to look at him as he grits out, "Rule six. You keep talking to me when you're upset. When you need something. Don't just go to the others. Don't just go to . . . *him*."

My head is too foggy, and I try to clear it, even while he rocks against my entrance. At first, I think he means Jasper, but there's too much hurt in his eyes—too much history.

Beau. He means Beau.

It's not a sex rule, and technically that's not part of our terms, but this is one I have no problem agreeing to. I *want* to go to Dom.

"I promise," I whisper, and his face lights with victory—like I gave him something important and not something that should be basic and fundamental to any relationship.

He leans down for a long, deep kiss, and I feel his cock begin to stretch me open as he forces himself inside. It's a strain, but my body leaps to take him.

"Considering how you were dripping in cum the other night, I'm guessing we're done with the rubbers," he mutters.

My mouth is parted, but I'm non-verbal. Every part of me focused on the feel of his cock claiming my cunt, inch by inch. Finally. He feels perfect. Hot and steely and he's pushing me in the best way. His heavy body leans over mine until I'm surrounded by him, filled by him, and—

The door slams open. "What's the hold up, Dom? This is meant to be your show."

I could almost cry at Beau's impatient voice—especially because Dom stops moving, his head snapping up. His eyes flash in warning, and it reminds me of a wolf protecting its kill from another predator.

"Give me five minutes." Dom sinks in another inch, and I cry out in relief, squirming under him. "I'll make this quick."

"No."

At the snappish tone, I try to turn my head up to look at Beau, but I can't see him from this angle. This isn't going to be like when he stumbled on Lucky and Jasper with me in the forest. Beau does *not* sound in the mood to share.

"No?" Dom's low voice is full of threat, and he runs a hand down between our bodies, circling my clit in a way that has me tilting my hips up into him on a sob.

"Beau, *please*," I beg.

He ignores me. "They're all waiting. I'm not going to make them wait just so you can give her an unsatisfying fuck."

That chilly cold snap to his voice reminds me of his anger after he almost shot me. The silent treatment he gave me.

I hate it. I hate it even as my nipples tighten at the sound of his voice, and the idea of him watching us right now makes my pussy clamp around Dom's dick.

Apparently, Dom isn't a fan of his tone either.

"You're a petty fucking shit sometimes, Beau," Dom growls.

He looks down at me with murderous frustration, but his fingers speed up over my slick clit. "Come on, pet. You can get there."

Pleasure coils inside me in a sharp, sudden rise. Dom shoves into me hard, until he's fully seated and his base grinds against me too.

"*Dom!*" His name comes out choked on desperate need, and I begin to pant.

Dom's eyes stay fixed on my face, ignoring Beau entirely, and his face is rapt with lust. "Fuck, little librarian. Just like that. Your greedy cunt is like a vice. I can feel it wanting to come all over my dick."

"Move it, Dom," Beau snaps, and Dom gives me a hot, wry look.

He slams his hips back in again, and again, and that's it— between his fingers and his perfect dick and that smirk, I come hard enough that my vision hazes and my head crashes back against the table. Every pulse of my orgasm clutches Dom deeper into me, and he grunts as he takes it.

"Perfect. You're perfect, Eden," Dom growls.

I'm gasping for air when he abruptly pulls out, shoving his glistening, throbbing dick back inside his pants. He looks down at me for a brief, branding moment, like he's imprinting the vision in his brain, and then he scowls.

Dazed, I watch in horrified regret at how much he struggles to get his zipper back up over the strain.

"You're a fucking asshole, Beau," he snaps. He stalks to the side of the room and grabs his rifle and his pack, and I hurry to fix my clothes.

My limbs are so shaky from the force of my orgasm that it's far harder than it should be. When I'm dressed, I walk toward the door where Dom and Beau stand glaring at one another, having a long conversation without a single word.

Dom's eyes sear my face in a quick, searching look. I worry he might ask me how I'm feeling, or if I'm okay, but he doesn't, and I'm grateful. I'm not sure what I would say, except that I am so, so glad we're finally on the same page.

"Come on, pet. You're staying with me."

His gruff command is reassuring—and I feel the double meaning in it. That bright, unsatisfied heat in his eyes promises me that this isn't over.

"Yes, sir," I murmur obediently, as much for Beau's benefit as his.

That heat flares for just a moment before Dom banks it, nodding at me to follow as he walks out.

I feel Beau's eyes on me too.

"Darlin' . . ." Beau starts.

I look up at him, letting him see every bit of the disappointment I'm feeling. It's one thing for him to have his own problems with Dom. It's another entirely for him to interfere with my relationship.

"You told me you wouldn't get in my way. That it was my choice," I say tightly.

Beau rubs the back of his neck, the hint of a scowl on his face. "We didn't have time. I—"

I purse my lips, and he cuts off.

"We'll talk about this later," I tell him, then arch a brow. "Right now, we don't have *time*."

And with that, I turn on my heel and follow Dom down the hall.

Chapter 58

Eden

Survival tip #255
Make your goodbyes count.

By the time we make it into the hall where everyone is gathered, the full weight of what we're about to do has descended on me and anxiety has me in its cold, sweaty grip.

Everyone is clustered into their allocated team—decoy, rooftop, or underground—and Lucky and Beau are doing quick headcounts of their people. There are maybe sixty of us in all. The Rangers, our civilians . . . and the people of Red Zone. With their bows and muskets and an unusual mix of swords, bows, and armor, they stand out, but the steely glints in their eyes belie their absurd-looking garb. They all have at least one firearm on them as well, and as many rounds of ammunition and grenades as they can carry.

Bentley reassured us that "most of them" could fire a gun.

It wasn't terribly reassuring.

Dom walks over to Heather and a stone-faced woman I haven't met yet and quickly counts our group.

Before joining him, I hesitate, looking at the others. I know they're confident in their plan, but this is still a large-scale raid. People are going to die today. A lot of them, most likely. My body is still shaky, and so many emotions tug at me.

I close my eyes against the rush of memories. Against the Sinners telling me my brutes had all died and confirming that, once again, I was left alone in the world. God, I can't do that again.

I start running through one of Jasper's grounding techniques. Five things I can see. Four things I can feel. Three things I can hear. Two things I can smell. One thing I can taste. When I finish, it's with the memory of Dom's kiss branding my lips.

I take a deep breath. The quick routine allows me enough control to pack my fear into a tiny, tight box.

In the dim lights, Lucky's beautiful hair shines, and I hope he does something to cover it. It seems too much like a target.

Lucky whistles appreciatively at his team.

"Looking *good*. I'm thinking we're going to work as a decoy just because they won't be able to help checking us out." He bites his lower lip and rakes his eyes over Jasper. "Especially you."

Jasper's wearing Lucky's spare kit, and he does look beyond gorgeous. Aaron rolls his eyes and picks up his pack, a sullen set still to his mouth, but Jasper just gives Lucky a scorching look and finishes checking his rifle.

Bentley sighs from his place beside Beau, looking at Lucky and Jasper regretfully.

Beau finishes up his counting and the tight, unhappy lines around his lips fall away as he grins at Lucky. "You just go stand around and look pretty then, Narcissus. I'll keep the mean ole Sinners off your back."

Looking at him now, the fight in the strategy room might never have happened. They're all so relaxed. So easy and self-assured. Is it a show? Or is it just their experience talking? Whatever it is, it has a visible effect. Smiles start breaking over faces, a few of them jostle one another in good humor.

I wish it would wash over me as easily.

Suddenly, it feels wrong to leave on a sour note with Beau. We can have a talk about what's happening between him and Dom later, but I can't let him walk into a battle with that hanging between us.

"Beau," I call. It's a question. An apology. An olive branch in a crowded room.

Beau's gaze drifts to me and the smirk softens. Relief breaks over his face like the sun over heavy clouds. "Come and say good-bye, darlin'."

I rush over to him and let him envelop me in his arms. My eyes sting, and I squeeze him back.

Don't let this be like last time. I can't take this again.

"It'll be okay, love. Just you watch," he tells me softly.

He holds me tight and hot against his hard chest, then tilts my chin. I expect a gentle kiss, something soft and reassuring—but that's not what I get. Beau pays no mind to the rest of the room. He devours my mouth with a hungry storm of a kiss. It's heated and not appropriate for the room full of strangers we're in, but it sweeps away my worries like a flood.

My head is swimming when someone impatiently tugs my head back, breaking the kiss. I don't even have time to be annoyed before Lucky's lips have replaced Beau's. His mouth feels different, more coaxing. He savors my lips and tastes my tongue, his beard bristling over my chin. The sudden difference is shocking and delightful, and I have the sudden urge to spend a whole night rolling between them, exploring every difference and similarity like a carnal banquet.

"Lucky, you really need to learn some manners," Beau grumbles.

Lucky laughs against my lips, rubbing his nose against mine as he backs up.

I take in a shaky, steadying breath, pushing my glasses up my nose. It does bring into focus a few wide-eyed looks, but I decide to ignore them. It's hardly the biggest event of the evening, surely.

"You will stay close to Dom, won't you?" Lucky asks in an undertone, and I finally see a hint of nervousness in him. For me. "No more kidnappings?"

I touch his chest, over his half-healed bullet wounds. "No more gunshots?"

Lucky's mouth kicks up on one side. "It's not my fault. Tragic hero is my—"

Beau cuffs him on the back of the head. "No. It's not your aesthetic. We're doing things right this time. You're the worst kind of patient, and I am *not* dealing with that again."

"You neglected me!" Lucky jabs his stomach, laughing. "Well, except for the whole bubble bath thing. That was cute."

My brows fly up. "Bubble bath thing?"

Jasper touches my shoulder, stealing my attention from Lucky's wicked grin. Unlike the other two, his face is sober as he looks at me. His eyes catalog every inch of my face, drinking me in like he's starved of the sight.

My own smile fades, and I shiver under the weight of it. If Lucky and Beau teased away my dark worries, Jasper fills the empty space with something deeply calm.

"Okay, let's get ready to move out. I want the teams split and spaced five minutes apart. Keep an eye on your buddy and alert your squad leader of any issue at all, no matter how small," Dom calls, heavy and resonant with authority. "Final concerns before we set out?"

One young man raises a shaking hand. "I'm claustrophobic. Can I switch teams? I don't want to be in the tunnels."

"For fuck's—" Dom bites off his curse and begins making some quick, final adjustments.

Beau's team is the first team scheduled to leave, so at Dom's irritated nod, he reluctantly lets me go. I feel his loss like a gouge in my side, and I bite back the fear that tells me it could be the last time.

With a last, sweet kiss on my cheek, he gathers his team and exits onto the street.

I wrap my arms around myself, chilled.

"That's it, then. Take care of yourself, darling girl," Jasper murmurs.

I nod slowly, looking back at him and letting myself soak in his reassuring presence for a moment more, like I'm charging a battery of fortitude for our journey.

Something like longing slips into the nooks of his eyes, deepening the longer he looks down at me. Suddenly, breaking the moment, he clears his throat and steps back.

He holds out his hand.

I stare at it—at the slender fingers and the elegant turn of his wrist, and I'm confused. Maybe even a touch hurt. He wants to . . . shake my hand? I think of kneeling for him, of him ordering Lucky to lick me, of him fucking Lucky into me and then watching us in horrified amusement as we sucked down too many drinks. I think of every conversation we've had this week, talking about anything and everything.

Ignoring Jasper's hand, I throw my arms around his neck, burying my face in him. He stands frozen still for a long enough moment that I begin to second-guess myself . . . and then his arms come fiercely around me.

In his arms, that feeling of safety, of steadiness and comfort fills me sweetly. I breathe in the soft skin of his neck and enjoy the strength he's not bothering to be polite about for once. I need him to be okay. There's too much unfinished between us. Too many nascent possibilities that need a chance to grow.

"I'll take care of him, Eden. I promise," he tells me, and reluctantly, I pull back.

My eyes burn, and my lip begins to shake again. He can't think I'm only worried about Lucky. Not now. Not after everything.

I smooth down the front of his uniform, struggling to take hold of myself.

"Take care of *yourself*." I try to force a smile. "I still owe you an essay."

Jasper takes a deep, unsteady breath, the barest smile brushing over his mouth. "It's *very* late."

My smile warms, becomes more natural, and Jasper touches the curve with his fingertips. His fingers feel like the softest kiss, and I press my lips back against them in goodbye.

Jasper swallows, his dark eyes searing, then he nods and walks over to Lucky's team.

Aching with worry, I turn back to Dom to find him watching me with a thoughtful expression. Our team is next to go.

Heather comes up beside me and nudges me with her shoulder. "Get your pack ready, babe. We have Sinners to smite."

CHAPTER 59

LUCKY

E den leaves with her team, tucked between Dom and Heather, and I'm caught somewhere between replaying the way she clung to Jasper . . . and praying that she'll be okay.

"It's time now, Lucien," Jasper murmurs beside me, and I nod.

Today is going to suck, no matter how I cut it. There are a *lot* of Sinners, and not a lot of us. We all need to play our parts perfectly.

But at least I get to use explosives. I have the danger pack all ready to go.

I run my eyes over my team one final time—and then again. I see the guy who didn't want to go down into the tunnels with Dom, but there's not a single face that looks like a baboon's ass.

"Where's Aaron?" I ask, and get a few blank looks in return.

Jennifer shrugs one shoulder. "I think Dom shuffled him into Beau's team?"

Dom is my new favorite. Beau can take him—he could probably use Aaron's *helpful advice* more than I could, anyway. Buoyed by the thought, I look over my team. I have Jasper, Jennifer, and seventeen people from Red Zone. I don't usually like missions where the team doesn't know or trust each other, so we need to bond. Fast.

How better to bond than over some good old-fashioned hazing?

"You!" I point at the new guy Dom just moved into my team, who jumps. "Do you have what it takes to face death and danger? To be on the front lines of adversity? To be at the very forefront of humankind itself in its battle for freedom and justice?"

Jasper mutters something and then walks away to pick up his pack.

The man looks like he's in his mid-twenties, but he twitches like an electrified beetle. Considering he's holding a wickedly sharp morning star, I'm hoping he gets that under control.

"Y-yes?" he asks, glancing at the Red Zone woman beside him who rolls her eyes. "I think I do. Yes."

Poor guy. He has glasses and that academic, bookish look that reminds me of Eden. He's perfect.

I grin. "Great, then. You can carry the danger pack. What's your name again?"

"Julian," he mutters, eyeing the pack uncertainly where it's sitting innocent and unobtrusive in the middle of our team. It has a cute smiley face keychain dangling from one of the zippers.

But everyone who *knows* is giving the bag a wide berth.

Julian scratches nervously at his patchy brown beard. "What's in the pack?"

Over his shoulder, Jasper gives me a reproving look—the one that tells me to *behave*.

I ignore it.

I sling on my own pack and casually double check my weapons. "Oh, rope, plastic . . . some other things." *Technically* true. I wave at him to hurry. "Chop, chop. Time's wasting."

Julian steps cautiously toward it. "Then why is it called the danger pac—?"

"Just a bit of flavor. Nothing to worry about."

I take his morning star from him and lay it on the ground—he can leave that one at home. Spinning him around, I lift the pack very gingerly up and over Julian's back and wince as it lands heavily on his shoulders. Turning him again, I secure the buckle around his waist and over his chest. He's starting to shake, so I pat his shoulder reassuringly.

"Just do me a favor and walk a good twenty feet away from everyone at all times." I frown, looking up at him. "You're not a smoker, are you? Nothing . . . flammable . . . on your person?"

Julian grows more and more gray by the word. "N-no."

"Thank God." I laugh.

Several members of the team start edging away from Julian, and his eyes get wider and wider. Better go before he bolts.

I give him two thumbs up as I back toward the door. "You're an inspiration, Julian."

At my gesture, we all file out onto the street, and as soon as we hit the wall of sooty black buildings and mortar-ravaged pavement, the darkness chokes my amusement.

The air is heavy out here. Whatever sanctuary Bentley made of Red Zone's base, Cyanide presses its weight against it on all sides in a silent siege.

I used to love cities. Every single one had its own personality, whether I was in Europe or the Middle East, Australia or here at home, and my friendships with those cities—with their flavors and music and people and histories—were some of my most valued.

This feels like walking over a friend's grave.

There are clothing stores that will forever advertise their last sale and strata of dust coating the bars of pubs. Some stores—like the pharmacies and supermarkets and liquor stores—are ravaged and torn apart. Toy stores sit like unhallowed memorials to all the children who won't ever get to play with their wares.

My mood isn't the only one affected. As I glance over my team of twenty, I see a mass of funereal faces, all of them scanning the surroundings closely.

"You shouldn't tease them like this," he tells me in an undertone, walking a step behind me . . . watching my back.

We don't often go out together like this. Dom and Beau handle most of the raids, Jayk is Jayk, and I usually hunt alone. Jasper's more of an indoor cat.

So this is nice. I mean, if you can ignore the terrifying bone-dead city, it's nice.

"None of it's real. It's just a harmless prank. A bonding exercise," I soothe, shooting him a wink, and Jasper sighs.

"Watch where you're going," he mutters, eyeing the shadowed, stained streets around us with healthy suspicion.

I turn around, and when I do, I'm smiling again. It might be my favorite part about how things have changed between us.

My smiles feel real again.

"That sounded like an order, soldier," I muse as I step around a haphazardly parked car. "Try to keep in mind that *I* am in charge here."

I feel the sudden silence behind me like the edge of a knife, and the small hairs lift on the back of my neck. My smile becomes a grin.

"Have your fun, Lucien. Perhaps you can even watch and learn how to obey an order," Jasper says silkily. He steps up beside me and gives me a dark-eyed look under his lashes, lowering his voice. "But don't be mistaken, you wretched brat. I don't need to be your superior to own you."

My mouth goes dry, and he holds my gaze for a moment more before he turns and taps the bricked building next to us. It takes me too long to recognize the chalk marking that tells us to turn left.

Cheeks burning, I lift my hand and gesture at the team to change direction.

Bentley and his men scouted the routes to the Den several days ago, marking the directions in chalk so we wouldn't get lost in Cyanide.

Night blankets us in darkness, but we follow the markings for two hours, using a few flashlights to shine our way. Dom, Beau, and I check in every fifteen minutes to make sure it's all quiet, and apart from flocks of pigeons roosting in burst-open buildings and the distant scurrying of random animals, it is.

I keep one eye on Julian, and every time he catches me looking at him, he sweats even more.

And yes, his nervousness makes me want to snort, but it also reminds me that he wasn't here for our briefing. He doesn't know the plan, and so I really do need to keep an eye on him.

Team Decoy isn't an attack force—we don't have the manpower to take out that many men. Our goal is to distract the Sinners and lead them away from the Den so that Dom's team can get in, collect the women, children, and whatever contraband they can steal, and get out.

We do *not* want Dom and Eden popping up like a Whack-A-Mole into an army full of Sinners.

So to draw them out, Team Decoy will set up explosives through the buildings along a nearby industrial street. We're going to set them off one by one, simulating the rippled drop of a drone strike. It should push the Sinners out of their Den—and hopefully make them scatter.

The drones targeted grouped heat signatures, after all.

It's a good plan—about as good as anyone could muster with this many vulnerable hostages, few resources, and even fewer men. But there are still a lot of ways this could go wrong. The midnight explosions should catch them off-guard, but they'll come out armed and ready for a fight. If we can avoid engaging them directly, we will. Team Rooftop can only do so much to cover our asses on the ground if we get jumped by that many men.

This one is all about the set-up and the timing.

Beau's voice clicks on over our Ranger kit radios in a burst of low static. "Team Rooftop has reached the target location and is in position, over."

They should be lined up opposite the buildings we plan to blow—ready to cover us while we set up and pick off any asshole Sinner if we get jumped.

"Team Underground not yet in position. Do not engage. Copy? Over," Dom's voice crackles back immediately.

I gesture at my team to slow as we approach a large warehouse with a big *X* marked in chalk on its side. There'll be another building a few hundred yards up the street just like it, also marked with an *X*, and there should be one more after that.

Glancing up, I see Beau's team spread along the rooftop of the building opposite us. Bentley chose this street because of how tightly the buildings are locked in beside one another, which should make it easy enough for Team Rooftop to follow us as we move.

I flick on the radio at my chest. "Roger that, Cap. Team Decoy is approaching the first target now. We'll check the bed for bugs and lay our plastic, then move onto target two. Confirming we'll hold fire until your signal. Over."

"Team Rooftop has eyes on Decoy. We're watching their six, Captain. Over and out," Beau confirms. He's lost the snippy tone he's had with Dom ever since we left Bristlebrook, and I'm glad they can pack it away for this, at least.

I hate it when Mom and Dad fight.

I gesture everyone over to huddle in the dip of an alley. Julian starts to move in close and everyone edges away from him.

Jasper gives me another exasperated look, and my lips twitch.

"Okay team, pair up and watch each other's backs. We're going to sweep the building. I want every room checked for civilians, Sinners, and cute baby animals. When we're sure it's clear, I'll set up the explosives and we move straight onto the second building.

You see a target, try not to kill them. We want to make sure who we're firing on first, okay? Any questions?"

We went over the plan a few times before we left, but funny things can happen to the brain in combat. The adrenaline can drown out those details fast if you're not used to it.

Julian raises a shaking hand, and I nod encouragingly.

"W-where are you getting the explosives from?" he asks trepidatiously, like he already knows the answer. He seems afraid to move, and he's holding the straps of the danger pack in a death grip.

I rub the side of my nose and say vaguely, "Oh, you know . . ." I click my fingers. "Can you stay where I can see you, though? For reasons."

Jennifer snorts with laughter next to me. Julian's eyes sink miserably closed, and reluctant smiles start cropping up over Team Decoy's faces, finally easing some of that twitchy tension in them. In most of them.

Julian is definitely still twitching.

We all move into the warehouse as Beau watches from above. It's dusty as hell, but that reassures me more than anything. This building hasn't been disturbed for years. It only takes fifteen minutes for the team to clear the building and gather downstairs, and a quick check in with Beau confirms the streets outside are quiet.

As Julian walks down the stairs toward us, taking ginger steps, I loosen one of the flares from my belt. He clears the stairs just as Jasper catches sight of me, narrowing his eyes on the flare in my hand.

I see the moment understanding hits. "Lucien, *don't*."

I light the end of the flare and throw it at Julian's pack, shouting wildly, "Julian, look out!"

The flare lights the room in a fiendish red, and it makes a loud bang as it hits the smiley face keychain square in the eye.

Shocked shouts lift up from the team, and I grin, dropping my own pack on the floor.

I'm about to reveal the joke when Julian *screams*.

He throws the pack off his shoulders behind him, then spins around, seeing the bright red flame atop the danger pack. In a startling display of heroism, he throws himself on the burning bag and tosses the lit flare in my direction.

I skid to the side to avoid it . . . and can't hold back my laughter as he frantically beats out the tiny flames.

Jennifer freezes at my laughter, halfway to the door in a panicked flight already, then turns to look at me with shocked, incredulous eyes. The rest of the team filters into the room, staring between me and the pack with varying expressions of horror and confusion.

"The . . . the danger pack. The explosives. It was on f-fire," Julian stammers, whipping his head around in every direction. "*You* set it on fire. Why would you . . .? Why are you *laughing*?"

His sweet, studious face is white, and it sets me off again until I'm bent over and gasping for air.

"I'm sorry. You didn't have it. I'm sorry, but your face—" I wipe a tear from my eye, snorting again. "I switched the chain onto my bag. You never had the danger pack—there's not one explosive in there. I wouldn't do that to *you*, recruit. That would be mean! The most dangerous thing in there is my sweaty old socks."

Jennifer presses a hand against her chest and flips me off with the other. "You motherfucker. You scared the *shit* out of me."

One of the Red Zone men snorts, then starts laughing, and the rest of them look somewhere between amused and scandalized. One of them hugs their friend when they can't stop shaking.

See? Bonding.

Jasper gives me a lethally unimpressed look. In the flickering, flaring light, he looks like hell's prince again.

Julian stands up on shaking, uncertain legs, picking up my old pack. "I-If I didn't have the danger pack, then w-who does?"

"Uh, Lucky?" one of the older men asks faintly, staring at something behind me. "*You* didn't have the danger pack . . . did you?"

I shrug. "Of course. I wouldn't ask anyone in my team to take a risk I wouldn't take." The man steps back slowly, his eyes widening. "Um. But why do you ask?"

"Fuck," Jasper swears, and it's so unlike him that I blink as he stalks up to me, then spins me around.

And I suddenly realize where all that flickering light is coming from.

When Julian threw it, the flare apparently managed to land directly on my pack—and it is currently flaring brighter and brighter as we watch in deathly, diabolic flames.

"The danger pack is on fire," I say dumbly.

"You infernal, ridiculous brat," Jasper hisses, then he shoves me toward the door and shouts, "Everyone *run*. *Now!*"

CHAPTER 60

JASPER

SURVIVAL TIP #308
If you elect to have a life partner,
try to choose one who won't get you killed.

W e *run.*
Our team skids out the door of the warehouse and
bolts down the street in a cloud of dust and limbs, *away* from the
burning bag of military-grade explosives we left behind us. Panic
seizes my lungs. Those explosives were meant to be used for several
buildings in carefully measured amounts, set off when we were a
safe distance away. We are *not* a safe distance away. How long do we
have?

Sweat gathers along my hairline, and I sprint faster.

Lucien flicks on his kit's radio, panting. "Uh, Beau! Hey,
buddy. Funny story, but—*run like your life depends on it.*"

I glare at him as we run, having no breath to snarl at him the
way I want to right now, and he nods like he's remembering something and flicks the radio back on to add, "Over!"

"What did—? Shit. Roger. Over and out." Beaumont's voice is
muffled through the radio, but at least he heard.

"Did not copy. Say again. Over," Dominic demands through the line.

Adrenaline courses through my veins. Jennifer jumps over a fallen bin in our path, and Julian stumbles over it, scrambling to get to his feet. I swerve around it, pulling him up as I go, and the sharp motion makes something creak uncomfortably in my back.

I'm not even sure where we're running, just that stopping means death.

"Hard right. In here! Go, go, go!" Lucien darts to the side and into a heavy-set stone building that I think might have been a bank.

I follow the turn and throw myself inside just as the shockwave shudders the ground and slams against the building in a great, rushing ripple. The remaining windows in the room explode, and Lucien yanks me down and out of the doorway, rolling on top of me as the deafening roar of the explosion finally hits my ears.

The building trembles, and I grip Lucien tightly, breathing him in and counting his heartbeats as brick dust rains down on us. He holds me back just as forcefully, panting into my neck.

The quaking settles, and Lucien pulls back, his beautiful blue eyes scanning my face. His hair is powdered with dust, and he's too pale by far, but he doesn't seem hurt. His lifeblood isn't spilling over my hands this time. There are no gaping holes that whistle with his fading, gasping breaths.

I can't hear anything but a high-pitched ringing in my ears, and I know we should move before the Sinners come to investigate, but the icy memories won't be banished.

Cupping his face, I kiss him fiercely. I need him. I need to feel his warmth and taste his breath and drown in each and every assurance that he's *alive*. I plunder his mouth until the heat starts to push back that frigid blast of fear.

Lucien pulls back first. I watch his lips move, but I still can't hear. After a second, he grimaces too, rubbing his ear.

He gets to his feet quickly, yanking me up and waving around to the team. We're dirty and disheveled, and Julian has a bleeding cut above one eye, but we're otherwise unhurt. The numb distance from sound is disorienting. The pressure in my head makes it feel as though it's about to burst, but I keep my focus on Lucien's rapid movements. Ill-thought-out pranks aside, he knows what he's doing.

Lucien pushes toward the door urgently, and fresh apprehension nips me into motion. What does this mean for our plan? We're nowhere near where we were meant to be positioned. Is Beaumont's team intact?

Is Beaumont?

We need to regroup and re-plan somewhere secure before the Sinners have a chance to catch up to us. This has gone too far off the rails.

When the last person clears the room, I head toward the door quickly, my rifle ready . . . and I notice everyone is standing in the middle of the street, curiously still. Is there too much debris? Lucien is framed by the doorway, staring down the street.

I shake my head, but the ringing only increases. It's unbearably loud, swallowing my ability to think, but I hesitate before clearing the door. A peculiar dread anchors my feet to the ground.

Something isn't right.

I grasp my radio right as Lucien drops to his knees and holds up his hands. Raw panic clutches me, and I rush forward, swinging up my rifle. As soon as I clear the door, Lucien's furious, fearful eyes stare up at me.

And the cold barrel of a gun kisses my temple.

CHAPTER 61

BEAU

Lucky's voice cuts off on the radio, and the sight of his team racing up the street is enough to convince me that we want to be here about as much as ole Daisy wants to be at the slaughterhouse. But damn it, why are they running *toward* the Den?

Dom crackles over the radio, demanding answers, but he's going to have to wait.

"Move. Over the rooftops and follow Team Decoy. Go!" I shout, and my team doesn't need any more urging.

One by one, they fly toward the adjacent building, leaping over the ten-foot gap to the next building, and running toward the next without pausing. Team Decoy might be the prettiest, but Team Rooftop knows how to *move*.

Except for one.

Bentley hesitates beside me, eyeing the gap.

"We don't have time. Pack it away and move," I order, and his shoulders roll like uncomfortable boulders.

I start to sweat, and I see Jennifer jump over a trash can like she's aiming for Olympic gold.

What on God's green earth did Lucky do this time?

Bentley backs away from the rooftop edge. "Ehh. Not much of a jumper, me. I sink like a rock. I'll hold the fort here."

Urgency whips me. "It's hardly a jump at all. You could walk over it. Move."

"No."

"Move, or I'll push you."

"Are you trying to save my life or end it?"

"Which will shut you up faster?" I push him, and Bentley flinches like he's a mouse staring down a cat's maw and not a six-foot-five human tank.

"Move!" I shout, and with a groan, he backs up and races toward the edge of the building, hollering as he jumps.

Wasting no time, I race after him and together we barrel toward the next ledge. He shouts as he goes over that one too, and on the street, I see Lucky turn into a bank, his team following inside.

Clouds roll over the moon, blocking out the main shine of our light. I see flashlights flicker over the rooftop garden on the next building, and it's only as we're clearing the ledge that I realize this jump is much larger than the two before it.

"Oh, shiiiiiit," Bentley bellows.

My stomach unanchors as we soar through empty space, flying over a distance I'm not sure we're going to clear.

Then I feel it.

The blast wave wallops us from behind like a steam train, the force hurdling us the last few feet over onto the building. Neither of us land clean this time. My insides feel bruised even before I hit the artificial turf of the rooftop garden, and Bentley and I slam into one another as we roll to a jerky, painful halt.

I heave in air, my lungs screaming as I stare up at the night sky. The clouds continue rolling, and the moonlight becomes the dazzling chandelier to this fucked up party of ours. I blink against the bright light, my hearing muffled and tinny.

Slowly, my team appears over us, holding their weapons and their flashlights right in our faces.

Only . . . I squint.

This is *not* my team.

CHAPTER 62

EDEN

It feels like a crypt.

I can't dislodge the haunting thought—it keeps whispering in my ear like a warning. We're swallowed by the underground, buried in rock, and the darkness is going to suffocate me. Only our flashlights glow in the forgotten tunnels, but their efforts seem weak and pathetic against the oppressive murk. This black has a bite to it.

The pistol is heavy in my hand as we walk along an abandoned rail line, and the weighty silence is only pierced by two dozen footsteps and the occasional kick of rubble. There's a chill clinging to my skin that I can't shake, some deep foreboding that tells me to *stop* and *go back*.

But that's just fear. It's just fear, right? The kind of fear any sane, rational woman might feel while walking through deserted, ghostly halls at midnight. It's less frightening than many things I've survived these last few months, certainly.

It's just . . . uneasy.

Dom's next step brings him closer to me, and he has the delicious warmth of a lit candle. He always runs hot, like a walking furnace I want to lock myself inside—it might be the end of me, but I need the burn.

"I have a question about your rules," I whisper and even that feels loud in the silence. The others are spaced out around us though, and it's more hushed than our footsteps.

Still, I need a distraction. Dom just so happens to be very distracting.

His golden eyes slice the gloom as he glances down at me. "So ask."

God, he's blunt.

My eyes narrow on his shadowed figure for a moment before I refocus on the tunnel. If I can flirt with Beau and Lucky, and even Jaykob, then I can flirt with Dom too, right? I'm allowed? He was inside me a few hours ago, so it feels like it should be allowed.

"You said you wanted me to address you as sir, but that I'm not allowed to speak unless I'm moaning your—I think you cursed here, so I'll redact that for politeness—unless I'm moaning your name."

Dom snorts softly, and I fight a smile. My skittery adrenaline leaps between nervousness and excitement like a ping pong ball. I adjust my grip on the gun.

"Well, I was thinking that's rather contradictory. When I come do I use your name . . . or do I call you sir?" I ask, carefully not looking at him. This feels risky. A sharp, offensive maneuver.

His head lowers toward mine. "Call me sir any other time you want, pet—but if you call me anything but my name when you come, you won't sit down for a week. That clear enough?"

My next breath is shuddery. Okay. Flirting with Dom is different. Jasper's compliments are rare and genuine, Beau and Lucky smile and tease me back, and Jaykob blushes. Dom doesn't even look at me, but I feel his body charge with lethal energy, and its shockwaves tingle over my skin.

"Yes, sir," I say breathlessly.

I'm not sure if my raid was successful or not, but now all I can think about is how much I suddenly don't *want* to sit down for a week.

Dom shines the light against the wall, illuminating a chalk marking that urges us forward. His radio clicks on abruptly.

Lucky sounds like he's panting. "Uh, Beau! Hey, buddy. Funny story, but—*run like your life depends on it.*"

Dom and I both freeze, and one by one the others around us do the same. Life *depends* on it? My unease slams back in. What's happened now?

Beau clicks on. "What did—? Shit. Roger. Over and out."

Dom's jaw is hard when he picks up his radio. "Did not copy. Say again. Over."

The answering silence is loud.

"Acknowledge, soldiers. Over," he tries again.

I stare at Dom's silhouette like my silent command will make them speak. What *happened*?

Dom slams his radio back in its pouch.

The tunnels feel like a coffin all around me. "What do we do? Do we go and find them? Wait?"

"No," Heather answers, coming up beside me. "We're not missing this chance. Whatever their problem is, they need to sort it out themselves."

"We're not going into the Den until we know it's clear," Dom claps back. He stops, then rubs a hand over his jaw. "It could have been anything. Going up there now could cause more problems. We move into position and wait for word. If we don't hear anything in fifteen, then we'll scout out what happened."

"Dom—" Heather starts, her voice razor sharp.

"He's right, Madison," I say firmly, trying to strangle the fear clawing its way up my throat. I can feel her desperation tainting the musty air. "Let's follow the plan."

She hesitates. "Fine. *Fine.*"

We turn back to keep moving when the tunnel shakes with a distant, sonorous *boom*. Rocks tumble from the walls, and my boots vibrate for a long moment before it stops.

Bombs. Lucky had bombs. Bombs are normal in this situation.

But Beau needing to run 'like his life depends on it' is *not*.

"What the fuckity fuck was that?" Ava snaps from somewhere to my left.

"That was a bomb," Sloane replies, grim and dark.

"Bombs were part of the plan. Keep moving." Dom's steadiness helps, and I clamp my mouth shut as I step after him.

We need more information. They're fine. They're probably fine. Lucky warned Beau, and they can't talk now because they're getting themselves to safety. Fear snakes through my veins, and without speaking, everyone picks up the pace.

Dom swings his flashlight up, checking the wall again, then lowers it to the ground in front of us so we can see where we're walking. He breathes in sharply. When I glance at him, the exhale comes out slow and easy, almost casual . . . but there's a stoniness to his expression that wasn't there before. I'm too jumpy already, and I'm expecting it now.

There's something wrong.

My eyes follow his, scanning the ground—and I see it. There are big, snaking tracks through the dust. Footprints. The Red Zone scouts did come through here a few days ago . . . but there's a lot more tracks than two people would account for.

Swallowing, I glance at Dom, and he tilts his chin just slightly. *No. Don't say anything.*

My palm becomes clammy around the Beretta I barely know how to use. I squint into the darkness, though I know it's pointless. I'm not sure how much my poor vision is contributing, even with my glasses on, but I can't see anything except the haloed radiance of our flashlight and the silhouettes of our team.

Someone could be three feet from me, and I would have no idea.

"Heather, you remember the night we met?" Dom calls back casually.

There's · a slight, almost imperceptible pause before she answers. "Pretty night. Full of fireflies."

To my right, Sloane coughs loudly, and pauses to lean on our sole Red Zone addition, Gemma. They straighten after a moment, and Sloane mutters, "Sorry."

Nervous energy broils inside me, and one by one, I sense it slowly envelop our whole group. I can't even say how I know it, because they continue on as normal, nothing outwardly different. And I don't know how, or what they've said to tip them off, and maybe it's only because *I* know there's danger that I can feel it, but I *know* the information has been silently passed around our group.

We're not alone.

Dom shines the light against the wall where there's a chalk marking of a big star next to a ladder that leads up to a large metal manhole.

"We're in position," he calls around.

My hand shakes, and I try to remember my two shooting lessons. I remember how to turn the safety off. Aiming is the difficult part. Oh God, what do I even aim *at*?

Dom steps closer to me again. "As soon as this is over, little librarian, we're finishing what we started."

His voice is low and full of heat . . . but not *that* low. Everyone would be able to hear him. Despite the situation, I shoot him a scandalized look.

"That— Right. Well. We can talk about that in private," I stammer at the same volume, and Ava's snicker echoes hollowly through the tunnels.

He glances at me. "You remember rule number three? That one's going to be useful later."

Rule number three? My mind scrambles. His rules. What were they? My brain was fogged with him at the time. There was "don't touch me unless I tell you to" and "address me as 'sir,'" but what was the third one?

We stop beside a large pile of rubble, and Heather skirts around it a few steps ahead of us. She snorts. "Give her a kiss, then pack the hard on away, Dom. We have shit to do."

Dom laughs. *Laughs.* Full-bodied, deep, and gravelly, that laugh paralyzes my panicked heart in my chest. With more casual ease than he should be capable of, Dom's arm comes around me, and he sweeps me into a low, romantic dip.

Dom dipped me. Dom *dipped* me. Who *is* this person?

My free hand clutches his chest, while my gun slaps up against his shoulder—thankfully, still with the safety on—and his head dips too.

He's really going to kiss me? Now?

When his lips brush over mine, he murmurs, "We're surrounded. Stay low and listen. Got it?"

"*No!*" I hiss, panicked.

"Now!"

Dom drops me on my ass, whipping his rifle up as he steps out from behind the pile of rubble and fires into the darkness. I cover my head with my hands as gunfire bursts in my ears, and I frantically look around. Can he actually see? Or is he just hoping for the best?

I peek my head around the half-shelter of rocky debris.

"Rule *three*, Eden," he roars.

It suddenly hits me. Rule three—stay where I put you.

Alarm pulses through me. I hear dozens of blistering shots slapping the air, one after the next. There are shouts—Ava, Sloane, Heather, Dom . . . and men, men I don't recognize. Their feet kick up the dust on the ground, and I can feel it coating my hair, gritting my eyes, and congealing in my nose.

And all I can see are vignettes in flashes of glittering light as flashlights are swung around and kicked haphazardly across the ground. My emotions swing just as wildly.

Flash.

Sloane shoots a man point blank between the eyes, spraying the air with shimmering blood.

Flash.

The Red Zone woman stabs a knife through a Sinner's wrist, and his gun falls from his hand. The next stab goes through his throat.

Flash.

An automatic gun fires off staccato shots.

Flash.

Dom brings the butt of his rifle down on a man's face. "Eden, run!"

Flash.

I freeze, falling to my hands and knees. Should I get up? Every familiar, animal part of me tells me to obey. To *flee.*

Flash.

A man has his arm wrapped around Heather's neck from behind, and she grapples with him with a furious screech.

Flash.

"Run, Eden!" Dom snaps.

Flash.

The rubble scratches my hands. No. No, no, no. I can't do this again. I can't leave her.

Flash.

The man kicks out the back of her knee, sending her to the ground. He raises his gun.

Flash.

I'm on him. How did I get on him? My body feels bruised, and he's thrashing underneath me. My gun has stopped shaking. I feel the cold storm rise in me, the way it did while I brewed my soup.

This is *right.*

Flash.

The lever. My other hand slams down over it, unlatching the safety as he clubs the side of my head.

Bang.

Silence.

I breathe hard, blinking against the throbbing pain in my head. I feel something hot and wet dribble down my temple . . . and realize the man is still and silent underneath me.

The dust begins to settle around me. The battle has stopped. *Everything* is still and silent.

"Eden? Are you okay?" Heather touches my shoulder, and I swing the gun around toward her as my heart leaps.

She raises her hands quickly. "Just me, babe. Be a waste if you killed me now after you went to all that trouble to save me."

Save her? I saved Heather?

I turn to look down at the man, and Heather grips my wrist, pulling me up instead. "No, no. You don't need to do that. You did good, Eden."

When I'm standing, she slides the safety back on my gun. I feel dizzy, and I wait for the nausea to hit—the revulsion or shame— only it doesn't come. I think I'm . . . okay.

"You're not hurt?" I finally think to ask.

When I see the outline of her nod, I pull her into a hug, my heart hammering so hard, I'm sure she must be able to feel it.

How did this even happen? How could they have known we were here?

"Hey, it's okay, I'm okay."

"Eden!" Dom yanks me off Heather by my shirt, and I fall into him. His eyes are battered gold in the gloomy light. "You didn't run."

"You said to stay. You said to run. Quite honestly, it was all very confusing in the moment," I stammer.

But what he said catches up to me. I *didn't* run. Heather is okay because of me. I did something. I didn't just save myself.

"You could have died," Dom snaps, and I choke on a laugh.

The thought doesn't scare me as much as it did even a few

weeks ago. It's not just myself anymore. The same things I want to live for . . . I think I'm willing to die for them, too.

My laugh becomes more genuine, and I lift up on my toes and give him a quick, exhilarated kiss. His breath catches as I settle back on my feet, and he stares at me as I put my glasses back on. Not that it does much in this lighting. I feel drugged, my brain swimming with thoughts and feelings, and my pulse still batters at my throat.

Dom's radio bursts to life, and my heart lifts. It's Beau or Lucky. If their radio is working and intact, they must be too.

But then I hear the voice.

"Hello, Captain." Whisper soft and deathly dangerous, I'd recognize that voice anywhere. It carves through my nightmares every night.

Alastair.

My victorious joy withers into ash, and the manhole above the ladder makes a yawning scream as it opens. Light shines down from it in a tricksome halo. Dom pulls me behind him, but no-one moves down the ladder. Of course, they wouldn't. It would be far too exposed.

"Come up now, Ranger. You know how this goes. We have your people hostage," Alastair's voice slides over the radio again.

Why *is* it Alastair? Why not Sam?

Dom lifts his radio up to his mouth. "How do we know they're still alive?"

His voice is even, but he's like stone beside me. Still alive? Horror thrills through me. It hadn't occurred to me that the radio might have been stolen from a body.

There's a loud crack and a grunt, and I hear Mateo snap, "Speak. Tell your friends you're alive."

There's no response for a moment, but then there's another fleshy thud, and a man yells. "We're alive! Why aren't you *saying* anything?"

I can hear him shout through the manhole as well as the radio in a discordant echo.

"This is not a negotiation. Come up, or I'll kill one of them for every minute you don't comply," Alastair says, and the line clicks off.

Heather grabs Dom's arm, and they immediately start arguing in low, rapid voices.

Alastair and Mateo have my men. I set Alastair and Mateo free, and they are *threatening* my men. Whatever storm had started to ebb in me rumbles with dark, furious thunder.

Moving as fast as I can, I dart for the ladder and begin climbing up.

"Eden? No, Eden, *stop*!"

The panic in Dom's voice rips at me, but I tune it out.

And crawl out into the bright, treacherous light.

CHAPTER 63

EDEN

SURVIVAL TIP #247
The truth will out.

I climb out into a large courtyard swarming with men. They stand on lunch tables and guard the entrances, and the overhanging stone balconies are lined with armed men. Fluorescent lights beat down at us from the four corners of the courtyard, dazzling me after so long in the dark.

Jasper, Lucky, Beau, Bentley, and the rest of our people are kneeling in a cluster, and there are at least two dozen guns trained on them. Jasper and Lucky are coated in pale dust, and Beau is bleeding from a swollen, split cut over his right cheekbone. Mateo hovers over him, his angel face still and cold.

I look between them, the storm in me so icy cold that I feel my lips turn numb. I didn't save the man he loves only for him to take mine. Guilt and horror and rage twist and wreck my insides.

At the head of it all, standing on a table, is Alastair.

He's looking much better than he did a few weeks ago. In a long-sleeved black shirt, his burns are hidden except for the swathe of pink, shiny skin peeking out from his collar and licking his neck around his tattoos. His color is good, *healthy*, and he stands with the comfortable ease of someone whose skin isn't scouring him with agony for every twitch.

Those pale, piercing eyes stare right through me.

"Eden. Wonderful to have you join us," he says serenely, then gestures with his rifle to go over to the others.

I throw down my gun before they can ask, as well as the large knife I had at my side. My weapons mean nothing against this many men. Once again, I have to use my brain, only this time, I'm not too numbed with grief to think.

How did this happen? Why *aren't* we dead already? How did they know where we were going to be? I can only see two possibilities—either Red Zone is bugged . . . or we have a rat. Nervousness skates up my spine.

Rushing over to Beau, I kneel beside him, then turn his chin so I can check his cut. His stubble bristles under my fingertips, and I can see the pulse in his throat. He's okay. Jasper and Lucky are okay. Even if it's just for this moment.

I reach around for my bag and feel the end of a rifle against the back of my head.

"Behave, *gatita*," Mateo mutters.

Beau tenses, his eyes darkening on the man behind me. "Back off her. Now."

Fear flutters through me, tripping up my heart rate, but the feeling is too drowned out by everything else for me to pay it much heed right now. I pull out an antiseptic cloth from my first aid kit and focus on Beau's scent. The warmth of him beside me.

"I would think that since I took such good care of your friend, you might allow me to do the same for mine, Mateo," I snipe, carefully dabbing at Beau's cheek.

There's a ripple of scoffs and raucous laughter, but under it, I hear Mateo sigh quietly. "You don't know what you're walking into here."

"Don't worry yourself over him, Eden. He might be dead in a

moment," Alastair cautions, and even as relaxed and measured as his voice is, it has the resonance of a church bell. My hand pauses. "If your friends don't come up, you will be too."

Dread washes over me. He says it mildly, softly, like our slaughter would be a thing of no consequence.

I drop my cloth and turn back to look at him, my mind racing and the storm in me roiling. What is this? Does Alastair want revenge for the men I killed? I know Sam will. Scanning over the faces above and around us, I can't see their leader, though. I'm not sure why he isn't here for this, but I'm glad.

If Sam were here, we'd already be dead.

I might not see him, but my eyes snag on another familiar face.

Aaron's vibrant red hair peeks from the group of men behind Alastair, and I suck in a breath as understanding crashes in on me. Aaron betrayed us. That's how they knew where we'd be.

Aaron is our rat.

My stomach clenches in resigned misery. I'm not even shocked. Aaron has been belligerent and miserable since I met him. But now, in between these older, hardened men, he looks like a boy playing dress up, his face set in a smirk I don't believe. His eyes are too fearful.

"It's—"

"I know," Beau mutters, following my gaze.

A dark head comes up from the manhole, and several rifles retrain on Dom as he climbs out, then the others follow him, one by one.

"Guns and weapons in a pile. Leave your packs too," Mateo demands as Alastair looks over them with a carefully blank expression.

Heather is the last one up, and she's bristling with snarling tension. Her mouth is set in a sneer, and she throws her weapons down with violent disgust. All the while, she glares at Alastair with undisguised hatred.

Beau's eyes are on me, silently urging me to look at him, but I ignore him.

I need to watch Alastair.

At Heather's appearance, his nonchalant expression freezes. If I hadn't been watching him for so long in the Sinners' camp, I doubt I would have noticed. Silent intent edges his gaze, like a snake spotting a fledgling bird for its next meal.

Only, if Heather is a bird, she's a raptor—and she looks just as likely to make a meal of him.

Her grip is tight on her pistol as she hesitates to throw it down, and those glacial green eyes are arresting.

"That one too," Alastair advises her politely.

"Motherfucker," she spits, her face flaming with her anger, and her pistol crashes down on the pile.

Dom touches her arm to draw her away, and at that exact moment, the ground at his feet bursts open, spraying dirt. Heather and Dom fall back, and it takes my brain a second to realize that Alastair fired on Dom.

I try to shove to my feet, but Beau grabs my arm and yanks me down. "Stop, Eden. He can handle himself."

Alastair and Dom stare at each other for a long, tense moment, and then Dom lifts his hands away from Heather. Alastair's cold expression doesn't change, but the tip of his gun dips away from Dom.

Heather spins to stalk back to the group, but Alastair shakes his head at her back. "*Stop.* Kneel beside me here."

My brows lift as he doesn't even attempt to hide his possessiveness.

Heather turns stiffly, her red hair snared with flickers of gold in the harsh lights. Instead of kneeling, she sits down, and leans back casually on one hand. With the other, she flips him off.

I bite down to hide my shocked squeak, even as familiar concern spikes. I think Alastair craves her too much to shoot her? I *think.*

I don't trust anything Alastair does anymore.

Dom faces off against him, seeming unfazed by the number of guns pointed on him. "What do you want, Alastair? We're not dead already, so there's something. Where's Sam?"

Dom is right. If Alastair and Mateo simply returned to Sam to rejoin the Sinners, then why hesitate to kill us? That would be the cleanest, smartest thing to do. We attacked the Den—I'm not quite sure how he can justify *not* killing us.

And then there's the Sam issue. Is he out of the city? If Sam were here, then I don't think he would let Alastair speak for him now. There was too much mistrust between them.

I try to pick over the possibilities. We need an edge, and there's *something* in that. I just wish I knew better what we've walked into.

Are the men surrounding us loyal to Alastair . . . or to Sam?

"I don't like Rangers." Alastair's tattooed fingers tap thoughtfully on his gun. "Brash and loud and not half as clever as they think they are. I prefer to deal with intelligent leaders."

He glances over our kneeling group. "You might understand why I don't put you in that category."

I can only see Dom's back. He doesn't move, but I feel that blow for him. Dom didn't do this. The plan was *good*.

God, why *is* Alastair hesitating to kill us? If he's on Sam's side, then the women at Bristlebrook would be easier to claim with us dead now. He has our weapons. We have nothing else of value to bargain.

The only answer I can think of is that he doesn't *want* to kill us.

I wrench out of Beau's grip and stand. "Stop it, Alastair. We came here to stop Sam, like you wanted. We're . . . we're allies."

Lucky curses, but I don't look over at him. This is a gamble; I know it is. If these men do belong to Alastair, then I've given him an opening, something that says *he's* masterminded this, and we belong to him.

But if these men belong to Sam, then I just confessed to trying to kill their leader.

At least, if they're Sam's men, I just outed Alastair too.

The air in the courtyard is brittle. Breathless.

Alastair's head tilts, and he looks over Dom to where I stand. Very slightly, he inclines his head, and I feel a violent rush of relief. He's taking my offering.

Does that mean he's on my side after all?

"Sit down, Ranger. I think I would rather discuss business with your Eden. I've seen first-hand how well *her* plans play out." He smiles faintly, and adds in a murmur, "She has a mind for scheming."

His voice is smooth as an unrippled pond, but I feel the guilt dig like poison fangs between my ribs. I hear his warning: I need to be very, very careful of what I say.

Alastair can expose my lies as easily as I can his.

Taking a steadying breath, I walk forward until I'm standing beside Dom, who doesn't budge.

"Dom," I whisper, but he just shakes his head.

"You don't know how dangerous he is," he growls back quietly.

"I know what he is." He's a snake, and I am, too. Dom shouldn't be trying to protect me right now. Alastair is my mistake. Slick with shame, I say, "Go with the others, Dom. Alastair and I have . . . an understanding."

At that, Dom gives me a sharp look, but I can't meet his eyes. Not now.

"Trust me," I whisper, hating myself.

After only a moment's hesitation, he nods. I could throw up from my nauseous guilt. Dom shouldn't trust a word I say.

Dom doesn't walk away, though . . . he sinks to a kneel beside me. My stomach jolts at the sight. There's nothing submissive about it. There's too much anger in him. Too much power and ease. Dominic would look dominant gagged and hog-tied.

Alastair gives me a considering look, and I hear the impatient rustles through the men surrounding us. How does he want to play this?

"Your timing is terrible," he says with mild disapproval, and I nod as though this was our arrangement all along.

"I know. I'm sorry," I agree meekly.

I'm hyperaware of Dom beside me, not even seeming to breathe. Of Heather staring at me like I've transformed into some shadow form of myself. I can feel Lucky, Jasper, and Beau behind me—can practically taste their confusion. My throat starts to ache, and my palms feel clammy.

I think I see a way out of this, but it might cost me everything.

Aaron pushes between the Sinners, spots of color blotching his cheeks. "No, *no*. That wasn't the plan. They were planning on killing all of you. I was in the room, Bentley and Dom and that *bitch* Madison had it all ready."

There's a dark rumble around the courtyard, and it reminds me of arriving in the Sinner's camp. That same sense of stomach-churning threat coats the air.

Alastair's eyes remain on mine, cold and dead and full of warning in his gorgeous face. "It doesn't matter what they planned. Clever Eden and I had our own deal. She was meant to bring them while we were gone and Sam's men were here alone so they could take care of that little problem for us. In exchange, I promised we'd leave their burned-out heap of a home alone."

The rumble quietens at Alastair's bored confidence, and Dom is stony silent beside me. Waiting. Listening. Does he believe Alastair? It's a pretty blend of truth and lie. I did make a deal, and he was meant to leave Bristlebrook alone. There's enough truth in it that I can feel the doubts rolling off our people.

Alastair's displeasure makes divots in his brow. "But she didn't contact me in time, and so our hand was forced . . . and now *I* have lost men. I don't like losses, Eden."

"Fuck you, bitch," someone shouts from the balcony, and they're joined by cruel, sneering jeers.

This situation is too volatile. It needs damage control, fast. I don't know what kind of hold Alastair has on these men, but I know I can't make him look weak. He's the only person who might open a door for us to leave.

"She's not loyal," Aaron spits, coming up beside Alastair's table. "She hates the Sinners. I've heard her. You can't trust any of them—you need to kill them."

There's a frantic fear in his voice, and I understand it. I wouldn't want Heather or my brutes alive and after me, either.

Sounds of agreement fill the room, and the ground starts to feel slippery under me. This is dangerous. Alastair might be willing to try to get us out of this, but I've seen his self-interest. If the mob turns against us, I know he won't risk his position.

"Trust," Alastair muses. His head tilts up, and the harsh lights limn him in silver. "It is so important in those we keep around us. Loyalty is *everything*."

Each word twists the hot, treacherous knife in my gut. My intestines feel knotted around it, and they slice with every turn. Loyalty is everything to Dom, too, and he's had so little of it given to him.

Alastair looks down at his gun thoughtfully, then with a slow, casual grace, he lifts it, and shoots Aaron between his eyes.

I slap a hand over my mouth to muffle my scream.

Aaron slumps in a heap in front of Alastair, the back of his head a blown out, bloody mess. Red pools underneath him. I gag a little, but only partially from the sight.

Alastair killed him like he was swatting a fly.

"You *are* loyal to me, aren't you, Eden?" he asks with gentle interest.

My heart throbs in my ears. In my chest and my throat. My angry storm feels like the tantrum of a petulant toddler next to Alastair's authority. He has this, I realize. Whether we die or not,

Alastair is a master of survival. He has the room read, his strategy set, and before we even stepped into the courtyard, we were already outmatched.

I press my palms against my stomach to stop my hands from shaking. "Y-yes, Alastair. We're loyal. You know I am."

Dom's golden gaze burns the side of my face, and my eyes fill with real tears at the questions I feel in it. The trust. He still thinks this is my ruse, and maybe it is, in part, but my lies will break him before it's done.

Alastair's stare is intense, and I know what he's calling for. Heather couldn't do it, and neither could Dom—their pride wouldn't allow it.

But I've spent my life being humbled.

I bend my head and *grovel*. "I'm sorry, Alastair. I'm so sorry, I tried. I tried to get away, and to send you a message that we were here, but there was no opportunity. I thought if we just came here anyway, we could still help—that you could still use us."

Dom stiffens beside me, and I feel ill to my stomach. In my soul. I might not have done all of this, but I did enough.

"That was a mistake," Alastair tells me, then glances around at his men. "But we all make them. I'm not like Sam, Eden. I don't like killing when there's no need . . . people tend to be far more *useful* alive."

Aaron's body is still in a gruesome heap at his feet, but I try not to look at it. The courtyard is quiet, captivated as they watch him.

"As it turns out, I didn't need you. The Sinners solve their own problems. Don't we, men?" Alastair asks with chilling calm, and there's a roar of approval so deafening that I shrink.

Alastair pauses until they've finished, his expression unchanging. "Why don't we show our friends here exactly what the Sinners do to their enemies?"

There's another roar, and then the sound of doors bursting open around the second level. The men around the heavy concrete inner balcony pull away, and there's the sound of scuffling and grunts. My breathing comes faster as I strain to see what's happening.

And then, one by one, men are lifted and forced over the edge of the balcony. One by one they fall, hard, fast, and then jerk, caught by the rope around their necks. Several necks snap with a brutal crack, but many don't. I count ten before I stop, freezing in place as, all around us, men strangle to death, hanged over the courtyard walls like a battle mural.

Their gags and gasps and grunts fill the air as they claw at their necks. Everywhere is flooded by bulging eyes and heels kicking against walls, and the vile smell of bowels releasing in death.

Then a final body is lifted toward the balcony, this one behind Alastair. It screams, thrashing wildly.

"No! No, don't. Don't kill me. *Please* don't. I'll do anything, I—"

They throw him over, and Sam's neck breaks clean, cutting his sniveling cries off mid-shout.

I cringe.

I remember him standing on a rock, bellowing about the new world he was claiming. Sam who terrified me with his stupid, belligerent rage. Sam who Bristlebrook has been planning against and cowering from for weeks. Now his weathered face is slack, and his blue eyes are staring and blank. All that evil potential, just dangling there, dead at the end of a rope.

I swallow back my nausea.

Alastair nods, like a music conductor who's heard the final note. "Sam won't be bothering any of us anymore. *I* am in charge now." He pauses, then looks at me. "Despite how things unfolded, I should thank you. I owe you my life after all. None of this would have been possible without you."

My eyes squeeze shut for a moment as I see it coming; it flashes in front of my eyes.

"*No.*"

I force my eyes open. This isn't something I can hide from. Not anymore.

Heather's casual pose has vanished, and she's pulled up onto her knees. I can't look directly at her. "You didn't, Eden. You wouldn't have."

"Eden?" Dom asks in a low, raw voice. He's starting to see it now. That this isn't *all* a ruse.

I *have* betrayed him. Something violent and toxic stabs me in my chest, and I know this will mean a slow, painful death for me.

Alastair shakes his head at Heather. "Eden is a good deal more pragmatic than you are, death wish. She dealt with the men in the camp who were problematic to me—you saw how they reacted to Sam's speech. They were no good to my cause." He raises a brow at her. "What do you think she and I talked about every time she tended my wounds? Why do you think Mateo and I didn't have any soup? We were in this together all along."

Alastair gestures to me with his rifle and adds the final, piercing nail to my coffin. "And then, of course, she set me free when you held me captive."

Dom flinches.

Truth and lies. Truth and lies.

I can practically hear Heather replaying it back in her head. How I tended his wounds. How I brought him the soup that he never ate. I'm not sure how she reasoned it to herself before—bad timing maybe—but I'm sure she sees the truth on my face now.

I *let* Alastair live.

"He killed Tommy," Heather screams at me. "How could you, Eden? I trusted you."

I blink hard, fighting not to cry. I can't. Not now. But God, the pain in her voice is like a thousand knives to sensitive flesh.

Dom's is worse.

"You didn't . . ." He sucks in a ragged breath. "Tell me you didn't set them free?"

Shame clogs my throat so thickly I can't breathe.

"A and M," I hear Jasper say behind me, and I can't stop myself turning. His beautiful face is soft with shock and realization. "That's what you meant in your journals."

Beside him, Lucky is shaking his head, over and over.

"Oh, darlin', no," Beau breathes.

They all know.

My tears do spill over then, and I look back at Dom. His golden eyes are disbelieving. *Hurt.*

"I'm sorry," I whisper through tears.

He stares at me, and the betrayal takes a long, long time to dawn on his face. When it does, it's crushing.

His jaw clenches as he swallows, and I see the sheen in his eyes as he looks away from me. I didn't know he could look so vulnerable.

I feel wrong in my own skin. Filthy. Dom shouldn't look like this. Just hours ago, he told me I was his best friend. He was flirting with me with dangerous energy, and confidently—finally— in control.

The way his shoulders curve in now is like a mountain tumbling down, and this time, when he slumps into a kneel, he doesn't look powerful.

He looks defeated.

My king has been dethroned.

I see the group of men behind Alastair start pulling together, muttering. There are similar ripples around us. Alastair's pale, calculating eyes sweep over them, testing the room, and his grim expression frightens me.

"Alastair is our ally," I insist quickly, trying and failing to keep the shame and panic out of my voice. "That's why I saved him. I saved him *twice.*"

It's as much a reminder to Alastair as the rest of the Sinners in the room. I hate myself for the desperation I can't hide. I need to think. I have to, but Dom is like a living, breathing wound beside me.

Dom's breath comes out heavy and hard, but I force myself to ignore the tormented sound. Alastair is in charge. We *need* these men to think we're on their side.

"Bristlebrook and the Sinners can live in peace. W-we want the same things. Alastair will free the women and children, and . . ." I trail off as Alastair stiffens.

He gives the slightest shake of his head, and the detached resignation I see in his face ices my veins.

Why does he look like that? What does that look *mean*?

"What the fuck is she talking about?" one man snaps.

Another grizzled man leans over the balcony. "I'm not giving up Sadie. I'll kill you first, Alastair."

Some of the men stay still and silent . . . but a good many of them don't. More shouts join in, angrier and hotter with every new voice, and I realize that in my distress, I've said the wrong, wrong thing.

But this *was* the deal. This was the whole point of getting Sam out of the way. A *new vision*, Alastair said. Does this mean he *isn't* freeing them?

How is he any better than Sam?

Alastair stares at me, and I see his mind working, gauging the pressure in the room like a barometer. I see the moment he makes a decision.

He smiles, small and sharp. "Settle."

The word is soft, and the measured pause after it even softer. The shouts stutter to a halt to listen.

"Of course the women and children stay here. She's going to ask for our food and medicine again next, I imagine. It must be hard to see, watching your betters have everything." Alastair raises one brow at me, and it's like a slap. "But if I'm meant to *trust* my ally, then they should show proper respect and not ask for more than was promised."

Loathing and dread swarm me. I hate him. I hate him for the way Dom's breathing has become ragged. I hate him for the way

Heather is glaring at me with furious tears. Alastair *did* promise to free the women and children. I trusted that. It was the only reason I saved him.

This is not something I can let go.

"You promised they'd be safe," I say, just as quietly as him.

His eyes narrow on me, but I hold his gaze, prickling with fear. There's too many of them, and they need us. I've done so many things wrong, but this has to be one that I got right, or else what was the point?

Finally, he says, "We aren't Sam. We take care of our people. Don't we, men?"

There's another roar of approval that I don't trust at all.

When I don't back down, a muscle in his jaw flexes and we stand off against one another.

His voice lowers even further. "I will keep them safe, Eden. I'm keeping my promises. This time, you should do the same."

The Sinners continue to scoff and jeer around us, and my dread overtakes the anger. The stench of death is thick in the air, and I'm suddenly very worried we're going to be adding to it.

It's as much of a concession as I think I'll get.

I bow my head and force more lies over my tongue. "I'm sorry, I shouldn't have asked again. I know you said no. Thank you for dealing with Sam. We're very . . ." I falter, and another tear slips down my cheek. "We're very grateful. We can leave now. We'll leave and we won't come back, I promise."

"I don't know that I trust you to keep that promise." Alastair's voice has a bite to it, and I wince, taking the hit.

I already promised him we wouldn't come to Cyanide.

"I think my men are right, Eden. We may be allies, but you need to learn your place. The Sinners own this land. We might want a different kind of rule than Sam, but that fact still holds true. We allow you to live in our territory by our grace." Alastair's eyes shimmer like snake scales, pale and bright against his dark, dark lashes. "Your medieval society has inspired me—consider me the new lord of Bristlebrook and Red Zone. In exchange for your ongoing safety, you all can offer me a yearly tithe in gratitude. I'll send a messenger about what I need."

That's not good, but it could be worse. It even seems . . . mild.

"Is . . . is that all?" I ask.

Part of me hopes that Dom will speak up now and take control. I've done my part. I saved Alastair's life, and he killed Sam, for all that matters. The women and children are still captive. We have no food for our starving people, or medical supplies for Red Zone. I've betrayed the woman who saved my life and somehow became one of my closest friends. I've broken the confidence of a good leader, and the trust of all my men.

But the civilians at Bristlebrook are safe, and we might just leave here alive.

Alastair looks almost amused for a moment. "I think we'll take some collateral before you leave, just to assure myself of your loyalty—two guests, I think, one from Red Zone and one from Bristlebrook. As long as nothing happens to us . . . nothing will happen to them."

Of course. There had to be new depths for my shame to spiral to. But at least I know what I have to do now. Some small measure of penance.

I nod.

"I'll stay with you, then," I say huskily. "Take me as collateral."

"The hell you will," Lucky shouts behind me, almost a snarl.

"Stay in line. One more move, and I'll shoot," Mateo warns.

"Shut your mouth, pet. Now," Beau yells.

Jasper says sharply, "*I* will stay. Leave Eden be."

Ducking my head, I fight back a sob at their instant defense, but tears are streaming down my cheeks now. Why would they fight for me now? After *this*? I've never felt so loved before.

Or so undeserving.

Dom is still utterly silent.

"No, it has to be me. It's okay. It is." I clear my throat and wipe my cheeks, then nod at Alastair.

But he doesn't respond. Alastair isn't even looking at me.

His eyes are fixed on Heather. "Thank you, Eden, but I don't want you. I want more meaningful collateral—your leaders. I want Bentley . . . and I want her."

No. He can't take her. She can't pay this price for me. Not to *him.*

Shouts from Red Zone rise up behind me. A chorus of "not him" and "please, don't." God, Bentley has teenagers to protect. Soren needs his uncle. What are they going to do without him?

Heather's red hair swings in its braid as she looks up at Alastair. She doesn't look afraid.

She looks bloodthirsty.

"Deal," she snaps.

"No!" I yell at her. "Madison, don't. Please. I'm sorry. I only did it because I thought— I didn't mean for this to happen. Please don't go with him."

Heather spares me only one glance, and it has as much naked hate in it as I've ever seen for Alastair. And so, so much hurt.

"I'm finishing this myself. Stay out of my way, Eden—I will *never* forgive you for this."

I'll never forgive *myself.*

Alastair lifts his hands. "The deal is done. Now get these brutes out of my sight. It's time for the Sinners to reign."

Author's Note

I feel like there's an awkward silence here. Is it awkward? I think it's awkward. Look. Yes. It's not . . . great. But everyone's alive! That's good, right? Yayyyyy!

Cough. I'm still sensing some tension.

There *is* a HEA at the end! I promise! (Don't hurt me!). The brutes and Eden had a rough trot this book, and dramatic end events notwithstanding, they've done a lot of growing. Some of them have. Kind of. A bit. They broke apart this book, and broke down, and book 3 is all about how they find a way to come together. So to speak.

One more book to go. We can do it!

But in all seriousness, thank you so, so much for reading. This was a really hard one to write for a lot of reasons. It was my first book writing experience as a full-time author. And it is *huge*, and heavy, and so emotionally twisty that it took a lot to get out.

Thank you so, so much for reading it and supporting me. It means everything, and I appreciate it so much more than I can say. Every one of you are making my baby author dreams come true.

If you liked it, please drop a review on Amazon or Goodreads. They make such an enormous difference to indie authors like me!

I can't wait to bring you the rest of the story in book 3 . . . and there may just be a spin off with some of our new morally grey characters . . .

CAN'T WAIT?

Are you desperate to know what exactly went down on the day the world died? When everything went up in smoke and our favorite characters' lives were changed forever? Do you want to see Jayk get his pride shredded? Beau realize he'll never see his family again? Jasper and Lucky desperately trying not to collapse into one another? Dom fighting for his men, the civilians, for *survival*?

Of course you do. You're a total masochist. It's okay, this is a safe space.

Head to my website (https://rebeccaquinnauthor.com) to sign up to my newsletter and you'll receive each episode of Day Death as they're created. Released as often as I can get to them and remain sane, we'll experience that deathful day from the perspective of each of our main characters.

I mean, who doesn't want to see six hearts shatter forever . . .

OUT NOW

Spicy Bites – Silk: 2023 Romance Writers of Australia
Short Story Anthology

Strap into your climbing gear and get a glimpse into the head of
Jasper, the sexy sadist himself. When Lucky nearly gets himself
killed in a stupid bet, Jasper decides that one very . . . spicy . . .
lesson is in order.

As a finalist in the 2023 Spicy Bites competition run by the
fantastic Romance Writers of Australia, I'm thrilled to be part of
this silky-smooth anthology that will definitely make you sweat.
Freefall acts as a prequel short story to the Brutes of Bristlebrook
series and can be read by new and old readers of the series alike.

ACKNOWLEDGMENTS

I get WAY too emotional writing these so I'm going to try and make it fast. Faster than my last one. This book was brutal to write for a lot of reasons. I was on an extremely tight deadline, it's *enormous*, and it was a very emotional book to write. I'm really lucky with my support network, and I had so many people helping to keep me afloat in different ways.

I will never stop being grateful to all of you.

Two people who need the biggest shout out in the world are Brianna Bancroft and A.K. Blythe. These two talented, incredible, unicorns of humans saved my LIFE with this book one hundred times over. They alpha read, followed me along chapter by chapter, wiggled out plot holes, dealt with meltdowns, fixed my wording issues—*all* of the things. Their advice and friendship means everything to me, particularly as they're such incredibly talented authors themselves (like, seriously, go read everything they've ever written). Love you always.

To Nicky, my sister, who read this book more times than I have, probably. I'm sorry for calling you at weird hours panicking. Thanks for always picking up. You saved my god damn ass.

To Charlotte, for your freaking fantastic beta help, cheerleading skills, socials help, and generally hyping me up 24/7, I effing adore you.

To Tegan, my mom bud and secret business manager, thank you for your beta help, your absolutely incredible swag sourcing skills, general handy help, advice, friendship and all the things.

To my betas Lisa, Shannan, Colleen, Amy, Renee, Noémie, Dimi, Chelsea, and Arielle, THANK YOU! Your comments made me laugh, made me think, and made every bit of this story so much better than it otherwise would have. It's a lot of work to beta and this was on a TIGHT deadline, so thank you so, so much for everything you did. I appreciate the hell out of you.

To my book wives, Letizia Firmani, Letizia Lorini, LH Blake, and WH Lockwood, you guys keep me afloat every day. The banter, the author struggles, the understanding, the humor, the friendship, I value the hell out of all of you so much. And thank you, Lety, for once again saving me and making this book gorgeous at the last minute. I love you to the moon and back for it. And once again, I'll reiterate, of my own free will—*gulp*—that Dom is yours. She's greedy, folks, and doesn't like to share.

To my editor and proofreaders, Kate, Libby, and Lilly, thank you endlessly. This one was tight and frantic, and you made this incredible. I really appreciate you going out of your way for this—and, of course, for doing such an amazing job.

To the superstar team at Blue Nose Audio who took my little baby author dreams and pushed them way up beyond any stratosphere I ever imagined, I don't even have words. Your whole team is warm and welcoming and so professional—on top of being super fun—and it's such a privilege.

To every one of my narrators, you brought these characters to life in a whole new way for me. The passion and commitment you put into your work is nothing short of art, and you can hear every single moment of vulnerability, and humor, and heat, and anger and I honestly can't even talk about it without getting emotional. I'm so freaking honored to have you performing my words.

To my ARC and street team, you are the hype team of my dreams. I love how much you love the brutes and I'm so grateful for your support. So much of my success is owed to you!

To my family, it will be super nice to see you again after a few months of total absenteeism. I promise not to make deadlines quite that tight ever again. Thank you for holding down the fort and building me up, always. My fiancé is my number one fan, big reader or not, and I love him as hard as Eden loves her brutes. Can't wait to watch you blush over this one, gorgeous.

Finally, to my readers, without you, there is nothing. Thank you for reading, reviewing, recommending, and generally just coming back for my words. At the end of the day, that's what this is all about.

About the Author

After spending her career publishing other writers' wonderful words, Rebecca Quinn decided to unleash her own. Turns out, she's a little debauched. Rebecca loves writing inclusive, character-driven reverse harem romance with heart, humor, and kinky heat —or romance with bromance, as she calls it.

Rebecca lives in a coastal town south of Sydney, Australia. She spends her days cuddling her young son and her fiancé, getting far too invested in her DnD campaigns, drinking too much wine, playing board games, and—of course—reading as many novels as she can get her grabby little hands on.

If you want to keep up to date with the next books in the series, bonus content, new series, filthy memes, and ridiculous chats, come get Quinnky with me on my socials, or sign up to my newsletter via my website.

36328571R00402